PIECES *of* SILVER

MIKE BRESLIN

Pie Shop Publishing

Copyright © 2014 Mike Breslin

The moral right of the author has been asserted

ISBN-13: 978-1-5004-8836-9

Pie Shop Publishing, London

Cover design: Bespoke Book Covers (www.bespokebookcovers.com)

Main cover image: LAT Photographic

Contact Mike Breslin: www.bresmedia.co.uk

This book is for Jassy: my wife, best friend, and travelling companion. Big thanks should go to Katherine McKenna-Price, my editor at Pie Shop Publishing, and my agent Leslie Gardner, at Artellus, for the many useful suggestions and for their help with cleaning up the manuscript – though I should add that any remaining mistakes are entirely down to me. I would also like to thank the many people in the motorsport industry who have helped with *Pieces of Silver*, far too many to list, and also the always-helpful staff at the Imperial War Museum, the Royal Air Force Museum at Hendon, and Brooklands. Last – and maybe sort of first – I'd like to thank the ever so slightly peculiar old man we met in the Red October Bar in Zwickau some years back. He told me a secret, and gave me an idea …

Prologue

East Germany, 1987

How deep was my greed? As deep as a coal mine. Why else would I have clanged down hundreds of metres of rusting ladder into the depths of the wetly-warm pit? Why else would I have ignored the signs that said the shaft was dangerous, on the point of collapse, filled with incendiary firedamp? Why else would I have trusted this old man?

He found a fissure in the wall of wood and with a tug of his crowbar he pulled one of the coal dust blackened planks away. It fell to the floor and the boom echoed down the long mineshaft like the slam of a cathedral door. He then angled the crowbar through the slot he'd created and pulled at its curled end. Almost immediately another plank came clear, crashing to the floor, and then another. Dust hung in the air, illuminated by my little torch so that it shone like powered gold. The echoes of the falling planks died in the depths of the mine, and soon all that could be heard was the trickle of water in the rock. The dust started to settle. And there it was.

Its silver aluminium glinted in the light of both our torches for long silent seconds, time when I found it hard to breathe for the dust and the excitement. My torch picked out the long curves, the sweeping, gleaming silver bodywork, and then the bubble windscreen. So Gramps had been right. One had survived. My eyes rolled to the roof of the shaft in a silent thank you. It was a record car – a streamliner. Back in the 1930s cars like this had sped faster than aeroplanes to break records on the then new autobahns. And in '87, during that decade of greed that had served me so well, a car like this was worth more than anyone in East Germany could possibly hope for ... dream of ... imagine ...

It wasn't perfect. No, not quite. There were a number of small holes in the bodywork, each barely half an inch across, each sucking the darkness into the shining skin of the car. It didn't occur to me then what they were,

1

what had caused them. Naive? Perhaps, but you must remember in those days I was into numbers, money, the hard sell. Not soft-bodied, long-forgotten people, prey to the crunch of metal, the lick of flame, or the hot hit of a bullet on a battlefield – then I had still to learn of all that. Of the story I can now tell.

The beam of the old man's torch locked on to something. A little painted flag behind the tight cockpit opening: red, white and black. As soon as I saw it I felt a little shiver of almost superstitious fear, mixed with a guilty excitement. For a stretched moment or two I could not take my eyes off the angular symbol, even though before me sat the most beautiful – the most valuable – car in the world. That is the morbid fascination of the swastika. But to others it is more. And the old man's face was a mask of streaming tears.

1936

Hot oil stung his face and covered the lenses of his goggles. He ripped them clear of his head and caught a glimpse of the road ahead through a funnel of trees and speed just before the buffeting, smoky air turned his vision into a pool of tears. Oil was still spraying from the louvre vents of the engine cover, and a long pennant of black smoke trailed over him, turning every breath into a choking gasp. The rasp of the exhaust faded and he felt the car stutter and die. He lined the Alfa Romeo up for the curve just as the flames burst from the engine bay.

He felt the lick of the heat against his face, smelt the scorching of his eyebrows, and then he ducked down low beneath the windshield, letting the flames stream above his head as he pressed firmly on the brake pedal. He tried to guide the car through the turn from memory, but when there are 170 corners a lap that can be as reliable as a battered old Alfa Romeo P3, and so now he was driving largely by feel. He felt the hammering of the bumpy road surface through the large wire-bound steering wheel, heard the hum of the tyres over the whoosh of the flames, and smelt the acrid reek of the blood-red paint burning to black just inches in front of him. Somehow he steered the car through the turn, but now the fire had truly taken hold, and it was almost impossible to keep his foot on the hot brake pedal.

Instant decisions, calculations in a heartbeat, are part of what it is to be a racing driver. The Alfa was still travelling fast enough to hurt: thirty miles per hour at least. So yes, it would mean a hard landing, a few broken bones perhaps – but better than roasting alive.

He could not see ahead, the flames too thick, but he could hear the collective gasp of the spectators over the roar of the inferno. He let go of the wheel and pushed himself up high in the padded leather seat, glad to get his feet out of the scorching foot-well. Then he climbed out onto the stubby tail, the spokes of the wire wheels a speeding blur close to his hands as he steadied himself, still standing on the seat, braced and ready for the dangerous jump to safety, careful not to touch the hot exhaust that ran close to where his right hand helped him to keep his precarious perch. The car bucked as it hit the grass verge and he instinctively held on tighter, only then seeing the way ahead through a brief break in the wall of flame that covered the front of the Alfa. There was a ditch, quite shallow, then a group of spectators standing behind a wooden rail, already breaking in panic as the flaming Alfa Romeo hurtled towards them.

His legs were still in the cockpit, so he gave the steering wheel a sharp kick as he balanced on the tail. The leg of his overalls caught fire but the kick was enough to pull the car back on to the road, and to send him flying

3

into the ditch in the opposite direction. He seemed to be in the air for a little age – a kaleidoscope of grey-green spinning before his eyes – before he finally landed on the soft grass verge beside the track. The air was driven from his lungs, but still he had the presence of mind to roll out the flames that were climbing the right leg of his overalls. His blurred vision cleared and he watched as the Alfa clattered through the white wooden marker posts at the inside of the turn, then hit a fir tree with a meaty thwack, the angled impact ripping a wheel clear of its axle and flinging it back on to the track.

That wheel was still trundling drunkenly across the roadway when he stood up, a little unsteadily, and started the usual damage report – hangover mornings, rough games of rugger, after a shunt, it was always the same. There was a minor burn on his leg, a twisted ankle, and the taste of the conflagration in his parched throat. *It could only happen to Westbury Holt.* Yes, he could almost hear them saying it – those in the paddock, those in the know – as he brushed himself down. The German spectators clapped when they could see he was all right and he bowed theatrically to them, which turned the polite applause into an appreciative laugh. West unbuckled his pale-green linen wind helmet and pulled his pipe out of the weave in his cricket jumper – both as much a Westbury Holt signature as the bad luck that had ruined his chance to impress the German teams here at the Nürburgring. Two track workers ran across the road and were now busy trying to put out the flames that danced from the engine bay of the Alfa Romeo with extinguishers and buckets of sand. He supposed it was fortunate they were stationed at this corner as the 'Ring was fourteen miles long, people had crashed here and never been seen again, they said. But they were too late anyway, and as he watched the black smoke block out a portion of the bright blue sky he knew that the German Grand Prix was the end of his racing for 1936.

"Do you need medical attention?" It was said in German-accented English, a man standing behind him. West just shook his head, then busied himself with stuffing his Dunhill briar with *Player's No Name* tobacco.

"It must be difficult, having to compete in such machinery after trying an Auto Union, Herr Holt," the man continued. West concentrated on the job at hand, shutting out that smug voice, and shutting out the sounds that echoed through the dark forest: the distant ripping of the Auto Union C-Types, the shrill siren-like whine of the superchargers on the Mercedes W125s, and the crackle of the burning Alfa. Then shutting out the memories, the one try-out, at Monza: very fast times, but dents to go with them. They hadn't liked that, from an Englishman, had liked it even less when he was quicker than the young Germans also on hand to try the car. He tapped down the tobacco in the bowl with the little blunt headed tamper on his pipe tool, then searched the pockets of the grimy white overalls he wore under his cricket jumper, but could not find his matches.

"Bugger it! Have you got a light?" he said, turning to face the man.

The German seemed to find that funny, glancing at the burning Alfa as a thin smile creased his face, but then he shook his head: "I do not smoke," he said.

There were two other men with him, West then realised, both in the military uniform of the Nazi motoring corps, the NSKK, complete with brown shirts and cavalry breeches, eagle-adorned black side-caps and the must-have fashion accessory of the moment, a swastika armband. One of the NSKK men tossed West a box of matches, and he threw back a nod of thanks. The other NSKK man carried a boxy cine camera, which he was now busy setting up on a tripod. If it had wheels in Germany then the NSKK would have something to do with it, and there were always plenty of uniforms here at the 'Ring. West didn't really understand the Nazi obsession with fancy dress, and he supposed he didn't really take to some of them – all pomp, whatever the circumstance – but that didn't matter; all that really mattered to Westbury Holt was that they made damned fine racing cars, and one day he hoped to get the chance to race one. And win with it. The man who was not in uniform was still looking at him, still smiling that thin, self-satisfied smile.

"Haven't we met?" West said, as the thought came to him.

"I was at your Auto Union trial, you were quick," the German said. West nodded, he didn't need anyone to tell him that. There was the snarl of a down-change blip from deep in the forest, and West wondered how long before the leading cars would come through again, he had lost plenty of time with mechanical issues even before the fire had started, but then it was a long lap here at the 'Ring. The tobacco caught and West sucked at the pipe, taking the chance to consider the man in front of him: tweed sports jacket, crisp white shirt, black tie, swastika lapel badge, black-banded grey homburg – set perfectly horizontal – and a face dominated by pale grey eyes magnified by thick rimless spectacles, the sort of grey they'd use to paint the inside of labour exchanges, West imagined.

"Anton Kessler," the German offered his hand – cold cod, but West enjoyed squeezing some grime-encrusted life into it, as he remembered who he was: *he's with the Party, propaganda*, they had told him, when he had tested the Auto Union. West grunted and nodded. The film crew were busy with the camera, feeding on the Viking fire of the Alfa. Once again West wondered what he had been thinking. Kessler was right, there was no way he was going to impress the German teams in that, especially as the rain he had hoped for had failed to show.

"The game has changed Herr Holt, *we* have changed it. The Alfa Romeo's no longer fast enough," Kessler said, seeming to read his mind.

"It was worth a shot," West said. "You never know your luck."

"Well, your luck seems well known," Kessler said. "Bad, most of it; that's what they say, isn't it? But it's true. You *are* unlucky – unlucky that you weren't born a German." West shrugged, he had sometimes thought as much himself. "But it's also a great pity," Kessler went on. "It really is, for we're starved of young German drivers, drivers who are fast."

"But you have Rosemeyer," West said, suddenly just a little interested in what Kessler had to say.

"Rosemeyer is Rosemeyer," Kessler said, after a heartbeat of hesitation. "There's room for others. Besides, some of these people have yet to realise there's so much more to it now than simply sport – they fail to see that it's heroes we need; not entertainers, not clowns."

"Well, they don't come more heroic than Delius," West said, with an edge of sarcasm, remembering how the German had beaten him to the drive – even though he had been almost a second a lap slower. *It's not all about speed*, the people from Auto Union had said, embarrassed as they said it, while the uniforms of the NSKK stood large in the background. *Then what is it all about?* he had replied. He caught the quick blink in Kessler's magnified grey eyes at the same time as he heard the harsh ripping noise of an Auto Union at full stretch. The excited chatter behind the fences dropped to a hush, and all heads were turned in anticipation of the leader's arrival. The engine note grew clearer and West picked out the crisp blip of the down-change before he caught the silver flicker through the trees. Then the car came fully into sight, Rosemeyer's car.

Just then, for some reason, West's eyes drifted to the burning hulk of the Alfa again, where the track workers were still busy bringing the fire under control. He caught the acrid smell of blistering paint and rubber and then dimly became aware of the sting of the small burn on his leg. The sun suddenly glinted through the billowing smoke and a melted rainbow seemed to sparkle upon the surface of the road.

"Oil …"

The word froze Kessler's satisfied smirk to his face. But West's warning was too late. The Auto Union crested the hill and raced through the turn, the driver in his red wind helmet bent close to the wheel, gloved knuckles flashing white across the top of the dash as he let the car dance to each jab of the throttle. He was on the limit, nothing in reserve, with Westbury Holt's oil spread out before him on the track like a welcome mat to whatever lay beyond. West felt the breath freeze in his lungs as he waited for the Auto Union to hit the oil. He knew this car, had had it tattooed to his consciousness for almost every waking moment since the day he had driven one, every curve of its long, voluptuous silver body, committed to envious memory. He also knew it took some driving.

Bernd Rosemeyer, as was his way, had the long tail of the Auto Union some way out of line with the front, and it was still in its skid when it hit the oil. The Auto Union slid wide instantly, two wheels running along the grass verge, the tail drifting even further out, and flying over the rough ground before crashing back down with a crunching thump that had Rosemeyer bouncing in his seat. For a moment West thought it would spin out of control and into the bank ...

... But somehow Rosemeyer held it. Then hauled the car back into line, onto track, and then drove past the still burning Alfa with a final flourish of revs that caused a blue-white ring of smoke to envelope the circumference of the outer rear wheel. Then, quite suddenly, all that was left of his passing was the pong of the fuel, a little like the smell of boot polish. West had caught sight of the look on Rosemeyer's face as he flashed past. The man was grinning ... West took a deep breath, then whistled softly to himself as he let it out.

"You think you could do that?" Kessler said, and West was astonished to see that he was now blinking at nineteen to the dozen, while also scribbling pencilled observations in a notebook he had taken from the pocket of his jacket.

"Given the car, given a little luck, I could do it better," West replied without hesitation.

"A shame you are not German then, isn't it?"

"Don't you think you should be getting them to warn the other drivers about the oil?" West said, nodding at the busy track workers, annoyed enough to let a little irritation creep into his voice.

Kessler shouted at the track workers, who were still concentrating on putting out the fire, but the roar of another V16 fast approaching cut him off. It was too late anyway. Konrad von Plaidt, the veteran driver, arrived with less speed than Rosemeyer, yet the car was still out of shape as he crested the hill. He was pushing, that was clear, his face was a mask of concentration and sweat and West also saw big-eyed terror behind the goggle lenses just as von Plaidt hit the oil – right then West knew he was going to crash.

There was a sudden increase in revs: then silence, a shriek of rubber on asphalt as the car slithered out of the slick, the harsh creak of compressed suspension, and then the metallic crump of the car hitting the bank. West watched as the rounded snout of the Auto Union struck the embankment, tearing into it and ploughing up a great wave of dirt and small stones before stopping short with a jolt that tipped it up on to its nose and into a series of lazy cartwheels. For one complete turn the driver was trapped in the cockpit, his arms hanging limply as the car was upside down, twenty-feet in the air, his legs pinned in place by the steering wheel, agony and fear filling his face. But as the Auto Union bounced tail first against the earth beyond the top of the bank von Plaidt flew clear of the cockpit and right then the figure in the white overalls was just another piece of debris.

Just like the loose wheel that bounced high over the spectators or the pieces of bodywork that shone like silver flakes in the sun. He landed against the wooden rail just half a yard from the spectators lined up behind it. A woman screamed. The car bounced once more, and then came to rest on its broken back amongst the fir trees, around thirty yards from the driver, a front wheel spinning impotently, fuel fumes blurring the air around it like a summer heat haze.

Kessler, his eyes still blinking madly behind the large lenses of his specs, had snapped his pencil in two. His intermittent gaze locked on to the rag-doll pile of stillness that was von Plaidt, some eighty feet away from where they stood, a leg bent into an impossible angle, so that the foot was close to the head. West stared with him, unable to move as the clicking of the movie camera ticked away the seconds of indecision.

"Perhaps you are not so unlucky, after all, Herr Holt?" Kessler said. Konrad von Plaidt stirred as he said it, letting out a groan that was clearly audible, and Westbury Holt turned away from Kessler, and the scene of the crash, just a little ashamed that he had been thinking the very same thing.

***

Sepp Nagel thought that the potato cakes sizzling as they warmed in the pan sounded a little bit like the fall of the rain on the pavement outside. They were his favourite, cooked with buttermilk, eggs, bacon and onion. Hanna was treating him, and after the effort she had made he hadn't the heart to tell her that he was far too excited to think about food.

"Nearly done," she said, "and there is still plenty of time."

He nodded and smiled at her, glad that his sister was there for him, glad that she was still helping him as she had for so long. But he could do without the buttermilchgetzen …

Through the chunky slot of the window high in the wall on the far side of the kitchen he could see the raindrops bouncing brightly against the pavement like silver coins. Every now and then flashing ankles would rush past, their owners little knowing that in this kitchen basement just below the level of a Zwickau street a boy and his dream were about to collide. *Boy?* Sepp thought. *Not for so very much longer.*

Hanna swished the potato cakes in the pan to a delicious little sizzle and then moved the coffee pot on to the table in what seemed like one fluid action, the rich aroma of the coffee briefly cutting through the stronger smells of frying bacon, onion and potato. Then she turned and scooped a potato cake from the pan with a spatula and slid it onto a plate, which she then placed on the yellow and white checked tablecloth in front of him.

"I'm proud of you, Sepp," she said, quite suddenly.

"It's not done yet, sister."

"No, but it will be, I'm sure."

"But so sudden. I had hoped I was doing well at the works – I believed I was – but I was told I would have to wait years for an opportunity in the racing department," Sepp said, slicing a small triangle off the steaming rectangle of the potato cake and considering his culinary geometry for a moment or two. Hanna had turned away, quickly, busying herself with putting some more buttermilchgetzen in the pan. He sensed she was keeping something from him, he could read her like a blueprint. But like the potato cake, the subject was too hot to bite, and he did not have the appetite for it anyway, and so he played with his food, and the thought, moving the golden-brown triangle around his plate with his fork.

"Konrad says you've been doing very well, so perhaps it is not so surprising?" she said.

"So you've spoken to him about me?"

"You know that, Sepp. I just asked how you were doing, nothing more," she turned to him now, then smiled. He could not resist it, and smiled back, and allowed himself to be content with that. The thought that she might have asked a favour on his behalf worried him. But he had thought it through many times now, and had *almost* convinced himself that even if this was so, as long as he proved himself up to the job it should not matter. Besides, to hear that a man like Konrad von Plaidt had noticed him was thrilling, even if he could not scratch the itch that it might be more to do with the fact that the racing hero had also noticed Hanna.

"But now you have a good friend, yes?" he said, hoping to bring out that blush again – with Hanna they were as red, and as rare, as rubies.

"He is Herr Ostermann's friend, you know that – all I've done is help him get over his accident," she said.

"Yes, three months on from the crash, but there is still much mending needed, I hear —"

"It will mean more money," she said, interrupting, obviously wanting to change the subject. "If you get the job on the race team, I mean."

"It will mean I have a chance to drive, sister."

"Sepp, please —"

"Like Lang," he added. Her smile hadn't dropped but there was that familiar exasperation in those blue eyes. Outside a tram squealed and clanged, the rain sizzling against its cables as it made its way up Nord Strasse. The frosted-glass-fronted cupboards were high, on a level with the window that peeped out flush to the pavement. She had to reach for a plate and he caught a glimpse of her fine ankles, the delicate, soft curve of the back of her leg. It was no secret that she was something, all the lads at the Horch Works, where he was two years into his apprenticeship, told him that, all too often. But soon he would get his chance to leave all those teases behind him. He would get his chance to work on the racing cars, and from there …

"You should concentrate on what's at hand," she said, spinning around with a white plate delicately balanced on fine porcelain fingers. "they are after a mechanic – not another racing driver."

"Oh Hanna, why so grown up all the time?"

"It's all I have," she said quietly. "And I know that they will not take kindly to some starry-eyed kid wanting to be another Rosemeyer – you remember that Sepp, I want you to do well."

"I'll remember," he said, grinning.

She was trying to look stern but her eyes, as always, gave her away. She served herself some buttermilchgetzen and sat opposite him. He normally took lunch at the works, in the canteen, but he had come home today to get ready for the interview with Dr Feuereissen, the race team manager, and Herr Kessler, who was something to do with the Party. *They* seemed to be involved in everything these days. Hanna was on her lunch break from Herr Ostermann's shop, the same old miser who was their landlord, the same old miser who was an old friend of Konrad von Plaidt.

"Eat up," Hanna said, flashing him a fresh smile that seemed to light up her face – the sort of smile she might have used to persuade Herr Ostermann to let her go to lunch just a little early; the sort of smile she used to persuade him to give them a week to find the next rent; the sort of smile that took her beauty to another level. Sepp often wondered how it could be that she was so beautiful and yet he felt so ordinary. After all they shared many features – including the cobalt blue eyes and the blond hair that some of those fools in the Motorised Hitler Youth would swap their own motorcycles for.

She wore a dirndl. The traditional rural dress the Nazis loved, with its long green skirt that shrouded her legs above the ankles like a dark drooping tulip, and its tight bodice laced in a lattice over the swell of her breasts, and its white blouse with puffed and gathered sleeves and crocheted collar. She hated it all, and always wore a coat over it whatever the weather when she was not in the shop, but Herr Ostermann demanded it, in the same way as he demanded she wore no makeup and that she tied her long golden hair back. Sepp could never understand why in this *new Germany* Nazis like Ostermann were so caught up in the past, in tradition. But, as Hanna said – quite often – they were in no position to argue. Not since Mother had died, joining Father. Not since they had taken on the debt Mother had let spiral out of control, not since they had lost everything but two rooms to live in, for which they now had to pay rent, and this basement to eat in. All of which was why, at just nineteen, just three years older than Sepp, Hanna spent much of her time pretending to be a woman, not a girl. Sometimes he would wish she would remember that he was in on the secret. She cut into the steaming square of her potato cake, then said: "And forget about Lang, just for today."

He smiled and nodded. *Lang.* Lang had given him hope. Herman Lang, the Mercedes mechanic who had become a driver, first wangling the odd test drive, then the odd race. It was how Sepp planned it, too. Though now, for once, he kept the thought to himself. She talked, told him all the things he should say, all the things he should not say – things to do with Rosemeyer, things to do with Lang – while he tried his best to swallow as much of the lovingly prepared lunch as he could. Two bites of buttermilchgetzen later and he could eat no more. Destiny and potato cakes, he decided, just do not mix. "Enough?" she asked.

He nodded.

"But you've hardly touched them?"

"I'm sorry …"

Hanna shook her head, but then said: "I understand." She took his plate from him, stroking his hair as she did so, just like Mother once did. Usually he hated that, but today he could forgive her. He stood up and reached for the jacket that hung on a coat hanger against the bright yellow painted plank door of the small larder. He had outgrown his own suit and the one he wore had once belonged to Father. She had worked wonders with needle and thread and now it fitted better than he could have hoped for. He was already taller than his father had been, so the sleeves were a little short, but she had his shirt cuffs gleaming like freshly fallen snow, while the jacket also helped to cover a tatty old waistcoat, with its small front pocket heavy with the pocket watch that had also once belonged to his father, and had long ceased to tell the time.

Hanna stepped back from the table and looked him up and down, biting her bottom lip and cocking her head to one side, clasping her hands behind her back.

"So, will my little soldier do?" She shook her head slowly, then leant forward to brush an invisible speck of dust from his lapel. Sepp looked down, catching his own reflection of newly trimmed blond hair and tie-choked collar in the gleam of his shoes. "That's better," she said. He pecked her on the cheek and they both laughed out loud. Somewhere upstairs a tap was turned and the water pipes running down the walls of the kitchen gurgled along with their laughter. They stared at each other for a moment, and he thought she would say again how much this extra money could mean. But instead she said, "You will do it." Right then he felt his love for her solid within him, like an extra heart.

There was the sudden sound of familiar, clunking, footfalls on the main staircase, which descended into the hall behind a door at the top of the stone steps that led from this basement.

"That's Strudel," Sepp said, "I can take the tram with him."

"Wait, Sepp," Hanna said, grabbing at the sleeve of his jacket. "There is still plenty of time." They heard the front door to the hallway slam shut.

"But Strudel, he —"

"He will be okay, he always is," she said.

"Not always."

"But today he will be, he must be – yes?"

Sepp nodded. He understood. It would not help his chances to be seen arriving with Strudel. Not today.

"Have some coffee," she said. "And cake?" There were some thick slices on a plate on the worktop, slabs of dense corn-yellow cake shot through with dried fruit, crusts dusted with a light snow of icing sugar. He shook his head, but she poured him a cup of coffee anyway. "Sit with me," she said. He sat with her and drank the coffee, while she told him once again what to say, and what not to say, during his interview, the tap dripping in the background.

Soon it was time to go. His coat and hat were in his room upstairs and once in the hall he took the stairs two at a time, the way he always took the stairs, a boy in a hurry. Their rooms were on the top floor. By the time Papa's, and then Mama's, affairs had been sorted this was all that was left, the right to rent the smallest rooms in the block they once owned, and the use of the basement kitchen – which many years before had a been a room for the maid of some old widow. Sepp collected his big grey raincoat, and his flat oilcloth cap, and then took one long and lingering look at the photograph of the Auto Union racing car on his wall. Old Kurt, Strudel's father and the caretaker of the building, shouted from an open doorway and wished him luck as he ran down the stairs. Hanna stood at the bottom of the staircase, with one last kiss for luck and some parting words: "This is a good chance, Sepp. Take it."

*

"Well it certainly brightens up a dreary day," said Westbury Holt.

"What does?"

"That flag."

Philip Grace, always 'Gracie' to West, tut-tutted and shook his head in exasperation. West, peering through the rain-streaked windscreen, shifted the pipe to the other corner of his mouth, laughed, then blipped the throttle as he snicked the Lagonda 3.5 Sport Tourer down a gear. The red flag, with its angular swastika within a yolk of white, was plastered flat against the wet and gleaming walls of a small house. The red had lost a little of its fire, faded in the sun of a summer now long past, but from what West had seen on the drive from Berlin the support for that funny little man was something that was far from fading. Each and every village had its swastika flags, almost each and every street. He accelerated through the outskirts of the village, feeling the rear of the car skip across the greasy cobbles. "I think," West said, "I might get one for the old man's town house."

"With your father's opinion on all things German I would certainly advise against that, friend Westbury," Gracie said, with a limp smile – he seldom seemed to see the funny side when it came to politics, which made it even more fun for West to rag him. He was still surprised – and intrigued – that Gracie had caught the train from Munich to Berlin to be able to accompany him on his drive to Zwickau, for although he was very interested in German politics, he had never before shown any interest in West's racing. But he supposed it was good to have someone to talk to, and someone to tease. The heavy car whispered its way along the wet road, the wiper blades squeaking as they swept wide parabolas across the split screen. Dancing along the tip of the long, black nose of the Lagonda West could just about pick out the dark towers of distant mine workings through the gloom.

"So friend Westbury, you're really going to do it – sell your soul to the very devil and all that, eh?"

"A chance to win, Gracie."

"But a Nazi car?"

"A German car."

Grace thought on that for a moment, then said: "The mark of a man is the mark in his pocket … Same for cars, one would suppose."

West shook his head and smiled, glanced at another of the swastika flags, then accelerated hard.

*

The rain was still falling and Sepp pulled the collar of the raincoat up around his ears. Nord Strasse's wet road surface shone like coal; the tram lines rich veins of silver shimmer within it. The street ran arrow-straight for a couple of kilometres, north to leave the city, south to pierce the ring road that encircled the centre. With its shallow camber and glistening asphalt it almost looked like a canal, Sepp thought, with the doors of apartment blocks and offices opening straight out onto the water. It was what he knew as home, a mundanity of red brick and dripping slate, sometimes grand, mostly not, ordered and uniform, forever Zwickau.

One of the red and white trams rattled past, the tilted cube steel framework on its roof scraping blue sparks from the wet overhead cables, and he broke into a run to catch it at the stop. He climbed on board and took a seat on one of the wooden slatted benches that ran down either side of the car. There were a number of people in the tram, one coughing and sneezing, and all the windows were steamed up, so that Sepp felt as if he was travelling inside a clattering cloud, and he was glad to jump off when it squealed to a halt close to the Horch Works. From the stop there was a shortcut he would normally take, cutting the corner by walking across the waste ground and the railway line that lay in front of the huge fat cylinder of the gasholder, but with his best shoes on, and the rough ground dappled with chocolate-coloured puddles, he thought it best to skirt around it today. There was still time, he had made sure he had plenty in hand. The wet wind carried the yeasty smell of the brewery from over the River Zwickau Mulde a couple of blocks to the east of Nord Strasse, while a small steam engine hooted as it swished along the shining rails to his left, its steam merging with the grey sky, as if it was source of the gloom.

Sepp's eyes were drawn to the small engine as it traversed the waste ground; they were always drawn towards machines and wheels, as if they were little white and blue moons, tugged by the gravity of the spinning parts. The engine was pale green, and any glint the old paint and the battered brass of its pipes might possess was lost to the grey and the rain. It *chuffer-chugged* by, smelling of burning coal, Sepp's gaze locked to it, but his mind firmly on the immediate future: what he should say and what he should do. He was a little nervous, he realised, it was a fluttering inside him, but the feeling that somehow today was the start of something bigger, his destiny, also made him confident. The path his life would take from here was as obvious and as set as that of the small shunting engine that chugged across the waste ground, locked on course by the deep grooves in its mesmeric wheels. Yet as it steamed by it revealed another scene, beyond the single railway that bisected the ground like a stitched scar, and three quarters of the way along the path that crossed the rails, the path that shortcut takers on the way to the Horch Works had etched into the waste ground over the years.

There was nothing interesting about this scene, just a group of youngsters stood in a tight pack across the path. They all wore overcoats, except for one, who from a distance seemed to be in black shorts and a brown shirt, despite the weather. Sepp looked away, he had reached the junction and he turned with the pavement on to Häuser Hohenzollern Strasse, so that the scene was now just about in his field of vision, like a dirty smudge on the top corner of the goggles he'd wear when he had the chance to ride a motorbike. But his course along the shining wet stone pavement inevitably brought him closer to the group and soon the red armband on the shirt of the one in shorts became clear, and difficult to ignore. The one in the armband was Hitler Youth, and he guessed the others wore a uniform under their overcoats. There were six of them, and they were in a tight crescent, which made him think there was something in front of them, but their backs and legs blocked his view. He could hear them now. They were all laughing, the sort of laughter he knew all too well, the brittle laughter of boys telling the jokes of men; jokes about the hates of men. He knew he should ignore it, and he made himself walk on.

He tried to think of the things he should do, the things he should say, at the interview, and concentrated on the huge sprawl of the factory to his right.

There was a shout, muted in the rain.

He ignored it. *Walk on Sepp.*

There was another burst of slightly forced laughter.

Walk on Sepp.

"S-s-s-sepp!"

The end of the stuttered shout was high pitched, almost like a whine. It was familiar – if rare. It was Strudel.

Old Kurt's son was not like other boys, other people. And the Nazis did not like that. But Hanna was right, they could not go on looking after him forever. He was a little older than Sepp, but in years only, for inside he was still a child. He was a simpleton, at a time when nothing could be quite so simple.

But Sepp could not help him today, and so he pretended he had not heard the cry, the slap of his shoes against the wet pavement now like slow and sarcastic applause. *He will be okay*, Sepp told himself, *they're just teasing …*

"Down boy!" came the shout from the waste ground, but Sepp ignored it, knowing there were other things to do this day, knowing that one day Strudel would have to learn to look after himself, knowing that …

He turned towards the shout, but did not stop walking, and through the lattice of limbs and the drooping curtains of open coats he could see Strudel, kneeling in the coffee dark mud in front of the tall boy in black shorts and brown shirt.

"Damn it!"

He knew he should ignore it, but he could not help himself, because he also knew there was nobody else who would help Strudel. He turned off the pavement and his shoes sank sigh-like into the soft, squirmy dirt. He would talk to them, ask them to lay off, they were just boys underneath the uniforms after all. All it would cost him would be dirty shoes, which he might be able to wipe clean with his handkerchief before the interview. Sepp walked across the waste ground, avoiding the muddy puddles. The lads had all turned away from him now and they were watching the figure in shorts and shirt, the one who was laughing the most. He had a gnarled stick in his hand which he was waving above his head. Some of the faces turned towards Sepp, flashes of pink in the grey. Then they seemed to recognise him, shrug and turn away. He knew them well enough, most of them. He was in the Hitler Youth himself, it wasn't quite compulsory, but most joined, and in the Motorised HJ – of which he was a member – there was the chance to race motorcycles, to show his speed every now and then. You didn't have to agree with their politics to ride their motorbikes, he had once said to Hanna.

Sepp was within twenty metres of the boys now. They stood close to a shallow scoop in the earth that was filled with oily black water, more pool than puddle, and dotted with a small archipelago of half submerged rusting-red barrels. It smelt of choking chemicals, there was an edge of ammonia, he thought, and the raindrops falling on to the surface made it seem like it was fizzing. The tall figure in the shorts lifted the stick high and threw it far away, the stick tumbling end over end before landing point first in the mud with a squelchy sucking sound. Sepp then heard the sound of footfalls on soft wet ground, and saw that Strudel was running after the stick. One or two of the lads nodded at Sepp as he came closer, then stepped aside to let him past. He got a better look at the one in shorts, a thick wedge of just-fair hair plastered to his skull, light brown shirt darkened and pasted tight to a well-muscled torso. His heart sank.

Sepp knew Wolfgang by reputation only. But this was enough to know he did not want to know him better. Wolf was two years older than Sepp, only just young enough to still be in the HJ. But to wear his summer uniform with no coat in this weather he must be a very special kind of knucklehead, Sepp thought. He caught the challenge in the Nazi's eyes, a flicker of fire, a warning. Somewhere inside him a little voice said this was the time to turn away. Wolf was not the sort to reason with.

"Good dog!" Wolf shouted, dismissively turning away from Sepp as Strudel ran back towards them, carrying the wet stick in his hand. Sepp had never asked just what it was that was wrong with Strudel, but most thought he was simply an idiot. He very rarely said a single word, because when he did it often came out slow, fractured with painful stammer, but his big brown eyes were like signal lamps – if you could read them. Sepp read *fear*.

"You alright, Strudel?" Sepp said, softly.

"Of course he's alright," Wolf snapped, "we're having a great time, aren't we?"

Strudel nodded mechanically. His cobweb fine hair was pasted to his small head by the rain so that the skin of his scalp showed through pinkly. His coat was open to show his threadbare red sweater and the brown trousers which were darker at the knees from where they had rested in the mud. Strudel was as small as a jockey, as pale as milk, as ugly as a rat; and when he moved it appeared *almost* as if he was a puppet, every movement a slight convulsion, as if his brain tugged at his limbs. It was a small thing really, hardly noticeable, and yet always noticed in a way people would not be able to put their fingers on. So, a small thing that gave him away, but a big thing, too. In days like these.

Wolf laughed, and the others joined in, always a chuckle or two behind. "Fetch it, then!" he shouted, and the stick took flight again, Strudel running awkwardly after it, arms straight and still by his side, his knees lifted slightly too high, his head held straight and stiff.

"Isn't it a bit wet for games?" Sepp said.

"Water never killed anyone," Wolf said.

Sepp didn't bother to correct him. Strudel was running back already, feet splashing flatly on the saturated dirt. He gave Wolf the stick.

"C'mon Strudel," Sepp said. "Let's go."

"But I've not finished with the dog?" Wolf said.

"Yeah, he can't go until he begs!" one of the other boys said, a short kid with the blue winter uniform tunic of the HJ showing behind the flaps of his coat, and dirty freckles on his face.

"He's not a dog," Sepp said.

"He's worse than that," Wolf said, grinning.

"Let's go, Strudel," Sepp repeated. But Wolf grabbed him by the arm and held on tight, Strudel's big eyes now bulging with new fear.

"But the hound has not learnt its lesson yet, *lad*." Wolf tugged Strudel to one side, then dragged him towards the black pool of water, stopping next to a pile of pale dog shit that looked as natural in this environment as a buttercup in a meadow. "Animals should know not to shit in this clean Germany," he said. Then he took a fistful of Strudel's thin, wet hair and forced his head close to the ground, so that he was on his knees again, his face close to the shit.

"Leave him!" Sepp shouted, both anger and fear racing through his veins.

"Animals need to be trained, eh boys?"

Sepp knew there was nothing he could do. Sepp knew he had tried his best. Sepp knew he had to go. Sepp knew. But the rage was boiling up inside him and he felt the dig of his fingernails in the soft flesh of the palms of his hands. He made to move away, as he knew he must, but he trod in a puddle and the muddy water spilt into his shoe.

Wolf pressed Strudel's face close to the pile of shit. Strudel resisted and there was a quivering tension between his head and Wolf's large hand. Strudel's eyes swivelled in Sepp's direction, filled with liquid pleading. Wolf saw, and said: "So you think a good clean German will help you, doggy – do you?" The Nazi eyed Sepp with malicious interest; the others in the group followed his gaze.

"He's as German as you are!" Sepp shouted.

Wolf laughed, and the others with him. Then he pushed Strudel's face into the shit.

Strudel spluttered and spat, then rolled aside on the wet ground, Wolf letting him go as he retched and choked. None of them laughed now. But Wolf stared at Strudel, a look of disgust painted across his face.

Before he had time to think Sepp was rushing the few metres to the scene. He pushed some of the other Nazis aside. There was shock on some of those young faces now, but not all of them. "Leave him alone!" Sepp shrieked, his high pitched scream sounding slightly ridiculous even to him.

"Oh, a dog lover, I see," Wolf said.

Sepp reached down for Strudel, who had curled himself into a tight ball, crouching beside him: "Come on Strudel, let's get you away from here," he whispered. But he could not move him.

"A dog needs discipline, persuasion …" Wolf started, and with that he aimed a swift and brutal kick at Strudel's rounded back, the hit of it hollow and horrible, and followed by a sharp gasp from the victim. Wolf glanced at Sepp, waiting for a response, a smile splitting his ruddy face.

It was too much.

Sepp's fist did the talking, without orders, without reason. Its peculiar, uncontrollable and unreasonable force pulled him from the ground and spun him to face the Nazi, so that he could watch as it connected with that square jaw, knocking back the head so that beads of water flew off Wolf's hair like silvery grapeshot. He felt the pain in his hand as the knuckles jarred against the hard bone of the jaw, and then he waited for the Nazi to drop. Waited long stretched seconds in a slowed down world. Waited to see that big, wet head drop to the sodden ground beneath him … But instead there was the empty smile, the dilation of black pupils into deep dark wells of hate … And the fist that seemed to spring from the chest of the Nazi like some helmeted jack-in-the-box, meeting Sepp's face at the speed of a Type C Auto Union.

Three punches connected with the rapidity and force of a jackhammer, forcing Sepp back towards the edge of the black-water pool, each hit springing his head against the extreme stretch of his neck so that he felt the rain fall against his upturned face. His mouth suddenly flooded with the metallic taste of blood. His cap flew clear. Dirty water splashed against his lower leg. He wondered what the racing manager at the works would think … He dipped his head to the right and ducked the next punch, letting it fly past his left ear and feeling the wind of its passage. The tall Nazi punched through and was stumbling forward with the momentum, passing on Sepp's left. Sepp clutched at Wolf's shoulder epaulette and pulled him on, at the same time sticking his left leg out. Wolf tripped over it, falling flat on the filthy ground, raising a great splash of brown liquid – and squashing the pile of dog shit beneath his sodden shirt.

The stink of the crushed shit filled the air. All eyes were on the prone figure, all expressions frozen in shock. Then they turned to Sepp, flexing fists, shrugging off coats to show the blue winter HJ tunics and the white-striped red swastika armbands.

"Leave him," a growl from the floor, then with surprising speed Wolf was up and pacing towards Sepp, who took a boxing stance he recalled from a newsreel of Max Schmeling, crouched forward with his fists close to his face. The tall Nazi came on, not raising his fists, staring into Sepp's eyes. Sepp met him with three quick jabs, straight on the chin, but it was like punching a bag of bolts and he found he was retreating towards the edge of the oily pool. Then he found that his heels were suddenly slipping in the loose mud at its edge, his arms flailing at the rain-laced sky, his trouser leg catching the ragged sawn-off edge of an old rusting barrel. When Wolf finally returned his punch Sepp was already falling backwards …

*

"I thought I could smell coffee."

"Hello Kurt," Hanna said, as his heavy boots clumped down the steep stairs. She poured him a cup without asking if he wanted one, Kurt always wanted coffee. It smelt good, almost covering the always-damp mustiness of the basement kitchen and the lingering aroma of the potato cakes, the remainder of which she'd wrapped in paper for a cold supper. She looked at the clock, there was still some time before she needed to get back to Herr Ostermann's shop.

"Cake too?"

She handed him a slice on a small plate and old Kurt was silent for a second or two as the cake was expertly dealt with. She put a fresh pot of coffee on the stove to brew. Old Kurt was not so old really, early fifties at most, a widower with a simpleton of a son whose birth had killed his wife. And a friend, too. Kurt looked out for them as much as Sepp and Hanna looked out for his son, Strudel. She felt a shiver of guilt at that thought, but she knew Kurt would understand, he was always the pragmatist when it came to such things. His hair was thin and steel grey, he had long given up trying to comb over the monastic bald patch, and his face was dominated by the nose of a drunken boxer – though he was neither a boxer nor a drunk. He had polished chestnut eyes, just like his son's, yet in his much larger and rounder face they did not look so big, and they were overhung by bushy grey eyebrows which reached to connect across the top of his nose, but did not quite make it. He might have been handsome once, but Hanna had never seen a picture of him when he was younger, and Kurt never spoke of the past.

"He's done well, I knew he would," Kurt said, a dandruff smudge of icing sugar at the corner of his mouth.

"He's not got the job yet, Kurt."

"No?" He raised his wire wool eyebrows.

Hanna shook her head and smiled, then changed the subject even before it was raised: "Is Strudel well?"

"Who can tell, he says nothing. If you could get inside his head you would find nothing but cogs."

"And appetite."

"Well, that he gets from me," Kurt said, letting his gaze drift to the last slice of cake. Hanna handed it to him without a word, and he ate it quickly. While he munched she thought of Sepp and how he would do. It was unusual for the team to take on one of the apprentices, Konrad had told her, but Sepp had already proved his worth at the works he had said, adding that his own word still stood for something with the team. She had felt awkward about that, but then they deserved some luck – and the chance for some of the nicer things in life – and whatever anyone said she had offered the racing driver nothing but friendship; although she sensed that was all about to change, and that she would be able to do very little about it. Of course, Sepp would not thank her if he knew, because he was stubbornly proud. But even if he had had a helping hand, she knew he deserved it. He had worked so hard for this; putting aside his views – their views – to race the motorcycles of the Hitler Youth, working longer hours than all the other apprentices at the Horch Works, studying the Auto Union racer until its image had to be imprinted on his brain. Yes, Sepp deserved it.

"But I worry about Strudel, that's true," Kurt said, his eyes now on the scattering of crumbs on the plate. She had asked Kurt once why his son was called Strudel, what his real name was, but Kurt had merely shrugged and said nothing in reply. "It is not enough to be harmless these days," he now murmured.

"He's lucky, he has friends," she said, feeling the breath of that little ghost of guilt again. But Konrad had warned her, there would be Party men at the Works today. It would not do Sepp's cause any good to be seen with the *idiot*.

"Jacob Levy had friends, many friends once," Kurt said. "But now he's in Osterstein. They say it's full again, it makes you wonder where they're finding all these criminals, eh?"

Hanna nodded, the castle had been the city prison for years, Rosa Luxembourg had once been held there, but it had never been as busy as it was right now.

"And I hear you have a *friend*, too?" Kurt said, in a tone that might have been accompanied with a wink.

"I know you have been a father and a mother to Strudel, Kurt, but are you really such an old housewife?"

"Gossip is cheaper than cake," he said with a grin. "But tell me, is it love?"

She felt herself reddening, a treacherous blush. "I do not know what love is," she said, forcing a smile.

"Oh, you know alright – more than anyone."

"More coffee, Kurt?" He smiled. On the street above car tyres hissed along the sodden road, a horn was answered by the ring-a-ding of a tram and shoe leather beat a tattoo against the wet pavement – someone in a hurry. She took the pot from the stove, using a cloth to protect her hands from the hot handle of the old coffee pot with its Norwegian coastline of chipped green paint around the lid. The front door slammed, shaking the window, and she wondered who it could be. A second or two later the door at the top of the stairs banged open and there was an avalanche of footsteps on the stairs.

Then the monster from the swamp was in the kitchen.

His coat was open and the old pocket watch dangled free on its chain. A long smear of fresh wet and black mud covered the left flap of the coat. His collar was flecked with a starburst of dirt, and his left trouser leg was torn up to the knee. His hair was matted with mud – looking like a bird's nest fallen from a tree – and there was the sign of swelling at his cheeks and above his right eye. One tiny bead of blood was bulging out of the corner of his mouth, and a pink smear across his jaw showed where earlier bleeding had been rubbed away. He was soaking wet. He smelt like a chemical works. And there were tears in his eyes.

"What ...?"

"I —"

"No – you fool, you silly little fool – I don't want to hear!" She looked at the clock, still some time. Sepp glanced at Kurt, whose mouth was wide open as if ready for more cake.

"But —"

"Quiet – I'm thinking!" she snapped.

His shoulders were hunched and she could see that her man of the morning had the beaten look of a boy. She melted for him. And then she took charge. "Take off your coat, wash off the mud – and take off the trousers, too." Sepp looked dazed, fish-mouthing and turning his head to the clock on the wall. "Now!" she shouted, rushing to the old dresser with its drawers of memories, Mama's things. "Clean your face with this," thrusting a wad of cotton wool into his hand, "and get that mud out of your hair." She turned the taps on full, the silver columns of water beating loudly against the base of the sink, and he did as he was ordered.

"My trousers, there was a rusty barrel, I —"

"*Shhhh!*"

She turned her attention to Kurt, knowing that Sepp's other pair of trousers would not match his jacket. "Kurt, take off your trousers," she snapped, watching as the shock morphed directly into panic on his face. "Now!" Kurt acted as if there was a gun to his head, standing up and slipping his braces off his shoulders and unbuttoning the fly before letting the trousers drop around his ankles to reveal long underwear as yellow as ancient parchment. Hanna snatched the trousers from him, spilling pfennigs from the pocket. They were close enough in colour, even if they might have benefited from a wash.

She helped Sepp to clean himself up, dabbed at his wounds with the cotton wool, then told him to put Kurt's trousers on. They were a little too long. But Hanna was able to pin them up, was able to comb Sepp's hair into something close to respectable, was able to scrape the last of the gritty black mud off the overcoat, was able to dab the tears from his eyes, was able to clean his shoes ... Was able to persuade him there was still time ... *But hurry Sepp.*

"We'll take my bicycle," she said. "There's no time to wait for a tram – you can hang on to me."

"But —"

"C'mon Sepp, look at the time!"

Sepp sat on the saddle and clung to her waist, he might have been quicker alone, but she would not risk another incident. In the rush she realised she had forgotten her coat and she was cold. She turned the bike off Nord Strasse, cutting the corner, feeling the tyres buck and slither against the wet cobbles and hearing the scrape of Sepp's shoe leather as he tried to steady the bicycle. She just about registered the big black and cream car as it swerved to avoid them, and she answered its blaring horn with a cathartic "Idiot!" before standing tall on the pedals and riding into the slanting rain, Sepp still clinging tight to her waist.

*

West drove the Lagonda along the greasy cobbles in what he hoped was the direction of the Horch factory, looking out for signposts as he went. The bicycle came from nowhere, cutting across the long nose of the car so that West had to haul the big wheel left to avoid it, stabbing at the brake and snatching a front wheel into a skid as he did so. He hit the horn as the tottering bicycle passed by the front-right wing of the car with inches to spare. The girl shouted something and the lad on the saddle leant back and mouthed an apology that would certainly have been accompanied with a shrug – had he not been clinging for dear life to the shapely figure in front of him.

"Lunacy!" Gracie shouted.

"But you'd have to admit, she wears it well," West said, with a grin.

A little later, and after asking for directions, they arrived at their destination. The Auto Union race shop was in the Horch Works, Horch being one of the companies that made up the Auto Union brand, one of the interlocking rings in the emblem along with DKW, Wanderer and Audi. It had been formed to take a share of the money the Nazis had put up to fund a German racing team, and to stop Mercedes from having all the fun. This was largely thanks to the Auto Union designer Ferdinand Porsche, who – some said – had personally persuaded the Führer that two German teams competing against each other would make winning all the more interesting. West parked the Lagonda in front of a flat white building with a gently curving roof, and next to a low, raked two-seater Horch coupe with wire wheels and a long bonnet, huge flowing fenders and big bug-eyed lights.

In front of the gates there was sodden open ground scarred with the criss-cross stitches of a railway line, while beyond this a giant gasometer dominated the skyline. The works itself seemed a bit of a jumble of styles, the buildings having sprung up by the decade to keep pace with the relentless development of the motor car. Rows of long sheds with curved roofs, or glass-panelled saw-teeth, were clustered about a grand five-storey white house with a tiled mansard roof that drooped down to form the cladding for the fifth level. Behind this building, and overlapping it in height by some way, was the main works; glass, and concrete, all square and modern save for the little classical flourish of a pediment top and centre of the building, bearing the words: *Werk Horch, Auto Union A-G.* Lights glowed dimly through the glass, giving it the look of a vast lantern, while every so often the flash of a welding torch from within would brightly pulse the grey afternoon. There was a familiar smell, like industry the world over, but also reminiscent of a burnt out clutch.

A young clerk with an umbrella collected them, shyly hesitating in offering West his handshake before leading him through the first white building – where there were secretaries and giggles – and into a partly covered yard beyond. They passed a group of workers finishing their lunch break on the ledge of a loading bay, where the rain hammered against the corrugated iron shelter like volleys of rifle fire. A youngster was pushing a broom around the bay beneath the shelter. He did not wear overalls, like the others, but a thin and faded red sweater and brown trousers with dark knees that appeared to be scabbed with wet mud. He moved stiffly, but the concentration on his rodent-like face was total, his big brown eyes bulging and bright against his alabaster pale skin.

Just then another worker, in buff-coloured overalls with the interlocking rings of Auto Union above the breast pocket, appeared from what West assumed was a workshop – he could just about make out the xylophone din of metal workers beating steel above the hammer of the rain. The worker's red hair poked out from beneath a mustard-coloured flat cap and his overall sleeves were rolled up over heavily muscled arms. He was carrying a huge pair of matt black and silver industrial scissors. He worked the blades, pointing them at the lad with the brush, and shouted: "Snip-snip … snip-snip." The rat-faced youngster suddenly froze, as if all the life within him had fled straight to his big brown eyes, now swollen in fear. The other men laughed, most of them. As West, Gracie and the clerk walked past the men, West heard his name whispered, and the ginger-haired worker in the Auto Union overalls and the cap nodded in his direction, still with a grin of pure sin stitched to his face. He put down the scissors, and the boy began to brush again.

The clerk led on, up some steps adjacent to the loading bay and down a wide tiled corridor which soon passed a door with a sign that West translated as *Race Team.*

"Hold on," Gracie said, "is there a chance we might take a quick look?"

"Why not?" West said.

"Later, I think. Now we must —" the clerk started.

"It will only take a moment or two, nothing more," Gracie said, pushing open the swing door. West followed him into the room, always keen to see racing cars, especially these racing cars.

"But they are waiting, and you are late already Herr Holt ..." the clerk said, panic prising his eyes wide.

The long room was white and almost surgically clean, an aspect accentuated by the harsh lighting and the gleaming tiled floor. It was certainly a far cry from the mews garage in Knightsbridge where West had kept the P3, and the ERA before it. The clerk hurried off, to get help West supposed. The rain hammered against the skylights but there was no other sound in this long room, and nobody else about, just the cars, shining dazzlingly silver in the glare of the overhead illumination. "Silver Arrows," West said, almost whispering it.

"More like bullets," Gracie said, matter-of-factly.

They were both these things, but mostly speed. Rosemeyer had won just about everything this last year in one of these, and West knew that if he was to win a grand prix then this car, or the Mercedes, was the only thing to have. The Auto Unions were arranged in a long angled line, like a half fishbone, eight of them in all, each the silver of naked and polished aluminium.

"But just the eight pieces of silver, friend Westbury? Surely it should be thirty?" Gracie joked. West just shook his head and concentrated on the cars. Most of them were without their wheels and sat on stands, some without their engine covers. But one sat low on its tyres, as if ready to go. Its nose was pointing towards them, round and muscular with a plectrum-shape grille, little lugs of mirrors either side of a small glass screen in front of a peeping segment of steering wheel, and then the crest of four interlocking rings above the radiator. West's heart beat a little faster just to look at this car.

He walked slowly around the car and studied it like a connoisseur sniffing round a Rodin, taking in every inch of gleam, from tail to nose. Yes, first from the rear, for this was where its creator Professor Porsche's touch was most evident. The louvre-slatted engine cover sloped back and down to a beautiful sculptured tail, almost as if this were the front of any other car – but then in any other car the front would be where you would find the engine. Horse before the cart, of course, but Porsche hadn't seen it this way, placing the huge six-litre, 520bhp V16 behind the driver, so that the portion of the car to the rear of the cockpit was twice that in front – he was not the first to do it, but he was the first to get it right. A long muscular spine grew out of the engine cover. It was rounded across its span, and straight like the root of a fossilised tusk embedded in silver, cut off where the cockpit started and crowned with a gleaming petrol cap, just above the point where it became the driver's headrest. The car sat on tall chromium wire wheels, reaching up to mid-thigh, and intricately patterned Continental tyres gleamed an un-scrubbed gloss black. The ceiling lights cast West's image across the aluminium bodywork, bending it like a trick mirror at a fairground. There was no number on this car, just clean, efficient metalwork – and a small four-by-four swastika flag just below the line of the deeply scalloped cockpit opening.

West suddenly realised that Gracie had wandered off a little and was now lost in the study of an engine that was perched on a stand, a huge dark block sprouting shining pipes, reminding West of an organ in a cathedral. Gracie considered it from behind his little round glasses, smoothing back great wedges of fringe for a better view and fiddling with the buttons on his leather-patched-at-the-elbow tweed jacket. He had never known Gracie to show an interest in things mechanical before, but then again that engine was a work of art.

"We have been waiting for you Herr Holt." The suddenness of it took West by surprise, but Kessler had spoken softly enough as he entered. He now held the door open for another, a man on crutches who was being helped by the clerk. West instantly recognised him as Konrad von Plaidt. "Never mind, we shall do the photographs first," Kessler said, nodding to the clerk who once again disappeared at great speed, and then looking West up and down, shaking his head in reproach of West's chosen outfit for the day he signed for Auto Union, which was pretty much his chosen outfit for any day. West smiled, and concentrated on the other man, secretly a little pleased that he had annoyed Kessler.

"We don't normally allow people to wander around in here alone, you know," Konrad von Plaidt said, smiling, "but I suppose you are part of the family now." He wore a precisely cut double breasted pinstripe and glossed black shoes, which made for a sharp contrast with West's habitual flannels, open-necked shirt, scuffed brogues and tatty old cricket sweater with the double pale-blue V of Cambridge at the neck. The German supported himself on two leather-padded wooden crutches and West felt a stab of guilt as he remembered that it was his oil that caused the damage, a stab that was twisted when the German put weight on his leg, and pain on his face.

West had seen this one before, in races and in pictures, and in the agony of the worst crash in a long and illustrious career, the crash that had given West his chance. But this was the first time he had met the famous Konrad von Plaidt face to face. "It's good to meet you at last Mr Holt," Plaidt said.

"Might I say the pleasure is all mine," West could not help but glance at the crutches as he said it, and Plaidt seemed to notice.

"Please! It's racing, not your fault – and forgotten." Plaidt chuckled, revealing perfect polished teeth and a smile that was replicated in the lines bracketing his eyes and mouth. His tan was deep, almost Mediterranean, and his hair shone with brilliantine, while his eyes were a smoky chestnut colour. His looks might have been described as matinee idol, but for a slightly weak chin, now blurred with a little fat – a result of his enforced inactivity since the crash, West guessed. He was thirty-eight, more than fifteen years older than West, with an Iron Cross won flying in the Great War, a host of top class victories in the 1920s, and a reputation for effective tactical driving that had helped gain him his place at Auto Union. His voice, in German, was warm and lilting – a light discussion over a glass of brandy with fine cigars in leather armchairs. West could follow it, as he'd been cramming at a small language school in Penge since the summer, and had enjoyed Gracie's surprise when he started to chat up a pretty fräulein in the Kranzler coffee house in Berlin the night before, but Plaidt chose to switch to English anyway.

"I have been looking forward to meeting you Mr Holt."

"West, please."

"*Ja...ja,* Konrad, too," Plaidt said, his face lighting up in a smile once more. "I saw you drive your ERA at Bremgarten, very impressive."

"You do me an honour, Konrad."

"No, the clock does West, that's all that honours us ... Or cheats us." Konrad's eyes drifted from West's, across to where Gracie was now peeking beneath a white car cover. The cover was elasticated at its edges and strained tight to the purest form West had ever laid eyes on, a hard femininity of curves at each corner of the smoothest of bodies. "Please, that is not for your eyes," Kessler snapped, as the clerk led a gaggle of photographers and a couple of notepad clutching journalists into the workshop. Gracie snapped the edge of the cover back over a peep of a spat-covered wheel, while Kessler began to organise the photographers, explaining how he wanted the swastika on the Auto Union to be clear in the background. Kessler was not officially a part of the team, West remembered, he was a Party man, but for this sort of thing he seemed important, and West thought it best not to antagonise him. Well, not too much ...

"Your friend?" Konrad lifted a wispy eyebrow as Gracie shuffled towards them.

"Konrad, Gracie – Gracie, Konrad." he nodded at both and they shook hands energetically. "He's just along for the ride, to keep me company," West explained.

"Gracie?"

"I know, a girl's name – friend Westbury's idea of a joke I'm afraid," Gracie said, "and I'm sure he has every idea of just how much bother it causes me," they laughed. "Real name's Grace, Phillip Grace. But tell me, what is that?" He pointed to the car beneath the cover.

"A streamliner, it's one of our record cars. But it should not interest you, or Mr Holt come to that. We save these for the senior drivers." His eyes were on West again, and there was a curious cock to his head as he leant heavily on his crutches. Then a shadow seemed to cross the older man's eyes, as if he was suddenly so very tired. West itched to have a good look at the streamliner, but sensed it would be pushing it, bad form for the new boy on his first day.

"Is it for Rosemeyer, then?" West said.

"Yes," Konrad said. "And for me, of course – when I am fit."

"Of course."

"And you are a racer, too – or enthusiast?" Konrad had turned his attention to Gracie again, while West studied the flowing lines beneath the cover.

"Neither really."

"Oh, you seem interested in the cars, I thought —"

"A philosopher, our Gracie's a philosopher," West interrupted, "but he's far too modest to say so."

"Sadly not, still just a student."

"So what brings you to Germany, Mr Grace?"

"My doctorate: *Plato's Republic and the Modern Fascist States*."

"Sounds interesting."

"Sounds a bloody bore," West put in.

"Boring to you West, but not to others. Come on, even you noticed how many Nazi flags we saw on the way here; it's everywhere, like a ..." He decided against finishing that, said instead: "Look, even this car bears the swastika." The three of them looked at the gleaming Auto Union.

"Ah yes, this one is just a show car, for pictures. We have to thank them for our racing when we can, they are generous people, and they pay for much of this – an open secret, of course."

"They are not so generous to all, Herr Plaidt," Gracie said.

"Perhaps, but that is not our concern, racing is our concern. Isn't that so West?" West simply nodded. "Besides, if it wasn't for them, what would we do? We don't all have the luxury of a rich father."

West smiled a thin smile. "You seem to know a lot about me, Konrad."

"Well, I've had plenty of time to catch up on my reading just lately."

"Those clothes will not do Herr Holt," Kessler snapped, tossing West some gleaming white overalls, and while he pulled them on over his flannels, choosing to ignore the NSKK badge at the breast, he listened in as Konrad spoke to Kessler.

"The boy, Sepp; how did he do?"

"Well enough, but Feuereissen and Fink have bees in their bonnets about the whole thing, they say he's too young, but he's a fine looking lad, and he has the right attitude. Whether he will make a good race mechanic, we will have to wait and see."

"He will," Konrad said.

"As I said, time will tell. Herr Holt, are you presentable now?"

West spent the next fifteen minutes blinking to the magnesium flashes as the photographers took their pictures of him in car; sat on wheel; shaking hands with Konrad; stood by car; grinning and leaning on car ... When the pictures were taken there was one thing left to do. Sign the contract.

West peeled off the overalls, put his cricket jumper back on, and tossed the keys for the Lagonda to Gracie, telling him to take a look around the town, giving him no chance to argue – there was work to be done, and no room for political discussions, no room for the fog of other things, no room for those small doubts Gracie had planted in his head on the drive down from Berlin. *Sport Gracie, nothing more.* West left it unsaid this time, and his friend just shrugged and left them to it, while Konrad advised him that the Marienkirche was possibly worth a visit.

*

West followed Kessler and Konrad out of the workshop and through a series of corridors, then up a grand wooden staircase. Konrad made heavy weather of the climb, clinging to the polished walnut banister rail and leaning on Kessler's shoulder while West carried his crutches. They arrived at the anteroom to an office where a stern old secretary glanced at West's flannels and cricket jumper as if they were the uniform of a convict. The room was wood-panelled to the picture rail, varnished dark so that the single bulb shone in a gleaming bronze band against it, while the remaining unpanelled section of wall and the ceiling was matt-white. The secretary returned to her work, peering over a large ledger, counting off lines with the point of her pencil. A big black typewriter sat to one side of the desk, a flourish of white paper curled through its rollers. The window was large, sequinned with raindrops, although through it West could see that the rain had now eased just a little, and the sun was peeping through a fissure in the grey.

Kessler asked the secretary if there was coffee and then showed West through to the team manager's office, again wood-panelled to the picture rail, with an oak desk in one corner at an angle to the big window. A leather briefcase hung from a hat stand by its carry-handle, along with a smart new hat with a sleek silk band, and an umbrella. A picture was fixed to each wood panel along the far wall, framed photographs at eye-level: Horch cars old and new, Auto Union racers, a high ranking Nazi taking delivery of an 850. In the opposite corner to the desk, just through the door, there was a bench following the right-angle of the wall, a small lacquered wood conference table, with room for four, in front of it.

They were joined by others, a solicitor and the team manager, Dr Karl Feuereissen: polite, sleeves rolled up, always looking at his watch. The signing was over before West fully realised what had happened and after the handshakes and more photographs – this time with West wearing a borrowed jacket and tie – Feuereissen asked West to leave his contact details, apologised that he was busy in the drawing office, and then left with Kessler and the solicitor. West made to follow, but Konrad said: "Wait a while, I thought we might have a cigar." Konrad took the polished wooden box off the desk.

"If you don't mind?" West said, taking his briar pipe from one trouser pocket, and his pouch of *Player's No Name* tobacco from the other. Konrad nodded and West proceeded to pack the Dunhill. Konrad showed him to the table and he slid in between it and the bench. It was a tight squeeze for his large frame and he instantly felt uncomfortable. Konrad clipped the end off a cigar, lighting it with a desktop lighter.

"It makes sense to smoke when Kessler's not around, there's a tip for you; he's the sort that takes after the Führer in as many ways as he possibly can," Konrad said, the tone was mocking, and it came with a lazy roll of the eyes.

"I'll bear that in mind," West said, then after a slight pause he added: "I take it Kessler's not a close friend of yours?"

"He's a necessary friend."

West sucked at his unlit pipe, checking that he'd packed it well, not too tight, and then he lit the tobacco with the heavy lighter on the table, puffing slowly to draw the flame on to the mix. About twenty seconds later he repeated the process, tamping then relighting the scorched fluffed up surface of the tobacco, and then drawing the flavour into his mouth, before puffing it out. For the long seconds this took there was silence in the room, except for the rattle-rattle-ding of the typewriter next door, but West guessed it was for more than a quiet smoke that Konrad had kept him here. The rich and woody tobacco aroma filled the office, cutting through the sweeter smell of the cigar, the smoke flooding the little space between them. He saw Konrad's nostrils twitch to the smell of his pipe. Outside there was the sharp blast of a hooter.

"I wonder, West, if I might speak frankly with you?"

"It's the way I like it.

"Good. You see, I want to make certain you understand exactly what is expected of you, not what Kessler says, but what I ... What the *team* expects." Konrad said, his eyes locked on West's. "You are here while I recover, a junior driver, nothing more. That means you do as you're told. That means at times you will not enjoy the best equipment. That means that at other times you will be asked to give up your car, for Rosemeyer, or later

– if you're still with us – for me, perhaps. But you know this, of course?" West nodded, it was what was in the contract, more or less. "There will be a few races at the beginning of '37 at least, and then you will act as reserve driver for the remainder of the year."

"And if I do well, if I'm quick?"

"That's not for me to say."

"But you must have an idea?"

"How quick?" Konrad said, with a slight smile.

"Oh, let's say – *exceptionally*," West also smiled as he said it.

"Exceptionally quick?" Konrad laughed. "That would mean beating Rosemeyer. But if it happened, well ..." He looked deep into West's eyes for a moment or two, as if trying to see into his soul. He shook his head, and then he said: "You know, I saw you watching me, on the stairs. But you need not worry, there is plenty of time before I am ready to get back into a racing car."

"I —"

"There's no need to deny it, we're both racers."

West nodded a single nod, then said: "I wanted to know; why did it take so long for them to call me?"

Konrad shrugged: "This is a German team, backed by the German Government. It's not a simple step to put a foreigner in an Auto Union, my friend. Necessary, perhaps, because there are not so very many German drivers who are skilled enough to drive a Type C well, but not simple."

"It shouldn't matter where a driver's from, if he's quick," West said.

"Perhaps you're right. But it does matter. The problem for the Nazis is that it is only now that many Germans are buying cars. We lack experienced drivers. And let's face it, some of these Hitler Youth motorcyclists are only interested in speeding towards martyrdom, and there is no room for that in grand prix racing."

"Master racers," West quipped with a grin.

"You would do well not to make light of the Party, West, these people are short on sense of humour. You should remember that, especially in front of Kessler." Konrad replied, suddenly serious. "And you should also know that there is little that happens in racing without the Party's stamp. That was why there was a delay, the decision to sign the illustrious Westbury Holt had to be taken at a much higher level than the Auto Union head office." West let the smoke from the pipe drift between them, through its lacy whorls he studied Konrad.

"How high?" he asked.

"How high can you think?"

West shrugged.

"Adolf," Konrad said.

"Hühnlein?" West said, referring to the head of the NSKK.

"Hitler."

West just looked at him, shaking his head slowly.

"It's true," Konrad protested. "The Führer takes a great interest in his racing cars and the men who drive them. You must remember, without Hitler there would be none of this success for Auto Union or Mercedes. Almost four years ago he decided that Germany should have a motor industry it could be proud of, and he saw that the best way to advertise it would be on the race track. So, you see, he has a stake in all this. But it's quite ironic, as it's *because* he has allowed Auto Union to race Mercedes, and *because* both need the fastest drivers to beat the other, that they sometimes have to look outside Germany."

"Then I suppose I should buy the man a drink sometime," West said.

"Just take my advice West, try to work with them, and try not to mock them. Oh, and perhaps you should think about getting a German car for the road, too," Konrad suggested, "it would look good, you know. What about a Horch?"

"I like the one by the gate, the ivory and black 853." Konrad smiled and knocked some hot ash into the ashtray. "Yours?" Konrad nodded.

"I've been unable to drive it for some time now, of course. It's just here for some modifications," Konrad said.

West was glad of the excuse to wriggle out of the confined space between table and bench – he hated feeling trapped more than anything in the world. He walked over to the window to take another look at Konrad's Horch. He looked beyond the yard to the space where the sleek coupe was parked, and then his gaze drifted to the factory gate. The girl was bent over the bike in the rain, her tied-back hair soaking wet and shining, her clothes sodden. At first he thought she was crying, but then he realised it was anger – and never had anger looked so absolutely, perfectly exquisite. "Beautiful," he whispered.

"Yes, wonderful lines, and she handles like a dream."

"I bet she does," West muttered, as Konrad joined him by the window.

"Oh, you mean ..." a slow grin spread across Konrad's face: "Mine too I'm afraid ... *old chap*." He put a particular emphasis on the last then smiled a broad smile. "And it is the sweetest thing in all of Germany, believe me."

She was stood up straight now, but still staring at the bicycle, hands on her hips, the swell of her breasts clear through the sodden cloth of bodice and blouse.

"You know, she's dangerous on that thing – almost caused me to stuff the Lagonda," West said.

"Doesn't sound like her, doesn't sound like Hanna at all," Konrad said, his smile wrinkling a little. "But come, I will introduce you and you can give her a piece of your mind."

"I think she would prefer help with the bicycle, old boy."

"Of course, you English, forever chivalrous. Bring that umbrella, before the poor thing catches her death of cold." West followed him out of the office then down the stairs, Konrad waving away any help, and West noticed he coped with them much better this time. They walked out into the rain and then on to the gate, the rubber feet on Konrad's crutches squeaking as they squished the cobbles. West did not open the umbrella, as Konrad had a hat, and he was not really the sort to overly worry about a bit of rain.

"Oh a shame, we are too late – she already has a champion," Konrad said, as they approached the girl.

West saw the rat-faced youngster he had noticed sweeping the loading bay earlier now tinkering with the chain of the bike, an oilskin roll of tools at his feet, concentration of the chess master at his face. "And who is this Sir Galahad?" West asked.

"Just an idiot," Konrad said. "He helps out here, sometimes. They say he is good with machines, and perhaps that's so, but he's not much use for anything else. They used to let him do some real work, but things like that aren't allowed now, Kessler has his nose everywhere. The lads treat him like a mascot, but he was told not to come here today." West thought he detected a note of irritation in Konrad's voice.

"They were teasing him, with scissors?" West said.

Konrad thought on that for a moment, and then smiled, as if suddenly getting the joke. "Ah yes, his is a worthless life, they say. And it is important that the German race is pure – that is where we get beauty like that after all," he said, nodding in Hanna's direction. "They will not let him have a family, the doctors will see to that, and the lads can tease, like lads will."

"You mean they're going to chop his old boy off?" West was suddenly horrified.

"Nothing so barbarous – that's saved for English racing drivers who stain the honour of good German girls my friend." They were close enough to the girl and the boy to be heard and Konrad dropped his voice a little. "It's just an operation as far as I know – proper doctors. It is the same in other countries; Sweden, America even ... Ah, my dear, are we having a little trouble?" There was concern in Konrad's voice, but there was censure in his eyes too, West realised. The simpleton made no sign that he had noticed their arrival, fully concentrating on fixing the bicycle chain.

The girl lifted her head and then West could see that she was just as beautiful close up as she was from afar. It was a natural beauty, the sort of beauty that's emphasised by wet hair, heightened by emotion. A raindrop traced the smooth curve of her cheekbone like a soft caress, until she dashed it from her face with the flick of an elegant finger. There was no make-up on her skin, just the rose-pink stain of exertion, anger, or embarrassment, he was not sure which. Her stance was suddenly different now, less defiant, and he thought the arrival of Konrad might have something to do with that. Konrad draped his coat around her shoulders and she reddened a little more at the cheeks, then he took the umbrella off West, opened it, and held it over her head.

Right then she looked directly at West, and in her brief gaze, for a mere moment, he thought he saw the *real* girl: a spark in the cobalt blue that seemed as vivid as lightning reflected in the iris, and a movement of the tiniest fraction of an inch at the corners of her eyes. But with this her whole personality changed for an instant of time, and there in front of him was not some simple, homely, sodden German girl, but an untamed intensity, a leopard lust for life.

*

The chain had snapped just as they had reached the gate. Sepp said he would come and fix it as soon as he was done, but he had been longer than she had expected, and now she realised he might be back at his work. She did not have money for the tram, her purse still on the table in the basement kitchen, left there in the rush. So she had thought she would have to walk back, pushing the bike all the way. She was already very late, and Herr Ostermann would not be amused, even less so when she turned up soaking wet. She realised she would have to go home and change first, and then make up some excuse. She might even have to flirt with him, she had thought with a shudder.

And then along came Strudel. Of course, he said nothing about what had happened to Sepp earlier and his part in it, she wondered if he even remembered, but from somewhere he found some tools – which took time enough – and then started to fix the chain. Strudel was always at the Horch Works, doing what he could to help out because he loved machines. But Sepp had told her the Nazis on the payroll were trying to get rid of him; it was typical of those bully-boys. But she knew Sepp could do nothing about that without causing trouble, and she hoped he had learnt his lesson now, too. To thrive in this world they both knew they had to live with what Germany had become, although she hated it and them, and particularly Herr Ostermann, who demanded she dressed like it was the eighteenth century because of something he had read in *Mein Kampf*. It was not really a problem in the shop, but here and now, with Konrad, and this other …

Hanna pulled Konrad's coat tighter to her – to warm her, to hide the dirndl – and slyly studied the tall, broad figure with the wet mop of thick, unruly hair and the ruddy face from under the umbrella that Konrad now held above her head, which crackled to the fall of the raindrops upon it. He had the height and the build of a man, and no doubt he was older than she was, yet he seemed all schoolboy to her – all big-eyed with something or other, some boyish excitement.

"Westbury Holt," Konrad had said, introducing him. She had felt her face begin to redden when Konrad had draped the coat around her, but she had made no effort to quench it, for she already knew that he liked it when she blushed. Yet now she felt he was being more familiar than he had ever been, and somehow this scruffy lad had something to do with it.

"Pleased to meet you," Westbury Holt said, and she forgave the clunky German on realising he was an Englishman. She forgave the scruffy clothes and the ridiculous pipe with its strange woody smelling tobacco, too. For in that happy, open smile, that large lit up face, there was so much sheer fun. And my God this one was handsome. "Can I help you with the bicycle?" he asked.

"No, my friend Strudel's doing a good job, Herr Holt."

"Westbury, please."

"A lift home then?" This time it was Konrad, cutting in, and she saw the young Englishman's shoulders sag just a little, almost as if he'd just witnessed a goal go against him in a football match. He didn't seem to notice the rain at all, and his old woollen jumper was already drenched, and hung heavy like ivory chain mail. She smiled at him and he cheered instantly.

"I need to get back to work," she said. "Herr Ostermann will be wondering where I've got to."

"Don't worry about Hans, I'll talk to him," Konrad said. "But just what *are* you doing here anyway?" She thought there was a trace of disapproval there, but she was not certain.

"It's Sepp, there was an accident and he was late for his interview, so —"

"Oh, how stupid of me, I forgot!" Konrad interrupted. "Sepp has been given a place on the race team."

"But that's wonderful news," Hanna said, instantly feeling both thrilled and relieved. Only she knew how much the job meant to Sepp, and how close he had come to messing up his chance. "Thank you," she added.

"No need to thank me," Konrad said, just as Strudel finished fixing the chain and stood up, wiping his oily hands on his dirty trousers.

"How can we ever repay you?" Hanna said. Konrad was about to say something, but then he seemed to change his mind. Instead he scrawled a note on an old envelope he'd taken from his pocket and gave it to Strudel. He told him to take it to the main office. Strudel set off in that strange jerking run of his, arms tight to his sides, feet splashing flatly in the puddles.

"So he has some uses after all," Konrad said.

"To be fair, he did fix the bicycle," Westbury Holt put in, glancing at Hanna as he said it, looking for a moment as if he might wink. A little later a car was brought out; a Horch tourer which smelt of polish and new leather and was possibly straight off the production line. Konrad joined Hanna in the back, a driver at the wheel because with his injuries he was still unable to drive. Konrad did not offer Westbury a lift, so she assumed he had his own car, and as the Horch drove away she looked back through the rain streaked rear window. Westbury Holt was still standing there, still watching, still getting ever wetter.

***

There was the soft crunch of another car on the fresh snow and Hanna dropped her hair brush on the work surface and sprang up on to the wooden stool to get a better view through the basement window, peering into the darkness of the December evening. Lick was looking up from one of the chairs at the kitchen table, his little glass of schnapps twinkling in the light from the single bulb, his ginger matted head cocked to one side as he pretended to try to get a sly peek up her skirt.

"Only looking!" He directed his apology at Sepp, still at the kitchen sink, trying to shave a beard that nobody else could see, braces drooping loose down over his trouser legs, a look of almost comical disapproval on that young face.

"Just drink your schnapps, Lick," Sepp said. Again Hanna noticed how much the new job on the race team had changed him: new friends, new confidence and new money – yes, very soon spending the winter days in the basement kitchen for the sake of warmth could be a thing of the past. And not just because of Sepp's pay packets either, as Konrad had already helped with some of the bills, and other things, like the *Volksempfänger* radio set in its gleaming Bakelite cabinet which now sat in the corner of the kitchen – because this was still the closest thing they had to a living room. Konrad had even said she should leave Ostermann's shop, there was no need to work, not now. Yet Hanna had stayed, because although she hated the work almost as much as she hated Ostermann, she was not sure if she was quite ready. Things were moving just a little too fast; and she did not feel quite in control. The car drove past, carving dark grooves in the settling snow.

Hanna jumped down from the stool and Lick winked at her. She was glad that the ginger-haired mechanic had taken Sepp under his wing, but he was an animal, and if he brought a puking Sepp home once more she had sworn to give him a good hiding.

"He's very protective of you, big sister," Lick said.

"Don't call me that," she said, as she stood before the half-length mirror she had hung against the pantry door, tugging at the pleated skirt of the blue floral-patterned dress to make the hem lie level. "I wish this would sit straight."

"Looks bloody fine to me," Lick said, helping himself to another splosh of the colourless liquid.

"And what would you know?"

"Enough to give you a better time than that old fart Konrad von-broken legs, I'd wager."

"Oh really?" She bent down low so that her nose was level with his, schnapps breath warm against her face. She looked deep into those honest, salt-of-the-earth eyes of his, held his confused gaze for some long seconds. Then she moved to kiss him, parting her mouth slightly. She waited for the flash of undisguised pleasure to light up his ruddy face, and then she drew away, tousling his ginger mop and laughing loudly.

"Bitch," Lick murmured. Sepp laughed, and then flicked a great dollop of shaving soap at his new friend, who then seemed to forget about the whole thing in two large gulps of schnapps. Hanna heard another car pull up outside and she sprang up on the stool once again. This time there was no mistake, she recognised it as the Horch tourer Konrad now used, its glossy black paintwork shining in the lemony streetlight. She jumped down from the stool, slipped stockinged feet into her shoes, shrugged her coat over her shoulders and was fixing her hat in place as she rushed up the stairs.

"Why rush," Lick said, "his lordship could always join us for schnapps?"

"Just you look after Sepp," she shouted back, "or you'll answer to me!" With that she slammed the door to the basement kitchen behind her, opening the front door to the apartment block just as Konrad's driver was about to ring the bell.

*

Lick wore a battered brown homburg he'd found on the tram, because he liked to wear hats – especially indoors, and especially if the hat did not really belong to him. He was knocking the beers back like there was no tomorrow and Sepp, and even some of the others, were having difficulty keeping up. The Auto Union boys had a corner of the bar at the Dresdnerstrasse Inn to themselves, at a long oak table polished bright by thousands of sleeves over many decades, now covered with a forest of foam-spattered empties which caught what light there was and reflected it into the ruddy faces of the eight drunken mechanics.

At first they had resented Sepp joining them. They were, after all, the elite of the factory. But he had proved himself quickly, and he truly believed he was no longer thought of as merely an apprentice with connections, but as a solid member of the team, someone they could all rely on. Even Herr Fink, the senior mechanic who treated the cars like holy relics – quite rightly, Sepp thought – had grown to accept him, and almost trust him. For the first time in his young life Sepp was proud, and it was a feeling that went well with beer.

A scratchy cloud of cigarette smoke hung over the group of mechanics, which Lick pierced with his right hand. "More beers for the heroic German racers Eva my love ... My only love ..." All at the table laughed heartily, as did some of the others in the bar, a small knot of coal miners and a couple of tram drivers at the end of their Saturday shift. A big log fire blazed away behind them. Sepp could feel the heat of it at his back, causing him to sweat in his new shirt and jacket, could smell the wood-smoke and hear the sharp crackle of the burning faggots. The shadows of the mechanics danced with the flickering flames against the wooden partition that shielded the lower part of the window. Above it, in the small glazed aperture on to the street, Sepp could see the snow falling. He blinked to hold his vision steady, and on opening his eyes again the room seemed to slide past him. He turned to Lick, and said: "Am I drunk again?" each word tripping over a tongue thick with beer.

"Let's hope so." Lick belched a full stop.

"But you were to look after me," Sepp said, a little plaintively.

"And have you ever felt finer?"

"I've never, *ever* felt finer," Sepp said, as sure of that as he was sure of anything. Eva brought two fat fistfuls of foaming beers over to them, a wary smile on her face, and one eye always on Lick – which didn't stop his hand reaching for an ample buttock, slapping it hard. There was more laughter, much of it from Eva.

"Do you really love her?"

"Of course not; I love your sister, everybody loves your sister."

"But now she has her man," Sepp said, with undisguised pride.

"That one!" Lick took a great gulp of *Zwickau Bier* that left a white foam moustache. "He's nothing, she will get bored of him, the filly has too much of a wild streak in her."

"You don't know her, Lick."

"We will see, I give it a month at best."

"And then she will be ready for Lick, eh?"

"Why not? I could tame her."

Sepp laughed out loud and a shadow of annoyance passed over his friend's face. He locked his gaze on Sepp, suddenly serious, or as serious as Lick could get. "I'll tell you something about Konrad von-arsewipe, Sepp," Lick held the tall tankard close to his mouth, almost like a microphone, a big hand impossibly squeezed through the handle. "That one is on his way out, he is past it. If it wasn't for his friends in the Party he would be on the scrapheap already."

"Nonsense, he is one of the finest drivers Germany has!"

"*Had*," Lick said, forcefully. "One of the finest Germany *had*. Now he's scared shitless. Any fool can see it."

"You are drunker than I am Lick, Konrad von Plaidt is not scared; the very thought is —"

"*Ach*, so you have signed up to the myth. Or maybe you misunderstand me? When I say scared, I don't mean he's frightened about mashing his legs again. No, what I think is that he's shitting himself because he can see his reputation going down the crap hole."

"He is still a hero, a great man, respected."

"Ah, but you are still young." Sepp thought to tell Lick that he was only three years younger than him, but he could not get the words in now. "But come on Sepp, he has taken a beating from Rosemeyer, you must have seen that? Look, who was he trying to stay with when he cocked it up at the 'Ring?" Sepp shook his head slowly then took a long swig of beer. "Rosemeyer's wiped his arse-crack with von Plaidt, and there are other faster drivers out there, be sure of it."

"Others? Who? The Englishman?"

"He's quick, that one," Lick said, suddenly coming over all thoughtful. "But I don't think our Konrad will fear him. You see you can be wild in this business, and you can be unlucky. But you can't be wild *and* unlucky."

"Is he unlucky?"

"They say so. He managed to put one of those fart-box English cars into the harbour at Monte Carlo last year. That's unlucky." They both smiled at that. "Anyway," Lick said, taking a *Merkur Rund* from the cigarette carton in front of him, "what Plaidt really fears is another quick German. Then he would be finished." With that he lit the cigarette, and was silent as he sucked contentedly on it.

"How quick is he, though, the Englishman?"

"Quick enough, I'd say."

"Rosemeyer quick?" Sepp said, both words coated in slur.

"Only Rosemeyer's Rosemeyer quick. But give this one time Sepp, time to get used to the Type C, for it's no easy beast that's for sure, and then – if he doesn't get himself killed first mind you – well then we might just see something. And by Christ if he gets to be Rosemeyer quick it won't matter if he's English, Italian or the chief fucking rabbi – he'll be in for good."

Someone opened the door and a sudden draught blew across the room, causing the shadow of the firelight to dance crazily across the ceiling. "Put that wood back in its hole!" Lick shouted, before lowering his voice to say to Sepp: "But it's a sad thing that there are no more German drivers like Rosemeyer to drive our wonderful cars, no? Then von Plaidt would really have something to worry about."

Sepp said nothing, just stared at the flickering shadows, clutching tightly at his beer until Lick said: "So that's what young Sepp wants is it?" Lick laughed, but Sepp could let it go. Destiny was with him and he would show them. Just then Eva came back to the table to collect some glasses, her strong perfume cutting through the fog of the cigarette smoke. This time she made no effort to keep her backside away from Lick and as she turned to scoop the empties from the table Lick folded his arms around her just-too-thick waist and pulled her tightly to his lap, letting out an ecstatic groan as he did so. The whole bar, landlord included, joined in the laughter as Eva half-pretended to struggle free, the fleshy slabs of her breasts above the low cut blouse quivering hypnotically. Sepp found he was staring, but could not wrench his eyes away. Lick let her go, looking at Sepp with drunken yet knowing eyes, as he said: "We must get you a go of one of those things, then ..."

Sepp was in the process of figuring out just what Lick had meant when the door to the bar burst open again and another group of young men came in, chased by a flurry of swirling snow. They stamped their feet hard to loosen the snow, found a table, and ordered drinks from a still grinning Eva – beers and schnapps chasers. Sepp recognised something in the voice of one of them, but the memory of it was sliding through his mind, as hard to fix as the outlines of his comrades before him, which now seemed to flicker as much as the fire-thrown shadows. No more beer ...

"More neck oil Sepp?"

"One more beer."

"Wolf, over here!" Lick shouted, and Sepp turned to see a figure in black walk towards them, hand outstretched. He recognised him.

"You know him?" Sepp asked, trying to lever himself out of his chair but falling back. Wolf was wearing the uniform of the SS and seemed as drunk as they all were, his cap high on his head like an engine driver, tie loose and cheeks red from the wind, the snow, and the booze he'd obviously had earlier.

"Nice threads Wolfie, good fanny magnet, eh?"

"Just got them Lick, we are celebrating my in ... *initiation* ..." he burped and screwed up his face to the taste of it. Sepp just stared, invincible in beer and more than ready to fight – if only the room would keep still. Wolf was swaying as much as the room, glassy red-rimmed eyes swivelling in an oil of inebriation before fixing, with a mantrap blink, on Sepp.

"You, eh?" Wolf slurred, his thin lip curling into a whip crack as he made a show of bunching one hand into a fist, holding its wrist with the other.

"Problem?" Lick asked.

"This one should choose his friends more carefully."

"What's that supposed to mean?" Lick said, after a puzzled pause.

"Not you, idiot – the other idiot. There are other things a good German can use his fists for, he should learn that, there can be glory in it," Wolf said.

Sepp vividly recalled the fight on the waste ground, and the memory was shot through with humiliation and anger. "What glory is there in torturing the weak, or beating up old Jews?" he said, raising his voice just a little too much, he realised. The boil of conversation around him seemed to reduce to a simmer, and he was aware of some worried and warning looks around the table at which he sat. Lick wore one of them.

"So, a Yid lover, too," Wolf said, a curious mix of triumph and hate in his eyes.

"He's no Jew lover, Wolf. Sepp's a good German – Christ man, him and his sister are like a Goebbels wet dream!"

"But a Jew lover, nonetheless," Wolf said, and now there was near silence in the bar. Someone coughed awkwardly from the far corner.

"Are you a Jew lover?" Lick looked directly at Sepp, shaking his head impatiently as if waiting for a kid to recognise a picture of a doggy for the fortieth time – *come on Sepp, say your bit and we can get on with our drinking.*

Sepp shrugged, he had the words ready somewhere in the pickle of his head, was settling them in their order – *No, just a Nazi hater*, or, *No, but I hate Nazis*, or … But what came out was: "Strudel isn't a Jew."

"No, that one has problems enough," Lick said. "But what has he to do with this?"

"Jews, idiots, all the same," Wolf spat the words, and some spit with them. "Untermenschen," he added, as Lick wiped a little spittle off his cheek.

"Now come on Wolf, we can't have our splendid SS heroes mixing up their Yids with their idiots now, can we?" Lick said. "This sort of matter requires precision."

"All the same …" Wolf repeated, then half swayed and half moved towards Sepp, fists at the ready. Sepp tried to stand, but Lick pushed him back into his seat with one hand, grabbing Wolf's arm with the other. It was enough to stop him, and the look he gave Wolf was as iron as his grip, unbreakable and unmistakable. Drunk as he was, Wolf obviously thought better than tangle with Lick. The SS man grinned, lightly patted Lick on the shoulder, and then rejoined his friends at the far table.

Sepp suddenly realised that his fists were clenched, he relaxed them. "I could have handled him," he said.

"You can't even stand up."

"No, but … Thank you then."

Lick laughed, drained his glass then drummed it on the table: "More beers and some schnapps, Eva … And bring those dumplings to daddy, I'm in need of nourishment!" Laughter shook the bar room again. Lick leaned over to Sepp, his elbow slipping on the beer-slick surface of the table so that his mouth almost collided with Sepp's ear. Alcohol fumes broke over him like a wave as Lick whispered, none too quietly: "Fine enemies you make my friend."

In the other part of the bar the Nazis broke into *Watch on the Rhine*, thumping out a ragged beat with their fists against the tables.

"I hate them," Sepp said.

"All of them? Will I have to fight off that skinny shit Himmler next, or that jolly Göring fellow?"

"They are just bullies — it's wrong," Sepp said, emphatically and even to him surprisingly clearly.

"You're right, there are some clowns, some hairy-arsed apes out there — Wolf among them, maybe. If only the Führer knew, eh?" Lick winked as he said it, and then turned serious. "But then, I suppose, someone has to do the dirty work."

"You're not ... Are you?"

"It's politics my friend, nothing to do with me," Lick said, shaking his head. "But this shit doesn't come from nowhere, you know. There is always a reason, always clever people seeing how things really are ... People in white coats, like Professor Porsche."

"Professor Porsche is a Nazi?"

"Who knows?" Lick shrugged, "But a genius ... In a white coat. And what of Herr Kessler? An educated man, no doubt about that, and he is a Party man through and through."

Some of those around the table had joined in with the song and Sepp found that his foot was tapping to the beat. Lick's eyes lit to the approach of Eva, her breasts bobbing to the thump of fists against tables. Someone handed Sepp a glass of schnapps and instinctively he flicked it down his throat. Suddenly the shadows in front of him seemed to spin like propeller blades and his head was as light as the foam on the beer that seemed to grow to a great height in front of him. A minute passed, or was it longer? The *Horst Wessel Song* had seemed to emerge from the first song without a break.

"There can be no reasons for such hatred, such evil ..." Sepp heard himself say.

"You think your dear Papa would be dead today if it wasn't for the Jews? They caused all the problems that made his company fold after the banks collapsed in '31, it's a fact. I read it. He was a good man. Then suicide." Lick thumped his fist on the table to emphasise the point and spilt beer splashed coldly against Sepp's hand. "No, they took his life Sepp, they take everything."

"That's rubbish — I can't believe you talk such crap!"

Lick laughed loud, his head back, Adam's apple bobbing so that he seemed to be gulping at the thick layer of cigarette smoke that hung over them.

"Crap?" he said, once more locking on to Sepp's eyes. "Maybe I do talk crap. But these are exciting times my friend, we are wiping the arse of Germany. Only the clean will survive ... and the strong. So, you be strong."

"I feel sick."

*

"Berlin," Konrad said, "will be better. We'll have a jolly time there – I'm still not too old, you know." He laughed and Hanna laughed with him; then stopped laughing when he stopped laughing. The snow still fell and the huge scoops of the headlights lit it up like a great swarm of white wasps panicking in the swirling wind. The road was coated in a thin white crust that crunched and creaked beneath the wheels of the Horch, the engine barely whispering its presence as Konrad's driver trod softly on the accelerator. Once or twice he corrected the steering against a skid, and she sensed Konrad's approval as he nodded beside her on the rear seat, his crutches stuffed in beside him at an odd angle. The car was going slowly, but she still felt as if her life was somehow travelling at the speed of a rocket. A rocket she had lit, but a rocket she sensed she did not control.

Her head ached from the glare of the snow and the effort of the evening in the Chemnitz restaurant: playing the lady, that creep Kessler looking on all the time, questioning her, studying her, seeming not to care what Konrad thought as he stared at her with his cold blinking eyes.

"Anton seems to like you," Konrad said, as if reading her thoughts.

"Really, do you think so?"

Konrad just smiled, and nodded. They drove on in silence for five minutes or so. The heater in the car emitted a soft whoosh and its spill washed over her legs, so warm that she could believe that the dark winter scene outside was unreal, that it might be projected on to the windscreen like a movie, black and white and silver-shining. They had turned towards Zwickau again. In the near distance the winding gear for one of the mines loomed out of the darkness.

"Sepp's doing very well," Konrad said, suddenly.

"Yes, thank you … Without you I don't think we, I mean he, could have —"

"It's nothing, Hanna, a trifle, truly. Auto Union should pay me more for it!" he laughed. "He is a find that one. The older mechanics are amazed at his aptitude, even Fink is impressed. He picks things up quickly and he works so hard, puts many of them to shame I shouldn't wonder. I have snapped him up to work on my car for this year."

"He will be pleased."

"The Englishman will be driving it to start with, of course, before I have recovered." He said it lightly, too lightly, she thought. The snow started to fall a little heavier, building up on the glass panels of the split windscreen so that the wiper motor was struggling to clear it, the arms stuttering as they swept through their narrow parabolas. She thought of the young Englishman with the engaging smile, the hearty laugh, the disregard for the rain, and the strange dress sense, and she realised it was not the first time she had thought of him since that day. The wiper blades stalled for a few seconds and thin lines of snow formed along their length.

"Sepp was very excited last week," she said, pushing that scruffy image to the back of her mind, "to meet the *great* Rosemeyer at last."

"Ah, the great Rosemeyer and his greatness, not a day goes by when I am not reminded of the great Rosemeyer and his greatness."

"I'm sorry," she said, a little taken aback by the reaction, for she had said it lightly. The driver changed down a gear for a corner, slowing the car almost to a walking pace.

"Damn this snow!" Konrad suddenly said, and she thought then that it was the first time he had raised his voice since she had met him. Then he smiled, white teeth caught in the glare of a truck's headlights. They drove on towards the town. Konrad had the driver move the heater lever through to its highest setting. The snow was thicker now, falling like feathers from a heavenly pillow fight, masking the chimney-scape of Zwickau from view. The wipers stopped again, but this time they did not restart and the snow began to dapple the windscreen, soon after almost covering it entirely. The driver brought the car to a gentle halt.

"The mechanism's jammed," the driver said. Konrad nodded and the young man climbed out of the car and a couple of seconds later was out of sight behind one of the bonnet flaps.

"It's rather a cliché, isn't it?" Konrad said, laughing softly, "but be glad that I'm a gentleman."

"Can he fix it?"

"I should think so."

Then she said: "Did I upset you, when I mentioned Rosemeyer? If so, then I'm sorry."

"No need to be sorry my dear, I'm a fool when it comes to the *great* Rosemeyer. You see, that one has no fear, and because of that we all fear for him. But we fear for ourselves too, because we cannot compete with that. Perhaps that is greatness?"

For a moment or two there was no sound other than the creak of the leather upholstery, then he spoke again. "You know it cannot last, this thing with Rosemeyer. A driver cannot keep taking the risks he does … It's only a matter of time."

"You don't think …?"

"Yes, sooner or later. That's why they will always need drivers like me. The crazy men do not last long. It's tragic. Very sad." He pulled one of his Turkish cigarettes from a silver case and struck a match, his face clear and handsome in the glare, but the expression as stern as any she had seen him wear.

"Do you fear for your place on the team, Konrad?" She surprised herself by asking it, yet she saw that he had taken it well, a look of interest on his face as he cocked his head gently to one side, the smoke from his *Murad* etching into the dark space between them.

"No, not really. Because I see the bigger picture, it's the benefit of the years, and I do not finish the race on the race track. Besides, this government has room for men of experience, Hanna, they see the worth of *heroes* – if you will forgive my immodesty." He chuckled at that.

"You approve of them, I didn't realise."

"Should it matter?"

"I'm not sure, but I don't like them. I used to think they were a joke, but now they are everywhere. No, I don't think I like them."

"Tell the truth, me neither my dear, oafs the lot of them. But they have their uses, it would be stupid of me not to be a part of it right now. You will see, I will keep my place on the team. You don't think I invited Kessler to dinner for his sparkling wit?" Konrad laughed. "He may not be a part of Auto Union, but he has more power than anyone else there. He is a direct link to those that hold the purse strings, and he understands the value of someone like me," he patted Hanna's thigh. "And that is valuable to us."

"But why is he so important?" Hanna said, noticing that Konrad had chosen to keep his hand on her thigh.

"He is the future, my dear. A typical Nazi: a small, failed man, who found his place in life by having a big chip on his shoulder. But that is all nothing. What is important is that he has a direct line to Goebbels, because he is part of the Ministry of Public Enlightenment and Propaganda, or some such nonsense: I'm useful to him, to them, and their new future. It's rather fortunate they need old heroes."

"It is?" she said, quietly.

"Yes. The joke is he thinks he uses me, but in truth I'm using him," he squeezed her thigh a little tighter. "And through him and his connections I will make a place for my family and myself in this new future. Of that I am convinced."

"Family?" Everyone knew there was no one now, not since he had divorced his wife, Bella, five years ago. There had been no children from the marriage.

"You know, I am very fond of you, Hanna," he said. Then the driver opened the front door and the blizzard whistled in. He gave them the thumbs up sign. "That should do it," he said.

***

1937

At this speed the buzzing of the aluminium around Westbury Holt was peculiar, more feeling than sound, at one with the funnel of blurring green through which he guided the Auto Union. The track ran straight, as it had for the last five and a half miles, and the outward portion of it – another six mile stretch – ran parallel to this, a matter of feet separating both. As a circuit Berlin's AVUS did not tax the driver – a simple autobahn blast, there and back. But at these speeds it certainly called for concentration.

The banking of the North Turn peeped over the horizon, seconds later filling it like a great brick wave rushing towards him. A glance at the rev counter and a quick calculation put his speed at close to 200mph, faster than he had even flown, and the air that spilled over his small windshield pressed his goggles tight to his face. He slowed the Auto Union for the high-banked brick surfaced left-hander, jinking right to start the left-handed loop and then guiding it into the band of track in the centre of the banking, marked out with two thick white lines.

The rear wheels of the Auto Union kicked against the brickwork as West held on to the wheel firmly, the car feeling heavy beneath him, the uneven track surface jolting his body painfully and flexing the aluminium around him, the steering pulling unnaturally thanks to the slope of the banking. High above him an NSKK man stared down from the lip of the banking, cigarette clamped between his teeth, like a spectator at a fairground wall of death. The new race control building, with its tall white cylinder of a tower striped with balconies, peeped over the edge of the banking at the end of the turn, while swastikas fluttered from flags along the wall-less lip of the track. West felt the tail of the car go light as the wheels scrabbled and skipped against the brickwork, he eased off the throttle a little, and then he was off the turn, plunging down its slope on to the pit straight. Slowing the car.

Speed makes a telescope of a man. Life at 200mph is lived some way ahead, and through the yellow and red smudge of a one-time-fly on the left lens of his goggles West could make out the activity along the wide pit apron long before he reached it. Sepp and Lick were ready with the big lever jack, Fink looking on.

West marvelled again at the way the youngster had come on, growing in confidence by the day and seeming to assume a certain amount of quiet authority with the others, even the older men, as his ability began to show through. Fink, the senior mechanic – a dour man who lived only for the racing cars – had told West that Sepp was an exceptional find, and West reckoned that praise from Fink certainly had to be earned; especially if it concerned someone who was charged with looking after *his* cars.

Further along a group of Nazi bigwigs were taking a close look at one of the streamliners, Konrad and Rosemeyer looking after them. Konrad was doing the talking, leaning heavily on his crutches as he did so. Kessler stood close to him, as if he was hanging on his every word. Konrad was dressed in a smart dark suit, hair carefully parted, shining with brilliantine, a raincoat draped over his shoulders. Behind him, and the group of VIPs, stood Hanna, watching West's Auto Union as it came into the pits. Gracie was there, too, stood behind the two mechanics, eyeing the VIPs. Although he had always insisted he had little interest in racing, these days he seemed keen on tagging along, even making the trip up from Munich, where he was based – West supposed he was simply looking for a chance to chat with an important Nazi politician, to help him with his dull as ditch-water dissertation.

West switched the engine off before stopping the car and a great wave of boot polish smelling fumes broke across him. He let the car roll to a halt, dabbing his foot against the brake pedal to a couple of scrapey squeaks. The fuel sloshed in the tank for a few moments and the hot aluminium pinged as it started to cool. Gracie turned to welcome him and clapped three or four limp and slappy sort of claps, then nodded his approval.

"How was it?" Sepp asked as West unbuckled his green linen wind helmet and took off his goggles.

"Absolutely splendid – good job lads." Sepp beamed. "How close to Rosemeyer?"

"Not very, but he will kick your arse here with the streamliner, you know that," Lick said.

"You are pushing too hard, too long," Fink said, the palm of his hand held over a slightly smoking rear tyre. "The tyres won't take it." He stared at the tyre, looking worried. But then he always looked worried, his range of expression starting with concern and ending with high anxiety. West just shrugged and grinned, which seemed to ratchet Fink's nervous state up a notch or two.

Bernd Rosemeyer came out of nowhere, no doubt glad of the chance to escape the questions of the politicians, and West was just as glad of the interruption. He was dressed smartly, yet casually – jacket and sweater, a garishly striped tie knotted in a thick Windsor, a green Tyrolean hat perched on his head. His big caterpillar brows were wide apart and expressive as he said: "Well, that looked good – you've picked it up a treat," his grin was in place, as it always seemed to be when he was anywhere close to a racing car.

"They've given me a terrific car, Bernd," West nodded at Sepp and Lick and for a moment it looked like the youngster would explode with pride.

"Yes, but I'm sure Lick would prefer beer before praise any day,"

Rosemeyer said, chuckling, and Lick nodded his instant approval.

"But what about AVUS, bit of a bore, isn't it?" Rosemeyer said, talking quickly. "All these people want to see is speed, speed, speed. All they understand is numbers – no finesse in numbers. Might as well be driving trains along here to my mind."

"I suppose you're right," West said, stepping out of the well of the cockpit. "Once you get used to the top end it's just a matter of holding on, making sure the tyres don't overheat, and trying not to fall asleep." He said it with a laugh and Rosemeyer clapped him on the back.

"It's a shame you did not see more of Tripoli my friend – now there's a race track."

"I would have liked to, but —"

"He has the luck of a Christmas goose this one," Lick interrupted, loyally coming to the defence of his driver. Rosemeyer nodded thoughtfully. Superstition was as rife with the German drivers and mechanics as it was at home – Lick had even decided that it was West's cricket jumper that was the cause of all his troubles. It had always seemed strange to West that he was the only one who thought it was all nonsense. The whole bad luck thing was getting to be a bit of an albatross around his neck, and to listen to some you would think he had killed and stuffed the bloody thing himself. Tripoli hadn't helped: two spins and a car failure – sand sucked into the engine. But then perhaps he should be glad of his reputation this time, for he knew how he had over-driven trying to stay in touch with Rosemeyer around the fast sweeps of the Mellaha circuit.

"Take no notice of this old woman, Bernd," West joked, but he could see just by the way that he looked at him that Rosemeyer thought luck was not something to joke about. Rosemeyer changed the subject. He swept his arm back behind him, presenting the streamliner.

"Well, what do you think of her?"

"Stunning, truly beautiful," West said, and meant it.

Rosemeyer nodded briskly then rubbed his hands in anticipation of his next run, for despite what he'd said about the track West knew, and understood, he was only really happy at the wheel of a racing car. There was a call for him to join the party of VIPs. "Ah, the hard life of a racing driver," he said with a shrug, before rejoining the small and animated knot of best suits and smartest uniforms.

"He's quite a card," Gracie said.

"Rosemeyer? Yes, quite something."

"You know who that is, friend Westbury?" Gracie pointed towards the group. West shrugged, he recognised the rather dapper man with the club foot and the mousy face, but couldn't place him.

"Goebbels," Gracie managed to say the name as if it was a swear word. Konrad was introducing Hanna to the little man. She looked stiff and unnatural, West thought, as she held out that slim hand in its black leather glove. She had come on some since the last time they had met and West could only guess at what cost to Konrad's bank account. She wore a tight-fitting, dark suit belted neatly at the waist, its skirt dropping down below the knee. Around her neck and shoulders was some kind of animal, or a whole herd of the things, mink he supposed – it was still a little cold and she had drawn the scarf close to her, hiding part of her face. A hat sat on her head at a rakish angle, dipping over one eye, her hair ballooning back behind it. He thought she had been watching him, before Goebbels had started to talk to her. In fact, he was sure of it.

"I hear Konrad is going to marry that one," Gracie said.

"So they say."

"Make a fine German couple, super for the photographers," Gracie added.

"I wouldn't know about that old boy."

Gracie smiled, then said: "See the fellow in uniform?"

West nodded; the man was very short, five-three maybe, and wore a pale blue uniform with yellow facings, it went well with his blue eyes and blond hair.

"That's Ernst Udet."

"The flyer?" West had heard of him: an ace of the Great War, a stunt flyer of repute.

"The very same," Gracie said.

"Thought he'd be taller."

"Thought he'd be too busy building up the Luftwaffe to hang around a race track, they say he's in charge of the development wing of the Reich Air Ministry, you know?"

"Where do you get all this gossip, Gracie?"

"Here and there, but I wonder why he takes such an interest in racing – that strange smelling fuel, perhaps? Just what is in that brew, friend Westbury?"

"I have no idea, and since when have you been interested in chemistry?"

Gracie shrugged and West turned to the car. Sepp had the engine cover off the rear of the Auto Union, taking out a spark plug to check it, lost in concentration, out of earshot.

"How is it?" West shouted.

"Fine, running clean," Sepp shouted back, before walking over, wiping his hands in a rag, a little of something familiar in his eyes. "It must be wonderful to drive so fast Herr Holt," he said, in almost hushed tones. West smiled at him, nodded.

"How's that sister of yours doing Sepp, she looks well?" Sepp looked puzzled by the sudden change of subject, his gaze shifting from West to the streamliner for long seconds. He either hadn't heard, or chose to ignore the question, for in reply he said: "What top speed on that last run, do you think?"

"Well, with the AVUS gearing 5000rpm is close to 200mph," West said. "But it must be much faster for the streamliners – maybe 245?" Sepp shook his head in wonderment, staring at the streamliner that sat some way along the pit apron, looking like a lad in love.

"Which means," Gracie put in, massaging his chin between thumb and forefinger and looking down the road, "that cars will approach each other at a combined speed of somewhere close to 500mph – and all that's there to separate them is that thin strip of grass."

"You know, I hadn't thought of it like that," West said.

"No, well I'm beginning to see that imagination does not loom large on the racing driver's list of attributes, friend Westbury." West laughed and pulled the pipe out of the weave in the old cricket jumper he wore over his overalls. "But tell me West, how come you get one of these ordinary cars and Rosemeyer gets that beauty?" Gracie added, pointing to the streamliner.

"Because I'm the new boy Gracie old chap, first come, first serve and all that – only fair after all." He took a good long look at the streamliner. It looked more Fritz Lang than Ferdinand Porsche, like a flying saucer on wheels. It was as smooth and as flat as a wave polished pebble, devoid of adornment except for the four-ring nostrils of the Auto Union badge on the nose. The cockpit was tiny, even too small to climb into directly, and there was a low hump behind it to smooth the passage of the air over the long tapering tail. The wheels were faired-in at the top and spats were fitted over the front pair to keep the car wind-tight. The car was big, and heavy – which was why it had not been seen before. For this was to be a special race, a chance for the German teams to show off in front of a proud Berlin audience. The local organisers had waived the maximum weight limit so that the cars from Auto Union and Mercedes could race in all their slippery finery – and so that German racing cars could race faster than any other cars had ever raced before.

West watched as Rosemeyer took off his jacket and climbed aboard, not bothering to slip into his overalls for this test run. A portion of the top of the car lifted clear on a framework, rather like a hatch, and Rosemeyer slipped into the gap between its underside and the bodywork. It was a tight squeeze. Once he was in the seat the bodywork was closed around him, so that his head poked through a tiny aperture at the top of the car. Rosemeyer signalled for the mechanics to push start the car. The engine burst into life, sending a cloud of sparrows skywards and forcing all those close by to thrust their fingers in their ears. Rosemeyer revved it, and the sound seemed to rip the very air.

"I would give anything to drive that," Sepp said, suddenly blushing as he seemed to realise others might have heard him. So *would I lad*, West thought, *so would I*.

*

Hanna stepped out on to the balcony of her room at the Hotel Savoy. Her bare feet were cold against the concrete, but it was good to be out in the air on such a fine spring evening in Berlin. A beautiful new dress from Paris, ivory-coloured and of silk and tulle, lay on the bed, waiting to be filled, waiting to become the person she hardly knew. The dress was a present from Konrad. There was yet another dinner tonight, where she would keep quiet and nod politely while Konrad talked to important Nazis and Kessler's photographers fed off the images of him and her; already she tired of that – that which Konrad said was so necessary. Hanna leant against the balcony enclosure and sighed. Four floors below, on Fasanen Strasse, other couples sat in cars or walked arm in arm – off to the theatre, the cinema, or a quiet dinner and dancing. But Konrad's work never seemed to stop, injured or not, driving or not. She sighed again, and reminded herself how much better it all was than working for Herr Ostermann. That usually did the trick.

She was wearing a burgundy silk dressing gown, another present, and beneath it only the glow from the bath she had just stepped out of – the en suite bathroom was by far the best thing about the Savoy. A towel was wrapped about her head in a turban that felt a little heavy and hot from the bath water it had soaked up. There was a light breeze, and it ruffled at the overlap of her dressing gown, finding its way to the naked skin beneath and tickling at her nipples, which hardened like bullets. She enjoyed the feeling, the intoxicating mix – part shame, part pleasure – and opened her dressing gown just a little more. They felt like little storm troopers, standing to attention in there. She chuckled at the thought. They also reminded her of what had happened the previous night.

It had not been how she had always supposed it would be, but then she had always supposed that such things happened after a man and a woman were married. But Konrad was an older man, and he knew the ways of the world, and she had not wanted to seem a mere girl to him. He was also a gentleman, and made sure she knew it was her decision. He had eased that decision with the cognac he'd brought along to the room. It was not unusual, he had said, for lovers to love. But surely it was unusual enough, else why the separate rooms? Of course, that was because people would talk otherwise. Some already did, she supposed, for it certainly *was* unusual for a girl of twenty to be with a man of thirty-nine. Unless that man was rich …

She wondered once again what Mother would have thought of that, as she stroked the soft silk sleeve of her gown with the tips of her fingers.

She heard music above the sound of the traffic, someone in another room in the hotel playing a record: something American, maybe the banned Negro jazz, she thought with a sudden thrill. There was a familiar smell in the air, and she was sure she recognised it: a nice, homely smell which sent her sifting through memories of years gone by, years long ago in Zwickau with Papa and Mama and Sepp. It was a little like damp wood burning, and spices, peat … Yes, familiar. A tiny curl of blue-grey smoke rose before her eyes, twisting to form a spectral question mark. She leant out over the iron rail of the balcony and looked below for the source of the smoke.

He was just one floor down, also leaning over his balcony; the smoke was from his pipe. All she could see of him was his back – hunched and stretching the wool weave of the off-white jumper so that the faded red shirt beneath just showed through – his wiry mop of hair, and the volcanically smoking bowl of the pipe. Beyond that there was just the busy street below, where cars queued to turn on to Kurfürstendamm.

"Herr Holt!" she called, wondering why as soon as the words had left her lips. He turned remarkably quickly, with no look of surprise on that open, boyish face of his, just undisguised pleasure. He craned his neck back to get a better view. She pulled the dressing gown closer to her body.

"Why, Hanna, what a pleasant surprise – a call from the heavens, no less."

"It's a nice evening. I thought I'd get some air before we go out, Konrad and I that is … We're going out," she spluttered, all of a sudden feeling in a bit of a fluster.

"A drink you say," he said, quite obviously pretending to mishear her.

"No —" But before she had time to say anything else he had grabbed at the thick black-painted drainpipe that ran down the edge of one of the concrete clad bays into which the balcony was inset, and had swung himself clear of the balcony, shinning the pipe without as much as testing it for strength first. Within a matter of seconds he pulled himself level with Hanna's balcony.

"You fool!" She laughed, despite herself.

"Well now, how about that drink," he said, speaking with the pipe clamped in one corner of his mouth, so that his words sounded cartoon comical.

"I said nothing about a drink, dear sir."

"But I've risked my life!"

"That's your business, why should I care?"

"Don't you?" he said, affecting a look of little-boy-lost. He glanced down at the street far below then changed the shape of his face to one of melodramatic fear, all big-eyed like a silent movie film starlet tied to a railway track. She laughed again, and wondered what those below would think of this little scene of a man hanging from her balcony, should they look up.

"You go ahead and kill yourself – I have to change," she said.

"But you can't mean that, I could really die here … And one so young!"

"Yes, that is sad. But it's a fool's fate, to die young," she said.

"You think so?"

"It's a scientific fact."

"Konrad tell you that?"

"I do have a brain of my own," she said.

The shape of his smile changed a little, and he seemed to relax his white-knuckled grip of the balcony's rail.

"Well then, my climb was in vain," he said. "For without that drink all is lost. Goodbye cruel world."

With that he let go of the rail.

For a split second her breath froze within her while her gaze locked on his foolish grin and the hands now held up in front of his face. He swayed backwards a little and she grabbed at both of his wrists, pulling him back towards the balcony and readying herself for the tug of his weight against her body, the wrench of his fall against her shoulders. She pulled him towards her, only then noticing that his feet were – of course – still firmly lodged in a bracket of the drainpipe, and his knees were also clamped tight to the pipe. She felt she could have pushed him clear of the building, but that impish grin and boy-like chuckle of his was irresistible, and although she almost hated herself for it she found that she was laughing along with him.

In the rush to grab him her dressing gown had parted slightly to show the glowing skin either side of her cleavage, and now his eyes were at her chest. She pulled the gown together and walked off the balcony, back into the room. Suddenly a drink didn't seem like such a bad idea after all. He heaved himself over the parapet of the balcony and followed her in. Without a word she poured them both a generous measure of the *Gautier* cognac Konrad had left in her room. She had quietly acquired a taste for the strong drink, especially before evenings like the one in front of her.

"You drink brandy?" he said, looking surprised.

"Yes, why not?"

He shrugged: "Your brandy?"

"Konrad's brandy."

"But your room?"

"My room," she said, nodding, enjoying the look of dawning realisation on his face, just a little surprised when his lower lip sagged a bit, in what she thought just might have been disappointment.

"Chin-chin," he said, with just a hint of sulk, she sensed, as his glass clinked against hers. He looked around the room with interest, though she guessed it must be the same as his: a bed, a dressing table with winged mirrors, two easy chairs, a table, vase of flowers and a couple of pictures – snow-capped mountains and the Führer.

"You know you really shouldn't be here when I'm trying to change, what would my fiancé say?" she said, taking a sip of the cognac.

"Oh, he won't mind." Outside a train whistled from the direction of the Zoo Station just a couple of streets away and she heard the squealing as its wheels spun against the track, steel on steel. He nodded at the dress lying on the bed. "Where to tonight, then?" he said.

"Dinner, with Herman Göring."

"My, my." He whistled his mock astonishment. "I'm impressed – but doesn't sound like so much fun."

"On the contrary, I've heard he throws a wonderful party."

"Well, they do say it's the party Party." He grinned.

"Everything's a game to you isn't it," she said, a little tersely, "but life's just not like that – you may find that out some day." He carried on smiling that now ever more annoying smile of his. "Anyway, a driver of Konrad's stature – a *man* like Konrad – has more to do than *just* race cars. But who knows? Maybe someday you might grow up to find it's the same for you," she said.

"Maybe, but let's hope it's a long time coming, shall we?"

"I'm sure it will be."

He shrugged, never losing the smile, just holding the glass up to the picture of Hitler, making a silent toast, winking and then taking a sip of the cognac.

There was a sharp knock at the door and she turned towards it.

"Hanna dear – it's me." Konrad's voice was muffled by the thick door. But by the time she realised she'd have to explain the presence of Westbury Holt the Englishman had gone, with a little wave, out on the balcony and down the drainpipe – unable to resist letting out a theatrical, strangled cry of a man falling. Hanna unlocked the door and Konrad walked in using his crutches for support. His expression was pained but, on seeing her, his face instantly split into a wide smile – and she realised, with surprise, it was because he had been met with a larger smile from her.

He was wearing evening dress, with a Party badge on the silk facing of his lapel. Her eyes rested on it, and he shrugged. "I have to make some sort of an effort for them Hanna dear." He limped to the far side of the room, leaning heavily on the crutches. "Kessler says it's important, many of the other drivers won't, he says, and what is a badge? You know, he likes you, says we make a fine couple."

"That's nice of him," she said.

Konrad sat on the edge of the bed, a slow smile of relief curving its way up his face as his backside sunk into the soft mattress. He looked at her for a moment or two, intently, that same smile frozen to his face. Suddenly it slipped, he nodded twice, and said. "There's something I have been meaning to talk to you about Hanna."

"Yes?"

"The way things are here, in this country. It is not ideal, you understand that?"

"Of course."

"But we must live with it, do what we can to make our way in the world, yes?" He didn't wait for a reply. "So there is something I will need you to do for me Hanna." There was the blare of a car horn far below on Fasanen Strasse, and the shout of a newspaper vendor. She was sure that the tobacco smell was still in the air and Konrad seemed to be sniffing at it.

"What?"

"Our marriage. There are procedures that we should go through, you understand?"

"What sort of procedures?"

"Paperwork, nothing more, a trifle," he cleared his throat. "You know, of course, I am a member of the SS?" She did, he had explained to her that all the German drivers had to join it or the NSKK, and how Kessler had persuaded him the SS was the wiser choice. She nodded. "Because of this there are things I will need from you if we are to be married."

"You mean an Aryan certificate, don't you?"

"Does that worry you?"

"No. It doesn't *worry* me, but —"

"Well, it should be easy enough, I mean, you —"

"Konrad," she said softly. "Should I really have to prove that I am a German for you to marry me?" Konrad shook his head, laughed softly, and patted the bed beside him. She sat down next to him and he rested his hand on her leg, squeezing it softly.

"Hanna dear, this is not for me. These are strange times, and if we can make it easier with a piece of paper … Well we would be foolish not to, wouldn't we?" She thought of the work it would mean, trawling through the records of past generations for something that should not matter, to show her blood had been pure Aryan for the past 200 years.

"I don't think —"

"Please Hanna," he pulled his hand from her leg and looked away from her, "this will be important for us in the future. And if there is to be a future for us then you must do it. It's as simple as that, there's no way out of it."

She hadn't expected that, and she felt shocked. "I understand," she murmured, and he faced her again, nodding slowly.

"I have heard good things about Sepp, you know," he said. "He is doing very well now; we all are, aren't we?" He reached out for an edge of the silk dress, rubbing it between thumb and finger.

"I should get changed," she said, and stood up.

"But what's this, a visitor?" he said, suddenly noticing the two unfinished glasses and the opened bottle of his favourite *Gautier* cognac.

"Yes, Herr Holt," she said. It might have been better not to mention it, but now she was strangely glad she had, and she saw a slight frown crease his forehead before she added: "He was told you might be found here, so he invited himself in for a drink."

"Did he now?"

"The boy's a fool," she said, surprising herself, and him it seemed, with the venom of it.

"Well he must be, if he didn't drink *this*." Konrad seemed genuinely astounded that anyone should not finish the fine liquor and set to putting that right, emptying the glass in two gulps. "Ah, that should help with conversation." She stood up and pulled the dress off the bed, it seemed as light a smoke.

"He has my drive, he drinks my cognac – or rather he doesn't – what's a fellow to think, eh?"

"Darling, please ..."

"I'm joking Hanna dear, now come, the car will be here for us soon, you must hurry. We must not keep our host waiting."

*

They would come in their thousands to see the Silver Arrows. Sepp had heard that nearly 400,000 spectators were expected to line the nine-kilometre straights of the AVUS autobahn. Most of them had arrived by now, family groups with hampers of beer, sausages, smoked mackerel and cheeses that filled the air with nostalgic aromas. Sepp and Lick helped to unload one of the streamliners, Rosemeyer's car, for despite and because of her beauty – her voluptuousness of curves – she carried a lot of extra weight. But Sepp didn't mind the extra work, for he could not get enough of these cars, the fastest on earth, the cars he was born to drive, and he still felt a thrill just to be close to one of them.

The streamliner rolled slowly onto the ramps and the mechanics took the strain, Sepp spreading his palms wide across the gleaming bodywork of the tail. Strudel helped, too. He had arrived with a truckload of spares from Zwickau early that morning. Sepp had not been able to discover whether the lorry driver had simply felt sorry for him, or whether he had hidden in the truck, or whether it was a mixture of the two. Luckily most were too busy to notice him. Then again he was a familiar face to those who tended the Auto Unions, so some of those who did notice him were even pleased to see him.

The streamliner rolled off the end of the ramp and then seemed to sink, almost sighing, to the level of its ride height. Sepp stepped back from the car and looked longingly at it once again.

"Come on dreamer-boy, we can't have you shooting your load all over Rosemeyer's chariot now can we," Lick shouted, "give us a hand with Cinderella here." He pointed to the racer that Lick and Sepp tended, the standard Type C for Westbury Holt, looking almost archaic in the company of the streamliners. Auto Union had brought five cars to AVUS, two streamliners and three of the regular racers. Mercedes had also brought five cars, but apart from a solitary and totally outclassed Alfa Romeo and a couple of Maseratis, specks of blood in a sea of quicksilver, no other team had dared to race them. Sepp felt a flush of pride at the thought. He reached over to steer Holt's Type C from outside the cockpit while Lick pushed from the other side, and once the inertia of its 750kg had been broken it wasn't so difficult a job. But then they had a little help.

"C'mon that man, put your back into it – we need to touch 300km/h!" Lick shouted, looking back at Strudel who was leaning on the tail of the car, bent almost parallel to the road, putting his back – putting his being – into the task of pushing the racing car. Sepp laughed. Ahead of them some of the other racers were already strung across the road opposite the stands, beyond a cordon of NSKK men and Brownshirts. Goebbels had arrived a little earlier and out on the track, some way distant, Sepp could pick out the throaty flutter of the hundred or so NSKK motorcycle combinations that escorted his limousine as it toured the course. The uniformed cordon opened for them, Lick giving a sarcastic little one-fingered salute.

"Look at them, as much use as chocolate brake linings," Lick said through the corner of his mouth. They pushed the Auto Union through the gap in the cordon, its tyres a crackling whisper against the concrete roadway, fuel sloshing gently in its tank.

"Halt!"

The voice was so authoritative that they pulled back without thinking, the car coming to a creaking stop. One of the Nazis, an NSKK man wearing more useless decorations than a Christmas tree, held the palm of his hand up, cold eyes locked on Strudel, staring. "And where do you think you're going?" Strudel looked up in confusion, then panic; Sepp knew that he had a particular phobia for men in uniform. "You have no pass, no team overalls – what is this, are you a famous driver?" The other Nazis laughed out loud.

"Leave him be, he's with us," Sepp said. He had always promised Kurt he would look out for his simpleton son, but he knew that wasn't the only reason he'd intervened.

"Not without a pass he's not." The Nazi strode forward and Strudel's eyes seemed brim-full with fear – of all the many uniforms these days, it was those Nazi-brown shirts he feared most, Sepp had noticed. The NSKK man grabbed Strudel's shoulder, spun him around, then shoved him away. Strudel staggered, then tripped, landing heavily on the concrete.

"I said, leave him!" Sepp snapped.

All eyes were now on him, and some of the other Nazis gathered around the little group. The NSKK man with the medal ribbons was flexing his fist, while Sepp was surprised to find that his fingernails were digging into the palms of his right hand.

"Enough of that," Lick said, and Sepp recognised that familiar rising panic in his voice. "We have to take the car to the start."

"Not without him." Sepp pointed to Strudel. Lick shook his head, sighed, and walked around the Type C to the NSKK man.

"Look, he comes with us."

"It's impossible."

"Impossible? You know what this is?" he pointed to Strudel, still cowering in a pathetic heap on the floor.

"An imbecile?"

"No, a talisman." The NSKK man shrugged and Lick went on. "You think Rosemeyer can race without his good luck charm close at hand?" he said it softly, putting a hand on the NSKK man's shoulder, patting his epaulet. The Nazi bit his lip in confusion. "You see, it's vital this one is here," Lick lied.

"Vital?"

"But you're NSKK, you must know what it is to be a driver, the superstition of these men?" The Nazi seemed to weaken, his chest filling a little. "And if the great Rosemeyer were to have an accident today because —"

"I understand," the Nazi suddenly snapped. "Let the idiot through," he said, though no other was standing in Strudel's way. Sepp still glared at him, but now Lick was pushing the Auto Union to the start again, Strudel up on his feet and at the tail of the car as if nothing had happened, concentrating solely on the job at hand. Sepp fell in with them.

"Thanks," Sepp said.

"You will have to learn to work with these people Sepp, otherwise everything will come to an end – you understand?"

Sepp nodded.

*

Goebbels sat in the tribune some rows below them, with his wife Magda. A large hat the shape of a fried egg hid Magda from Hanna's view, but there was no hat for him, just brilliantine-slick hair, brushed back from a high forehead. She didn't like the propaganda minister, didn't like the way he looked at her, and so she was glad they sat some rows behind him, but Kessler had been annoyed when they had been shown to their seats. Every now and then Goebbels would lean over to Korpsführer Hühnlein to ask him something about the cars. Konrad had told her that Hühnlein was a great friend of Hitler's and the Führer had personally put him in charge of all German motorsport. Not a bad job, Konrad had said, when things go right, but on the rare occasion the German teams had been humbled no one would have wanted to be in his jackboots as he telephoned in his post-race report to the Chancellery or the Berghof.

Konrad sat beside her to her right, talking to Kessler to his right, who was wearing the uniform of the SS. Every time the Nazi looked in the direction of Goebbels, looked towards the power, he blinked a little more, the lens of his heavy glasses magnifying the movement, making it grotesque. He reminded her of a cold, deep sea fish startled by the light. Earlier she had met his family, three boys in Hitler Jugend outfits, stiff as toy soldiers, each a year older than the other; a plain and stout wife excited by the company, the celebrities, but kept from them by her husband, and his 'serious work'. They had been sent to sit elsewhere, among those other thousands who dressed and thought alike.

Every now and then Konrad would turn to check that Hanna was all right, sometimes squeezing her hand. He wore a light woollen suit, the black and white silk bow with crossed swords that marked him out as a war veteran pinned to his lapel alongside the Party badge. SS officers and Party officials were all around them. She caught sight of Sepp and Lick, pushing Westbury Holt's car out to the start line, her brother's hand on the wheel as he guided it into its position, his shoulders held back and his head high – he looked so proud and she was so proud of him. Strudel was with them, completely immersed in the job of pushing the car.

"We will have to do something about that one," she heard Kessler say to Konrad, "I thought I'd made it clear?"

"He should not be here, I don't understand it. I will have a word with Fink," Konrad said, before pointing to the streamliners, diverting Kessler's attention. The noise in the grandstand was changing now, Hanna realised, the chatter louder, faster, arms shooting out like salutes to point to favourite drivers, beautiful cars.

The racing cars gleamed in the bright sunshine a hundred metres away from Hanna, like little silver trophies arranged before her. There were just six of them for this event was to be held over two heats and a final. Konrad was still talking to Kessler so she consulted her programme, checking the names against the numbers: Caracciola and Seaman for Mercedes, the former in a streamliner, and Rosemeyer, Holt and von Delius for Auto Union – Rosemeyer in the streamliner and the other two in the regular racers. There was one other car, a blood red Alfa Romeo, a gate-crasher in colour and class. She spied Westbury Holt walking to his car, still with that tatty off-white sports jumper over his white overalls, his head encased in a light green linen wind helmet which, she realised with a giggle, made his nose look rather big. He shook hands with Seaman, the other Britisher who drove for Mercedes, and then he walked, in that almost mockingly casual way of his, to the car. There were jokes, Westbury and Lick laughing at something, Strudel looking lost now that the task of pushing the car into place had come to an end. Sepp, however, had his eyes fixed on the streamliner – *I know your dreams little brother, one day perhaps ...*

Westbury Holt was waving into the crowd. She looked about to see who it could be, a girl perhaps, that would be interesting. But there was no one waving back, yet still he kept waving, grinning. Suddenly she realised he was waving at her. But she did not wave back, *let him look like the fool he is*, she thought, smiling slightly. Eventually he stopped. *So there is a limit to his persistence ...* But then he turned to Sepp and pointed to her part of the stand. Then there were two distant faces, two distant smiles, two distant waves. She waved back, and even from a hundred metres she could see the satisfaction, the triumph, on the Englishman's face. Konrad turned to her, coughed gently.

"He is a handsome lad isn't he?" She turned to him, realising that he had stopped talking to Kessler a little time ago. West and Sepp had stopped waving and the Englishman was climbing aboard the car. "Your brother, I mean —"

"Oh yes, the second most handsome man in Germany," she cut in. Konrad smiled, nodded gently. There was a sudden ripple of applause along the length of the grandstand as the two greats of German motor racing, Rosemeyer and Rudolf Caracciola, climbed aboard their streamliners, each using a hatch in the top of his beautifully sculptured machine to help him into the confined space. The Mercedes looked similar to the Auto Union, although with its front engine its nose was longer. That's where the three-pointed star sat proudly, but there was also a large black swastika behind the driver's head. "The others will have no chance against those beauties, will they?"

"No," Konrad said. "Not unless the streamliners fail." He flicked open a silver cigarette case, one that was inscribed with a long ago victory. He lit his cigarette, sucked on it, then said, "I don't envy them today."

"I can't believe that."

"You should, there is nothing more to this than holding on – or getting hurt if it goes wrong. A fool's game." She felt an unexpected shudder travel the length of her spine. "Are you all right Hanna?"

"Yes, perfectly."

"I'm sorry, I should have known better than to speak of such things – you are such a delicate little flower sometimes, aren't you?"

"Not so delicate really Konrad," she said, "and whatever you say, I bet you wish you were out there in a car rather than sat here with this blossom in the stand?"

"Perhaps, but the view here is quite magnificent." He looked into her eyes, and smiled. It was the smile of a secret shared. Last night he had come to her room again. With his injuries it was difficult, but he had shown her how it could be done, and in the midst of passion he seemed to forget his pain. She was pleased that it helped him. He took precautions, of course, because their wedding would have to wait. It would take time to gather the documentation for the Aryan certificate, and once over her initial annoyance she had actually found she was glad of that. Things were moving fast, too fast, and marriage could wait just a little longer, she had decided. She was in no great hurry to prove she was German.

Konrad continued: "Besides, there is other work I have to do, talking to these people." He spread his hand over the black caps, the brown caps, the grey caps and the civilian hats in the rows in front of them: "Showing them that our racing cars are just as important to the Fatherland as aircraft and tanks. It is prestige through speed, this will be the fastest race my dear, the fastest race ever – and the world will see that."

Quite suddenly there was a great roar from below as one of the engines came alive, a sharp *wharrp-wharrp* followed by a harsh rip that echoed through the stand, seeming to shake the hard seats on which they sat. Another engine was fired up, and then another, almost simultaneously, great licks of flame shooting from the exhausts. Very soon the entire grid of cars was shaking to the rasping, irregular, breath of the engines, like a herd of sleeping monsters, snoring loudly. Little curls of smoke rose up from the engine covers and the pipes, and a soft blanket of heat haze settled across the cars. The smell of the burnt fuel broke over the grandstand, a little like boot polish, reminding her of Papa in his suit, of childhood Sundays in church. The congregation stood, the service was about to begin.

*

The needle swept across the rev counter in jerky little stutters, vibrating against the glass as it did so. Once it was more or less settled at 1500rpm, enough to keep the sparkplugs clean but not enough to overheat the engine when the racer was deprived of the airflow that cooled it, West kept his accelerator foot as steady as possible. He felt the tremor of the engine through the sole of his shoe, as he sat forward in his cushioned seat, hunched up over the wheel slightly with his arms well bent. It was the only way to sit in these things, with their big steering wheels and tight cockpits, up close to the dials and the big central clock of the rev counter that counted out the revs to just 5000 – this motor was all torque, plenty action. The whole car shuddered in time to the engine, the rim of the steering wheel buzzing through the palm of his thin gloves. He kicked out at the clutch and clunked the gearstick into first. The other racers were either side of him, streamliners in front. He knew that there was only one chance to get himself noticed in this race, and that was to lead early on – those beautiful, heavy beasts would be bloody slow off the line, so West aimed to make a race of it at least until they came up to speed. He adjusted his goggles, gripped the wheel, and locked his eye on the rev counter, trying to match the dancing needle with the tiny spasms of his throttle foot. The noise around him grew, the needle danced crazily to the vibration, wafts of fuel fumes spilt into the cockpit …

A small cannon fires to signal the start, hardly audible over the engine noise, but West feels its shock wave. Clutch out and away, the squeal of rubber against the concrete, the car twisting about his hips before it grips in an instant, shooting forward, sucking him down into the well of the seat. It's a good start and he passes through the narrow gap between the streamliners as they lurch into motion. He selects second gear with a crisp crunch and glances in the little mirror that buzzes at the rim of his cockpit. Delius in the other standard Auto Union racer has also slotted his Type C through the gap between the streamliners and is close behind, looking for a way through already. West lets his car drift slightly to the right, closing the door. Up to third gear, accelerating steadily but not violently, giving the tyres the chance to grip the road, and then into top, the airstream is pressing his goggles tight to his face, the trees either side of the course blur into a green smudge, the patter-patter of the jointed concrete road surface turns into a regular buzz. Soon he is approaching top speed. The road channels through the greenery for six miles; it's just twenty feet wide. The home straight runs parallel with just a thin strip of grass separating both – after all, at other times this is a regular autobahn for Berliners. *Now what was it Gracie had said about combined speeds?* West thought, before deciding it was probably best not to remember.

West is up to top speed when the first of the streamliners passes, the wide Mercedes moving the air in front of him and causing the racer to weave alarmingly across the track as the spill of its slipstream passes over it. West holds it and is ready for more of the same when the next comes by – Rosemeyer this time, one hand off the wheel, a casual wave at over 200mph. Typical Bernd. The streamliner shaves the edge of the circuit, a rear wheel kicking up a small stone that ricochets against the bodywork of West's car at the speed of a bullet. West shakes his head and laughs. He has done as much as could be expected of him, now is the time to get a rhythm going to make sure of a finish and his place in the final. Delius has dropped back some lengths, only to close up when they reach the south curve. It seems to take an age to slow the car down for the long, looping hairpin. West changes down just one gear as he brakes – with a habitual heel and toe blip between a double dip of the clutch – because after the start he only needs third and fourth here; with the torque available he could probably drive the entire lap in top. He guides the car through the long turn and then, halfway through, he treads on the throttle a little, to liven up the day of the thousands of spectators crammed into the enclosures. The rev counter flares, his arms cross to collect the skid, right foot flexing, easing, then feeding in the throttle, back on to the straight after the long loop, the regular rasp of the engine only punctuated by the meshing, clunking hiccup of his single gearchange.

Home straight, back the way he came, the track West's just blasted down just metres to his left. There's a slight wiggle from the rear as he presses the throttle just a little too firmly as the car accelerates past 100mph, the wheels spinning even now, such is the power, but once he's up to speed it's just a matter of sitting there and concentrating on that filament thin ribbon of road and the postage stamp sized patch of pinched horizon racing to meet him at something close to 190mph. There is one slight kink in the road along the way, the steering wheel turning through barely a second of its clock face travel, a shiver of West's wrists, nothing more, and he's through.

It's a good four minutes before the great wall of the north turn finally looms into view. West has been told to keep the speed down to save the tyres, but Fink was always too cautious, he thought, and he had figured a few more revs could not make much difference. Anyway, if he could not beat the streamliners, at least he would beat von Delius, the man who had taken *his* drive after the Monza try-out last year. The car behind is but a silver scratch on the surface of his mirror by now, as West brakes for the turn, knocking off a little speed.

He hits the north turn: the front of the car slithers against the brickwork as he steers, forcing him up high to where the sixty-foot wall gains steepness, from around forty-five degrees to an almost perpendicular eighty. The top of the slope sucks the momentum from the car, stopping it from plunging over the lip and into the Berlin streets beyond. West wrestles with the steering, feeling the staccato patter of the bricks through the wheel. The cross-section of the banking is flat, not concave, so there is not the same centrifugal forces he is used to at Brooklands, but still he feels the blood drain from his head a little, and his vision blurs from this and from the effects of the bumpy track. He uses the slope at the exit to help with his acceleration out of the turn and hits the straight like a dive-bomber, the main grandstand blurring by in a mess of pink faces and fluttering red flags. He catches a snatch of the commentary over a loudspeaker – *"Rosemeyer, Caracciola as one!"* – then it's flat out again, another six miles to the south curve ...

Delius had dropped back a long way by now, probably saving his car for the main event, taking Fink's cautious advice, and so West's race became a lonely one. Another lap: the same blur of trees, the same ripping roar of the engine, the same judder of the fly-spattered windshield. But then: *what's this?* Something different ... a cough, a sag in speed ... He's imagined it. But no, there it is again, and again. Soon the car is misfiring dreadfully, power seeping away, and the other Auto Union Type C sweeps by, then the Mercedes W125. Then, a minute or so afterwards, ignominy of ignominy, the blood red Alfa, Satan's own grin tattooed to the sun-bronzed face of its driver, his yellow silk scarf fluttering like flame. The car slowed a little more, so that West was forced to drop down a gear in the hope that the surge of revs would clear the problem. No chance, the stricken Auto Union could hardly muster the power to climb the banking, and was slipping under its own weight by the time that West had brought it through the 180-degree turn. Sepp and Lick stood at the edge of the pit box, quite far out on to the track, faces painted with puzzle. West coaxed the machine into the box just as the two streamliners thundered by as if they were tied together, their passage seeming to shake the sky as if it was shivering sheet metal.

"Plugs fouled!" he shouted as he switched off the ignition, taking the cup of water Sepp handed him and gulping it down. He felt the car lift beneath him as the big jack levered the rear into the air, then he heard the hammer of the wheel mallets on the spin hubs, and the clatter of discarded tools. They would be taking the opportunity to change wheels – fresh tyres are always welcome – and he could smell the baking rubber as the wheels fell to the ground with a rattle and thump. Fink inspected one of the tyres, and then shot West a warning glance. Meanwhile Sepp had the engine cover off and was attacking the hot iron with a plug spanner, popping off the rubber cups and twirling the spanner at the speed of a propeller. Whole minutes were lost as West craned his neck to check the progress, whole minutes before the slam on the aluminium body, the clunking insertion of the starter, the shrill whirr of its spin, the roar of the reawakened motor, the tap on the head and Lick's pointed signal and mouthed shout to "Go, go, go!"

West was soon up to speed again. He'd faced disappointments before in his racing career and he knew that until the flag had fallen there was no point in worrying about it. *The game goes on, old man. Yes, the game goes on.* But now he could only hope that one of the cars in front would hit trouble if he was to qualify for the final. Yet while he could hope for that, he could also try to lodge the fastest time for the non-streamlined cars, and so he squeezed far more out of the car than he had all weekend, holding his foot down for longer, making a point of forgetting the warning from Fink: *The tyres will overheat*, he had said. But the man was carved from caution, West thought, and where there was caution there was always a tolerance, some leeway: an extra ten miles per hour here and there, for just a little longer, there and here …

Suddenly there was a strange noise from the rear of the car, a buzzing, a vibration that he could feel through his left shoulder and down his arm. He put it to one side. In the distance, on the opposite side of the road at the vanishing point of this funnel of speed, a pinprick caught the light like a signal mirror. He guessed that it would be the two streamliners, Rosemeyer and Caracciola, and they would be passing by in seconds. Just then the slight buzz behind him turned into a rasping *thrupp* followed instantly by a muted pop. A long, hard thread of rubber whipped over his shoulder, slapping painfully against the crown of his linen wind helmet. He knew instantly that one of the rear tyres had failed.

In the space of a heartbeat the car pitched left, spearing towards the narrow grass strip between the two straights. Everything happened at the speed of fright, but his senses were sharpened by the jolt of adrenalin and he could hear the long grass of the central reservation brushing against the belly of the Auto Union as the car crossed on to the opposite carriageway, and could feel the deflating tyre shudder and squirm on the rim. He turned the car right before it could leave the road, making sure the movement on the wheel was small, and in an instant he had it more or less straight – if on the wrong carriageway – fighting it with deft little shivers of the wheel. He thought it was under control, thought he could start to slow it now …

And then he thought of the two streamliners: speeding towards him. Point of death; what to think in that finely split second: life like a flickering film in front of you? Lost chances of heartfelt goodbyes? Or mathematics, combined speeds: maybe 160mph, plus 240mph? He gripped the wheel and tried to keep the Auto Union as straight as possible. Another thought: all those Nazis with their daggers and Lugers, and here's Westbury Holt about to wipe out two of the Third Reich's most popular heroes …

The double dots of quicksilver grow like shining explosions. They are on him almost as soon as they form into recognisable shape. A part of his brain tells him to close his eyes before they hit. Another part fights it, so he is able to watch, but mostly feel and hear …

Two silver smears, like cutting sword strokes blurring through the air, then the hit, like an iron bar on a steel drum, two near simultaneous sharp strikes, *boom-boom*, and he is inside that drum: deafening, painful.

A moment later the bodywork still vibrates from the passage of the two streamliners that have bracketed his hobbled car – just inches either side of him – while there is a ringing in his ears and even a fluttering in his lungs from the steely-hard noise of their racing engines. He slows his car, amazed that it is somehow not in a hundred pieces, braking gently at first, for he is still travelling at speed, still trying to control it, the car slewing from side to side, the horizon dancing giddily along the lip of his cockpit, the streamliners already dots in his mirrors. Through the right mirror he also sees the failed tyre peel itself from the wheel, which then throws up a rooster tail of sparks as the naked steel rattles along the road.

He finally brings the car to a clattering, skidding halt on the slender strip of the grass central reservation. He looks at the narrow road alongside. There is barely room for three cars. He shakes his head in admiration. Rosemeyer and Caracciola have both worked a miracle to miss him.

"Well," he said quietly to himself. "I think I've made my mark on this race."

*

They had fallen in with two NSKK men, sharing a table in the Prater beer garden, which had just reopened after its winter hibernation and smelt almost as much of fresh paint as it did of hot sausage. They were ordinary men, really, ordinary men wearing swastikas; but ordinary men who loved cars more than politics, ordinary men who were happy to talk to two who worked on the Auto Union racing cars, and even buy them beer. They had left the table under the chestnut trees and had then walked through streets Sepp did not know. Now they had stopped in front of a UFA cinema. One of the NSKK men, a bald Berliner, had promised them a treat, but Sepp had said he wanted to see the film. Maybe he did, but maybe he was scared of what the Berliner promised, too. He would admit that, to himself.

"More like you want to grease your driveshaft to all those healthy Nazi girls in their short skirts and tight blouses on the newsreel, eh?" Lick said with a lascivious laugh.

"Ah, 'strength through joy' is it," put in one of the merry Nazis. "But come with us friend, the real thing is much better. Berlin has some of the best snappers money can buy – if you know where to look."

Sepp declined, again. Lick put his arm around his shoulders, where it hung heavy like a python, he tipped the black NSKK side-cap he'd borrowed off one of his new chums on to the back of his head. The other three were quite a few beers up on Sepp, because he had lagged behind, not in the mood for it. Also, he no longer believed he had to drink as much as

Lick and the others to fit in, and he was glad of that. Proud, even.

"C'mon pal, it will do you good," Lick said.

"No, you go on. I want to see the film."

"It wasn't your fault, it was probably a dodgy tyre, it happens. And with that one's jinx ..." Lick said the last with a theatrical shudder.

Sepp nodded: "Still, I'd rather not."

Finally they left him to it, shaking their heads and shrugging. Of course, he knew Westbury Holt's spectacular retirement was not down to him. But while Sepp also believed it was a faulty tyre, Herr Fink had not been so sure, blaming the Englishman for overheating the rubber. That had been a strange aspect of the event; it was the fastest race ever and yet the tyres had not been able to cope with the speeds for any length of time. None of the cars had been able to race flat out for long, and in the end the most cautious of the men in the streamliners had won the final.

The cinema was stern, grand, faced with concrete slabs, but with bright lights flooding the entrance and long frosted glass rib windows that shone like the slots in a radio set. A huge swastika flag hung over the door. Sepp paid with a handful of change and took a seat near the back. The theatre smelt of cigarette smoke. It was half-empty, it was a pleasant spring evening and most were on the streets, or in the bierkellers. Perhaps some of them celebrated the victory of Lang in the Mercedes, maybe others talked about the extraordinary escape of Rosemeyer, Caracciola and the Englishman. When the incident had been described to him Sepp could only feel relief that there had not been the most horrific crash.

The show had started, a mote-laden cone of light bathing the far wall with the flickering image of fit Nazi girls, blonde and wholesome and squeezed into white gym kit, playing with medicine balls. He thought of Lick's comment and felt a stirring in his loins. He shifted in his seat, wondered what it would be like. Lick had said that to not visit a brothel in Berlin would be like not taking coffee and cake in Leipzig, but Sepp wasn't sure about that. It seemed wrong, yet he knew he had done well not to say that to Lick. Besides, he had other things to occupy his mind, things that were more important to a boy – a man – with a simple dream.

Yet earlier that day, as he'd watched Hermann Lang take the flag to win the final at the AVUS – the mechanic who had worked his way up to race for Mercedes – his dream had seemed far from simple. Even as he had touched the car that could make him one of the fastest men in the world – yes, even as he'd touched it, it all seemed out of reach. But one thing, at least, he had now driven a racing car. When a mechanic was needed to bring a Type C around to the pit area Lick was always sure Sepp got the job, and he had been thrilled on those rare occasions.

Yet that was hardly racing. Perhaps Hanna was right? Perhaps it was time to grow out of these *silly dreams*? Perhaps. The screen was filled with soldiers now, the crunch of goosesteps overplayed with martial music boomed from the speakers. He wondered how long before the feature, a German comedy called *The Man Who Was Sherlock Holmes*, would start. Someone shuffled past him with a grunted 'excuse me' and he was forced to stand for a moment. On the screen the image of the Führer had been replaced with that of a middle-aged man, kindly eyes and moustache, wearing the long white coat of a doctor, a stethoscope hung around his neck like a medal. A girl was with him, of a type, blonde and firm – easy to imagine she had rushed straight from the game with the medicine balls.

The girl and the doctor bent to peer into a glass tank, their faces visible through it. Inside the tank there was a pair of scorpions, each of which moved in little darting spasms. The camera moved closer and the girl's eyes bulged big through the glass. "Now watch my child," said the doctor in tones of hushed reverence. Sepp watched too, with growing fascination. The scorpions fought and the girl grew more excited. It was a one-sided fight that, ironically, had no sting in the tail. The larger scorpion triumphed and the doctor looked hugely satisfied, an expression of smug wunderbar stretched across his face as the weaker creature died in a series of dramatic convulsions.

"You see, that is the way of life. At all levels," he explained to the girl. "From the lowest creature to man himself, it is a struggle, and only the strong will survive. It is the natural way of things."

"I see Doctor," she said, sweetly.

The short film finished and there was a general shuffling around as people made themselves comfortable for the feature, a match flared in the row in front of him and a woman coughed. All of a sudden Sepp felt better, as if he'd woken up to find the answer to a tricky problem that had been unresolved at bedtime. He could do it. He was strong. He was fast. Like Rosemeyer, like Lang. *This is Germany* ... And there is no cheating the destiny of a man in Germany. Somehow he would find a way to show how quick he was. Whatever it might take, he would find a way. He rushed out of the cinema. "Must be a good film," remarked a young sailor to his girl in the lobby, as Sepp brushed past them and took his grin out into the Berlin streets.

***

"The old man's cut me adrift – not a farthing."

"Well, you know how your father feels about the Germans," Gracie said. "War leaves more than empty trenches, friend Westbury."

"The trenches have been filled in."

"But it's the other empty spaces that need addressing," Gracie said. "The Nazis know this. They know how to use it to their advantage, too. I'll give them that."

They were walking across a large square lined with brightly painted buildings most of which were bedecked in swastikas. The Odeons Platz, Gracie had told him; always the tour-guide. There seemed to be even more swastikas here than elsewhere, West thought, as they angled across the square and then past a towering statue-stuffed loggia where eternal flames flickered in front of yet more swastika flags – it was called the Feldherrnhalle; Gracie had given him the full Baedeker on it. West had arrived in Munich that morning. There was a Nazi brass-hat who wanted a Horch instead of a Mercedes. West had sold the Lagonda on his last quick trip back to England, it was the only way he could lay his hands on good-for-something currency, and so he'd jumped at the chance to deliver the Horch to the Party HQ at the Brown House in Munich. The Nazis liked to have their cars delivered by the racing drivers, and while West was not Bernd Rosemeyer, the customer was not Rudolf Hess, either. It also meant West could pay Gracie a visit as he had long promised to do.

The corner of Gracie's mouth was twitching a little, as if he was enjoying West's recent fall into poverty. Though in truth he was only really poor once he stepped out of Germany, his junior driver wage of 200 Reichsmarks a month was more than enough to get by otherwise. He was not entirely sure he was happy about spending the rest of his life in one country, though; a man can tire of beer and sausage and swastika. But then West had always known that the old man would not take kindly to him driving for a German team; he hated the Germans with a passion that only those who had gone to war might understand, West supposed. His father was a patient old bastard, but even he had his limits. West had felt perversely proud to have found them; and then a little sad. They took the street to the left of the pompous building and immediately walked past a monument of some sort, in line with the portico of the Feldherrnhalle, the sort of bronze that was everywhere in Germany these days, and couldn't hold West's attention.

"Halt!"

The shout was loud enough to earn an echo, and it was the sort of shout you could not ignore. It was enough to make West and Gracie pull up in a scuff of shoe leather. They turned to find its source, which was marching towards them: a head that was a ball of ugliness and anger, in about equal measures, squeezed into a black coal scuttle helmet that gleamed like anthracite. Beneath the helmeted head the man wore the uniform of the SS.

"You are supposed to salute," the SS man said, with a sneer of contempt, his gaze flicking up and down West's usual attire of cricket jumper and flannels like the tip of a slashing sabre. West's scruffiness was possibly all the more offensive because the man seemed to be in his best ceremonial uniform: as black as night in a cave, with white gloves and red armband flaring brightly in contrast.

"Salute you?" West said, realising the tone was more mocking than inquiring just as the words left his mouth. He turned to Gracie, expecting him to cringe, or at least look a little worried, but he was surprised to realise there was actually the hint of a smile there, tugging lightly at the corner of his mouth.

"Salute the memorial – as well you know!" With that the policeman grabbed West by the arm, while behind him his colleague, who had kept out of it until now, standing in the shade of a deep doorway that seemed to act as their sentry box, looked on with interest, a white-gloved hand resting on the flap of his holster. "I think you might enjoy a day or two in the cells, lad!" the first SS man said.

Just the thought of being locked up in a cramped cell – an image of a crushingly tiny box of a room flashed inside him as soon as he heard the word, such was his aversion to enclosed spaces – was enough for West to react. He grabbed the arm that held him with his right hand and bunched his left into a fist, at the same time looking for a direction to run in. Shock filled the face of the SS man, and his eyes puffed up like a pair of panicking exotic fishes.

"Steady on there, old man." The words were Gracie's, as was the steadying hand on West's shoulder, pulling him away from what seemed, for a brief moment at least, like inevitable confrontation. Then Gracie turned his attention to the SS man. "I'm sorry; we're visitors here, what seems to be the trouble, sir?"

Gracie's conciliatory tone seemed to snuff the spark of anger. "Foreigners eh?" the SS man said. "Well that *might* explain it." He took a deep breath which filled his chest, then shook his head: "This marks the spot where the martyrs of the movement fell in 1923. It's a site that's sacred," the SS man explained, in a proud, yet also slightly embarrassed, manner, and West followed his gaze to the large tomb-profiled bronze slab set on a stone plinth and surmounted with an eagle clutching a wreath-enclosed swastika, now toffee bright in the sunlight. "Everyone must give the German salute to the memorial to the fallen, it's respectful ... It's the law," the SS man added, quite sharply. "So next time you walk this way, make sure you salute the memorial – got it?"

"Got it," Gracie said, as a woman passed by, her arm snapping into a stiff Hitler salute as of it was attached to a cord tugged by a puppeteer in the sky. West and Gracie walked away, without saluting, as they were already past the memorial.

"You knew about that, didn't you?" West said, once they were out of earshot of the SS man.

"Possibly," Gracie said, grinning now. "I normally take the side-street to avoid it. Others do the same, which has to be a good sign."

"Never had you down as a practical joker, Gracie," West said.

"A practical *demonstration* friend Westbury, that's all. It's important you're aware of just how easy it is to get arrested in this country."

"Right now I'm more interested in just how easy it is to get a beer."

"Well, the good news is that in Munich that's one of the very few things that's easier than getting arrested."

A short time later they were sat at a long table at the Hofbrauhaus. Foaming beer in tall, grey salt-glazed stoneware litre steins, each with the blue crown and HB stencilled upon it, stood in front of them. The huge beer hall smelt just a little of spilt beer, and a little more of hot wurst, smoke, sweat and the past. It was the sort of place that seemed immune to the passage of time – though some kindly soul had supplied enough swastika flags to remind drinkers they were in the 1930s, and not the 1580s.

"The whole thing started here, in a way, you know," Gracie said, taking a sip from his beer that left a froth moustache – more Stalin than Hitler – above his lip.

"Well, if it all started in a pub then surely it can't be all that bad, Gracie?" West said, as he took in his surroundings. The huge beer hall was not full, yet the shouts and laughs of other drinkers boomed through the arches of the vast vaulted ceiling, while light that was filtered through blue glass splashed on to the wooden tables and the pale wood of the ceiling supports, or illuminated the scratchy smoke from cigarettes, cigars and pipes.

"Hitler made his name ranting and raving in the room upstairs," Gracie said. "Some wish he'd stayed there. Mind you, without Herr Hitler some others might not have their silver toys to play with."

"I thought we'd agreed that was off the agenda, old boy?"

"Quite. But surely you don't mind talking about racing?"

"Since when have you been interested in racing?" West said, beginning to stuff his Dunhill with *Player's No Name*. "I've been meaning to ask you that for a while, actually."

"I'm more interested in others who are interested in racing, if truth be told."

West lifted his heavy stein and gulped down a couple of inches of the stone cold Hofbrau, before saying: "Just why are you *really* here, Gracie?"

"Good beer," Gracie grinned, then wiped his upper lip with the back of his hand, taking care of the remaining flecks of beer foam and the grin in one. Suddenly he looked serious, and he lowered his voice as he said: "You know I've always been interested in politics, friend Westbury."

"And politicians?"

"That depends. The politicians at home are harmless, nothing more than lap dogs, but they breed them with bite over here." He looked around him, almost seeming to suggest that by 'here' he actually mean the Hofbrauhaus. "You know, I was talking about you some weeks ago, to a friend at home," Gracie said.

"You have friends?"

"A colleague," Gracie smiled.

"You have work?"

"It pays the bills, how else do you think I can afford to stay in all those German hotels?"

"I'd never considered it."

Gracie smiled, then took a quick look over his shoulder, checking to see there was no one close enough to listen in. The nearest table that was taken was three away, where four workmen argued loudly about boxing. "You know," Gracie said, "there are ways you might earn a little useful money – pounds that is."

"Work?" West formed the word as if he was speaking around a nugget of dog doings.

"Not so much working, more …" Gracie seemed to fish for the right word for a moment "… More, *observing*."

"And just what do you mean by *observing*?"

"Well, has it never occurred to you how many uniforms there are around when you're racing in Germany?"

West shrugged: "They like dressing up."

"There's more to it than that, old boy," Gracie said, as another group of drinkers clanked steins and laughed in a far corner. "I'm sure that even you are aware that the Nazis are building up their armed forces?" Gracie said.

"That's their business."

"Well, not quite. They're supposed to be restricted by the terms of the Treaty of Versailles. But let's not get into that now. Suffice to say they're developing a lot of their technology on the quiet, the very quiet. But then again, just some of it in the full glare of the limelight."

"What's this got to do with me?"

"Well, one of the ways in which it's believed they're testing their technology is on the race track."

A waitress in a dirndl, her breasts as close to overflowing as the froth on the grey steins she carried, passed the table in a swish of rounded hips, and West allowed himself to be distracted for a moment or two. Then he said: "I race cars, Gracie, not dive bombers."

Gracie eyed him, that new, mischievous look – like the one before they'd walked by the memorial at the Feldherrnhalle without saluting – in his eyes. He lifted his stein in both hands and sank its contents in a succession of Adam's apple bobbing gulps, then gasped and allowed the base of the stony stein to thump against the table.

Westbury Holt could recognise a challenge at a thousand and two paces so, of course, he matched him – as he did for the next two steins …

"So, you're a spy?" West said, after Gracie admitted defeat and started their fourth stein with a sip and a hand held up in surrender.

"An amateur really," Gracie said, making sure again that they were out of earshot. "The dissertation is real enough, and it gives me an excuse to travel around Germany, read the newspapers."

"The papers?"

"Yes, the stories might be far-fetched, but when you see an advert for skilled machinists placed by an aeroplane company, then that's what they call currency in this trade, old chap."

West shook his head. "Never had you down as The Thirty-Nine Steps sort," he said.

"I was approached at Cambridge, and I wasn't the only one, I can tell you … Well actually, I can't tell you. But you would be surprised."

"I'm more surprised that you seem to think I might get involved," West said.

"I'd hoped you might consider —"

"But it's you who keeps telling me what an unsavoury bunch of people these Nazis are, why would I want to upset them? I simply can't afford to lose this drive, you know that."

"We could make life a little easier."

"*We?*"

"Perhaps change a little currency, and as I've said, we'll pay you, too – in pounds, of course."

"I don't need the money that much."

"I know your situation, friend Westbury. Your debts back home have got out of hand since you've been in Germany, what with Pater not being on hand to bail you out."

"How do you know that?"

Gracie shrugged.

"I'll pay them all, just need to start to earn some proper cash, that's all," West continued.

"If their patience holds, that is …"

"What are you getting at?"

Gracie shook his head and smiled widely. "Oh, come on West, all you need to do is keep your ear to the wall, nose to the ground, lips to the stein, and life will be easier for everyone – besides, haven't you an ounce of patriotism? We could be at war with these people sometime soon."

"Do you really believe that?"

"It's merely indulging in gossip, friend Westbury," Gracie said, ignoring the question. "Then some idle chitter-chatter with yours truly from time to time – and who's to think anything much of a couple of chums getting together for a few drinks every now and then, eh?"

"And just what sort of gossip do you want? What Rosemeyer has for breakfast?"

"It will be enough to know who you see, tell us who you meet – especially if they're in the uniform of the Luftwaffe."

"Well, that should be simple enough," West admitted, wondering then if Gracie had forced the pace with the steins to make him more receptive, but doubting that was in him. They were both still sober, but merrily so.

"You might want to ask some questions about the fuel you're using, too, if you get the chance," Gracie then said, in just a little too offhand a manner for West's liking. "If there is to be a war then Germany will be stuck for a fuel supply for its aircraft, and you can bet they're looking at all sorts of concoctions and potions – such as that strange smelling brew that your cars run on, for instance. You know, it might be useful for you to develop an interest in chemistry."

West nodded, but made a point of not actually saying he'd go along with it. And yet there would be no harm in a little gossip, he supposed. What would it matter if he chatted about work with an old pal? But then he suddenly remembered the little incident earlier in the day, and that same image of a tiny box of a prison cell jumped into his head, causing a little flutter of something close to panic.

"Tell me Gracie," West said, "why the little *demonstration* at the Feldherrnhalle earlier?"

"I thought it only fair to show you that nothing is quite safe here, friend Westbury, not walking down the street, perhaps not even gossip. So just you be careful, old man."

***

Hanna sat on the pit counter, swinging her legs slightly and letting her heels tap against the tin sign that was fixed to it. Bored. Again. She wondered if Konrad had brought a bottle, a drink was always welcome at times like these, but she knew this was hardly the time to ask, as he was talking to the press, leaning heavily on his crutches. Coming back to the Nürburgring today seemed to have reminded him of the pain of yesterday. Then she had sat in these same pits to watch the race – the Eifelrennen – stopwatches and clipboard in hand, which helped alleviate the boredom a little. Konrad had driven the first two laps of the race, but when the pain proved too much for him he had brought the car in, handed it over to West, then collapsed in agony against the pit counter as the magnesium flares flashed and the camera shutters clicked.

They were still flashing and clicking now and Konrad was smiling through the pain, reporters hanging on his every word as he modestly told of the effort of driving the Auto Union when he was, "perhaps not quite recovered". Earlier the photographers had had their slice of her and him, "the perfect German couple," as Kessler had then put it. The Nazi was in the background now, nodding his approval as Konrad spoke. She had worried for Konrad yesterday, but just a few painkillers and a couple of glasses of his *Gautier* cognac after the race, once back in his room at the Hotel Eifeler Hof in Adenau, and he had been back to his old self.

Westbury Holt stood to one side now, getting ready to drive one of the racing cars, putting his tatty off-white sweater on over his overalls. He had seen little action the day before, the gearbox breaking just a half a lap after he had taken over from Konrad. She had never seen him as angry as he was when he walked in then, but he seemed back to his jocular self now, and she found she was glad of that. They were to shoot some publicity film but first West, as junior driver, was to take Konrad's car around the circuit for one lap to warm it up and check the repairs. West stood close to where Lick and another mechanic, both looking the worse for the celebration of Rosemeyer's victory in the race, were decanting fuel from a large barrel with a pump affixed to it into a smaller churn that sat beside it. The fumes were beginning to sting Hanna's eyes a little. Opposite, across the broad expanse of the pit straight, a long comb of Hitler Youth boys were working their way along the stand, a lad to a row, filling sacks with rubbish as they went. Sometimes the youngsters would steal a glance of their heroes but they would not neglect their duty for long and the long fawn line of boys was never less than perfectly straight, their work the rustle of the rubbish sacks, the clatter of slamming seats, jokes and happy laughter.

"What exactly is in that stuff?" West asked Lick, nodding at the fuel churn and making a point of sniffing and grimacing at the acrid pong of the potent brew. The racing fuel smelt more of raw alcohol now, rather than the strange – sometimes boot polish, sometimes burnt almond – whiff it gave off when the cars were running.

"Damned if I know," Lick said. "Ask Fink, he's quite particular about what they feed his babies."

An engine burbled in the near distance, someone revving it every now and then, its rasping snarl tearing at the grey air. It would be one of the mechanics readying the car at the Auto Union Hallen, the team's HQ and garage at the circuit, situated further up the pit straight between the Sports Hotel and the main grandstand. The engine revs suddenly rose once more, though it was more sustained this time, before there was the unmistakable sound of squealing rubber as an Auto Union snaked on to the circuit. The tail of the car kicked out in a wide, graceful arc – just like Rosemeyer, she thought – before the driver took second gear and pulled the car straight. The car braked late at the box, but without skidding, to a cheer and a ripple of applause from the Hitler Youth lads in the grandstand.

Hanna recognised the driver instantly. It was Sepp, his flat cap turned backwards so that it looked like some peculiar cloth-coated streamlining device, at one with the profile of the car. West smiled and shook his head in mock censure, Lick and the other mechanic laughed and clapped him on the back as he climbed from the cockpit, but Konrad looked annoyed – perhaps because the little show had distracted the journalists. Sepp greeted her, then leapt over the pit counter to collect some tools. She turned to face him, swinging her legs clear of the counter.

"I thought you'd been warned about that?"

"That was nothing."

"It looked fast to me."

"Oh no, that's not fast, that's just show. When I'm given the chance, then I'll go fast – you'll see," he said it with such surety, such utter self-belief that she had to smile with him.

"What would Herr Fink say?"

"He's not here," Sepp said. The senior mechanic was still with the other cars at the Hallen.

"Been busy?" she asked.

"You bet," he said. "I don't know what they did to that gearbox, there were broken teeth everywhere."

"Well, it's not so easy to drive with such injuries, little brother."

"Herr Fink seems to think it might just as well have been Herr Holt," Sepp said, a thoughtful look on his face. He took off his cap, then ran his greasy hand through his blond hair, leaving a dark streak in it before putting the cap on the right way around. "Have you asked him?" Sepp said, and she knew instantly what he meant, because he asked her the same thing every time they were together these days.

"Konrad will do what he can for you," she said.

Sepp grinned again, then he was leaping back over the low counter, an oily tool roll clanking in his hands. She shook her head a little sadly and turned to face the main straight again. Yes she had asked Konrad, but how could she explain to Sepp that he would have to be patient if he wanted his chance to drive some laps in one of the cars. Sepp was always in a hurry.

West strapped on his wind helmet and goggles as he walked over to Hanna. "You been round yet?" he asked her.

"Round?"

"You know ..." he made a funny circular movement with his head then glanced suspiciously from side to side like a melodrama spy, "the 'Ring."

"Once, with Konrad in the Horch, it was very —"

"No, that doesn't count – in this," he rolled his eyes in the direction of the Auto Union. "Fancy a ride?" he whispered.

"But how can you —?"

"Leave it five minutes or so and take a stroll down to the end of the straight."

"But —"

"Well, only if you're up to it, of course." With that he was away, diving deep into a conversation about the replaced gearbox with Lick. Her jaw had dropped and she had to make a conscious effort to close her mouth tight. *Only if you're up to it*...Damn him.

She heard Lick say: "More broken teeth than you'd find in a Rabbi's gob after the Brownshirts have paid a visit; what was the old boy up to?"

West shrugged, but didn't reply, while Hanna eased herself off the pit counter then strode over to Konrad, piercing the ring of conversation as politely as possible.

"Konrad?"

"Yes darling," Konrad broke off from his interview with the reporters and the film people, Kessler shot her a look of annoyance; it was a look she was getting familiar with.

"I'm feeling a little ill – the fumes ..." she glanced at the fuel churn. "I thought I might take a little walk?"

"Yes, yes – you go on." He nodded vigorously then went back to his conversation. She turned and walked. Five paces before he called again, chasing after her, swinging from the crutches. "I'm sorry, wrapped up in things as usual – but you're not well, shall I get one of the lads to take you back to the hotel?" he looked genuinely concerned and she felt touched, and a little guilty for the white lie she had told.

"No, really, a walk will do me good."

"Konrad! Time is short," Kessler shouted, leather gloved hands resting on his hips

"A moment, please," Konrad snapped back, before turning to her again: "If you're sure then ... But don't get lost now." He laughed and pecked her on the cheek, then went back to his conversation.

She walked up along the row of pit stalls. Despite the activity in the Auto Union pit and the grandstand opposite the circuit felt strangely empty, sound seemed to carry further because of it, a wheel hammer dropped on the floor, the shout of a Hitler Youth leader, the cry of a crow. The pit straight was a wide expanse of jointed concrete slabs, some stained in long island-like maps of black oil, others tattooed with the dark grey stripes from yesterday's rubber-melting start. She strolled past the other pit boxes, with their low counters and car numbers painted above them, and on past the race control tower with its clock hanging over the start finish straight and its balcony dressed in the colours of *Continental Tyres*. The road split here, the fork fenced off with low removable pylons, which meant that cars could do quick circuits of the south curve and return to the pits without running the entire fourteen-mile lap. She walked behind the control tower and took in the view of the castle, its dark tower peeping over a fringe of trees, from here she would be out of sight of the Auto Union pit. There was the sound of an engine starting.

The Auto Union ballooned in size as it sped down the narrow concrete straight behind the pits and Westbury Holt pulled it up close to her with a couple of rasping blips of the accelerator. "Climb aboard!" he shouted over the din of the engine. She looked into the well of the cockpit, there was hardly the room for him in there, never mind a passenger. "Well come on then!"

"You're not really serious are you – there's no room?" she shouted, above the burble of the engine.

He just grinned: "Are you coming or not?"

"But I —" He revved the engine to drown her complaint, "but I —" another loud rev and she looked around to see if anyone was looking. Then she shook her head, cursed herself quietly, and climbed into the car, hitching her skirt up high and ignoring the comic roll of his eyes as she did so. He had to shift back in the seat and it was a tight fit. She was squeezed half onto his lap and half onto a tiny portion of the seat, her right arm draped over the side of the cockpit opening. West threaded his arms around her waist and managed to get a good hold of the wheel while she gripped the thin sides of the cockpit surround for support, feeling the buzz of the engine tingling through the metal at her fingertips. It felt alive, a living beast. West squeezed himself tighter to her and revved the engine again, the needle in the large clock on the dash stuttering across the dial.

"Hold on," he shouted as the needle dipped, then he kicked out at the clutch pedal, the inside of his left leg rubbing against the top of her thigh. There was a clunk and then more noise, then they were away, the sudden jolt pushing her back into him so that she could feel his breath against her ear. Only then did she realise she was at his mercy in more ways than one.

She wore no goggles and at first the wind blasted her eyes painfully, so she hunched lower behind the windshield, close up to the steering wheel, blinking away the tears, while he looked over her left shoulder for a view of the track ahead.

Within seconds she had forgotten the man. Within seconds she could think of nothing else but holding on, and savouring the sights and sounds that rushed at her. In some places the car seemed to be facing off the track as West twirled the wheel this way and that as fast as an untied helm in a storm tossed sea. At other times the world seemed quiet as the car would take to the air, and then land with a bone-crunching jar and a more welcome scuffy kiss of tyres on asphalt. It seemed like corner after corner, hill after hill, was there no end to it? There were dark patches of forest where he would thread the silver needle through the green tapestry, open meadows where they would tag the hedgerows, kicking up whirlwinds of grass at the side of the track, and concrete speed bowls where the centrifugal force would push her tight against him. There was no respite, she was scared – she knew – yet also exhilarated.

Then, as they sped along the long, long undulating stretch that headed back towards the pits, arrow straight between the hedgerows, she felt him. At first she thought it was somehow a part of the seat, hard and sticking out into her lower back. But as he shifted to get a better view on the approach to a small humpback bridge it seemed to press harder still: granite, unyielding – and she caught sight of his grin in the little lug of a mirror on the edge of the cockpit. She did her best to ignore it, but all the same she was aware of the treacherous blush that was beginning to warm her throat. *Damn it … Damn him … The fool …* Finally he pulled up before the long sweep that led into the pit straight, leaving her with a long enough walk back to the pits. The car burbled at low revs as she climbed out, brushing down her skirt. She felt weak, as hanging on had been harder work than she would have imagined and her fingers were numb from the effort, and from the cold from being out in the airstream. "Of course," he shouted over the noise of the engine with a grin, "that was a slow lap, you know."

"Of course," she nodded, wondering if the words had actually come out.

"And now you can do me the honour of accepting an invitation to dinner."

She said nothing. The world still seemed to be rushing past at 100mph, and her vision was still blurred from the tears the fast and cold air had caused. And then there was that invisible spot on her lower back she ached to scratch, to touch. She was trying to form the words in her head, something like: *Konrad and I would be delighted …* But in the end she simply shook her head.

"You'll change your mind," West said with a laugh. "And I never give up on a debt." With that he gunned the engine and took off in a cloud of tyre smoke, throwing a casual wave behind him.

***

Sepp's head was swimming with new ideas; bright fish of thought colliding in a confusing jumble of fear and ferocity. And yet … and yet there was something else there, too: something that seemed to speak to his very soul. These days he knew how good it was to be a part of something great, now he was learning that he always had been.

The pad on the dusty old table in front of him was scrawled with lines transcribed from the fat blue hardback book that lay flat against its spine beside it. The words were in a hand that was undoubtedly his, yet it looked as unsteady as drunken graffiti on the wall of the pisser at the Dresdnerstrasse Inn. The naked bulb no longer worked, but at this hour, early evening, the summer light flooded through the basement window in a wide mote-laden shaft that reminded him of the still of the Marienkirche. Outside, kids screamed in praise of summer and bicycle bells answered the clang-clang of the trams.

Thanks to Konrad's generosity, and the extra money Sepp now brought in – his pay had gone up fourfold as he'd proved his worth to the team over the past months – they had neglected this basement kitchen, moving into one of the better apartments upstairs complete with kitchen, bathroom and two bedrooms, where they planned to stay until Hanna and Konrad were married. But sometimes he still liked to visit the basement kitchen, to remember the dreams of youth not so long gone – to remember to keep dreaming those dreams.

He had set a pan of water on the stove for coffee, but it had boiled to nothing as he devoured the book, the steam licking at the light, over-heating the room and filling it with the familiar smell of hot metal, before he had finally turned off the hob. He should open the window, he thought for the fifth time in as many minutes, then he refocused on the page in front of him.

Sepp couldn't make sense of some of it – how could a *book* be filled with such hate, and yet speak of purity and, yes, destiny? But then could so many Germans really be wrong? He wasn't sure, so took from the book what he could see, those things that meant something to him – things about destiny, things about Germany – until there was line after line on the pad. Somewhere beyond the veil of his concentration the tap-tap of shoes on the pavement outside was followed by the slam of the heavy front door. *Could I have really been so wrong about this?* he asked himself for the umpteenth time. And then the door at the top of the little staircase swung open to a scream of tortured hinges and the light from the hallway flooded a corner of the kitchen, a patch that was filled with Hanna soon after. There was another set of footfalls in her wake – creased trouser legs now in sight beyond her lovely big eyed look of curious shock.

"Well … So what are you doing down here little brother," she said, "and what's this, a dirty book?"

Sepp swept the heavy book and the notepad off the table and into the rough canvas shoulder bag he used for work. "It's nothing," he said, quickly buckling the strap in place, wondering at the strange irony of it all, hiding the one book that these days certainly need not be hidden. The trouser legs stumbled down the last few steps.

"He's had a shock." Hanna had read Sepp's inquisitive glance before he had time to form the question. "The doctors have had him."

"The doctors?"

"The snip," she said.

Sepp read the fear in Strudel's eyes, which still shone wetly with tears. His hands were clasped tightly together over his crotch.

"I have chocolate," Sepp said, after some moments of hesitant silence, pulling a paper-covered slab of *Stollwerck* from the front pocket of his work bag. "It's melted a bit, but he's —" Hanna snatched the chocolate from him and sat Strudel at the table. If there was one thing Strudel loved as much as machines it was chocolate. He ate it mechanically and very quickly, with no sign that he was enjoying it, except a little light in his eyes, the half melted bar messily smearing his lips. It reminded Sepp of the way a dog would eat a treat, he thought – with sympathy – and then just a little disgust. *Is he anything more than an animal?* Sepp thought, surprised that it had come to him like that.

"Why here?" Sepp asked, throwing the thought into a dark corner of his mind, wondering if he might find it some other time.

"He was wandering the street, crying and clutching his … You know," she glanced downwards. "The children were laughing, the adults turning their heads. I had to do something, and that nosy old bitch Frau Hansen is up with old Kurt, and I didn't want her to put her two pfennigs into the pot."

Sepp nodded, that was fair enough. Their neighbour did not miss a trick, and would have been on the landing asking questions as soon as Hanna and Strudel were at the door to the apartment. Besides, Strudel had always liked it down here. They all had.

"Does Kurt know?"

"Yes, I spoke to him earlier. Says it was inevitable, said he had told

Strudel to keep his head down, keep out of sight. But is that a life?"

Sepp shook his head.

"How can they do it?" Hanna said.

"I suppose they have their reasons."

"Sepp!"

"I mean, they're doctors, they know what they are doing … It's for the future … Isn't it?"

"Some future, you should spend more time in Berlin little brother, there's the future for you. There are signs that say 'No Jews' at Wansee, can you believe that? People are going missing, just disappearing, all the time, and then this …" She looked at Strudel.

"I know there's much that's wrong Hanna, much, but …" he let it tail off, it was all too much a part of this new confusion.

She looked at him, her gaze locked on to his. There was a slight shake of the head, almost imperceptible like the stir of a heavy branch in a light breeze, and then she sniffed at the burnt air. "My God, let's get some fresh air in here." She stood on the old stool and opened the basement window.

He was glad of the distraction, his thoughts too confused, too jumbled, for him to argue. He made use of it to change the subject, asking her what he always asked her: "Have you talked to Konrad about my try out?"

"I've asked him, you know that," Hanna said, as Strudel noisily licked the last of the melted chocolate from the corners of the wrapping paper.

"And?"

"You must wait a while longer; he says it's not the right time, yet."

"And when *will* it be the right time?"

"Please Sepp, I really don't know," she reached over and placed her hand on his. "I will try my best for you but you must be patient. Konrad has a great deal on his mind right now." Something in the way she said it had the brotherly antennae twitching, the hint of Hanna's frustration that had lived with him for so long. She held her face to the broad band of light that shafted through the basement window, her hands at her hips. "My, look at us, shut up down here like fugitives; let's get some sun boys, shall we? We can walk by the river. C'mon!" With that she thumped up the stairs and Sepp and Strudel followed, Sepp slinging his bag over his shoulder.

They walked down the street, then turned right at the Johannisbad. Hanna curled her arm through Sepp's, as natural as it had always been, but when he caught the envious glances of those young men looking at him and her, he could not help but feel a flush of pride. Let them think that. They headed towards the river, dropping down from the road before the bridge and making their way slowly north along the path that ran along the top of the flood defences. Yes, this was a good move, Sepp thought. The Zwickau Mulde was an old friend, flowing slowly to his right, calming his thoughts.

Before he had been given the job on the team he had come here often, to dream of racing, but he had not walked along the riverbank lately. Being near the river again made him less confused, more sure of his destiny. The path his life would take from here now seemed as obvious as that of the river that flowed south besides him. Good friend Zwickau Mulde.

They walked slowly, still arm in arm, stopping for a while to watch the evening fun at the swimming pool. Strudel walked in front of them, moving in that slightly jerky way of his.

"He seems happier," Hanna said, though it was difficult to really tell what Strudel was thinking or feeling, if anything at all, Sepp thought.

"He just needs his chocolate, he'll forget about the whole thing in a week," Sepp said, as they walked on. The trees on the far bank were reflected in the slow moving river, a man doffed his cap to them, the shrieks and splashes from the Lido slowly diminished into the distance. "You know, Lick thinks the Englander is running out of chances, they might get rid of him if he doesn't have a good result soon."

"Really?" she seemed concerned, and that surprised him, she seldom took an interest in the racing these days. "But I thought you said he was quick?"

"He's quick all right. But Konrad will show him who is boss, once he's fit – you needn't worry on that score."

Hanna said nothing.

"And if Delius is back to his best after his accident then there seems to be little need for Holt now," Sepp added, remembering the nasty crash Ernst von Delius had had during the Eifelrennen after a bird had flown into his face when he was at speed. "Herr Fink will not be sorry to see him go, that's for sure. He thinks he's far too wild."

"What about you, what do you think?"

Sepp just shrugged.

Hanna was silent, and he noticed that she turned her head away from him. "Don't you like Westbury, Sepp?" Hanna said, still not looking him in the eyes.

"I like him well enough, but he's not serious, so he will never be successful. He plays the fool too much, people like that don't realise how lucky they are."

"Rosemeyer plays the fool," she said.

"Rosemeyer's Rosemeyer … Besides, it's not enough to be just quick; pretty soon I think Konrad will show the Englander that."

"Let's hope so," she said, quietly.

They walked on a little further, Strudel still ahead of them, his arms stiff by his sides, attention wholly focused on a small white and rust motor boat that was slowly nudging its way upstream, a creamy wake curling from its stern.

"Tell me Hanna, how are things with you and Konrad?"

"Fine … Good, everything is fine."

"It's just that you rarely talk of him now."

"Don't I?" she shrugged, suddenly letting go of his arm. "Maybe there's not much to say, he spends more time with that creep Kessler than me."

"But that's work."

"Yes, work."

"And the wedding?"

"I'm still waiting for my Aryan certificate."

"There's not a problem is there?" She shrugged. He had wanted to ask her about the certificate for some time – about the blood that ran through his veins, too. "You have applied?" She shrugged again, then walked on a little quicker, a full half-metre between them now.

"Hanna?"

"There is still much to do; it's no easy matter proving Aryan ancestry back to 1750, little brother," she said.

"But you have started; you have some birth and wedding certificates?"

"There's plenty of time," she said, "I'm still young you know, and anyway, I have to be sure I'm ready for marriage."

"That's nonsense, Hanna," he said, finding it difficult to believe what he was hearing.

"Is it? What do you see, what do you know little brother – is there anything you know beyond nuts and bloody bolts!" Her face was flushed with that familiar anger, the type she saved for bullies and debt collectors not so very long ago. They walked on quietly again, her head dipped slightly. A couple passed by, faces so close that their smiles almost seemed to interlock.

"He was asking about you again," Sepp said after some long seconds of silence.

"Konrad?"

"The Englander."

"Was he?" she replied, trying hard to make it sound like 'so what', Sepp thought. Suddenly he took her by the shoulders, turned her, and looked into her eyes. "Hanna, you know I love you more than anything in the world, don't you?" She nodded, the corners of her mouth turning up a little. "There is nothing I want more than your happiness – and that even includes racing, even driving the streamliner, believe it or not. But please, please be careful."

"You don't need to worry about me Sepp, I can look after myself."

"But you are so close to everything you have ever wanted, all the things we always talked of."

"And so are you, is that what you're worried about?"

"Hanna, please! That's not the way it is, I'm sorry, it's just —"

"It's just that it's my life little brother, and you, Konrad, Kessler, the Nazi Party and everybody else would do well to remember that."

He smiled at her, it was the only antidote he had for the venom in her sting when she was like this. Long seconds later she smiled back.

"Come on you, let's get this one back to where he belongs," she said, nodding at Strudel. "Then you can show me your dirty book!"

Sepp felt the weight of the copy of *Mein Kampf* in the well of his bag. He would have to return it to Herr Kessler soon – maybe he could help him to understand it better?

***

Caracciola's Mercedes W125 sped down the home stretch, looking like a silver toy against the vastly wide pit straight, moving like a silver bullet. From their vantage point on the top of the pit stalls West and Gracie would be able to follow the car down the straight and around the loop of the South Turn, and then as it sped back in the other direction behind the pits, before taking the left-handed North Turn. This fed the cars on to what West thought of as the Nürburgring proper, where the road carved its grand arabesques into the greenery. He wished once again it was him out there, starting a racing lap of the 'Ring.

But Westbury Holt was not in a racing car. Westbury Holt was not on the bench. Westbury Holt was not even in his overalls. With Konrad now just about fit enough to drive there had been pressure for the veteran to start the German Grand Prix, and with other German drivers eager to have their chance West had not even been listed as a reserve. He half understood why. He had tried to match Rosemeyer at the Vanderbilt Cup race on Long Island, near New York, and ended up in the fence, throwing away a sure second place. He now felt as if his big chance was slipping from his grasp.

"Well, I must say, you've found us a splendid perch," Gracie said. He had been surprised when Gracie had turned up, although he was finding his friend was full of surprises these days. Despite his waning influence with the team he had managed to find them space on the roof of the pit stalls to watch the grand prix, and most importantly space far from Kessler, who had warned West about Gracie – the man asked too many questions, he'd said, to which West had had to agree. In truth West was in no mood to watch a race; no mood for crowds, and no mood for Gracie. They had met on five occasions since Munich, and West had told him what he'd seen, who he'd seen. But each time Gracie had seemed less impressed than the last. West watched as another W125, von Brauchitsch's car, braked for the left hander that led into the long looping right-handed South Turn. Gracie started to say something but his words were submerged beneath a tidal wave of air-ripping noise as another Mercedes, the car of Lang, passed them on the back straight, very close to where they stood so that they could look down and into the cockpit. It was crowded on the roof of the pit stall, it was crowded along almost every inch of the 'Ring, but there was room for them to move from the front to the rear of the space, and in the lull between the passage of each car it was just about quiet enough to talk.

"I was wondering, friend Westbury," Gracie said, as the air still crackled to the passing of the racing car. "Have you been able to find out anything more about the magic potion?" As he said it he sniffed at the air, which was dripping with the acrid smell of the burnt fuel, somewhere between singed almond and shoe polish.

"If anyone on the team knows, they're not saying, and I've done as much asking as is wise for someone in my position, Grace," West said, hoping that by dropping the jokingly effeminate second syllable he might realise this was just not the time. But Gracie didn't seem to notice. West *had* told him all he knew: the names of the brass he might see at the factory or the track – especially those in the uniform of the Luftwaffe – and even the small technical details he could discover through idle chat over a coffee or a smoke with Lick, Sepp and sometimes even Fink. There was nothing in it that would win a war, he knew, but then he believed there would not be a war. As far as he could see the Germans were having far too good a time for that, especially those at the wheel of a Mercedes in this particular race.

"What about the people from Shell?" Gracie said, angling his head so that his mouth was close to West's ear. The Mercedes of von Brauchitsch was now coming up the back straight, so it was no use West answering, and he merely shook his head. The chemists from Shell mixed the stuff, but they were seldom around, and would not talk to him when they were. It was the mechanics who put it in the car, but none of them knew too much about what was in it, beyond benzol and alcohol. Gracie turned away from him and they both watched as the Mercedes was pitched into the North Turn, the car understeering before it clipped the apex and powered out, the tail snapping well out of line for a moment before speed pulled it straight, the harsh whine of the supercharger diminishing as the silver car disappeared from view.

The field was spread by now, and while the engines could still be heard, the predominant noise was the swarming hum of the excited spectators, thousands and thousands of voices all talking at once. It seemed impossible that four words could mean much in the midst of that surging babble, mere droplets in the Zambezi, but what Gracie had to say next certainly caused a ripple in the mind of Westbury Holt.

"We need a sample."

"Impossible," West said, without hesitation, just as two cars hit the pit straight as one, a Mercedes and an Auto Union, in close combat. He turned to watch as von Delius passed the pits, Richard Seaman in his Mercedes chasing him down. He could see Fink out on the edge of the vast concrete pit apron, biting what was left of a thumbnail and pacing like a father-to-be outside a maternity ward. He loved his racing cars so much that he hated to see them actually racing, especially when a Rosemeyer – or perhaps a Westbury Holt – was at the wheel. He preferred them driven well within their limits, liked a tactician like Plaidt far more than a barnstormer like Rosemeyer, or even worse an unproven charger, like West. Fink looked extremely worried, for Delius was pushing hard.

"Impossible?" Gracie said, as the two cars sped down to the South Turn. "Really? That is a pity."

"I've not been close to a racing car in weeks, and the way things are looking it'll be months before I'm back in one," West said, unable to add the *maybe never* he felt within.

"We could make it worth your while."

"Even if I could get near enough it would be a damned stupid risk, Grace. Besides, I thought you said it was just gossip you're after?"

"Gossip's pin money, friend Westbury, a small sample of that evil smelling brew would clear your debts back home with the swish of a fountain pen."

"You could do that?"

"Not me, but it could be done, yes."

"Well then it's a damned shame I can't get anywhere near the blessed stuff then, isn't it?"

Gracie nodded, and another car thundered past the pits. He allowed the noise to pass, the quiver in the air to still, and then said: "Sorry, I forget: just why aren't you racing today, old man?"

"I never said," West replied, then leant heavily on the steel rail.

"Not quick enough?"

"It's not that, it's —"

"Politics?" Gracie interrupted, grinning now.

West sighed. "Perhaps that's partly the case. But there's more to it than that. The Auto Union's a damned beast of a machine, and as yet I've been unable to tame it."

"My, this is a first, Westbury Holt admitting there's a car he cannot drive – what next, a fräulein he cannot bed?" Gracie tossed a glance at Hanna, who sat below the pit roof on a tall stool, stopwatches and a clipboard in hand.

"Don't push it Grace."

Gracie grinned that new grin of his, and the cars of Delius and Seaman came back into unhindered sight exiting the South Curve, the tail of the Auto Union flapping widely as the little man trod on the power, then fought for control, using all his strength on the big wheel, his shoulders bobbing, so that for a moment it almost seemed as if the car played puppet tricks with little Delius – as if he was a man on a wheel, not a man *at* a wheel.

"So, that's the way to drive an Auto Union, is it?" Gracie said, pointing at the Delius car. "He seems to be …" The rest of his words were lost in the quaking passage of the two racing cars, seemingly tied together in seismic tandem, their motion felt as well as heard, a fluttering in the lungs.

"He's pushing too hard," West muttered, but he knew no one would hear him. He watched the cars dive into the North Curve, Delius ragged again, the car teetering on the brink of a spin. Delius had been over-driving since his accident at the Eifelrennen earlier in the year. A part of him was pleased to see him struggle, pleased that he tried so hard, for perhaps it meant there was also a question mark over Delius's seat. Pressure can lead a man to take too many risks, West knew. But with the thought came a soberer one, for Westbury Holt also knew that the Nürburgring never did a desperate man a favour.

With the Silver Arrows now out into the country for the bulk of their seventh lap there was a lull, filed with the odd Alfa Romeo or Maserati, and then the fast men were through again: Caracciola, Lang and von Brauchitsch – Rosemeyer far behind having lost time with a shredded tyre. A little later came Konrad, trailing the wildly, yet quickly, driven Alfa Romeo 12C of Tazio Nuvolari. West watched Konrad drive into the South Curve and come out on to the straight behind the pits: "Watch Plaidt; always cautious, but just quick enough," he said to Gracie, raising his voice over the growing snarl of the approaching cars. "They like that; it means he always finishes."

"He didn't finish here last year," Gracie said, and West remembered the crash that had given him the chance that was now slowly slipping away.

"He made the mistake of trying to fight Rosemeyer on Rosemeyer's terms, but he's learnt the hard way that he's better off driving his way. It means he picks up the finishes, and the foreign currency for the team when they're abroad, and to some that's all that matters."

"Couldn't you be cautious?"

"Of course not, what an idiotic question. I *need* to be fastest."

Gracie just shook his head.

He would never understand. The acid of competition wasn't in his blood. It didn't burn as it did with West. But he thought about what Gracie said for a while. Yet they had plenty of drivers who *could* be cautious, what they really could not ignore was another Rosemeyer. Someone with pure pace. "If only I could unlock the secret to that car," West said.

"There's a secret? Surely you just keep your foot down, old man?"

"Not quite, the Auto Union's a bugger of a machine. But figure it out and it will fly – I just need more time at the wheel, then I'll be fine. I'm sure of it."

"And then you'll be close to the fuel again, friend Westbury?"

West chose to ignore that, life was complicated enough right now. He glanced down to where Hanna was sat on her tall stool below. For some reason she was looking back down the straight, a slim hand shielding her eyes from the sun. He realised there was a strange sound in the air, a sound he knew well from his years of racing, and not a sound he relished. It was thousands of questioning voices; a loud murmur of morbid excitement mixed with a respectable edge of concern. Someone had had a big one.

Fink had marched out on to the edge of the pit straight and was looking down the road, Sepp and some of the other mechanics with him, including Lick, pushing a yellow flat cap to the back of his head so that his red hair gleamed in the sunlight. In the stands opposite all heads were turned to the right.

"A terrible crash!" the commentator announced, but the news was late, everyone knew. Death hung over the circuit like a cloud; the racing engines suddenly seemed quieter beneath it, and the silver skins of the cars somehow dulled to grey. Yet they raced on.

About fifteen minutes later West spotted a reporter he knew, walking along the edge of the pit stalls, coming from the direction of the accident, a lap chart attached to a clipboard in one hand, a notebook and pencil in the other: looking for a quote – or an epitaph. The reporter looked up and saw West. He recognised the question in his eyes, and he said: "It's Delius." West had already guessed as much.

"How bad?" West asked.

The reporter just shook his head, then scored a line through a name on his lap chart.

"Seems you're back in the game, friend Westbury."

"No need to look so damned smug about it, Grace."

"At least I'm honest enough to admit that I'm not overly distressed with this particular turn of events, old man."

***

West accelerated out of Monte Silvano and on to the final straight for the last time. To his left the azure of the Adriatic shone and sparkled in the bright sunshine through the gaps between the houses, to his right caramel coloured buildings scuffed by at 80mph … 100mph … 120mph. The wheel shuddered violently, once more rubbing painfully at the mincemeat that had once been the palms of his hands, his back ached from the unforgiving ride, his head throbbed with the eyestrain that comes from squinting through the blazing sunlight, while the heat from the engine behind him and the sun-cooked bodywork around him turned the cockpit into an oven. *Take a six-litre 520bhp racing car, add sixteen miles of twisting mountain road – let's say around Pescara – and one raw (some still say) English racing motorist,* West thought, with a cracked smile. *Dust liberally and bake under the Italian sun for three hours …*

A curtain of dust kicked up by a backmarker he would not now have to lap still hung in the air and he glimpsed the stands at the finish line through it. In his mirrors he could see the white indicator stripes flashing on the tyres, showing they were close to worn out. His biceps were pumped-up with pain from steering the heavy car around the mountain. His right foot was burnt, the heat conducting through the pedal and smouldering straight through the sole of his shoe. It had been hell to keep it flat along the two four-mile long straights during those last laps, but he had done it. He braked for the final complex of corners, a detour into side streets designed to slow the cars along the start-finish straight, and caught a whiff of nearly-cooked brake linings before shuffling the Auto Union through. Then he accelerated back on to the main straight to take the finish. People ahead took shape, fascists in black uniforms, Auto Union mechanics rushing out to meet him, spectators with their bronzed faces split with white smiles, cheering from the great bank of the grandstand to his left. He opened his mouth to acknowledge them all, and felt sure he heard it creek like old leather. God, he was thirsty. He held up an arm, heavy from fatigue and burnt from the sun, waved to the crowd, then let the car roll to a halt. He wondered if he had ever felt so tired after a race, or in so much pain without crashing … Or so satisfied.

Second. Second to Rosemeyer. *Good effort old man.* He whipped his goggles off and was suddenly surrounded by people eager to congratulate him, a piranha school of fluttering handshakes attacking his face. Someone passed him a bottle and he gratefully lifted it to his cracked lips. The coarse red wine went straight to his head. Before he knew it he was out of the car and was being half-carried, half escorted, to the rostrum, drinking more wine as he went. Before the race he had knotted his cricket jumper around his waist and now he had to hold it tight as scamps shot out from behind the legs of the policemen to try to take it as a souvenir. "How close to Rosemeyer?" he mouthed the words at Lick who he sighted over the crowd.

"Much closer," Lick shouted back, "but he still has a few seconds a lap on you – and he had a problem, too." West nodded, he would not let it spoil his day, and a few seconds over a sixteen-mile lap wasn't *that* bad. "And did you notice how much quicker you were without that cursed rag on," Lick added, laughing, pointing at the grimy cricket jumper. West shook his head and smiled, then made his way through the pressing crowd to the rostrum. He was pleased to have Lick on his crew still, but it was a shame that the best mechanic, Sepp, had been put in charge of Konrad's car. But he could not moan, the death of Delius had given him his chance, and now he had taken it. The week before he had shared fourth place at Monaco, where as a junior driver he had been obliged to hand his car over to Rosemeyer, who had had steering problems with his own Type C. But West had been going well enough before that, and he felt he was finally beginning to show his worth.

On the rostrum Rosemeyer looked satisfied with a good day's work. He handed West another bottle of wine, and his congratulations, and West drank deeply and gratefully. Konrad had come sixth, he was told, and over the heads of the crowd West could see that he was being carried to the Station Hotel, completely exhausted. Some visiting Nazi officials stood with them on the rostrum, along with a knot of Italian Blackshirts and overstuffed dignitaries. West's head spun from the wine and the heat and he did his best to concentrate on the speeches when all he wanted was to lie down in the shade somewhere, and then take a long cool dip in the sea.

Finally, the national anthems were played. Arms shot up in Nazi salutes and without thinking his went with them, a reflex action. He held it there for long seconds as the *Deutschlandlied* blared out of the loudspeakers and cameras click-clacked in front of him … It seemed like that music would never end. Then he realised he was saluting. He cursed himself, and then made a mouth of his upraised right hand, so that it chattered like a mute and naked glove puppet – and the children laughed.

*

Hanna sat in the cool of the lobby of the Station Hotel, she had been told that someone would be there to collect her soon. She stared listlessly at the potted palms that shivered to the light breeze. The door was wedged open with a brass umbrella stand and every now and then she'd catch a sniff of sea air, the cry of a seagull, or the curse of a workman helping to dismantle the grandstand. There were many workmen out there. Mussolini, Konrad had told her with a smirk, always made sure there was work for all the cooks and never worried too much about the taste of the broth. She sat on a crescent-shaped sofa, which faced the huge wood and wrought-iron reception desk. She turned her attention to the little flags of key fobs hooked on the board behind the desk: who's in, who's out? Konrad was out already, a dinner for the drivers, the managers and the politicians, hosted by the *Reale Automobile Club d'Italia*, a men-only occasion. He had gone with Kessler, although she could see there was tension between them. Konrad coming in behind the Englander had not gone down well at all in Berlin, she had heard Kessler say. She'd protested about not being invited to the dinner, of course she had, but she was secretly pleased – until Konrad told her that there was a delegation of local ladies on their way to entertain her.

Everyone stayed in this one hotel – off the seafront and the main straight and, apart from the mosquitoes, rather grand in a well-worn way – so it was no surprise to see Westbury Holt. Hanna was wondering what she would be put through this evening when she spotted him, ambling down the wide marble staircase, limping a little, hands wrapped in bandages, wearing knee length tropical shorts, a red shirt open at the throat and tatty tennis shoes, his pipe clenched between his teeth and, of course, that old off-white sports sweater tied around his waist.

"Westbury," she called, hearing her own voice with some surprise.

"Why hello there – now don't we look pretty!" Suddenly she wished she'd worn the stockings after all, her legs looked so pale against those of the Italian girls. "Going somewhere nice?" he asked.

"No."

"A crying shame, you look like you should be."

"Thank you," she said politely, modestly, the way Mama had told her to take a compliment, long ago. "And you're going to the dinner – *like that?*"

"Why not? It's the height in Paris don't you know." They both laughed. "Actually I thought I might give it a miss, I'm dreadfully damaged after the race."

"Then shouldn't you be taking it easy in your room?"

"That's what the sawbones said, funnily enough ... But I thought some fun. Fun is always the best medicine." He turned to leave, took three steps and turned, holding his finger up in front of him and corrugating his brow with all the subtly of an actor in an old silent melodrama. "I say, I've just had the maddest idea, absolute lunacy."

"Which is?" she said, not bothering to remove the hint of suspicion.

"Why don't you come with me?"

"Where?"

"Dinner, a little place I know. You owe me, after all."

"Owe you?"

"Our little secret – don't tell me you've forgotten the world's fastest taxi service?"

"There was no mention of a tip," she said. "Besides, if I were dining out with a strange man surely I would need to inform my fiancé." A family group of Italian tourists burst through the doorway carrying armfuls of luggage, they were in the midst of a huge argument. The father jabbed at the bell, shouted.

"So that's it? Married already," West said, ignoring the commotion behind him. "Well then madam, there is nothing that can be done for you. Good day." She watched him go, using a gilt-framed mirror to check for when that ill-fitting mask of mock seriousness would slip into a smile. His eyes were on her too, she knew. The cheek of the man ...

"Wait!" she shouted, then she darted over to the reception desk, scrawling a note on hotel paper – *sorry, headache*, and so on – interrupting the family argument to tell the receptionist to pass on her apologies.

He drove fast. She knew he would, he would know no other way, hands ripped to shreds or not. He followed the route the race had taken earlier that day. The car was a small dark green MG. He had had to borrow it as he'd still not replaced his Lagonda, he had explained. With the roof down the last of the day's heat was forgotten and she soon began to enjoy the scenery, completely confident in the skill of her chauffeur. The road curled this way and that, gaining height quickly and leaving the sparkling Adriatic way behind them, passing meadows of sun scorched grass dotted with green-black trees. Finally, they reached a village, Spoltore, where the hard edges of the houses marked the serpentine flow of the road: a road painted with parallel and overlapping flourishes of freshly laid rubber, the smell of the scorched racing tyres still heavy on the hot air. Some of the sandy-coloured brick houses had rugs stretched over the porch to keep out the last of the strong summer sun and two old men sat on low stools outside one of them, almost in the street, perhaps talking of the day's event. A ragged dog slept in the middle of the road in the shade of a house – glad, no doubt, that those ear-splitting monsters of the day had gone now, leaving him in peace.

West pulled the little MG up by the side of the road, opposite a steep and dusty bank patched in places with mats of dry grass, and in front of a small osteria. Children appeared from nowhere, perhaps to gape at the sportscar, or more likely the sunburnt young man in the funny clothes, for they would have seen more exciting cars than this already this day. Hanna followed him into the small rustic eating place, which was open on one side and crowded with little tables decked in red and white checker cloth.

The little old lady who seemed to run the place – all in black from headscarf to little boots, a face lined with laughter, sun and good living – seemed to know him, West bending low so she could kiss him on both cheeks and then fuss over his bandaged hands before setting them down at the very best table. The osteria was clean, but basic, with many of the tables outside placed under a vine-choked trellis. She had expected more, but then he was hardly dressed for haute cuisine.

"How did you find *this* place?" Hanna asked, with a frown.

"Actually, it found me," he said. "See this wall? The stone's lighter, it's all new." He ran his hand over the low wall that separated the tables from the road. "I demolished the old one with my ERA a couple of years ago, in the Voiturette race, damn fine job I did of it, too. Overcooked the turn as I was trying to maintain speed up the hill, hit the bank over there at close to sixty, and then bounced back through the wall. I almost ended up in the kitchen," he laughed.

"Didn't they mind?"

"Not a bit of it. They poured so much wine into me that by the time I finally made it back to the pits I had to be carried, the lads thought I was in a bad way from the prang. Touching really." They both laughed. Then the old lady brought a cool stone jug of red wine, placing it on the table and winking at West, a wink Hanna tried to pretend she didn't see. The wine was rougher than the local Montepulciano d'Abruzzo she had enjoyed – alone – at the hotel, but it was good enough, and it was somehow honest, too. It seemed it was made for gulping rather than sipping and Hanna followed West's lead – after encouragement from the old woman. Hanna couldn't speak a word of Italian. West could; but the word was *si,* always with a shrug. It seemed to mean *everything, if you please,* and very soon the table strained under the weight of huge earthenware dishes containing string-like pasta in a spicy tomato sauce and a salad that seemed fresh from the earth – big slices of juicy tomatoes, olives, onions and cucumber – and loaves of fresh bread. West ate his starters like he had never eaten before, a schoolboy fresh off the football field. And before she knew it the main course was placed in front of them, a simple pot-roasted leg of lamb cut into pieces and served on a bed of oven-toasted coarse bread, along with a deep dish of golden roasted potatoes.

"Could you really eat more?" she asked incredulously as he took a portion of the meat, to the undisguised delight of the old lady.

"Of course, nothing builds up a man's appetite quite like hurling an Auto Union around a mountain." He grinned, and hacked at the lamb with the edge of his fork before shovelling it into his face. "Bella!" he shouted, after a few chews and a quick swallow and the old lady's face lit up like a lantern. His eating was intense, wholly purposeful.

"Has anyone ever told you you're not great company when you're eating?" she asked.

He held up his free hand, to indicate he would answer when he'd finished the mouthful he was relishing, kept the hand up as he chewed for some long seconds, finally swallowed, then opened his mouth to answer – only then to fill his mouth with another fork full of food, and his eyes with laughter. She laughed with him.

After a plate and a half of the lamb he slowed, took two half-hearted bites of a roast potato, and then let his fork drop with a clatter against the edge of the plate. "Stuffed," he said, patting his stomach. The old lady brought more wine. Without Hanna noticing the sun had dipped behind the mountain and candles were placed on the table, West crammed tobacco into the bowl of his pipe and lit it from one of the candles.

"Now then, what shall we talk about – and have some more wine won't you?" He filled her tumbler with four great ruby sploshes from the old jug. The village was quiet: just the pulsing rhythm of the cicadas, the odd snatch of distant conversation and laughter, and someone practising with an asthmatic accordion someway down the hillside.

"Why don't we talk about you?" she asked.

"Fine – you ask, I'll tell," he said, before taking a long and luxuriant suck on the stem of his pipe, leaning back on his chair, balancing on the rear legs so that its back rested on the low wall he had once demolished with his ERA.

"All right then," she said, "I wanted to ask you … Today, after the race. Why the salute?" There was no change in his expression or posture, other than the slightest of frowns, breeze-ripples on a millpond.

"Why not?"

"Was it a mistake?"

"No. It was nothing. Just a thing I did, that's all. What's it matter anyway, it seemed to make those stuffed shirts happy enough – besides, I made a joke of it."

"It matters to some," she said, quietly, "don't you care what people think?"

"Not if I don't like them."

"Do you care what I think?"

"*Ahhh* … That depends, will it mean hard work?"

"Oh yes," she said, laughing suddenly, "very hard work."

"Well then, I will just hate you; that's much easier."

"And I will hate you too, Westbury Holt." Now they were both laughing and she followed his lead in taking three great gulps of wine, draining the tumbler and feeling the hit of it in her head like the swoop of a swing. West refilled the glasses.

"And who is this man I hate?" she said, hearing herself giggling. He leant forward and looked into her eyes through a veil of blue pipe smoke. It was then that she noticed what it was about those eyes of his – they were always smiling.

"This man," he said, slowly and clearly, "is the fastest racing driver in the world."

"Faster than Rosemeyer?"

"Maybe," he said thoughtfully, "but definitely soon, I'm sure of it.

I just need a little more time, that's all."

"And faster than Konrad?"

"No contest my dear. And while we're on the subject —"

"We are *not* on the subject; the subject is this new object of my aversion."

"Ah yes," he laughed. "Mr Westbury Holt Esquire: Harrow, Cambridge and playing silly buggers in racing cars – know the chap rather well actually. Born just before the Great War, which really was actually fairly *great* as far as he can remember, lots of women in big blouses fussing over him, walks in the park, feeding ducks as high as his eye, and then some man arrived in a uniform. Then things changed a little. A nice enough chap, but a tall stranger all the same, a man with tears in his eyes and friends who talked in hushed voices of muddy places far away. And soon a little life scented with flowers and perfume was all tobacco and brandy ... That must have been when Mater died ..." He trailed off, the curls of smoke from his pipe lay blue across his eyes. The candle flared and West took a gulp of wine. "So," he said, quite suddenly, "the man in uniform packed young Westbury off to prep school, which he hated. Harrow was even worse. Poor child had a bad time of it, a rough bunch would lock him in a tiny cupboard under the stairs for hours, and he never could understand why." A huge smile split his face before she had the time to show any spark of sympathy, any trace of empathy for a mother lost. West took another gulp of wine, then said. "And then he discovered sport, and that was pretty much that. Happy ever after; as they say."

"That's it?" The rough wine was beginning to stain his lips a little and she ran her tongue over her own to check for the same. She thought he seemed to read something into that.

"Oh, you want more. Well, let's see. Ah yes, *sport.*" He took a long pull on his pipe and savoured the flavour with a series of little tut-tutting noises. "Yes, rugby and cricket mostly. And this boy had found something out all right. Yes, *I really* liked to win. And where there was risk he found an edge to help him win, running at the brick-built forward without checking his pace, facing the fastest of fast balls without fear. Suddenly Westbury Holt was someone, and he liked that."

"And your father?" she asked.

"Oh, he liked that too, and in the holidays he would make sure that Westbury had all the sport he needed. But he was a busy man, building up the family firm and all that. By the time I went up to Cambridge I hardly ever saw the old man to be honest. I chose philosophy over economics, he had wanted me to take the latter, but I hadn't really cared either way. I was just determined to have fun and I supposed philosophy would give me more time for rugby. He didn't seem to mind as it happened, or at least the money still came in. Well it did until ..." he paused, took another puff on his pipe, and then said: "I met Gracie about then too, you know Gracie, of course?"

"Yes." She nodded, remembering the studious looking Englishman who would sometimes accompany West, and wondered just what he had been about to say before he changed the subject so abruptly.

"I actually studied quite hard for a little while, thanks to him. He used to say I was there just because of Father's money – true of course – so I worked doubly hard to be better than him, but in the end even that was just a game. And sport was a better game, with real answers, easy rights and wrongs. Much simpler." He took another deep puff of his pipe and leant back on his chair, the old wood creaking. Hanna looked at the Patek Philippe wristwatch Konrad had bought her in Monte Carlo. It was getting late, but she had not looked at the watch just to see the time. It was one of the nice things in life, a reminder.

"So then, a thoughtful person *this* Westbury Holt," she said.

"Is he, you think so? Well, not to worry, here's where the fun really starts. I actually grew rather bored of rugby and cricket. Never been one to rely on other people, or to share the glory some might say, so team games always had their limitations. But then I joined the University Aero Club and learnt to fly, absolutely adored it. One thing led to another and I persuaded dear father that this was the career for me. He had his heart set on me joining the company but I suppose he thought that if he let me get it out of my system that would be that. He gave me the money for a crate and I popped down to Brooklands with Gracie to pick one up. And that's where I saw racing cars for the first time. The combination of speed and competition was simply irresistible, and I ended up spending the money on a Sunbeam that almost killed me the first time I raced it. Dropped out of Cambridge the year after and I've been living the life of Riley, Delage and ERA ever since."

"You are a very lucky man, Westbury."

"Westbury Holt, lucky?" he laughed.

She didn't think he'd understood her.

"And how lucky is the future Frau von Plaidt?" he said, his eyes gleaming in the candlelight as he leaned across the table towards her. *Future frau*, how lucky she was indeed, as she told herself over and over again. Was she to tell him, Westbury Holt, of the stalling games she played? *No, let him see what real life is first* …

"My father killed himself, when his business failed after the collapse of the banks. Mother died soon after, no – a long time after. But it always seems so …" she spoke softly, in a low monotone, as if mumbling the words of a familiar prayer in the dead of the night, not looking into his eyes but fixing her gaze to the red flicker of the flame on the surface of the wine jug. "Then it was just me and Sepp. We never asked for anything. But we

survived. And now Sepp is close to realising his dreams. And I ..."
Suddenly her vision blurred and she felt the salty sting of tears in her eyes.

*

She'd felt foolish, and blamed the wine. So he had ordered some of the old
woman's homemade *cent'erbe*, a strong green liqueur, saying it was dangerous
to stop drinking at the melancholy stage. Hanna didn't argue. Didn't argue
when he said, "I'm too drunk to drive you know, but luckily it's downhill
most of the way," either. And now the world spun away from her on either
side at a giddying speed and the tyres of the little MG screeched above the
gnash of its engine. Soon the scent of thyme and oregano gave way to salty
snatches of sea air and the hills opened up to reveal the jewel studded night
in all its glory. On reaching the coast road West turned left rather than
right, steered away from the bright lights of Pescara, accelerating hard. She
said nothing, glad of the clean air moving fast through the car, clearing her
head a little. After a few minutes he turned down a side street between
some shuttered-up houses then a little later parked the car at the end of the
road. She could hear the sigh of the surf close by.

West climbed out of the MG without opening the low door. "C'mon
then, last one in's a rotten egg and all that," he shouted, peeling off his
sweater and dropping it at the dusty roadside before disappearing over
a low wall.

"Come back, where are you?" she shouted, and then she climbed out
of the car herself and followed him over the wall and onto the beach. The
sand glowed milk white in the moonlight and soon enough so did West as
he pulled off his red shirt. "Come on, I won't look; promise!" With that he
turned, unhitched the belt of his shorts and dropped them to the sand, then
ran into the surf, his backside glowing bright white against the dark sea.
There was a shout of joy, three huge phosphorescent fringed splashes, and
then West was underwater. She laughed, and shouted: "You're mad!"

"Come on in, the water's lovely!"

"No, you're a maniac."

"Oh come on!"

"No! Definitely not!"

"Nothing to be scared of you know – I won't bite!"

With that she reached behind her to unhitch her summer dress, letting
it fall to the floor around her ankles. Her French brassiere followed and for
a moment she stood there, enjoying the light Adriatic breeze as it licked at
her naked breasts, thrilling to a feeling of a drunken freedom she had never,
ever, known before. Her knickers were also French, silk and loose and light,

another Monte Carlo offering from Konrad. They would stay in place.

She unbuckled her watch, dropped it on top of the pile of clothes, and ran to the water, diving under to cover herself from his gaze as soon as the gentle waves had reached the level of her knees, she tasted the salt against her laughing lips. The water was chilly, just right to clear a wine fuddled head, and they swam like children, a circling game of tag with him never quite touching her – though she felt sure he could have for his arms were well muscled and his swimming stroke assured. Every time he swam towards her she would kick out and swim away, laughing so much that she took great gulps of the Adriatic. When she swam backstroke she could clearly see the sparkle in his gaze and the crescent of gleaming white of his shark-like grin. She would kick out, leaving a foaming white wake, and he would swim towards her, slowly, slowly, teasing, teasing ...

Finally, she had had enough of the game. They had drifted quite far out now, so she swam for shore, using the over-arm Sepp had taught her in the Zwickau Lido a summer or so before. She heard the gentle splash of his easy passage a metre behind her. Soon they were in the shallows and she was able to stand, the wet, gritty sand squashing between her toes. She splashed to a point of indecision, neither land nor sea, then turned to face him. His body was stark white in the moonlight, except for where the sun had browned his arms, face and throat, and if it wasn't for his body hair – wiry at his chest, an isthmus of curls along his flat, muscular belly – it might have seemed as if he wore a pearly shirt. His eyes were flicking along her body, her silk drawers were plastered wet to her and she knew the sea would have soaked them to transparency. There was nowhere to hide. Suddenly, very suddenly, there was a stirring in the nest of wiry curls beneath his belly, and they both stood stock still to the awakening. In a matter of seconds it was pointing at her face like a long-armed salute, stiff and uncompromising. He looked down.

"Heil Hitler," he said, and they both laughed. He took her laugh as a signal and moved towards her. It brushed gently against her belly, her breasts against his chest, strong arms around her, then the moment when she could say no, the soft brush of wet, salty lips at exactly the same time as a small wave broke around her toes. She hardly moved her lips, hardly moved them ... But it was enough for him she guessed, enough to confirm what they both knew, yet he looked deep into her eyes before holding her tighter, then kissing her harder: rough, hungry, almost violent, a ferocity she had never known with Konrad, a ferocity that seemed to pull the breath from her lungs ... And she responded. His right hand moved to her breast and she felt the rough cloth of the sodden bandage across her nipple. His left hand lay flat against the cool wet skin of the French knickers, a finger flicking over the thin elastic edge, peeling them from her softly, wetly. The knickers fell damply and she felt them clinging to her ankles like seaweed.

All the while his mouth worked hers, salt and wine, as he pulled her to the ground.

She sank into the wet sand and he lay above her. For a little while he was granite in her fingers as she guided him to her. And then he burst through the warmth of her. Every so often the thrust of his hips was the break of the soothing surf around them, the foam frothing around her head, whispering its shared secret, his breath, her breath, mingling with it. The silica in the wet sand that plastered his arm glinted in the moonlight, one particular star would peep over his shoulder, disappear, reappear, and disappear ... She felt as though the sea flowed inside her, welling up from the base of her belly, filling her legs until they were heavy, and he's faster now, breathing quicker, and she hears her own rapid pants, strangled screams, sobs. The sea surrounds her, seems to well inside her, a tiny wave breaks around her head and at the very same instant she feels the floodgates rupture within her, a tidal wave inside. She hears her own screams, sees the chalky crescent of his grin, and an instant or two later he is done. She feels him relax within her as he lies heavily — breath and heartbeats as one — on top of her. He peels himself from her and collapses in a heap on the wet sand beside her.

"Do you still hate me, Westbury Holt?" she whispered, some silent minutes later.

"More than ever, darling ..."

*

The mountain air tasted thin yet very good, the champagne of all air; but Sepp needed thicker sauce for this work. He was gulping down great draughts of it as he pumped at the long handle of the bottle jack. "Idiot," he mumbled under his gasping breath as the tall side of the grey Büssing NAG lorry emblazoned with the rings of Auto Union tilted away from him. The other trucks would have made it far up the pass by now, while they had wasted time looking for a jack Strudel had stowed in the wrong place before they had left Zwickau for Pescara, a job Sepp himself had trusted him with. *Just wait till I get back, I'll roast that little simpleton,* Sepp thought, as the sweat broke through the thin cloth of his vest. The sun was high, glaring off the naked rock face, and although it was much cooler in the mountains than it had been in Pescara the day before it was still hot enough for work like this.

"Idiot," he grumbled again, and this time Lick's face cracked into a wide grin. He was sitting on the spare wheel, a tasselled fez he'd won in a card game, part of an Italian Blackshirt's uniform, was on his head.

"You're not still blaming our lucky charm are you, Sepp?"

"He's ... an ... idiot," Sepp said between pumps on the jack handle.

"Maybe we should give him to the SS to play with, then," Lick said mischievously. Sepp was in no mood to answer. The wheel suddenly jolted a little and he was able to undo the finger-tight nuts and, with Lick's help, pull it and its punctured tyre from the hub. They fitted the spare quickly – changing wheels was a speciality act for this pair after all – and then they ate lunch in the shade of the lorry for quarter of an hour, slicing chunks off a spicy Abruzzo salami and eating it with good fresh bread, then washing it all down with apple juice mixed with water.

Bellies full. Bernd Rosemeyer had won and Westbury Holt had come in second. The weather was just fine for a long day on the road. Life was good. Lick belched his contentment, then made a play of listening out for an echo. He grinned, and said: "Did you clock the look on old Blinky's face after the race, Sepp? Quite a picture it was."

"Herr Kessler?"

"You know it Sepp – stop being so damned respectable, it turns my happy stomach, so it does."

Most of the other lads called Herr Kessler 'Blinky', behind his back, because of the way his eyelids batted when he was excited. As far as Sepp was concerned he could not make the man out. He was serious, but there was nothing wrong with that, and he was intelligent, too. One of the white coats, in a way, but one who worked with words rather than machines, one of the white coats who were doing all the thinking in this new Germany, and for that he should be respected, shouldn't he? Hanna said she loathed him, though. Sepp had still hoped to talk to Herr Kessler, about some of the things he had read, yet something always stopped him, some kind of fear he supposed, something he could not put his finger on.

"Now there was one unhappy lab rat," Lick continued.

"But why, we won?"

"Rosemeyer won, yes, and our Jonah of an Englishman second. Good for all, you'd think. Only Blinky has tied his colours to another's mast and, if I may speak frankly dear Sepp, von Plaidt hardly set the world on fire, did he now?"

"Konrad is still injured, you know that Lick."

"It's been a long time now Sepp, that excuse is wearing as thin as Eva's claim to virginity," the mention of the barmaid's name brought a salacious grin to Lick's face, "and he can only rely on friends like Kessler for so long."

"That's nonsense Lick, he's a hero."

"You're right. And the Reich needs heroes. But I'll tell you something, a racing team needs wins, and for my money that's Rosemeyer and Holt."

Sepp watched an eagle catch a thermal and rise majestically above them. He understood what Lick meant, but he would not like to admit it.

Rosemeyer was the darling, the best, the people's favourite. But it was said the Nazis did not approve of his antics and his attitude. Sepp himself had been there when Kessler and a group of Party dignitaries had caught Rosemeyer doing his impression of the Führer, a comb beneath his nose, his hair swept to one side.

"Konrad will get quicker," he said.

"He'd better, or German hero or not, I've a feeling our unlucky Englishman is going to get himself even more chances to kill himself." Lick belched again, then got to his feet. "Mind you, if he pulls a stunt like he did the other day then I'm not so sure Fink won't kill him first."

"What stunt?"

"Trying to borrow some of the race fuel for that little fart cart he's running around in, that's all."

"But he knows better than that, it's too —"

"Yes, but who can figure the thinking of a mad Englander, eh? Fink sent him to an Italian filling station with a flea in his ear and a good German boot up his arse," Lick said, and Sepp laughed.

Some time later Lick's heavily muscled arms worked hard to steer the big truck with its load of Type C Auto Union through the staircase of corners that climbed the pass. It was heavy work, Sepp knew, and Lick looked like he was struggling with a rusty old stopcock on some pipeline every time he turned the flat wheel, the gothic grey peaks of the jagged mountains sliding by geology-slow as the truck crawled up the steep incline. The mountains reminded Sepp of cathedrals in the rough, but he thought they were more beautiful for the lack of stained glass, more magnificent for their lack of reverence to anything other than the power of nature.

"Arse!" Lick shouted, as a sudden herd of sheep emerged from the roadside and broke either side of the lumbering truck, forcing him to brake and spend his hard earned momentum. The shepherd waved but made no effort to hurry his bleating sheep on. Lick gave him a sarcastic grin.

"God, give me an autobahn!" Lick shouted, looking to the sky. "You know Sepp, I'll be glad to get out of this tin-pot little country."

"I thought you liked it?"

"Oh, the plum's worth the effort I suppose, but the rest ..." Lick made an obviously Italian gesture with his thumb sandwiched between his fingers. "Put that lovely fanny aside and it's just lazy old men sitting on their arses, and youngsters poncing about in comic opera get-ups." He adjusted the tilt of the black fez on his head, its golden badge depicting an eagle clutching a fasces glinting in the sunshine.

"There's plenty of dressing up back at home, too," Sepp pointed out.

"True enough. But at least in Germany you can really feel things are happening, really feel it. Don't you think so?"

"Perhaps; people have work, that's good."

"It's more than good Sepp, you have to give them credit there."

"I suppose I do," Sepp said. "But—"

"They're not soft on the crooks either," Lick interrupted. "Though I will admit that sometimes they do go a bit over the top; with the Yids maybe, and the commies and the queers – and let's not forget the idiots."

"That's what I'm not sure about," Sepp mumbled.

"And the *idiots*," Lick repeated, a smirk on his face. Sepp huffed, remembered what he'd said about Strudel a little earlier, and shook his head. "Oh, but I meant to tell you," Lick added, still smirking. "That particular idiot was not responsible for stowing the truck's bottle jack in the wrong place, you know. I saw Ludwig using it yesterday, so I suppose he's to blame, yes?"

Sepp shrugged a 'so what', but felt shame burn within, while Lick crunched the gear-stick back into first as the last of the sheep passed by. He continued: "But things are happening back home, alright, and not just sheep-free autobahns – you can't deny it?"

"Yes, you're right. But don't you see? It could be so much better. Without the bullying, the hatred, I think we could have the most marvellous country known to man. I really believe that."

They suddenly crested a rise and a little later the lorry tipped over the other side, so that Lick had to hold it back on the brake, his right leg obviously straining with the effort, the big tyres humming heavily against the road surface.

"Omelettes and eggs it is …" he suddenly said as he lined the lorry up for a curve, "… omelettes and eggs."

"And that's it?"

"I'm no professor, or chef come to that, but my hairy arse tells me that we're in good hands. Eggs will be broken, smashed even, but the children of the Reich are in for a hearty breakfast one sunny morning soon, my friend."

"It just doesn't seem right, treating people like that. Like the way they are with the Jews," Sepp said quietly. "So, they may have wronged us in the past, but still —"

"It's a new *right* Sepp, that's all," Lick put in with a note of clear exasperation. "It's not nice, but neither is medicine. And that's the way to think of them, like doctors, clearing out the pus and dirt, so Germany can be clean again."

Sepp said nothing else, and Lick started to whistle *Horst Wessel*. Sepp liked the tune, so he joined in.

They drove on for the rest of the day, through Austria and into Bavaria, and they were getting close to their overnight stop at Garmisch when the sun started to go down. Lick was at the wheel again, yawning like a bear – it had been a very long day on the road. "Well, suck my cock mother superior, what have we here?" Lick said, as he suddenly slowed the truck.

She sat on a white kilometre stone at the edge of the road, one leg crossed over the other, hands busy massaging an ankle. Her face was turned up towards them in their high cab, round and full, as simple and as beautiful as a moon. Lick pressed the brake even harder and the lorry shuddered to a tortured halt. He switched off the engine and the cab shook to a burp of pre-ignition before there was an all too sudden silence. She stared at Sepp, eyes big and pleading. Her hair was blonde and in pigtails, her cheeks rouged by the sun.

"Well go on then," Lick barked.

"Why me?" Sepp recognised the panic in his own voice.

"'Cos she's your type, that's why, now get out there."

"I haven't got a type."

"Yes you have: big tits, strapping thighs, hungry plum, good German kinder factory – her!"

Sepp sighed and reached for the door handle, then clambered down from the cab.

"Are you all right fräulein?" he said.

"Yes, yes ... I'm fine," she started, but he could see she had been crying, her big blue eyes wet and shining. Her lips were a little thin, and she smiled with a closed mouth, which puffed up her reddened cheeks a little more. It was an honest and simple face, he thought. She rubbed away her tears with a handkerchief while Sepp fish-mouthed mutely, trying hard to think of something to say and feeling the treacherous burn of a blush as it travelled up his neck to his face. Lick would be enjoying this.

"You're not from Bavaria, are you?" he said, finally, unable to quite place the accent.

"No, I'm from Essen ..." As she spoke he could see that one of her teeth was slightly discoloured and showed up clearly in what was otherwise a gleaming mouth. Her name, she told him, was Trudi, and then she carried on talking, giving him her life story, an ordinary German life of an ordinary German girl. She spoke quickly and he let her words break over him as he nodded to every sentence, and tried desperately to take his eyes off those wonderfully sculptured pins, smooth and muscular, disappearing into those tight black hiking shorts. Only then they would move up to those great swells of womanhood which seemed on the point of bursting out of her white blouse. He remembered something Lick had once said about another, similarly proportioned, girl: *like a dead heat in a Zeppelin race.* A loose black tie drooped low along the line of her cleavage like a long, thirsty tongue, and above her left breast there was a small blue and white badge at the centre of which was a black swastika – the badge of the BdM, the girls' wing of the Hitler Youth. He guessed she was around seventeen, a year short of the age a girl would be too old for the Band of German Maidens.

"... That's how I came to be here," she went on as Sepp nodded dumbly, "with my group of the BdM. We have been hiking here; it is a special prize for collecting the most old toothpaste tubes for the Reich. I twisted my ankle, and now I feel so stupid – so stupid!" There was a diamond dampening at the corner of her eyes again.

"Please, please don't cry – where are the rest of your group?"

"They have gone to fetch the car. I said I would wait here."

"No, we can't have that. Here, take my arm." He reached down and pulled her clear of the kilometre stone, suddenly feeling stronger thanks to the activity, feeling the blush drain from his face.

"You are very kind." She put her hands across his shoulders and he felt the brush of her breast through the thin cotton of his shirt. She seemed to press closer to him and he could smell her simple womanly odour, nothing more, nothing like the gallons of perfume those Italian girls would drench themselves in. He had to help her into the cab, clumsily pushing her backside as Lick pulled her by the arms. She looked back and smiled at him, as he felt the firm softness through the seat of her shorts. He felt himself beginning to blush again, and he was glad that Lick, for once, said nothing.

Lick continued to be remarkably well behaved as they drove on, whistling softly and letting them tell each other about their lives. She sat between the two mechanics, and once she realised who they worked for her voice was filled with a hushed awe which Sepp could not help enjoy. Finally they met a beige Opel Olympia coming the other way, and she recognised it. Lick waved it to a halt and Sepp helped her down from the cab then took her arm to support her as she hobbled to the car. Two other BdM girls helped her into the little Opel, giggling a little, while a middle-aged woman in the driver's seat looked at him just a little suspiciously. Sepp felt another blush fermenting at his throat. The door of the car was shut and Sepp gave a little wave as he walked back to the truck.

"Well?" Lick asked.

"Well what?"

"Don't tell me you didn't get her address at least – Christ boy, will you want me to wipe your shitty arse for you next, or what?"

"I —"

"Quick, before they go." Sepp jumped from the cab and reached the Opel just as it was halfway through a three-point-turn. She wound down the window and pressed a piece of paper into his hand. He heard a ripple laughter from inside the car, and then it moved off, crunching the broken stones at the side of the road. There was an address in Essen on the note.

***

It felt good to be in Paris with some useful cash in his pocket. Proper money: francs and lira. Cash he could spend outside the Reich. With his cut of the prize money from Pescara he would not have to rely on Gracie's hospitality, nor the foreign currency he received for shady services rendered to His Majesty. Spying was not the game for Westbury Holt, the rules were too complicated, and he was glad to be out of it. He had come close to getting caught in Pescara, trying to take a little of the fuel, then using the woeful excuse that it was for the borrowed MG. Fink had not been amused. That, he decided, was it. He would not take the risk again. He would still take money off Gracie, of course, but he would do it on his terms – and so he asked the waiter if there was a backgammon set as he ordered a bottle of house red.

It was raining outside, the fall of it sounding like background static on a radio set. Paris always looked good in the rain. Especially from a window table in Café Les Deux Magots, where his view out on to Boulevard Saint-Germain, its cobbles and cars made shiny with rainfall, was filtered through crisp lace. Gracie liked this place, and that's why they had agreed to meet here. Although Gracie was not a fan of what he called continental philosophy he always liked to drink in the haunts of the French thinkers. The café was about right for philosophy, West supposed, the ceiling high enough for thoughts to float before they popped, the space big enough for tiny echoes, to make it seem like you could listen to – and maybe even respect – your own words. It was the sort of place a man could comfortably drink alone, but to win francs at backgammon you need a victim, and West's victim was late.

It was not like Gracie to be unpunctual, and West glanced at his new Breitling, it was ten past three. He suddenly found he was thinking of Hanna again. He had hardly seen her since Pescara, and he had not had the opportunity to speak to her. Usually that was just the way he liked it with a girl after he had gone all the way and then some, but he was beginning to feel she was avoiding him, and that itched, maybe even burned.

The café was half full with people stretching long lunches into dinner, and the air was filled with the smell of good coffee, the sound of bubbling conversation and the clink of cutlery on china, while the smoke from cigarettes and pipes merged in tangled arguments. West began to stuff his Dunhill with *Player's No Name*. A middle-aged man in a business suit approached his table.

"Excuse me sir," he said, in halting English, the accent German. "I am sorry to interrupt you, but my son is an admirer of yours."

"He is?" West said, in German, genuinely surprised that he should have an admirer who didn't wear a skirt.

"I wonder if …?" With that he handed him a fountain pen and a postcard of Notre Dame. West signed the back, while others looked on, probably wondering who he was, and as the German thanked him and left, Gracie arrived. He was wet from the rain, and as the warmth of the café hit the lenses of his spectacles they steamed up slightly. Gracie took them off and wiped them with the tongue of his tie. West noticed immediately that there was a slight smoulder in his eyes.

"Quite the star," Gracie said, with an acidic hiss to the S.

"Sorry?"

"French?"

"Of course not," West said, realising he was referring to the man who had asked for his autograph.

"German then? Perhaps he saw your picture in the German newspapers? I hear it made the Italian papers, too."

West shrugged. "What picture?"

"Friend Westbury with his arm in the air, saluting like a proper storm trooper; ring any bells?"

"I've not seen it," West said, slightly annoyed at the tone in Gracie's voice. "And who cares, anyhow?"

"People are beginning to care," Gracie said, as he took his seat opposite West.

"That's their concern, and come on Gracie – it was just a joke."

Gracie's face rapidly morphed through disbelief, frustration, and then anger. "It's not a joke for millions of people," he said. "Ask anyone here what the Germans have been up to in Spain, and the Italians in Abyssinia. You have to realise that Hitler and Mussolini are not comedians, here are two of the biggest egos on the planet – even bigger than yours friend Westbury – and they are right now deciding which way history should go."

"It's politics Gracie —"

"It's life, and death quite soon, you need to know which side you're on."

"Oh don't talk such rot," West snapped, suddenly angry, "no one in Germany wants a war and Hitler's not daft enough to start one. I know, I've been over there for months and I've seen how things are."

"You've seen what you want to see."

"Bugger off Gracie, I've seen enough," West spat back. "Christ man, I'm no lover of the Nazis, but there's nothing I can do about it, it's up to the Germans to decide who runs their country. I'm a racing driver, nothing more. But I will tell you one thing, there are plenty of decent Germans."

"Tell that to the Jews, or the communists, or the …"

Just then the wine and the backgammon arrived, and West missed the last of what Gracie had said. West opened the lacquered wooden case and set up the game.

"Besides," West said, as he lined up the first of the wooden counters on its brightly painted point, "I've done my bit – wouldn't you say?"

Gracie just shook his head. "There's only one glass," he said, then shouted "garcon!"

The waiter came back and Gracie asked for another wineglass, which he brought and placed sharply on the table, then half filled, all without a single word, as West placed the remaining counters on the board.

"I heard something here one night that's interesting," Gracie said. "French waiters are rude because they are *being* French waiters. But I'm not sure what the excuse for your ignorance is friend Westbury. I'm glad I'm angry about it, though, because it makes what I must ask of you next a little easier, old boy."

"Sorry, if it's to do with your *gossip*, then I'm done with that game. I simply don't need the money now, Gracie."

"It's not about money anymore, *Holt*." The use of his surname like that was like a drawn pistol.

"Come on, let's play backgammon." West said, keen to change the subject now, forcing a smile. He threw to decide who would start the game: a two.

"High stakes?" Gracie said, the edge still in his voice, as he threw a five.

"Of course," West said, drinking a little of his wine.

"Well then, here's my first throw." With that he picked up the leather covered cup, placed the dice within it, and started to shake it, so that the dice rattled. He kept rattling the dice as he spoke. "You say you're unable to supply us with a sample of the fuel?" West nodded, he had explained as much over the telephone. Still Gracie shook the dice in the cup. "Well I'm afraid that's just not good enough."

"Well, there it is," West said. "I tried my best. Anyway, why not just wait until the Donington race, you could stop the fuel truck at customs, it would be easy, surely?"

"Easy to start an international incident," Gracie said, still shaking the dice. "So I'm not sure the Government would agree to it just now, you see things are rather delicately balanced in that world you refuse to live in, friend Westbury. And you can also be sure the fuel will be guarded very well indeed once it's in England."

"Perhaps, but that's your concern, I'm done with it."

"It might be wise if you made it *your* concern. You see *they* have a very effective way of letting the Germans know just what's happening," Gracie said, still shaking the dice in the cup, the rattle seeming to grow louder by the moment, like a snake in a Western flick. "They know of many of the German agents who operate in Britain. They let them stay there, and they feed them harmless information, and sometimes juicy titbits, to keep them useful – because they are tools that can be used in the future."

"Tools?" West said, and the dice still rattled.

"Nothing more. One day they might be fed misinformation that will be useful to us, but for that to be believed they have to be effective, and so every now and then they're given something *substantial*."

"Substantial?"

"Like the name of an agent working for us." He still rattled the dice. "You do understand it's very important we know exactly what's in this fuel, don't you?"

West found he was gripping his glass very tightly, yet he could not quite get a grip on what Gracie was implying. "You're saying, that if I don't spy for you you'll let one of their spies think I am a spy?"

"Well, I hadn't realised it was quite as complicated as that," Gracie said, still rattling the dice, "but I suppose that's about the size of it."

"You are a bastard, Grace."

"It was not my idea."

"No? So I take it you protested on my behalf?"

"Sorry old boy, they're not the sort to take no for an answer. But then I did warn you there would be dangers."

"Yes, but not from your side!"

"*Our* side, surely?" Gracie said. With that he stopped shaking the dice and reached into his pocket with his other hand, pulling out something metallic, which gleamed in the light from one of the wall-mounted lamps. "Here, you'll be needing this," Grace said, as he pressed the steely cold object into West's hand. Then he threw the dice, and they clattered out across the board, landing on a double six.

"Now that's what they call Westbury Holt luck," West murmured.

***

The strange looking young man stared at it with bulging brown eyes. He wanted it, this was quite obvious, but was his fear of old Fink stronger than his desire for a bar of chocolate?

"I have another one," West said, pulling out another square slab of *Ritter*.

That was enough.

Strudel would do anything for chocolate, Sepp had once told West that. And Strudel knew his way around the Horch Works better than anyone, even those who worked there. He looked like a rat, West thought. But it went beyond mere looks, for Strudel knew the factory like a rat would know its sewer: he knew the parts of the wall where a man could slip over, unseen; he knew the places where doors were not locked. He also knew the ways into the workshops where the racing cars were kept.

And what did West know? He knew that there was fuel in one of the cars. He had been called to the factory for a meeting, he hoped it was to do with how his race performances had improved, but he knew it was also an opportunity. This was why he had turned up early: early enough to volunteer to help shake down an Auto Union which had just been fitted with a new gearbox on the road outside the factory. A small crowd had formed, for although the cars were often run on the streets – even though there was a rolling road in the works – it was still quite a thing to see and hear. In the front rank West had spotted the strange looking simpleton, staring at the car as he took it through the gears, before spinning it on the throttle at each end of the tight street. The expression on the simpleton's face as he watched was one of wonder and awe, and of honest happiness. For a sliver of a moment West had envied him.

West also knew that there was little time, for he had to meet with Feuereissen, Kessler and some suits for lunch in an hour from now. Konrad would be there, too, and just maybe Hanna – he hoped. It was an important meeting he had been told, which meant it was sure to drag, and by the time it was over the car would almost certainly be drained of the special fuel. So now was the time to act. But there was no way he could go through the front entrance. Someone was bound to ask what he was doing there. He had already tried it once, to retrieve his pipe which he had left in the car on purpose, but then Fink had stopped him, and had found it for him – always the protective father when it came to his cars, not wanting anyone to play around with them other than his trusted band of mechanics. Now there was only one way left.

The sky was grey and the air tasted of iron, and seemed to quiver like thrummed sheet metal to the sounds of industry within the works. Strudel led him along a side street to a point where the grimy brick wall of the Horch Works gave way to rusting railings. One of the railings was loose, and had been pulled out of the bottom bracket. Strudel angled it outwards so that he could squeeze through the resultant gap. West doubted he would fit, but the ratty looking youngster was insistent.

"C-c-c-c-c-c-come," Strudel stammered. West was surprised to hear him talk, he had assumed he never did, and he hoped he wouldn't make a habit of it after this little adventure. He peeled off his cricket jumper and trusted to Strudel's judgement, angling his head through first, then his body. There was a moment when he thought he was trapped, and he wondered then, with rising panic, how he would explain this to Kessler. But then, with the help of a surprisingly strong tug from Strudel, he was soon out the other side. His shirt was mossy with rust from the railings, but he wiped as much of it off as he could, then pulled his jumper back on.

Strudel led him through a maze of alleyways that angled between the many different sheds and workshops surrounding the main factory at the Horch Works. The smell of hot, worked metal laced the air like grapeshot, while heavy clangs and thumps, or lighter pings and pangs, surprised West at every tight alley corner in aural ambushes that did little for his nerves. They met with just two other men, one who nodded and one who touched his cloth cap on recognising West, but neither seemed to even see Strudel, who blended in with the surroundings in the way a pigeon can blend in with a cathedral, becoming a thing of stone, a part of the place.

When they came to the rear door of one of the race workshops West thanked Strudel, and gave him the second bar of chocolate – called *Ritter Sport* as it had been designed to fit into the pocket of a sports jacket, but slipped into the pocket of West's flannels just as handily. With that Strudel's brown eyes bulged as big as Easter eggs, but he made no effort to move, just stared at the chocolate, and then at West, like an expectant spaniel.

"Off you go then," West said, nodding sharply.

Strudel waited a few moments more, an unsighed sigh in his eyes, then turned and walked off in a vaguely jerky way. The door to the workshop, painted sky blue and pierced with a frosted glass window, was unlocked, though a sign that said *strictly no admittance* was stencilled on to the blind glass.

When the door swung shut behind West the creak of its hinges seemed like the scream of an eagle in the sudden quiet of the workshop. This particular 'shop was adjacent to the one he and Gracie had poked around in the November of the year before, just before West had signed on for the dream drive he was now putting at risk. But he knew that he had no choice, the deed had to be done, and he even felt a little flutter of excitement as he pulled the cold metal object from the pocket of his flannels.

The object was a hipflask. It was made of pewter and was curved in cross section, as sleek as a slice of Auto Union streamliner. It was also empty. Tucked under his belt West wore a short length of rubber hose, which he now pulled from its hiding place. Gracie, or more likely the shadowy people he worked with, had made sure the nozzle of the flask was wide: now it was just a matter of siphoning off a little fuel.

There were three cars in the workshop. Konrad's car, which bore the number eight, he had shaken down a little earlier so he knew this definitely had fuel in it. He took a deep breath, wished there was some whisky in the flask so that it could have been a deep slug, and then started to unscrew the filler cap that sat high on the car behind the driver's headrest. The squeak of the metal on the threads seemed high and loud, like a baby elephant chased by a lion, but he was committed now, and unscrewed the shining chrome filler cap as fast as he could, seeing his own distorted reflection in it.

A laugh.

It was in the corridor, and he recognised it, but could not quite place it. There were footsteps, too, heavy working boots clumping purposefully.

"Those BdM tarts are all the same, loose as Rosemeyer on ice ..." carried the voice from the corridor.

The main doors swung open just as West had re-tightened the cap. He stuffed the hose into his pocket but was still holding the empty hipflask as Lick and Sepp walked in. Sepp's face was red, and West guessed Lick had been teasing him about something or other, but his embarrassment turned to surprise on seeing West in the workshop.

"Came for this," West spluttered, thinking on his feet. "Must have slipped out of my pocket in the car." He held up the pewter hipflask.

"You take that in the car with you?" Lick said, with a grin. "Well, that explains a lot." But Sepp wasn't smiling.

*

Old Kurt's coffee break had run into a second cup and a full half-hour of doing what he liked doing best – staring out of the window down into the street. "It will not paint itself," Hanna said, obliterating another swathe of the grimy white paper with a broad smear of fresh and gleaming, bright green paint.

"Christ girl, that stuff is giving me a headache!"

"Then open the window a little more."

"That will not calm the colour!"

She laughed, then dipped the wide bristles of the brush into the paint pot again. She was happy to have something *real* to do at last, happy to be back in Zwickau, and happy to have an excuse not to go to the lunch with Konrad. For Westbury Holt might be at the lunch and she had been avoiding him just as she had avoided the debt collectors in those dark days after Mother had died. The excuse was valid enough, though, the apartment had desperately needed decorating, and besides, Konrad's invitation for her to join him at the lunch with the Auto Union management and Kessler had been half hearted at best. She sensed all was not well, and it worried her.

Roping Kurt in to help with the decorating was easy enough, but so far he had been more company than help, though she was still glad of it. She only wished Sepp was there, then it would be just like old times. She hoped that Sepp would like the colour, as she thought it was sure to be his apartment eventually, because even though she did not want to leave this place, she knew it would never do for Konrad, freshly painted or not. Strudel was not here. Some weeks ago he had been told not to visit the works in no uncertain terms – the sort of terms which were all so certain these days. Then, after a nasty scuffle in the street with some Brownshirts, Kurt had thought it best that his son should stay inside for a while. That was Kurt's answer to most things. But there was no stopping Strudel, he could always find a way out, and back in, too, according to Sepp, who still saw him wandering around the Horch Works and even the racing department from time to time. She had thought it best not to mention that to Kurt.

"So then," old Kurt said, "you never did tell me about Sepp's girl?"

"There's not much to tell."

"Pretty?"

"Pretty."

"Good for him."

"But very young … A child, he could do …"

"Yes?"

"Nothing Kurt, it's not my place – or yours come to that."

Old Kurt took another slurp of the coffee then turned to the window again, a smirk on his face.

"Ah, your special man is here?"

"Sepp?"

"Konrad," Kurt said, shaking his head a little as he smiled. Then she heard the big Horch as its tyres scuffed against the kerbs far below. "Ah, I see he is walking better, perhaps he will be his old self again soon, eh Hanna, as quick as before?" Kurt said, a wicked twinkle in his eye.

"He is still quick, Kurt, you will see – they all will."

"A good reply, you've been practising."

"And you've been listening to gossip, again."

There was the ring-a-ding of the bell-pull and Hanna wiped her brush then placed it in the jar of turpentine before walking through to the narrow corridor where she pulled the lever to open the front door. She listened as Konrad politely greeted Frau Hansen on the ground floor – the nosey widow would be at her door at the first hint of a visitor – and then made his way up the stairs.

"I'd best be off then, see if I can find out where Strudel's got to," old Kurt said – like everyone else he never used the name he'd given his son, as if it was reserved for someone else, someone who had never happened. "Give me a shout if you need any more help," he added.

"You can be sure of it," she said, as he left, clumping up the stairs to his own apartment, the line about finding Strudel just a polite excuse, she knew. Hanna met Konrad on the landing and instantly she knew something was wrong. He walked with a slight stoop and there was no kiss for her, not even a peck on the cheek. Without saying anything she followed him into the main room. She could clearly hear the taunting *told-you-so* crash of sea surf in her conscience. Konrad slumped in an easy chair that was draped in a protective white sheet, so that it looked like a crouching ghost, and he sat there for long silent seconds as the last of his spirit seemed to seep from him. She had never seen him look so totally deflated.

"Do you like it?"

"Green, yes," he said, as he sniffed at the air, which was still laden with heavy, earthy, paint fumes.

"What's wrong?" she said, after the deepest of deep breaths.

"They are losing patience with me."

"They?"

"The team."

"What do you mean?" she could almost hear the relief in her own voice as she said it and suddenly she hated herself as much as she ever had, and she had hated herself with a passion since Pescara a month ago: a passion of shame, a passion of regret, but also a poison passion of longing for that night once more, which always started the whole cursed cycle of passion all over again.

"They say Holt is quicker, and with the Mercedes being so much better this year, they need pace rather than stealth." Konrad said. "There is a chance he will take my place as the senior driver alongside Rosemeyer."

She knelt down beside him, taking his hand. "Would it be so bad?"

"Kessler thinks so, it is how it will look, beaten by an Englander, by a fool – I must not let it happen, or I will be forgotten."

"*Forgotten*? That's Kessler's word."

"He understands the currency of heroism, Hanna. So, I have to beat Holt. That is all. They have decided, and they have been fair – well, Kessler has told them to be fair, I suppose. They say I have the last two races to show I can still do it. It is as simple as that. The driver who performs best, the one who finishes in the highest position in either of the two races will be the senior driver alongside Rosemeyer, for the record runs, and then for the whole of next year."

"And what of the other?"

"A second driver, like Holt is now – with far less money, of course."

"Well, you have plenty of other business interests," Hanna said.

"That's true, the money is a small thing, I suppose, it's more the prestige. It's important, now more than ever, in this new Germany," he sighed, then added: "And yet it seems being German is not enough after all, not with Rosemeyer, and now Westbury Holt, around. If only …"

"What?"

He paused for a moment, and suddenly there was steel in his gaze, and she thought he nodded, as if agreeing to an unheard suggestion, and then he said: "Nothing, I must just hope I can beat Holt."

"And you will, won't you?"

"Perhaps. Perhaps not. I should have put him in his place by now. Maybe I've been fooling myself all along, telling everyone I have the advantage of an old head, when the problem is simply an old heart."

"You know that's not so, Konrad."

"You are so sweet," his face suddenly lit up with a broad smile. "What would I do without you Hanna?"

"You would do fine, but how about some coffee – if Kurt has left us any?" She strode into the kitchen. It was a big room but she did not like it, it was somehow cold and the next target for bright colouring – when she was here with Sepp they would even now sometimes use the basement kitchen. She filled the pot, shouting against the metallic beat of the silvery pillar of tap water on the tin bottom as she said: "You know, perhaps it would not be so very bad, not to be a lead driver."

"There is only room for heroes in this land now," he said. She placed the pot on the stove, then walked through to the living room again.

"Then you must beat him," she said, with as much conviction as she could muster. But she could not look in his eyes, and instead she broke the smooth green surface of the paint in the pot with the bristles of the paintbrush. She would ask him once more if he would arrange a test drive in an Auto Union for Sepp, she would ask him after she gave him the good news. It was what she could do for her brother at least, and by doing something good for him, she could almost feel good about herself.

***

Finally he'd figured it out. Finally Westbury Holt had worked out the secret to pedalling an Auto Union Type C quickly – *Rosemeyer* quickly. But it had been of no use to him. Because while getting the fuel from the car had not proved too difficult after all, it had meant giving up on the chance of a *very* good result.

That had been yesterday, and now he was in Berlin, a hipflask of special fuel in his pocket and a rendezvous to make in the city centre sometime within the next hour, the details of which were committed to memory, rattling around his skull like the steely shuffle of the U-Bahn carriage in which he sat. He looked at his watch, he was running a little late. Yesterday he had overshot a turn. It was as easy as that. Then he had driven on into the Czechoslovak countryside, leaving the puzzled spectators to scratch their heads. But the edge of the track was not well marked, narrow roads through countryside and villages are not laid with motor racing in mind, and drivers had been known to overshoot before.

West had then driven on to a point where there was no one about, stopped the car and climbed out. He had siphoned a little of the fuel into the hipflask, and then thrown the rubber pipe, which he'd tied around his waist beneath his overalls like a hidden belt, into the weeds. When the race was finished he was down in fifth, with Konrad fourth, but that was something he was now absolutely certain he could put right at Donington – he now just needed to finish third or higher, and ahead of Konrad, and then the senior driver role was his. Fink had looked as dubious as a father, his daughter brought late home from a date, when West had explained he'd had fuel pick up problems. In reality it had been just the opposite, and West smiled at that thought.

The underground train was slowing for his stop, Friedrich Strasse. He had taken the U-Bahn from Tempelhof Airport, to where he had cadged a lift from Brno in a light aircraft belonging to an industrialist who liked to follow the races in style. It meant there was no border crossing to worry about, and all he had to do was entertain the old fart and his old wife. They were even waved through the formalities at the airport. In fact, it had all gone swimmingly so far, maybe even a little too smoothly ...

It was midday and the underground train was not full, in this carriage there was one other man and a woman. Others had come and gone, and the woman had been with them for the past two stops, but the man had been there since Tempelhof, on the other side of the carriage, sitting up straight on the wooden bench. He carried no luggage, just a newspaper, and West supposed he must work at the airport, or maybe he had deposited his bags at the left luggage office, just as West had. He had noticed him because of the newspaper. It was the *Berliner Morgenpost*, and it was folded to show a sports page, on which West could just make out the name "Caracciola". It would be a report on yesterday's race.

As the train continued to slow West stood up to leave, glancing again at the man with the newspaper, thinking to ask him if he might borrow it, just for a quick look-see: nice to know if his fast times at the Masaryk Grand Prix had been noted. And then – just as the train came to a stop, electric motors whirring then clunking, doors rattling open – it suddenly dawned on him: this man was either a *very* slow reader or he was simply pretending to read, for the paper had been folded just like that for well over half an hour. As West thought it the man also stood up, stuffing the paper beneath his arm. West made eye contact and the other man looked away. He was a big fellow, looked like he could handle himself, looked like he could handle West, looked like he could handle a Luger. He stuffed his head into a hat and followed West off the U-Bahn carriage, his cold steps on the stone echoing West's progress up the stairs. There was a ticket barrier in the main foyer, and a belly-high wooden rail that divided the space. A man in a dark suit and hat stood the other side of the barrier. He had just walked past the ticket inspector so would also have been on the same train, West supposed. The man nodded, very, very slightly, at a point to West's left, over his shoulder, where he thought the head of the man with the newspaper would float. If he had not been alerted by the slow reader he would never have noticed that nod.

West went through a gap in the barrier, showing his ticket, and then made a point of glancing at his watch and picking up his pace. He jogged up the steps and out on to the busy street. The traffic was heavy, which suited West just fine. He stepped out into the flow of cars, buses and trucks, trusting to his racetrack-honed judgement and reactions, but still causing a taxi to brake hard, its nose dipping, horn blaring. He skipped by it like a matador, with an inch to spare, then stopped suddenly, tottering on his toes, to let a big blue Opel beer truck thunder by with an elephant blast of its horn, before passing behind it and dodging in front of another car, feeling its slipstream brush his back as he stepped on to the safety of the pavement opposite.

The sound of more horns was enough to tell West they followed and as he hurried down the pavement he tried to get his bearings, the details of his rendezvous still bright in his mind. He did not run, but walked quickly, making a point of glancing again at his wristwatch, as if he hurried because he was late for an appointment. At the corner of the street he looked in a shop window, to see the reflections of the two suited men floating between the lamps on display, walking quickly, their eyes burning onto a spot on West's back with an intensity he could almost feel.

West waited until he was around the corner. Then he ran. He could hear the slosh of the fuel in the hipflask in the pocket of his flannels as he sprinted, a reminder of the trouble he was in, and yet the familiar flood of adrenalin was far more potent than the high octane brew, and it was this that drove him on. There was a bus ahead, a long-nosed cream-coloured double-decker that was pulling in to a bus stop. The bus pulled up in a loud squeak of brakes and seemed to sigh to a stop as it came to rest by the kerbside. There was one man waiting for it and West stepped on behind him. Once on board, his fare paid, West did not risk a glance through the rear window, he just sat down as soon as he could so that he could not easily be seen from the outside, a large woman in a ludicrous lime-green hat having to move her equally ludicrous lime-green shopping bag to give him a seat.

West rode the bus for twenty minutes before he decided it was safe to get off. He had lost his bearings now, as this was an unfamiliar part of Berlin, but he knew it would be easy enough to ask directions. The street he was in was busy, lined with trees. He could hear the sounds of a railway station nearby, a steam engine working up speed, a sharp whistle. He took a deep breath, savouring the aroma of bratwurst, realising he was hungry. Then the car drove up on to the kerb in front of him.

It was a Mercedes 260D, a cloud of sooty diesel fumes belching from its pipe as it clattered onto the pavement, the underside of the chassis throwing up bright sparks as it scraped against the stone kerb. The front and rear doors of the car were thrown open at the same moment and three men leapt out at a speed that defied their bulk, while another remained seated in the rear of the black car. He recognised one of them instantly, the man from the U-Bahn, and as he turned to run he realised they must have called for the car – following a bus would have been little trouble then, West realised, just before a woman with a pram seemed to spring out of nowhere, blocking his escape.

West sidestepped the chrome and canvas obstacle, and the woman gasped, but the sharp turn away had slowed West and thrown him off balance, too, and now he teetered on the edge of the kerb ...

He felt the heavy hand on his shoulder. He spun on his heel to face the man, letting his fist fly in a long loop, until it connected with a knuckle crunching crack against the chin of his assailant. But the big man did not fall, just staggered back a little, his hat spinning into the gutter, and by then the others were on West, his arms held while a fist buried itself deep in his gut. He doubled over in pain, winded and choking for breath, as the other people on the street looked away and hurried on. He knew there would be no point in shouting for help, and he doubted he had the breath left to do so anyway.

They dragged him into a nearby alley, the toes of his shoes scraping on the rounded cobbles. It stank of decaying food and a broken pipe splashed red-brown water against the dirty stone. They let him drop to the floor, half in the puddle the broken pipe had filled. One of them kicked him in the ribs, but he managed to turn from it before it could do too much damage, though it still hurt like hell on a hot day. Another kick landed directly on the hipflask in his pocket, and he heard its contents slosh within, felt the steel impact hard against his thigh.

"Find it," said one of his attackers, and before he realised what was happening his pockets were filled with foreign fingers. They took his wallet, they took his passport, they took his pipe. They took the hipflask.

"What's going on?" The words were sharp, and they came from the entrance to the alley, where the car was parked on the pavement, some distance from the men who pressed him tight to the wet cobbles. The voice was familiar. He managed to painfully twist his head around and look up to see one of the men smile a conspiratorial smile, and then nod. Then he saw Kessler. The other men walked back to their car. West sat up and tried hard to get his breath back, checking himself for injuries, as he always did after a crash or a kicking. A minute or so later Kessler walked over to him.

"It's a good job I came along," he said. He now had the hipflask in his hand.

"Yes, you're timing's impeccable. I suppose I owe you one, old man," West said.

"Well, that depends." With that Kessler opened the cap of the hipflask and sniffed at its contents, his face souring into a grimace, his head seeming to involuntarily tip back away from the flask. "They said you ran; it made them suspicious?" he said, holding the flask away from his nose.

"They were following me," West said, picking himself up and brushing himself down. "I thought they might be thieves."

"This is Berlin, Herr Holt. No one will rob you here."

"Still, it was fortunate you turned up, eh? What are the odds on that – Berlin's a big place?"

"Yes, it seems you're a lucky man, Herr Holt."

"Well, that's a first – who are they?" He nodded in the direction of his attackers.

"Well, it has all turned out fine," Kessler said, ignoring the question. "This has obviously been a misunderstanding, perhaps they took you for someone else?" West looked down at his cricket jumper, and thought that unlikely. "But you must be shaken up, why not take a drink, Herr Holt?"

"You first, please," West said.

"But I don't drink." Kessler said with a suitably dry smile, and with that he handed the hipflask to West. The other men were still at the opening to the alleyway, stood around the car, looking on, one with a hand inside his jacket, like a plain clothes Napoleon. As West took the flask Kessler began to blink, steadily.

West did not hesitate, but took three deep glugs from the flask, feeling the burn of the liquid in his throat. He coughed a little as he took the flask from his lips, and he felt his eyes begin to water.

"You sure you won't have some?" he said to Kessler, a slight rasp in his voice. Kessler wore a puzzled expression, and he had stopped blinking. "You should try it, it's good stuff." West lied about that, for the whisky in the replacement flask was a very cheap blend. But better for the old constitution than racing fuel, and as the warmth of it spread through him he began to appreciate it. Kessler would have caught the smell of the near raw alcohol when he took a sniff, and it was certainly similar to the smell of the racing fuel, which also contained alcohol – especially for one not versed in the subtleties of liquor. West grinned and winked at a still bewildered Kessler as he took another burning swig of whisky from the hipflask.

***

For most of them it was their first time in Britain, so it was a shame that their initial impression would be of a rainy and grey day at Croydon Airport. The Lufthansa Junkers was reflected in the wet pavement, its three propellers still spinning slowly as Konrad held his hat to his head in the face of the stiff breeze that whipped across the runway apron. Hanna clutched at his arm, her head dipped from the rain and wind so that all West could see of her was the brim and the crown of her dark hat. He had not had the chance to get close to her on the aeroplane, and he had only seen her on two occasions in the six weeks or so since Pescara, with not even the sniff of an opportunity to speak to her without Konrad in attendance. All other attempts to contact her discreetly had come to nothing.

London's busiest airport was served by a modern white building which housed the customs office, the control tower and the main booking hall, into which they now entered. West was surprised to catch sight of Gracie waiting there, but then he remembered he'd wangled a job with the circuit, largely because he said he was a friend of Westbury Holt's and that he knew some of the Auto Union people. The job entailed helping with translation and with any other little difficulties the teams might face. West wondered what Kessler would think of that, for that one had little time for Gracie and Gracie's curiosity.

The booking hall was not big, but a glass dome high in the roof made it seem airy and light, even on a day like this, while widely spaced stark rectangular white columns which supported a gallery gave it a classical grandeur at odds with the busy frontage of the newsagent's shop and the hectic clunking of rubber stamps on the airline counter tops that lined one side of the hall. Bench seats sat on the highly polished parquet floor and there was a tall, octagonal-sectioned, polished oak structure studded with clock faces – which showed the times of flights departing and arriving – in the centre of the space. The hall smelt strongly of ink, furniture polish and damp clothes. There were few other people in the booking hall and those that there were eyed the large party of Germans, West among them, curiously. There would be very little chance that most of them would know who they were or what they did and West was surprised to feel just a little like a stranger in his own land. There were also a couple of reporters in beige macs and felt hats, one he recognised as the youngster from *Motor Sport*, and a single photographer. The continental motor racing scene hadn't suddenly become big news since he had last left the country and he wondered what his German colleagues, some of them household names in the Fatherland, would think of that. There were quick handshakes with the reporters before a few brief, polite questions.

"You're familiar with the Donington circuit, Mr Holt?"

"Yes, I took the Alfa round last year, got myself closely acquainted with a deer and that rather stuffed it – literally, as it turned out." They both smiled, he thought they would be thinking *Westbury Holt luck*.

"How will the Auto Unions fare, do you think?"

"Oh, who knows, the local chaps know the course well, but ..." He let that *but* hang there for dramatic effect, and they seemed to enjoy it. In a few days Britain was about to see *real* racing cars for the first time, and he wasn't about to spoil the surprise. "... Let's just say it should be quite a show, shall we?"

"And your chances, Mr Holt?"

"Well, we'll have to wait and see, we showed good speed at Brno – who knows what we might have been able to achieve without the fuel issue," he just about managed to keep a straight face as he said it.

"There is talk that you may be taking Konrad von Plaidt's place as a senior driver?" the younger reporter said.

"Well, I'm not sure Konrad would agree with that for a start," they laughed politely. "But if that's enough gentlemen, I have some other matters to attend to."

The reporters thanked him for his words and there was the click of a camera and the flash of a magnesium flare as the photographer captured the moment with his bellows-lensed Leica. West was blinking the dazzle from his eyes as Gracie appeared. They shook hands. Despite the threat in Paris – maybe because of it – West had found a new respect for Gracie, and their friendship had just about survived, mainly because he was always glad of an Englishman to drink with in Germany, but also because Grace was the only one who would laugh at West's jokes about the Nazis. Besides, although he would never admit as much to Gracie, he had quite enjoyed the little escapade, and he had particularly enjoyed getting one over on Kessler and his charming group of friends. But whether he would ever trust Gracie again was quite another thing.

"You did well, friend Westbury, the boffins are very pleased," Gracie said, after making sure there was nobody in earshot.

"I was damned lucky, and that must be a first, eh?"

"How so, old boy?"

"Gestapo, I think. Kessler was with them. And if those ugly buggers had got to me before I'd managed to make the rendezvous on the bus and switch the flask it would have been a very different story, I can tell you."

"I told you you'd have no difficulty spotting Mrs Frobisher, didn't I?"

"Well, she certainly stood out in that hat. She moved the bag and I did the switch when it was on her lap."

"Yes, it's tried and tested. But how did they get on to you?"

"I've no idea. But I don't think Fink was buying the fuel problem during the race, I suppose he told Kessler and then he put two and two together and came up with an excuse to kick a man in the ribs." With that West felt a twinge in his bruised lower rib, and sucked in air thorough his teeth. It was going to be hell to have to drive an Auto Union with the injury, but Gracie showed no sympathy. "You were right about getting the switch done in Berlin, though," West continued. "They ripped my stuff apart on the way out of Tempelhof, they even tasted that awful whisky – say, Gracie, can't His Majesty's coffer's stretch to a decent drop of Talisker?"

"I'll fix you up with a good dram later, old boy."

"That's the least I'm expecting, with what I went through to land that little brew I would think I'm owed a distillery."

"You'll be rewarded, friend Westbury. As I said, you've done well, and we've got what we wanted, for now."

West was about to ask him what exactly he meant by *for now* but the tap-tap of her shoes against the parquetry was a bigger and better draw. Her arm was in Konrad's and West felt a stab of something he wasn't ready for – a sensation that surprised him. Konrad was limping quite badly again, and he wore a thin smile beneath brooding eyes. He was looking a little pale. The couple greeted Gracie, they knew him slightly, and then Konrad turned to West. "You know this circuit, I presume?" Konrad said, an unmistakable strain in his voice.

"No, not really," West lied. He spotted a tiny glimmer of hope in the German's eyes.

"I've heard it's a challenging track?"

"They say so."

"We will be going straight up to Derby with Herr Kessler, I have public relations work to do," Konrad said, looking at Hanna, "a shame, as Hanna so wanted to see London."

"Well, all's not lost, why doesn't she follow on later?" West suggested. "I could show her around … With Gracie, of course," he added quickly, "he's a whiz of a tour guide, a walking Baedeker."

"Well —" Konrad started.

"I think I would rather travel up with Konrad," Hanna suddenly broke in, and Konrad looked as surprised as West felt.

"If you're sure, darling?" Konrad said. She nodded, and turned her head so there was no way of catching West's eyes. "But here's Anton now," Konrad said, and they turned to see Kessler walking into the hall, two men wrapped in long coats either side of him. West had never seen either of the men before.

"Who are they?" West asked.

"You'll find out, soon enough," Konrad said, and it was the first time West had seem him really smile in weeks. Konrad moved to meet Kessler and Hanna made to follow, but West grabbed her arm.

"What was all that about?" he said, under his breath, one eye on Konrad and Kessler who were already deep in discussion some yards away.

"What do you mean?" She still didn't look him in the eyes.

"You're avoiding me. I thought we had something?"

"Then you are as foolish as they say, Herr Holt." With that she shook his hand clear of her arm.

"You'll change your mind," he said, knowing that she could still hear him as she walked away, "but don't leave it too long now." He was amazed to find his heart was beating faster, and his breathing was irregular. But it wasn't because Kessler was pointing him out to the two unfamiliar men in the long coats.

"You should be careful, friend Westbury," Gracie said. "They might be watching you closely now." West had almost forgotten he was there, but now he forced a smile and nodded.

"How about the Grill Room at the Savoy for dinner? On you, of course," West said.

*

All my love, all my love, all my love … Sepp read it over and over, that one little line, then he whispered softly to himself as he read the signature, "Trudi". The letter, spread flat by his plate, had arrived just before he had left for England, and he had read it and read it time after time throughout the following days. Read it so much that every word had developed a thousand meanings. Each time he read those three little words at the end of the letter he felt a slight tremble at the base of his belly. Was this love? He would ask himself then, so surprised that it tasted so much like fear. If it was he would tell her – but he had to be certain. Sometimes she almost scared him; she seemed so sure of it all, as if it was as clear as the alpine air on the very day on which they had met. He had asked Hanna, but his sister had just laughed. And how that had hurt.

Trudi wrote as she talked, without punctuation, a girl in a hurry, cramming in thoughts as they came to her. She told him where she had been, who she had met, what they had talked about. She told him she couldn't wait to see him again, that those two days in Essen in the middle of September were the happiest of her young life. And she had written of the Führer. She always wrote of the Führer. Half of the letter, at least, was on the subject of Adolf Hitler, and although he knew it was ridiculous Sepp was beginning to feel just a little jealous.

They said that all German girls loved the Führer, though he knew that Hanna for one did not. Otto at the works, whose brother worked at the Chancellery in Berlin, said that every day Hitler would receive a great sack of presents from the grateful, adoring womanhood of the Fatherland. From cakes to portraits, locks of golden hair and even girls' underwear – washed and unwashed.

Sepp sat at a long wooden table covered in a crisp white linen cloth, a glass of milk and an empty plate in front of him, stodgy smells of over-boiled cabbage wafted in from the nearby kitchens. He looked up from the letter and out of the big window. The green meadow rolled down to a portion of the track; the sky was pearly grey, with an iron-dark cloud drifting through it like the hull of a battleship. A group of deer stood still at the edge of a dense and dark wood, like sculptures in mahogany, until the rasp of a racing engine startled them into life and they darted for cover. The gothic Donington Hall and its surrounding parkland made for a wonderful setting for a race, and who would have ever thought that Sepp would stay in such a grand house, even if it was with the other mechanics in a large dormitory? Lick wasn't among them, though, as because the turnaround between the Czechoslovak and British races was so tight, he and some of the others would not arrive until the day before the race. Sepp was surprised how much he missed him.

He looked at the letter and found he was thinking of the Führer again. There had been so much in *Mein Kampf* that had struck a chord, yet so much that worried him. Somehow, he knew, he had to be missing something, something that they all saw – Trudi, Lick, those thousands of torch bearing acolytes at Nuremberg. Surely they couldn't all be wrong? It was badly written, he thought, but then one man cannot be good at all things, he supposed. As he was thinking this the other mechanics sat down with him, boisterous and hungry, Mercedes and Auto Union boys mixing together, each making jokes at the other's expense. They all carried trays of food, plates piled high with crumbling over-cooked potatoes, cabbage, peas and lamb chops immersed in a light brown gravy and a drizzle of mint sauce. One of the mechanics on Rosemeyer's car, Wilhelm, nudged Sepp and winked as he took his place besides him. Sepp greeted Wilhelm and then he realised Herr Kessler was sitting on the table behind him. He was sharing it with some of the Auto Union management, but not sharing in their conversation, his interest entirely on a book he held close to his face, his eyes blinking steadily, yet regularly, behind the thick lenses of his spectacles. The two new mechanics took seats at the end of the table, saying little. The others had not taken to them, NSKK men given the opportunity to work in the big time, but Sepp had welcomed them – he knew how important it was to be given a chance, and he dearly hoped his next one came along soon. Still, he had been very surprised when they had been assigned to Westbury Holt's car, and he knew that Lick would not be pleased that on top of that he had been switched to Konrad's car, alongside Sepp.

"Good job your pal Lick's not here Sepp lad," Wilhelm said, "gives me a chance to get a piece of the action."

"Action?"

"Betting – oh, but you don't do you?"

"Not really, who's favourite – Rosemeyer or Caracciola?"

"Ah, we have something far more interesting to bet on this time young Sepp, we have the tortoise and the hare, and there is much at stake. Are we to have the crazy Englander wreck-meister with no luck as a senior driver, or the old man who now seems to have little stomach for the fight?"

"That's no contest," Sepp said, suddenly angry, "Lick wouldn't take such a bet – Konrad will beat the Englander for sure."

"Ah, that surprises me Sepp, one of such passion, I would have thought you would side with panache over tactics any time. But then you are all but family now —"

"You don't mind, do you?" The Englishman, Grace, had spotted Sepp and placed his tray down beside him, cutting into the conversation and robbing Sepp of a chance to come to Konrad's – and his own – defence. And actually, he did mind, but he wouldn't say so. Grace asked too many questions for his liking, and never seemed that interested in the racing, far worse a crime. Grace took his glasses off and cleaned the lenses with a handkerchief. There wasn't an inch of the man that didn't look scholarly, from those spectacles to the notebook jammed in the pocket of his tweed jacket. Over the months since he had first turned up with Westbury Holt – such unlikely friends Sepp always thought – he had improved his German at a remarkable rate, enough so that now he had offered his services to the circuit, acting as interpreter and liaison between the track and the German teams. Sepp suddenly remembered that West had told him Grace's study was something to do with politics. Perhaps he was the one to ask? The Englishman cut off a slice of potato and popped it into his mouth.

"Herr Grace?"

"Yes Sepp," between chews, "but it's Phillip, please."

"You're an intellectual?"

"Perhaps, but whisper it, you can be shot for less these days you know," Grace laughed but Sepp could see nothing funny in it, though the next thing he said was at a near whisper anyway, for it was not good form to speak politics with the lads around.

"Tell me, what do you think of our Führer?"

Grace's face lit up, he was obviously thrilled with the question. "Honestly?" he said.

"Honestly."

Grace took another slice of potato, which crumbled into a near mash as he cut it. He put it into his mouth and chewed quietly before swallowing it, a look of undisguised mischief at play beneath those shallow lenses. After some long seconds he said: "He's a dangerous fool."

Sepp said nothing, just looked at him, the answer had taken him by surprise, but the most surprising thing of all was his own reaction to it, a sudden flare of anger that burnt bright for a second of silence.

"You seem upset, Sepp?"

"I've never heard anyone else say such a thing," Sepp said, shaking his head.

"Best get used to it."

"It is your opinion, nothing more."

"No, it's how it is. You did ask me to be honest, didn't you? No doubt you've read *Mein Kampf* – but of course you have, shouldn't wonder they force feed you it at school, eh?" His tone was patronising and the others were beginning to take an interest, Sepp wished he'd never said anything, but the Englishman wouldn't stop. "It's all a bloody mess, those endless rants for one thing, now there's a man with a colossal chip on his shoulder. And don't get me started on the philosophy, if that's the right word for it," he sniggered. "Take *will*, what exactly do you think he means by that?"

"He means the strong can will —"

"He means the strong, he means the Party, he means the German people, he means everyone and no one." Grace's smile as he said this was superior and Sepp felt that certain anger well up inside him, the same sort of anger that had landed him in trouble so many times before.

"Perhaps you have to be German to understand Herr Grace," Sepp said.

"So is that what it is to be German, to be confused!" he laughed, loudly. "This *will* of your Führer is both Schopenhauer and Nietzsche, both the one and the many. This *will* is whatever *will* suits Adolf Hitler best at the time." Grace wore a gleeful look as he said it, and for some reason Sepp could not help taking it personally, maybe because there was so much he didn't understand, maybe because he could not help but feel that this silly, bespectacled little man was laughing at his people. Whatever the reason, what he said next surprised him as much as it surprised the Englishman.

"Are you a Jew, Herr Grace?" The smile dropped from Grace's face and he shook his head very, very slowly. There was an awkward cough from the far end of the table and the clatter of cutlery against a plate. Sepp noticed that the two new men were staring at Grace.

"If I were Jewish," Grace said firmly, seriously, never taking his eyes off Sepp's. "I would never set foot in your country as it is today, Sepp." Sepp held his gaze, he heard the scrape of chairs against the floor. He wished Lick was there, Lick would put him right. Finally, after a little age, the Englishman turned to his meal again, slicing a piece of meat from the chop. Sepp made to move.

"Aren't you enjoying our conversation?"

"I —"

"Do you believe in God, Sepp?" Grace asked quite suddenly, stopping Sepp in his tracks.

"No. I stopped believing when father …" the word stuck in his throat, "… died. How could a good God allow that?"

"Me neither. But you say, a *good* God. So I can take it that you believe in good and evil?"

"Doesn't everybody?"

"Good, that's good. You, and others like you, will have to decide whether Hitler is a good man Sepp. A great deal will depend on it."

There was a sudden burst of laughter and Sepp was relieved to see West, walking in with a cricket bat in hand, bouncing a beaten up onion against its broad willow blade. Rosemeyer was with him. Earlier West had taught him the rudiments of the game but with no ball they were forced to steal onions from the kitchen. By the time Bernd had got into the swing of things there was enough pulped onion to bring tears to the eyes. Rosemeyer greeted the mechanics with a grin and a joke.

"Come on Gracie," West said. "Bernd says he has something to show us, why don't you come along, too, Sepp?" he added. Grace dabbed at the corner of his self-satisfied smirk with a napkin and pushed his half-empty plate to one side. Sepp followed the two racing stars and the academic out of the room.

Rosemeyer led them to the rear of the house, talking excitedly as he did so. "Back in 1917, during the war, they used this place as a prisoner of war camp for officers," he said. "Anyway, seems some of our countrymen grew tired of your English hospitality, West." Rosemeyer showed them the tunnel in the corner of an old disused room. It was a bit of a minor tourist attraction, he explained. It disappeared through the tiles in a vertical shaft, quite narrow, barely room for one regular sized man. The colour of West's complexion had grown decidedly pale as he looked at the dark little hole in the ground.

"You alright old chap, look like you've seen a ghost?" Grace said.

"Small spaces, can't stick them – that's all," West said, and Sepp thought that it was the first time he had seen the Englishman look less than assured, and more than nervous.

After that West and Rosemeyer found some more onions and headed back outside for another game of cricket. Sepp followed them out to the rear of the house, not wanting to return to the conversation with Grace, scrunching the fine gravel of the narrow pathway that looped around the many flower beds, taking in an autumn air heavily scented with the smell of chopped onions, wood smoke, and just a sniff of race fuel.

"You handled the Englishman well, Sepp." The voice was Kessler's, it startled him. He was coming through a side door and crossing the lawn.

"You heard?" Sepp said.

"I hear much of what's said," Kessler said. "It is part of my work, the team is supposed to represent the Reich, I need to see that *everyone* does. That is why I must thank you for telling Herr Fink about Holt being in the workshop alone."

Sepp said nothing, he was still not sure what he really felt about that; but he had felt he should tell someone. "I just thought —"

"Yes, you *thought*," Kessler interrupted. "And by thinking you alerted us to something which, while in truth we have not yet been able to prove, could turn out to be an extremely serious matter indeed."

"You mean you really believe he was tampering with Konrad's car?"

Kessler smiled a thin smile, snorted a little laugh: "Ah, that. Well Fink could find nothing amiss, and that one knows his babies alright."

Sepp did not really believe West would sabotage Konrad's car in any way, and if he had then as Herr Kessler said there was no sign of it, and he had been told it had run well enough at Brno. In fact it was West's car that had problems there, mysterious as they were. But then why else was he in the workshop? If it was to collect his hipflask then why hadn't he asked Herr Fink to fetch it? He had always known Westbury Holt was a competitive animal, but he found it hard to believe he would go that far. Then he wondered how far *he* might go for a senior drive, or any drive …

There was a pulpy thud and suddenly an onion flew over their heads, just missing Kessler. "Idiot," Kessler muttered. Rosemeyer was laughing loud, preparing for the delivery of the next high speed onion from West. Kessler shook his head and continued: "Yes, you are a thoughtful lad Sepp," he said, as Sepp shifted uncomfortably, wondering what the others would think to see him with Kessler. "Like myself in many ways; one who understands the mechanics of things."

"It's my job, Herr Kessler."

"Quite so; I have an engineering background, too, you know."

"I didn't," Sepp said, as two halves of an onion landed close to their feet, gales of laughter following soon after – familiar laughter, Rosemeyer's laughter. Kessler ignored it.

"Walk with me," Kessler said, and before Sepp could think of an excuse they were walking away from the laughter. "Let me tell you something about myself Sepp. The way things work has always intrigued me, but there was little work for engineers in my younger years, thanks to the Jews all that I could manufacture was protest, ideas. But I am lucky there is room for a man of my talents now, one who knows which levers to pull, which switches to flick; one who understands the machine that is man." They walked onto the grass and Kessler continued. "You see, these people are just racers, just small players in a game, and it is up to me to move them, to control them. It is thrilling. You understand that?" Sepp was not sure, but he nodded anyway. "Let me tell you something else," Kessler continued. "Mercedes and Auto Union, both German teams, both racing for the Reich, but why are there two German teams, Sepp, would it not be easier just to finance one, and still win for the glory of Germany?"

Sepp started to answer him but Kessler held up a hand in a half salute to stop him. "The Führer is a great believer in the battle that is life, Sepp. In the survival of the fittest, strength comes through conflict. And we all have our conflicts to fight in. For me, my work is the manufacture of heroism, but there are others who do the same, the fight is on many levels, like war in the air, the land and at sea."

"I understand," Sepp said.

"It would help if your sister could grasp these concepts as quickly," Kessler said, slightly quieter now.

"I'm sorry, I —"

"It's nothing," Kessler said. "It's nothing." He nodded sharply, then quickly changed the subject. "You know, I have not forgotten my engineering Sepp. It's just that the machine I now work on is the greatest of all, you know what it is?"

"The Streamliner?" Sepp said, risking a small joke and smiling a small smile.

Kessler chuckled, a rare thing, and shook his head. "People, Sepp, the German people … The *race*, they say: fittest, fastest, greatest. You know, we are building a superb machine Sepp, a machine that is the people, could anything be grander?" Sepp looked at him and realised he was blinking quickly, almost like eyelid Morse code, but there was something in what he said: *the fastest*. "But I need not tell you these things, I see you are finding out for yourself. As I said, you are a thoughtful one."

Suddenly there was the unmistakeable sound of breaking glass from behind them and they both turned to see Rosemeyer and Westbury Holt doubled in laughter, the kitchen window shattered.

"If only others were so thoughtful."

"I'm sorry, Herr Kessler?"

"Or perhaps if someone like you were another Rosemeyer, eh?" With that Kessler laughed, and Sepp felt the treacherous burn of a blush on his face.

*

West looked at his watch, time to pack up for the day soon. Practice had gone well, he was close to Rosemeyer and also to von Brauchitsch in the quickest Mercedes, while Konrad was behind him, faster than expected, but still slower than West. The two new mechanics had not performed too badly, though they seemed to communicate more with Kessler than they did with West. He had talked to Feuereissen about it, hoping to get Lick assigned to his car again when he arrived, but the team manager had made it clear there was nothing Auto Union could do about it. 'Orders from above', he'd said, glancing at Kessler as he said it. It meant Konrad would have Sepp and Lick on his crew for the race. Yet the two NSKK men worked and had been trained at the race shop in the factory, Feuereissen promised, and they had manned the pits at other races in the past. His explanation smelt like apology, but West knew there was little point in arguing, it was out of Feuereissen's hands.

West hadn't seen Hanna since their brief chat at the airport and he found he was thinking about her more than he would ever like to admit. Usually his head was full of *so what … plenty more fish … her loss*. But none of it rang true. He made another huge effort to put the mental image of her aside, but it was like a brand on his consciousness, a constant burning that drove him to distraction. He sighed, and then peeled off his driving gloves.

The pit boxes were at the top of a hill and the last of the competing cars pulled in from its practice laps behind him, a dark green ERA that looked boxy and angular alongside the rakish Silver Arrows. The looks had not been the only difference. The British cars and drivers had been completely humiliated by the German teams in practice and those Englishmen that had seen the Silver Arrows shooting the Melbourne hump just before the pits were already talking about the cars in hushed, reverential tones. West felt proud to be a part of it.

The mechanics were packing away equipment. Opposite, the corrugated iron roofed grandstand was empty and the sun was already beginning to dip behind the dense tree line. West could just about detect a trace of wood smoke from a nearby farmhouse over the almond and boot polish reek of the racing fuel. There was an autumn chill in the air and he shivered. The others wore long overcoats over their overalls, mechanics and drivers alike, except for Sepp, who worked on Konrad's Auto Union without a thought for the cold. There was a burst of familiar laughter from behind him and West turned to see Konrad in conversation with Rosemeyer, the latter shaking his hand vigorously, congratulating him, it seemed.

"Well Sepp, seems we're soon to be family," Konrad said, as he joined Sepp and West by the Auto Union.

"The papers are all in order?" Sepp's face lit up. West was surprised and also a little disappointed at Sepp's reaction. He made a small effort to offer his congratulations, shaking Konrad's hand. He had known it was coming for a while, but he supposed a part of him had hoped she would change her mind.

"Everything is sorted, now we just need to name the day."

"Ah, but that is good news, very good news!" There was relief on the youngster's face as he said it.

"But that sister of yours drives a hard bargain Sepp, though I'm sure I don't need to tell you about that," Konrad said. West felt flat, and he looked away, pretending to study the Auto Union with the sort of close attention that he hoped no one was devoting to him. "She has asked me for a *very* special present," Konrad added. "And so now you will get your chance."

West turned to see Sepp's eyes seeming to balloon to twice their size while his jaw drooped slackly. He dropped the spanner he was holding and it clanged dully against the asphalt. Konrad laughed, patting him on the back. "Let's just wait until some of these others have gone, shall we? It's easier without the pressure, believe me – besides, this is, shall we say, *unofficial.*" He winked at Sepp as he said it.

They waited for twenty minutes, Sepp pacing up and down in front of the last remaining racing car on the pit apron, Konrad's spare goggles and wind helmet in his left hand as he swung the detachable steering wheel in his right. Once the last of the other mechanics and drivers were gone there were just the three of them and an odd assortment of track workers, and the two new mechanics – despite West telling them they were done for the day they seemed to keep finding small things to do. He supposed he should be pleased they were so keen, but he could not help feeling they were there to keep an eye on him. After the incident in Berlin it was a feeling he was getting used to – there's nothing quite like a kick in the ribs to bring on a dose of paranoia. West had a dinner date in Nottingham that evening, and this time overalls and cricket jumper just would not do. But that could wait, and he would wait: because he had a feeling that seeing Sepp at the wheel might just be worth the wait. He'd seen a little of Sepp's driving already, when he'd brought the car around to the start, or warmed it up, and he knew the lad had flair at least, but anyone could slide a car on the power at slow speed. You could only really judge a driver by putting a stopwatch on him. The watch is all: the watch, it never lies ...

Konrad waited for as long as possible, so that the pale autumn light was beginning to seep away. "Don't you need to be somewhere?" he asked West, but West just shrugged and said: "Don't mind me old chap."

Konrad shook his head, then gave Sepp the nod and the youngster bounded into the cockpit of the Auto Union almost without touching the sides, fixing the steering wheel to the splines of the column with practised assurance.

"As you're still here ..." Konrad said, gesturing to West with a look of obvious annoyance.

"Why, of course," West grinned, taking up station behind the long tail of the Auto Union, because the electric starter had been packed away. They both bent low and heaved against the car, hearing the creak of its wheels, the gentle slosh of fuel in the tank, the whisper of the rubber on the asphalt, the squeak of moving parts as Sepp kicked at the clutch. Then the cough of the engine, and the roar as it cleared. Fumes of exhaust and unburnt fuel burst over their heads, instantly bringing tears to their eyes, and then the tall rear wheels spun against the road surface, blue smoke shrouding the tyres as the tail yawed lazily to the left and to the right. Long licks of flame shot out of the pipes and the car straightened, heading for the first turn with Sepp tossing a confident white-gloved wave behind it.

West knew this track well enough, knew a version of it from the year before, and knew it in the Auto Union after the days of practice he had taken part in this week. He watched as Sepp flicked the car through the left hander at Red Gate and then accelerated under the boomerang of the Dunlop Bridge and into the dense wood beyond. He listened as the car drove through the sweeping series of curves down towards Hairpin Bend – which wasn't a hairpin and never had been – opposite Donington Hall. He listened as Sepp took the car through Coppice Wood, the engine noise distant now, sometimes disappearing altogether, muffled by the overreaching canopy of trees, which were dappled with the rustle-rust of autumn. He tried to place Sepp's position on the track in his mind's eye, would he be through the wood yet? Then he caught the strengthening sound of the car accelerating up the back straight, little hiccups of gear change breaking the exhaust note's reach for the very height of noise.

They both rushed through the pit stalls to watch as the Auto Union passed behind them. It was going full chat, no doubt about it, and West had to marvel at Sepp's bravery – 150mph on this bumpy, narrow track took some getting used to. The car streaked by, a silver blur, rising, then dipping over the crest in the road in a cloud of dust. West looked at Konrad. Konrad looked away, reaching into his coat pocket for the stopwatch. They heard the crisp, clean blips of the throttle as Sepp took it down through the gears for the long loop of Melbourne Corner. They heard the squeal of tortured rubber, then the *barp-barp* rasp of the engine as once again he was feeding in the power, heading up the steep hill towards them, ready to shoot the jump.

Konrad had his thumb curled over the button of the stopwatch, West had his eyes locked solid on the lip of the brow. It would take nerve for the youngster to take it flat first lap. The Auto Union burst into sight over the brow, the revs rose to an air-ripping peak, and a foot of the darkening horizon suddenly appeared beneath the car. The car seemed to hang in the air for a little age, flying for a full thirty feet, its nose pointing straight at West and Konrad in the pits so that its flight would take it to the right hand side of the track, ready for the entry to Red Gate. For a moment 750kgs of good German metal headed straight for them ... But as time seemed to stand still West caught the grin on Sepp's face, and he felt an affinity there and then – and he also knew for sure he would hold it, control it, drive it. The front wheels touched the ground first, followed almost instantly by the rears, all four tyres giving out little scuffing yelps as they kissed the asphalt. Already Sepp had the nose sorted for the left hander. Konrad looked worried for the lad, West thought, as the other man pressed the button on the stopwatch.

"You know, it's a shame your friend Kessler's not here to see this," West shouted over the tearing snarl of the V16, but Konrad didn't seem to hear him. He looked round to see his own pair of mechanics, but they were studiously busy sorting through equipment, and seemed to have no time for this fine show. It made him wonder if they were racers; it would be a worry if they had no passion for the game, if their passions lay elsewhere ...

Sepp pitched the car into Red Gate and West could see his hands judder on the big steering wheel as the front wheels began to bite into the turn. He took the tight corner in a gentle arc, yet the forces on the car still caused the aluminium body to flex, shudder and pop. The Auto Union drifted to the outside of the turn and a little cloud of dust was spat up from the rear outer wheel as it hung in the slide. Sepp floored it, white gloves a card trick blur of correction in the gathering gloom, flames spitting out of the pipes, then the rasp and the crunch of the engine as the car once again accelerated into the trees, out of sight.

"Rosemeyer couldn't have done it better ... Christ ... I couldn't ..." West whispered softly to himself. If he had merely glanced at his watch there and then he might still have timed that lap, but he didn't. He chose not to, telling himself he preferred to listen to the progress of the car, as the snarl of the Auto Union faded into the distance.

Another lap done. Sepp flew the Melbourne hump in style again, as if he had been doing this all his life, and set off on another circuit. West turned to see Konrad click the watch in his right hand, another watch already ticking away this next lap in his left. It was difficult to read his expression as he kept his eyes locked on the stopwatch, just glancing up to study Sepp's progress through Red Gate.

Konrad gave him five laps, each of which, to West's trained eye, looked perfect through Red Gate at the very least, then finally he called him in and Sepp acknowledged with a flick of his right hand as the car landed from the jump. He let it overshoot at Red Gate, on to the access road for the stables, and then turned it with a finely executed throttle spin in the narrow road, painting dark roundels on its surface, before driving back up the track to the pits. His smile was wide. He pulled the car up in a small skid and switched off the motor, which burped and spluttered before dying. The hot metal ticked loudly and the warmth from the brakes and the engine licked around them. Sepp pulled the goggles up on to his forehead and looked at Konrad expectantly, confidently even. Konrad slapped the aluminium bodywork of the car and laughed out loud – but the laugh sounded false and brittle in the crisp autumn air.

"Good job Sepp!"

"Was I fast? It felt fast. Faster than I've ever been ..." He was talking quickly, as many do when they climb from a racing car.

"Fast?" Konrad corrugated his brow and West saw the grin begin to slip from the youngster's face. "But this was not about speed was it, just a try out, no?"

"But you timed ...?"

"Yes, but please Sepp, don't worry about that."

"What was his best, Konrad?" West put in, quite sharply.

"Two minutes twenty-six."

Sepp went pale, then slumped against the steering wheel. That sort of time would put him down with the British cars: the ERAs, the lone Riley, the also-rans.

"It looked quicker," West said.

"The watch never lies, my friend, you know that." Konrad looked him straight in the eyes for a long, lingering moment, then turned to the crumpled Sepp in the Auto Union.

"Take the car back now, Sepp," Konrad said.

The young man nodded but said nothing.

"And Sepp," Konrad added, "don't worry, there will be other trials." He gave him a fatherly smile and then they bump-started the racing car again and Sepp drove it slowly – very slowly – back towards the stables.

"You sure that's right?" West asked Konrad, nodding at the

stopwatch as the Auto Union trundled out of their line of sight.

"I'm sure. Completely sure."

*

It was how Hanna had always feared it would turn out, one day. Utter disappointment. Sometimes it's best just to dream Sepp, she had told him, but he had looked at her blankly, and tried to sound philosophical when he said it was just not meant to be. Eyes dead. She wished stopwatches could be wrong, she wished her husband-to-be could be wrong ... And she longed for someone to bring the laughter back. She had always hoped for Sepp, helped him, and now his dream had died she felt something had died in her, too. She wondered if he had written to Trudi about what had happened, and hoped that he hadn't – the silly child could hardly help him.

She sat in the pit stalls, on a high chair behind the counter. Opposite her the British spectators were crammed into the covered stand and others crowded five-deep against a wicket fence. Sandwiched between the pits and the grandstand the cars were ready for the race. Word of the spectacle of the German cars had travelled fast and far; to her left the sun glinted off thousands of windscreens, while the excited chatter of the multitude seemed to fuse into a babble, then swell into an insistent surge as the time for the start grew closer. Tinny loudspeakers announced the grid for the race, familiar names in an unfamiliar accent: *Manfred von Brauchitsch, Bernd Rosemeyer, Hermann Lang, Westbury Holt, Richard Seaman, Rudolf Caracciola, Konrad von Plaidt* ... then the other names, some she had never heard before.

Hanna often tired of all the talk of how great it was to be German, all that unconcealed and hugely encouraged nationalism. But when she looked at those Silver Arrows, parked up in front of her in their rows of three-four-three, she could not help but feel a swell of pride in her chest. Compared to the cars lined up behind they looked like cinema space rockets, sleek and futuristic, glinting in the pale October sunlight, seemingly speedy even before their engines had fired. The gap between the German and British cars in the practice sessions had been vast in motor racing terms. The best of the rest more than ten seconds a lap off the slowest of the Silver Arrows from Auto Union and Mercedes, and over a race distance that translated to just about half an hour: fourteen laps, or about sixty-five kilometres, Hanna calculated quickly. The English drivers would only see the Silver Arrows when they lapped them: again and again and again ...

Sepp was finishing the final checks on Konrad's car, diligent and systematic as always, and she was thankful that his strong sense of duty would help him get on with the job at hand despite the crushing disappointment of the day before. Not for the first time she wondered where he got it from, that sense of duty. Lick was with him now, having arrived during the night, and she was glad of that, because she knew he would look out for her brother – though she was not so glad that he had brought a day-old copy of the *Völkischer Beobachter* with him, with a story on the upcoming wedding of Konrad von Plaidt. Kessler's work, she knew. Of course, it was hardly news to her, but seeing it in black and white, with a photograph of her with Konrad from earlier in the year, had shaken her. It was written in stark printer's ink now, not in pencil, and there would be no changing that. The deed was done, a decision made.

She stifled a sigh, would not allow it, but her eyes were not quite so obedient and they strayed to the far side of the grid. The figure behind the steering wheel was waving to someone in the crowd, then snapping his goggles to his face and rolling up the cuffs of his cricket jumper a little to show the sleeves of the white overalls beneath. He hunched forward slightly and gripped at the wheel as the two new mechanics carried the bulky electric starter to the rear of the car. They looked nervous, she thought, and one of them glanced furtively in the direction of Kessler, who nodded sharply. Suddenly West spotted Hanna, assumed she was watching him. He smiled that smile of his, that smile so full of life, that smile so knowing. *The arrogance of the man!*

She acted quickly, jumping down from the high chair and rushing to Konrad's car. Her husband-to-be was at the wheel, gripping it very tight, a front tooth crushing deep into his bottom lip, a fine – almost invisible – line of sweat glistening at the edge of his wind-helmet. Kessler was standing alongside the car, watching the new men tending to West's Auto Union, blinking as he did so. Hanna kissed Konrad on the cheek, then the mouth, as extravagantly as she could for whoever might be watching. His lips were as dry as parchment, but he smiled – the emptiest smile.

"Are you alright, Konrad?"

"I'm fine my dear, don't worry," he said in a slightly strained voice.

"Are you sure?"

"He is about to drive the race of his life," Kessler said. "It is only right that he is a little nervous."

"Please Konrad, be careful," she said.

"I will do what has to be done – no more, no less," Konrad said, and the frequency of the blinks behind the thick lenses of Kessler's glasses increased. Hanna nodded, then walked back up the grid to her seat in the pit stall, glad to be away from Kessler. She wondered if West had been watching when she had kissed Konrad; right now he was looking straight ahead to the first corner. She thought she knew what Konrad had meant by 'no more no less', he had explained it enough times. There are two ways to win a race, he had told her, flat out all the way, if you are young and fit, and show no fear. Or the canny way, sparing the car, the tyres, the fuel, and jealously guarding the advantage of the one less pit stop that this would give you during the race. She looked down at her lap, where the watches and a lap chart sat on a clipboard. To her left was the packed lunch the hotel had made up for them. A pork pie the size of a small hat with a wedge Sepp had refused sliced from it, some white-bread sandwiches of pink ham and a tall vacuum flask filled with hot, sweet tea. She unscrewed the top of the flask and poured herself a mug of the milky brew.

She was nervous, more nervous than ever at a race. She jumped as the first of the engines started with a rasping, distant shriek, causing her to spill a little splash of tea on to her lap chart. She cursed herself below her breath. The other engines burst into life one by one, but just the cars to the rear of the grid, each one starting, popping, then ripping away furiously, a cloud of smoke billowing up from the tailpipes of the tall racers. All the while the German cars sat there: still, silent, mocking, some of the mechanics with knowing grins tattooed to their faces. Then the mechanics slotted the electric starters into the Silver Arrows and the beasts were roused.

The collective roar of the German cars was a great wave of noise that seemed to quake her very being and she was forced to thrust her fingers into her ears. It drowned out all other noise, the English cars now mute and smoking to the rear, the spectators open-mouthed in silent astonishment. A little later a stout man in a grey hat, a curling pipe clenched between his teeth, raised the Union Flag and the drivers' heads, shrouded in white, yellow, green and red linen, snapped left to watch his every move, his every twitch for a clue for when the flag would fall. The noise of the massed cars grew and they seemed to be straining at an invisible leash, vibrating furiously to the deep and rasping breath of their huge engines. Smoke billowed from the exhausts in little clouds, one or two of the cars crept slightly, drivers leant forward, eyes twitching from starter's flag to rev counter and back again, a strong burnt almond smell washed over her ...

Then the stout man's arm snapped to his side and the flag unfurled, fluttered momentarily ... The silver cars seemed to hesitate for a fraction of a second as their tall rear wheels spun furiously, leaving long black smoking streaks on the track surface. The smell of molten rubber broke over Hanna like the blast of heat from an opened furnace. She blinked the smarting fumes from her eyes and watched as the field raced out of its own smoke and headed into the first corner.

*

The anger had slowed West at first, goaded him into over-driving, but now he had focussed its white heat on the job in hand. It was a neat trick, he would give Kessler that. No one watching would realise just how slowly the new mechanics worked on his car at the pit stops; a few seconds lost looking for the wheel mallet; some more in locating the fuel churn awkwardly; a handful more in taking their time to jump away from the car, while the third mechanic in the team shook his head in frustration. Christ, he might have lost about thirty seconds all told … But he had found those seconds now, with the race three-hours old and approaching its climax. And now Konrad, one less stop in his pocket, was in sight – and it was looking for all the world as if he was going to make a proper fight of it. Konrad was third, and West was fourth. So the mathematics of it were easy enough: West just had to beat him.

West took the series of sweeps that led down the hill in the same way he had the last seventy-eight times, throwing the nose into the apices and steering with the throttle, his gloved hands blurring to the steering correction as the long tail of the Auto Union swung this way and that as if it was sweeping the surface of the track clean. He shot the little bridge, and the revs spiked momentarily as the car stood on tiptoes. And then the gap between the two Auto Unions seemed to close, and he could clearly see the oil stained detail on the rear of Konrad's car, the blurring pattern of the tyre treads, and the grey-black puffs of smoke from the vertical exhaust stack as he changed gear. The gap between the cars shortened again in the space of two corners, almost as if Konrad's Auto Union were magnetic, and then, quite suddenly, West was on his tail – and he knew that Konrad would now have to drive with one eye on his mirrors.

For half a lap West ran as close to the other Auto Union as was possible without running into it. He could feel the heat from its exhausts wash over him in the buffeting of its slipstream. He caught the crisp bark of the engine on the down-change, and smelt the oil and the hot tyres while the poisonous taste of the exhaust fumes snatched at his throat, causing him to close his mouth tight, crushing his lips together. The next time they shot the hump by the pits they were still nose to tail, and Konrad was quicker than he had looked the lap before, a full foot of fresh air under the spinning wheels. Then down the hill to the Hairpin he gave it more again, and West was impressed with his line and the attitude of the car as it picked itself up over the crest in the road and flew sideways for a yard or two. West did the same, as he had on every lap, and tucked up close to the other Auto Union once again. Through the right hander at McLean's Konrad let the tail hang out a little more, driving it on the throttle so that a thin ring of smoke wrapped itself around the outer rear wheel. West did the same. The two cars thundered through the wood as one, the din of their passage seeming to shake the trees, and still Konrad was looking to his mirrors.

Konrad's line through the next turn, a tight right hander back on to the long straight, was neatly spectacular, the tail sweeping behind the car as if it was a lazy old pike in the shallows, the wheels clawing at the edge of the track and raising a curtain of fine dust. West was right behind him, almost the very same line, almost the very same attitude of the car through the turn, but as it came to the exit he gave it a little more on the throttle pedal. He'd timed it just right, and as the car kept its near sideways angle across the road, with West's arms crossed in exuberant steering correction, he caught sight of Konrad's goggled eyes in the other car's mirrors. Just then he took his right hand from the wheel and waved at Konrad. The car bucked against his left arm and he was out of the slide in an instant. But there had been time enough for him to catch the look of sheer astonishment on Konrad's face. *Well, that should show him what he's up against – now let's reel this fish in.*

They thundered down Coppice Lane with the daylight of two car lengths between them. West's Auto Union bucked against the rough tarmac, so that even on this long stretch of straight road his hands were constantly working the wheel in little shivers of correction. The rough surface was transmitted through the steering and he felt every dimple, every pit, like a small but solid kick to his arms and shoulders. The inner skins in his gloves seemed to slide against his palms, just a little, and he knew his hands were blistered to bloody mincemeat through the effort of driving the beast, he also knew his badly bruised rib had been given a proper shaking, but there was no pain. That would come later.

Into the Melbourne loop at the end of the straight Konrad left his braking very late and the tail of the car waved through the entry to the corner as its front dipped. West matched him, his front wheels juddered over the bumps and clouds of smoke billowed off the brakes as he frantically pumped at them. Both cars powered out of the loop and on to the climb towards Melbourne Rise, the tail of Konrad's car flicking this way and that under power, like a fencing foil probing and feinting in front of West's face. At the top of the steep hill they shot the jump and headed into their last lap. Konrad took Red Gate smoothly, but quickly, and powered through the wood and down the hill, drifting the car through the serpentine section before shooting the rise at the bottom, all four wheels off the deck, but West was with him all the way – ready to make his move.

They blasted into the tunnel of trees that was Coppice wood, the low sun dappling the way with leopard light in places, the road as dark as oil in others. Konrad still had eyes for his mirrors but as they came to McLean's for that last time he slowed suddenly, and much sooner than West had anticipated, forcing him to jump on the brake for a split second. Then the German turned in some feet short of the usual turn-in point, clipping the dusty, broken, stone-strewn inside edge of the corner with his right side wheels and powering hard. Before West had realised the trick he was hit with a hail of stones and dirt thrown from the rear wheel of the other Auto

Union like the blast from a shotgun. His small flat windscreen shattered into little pieces as a large rock, as big as half a brick, hit it, while the left lens of his goggles fractured into a glassy spider web in the pepper pot blast of smaller stones. Instinctively he whipped the goggles from his head and the car slewed from side to side of the road, two wheels pawing at the grass verge for a moment as he struggled for control.

But he held it. Then narrowed his eyes to little slots against the hit of the airstream and bent as low as he could in the cockpit, following the smell and the heat of the other car as much as the blurred silver shadow still just a few car lengths in front – for the strange line Konrad had taken had compromised his exit as much as the volley of stones had compromised West's entry. West took the Auto Union through Coppice Corner on instinct as much as anything else, and then tucked up tight into the slipstream of the other car.

Even with Konrad's car taking the brunt of the pounding air West's eyes were streaming tears, and his vision was clouding like water mixed with *Pernod*, the world rushing by in a wet-grey blur, the insistent ripping roar of the Auto Union in front his only reference point. He felt the track beneath him, its familiar jolt and switch of camber, the pattering of the tall wheels over the lumpy road surface, and he guessed when the time was right. The car suddenly stood tall, and then sagged low, and he knew he was heading downhill towards the Melbourne loop. He jinked the car to the right as they came into the braking area, the speeding air hit his eyes like breaking surf so he ducked even lower in the cockpit, but he kept off the brake until the last possible moment, so that he pulled level with Konrad's already slowing car. Textbook stuff: up the inside, on the brakes. West knew he held all the aces as they headed into that last corner. It had almost been too easy …
It was then that West sensed that the other Auto Union was moving towards him …

*

For that last lap, and for the first time, Hanna had neglected her chart. The race had long been sealed at the front, Rosemeyer well ahead, but now all eyes were on the battle for third place, though only those within the team knew that a position as senior driver was at stake. She watched them shoot the Melbourne hump, graceful and powerful like silver salmon against the river, and then pitch into Red Gate, the long car bodies popping and flexing like storm teased boats. All necks were craned to catch the last glimpse of them as they disappeared into the trees: every spectator, every marshal, every mechanic, while Lick punched the air in sheer delight and let off a volley of artful expletives. Fink was long finished on his fingernails, now biting at raw skin. Only Sepp looked uninvolved, staring at the corner long after the two cars had passed. Hanna walked through to the back of the pit stalls with many of the others, and she waited.

She heard them first, the overlapping ripping snarls of the two engines, and then she caught sight of them, silver beads swelling by the hastened heartbeat. Both cars went light over the brow and their rear wheels spun off a thin thread of white smoke, and then the second of the Auto Unions pulled out from behind the first and was alongside in a silver flash. It was Westbury, and she could see his windshield was smashed and he was bent low in the cockpit. The cars dipped as they braked, and she knew the game was up, she knew there was no way Konrad could hold him off now, and she felt strangely relieved. Then those words, a sudden memory lighting her consciousness like the burst of a firework within: *I will do what has to be done. No more, no less* ...

As the words Konrad had spoken came to her she watched in utter disbelief – as her husband-to-be turned in on the other car. She could not believe she was seeing it, she could not believe he could do such a thing. But she could also see that Westbury was not about to be intimidated, and he held his line stubbornly.

There was a light clink and then a cymbal shiver of wheel kissing wheel, and then a puff of blue smoke and sharp howl of rubber on rubber, before both cars speared off on divergent paths as if they'd come to an invisible fork in the road. They hit opposite sides of the track and threw up twisters of grass and dirt as they left the asphalt, both now curling into spins. Hanna's eyes were locked on Westbury's car as he fought for control on the steep slope of the grassy infill of the hairpin's loop. It completed one 180-degree rotation, and then snapped straight for a moment; the tail of the Auto Union kicking left then right, his white gloves pumping to the rapid steering corrections like the arms of a running man.

A sudden silence had descended upon the circuit, and she waited for the ghastly shriek of tearing metal to fill it. Time was trapped in a frozen heartbeat as the car bounced across the grass at high speed, then turned sideways on, the wheels ploughing twin brown furrows and throwing up a wave of dirt before it. A white-painted marker board was splintered, and then the Auto Union dug in. For a sliver of a moment it was on the point of tipping over into a driver-crushing roll, canted over like a tossed toy, the wheels on its right side high in the air ...

But then Westbury managed to correct the slide. The Auto Union crashed back on to four wheels and carried on bouncing and skidding down the steep grassy slope. There was a hedge that ran the length of the grass peninsula like a dark green stripe on a trooper's trousers, and now the car was headed for it at an angle, its front wheels slipping as he tried to avoid it.

But he was unable to straighten the car in time and it hit the hedge, sending a shiver along its length and a flurry of foliage into the air, before the 750kg projectile burst through it, sounding like a rogue bull elephant crashing through the bush, crushing a section of the hedge beneath its wheels, which then acted like a sprung ramp and launched the car high in the air.

The Auto Union flew for many metres then landed awkwardly on its heavy rear, which crumpled as it dug a deep groove in the ground. But the impact with the hedge had slowed it a little, and he was able to steer it back on the track at the point where the loop finished, almost as if Westbury had taken a dangerous shortcut. He was hard on the brakes now, and facing the wrong way. Plumes of smoke erupted from the brake linings and the skidding tyres as he tried to bleed off more speed.

"Well held that man!" an English voice cut through the cheers as the Auto Union just managed to slow, its outer wheels kicking up dirt at the far edge of the track. He collected it, then kicked at the throttle to spin it on the power; now completely in control. Hanna exhaled the breath she had held for those long seconds … and then she realised that she had no idea as to what had happened to Konrad in that dangerous time after the cars had collided. No idea whatsoever.

*

This time the Westbury Holt luck had held … West fed in the power and drove up the steep hill to the finish. The cockpit was full of foliage, and a fletched branch was stuck in the weave of his cricket jumper, like an arrow lodged in chain mail. The front right wheel was slightly buckled, the radiator was holed for sure – he could hear the hiss and see the steam – and there was bound to be other damage. But there was not far to go, so he was not about to let that worry him, not about to let it lose him the lead he'd gained over Konrad during that wild ride down the grassy slope and through the hedge.

He had fleetingly caught sight of Konrad's spin in the corner of his eye as he'd endured his own adventure, but he did not know where he had finished up. That was Konrad's problem; he should have known that a driver like Westbury Holt would not be the type to give way to intimidation, certainly not when so much was at stake. It had been a miscalculation born of fear, West knew, fear for what Konrad was about to lose. West powered up the hill and shot the hump as he had every lap, making no allowance for any damage the car might have suffered. Then, as he passed the chequered flag, he glanced in his mirrors to see Konrad's Auto Union roll over the hump at greatly reduced speed. Well beaten.

When West pulled in to the finishers' enclosure Lick was the first to the car, pulling some branches out of the grille, his face split with an insane grin. West's two new mechanics looked on with forced smiles, shifting uncomfortably as he gave them an ironic thumbs-up. "How close were the times?" West shouted to Lick – he knew by now that he didn't have to mention the name.

"*Close*? You were there, you just about equalled Rosemeyer's time for four laps when he was flying. Without those pit stop *problems* you would have smacked his holy arse for sure!" West smiled, and nodded, pleased that Lick had noticed the performance of the new men. Lick added: "You're third, too; betters Konrad's placing at Brno that does all right. So it looks like you've booked a seat in the streamliner, my unlucky *senior* driver!"

As Lick said it Konrad's car pulled up beside him, one tyre was punctured and there was a line of dents down the body of the car where it had, West assumed, rattled along the boundary fencing, while chips of white paint speckled the wire of the rear left wheel. West watched him climb from the car and pull off his goggles to reveal white panda eyes where the lenses had been, the rest of his face caked with grime, oil and dust. Beyond that dark mask there was something else, the face of a crushed man, a beaten man. At any other time even Westbury Holt might feel sorry for him for that. But when a man runs you off the road at over 100mph …

"I didn't see you," Konrad said as he climbed from the car, avoiding the questioning looks from a watching Kessler.

"Of course not," West said, coolly, fingering a cut that he had just noticed above his eye, where the stone thrown from Konrad's rear wheel had hit. He knew the team would believe the man's story: Konrad von Plaidt would never deliberately move over on another driver. It was not his style, everyone knew that. But West didn't really care; he had beaten him, and that was all that really mattered. That was all that ever really mattered. West nodded then quickly turned away, and the German was soon lost in the crowd that pushed its way past the cordon of uniformed RAC men. West stood on the Auto Union's seat to look for a way through, his eyes still smarting and watering from the wash of the racing wind, the acrid pong of his burnt brakes filling the air. Hanna sat in the pit stall. He looked over at her. She held the two ends of a snapped pencil in each hand. She took his gaze, and he would have sworn he could just about make out a spark of defiance in her eyes. Suddenly there was a shaft of understanding as strong as steel, but as transparent as glass, between them. West only hoped that no one else had noticed. After some long aching seconds she nodded slowly. Once. Then twice.

***

1938

Nebelmeister ... Rosemeyer's right foot didn't flinch as they hit the bank of fog. In a matter of seconds West could see nothing but the faint play of the Horch's headlamps on the cotton-grey wall in front of them, though he knew that heavy barges gouged down the Rhine to his left, fairy tale castles stood sentinel on the hills to his right, and ahead of them the road was littered with everything from bicycle to bus.

Nebelmeister ... The fog master, as much a part of the Rosemeyer legend as the Horch 853 Coupe they were travelling in: all gleaming steel-coloured lacquer, pig-skin upholstery, walnut and brass, a car he had had built to his own requirements, quite possibly the fastest tourer in Germany, with a registration that every German schoolboy knew by heart: IA 227 227.

West also had a Horch now, it was an easier way for Auto Union to pay him senior driver salary without forking out cash from their precious foreign currency reserves. But at the moment that was being driven by Lick, and was very possibly being followed by the Gestapo. Since the incident in Berlin they had been on West's tail quite a few times, which had made meeting up with Hanna doubly difficult – and twice as exciting – and he knew they were sure to follow him after this particular factory visit, to see where he might go, who he might meet. But there was only one person he wanted to meet, and she was waiting in a small chalet in the Black Forest. It had been a bugger of a job to arrange, but with Lick – glad of the loan of the fancy 853 – drawing off the Gestapo Mercedes, West would be able, at last, to enjoy some quiet – well, not too quiet – time with Hanna.

The drivers had been visiting a plant for 'agricultural haulers' just outside Köln, something to do with one of Auto Union's favoured suppliers, and although Konrad was, as usual, the star turn at the microphone they all had to do their bit: shaking hands, signing autographs, and grinning for photographers. West hadn't really been invited, he'd learnt about it from Lick, as the team was taking a racing car there to put on display. But it had suited his plans to meet Hanna, and so he had turned up, much to the chagrin of Kessler. It had been boring and he had wandered off for a moment. He hadn't meant to snoop, though he supposed it had become a bit of a habit. But Kessler had been less than pleased when he was told that West had been found having a good look at the tractors – with their steel grey finish, bold crosses painted on the turrets, guns angled high like stiff Nazi salutes.

"It's because of the Versailles nonsense," Rosemeyer had explained. "They don't mind if we have an army of agricultural haulers, but tanks ... Well, that's a different matter entirely. But everyone knows what they're up to; it's hardly a secret by now, is it?" West knew he was right about that, there had certainly been nothing that would excite Gracie and his shadowy friends there, and he was not sure if he would have told them if there had been. Their games had already made life awkward enough for Westbury Holt.

It was just after Rosemeyer had explained the agricultural haulers that they had hit the fog bank. West could just about pick out the winged-ball mascot at the end of the bonnet, and a few feet of cobbled road beyond, nothing more. But Bernd was clearly at ease, slowing for turns – just a little – and swerving smoothly to pass other road users before West had even seen them. West had found it hard to believe when he'd been told about it, but here was proof right in front of his eyes – about the only thing that was. For Rosemeyer it was simply as if the fog was not there. Now and then Bernd would look at him, and West knew he was looking for fear, and these days he could take that as a compliment, and do his best to hide any concern ... With his foot pressed tight to the bulkhead in lieu of his own brake pedal.

"You know, West," Bernd suddenly said, "I'm glad I have been able to get the chance to talk to you. I know you were promised a run in the streamliner ..." So here it was, thought West, the reason why Bernd had been so happy to give him a lift – and had also been so unquestioning as to why he'd been foolish enough to lend an ape like Lick his own 853. But, much more importantly, maybe also the reason why he hadn't been allowed to drive the streamliner during the record week in October, as was his right as a senior driver.

"It seems *someone* didn't want me to get a crack at it," West said.

"And you think I could be that *someone?*"

"Figures, doesn't it? Wouldn't look good if I was faster than the great Rosemeyer in the streamliner now, would it?" West said, making it sound as casual as he could.

Bernd laughed loud: "Believe me, I'm far more scared of the streamliner than I am of being beaten by *you!*" he said, between chuckles. "Besides, you credit me with far too much power."

"Kessler?"

Rosemeyer simply nodded, the laugh drying up as he shifted down for an unseen kink in the road. "Of course, but you knew that didn't you? And please don't be too hard on the team, West, you should know that the pay masters are also the puppet masters."

"I'm beginning to understand that."

"You must learn to go with the flow."

"What, perhaps join the SS?" West said, knowing that Bernd, like Konrad, was a member.

Rosemeyer laughed: "That? But it's nothing. Like boy scouts; that's all. I've been in it for ages. You know, after my last win I was promoted again, but there have been so many wins that I'm not quite sure whether I'm an Obersturmführer or a Haupsturmführer!"

"Isn't it all a bit *political?*"

"Just dressing up; and I rarely do that. But it sometimes smoothes the way, you know. Like being in a club, I suppose."

"Friends in low places?"

"The best sort, I'm finding," Rosemeyer said, smiling. "But enough of all this nonsense, I have some good news," he said, as he lined the car up to pass another unseen obstacle. "There is to be another record run. Mercedes are sore after losing every record to me ... to us ... in October. They have been talking to their friends in Berlin. And believe me West, this time I will do all I can to make sure you get your chance. Lord knows it's work enough for two drivers." Then he grinned as he added: "Two *quick* drivers, that is."

"Thanks Bernd," West smiled. "I appreciate it."

"Thank me after you have been in one of those things West – my God, it's a scary ride all right." For a moment a shadow seemed to pass over Rosemeyer's face, and his heavy eyebrows pulled together as a frown formed, but that soon dissolved into his usual childlike smile as they suddenly emerged from the bank of fog. "Oh, and don't expect to get a run if conditions are bad."

"No, that's quite obviously your thing, old man," West said.

"Not so much that, just that I think our friend Kessler could do much more with me as a dead hero than a live one," he laughed as he said it, but it was a brittle laugh.

After the fog the sky seemed bright, yet it was a uniform grey, a January day. At the side of the road a policeman on a bicycle tried to sort out the aftermath of a collision between a milk cart and a car, and Rosemeyer slowed for the tumbled churns and the cloudy white slick across the road. West watched him shift down the gears and wondered then if he was scared of driving the streamliner. It seemed ridiculous. Yet he found he was pleased with the thought. Right then Rosemeyer accelerated brutally and drove through the milk slick at speed, causing a great wave of white to splash over the policeman. Bernd laughed, laughed loud, and then started to tell the story of how he had once landed his wife Elly's aeroplane – she was a famous aviatrix – on the start-finish straight at the Nürburgring.

***

The frost on the road surface shone like diamond dust in the wide white sweep of the headlights. The sun should be up by now, Sepp thought – perhaps it was too cold for it? Westbury Holt was another not comfortable with this hour of the day, there was no sound from the other seat and Sepp wondered if he was asleep. He was a cool one, that was for sure, for today he was to pilot the streamliner. Still, at least it gave Sepp the chance to drive the KdF-Wagen prototype again.

The indistinct form stirred in the passenger seat, there was the sudden flare of a match, which West pressed into the bowl of his pipe. A little later a dull glow suffused the little car, just as the porridgey grey light of the morning started to fill the long dark canal of the autobahn. "You drive it well," West said.

"It's just a straight road."

"I'll try to remember that later on," West said, and took another long puff at his pipe. Sepp knew what he meant, at streamliner speeds the merest kink in the road would be a huge challenge. West suddenly took the pipe from his mouth, quite sharply, as if he was about to say something, but then he seemed to change his mind and it was back between his lips again, lazy curls of smoke filling the cabin of the car.

Sepp concentrated on driving the KdF-Wagen, or *Volkswagen* as some were beginning to call it, and he felt enormously privileged to be able to do so. They said that the Führer himself had helped to design its beetle-shaped body, but underneath its genes were all Auto Union – for Professor Porsche had used the same rear-engine layout and a suspension philosophy similar to the racer when creating it. Some of the factories in the Auto Union group had turned out prototypes of the KdF-Wagen, and some of the racing drivers had helped with the testing; though it had been left to Lick and Eva to christen the back seat, he remembered with a smile. All the top drivers were allowed to run around in these little cars; a picture of Rosemeyer, Caracciola, von Plaidt, and even the Englander Westbury Holt with the KdF-Wagen would certainly help their sales, while the Führer himself had often ridden in the back of a convertible example.

Sepp found he was still thinking of Hitler when they reached the start line for the record attempts, a length of the autobahn between Frankfurt and Darmstadt, where hatted silhouettes worked in tents, checking timing gear and brewing coffee. A vast Zeppelin hanger dominated the scene to their right while there was a forest the other side of the road, pine trees dark and still like iron, for there was no wind. Just twenty-eight days into 1938 and brass monkey weather, and they wanted yet more records.

Mercedes were already there, the mechanics working under the glare of arc lights, but there was as yet no sign of the Auto Union truck. The new Mercedes record car had been unloaded from its transporter. It seemed huge, completely streamlined, with covers over the wheels and a bubble style windscreen. Two huge nostrils of air vents snarled from the front of the car, beneath a big three-pointed star on the long, long bonnet. Behind the driver's headrest a swastika in a black ring was the only other embellishment on the silver surface.

They climbed from the little KdF-Wagen and for a moment Sepp might have believed he'd stepped into some cold place in the future where the streamliner and the Volkswagen, spaceships from either end of a universe of speed, had landed on earth for a visit. West puffed out little white clouds of frozen breath as he cast a professional eye over the streamliner. He wore a long leather coat but no scarf, so the blue and white V of his jumper's collar showed through. He wore no hat either, he was the only one without a hat, and his thick, wavy hair stuck up untidily. "Looks the part," West said, taking in the lines of the Mercedes streamliner with a cold curiosity. Sepp nodded. "You still like to get behind the wheel of one of these Sepp?"

Sepp shrugged: "There will be no chance now, I had my opportunity and I failed. I have to let it go."

"Nonsense, there will be other chances. Konrad's sure to wangle another run for you ... I mean, now that he's family."

"Yes, one day. But there's little point, the stopwatch doesn't lie." He wished that the Englishman would not mention it, wished that he had the decency not to talk of that day – Konrad didn't.

"You didn't really expect to be quick straight away did you, Sepp?" West said, rather quietly.

"I had my hopes," he said. "I mean Herr Rosemeyer was, wasn't he?"

"Rosemeyer has a lot to answer for," West said, smiling.

"But he was quick in his first try out with Auto Union, with only motorcycle racing experience."

"Some say that's his advantage," West said, suddenly stamping his feet for warmth, "there was nothing he had to unlearn, and the Auto Union's a strange beast, believe me Sepp, a bloody strange beast. It took me months to figure out just how to get the best out of it."

"But my experience was similar to Herr Rosemeyer's, and I even had an extra advantage, for I had driven the car, quite often."

"Thanks to Lick."

Sepp nodded.

"Sepp ... There's something I should tell you ..." Sepp eyed him with interest, the tone of his voice was strange, unsure, like never before – but then that was often the way with these men, before a race, or before they drove the streamliners.

"Yes?"

"Oh, it's nothing," West said, turning away, suddenly adding, "just you're lucky to have such a good friend," as if it was an afterthought.

Sepp nodded, Lick would be on the truck on its way down from Frankfurt, but inside he was glad that he wasn't here. He'd let slip about that night over Christmas with Trudi, and Lick loved to tease him about it, only shutting up when Sepp's face was as red as a fire engine. He thought back to that night with her, when she had come to the bed her parents had made up for him on the sofa in the living room of their Essen home. He had not wanted to, but she had been insistent. It had not been as he expected, she talked the whole time and he felt sure that her father would burst through the door with his old service bayonet and notions of saving his daughter's virtue. She had climaxed, whispering *Heil Hitler* as she did so. That's how Lick knew of it. 'Was it normal?' Sepp had asked. 'Increasingly so', Lick had said, before laughing like an old, cracked drain.

Sepp heard the whisper of rubber tyres against the road surface and the clump of heavy boots as a group of mechanics tried to push start the Mercedes streamliner. The engine churned stubbornly in the cold, but did not fire and a great wave of unburnt fuel vapours burst over them, choking them slightly. The activity brought him back to the now. West still smoked his pipe, looking at the Stuttgart streamliner with mild interest.

"None of it matters now anyway," Sepp mumbled quietly.

"No, why not?"

"I have to go into the military soon, when I'm eighteen. It's the law." It was a part-truth, for he had volunteered before he needed to, keen to prove himself in some other way now that his dream was dead.

"Christ, poor bugger!" West looked genuinely horrified for him. "For how long?"

"Just two years, to start with. I have joined a special regiment, part of the Luftwaffe."

"As a mechanic?"

"No, fallschirmjäger."

"Whatschirmjäger?"

"Paratroopers."

"And what might they be when they're at home?"

"They jump out of aeroplanes," Sepp said, matter-of-factly, but with an inner thrill all the same.

"My God, have you told the boy Rosemeyer about that, he'd love it!" West laughed.

It was fully light now, as if a milky-grey liquid had dribbled into the darker vessel of the sky as they talked. The Mercedes mechanics were still tinkering with the streamliner. Groups of officials in NSKK uniforms and long black coats stood in knots, blowing clouds of freezing breath and stamping feet. Talk and laughter was muted, the overwhelming noise being the ping-ping syncopation of the tools on the cold grey steel of the streamliner. Just then a truck with the Auto Union rings on its tall flanks arrived and pulled up with a squeal of brakes. Lick grinned from the cab.

*

The Auto Union mechanics were unloading the streamliner and West stood by as Sepp rushed to help them. The car wore a new suit of bodywork, sleek and naked silver – except for the crooked birthmark of the swastika – and built up so that it was level with the wheel-tops, with perpendicular flanks hanging down to almost brush the road. It looked huge, and it had lost much of its curvaceous beauty. There was a sudden bustle of activity among the Mercedes people and West realised that Caracciola was preparing for his run. Rudi waved to him, and West gave him the thumbs up. Caracciola was a dapper little man with swept back hair gleaming with brilliantine. He had his airs, that was true, but West thought he was cheerful enough, with a smile that would gouge huge creases into cheeks that bulged with ready laughter. There was no smile today, though, as he sniffed at the cold air and pulled on his driving gloves and wind helmet. Caracciola's racing suit, buttoned up tight to his throat, was spotless white and it gleamed like a flare in the drab morning. Everything else was grey: the road and the sky fused at the horizon, the long winter coats, even the record cars – the lustre of their finish sucked from them so that they looked almost leaden.

Caracciola inched his way along a wooden framework before dropping into the tiny little hatch of the W125 streamliner. The Mercedes was push-started once again and Rudi set off on his warm up run, the car soon vanishing into the all-grey horizon where the narrow two-lane road seemed to be pinched into a thumb's width. There was a hint of fuel in the air, some nervous chatter, and the tick of metal cooling from one of the trucks – for a moment West thought it was the sound of the watches, all the sophisticated timing gear, counting off the Ks Rudi spun beneath his wheels.

Konrad arrived, with Kessler, and West nodded in their direction but made no move to greet them. West had hardly spoken to Konrad since Donington, but he'd made no fuss about it either; taking his place as a senior driver, and secretly taking Hanna, had been more than revenge enough for that clumsy – and desperate – move at the Melbourne loop. Rosemeyer turned up a little later in his Horch. Bernd came over to say hello, complain about the cold, and agree that "yes indeed, we must be mad".

West pulled a carpet bag out of the Volkswagen and found a space in the back of the Auto Union truck to change into his racing overalls, pulling the cricket jumper over the top of them.

"Are you sure about that?" Lick asked him as he fished for a spanner in a vast tool chest.

"It's bloody cold Lick," he said, sharply, not in the mood for superstition. Lick just shrugged, and threw him his overcoat.

Some little time later Caracciola and Mercedes had taken the first of Auto Union's records from October. But it was a shaken, ashen Rudi who climbed from the streamliner – and just then West was surprised to feel that a walnut-sized ball of fear had started to tighten itself within his gut. As he pulled on his driving gloves he walked to the fringe of a conversation that Caracciola was having with Rosemeyer.

"There was a sudden crosswind at Morfelden, you would be advised to leave it for today," Rudi said.

"You hear that West, you might be unlucky," Rosemeyer said as West joined them.

"Or lucky," Caracciola said, shaking his head.

"Then again, perhaps Rudi's just trying to put us off," Rosemeyer said with a laugh. "But hold on, something's up," Rosemeyer turned his head in the direction of Kessler and the team manager, Feuereissen. They seemed to be arguing, brisk feathers of frozen breath mingling in the grey air. West, Bernd and Caracciola watched as the dispute continued, unable to pick out the words, and then Feuereissen walked over to them, a scowl of disbelief on his face.

"What is it? Are we to pack up?" Rosemeyer asked.

"No, this will be our only chance, I'm sorry. Kessler says they will not allow another day, though I must say I can't see what the hurry is."

"It's not a problem," West said. "Let's get moving."

"Did you not hear what I said about the crosswind?" said Caracciola.

"Of course, but it's easy to be cautious when you've a record in your pocket," West said.

"That's idiotic," said Caracciola, obviously annoyed. "Anyway, this is not a job for a novice; these things are death-traps at the best of times."

"Well he has a point there," Feuereissen said. "What do you think, Bernd?"

"Now hold on a minute," West started, turning to Rosemeyer. But Bernd was looking out of the small ring of the conversation, to a point where Kessler was busy scribbling notes into a pad.

"You know, if it's as Rudi says, then perhaps I *should* drive it," Rosemeyer suddenly said, not looking at West, still looking at Kessler.

"I suppose that would make sense, if any of this makes sense," Feuereissen muttered.

"Bernd? But it's my turn – that was agreed," West pleaded.

"I'm sorry —"

"But the crosswind?" Caracciola cut in.

Feuereissen shrugged. "They say there is just this day, and they say we cannot waste it."

"But why Bernd, I'm ready for this?" West could not keep the frustration out of his voice.

"I insist," Rosemeyer said, sharply now, his eyes smouldering as he turned towards West, who felt a sudden surge of anger and frustration flow within him.

Kessler had walked over to join them. "What's the problem?"

"Bernd thinks he should drive, what with the changing weather," Feuereissen said.

Kessler considered this for a moment. He blinked three times in sharp succession, and then nodded. He did not seem too displeased with the outcome, West thought, but then he doubted he would have been too pleased that West would be driving today in the first place.

"Well, that's settled then," Rosemeyer said, and then he walked towards his Horch to find his gear.

"You would do better to listen to me," Caracciola shouted after him, "you can be sure someone has." He glanced at Kessler.

West knew there was nothing he could do. The decision had been made, but it did not stop him burning up inside. To come so close to this, to the chance of being the very fastest, and then have it taken away, was just too much. He watched in a detached way, feeling like an outsider, as the mechanics pushed the Auto Union into line, having to turn it on rollers because with the wheel-spats they were unable to steer the wheels more than a few degrees either way. The sides of the body looked too high to West, all the curving beauty of the earlier car now lost. But more than that, much more than mere aesthetics, he could not help but wonder at how those flat flanks would cope with a side wind. Yet he felt nothing but a nauseating regret that it would not be up to him to find out. Regret and anger. Kessler was suddenly standing alongside him, and West noticed that those grey eyes of his were blinking steadily behind the thick spectacles.

"You understand, of course?" Kessler said. "If there is a wind the driver will need experience with these cars. But to be perfectly honest, I was more than happy for you to have your chance."

"You were?"

"Maybe he is doing you a favour, eh, Englishman?"

Something in the way he said it, the syrupy hint of a dark joke perhaps, made West feel uneasy. He shrugged: "Maybe," then walked back to the truck to change out of his racing overalls.

*

Feuereissen suggested that West should watch the record attempt out on the course: to keep an eye on how the car was performing at speed, and to look out for any sudden changes in the weather. The streamliner had gone well during a recent test on a stretch of the Halle-Leipzig autobahn yet there were still worries about how those tall flanks would stand up to cross winds. But West thought it was as much to do with getting him out of the way – a disappointed man is rarely good company, or much use. Feuereissen told Sepp to accompany him, as the youngster had a good head for the technical and two sets of eyes are better than one. West allowed Sepp to drive the Volkswagen again, he always felt slightly ridiculous at the wheel of one of those things anyway.

"Can you imagine driving along here at over 260mph, Sepp?"

"I imagined nothing else for a long time."

West too, but now he had had his chance taken from him. But at least he could hope for a run later in the year, and with that in mind he studied the road carefully, and tried to imagine how it would be at 200 plus. It was then he realised that in parts it wasn't even really straight, for there were long swooping curves that would take on a completely different character at aeroplane speeds. And then there was the lack of width: door-handle to door-handle you'd be hard pressed to fit three of the little Volkswagens on this strip of road. Yet he would still have given anything to have a crack at it and the frustration he felt at having his chance taken from him still simmered within.

They found a good spot, taking a curling slip road off the autobahn and parking the curved little car just off the Langen-Morfelden overpass, where there were a couple of uniformed NSKK men blowing into their hands for warmth. West and Sepp stood on the bridge, the concrete autobahn stretched out in front and behind them. The forest crept close to the road on both sides, but there was also a large clearing to the right, and West could see that the breeze was already beginning to stir the grass. He looked to the treetops, a lazy nod of confirmation from the pines, and the little marker flags that fringed the road before the bridge, flapping languidly. The breeze was definitely up, Caracciola was right, but West didn't think it was enough to be a problem, and once again he silently cursed Rosemeyer for stealing his chance. Tucked down by the side of the road another NSKK man crouched with a field telephone, one of many who would report progress along the run. Sepp had brought along a Thermos of coffee and happily it was the real thing, something he must have picked up abroad, as good coffee had been an early victim of Germany's closed economy. He handed West a steaming mug and a homemade biscuit.

"Hanna make this?"

Sepp shook his head vigorously: "No."

West thought he saw the beginnings of a blush at the youngster's throat. Hanna had said not to talk of her to Sepp. But he couldn't help but want to know how she was, beyond those happy hours, those crammed evenings, they still somehow managed to steal together.

"How is she, Sepp, I've not seen her for a long time?" West lied.

"She's well, happily married," Sepp said, just a slight glower passing across his face.

"Good, glad to hear it."

"Here he comes."

Nothing had prepared West for this, certainly not sitting at the start line on previous record attempts. The speck on the horizon suddenly swelled to ten times its size and the air seemed to quiver around it. West would swear that the tall trees dipped to its passing, and then the little marker flags snapped rigid against their flexing poles as the shock wave hit them just before the car had passed, the sound of its engine seeming to turn the air to shuddering steel. Then gone.

West and Sepp spun on their heels but already the car had almost disappeared into the distance, shrinking to a silver speck just as a terrific crash seemed to shake the bridge, both deafening and bewildering at once. The two NSKK men stood with their mouths open, jaws hanging slack, and West guessed that they were a faithful mirror of the driver and the mechanic standing on the bridge just a little way along from them. One of the Nazis shook his head, and then let slip just about every swear word known to the German language in a long stream of unbroken curse.

"My God," Sepp said, hugging his coat close to him.

"That should be me," West muttered, very quietly, so that Sepp could not have heard. Then he looked at his watch, and tried to calculate when Rosemeyer would be along on the return run. They didn't have to wait very long, West visualising the scene at the far end as the mechanics spun the heavy car around on the rollers, quickly checking the bodywork for any sign of warping, Rosemeyer no doubt joking with them as they did so. When the car reappeared West was almost ready for it but it still passed through his field of vision in a blink, and still he nearly wrenched his neck on turning to follow it the other side of the bridge. At that speed it was impossible to tell how the car was behaving, only Rosemeyer would know that for sure, and West knew that those first two passes were nothing more than a warm up. They waited for the record run.

Sepp offered him more coffee and they silently toasted the sight they had just witnessed. There was a hint of the streamliner's passing on the air, heat and burnt fuel, but that was soon wafted away on the light breeze. They waited for around fifteen minutes and there seemed to be no real sound for a while in the wake of the mighty whoosh of the streamliner, save the excited chatter of the two NSKK men, and the sough of the wind in the treetops. Just like the rub of skin on bed sheets, West thought, suddenly thinking of Hanna, just like the rub of crisp clean bed sheets ... Funny how pines can sound like ...

"Sepp, those trees ..."

"What?"

"Look at them; do you think the wind's up?" He recognised the creep of panic in his own voice as he quickly switched his gaze on to the grass of the clearing.

"I'm not sure, seems the same ... Doesn't it?"

Suddenly the colour of the grass visibly paled as it whipped into a swift swirl, stirring like a whirlpool on the surface of a lake.

"It's up, the wind's up!" West leant far over the concrete parapet of the bridge to shout a warning to the NSKK man with the field telephone.

"It's too late!" Sepp yelled.

West let himself drop back from the parapet just as the streamliner burst into view. From then on everything happened at the speed of a thought, yet the violent progress of the crash seemed to imprint itself on West's consciousness in a series of ghostly still photographs.

The side of the car seems to buckle slightly as the wind off the open ground hits it. The streamliner veers across the road, shedding its silver skin, before flipping and spinning through the air, silver-foil-like aluminium crumpling and fluttering in its wake. A figure in white, Icarus against the grey, flies from the disintegrating machine like a cork from a champagne bottle. The car is bouncing towards West and Sepp on the bridge at barely diminished speed, and their eyes flick from it to the white figure flying to the trees. The sound of the crash reaches them: *boom* then *screech*, the pop of bursting tyres, and a long staccato series of hollow thuds backed by the wail of tearing metal. The wreck of the streamliner, now just an ugly bedstead of a device with twisted wheels, naked and overturned, trailing a grotesque tinsel of twisted aluminium, veers to the right and hammers into the earth embankment of the bridge. The final crash sends up a great plume of dirt and debris which washes over the parapet, forcing West and Sepp to duck as an engine part whistles past their heads at the speed of a bullet.

Then the world is still.

"The car has crashed!" It's the NSKK man far below, bellowing into the field telephone. Sepp's already sprinting down the length of the bridge as West tries desperately to come to terms with the scene of devastation before him: the long black stripes where the Auto Union has veered out of control, the smouldering wreck of the car, the paper chase trail of torn aluminium right across the road. Suddenly he remembers that figure flying through the air and a great wave of nausea rises within him. He chases after Sepp.

Sepp crashed through the trees at the side of the road and West followed the thud of his boots against the soft, springy earth as much as the brief glimpses of his back between whipping branches. It smelt of dank ground, dark places ... They ran on. They ran as quickly as they could, undergrowth snagging at their legs, until suddenly Sepp halted in a scuff of dead leaves and broken branches, still some way ahead of West.

"He's here!"

"Is he all right?" West shouted.

"I think ...Yes he's all right, I can't believe ..." But Sepp stopped as West drew alongside him. There was Rosemeyer, sat against a tree, not a mark on him. Suddenly the wind shifted the branches above and as the light played across his face he seemed to smile. West half expected a joke, the crease of a grin, and from Bernd – *well, I had you that time, eh?* They rushed forward, and those blue eyes of his looked beyond them.

"Herr Rosemeyer?" Sepp said, quietly, as West took Bernd's wrist and felt for a pulse.

"It's no good Sepp. He's gone," West said, suddenly remembering the words he'd muttered on the bridge: *That should be me.*

***

Hanna leant against his chest, listening to the soft pitter of the rain on the window, listening to the life of him. His heartbeat was strong, steady, and she wondered how it would race when he was in the Auto Union – possibly as much as hers was now. She loved these rare stolen moments, when she could give the maid – that nosy bitch Inge – the evening off and they would stretch their time together beyond what was safe. It was this that excited her, more than anything else. It was this that made her feel alive. Konrad would be back in an hour or so, and soon she knew she would feel sad, sadder than the last time, for each time it seemed to get a little worse. She savoured the slightly musky smell of his fresh sweat and played with the fine, curly hairs on his chest, twisting one around her finger as he sucked contentedly at his unlit pipe. He seemed back to himself, and she was glad, for everybody in her life had been a little different since Rosemeyer's death just a few weeks ago.

They had made love with the light on, the way they always did, while the rain washed the cobbles of Bayernallee beyond the tightly drawn curtains. She would have to tell Westbury to go soon, it was always such a risk to use the Charlottenburg apartment, but this just made it all the more thrilling, too. And so she tried to play the usual trick on herself, letting her eyes wander around the room, taking in the things Konrad had bought for her here in Berlin and elsewhere. Reminding her of the life they had already built, the risk she took. Reminding her of the things she could lose, from the beautiful lacquered dressing table on which sat brass-shining bottles of French perfume, to the walk in wardrobe with its thick folds of Parisian fashion and shoes from Ka-De-We or Grunfeld's lined up like sleeping soldiers along the length of the skirting. Conning herself, even though it never worked now, for something was missing, and she knew that all it would take was a word from the man beside her, a sign, to show her the way out. But that was still to come, if it ever would. She thought about it often, but in her heart she knew that Westbury Holt loved life more than he could love any one thing – any *one* – and she doubted, with an inner sigh that was almost crushing, that he would ever make the same mistake she had.

"Have you seen much of your brother lately?" he said, quite suddenly, startling her.

"Why do you ask?" She said.

"The accident. I was worried, it shook him." He stroked her hair as he said it. Outside she heard the whisper of car tyres against the wet cobbles.

"He has been very quiet. But he's been like that since England." She thought she felt him stiffen a little, and then he shook his head slowly, almost as if he was about to tell her something but thought better of it. They lay in agreeable silence for some minutes, but mention of the accident had awakened something in her. She remembered the funeral at the

Dahlem Cemetery, wreaths from Hitler, Hühnlein standing up to talk of heroism and sacrifice for the glory of the Reich, Elly Rosemeyer stopping him short. That had taken nerve – though Konrad had thought it stupid. Since the death of Elly's husband Hanna and Konrad had truly become the new darling couple, a picture-perfect partnership – Kessler had said that, and he had always wanted that – and it was getting more and more difficult for her and Westbury to meet, especially in hotels. She hated it, but she also realised it was what was expected of her ... It was what Konrad expected, what the Party expected, what Sepp expected, what *Kessler* expected. Kessler? He had smiled at the funeral, she was sure of it, when they were getting in the car to leave. A shallow smile, but it was a smile she had seen before, a smile of triumph. It was then that she clearly saw her place in this world. Konrad was Kessler's ticket. Kessler hoped to climb within the propaganda ministry, riding in the slipstream of Konrad's glory, basking in the wash of the bright light of the image he had helped create of this perfect German couple. A man dies, a great man to most, a fool to some, and she saw Kessler smile. It was the way of now.

"Tell me Westbury," she suddenly heard herself saying, "what has it done to you?"

"What?"

"Bernd's death, what has it done to you?"

"What has Konrad said?"

"I asked you."

"And I'm asking you," he said.

She sighed. "Konrad has said very little. Except that he knew it would happen, sooner or later, said Rosemeyer took too many risks – he says the same of you, says that if Bernd had not insisted on driving it would have been you. He was not upset, but he was ... *respectful* ..."

"He's relieved."

"I never said that," she snapped back, suddenly sitting up in bed so that her breasts flopped full in front of her. He laughed, and she smiled with him, it was irresistible – damn the man.

He put his unlit pipe on the short octagonal bedside table, and then he said: "You know, I might have a quick chat with Uncle Adolf. I'll suggest he sends old Konrad off to Timbuktu or somewhere, he'd make a great ambassador, would thrive on all that civility. Best of all, it would leave us alone to have fun."

"And what makes you think the Führer will listen to you?"

"Oh, we're very much alike. I'm just a little more serious about politics, that's all."

"Is that so," she giggled. "But you should know that if Konrad goes to Timbuktu I will have to go with him, I am the dutiful German wife now."

He smiled, but at the same time the slightest of shadows

seemed to cross his eyes, she thought, she hoped – yes, she hoped.

"And you, you still haven't said, what did it do to you – you still haven't answered?" she said, as he started kneading one of her bullet hard nipples between thumb and forefinger, while she did her best to ignore it. "Well?"

He was suddenly silent and he slipped back off the elbow he was leaning on and into the deep, soft embrace of the mattress, the folds of the crisp, white sheet lying like a thick belt across his middle. He stared at the ceiling for some long seconds, then turned to face her again. "Hanna, I am going to tell you what I thought. I am going to tell you exactly what I thought for one reason. So you know I am capable of telling the truth, however hard that may be." He looked deep into her eyes as he said it. "When you see that I can tell you this, you will know that what I have to say to you after will be true as well. You can be sure of it." He looked serious, as serious as he'd ever looked. She nodded slowly.

"Then I will tell you how I felt."

"Yes?"

"I felt cheated."

"You felt *cheated?*"

"To begin with, yes. I have worked for over a year for one thing, to beat Rosemeyer, and then he goes and kills himself on the day when it was my turn to be the fastest. I felt cheated. At first I simply felt cheated because I thought he had stolen my chance, but now I see that he saw the risks for what they were, and I suppose I should be grateful, it was a brave thing he did. But that was before he died. I truly felt all the more cheated when we found him dead. For now it was impossible for me to beat him. I felt other things, of course I did, but the first thing was this. That's the truth."

"Are you really so competitive, Westbury?" she said, softly.

"Seems so – would you hate me for that?"

She said nothing and they lay there in silence for a little while. There was the sound of a car pulling up outside, into the shared parking area in front of the plush apartment block, the gravel of the driveway spilling around its wheels.

"And what else were you going to tell me, Westbury?" she said.

"That's a Horch!" he snapped, and a panicky grin spread across his face as he leapt out of the bed and stepped into his shorts and trousers and hauled on his cricket jumper. She dressed too, grasping immediately the drama at hand – it wasn't the first time this had happened. He kissed her fully on the lips and said, "Next time," then left with his shoes in his hands, while outside the car door slammed shut. Westbury knew the safe way out, the clanking fire escape at the back of the building, so she need not worry about them meeting on the stairs as she opened the window, letting in cold, damp air, and then quickly made the bed, pulling on her dressing gown at almost the same time. She looked out of the window, to see if she could see Westbury as he came from the side alley. There was a man in a hat and coat walking smartly along the pavement, but Westbury had neither hat nor coat, he had never cared about the rain, so it could not be him. Just a passer-by, she supposed …

The door to the apartment creaked open, and just then she caught sight of the pipe on the bedside table. She dropped it into the drawer of her dresser as the new-leather creak of Konrad's shoes made its way through the large lounge and along the hallway.

"I'm home, darling. And what a boring evening that was …"

*

Westbury Holt was extremely uncomfortable. In the first place he always felt naked wearing his racing overalls without the old cricket jumper, and then they had nagged and nagged him to do the top button up, buckle his wind helmet under his chin, and place his goggles just so – above and parallel to his eyes. He looked like every other driver in the great hall, Mercedes and Auto Union alike, and yet he felt like a gate-crasher. He tried to stand to attention like the others, but he knew he was slouching, and in all the world all he wanted was a smoke. All he had had that day was a rough little fag he'd scrounged from Lick and he cursed himself once again for forgetting his pipe the night before. To cap it all he was about to meet Adolf Hitler.

The day hadn't started so badly. After the close escape at Hanna's he had gone to the Eden for a few drinks. There was no point in trying to sleep, he knew. He had come close to telling her, very close, and next time his feelings would be flushed out in the open for sure. Then it was up to her. He had drank with a group of motoring writers he'd met around the tracks, all here to cover the motor show, and had got back to his room at the Adlon just in time for half-hour's shuteye, before shaving then spending a little more time than usual getting ready. He had not been tailed at all yesterday, he felt sure of that, and he wondered if they had, at last, given up on him. He hoped so, for it would make it far easier to meet with Hanna, but he would also miss the sport of losing his shadow, which had kept him royally entertained during the dull months of the off-season. West often wondered if the Gestapo men ever admitted to losing him, and he suspected they didn't.

That morning they had given the Berliners a great show as the Silver Arrows sped through the streets of the capital at race speed, skidding over wet paving stones between forests of Nazi salutes and tall columns crowned with eagles. They thundered under the Brandenburg Gate, their slipstream causing the vast swastika flags that were draped beneath it to whip up then snap straight. And then it was flat down the Unter Den Linden, tyres slipping in each and every gear, the engine note cracking and echoing off buildings as they raced between the Doric columns and the young lime trees – replacements for those that had been felled to make a wider marching space. It had been great to get behind the wheel of an Auto Union again, the first time since Donington over four months ago for West, and he had given the locals a good show: hanging out the rear on the tight corners, even tail-sliding into the ante-hall of the Berlin Messe, the exhibition centre, with a shrill screech of tyre rubber against the polished floor.

West knew Hitler was on his way when he heard the band outside strike up with the Badenweiler March, as they always played that catchy little ditty when the Führer arrived. They had arranged the cars in two opposing lines, Mercedes facing Auto Union with the drivers paraded in front. Hitler made his way down the opposite line first – and West tried his damnedest to make Dick Seaman laugh by pulling faces as the other Englishman met the Führer. One of the SS guards scowled at him for his efforts, but he simply grinned back. Soon it would be his turn.

The hall was clean, cream-coloured stone with big windows and bigger doors, the scale of a cathedral, the residual incense of the engine smoke of ten now dormant racing cars still lingered and licked at its tall ceiling, adding an extra ecclesiastical air. At one end a vast red curtain adorned with swastikas with gear cog surrounds blocked off the main hall where the 1938 Berlin Motor Show exhibits gleamed under bright electric lighting. Black uniformed SS guards of the Adolf Hitler Leibstandarte lined the walls, each snapping noisily to attention as Hitler and his entourage passed by. Meanwhile the band played on for the benefit of the queuing public outside, the martial music muted by the cold stone. Every now and then a camera flash would flare and gleam in the silver bodywork of the cars, or a church cough would rise above the murmurs of the small group, with Hitler at its head, which moved from driver to driver.

Konrad was next in line to meet the Führer, his arm held out stiffly in salute, as he clicked his heels in Prussian fashion. Konrad's overalls were pressed into razor sharp creases and they bore the lightning-flash runes of the SS at the breast. West could clearly hear the conversation in the church hush of the large space.

"Herr Plaidt, I trust you have now fully recovered from your accident?"

"Almost completely thank you, my Führer."

"Good, good, we will need your experience more than ever now."

"I will soon be fully up to speed, my Führer."

"And some said you tired of the game, but I thought not. Old racing drivers are like old soldiers, are they not?"

"That is just so, my Führer."

Hitler seemed pleased, nodding his head contentedly. He was a great motor racing enthusiast, and it was his speech at this show in '33 that had been the start for the German teams, not to mention the little Volkswagen and the octopus of autobahns that was spreading its tentacles across Germany. The little group moved to West's car next. He did not salute. There was no doubt that Hitler knew of him, but Kessler, who stood at the Fürher's shoulder with Hühnlein, an ornate dagger dangling on a lanyard from his uniform belt, still took long-winded pleasure in introducing Westbury Holt, blinking steadily as he did so. "Herr Holt is now settled in the team, my Führer, and he has proved to be a competent driver. Thanks to the excellence of German engineering he was able to score a fine second place finish at Pescara last year."

West wanted to say, *sorry, have we been introduced?* but he bit his tongue as Hitler reached out for his handshake. They shook, and Hitler gripped his hand … And his gaze. The Führer wore a long ankle-length toffee-brown uniform coat with bright brass buttons and broad grey lapels. There was a swastika armband blood red against his left arm and the glassy peak of a red-banded brown cap pulled low over his eyes, so his head tilted back ever so slightly as he looked at West. Stared at him. His face was fuller than West had expected, and there was a little bulk around his middle – photographs served him well. The trademark toothbrush moustache was trimmed to geometric perfection, but still looked ridiculous, West thought, and his complexion was surprisingly sallow. Bags hung heavy from his eyes, but his stare never wavered, he never even blinked, and West found himself, ever so slowly, growing more and more uncomfortable.

Finally Hitler broke his gaze and simply nodded, making no effort to speak to West, but brushing past him to take a closer look at the racing car. He stroked the rounded nose of the Auto Union as magnesium flares flashed in the background and camera shutters chattered. West turned to see something close to a smile on his face as he caressed the machine. Hitler couldn't drive, but he obviously loved his cars, and for a moment he looked like a happy kid there, with the Auto Union – but the sort of kid who'd break your toys given half the chance. The Führer nodded again, then moved on down the line, the creeping cluster of brown, grey and black uniforms following him. Half a minute or so later West caught a strong whiff of cologne and turned to see Konrad beside him.

"Well, so what do you make of him?" Konrad said.

West shrugged, then said: "I could murder a smoke."

"The Führer doesn't approve," Konrad said. "How have you been

West, we haven't seen you for some time now?"

"I've been around, twiddling my thumbs, waiting for something to drive."

"It's the same for us all," Konrad said, quietly.

It was only the second time they had spoken since Donington, which West was sure had suited them both just fine.

A little later, at the far end of the hall at the foot of the huge red curtain, Goebbels gave a speech about how great everybody was, and then Hitler climbed onto the dais, which was heavily embossed with the cog-wheel surround swastika of the DAF, the Nazi labour movement. A murmur of excitement swept across the large room like a breaking wave. He had taken off the long coat to reveal a brown uniform tunic, with an Iron Cross he had won – so they kept saying – on the Western Front on his left breast. There was a swastika armband on the left sleeve of the tunic. Hitler held his right arm in the air and instantly a hush descended on the gathering.

He spoke. Playing the audience like a pro, a showman, with well-timed pauses in which you could have heard a party badge drop to the floor, interspersed with almost maniacal tirades. While he spoke he kept his left arm by his side, using his right arm to gesture. It lasted a full seventeen minutes, by which time West was thoroughly bored. Soon after the speech the curtains were drawn back and the glass and steel of all the cars on display in the great hall glinted like sudden treasure in the harsh white lighting.

*

Sepp would never have believed it was possible. Never would have believed that listening to one man speak could generate the same excitement within him that racing cars had ... Once, not so very long ago. The hairs still stood up on the back of his neck and his mouth was dry, his tongue almost sticking to his palette. He felt that the words had been for him alone, and yet for everyone, and he could not wait to tell Trudi about it. He had been in the presence of a great magician, there was no doubt about that – even Lick was struck dumb with awe. The pair of them now hurried between the stands, dodging salesmen and news photographers, to take their positions by the streamliner. Konrad followed them. The record cars from Mercedes and Auto Union had pride of place in the great hall, along with the little KdF-Wagen and its derivatives, and the Führer would pass by their stand first of all.

The streamliners from both companies stood on waist high marble plinths, so that more than ever they looked like the perfect silver sculptures they were. They were in front of tall panel windows, with long red curtains, rolled up to let the grey morning light into the hall. Ornate standard lamps with upturned buttercup shades stood behind the cars, bathing them in a deep-water sheen, the swastikas behind the cockpits starker and prouder than ever. The Auto Union was the earlier October car, as the other was in silver shreds, an unworthy monument to the great Rosemeyer. Sepp and Lick took up station at the rear of the car, while in front of it stood Konrad, next to a bronze bust of Rosemeyer sat on a stone pedestal, a huge laurel wreath draped around it. Konrad had removed his wind helmet and smoothed back his hair, and on his signal they raised their arms in stiff salutes as a photographer stationed himself beside them, kneeling low, ready for the Führer.

Konrad greeted Hitler for the second time that day and showed him around the beautiful streamliner. The Führer folded his arms up tight to his chest and concentrated as Konrad described an arc over the flowing wheel-fairing with the palm of his hand, explaining how the slippery surface helped the air to pass over the car at 250mph plus. Hitler smiled like a proud, proud father. Sepp had seldom seen that before, in pictures, on the newsreel – for then Hitler only ever seemed to smile when he was with children. But then in many ways these machines were his children, Sepp thought, for without him there would be no racing, no records, no autobahns, no Volkswagen, no Trudi, no hope ...

Suddenly, before Sepp knew what was happening, the Führer had picked him out, he looked around to make sure it was true, but still Hitler beckoned him forward. Sepp felt a shiver of excitement run down his spine. He dropped his salute and walked forward. Then, extraordinarily, he felt sure there was some spark of recognition in Hitler's eyes – and just an instant later he felt completely trapped in their gaze.

Those eyes were deep Nordic blue, bringing clean cold fjords to mind. Deep pools of blue, as Hitler seemed to stare at Sepp for an ice age. There was something in those eyes that seemed to penetrate to the very heart of Sepp, and for a strange instant – that should have been uncomfortable but wasn't – Sepp thought that this man could read every one of his deepest thoughts and feelings. He had to trust those eyes.

"You are one of the mechanics?"

"Yes, my Führer," Sepp said, surprised at how calm it sounded.

"And do you ever dream to drive?"

Again, Sepp thought the man could see inside him; see the ghost of hope that lived within him. But that hope was spent, and he said: "No, my Führer. I am to join the Fallschirmjäger, quite soon."

"Ach, but that is good, we need soldiers with technical ability." He paused, but still stared at Sepp. As a child, in quiet moments in the

Marienkirche in Zwickau, Sepp would stare at the dangling crucifix, looking for some sign of life in the Christ eyes, looking for some sign of good, of truth. He only ever found paint. But now he had found truth in eyes.

"Racing is like politics, games the older generation play for Germany," Hitler continued. "But destiny is with the German youth. Germany is yours to build. You see that?"

"Yes, my Führer."

Hitler nodded again. The nod seemed to carry the weight of a sacred blessing. And then he moved on to the Mercedes streamliner, entourage in tow, where Caracciola greeted him.

"Christ Sepp, am I still fit to wipe your worthy arse?" Lick said.

"Well brother in law, it seems you have the Führer's ear!" Konrad slapped him on the back. He tried not to smile, he really did, but soon his mouth was aching from the grinning. For at last he knew. At last he knew for sure that his destiny and Germany's were one. But it had taken a great man to show him.

"Is Hanna here?" he asked Konrad.

"Yes, she is waiting in the café at the entrance, she had a headache, go to her if you want, we can hold the shop here. She'll be thrilled for you, I'm sure."

"Thank you, I won't be long," Sepp said, hurrying away.

By the time Sepp had reached the main entrance it was like swimming against the current. The Führer had finished his quick tour of the show's highlights and the German people had been allowed in. Sepp had to force his way through the mass of humanity, with its excited babble, and the more it frustrated his efforts the more he dug his elbows in to prise a way through. He had to see her now. If one person would understand what this meant it would be Hanna, for they had shared everything, and now he wanted her to have a part of this too: his destiny – the greatest destiny a man could ever hope for. Finally he forced his way through the great doors of the hall. He pushed his way to the side of those trying to funnel in, then allowed himself to spin out of that molten mass of people. He took his bearings, finding the entrance to the café. The door was of thick frosted glass in heavy oak, stout brass bars for handles. He heaved it open to see that the place was almost empty, as most had gone into the show. Waitresses in traditional dirndls cleared tables and a salesman in suit and tie sat with a bowl-shaped glass of foaming Berliner Weisse in the far corner, looking at his watch between sips.

Along the length of the frosted window ran a deep shelf, with tall padded stools in front of it. Hanna stood there, a glass of Sekt within reach, though it was early in the day for wine. She was talking to Westbury Holt. Neither of them had seen Sepp and he stopped in his tracks, said nothing, as she opened up her bag. West was now wearing his cricket jumper again, the same as always, the only thing that was missing was his ... She pulled the briar pipe out of her bag. Before that Christmas night with Trudi he would not have recognised the look they gave each other. And now joy swiftly turned to anger and he wanted to be out of that place.

"Sepp!"

"Hanna," he said quietly, as they walked over to meet him. Her face had reddened slightly.

"How did it go?"

"He spoke to me."

"Hitler?" West said. "Well bully for you."

A Hitler Youth lad seemed to appear from nowhere, a strange looking kid of about fifteen, tiny ears and a squashed up nose, a reddening face that looked half finished. He crashed a boot against the parquet floor and flicked out an overdone Hitler salute in the direction of West: "Heil Hitler!" West laughed out loud and the salute drooped a little, but the youth still kept the stern expression on his half-done face, and held out his autograph book for West to scribble in. At that moment Sepp hated Westbury Holt more than anyone, or anything, in the world.

***

Hanna sometimes prayed, but there was no belief. She prayed because her mother had always told her to, and because it could do no harm. But she knew it was merely superstition – it was the very same for her as not walking under a ladder. Yet these last few weeks she had prayed a little more often. For she felt she was losing her Sepp.

She had hoped that meeting him in Zwickau might help. Konrad had provided the money as he had always promised and at last they had been able to buy back the rest of Papa's apartments from Herr Ostermann. It was all arranged and now she was to meet up with Sepp before they went to the block, where Ostermann waited with old Kurt, together. Konrad had insisted the paperwork should be in Sepp's name, it was the sort of old fashioned nonsense he thrived on, but she did not really mind. Because she did not feel she deserved this favour. And because now she was not so sure she even wanted it.

Hanna and Sepp had talked about this day often, on cold evenings in the basement kitchen, how they would somehow gain back all they had lost, although she had always thought for Sepp it was just a way of justifying his other dream, the dream that had *been* him until that day in England five months ago. Now she wondered what it might mean to him, beyond an extra income for that child Trudi to squander. She put the thought aside, slightly ashamed of it, and then tried to enjoy the sunshine.

It was as good as a March day in Zwickau could get. Very good, that is. She had taken the train from Berlin that morning, travelling first-class back to her past and finding that her mood lightened by the kilometre. For some reason Sepp had asked her to meet him outside the Marienkirche, which had puzzled her, but they had not spoken for long so she had no chance to ask him why before he put the telephone down, saying he had things to see to. His tone had been a little cold, she had thought.

Zwickau was changing. Outside the station there was a recently erected statue of a coal miner with his pickaxe raised, on a very tall narrow stone plinth, higher than a house, hacking at the clean air. She thought it a mocking mirror image of those who worked far beneath the earth, but she guessed that these days most would see it as heroic. There was also a huge swastika clamped to the ribbed facade of the station, clutching it in its angular talons, and as she walked towards the Marienkirche she saw that more and more Nazi flags were now fluttering from buildings. Some people recognised her: some of those she knew from the past who she greeted and chatted to, and others who might have seen her in the newspaper or perhaps even on a newsreel, on Konrad's arm, opening an autobahn or watching a parade.

Although you could see its baroque bell tower from far away the Marienkirche always seemed to be hiding when you came nearer to it. Along with the house that was the birthplace of Schumann, the great composer, the cathedral was the small city's pride and joy, and had been for over 800 years. It was squeezed into a tiny square, old houses encroaching close to its walls. Industry's breath had darkened the old cathedral and its intricate Gothic cladding, yet all the statues that lined its walls were bright faced from the wash of the rain, all those unsmiling but familiar faces that had peopled the childhood fantasies of Hanna and Sepp. She tipped her head back to look at the bell tower, a later addition after the original had collapsed some centuries ago. She had always fancied it looked eastern and exotic, with its bulging black tiers, and as a young girl it had been easy to imagine it as a place in fairy tales. The gold cross at its summit sparkled and winked in the sunlight.

Hanna was early, and she knew that Sepp would arrive on the hour, on the very minute, so she had time to kill. She realised she had not been inside the church for years and so she pushed through the creaking wrought iron gate and then shoved at the heavy door and stepped within. It smelt damp and cold, but she did not mind, because it was simply the smell of this special place. Shafts that shone through the tall windows striped the grey space with heavy mote laden columns of light. One person sat in the front row, just a grey overcoat, a man in prayer, she guessed. From habit of old Hanna slipped a five Reichspfennig coin into the box and lit a candle, hers the only flame to flicker, all others long since burnt to nothing, snubbing out in the film of dark water in which they stood. She walked beneath the vaulted ceiling which supported the giant organ, the sound of which could almost shake the ancient stone, and then down the nave, her footfalls throwing hollow echoes through the still of the Marienkirche. As she came closer to the figure she realised the man was not at prayer, but was staring up at the crucifix that hung from the heaven-high ceiling over the transept. His blond hair flickered in the dusty light.

It was Sepp.

"It's just paint, you know," he said. His eyes were fixed on to the brightly painted face of Christ.

"I thought we were to meet outside?"

"I knew you would come in," he said.

"You did?"

"I know you," he said, very quietly, and because he still stared at the crucifix Hanna could almost believe he was talking to the painted Christ.

She slid in to the pew beside him, the hard wood cold through the seat of her dress. "You haven't been in touch much lately," she said.

"I have had important things to attend to."

"So important you've forgotten your sister?"

"I have asked Trudi to marry me." He said it suddenly, no preamble, and for a little while she was completely lost for words. "Well?"

"Sepp ... But it's so sudden, you're still so young."

"I'm old enough."

"But still —"

"There's more," he waved her silent. "I have joined the Fallschirmjäger."

She nodded, they had talked about it before, often in the months following Donington. She had long understood his mind was made up and it had always been just a matter of when. A cloud must have floated in front of the sun, cutting out the light that filtered through the old glass a little.

"What does Trudi think?"

"She understands that I have to do my duty to the Fatherland," he said, still staring at the painted Christ. He had yet to meet her eyes.

"Duty? Not so very long ago military service was something you wanted to avoid, or at least get over with as soon as possible – do you forget that Sepp?"

"We all need to grow up, to see that there is more to this life than the wants of individuals – all of us Hanna." That last was loaded with such intensity that a shudder travelled the length of her spine. Just after he said it a heavy beam of sunlight found his face, lighting it up, and he finally turned to look at her. She had never seen him like this before. She remembered a frenzied preacher she had once seen on the streets of Chemnitz, long, long ago. There was something of that man in Sepp's eyes right now.

"How long will you be away from me, Sepp?"

"That depends." He stiffened as he said it.

"But you must know how long you will have to serve, and there will be leave?"

"No, you don't see – it depends on you."

"I'm sorry?"

Sepp laughed loud, very loud, very sudden, a hollow stage laugh that might have shaken dust from the rafters as it echoed and boomed through the cathedral.

"Sepp please, what's wrong with you, this is not the place, it is wrong, someone will hear!"

"Wrong ... Wrong ... Wrong!" he shouted, then shook his head slowly, "what is *wrong* Hanna dearest?"

"Please Sepp, let's leave – old Kurt and Ostermann will be waiting for us."

"I asked you a question, sister: what is *wrong?*"

The tone unnerved her, it was as cold as the hard wood on which she sat, and she realised that he now stared at her in just the same way as he had stared at the painted Christ. It was the look of a man who had seen a trick for what it was, the questioning look of a man who knew the answer. But there was a trace of anger there, too. Suddenly she felt the tears burning at the back of her eyes, but it seemed to leave him unmoved, and she turned from him, reaching for a handkerchief.

"Upset are we sister, you need to relax – why not smoke something?"

"Sepp, please, don't be absurd, you know I don't smoke – what's wrong with you?"

"Smoke a pipe, perhaps?"

Then she knew. She remembered his expression at the motor show, a cold sigh of resignation seeped through her body. There was a long, silent pause. Then: "It is *my* life Sepp," she said, softly.

"No, it is not. All of our lives belong to Germany."

"You are beginning to sound like one of them, Sepp."

He said nothing.

"So, you know," Hanna said. "Will you tell Konrad?"

"I'm not sure, it's not my place to do so, is it?" he said, paused for a moment, and then added: "But know this Hanna, what you are doing is wrong. It cheapens you, and it is the sort of behaviour that cheapens the Fatherland. If you continue I will never see you again, you have my word on that." His stare was ice cold, intention as solid as the old stone that surrounded them. There was a deathly silence.

"You can't just stop being my brother Sepp, that's ridiculous."

"I can, and I will. The choice is yours. Now, if you will excuse me I will go to the apartments to meet Herr Ostermann. Think about what I have said. Then come."

"But Sepp, it was all for you, always – can't you see that?" she whispered, but he had slid along the pew by now, and stepped into the aisle, and the cold click of his shoes on stone echoed through the empty cathedral.

*

There was a strong smell of cooking cabbage, and Sepp could hear the saucepan bubbling away in the adjacent kitchen. "You will have schnapps with me?" Old Kurt did not wait for an answer and the next thing Sepp heard was the splash of generous measures into two tumblers. Kurt had agreed to stay on, as caretaker, and Sepp could ask for no better man for the job. Old Kurt smiled and raised his glass: "I've waited for this day, you know. This place has always belonged to you and Hanna as far as I'm concerned – it's a shame she's not here."

"Perhaps it's not so important to her now, Kurt," Sepp said, unable to keep the edge from his voice.

"What do you mean?" There was unmasked concern on the older man's face, and the glass hovered before his lips.

"Some things were said, it's nothing."

"I hope you're right there," Kurt said. "You should never fall out. Not you two, you belong together, like coffee and cake. She loves you more than anything in life. You know that, don't you Sepp?"

Sepp nodded, but did not answer.

"You should never forget what it was like for you two, alone, without her you would not be the man you are today Sepp, believe me."

Sepp nodded again, but lightly, and then turned to look out of the window down the length of the street. A tram rattled past, but most chose to walk in the sunshine. In the distance a figure with a vaguely familiar gait walked along the pavement carrying a package, or maybe a shopping bag. The contract lay on the table, with Sepp and Herr Ostermann's signatures scrawled across the bottom. He had not been sure about accepting Konrad's generosity, even less so since he had discovered Hanna's secret. But Konrad had insisted, and Trudi had persuaded Sepp to accept it, too, and finally he had decided to give Konrad a large cut of the rental income they would make, there was honour enough in that – a business agreement. His father would have approved, he thought.

"You know Sepp," Kurt went on, "that one is a remarkable girl. She has been both a mother and a sister to you – and the same to my son Strudel, too – maybe you don't see that so much now?"

"I see what there is to see – it's time she grew up."

Kurt shook his head, sighed deeply, and took a gulp of schnapps. Then, obviously realising the subject of Hanna was closed, he said: "You know the Haarzopfs have gone?"

"Gone?" Sepp asked, remembering the Jewish family who lived on Moritz Strasse.

"Disappeared, they say they have left the country."

"Then it's for the best."

"Yes, much safer for them."

Sepp said nothing, and the older man eyed him curiously.

"I have something for you," Kurt said finally, disappearing into the back of the apartment. Sepp looked out of the window again, there was still no sign of Hanna, but the figure with the shopping bag was nearer and he realised it was Strudel. He had seen little of him lately, the simpleton was not allowed near the works now, and if he was found there they had been told to throw him out – for his own sake, and for their sake. Herr Kessler had been insistent on that, and Sepp thought that it was for the best. Strudel was walking along the pavement, a postal worker in the dark blue uniform of the Reichspost was coming the other way. Sepp supposed Kurt had sent him on an errand to make sure he was not around when Herr Ostermann had arrived with the paperwork, and he could understand why, could understand the embarrassment Strudel must cause him. Suddenly, on seeing the postman, Strudel ran across the street without checking for traffic, spilling two apples which rolled in the road. A car horn sounded a warning and one of the apples was juiced beneath the wheels of a Ford Eifel a second later. Old Kurt always warned Strudel to keep clear of men in uniforms, but sometimes he took it a bit too far.

"Idiot," Sepp said softly to himself, shaking his head.

"You say something?" Kurt had come back into the living room carrying a beaten up old cardboard suitcase, it was obviously heavy and it clanked as he placed it on the polished seat of his worn old easy chair.

"What's this?"

"There may be war."

"Some say so, but I don't think so. No one wants it."

"There may be," Kurt said again as he slipped the catches on the suitcase. The case opened with a creak to reveal a number of small newspaper-wrapped packages and a fan of cracked old photographs. Kurt wiped one of the pictures against his trouser leg and handed it to Sepp. It showed three soldiers in uniform, each wearing a cap without a peak and carrying a rifle.

"Handsome hero, that one, eh?" he said, pointing to the man on the left of the picture.

"You?"

"Western Front," Kurt nodded. "It is where I learnt to keep my head down." Sepp smiled, wondered whether it was the poor quality of the picture, or was there really age in that face, even then? "And this," Kurt went on, pulling out a large package, "is my little souvenir." Sepp watched with curiosity as the older man peeled off the layers of newspaper to reveal a strange green stump of a thing with a spike sticking out of it, like the muzzle of some iron swordfish, ugly and brutal. Its paint was old and had dried in dribbling blisters, and was now peeling in places. Kurt handed it to him and he turned it to see that it was hollow, like an iron gauntlet, with a leather wrapped handle inside.

"It's a punch-dagger. Unique I would have thought. I took it off a dead Tommy, probably the man who made the damned thing, near Bullecourt, it was."

Punch-dagger. Sepp's stomach turned at the very name. Never had he seen such an ugly weapon. Never had he held such a grimly fascinating tool of violence. He placed it over his right hand and slid the body of it under his jacket sleeve. He gripped at the handle, tightening his fist around it, hearing the leather creak. The spike was naked steel, as thick and as pointed as a pencil and as long as two joined together. With his hand inside the deep gauntlet of the dagger it almost looked as if the spike came straight out of his wrist, as if he had lost his hand and had had a long and pointed probe grafted to the stump. He let the spike twist a figure-eight through the air, feeling the weight of it, and then he made to punch, a right hook. He thought of that spike sinking into someone, and he shuddered.

"Kurt, but this is a terrible thing," he croaked.

"War is terrible, Sepp."

"But this …" he shook his head, his eyes fixed on the gleaming tip of the spike, wondering if Kurt, their old Kurt, had ever used this weapon.

"I want you to have it, take it with you when you join up."

Sepp laughed: "What will I do with it?"

"Who knows? But you might thank me, one day."

"I can't … Besides, war would be different now old friend. We would drop from the sky with modern weapons, this is medieval – how could I even carry such a lump of iron on to an aeroplane!" Sepp laughed again as he said it, but then realised that he'd upset Kurt, who was about to take the punch-dagger from him.

"I'm sorry," Sepp said. "You're the old soldier, and you know more about this sort of thing than I do, so thank you, Kurt. But for God's sake, can you wrap it for me, or I'll cause holy hell on the tram." They both laughed and Sepp decided he would hide the murderous hunk of iron away somewhere, no use in offending Kurt. He looked out of the window again as Kurt wrapped the punch-dagger in newspaper. There was still no sign of Hanna. He could hear Strudel, coming up the stairs, still running from the postman's uniform.

"I have to go," Sepp suddenly said.

"Can't you wait for Strudel, he would be sorry to miss you?"

"No, I must get back to the works," he lied, making a point of looking at his watch. Just then Strudel burst through the door with the bag of shopping, his rat-like face lighting up on seeing Sepp, brown eyes shining bright.

"S-s-s-s-epp! T-t-t-t-tell me about the T-t-t-t-type D," Strudel stammered, excited.

"My god! It talks," Kurt gasped, astonished.

"Sorry, I must be off," Sepp said, taking the hastily-wrapped punch-dagger from Kurt, ignoring Strudel, and leaving quickly, his drink untouched.

***

Frau Schuster's shop on Tauentzien Strasse was a haven. The clothes were not quite as stylish as those Hanna would see abroad or in the big department stores like Grunfeld's, but she liked to spend time, and Konrad's money, in this particular place. She was still angry with Sepp, but she could not hate him, that was not in her. But she also believed she could not stop seeing Westbury, even though she did not know if he loved her, or if it was even in him to love someone. For now it was best not to see either of them, and hope she would somehow never have to make that awful choice between one or the other.

She stood in the fitting room in her underwear, half naked. There were three dresses to try and she was wondering which would be first, all part of killing a day to death, with small and decisive stabs of indecision. One wall of the changing room was a mirror and she studied herself in it. She was still young, and her breasts were full and round, her waist trim. She had everything a girl could want, some of it a gift of life, much of it a gift from Konrad. She knew she should be happy, and she tried to imagine herself talking to that girl in the basement kitchen two years before, how envious she would be of all the things Hanna now had. Then she thought of Sepp, and his recent words burnt within: *the choice is yours.* Slowly the inner image of him morphed into that of Westbury Holt.

When she pictured Westbury in her mind's eye her breath seemed to catch in her throat. It always amazed her, the effect just the thought of him had on her, and she was now aware of the arousal bubbling within her. Without thinking she closed her eyes. She reached down to the top of her drawers, her fingers slipping beneath the elastic and silk, sliding across her warm smooth skin, and angling to the soft hair, the touch of it electric ...

There was a sharp knock at the door, and she pulled her hand away, opening her eyes and catching the shock and shame in them in her reflection. A blush began to burn her cheeks.

"What is it," she said, her voice sounding dry and cracked.

"Frau Plaidt, there is a man here to see you, he says it's urgent."

"Who?"

"He says you will be glad to see him, but —"

"Oh, I ..." She hesitated. Hanna remembered talking to Westbury about this place, but she had never dreamed he would be foolish enough to try and find her here. She felt herself reddening even more, and the burn of it annoyed her. But a part of her was pleased he had tried to find her. She thought to ask Frau Schuster to show him in, but she knew the widow would never do that, she was far too respectable. And so Hanna said: "Tell him I'll be right there."

There was a gown hanging on the back of the door, the sort of detail Frau Schuster would always see to, and the sort of clinging silk flimsy that would drive Westbury mad for her. She pulled it over her shoulders and tied it loosely, and then she remembered Sepp, with a double-bladed stab of guilt and regret, and she tied it tighter. The counter was just outside, and she wondered if Westbury would be flirting with the shop girls. It was a stupid risk, him coming here, and she would have to pretend she was angry with him, she knew.

She strode out into the shop, trying hard not to smile, and then suddenly not having to try at all. For there was Kessler.

"Hello Hanna," he said.

For a long drawn out moment, during which Frau Schuster and the shop girls tried to look elsewhere, tried to look busy, Hanna was lost for words.

"What do you want?" she finally said.

"I need to speak to you."

"You might have waited —"

"My time is precious, and I am not in the habit of standing around in dress shops." With that he quickly surveyed the boutique, a look of slight disgust on his face as his gaze passed over the racks of dresses and the sofas, all reflected into an infinity of softness by the many mirrors.

"How did you know to find me here?"

"Your housekeeper said you were shopping and, of course, I see the bills – the larger bills, that is."

"You do?"

"I see a great deal, Hanna." With that he blinked four times in rapid succession, and then turned to Frau Schuster, who must have been looking on through a mirror as she also turned. "Is there somewhere I might talk privately with Frau Plaidt?"

"That will not be necessary," Hanna snapped.

"It would hardly be proper, Herr ...?" Frau Schuster said.

"Kessler." With that he opened his wallet and showed her the light blue SS ID card within, and the widow's face visibly paled.

"There's my office, sir – it's through there."

The office was tiny, a little rat hole to share with a little rat. There was no window and one door, which Kessler closed behind him. As well as the desk with its big ledger and roller card index there was a worktop scattered with rags of material and glistering with loose pins, on which sat a *Haid & Neu* sewing machine. There was also a small chaise longue. Hanna sat on it, instinctively pressing her legs tight together, which did nothing but give him the room to sit by her side. She stared at the wall, which had been pasted with old sewing patterns and sketches of dresses and blouses and skirts. The room smelt of glue.

"I've asked you once already, what do you want?" Hanna said.

"I have some good news for you."

"You have?"

"Westbury Holt is *not* a spy."

The shock of it forced her to turn her head, to face him. His breath smelt bad, but in an unusual way, and she had not noticed it before, perhaps because she did not like to get too close to this one. It was the sort of breath that made the idea of things that caused bad breath, drink and cigarettes, a good idea. It reminded her of hospital.

"Westbury, a spy ... Westbury Holt?"

"*Not* a spy, I said."

"Whoever thought he was, he's a racing driver, and nothing more – nothing at all."

"*We* thought he might be," Kessler said, the emphasis bringing to mind the SS ID he'd shown Frau Schuster two minutes or so ago. "But it seems that what Herr Holt is after is something far baser than industrial secrets. His rather strange behaviour, his secretive ways, it all suddenly made perfect sense. I must admit it was a great disappointment to us, Hanna, a double disappointment, in fact."

"I'm sorry, I don't follow —"

"No, we *follow*," Kessler said, obviously very pleased with his little joke. But the punch line came wrapped in knuckle dusters: "We've followed him almost everywhere, dear Hanna."

"So you know," she said, surprised that what she really felt was relief.

"Yes, we have known for some time."

"Have you told Konrad?"

"I don't want to tell Konrad."

"Why not?"

"I have worked hard to make you the couple that you are, it has been good for my career. It has been good for us all, Hanna."

"But it's a sham."

"Konrad doesn't think so."

"Konrad doesn't know."

"And we can keep it that way. No one needs to know. You just need to stop seeing Holt."

"It's not as easy as that."

"It is."

"I love him." It came out before she had time to stop it, and she felt a stab of instant regret. She had told no one, not even Westbury, but now she had told the last person in the world she would have wanted to know.

"See, you are just a girl. There's no such thing as love. It is merely the sugar to biology's bitter pill."

"Do you say that to your wife?"

"She knows me."

"Does she love you?"

"There is no such thing, as I have said. But if you insist on such schoolgirl nonsense, then do you think Holt loves you?"

"I don't know," she answered, honestly.

"Stay with him and you will lose everything, and do you think he will pick up the pieces?"

"He has money, now."

"But what will *you* have when this one goes the same way as Rosemeyer?"

"Why do you say that?" There was a certainty in the way he had said it, and it chilled her.

"It is inevitable with that type, nothing more. But you must see, there is no future for you with him. You must call it off. I demand it."

"*You* demand it?"

He snorted a little laugh, then patted his hand against his leg, the slap of it loud in the tight little office.

"I knew it would come to this," he said. "Your brother ..."

At the mention of Sepp panic flared within her, and she noticed Kessler's eyelids bat quickly, a sure sign that he knew his poisoned arrow had hit home.

"If you persist with this girlish thing then there could be trouble for him," Kessler continued. "We can make things rather difficult for a young recruit. It is an easy process, rumours cost nothing, and for such powerful fuel their manufacture is easy: maybe the boy's a queer, maybe there's a trace of Jewish blood?" Kessler held out the milk pale palms of his hands, as if weighing the options. "Life could be hell for Sepp, you wouldn't want that now, would you Hanna?"

"We are not as close as you think. Not now." She swallowed hard as she said it, then turned away from him.

"That's not true," Kessler said. "I know people Hanna, I know how they work, and I know how to work them. It's all about switches and levers, and Sepp is your lever."

"You have no right to interfere in my life."

"I have every right. You are a married German woman, not a girl, and with that comes grave responsibility. It's time to tell Holt it's over."

Hanna said nothing and they sat in silence for some long seconds, awkward time measured off by the ring of the shop bell and the sound of typewriters, distantly rattling away in the office upstairs.

"You know, you needn't stray so very far," Kessler finally said, quietly now, the words dry with a sort of croaky excitement. "Konrad's getting old, I understand this, and I also understand the quite natural needs of a young German woman," he added, as his hand slithered through the opening in the silk robe and rested cold against her thigh.

Quite suddenly Hanna could not move. It was as if the very touch of his icy hand had frozen her. He took it for encouragement and he slid his hand up her thigh a little. His eyelids flickered beneath the thick lenses of his glasses, and the tip of his tongue traced the dry edge of his thin upper lip.

The anger came suddenly. The paralysis of fear and disgust burnt away in a jet of flaming temper. She meant to slap him, but she could not control herself and instead she allowed the long nails on her right hand to scram a comb of angry red into his cheek. He let go of her thigh and sprang away from her. He was blinking even faster now, as he rubbed the rake of broken skin on his face. He stood up and bunched his fists, but then shook his head, the blinks slowing a little.

"One day, bitch ... One day."

*

Gracie had told him that many of the waiters in the Adlon also worked for the SD, the Nazi intelligence agency, as a side-line. But West liked the Adlon, and he had always stayed there when he was in Berlin – since the money had started to come in, at least. But he knew those waiters would be on the phone to Prinz Albrecht Strasse as soon as there was anything unusual to report – and it didn't come much more unusual than Westbury Holt in a dinner suit. Then again, from what he could tell, they had lost interest in him. He had not spotted anyone on his tail for a while, though he wouldn't admit this to Gracie, otherwise he'd be back on His Majesty's payroll before he could say 'cloak' or 'dagger'.

"Have you honestly thought this through friend Westbury? You can't just steal another man's wife then throw her away when you get bored of her, you know."

"One can get bored of old chums, too, Gracie old chap, now stop being such a woman and help me with this infernal bow tie would you," West said. Gracie shook his head and smiled. West knew what he was thinking. Westbury Holt, love and marriage, happy ever after, pull the other one and mine's a stiff gin while you're at it. "Damn it!" The bow tie seemed to unravel in West's fingers and Gracie chuckled.

"Here, let's have a look at that," Gracie offered. They were in the marbled lobby of the Adlon and there seemed to be more guests than usual, rushing back and forth, many of them enmeshed in excited conversations. Yes, excitement was in the air. West could feel it too, but for better reasons he'd wager – Hitler had stolen Austria, he would steal Hanna, and who the hell would make much fuss about either crime in the end? She had telephoned him at the hotel earlier – the first time in a while and he had almost begun to worry – and she had said she needed to see him, tonight. It was the chance he had been waiting for. He thought she felt the same way as he did. No, he was sure she did.

"What makes you so confident she will want to leave Konrad, anyway? She has his money, his fame, his friends in high places, his family house in the Rhineland, his apartment in Charlottenburg, his —"

"Oh, I'm sure she will, don't ask me how, it's just something in the way she talked on the phone, a hint I suppose. Besides, since Donington it's all been very different. I was close to asking her last time we — Ouch!" Gracie pinched his neck with the tight collar.

"Hold still would you. There – now don't we look a picture." West glanced in the mirror that lined the lounge, seeing himself framed precisely between a pair of stout square pillars of yellowed marble: no, she couldn't resist this, of that he was quite confident. The dinner suit looked good on him; they always did, although he hated to admit it. "Well," Gracie said, "I suppose she must mean something to you if you're willing to wear that rig, old man."

"Exactly."

"Where are you taking her?"

"The Germania Roof; that should make an impression."

"Have you booked a table?"

"Not yet."

"You know, you'll be lucky to find a table tonight old chap. It's always sardines in there, and Germany's having a grand old party tonight, celebrating the Anschluss, and laughing at our feckless politicians."

"Gracie please, no politics, I'm in a good mood. Besides, I have this." West reached into the inside pocket of his dinner jacket and pulled out the little diamond-studded brooch, letting the small jewels twinkle in the lamplight. Gracie just shook his head a little. "Brauchitsch's loaned it to me" West went on. "He owes me a favour, you see, and he's in some sort of dining society, says if you flash this at the maître d' you're guaranteed a table at the Roof, some sort of arrangement they have. Like being a member, I suppose."

"You know, you are storing up a great deal of trouble, friend Westbury," Gracie said.

"As long as it helps gets me a table tonight, I can deal with the trouble later."

*

"Off somewhere nice, Frau Plaidt?"

"Just for a walk, Inge," Hanna said, as she placed her hat so that the diagonal of the brim shaded her right eye, and then downed the remains of her martini. Konrad's maid, Hanna had never felt that she was *their* maid, tried to smile, but it was more of a sneer. It suited her.

"If Herr von Plaidt calls, what should I say?"

"Say I have gone for a walk. Why should you say anything else?" Hanna said, that second martini sharpening the edge of her voice, while also fortifying her for what was to come. She walked out of the apartment, down the stairs and past the concierge, who greeted her formally, then out on to Bayernallee. She knew that West waited down the street, on the corner with Länderallee. The clean and bright spring sunshine was softening now, what clouds there were shot through with the pink of the dipping sun, so that they almost looked like visual echoes of the cherry blossoms that lined the street. A lace curtain twitched in one of the upmarket apartment blocks, but Hanna ignored it. Either way this was the last time they would have to go through this nonsense, she thought to herself, but found little comfort in that. A sudden image of her brother flared within, as clear as if he had stepped out on to the pavement in front of her. Of course, Sepp could never know what she was doing right now, he was many miles away. Yet somehow she felt as if he was looking on, as if he was the spying face behind the curtain, watching her walk up to the waiting Horch.

"Hello Westbury."

"My, don't you look a picture," he said, jumping out of the driver's side of his Horch and rushing around to open the passenger door for her.

"I thought we could go out in town?" he said as he started the car.

"I'm not sure," Hanna said, suddenly aware that something was different – they never went anywhere where they might be recognised. "Let's go to the Tiergarten, there is something I need to discuss with you."

She was surprised to see he had dressed up. He looked smart, magnificent even, and as he drove in that decisive, confident way of his – dodging between the other cars on the Kaiserdamm as if he was in a race – Hanna felt as if she wanted it to go on forever, and she found that she had to fix the increasingly blurring image of Sepp into her inner vision.

He drove into the Tiergarten and they passed the place where the workers who were moving the Victory Column to its new home had downed tools for the day. West parked up and they took a narrow path into the heart of the park. The rhododendron bushes were beginning to bloom, and the birds sang of new life, and she could not refuse his arm when he offered it. They walked along a soft, peaty path, every step cushioned, not a word spoken, hardly a soul seen, until they reached a leafy glade where the early evening sun seeped syrup-soft between the hard shadows of the trees.

"You said you wanted to talk to me," he said.

"Yes, but let's sit for a moment."

She sat on a bench, West beside her. He started whistling, she could not place the tune at first. He seemed restless, tapping out the beat on his leg. Then she had it, the *Hitler Youth Song*.

"You know what that is, the tune you're whistling?"

"No, just something I picked up; catchy," he said, looking at his watch. "Look, let's go somewhere else, I need a drink."

"You seem nervous?"

"Do I? It's just that I wanted to get a table at the Germania Roof."

"You haven't reserved?" He shook his head. "Well, then there's no chance now, besides, do you think I'd be seen there with you?"

"I'd hoped ..." he started to say something, then seemed to think better of it, before adding: "von Brauchitsch loaned me this. He said I should wear it and the maître d' would be sure to find a vacant table. Something to do with some dining club he's in, apparently." He grinned as he pinned the diamond-studded brooch to the lapel of his dinner jacket. It sparkled in the tree-filtered sunlight. In the space of seconds Hanna had turned through the whole gamut of emotions. First, a selfish pleasure that she thought he had bought her something; second, relief that the stupid, blind fool had given her a way out; third anger, because he couldn't see what he had done – that he had done it.

"What's wrong?" he said, looking as worried as she had ever seen him look. His coat flaps were open and the swastika, studded with five tiny diamonds, shone like a malignant constellation against the night-black of his silk lapel.

"You really can't see can you, Westbury?" She had raised her voice.

"See what? Please Hanna, don't tease me, not tonight."

"That." She pointed at the diamond-studded swastika. "You don't see what *that* means, what it is doing to people, what it has done to my brother."

"Sepp? But he's all right, isn't he?"

She shook her head. "He'll be fine, now ..." she hesitated, there was real panic in his eyes, a child with his sandcastle crumbling in the surf, looking for a way to push back the tide.

"Please Hanna, it's nothing – I'm no Nazi, you know that, I can't abide them," he said plaintively.

"No, but you like this," pointing to the diamond-studded swastika, "just so long as it gets you into nightclubs and racing cars, isn't that so, Westbury?"

"Come on Hanna, you know it's not like that, I've no time for politics."

"You close your eyes, your ears, and your mouth. Westbury, you are all those monkeys in one, when it suits you. Do you know that? And as you drive your silver racing car, with its swastika painted on the side, everyone else may say – in Paris, in London – surely it can't be so bad over there. It's normal – *chaps* like Westbury are racing there after all ..." She felt the anger alive within her. "Well, you have to know Westbury that nothing is so normal here anymore and ..." She started crying. It came from beyond the words, and she knew it was a purer honesty. And it came suddenly, tears springing from her face, sobs wracking her shoulders. West pulled his handkerchief from his top pocket and dabbed at the tears on her cheek, but she pushed him away.

"I'm sorry, I didn't —"

"Think?" she sobbed. "You are a fool Westbury, a blind fool, and I want to go home." She turned away from him, fixing the picture of him that she would mount in her memory at that very moment: the dropped jaw, the panic, eyes without their laughter. She walked away, twigs crackling beneath her feet, birdsong mocking the moment, a little boy's laugh, far away. West ran up behind her, grabbing her roughly by the shoulder. She spun to face him.

"But you can't go!"

"I have to."

"I love you, Hanna."

She looked him in the eyes and a part of her ached to believe. She stared into those eyes for long seconds, and then she said: "I came here today to ask something of you Westbury. It was a test, to see if it was me you wanted, you loved – because I know how much one is willing to give up for love, and what one will do for love, you see." She looked down at the floor, and took a deep breath, sniffing back a sob, and then added: "I will still ask it of you, but perhaps it's now only because I know you will not do it."

"What is it Hanna, please tell me, I will do any'—"

"Give up driving the Nazi cars," she said, before turning away from him and walking briskly away. He followed her to the road, where she hailed a cab, West always talking, promising, but she had said her piece, and she did not even say goodbye when she climbed into the taxi.

*

"I say friend Westbury, you look like you've seen a ghost."

"Quite."

Gracie was standing at the hotel bar, slowly sinking whiskies, getting drunk in that quiet way of his, a notebook at one elbow, a cluster of empty tumblers at the other. The bar was like the rest of the Adlon, yellowed, rectangular smoky-marble pillars and tasteful enough pieces of art. It smelt strongly of cigars. The only free place at the bar was alongside Gracie and

West took it. The bright light reflected harshly off the ivory-hued marble top. West's bow tie dangled untied across the top of his shirt, his top button was undone, and he felt as if some part of him, some kernel within he had never suspected existed before, had been crushed to a nothing; leaving a cold emptiness so tangible that, paradoxically, it filled every corner of his being. So this was rejection. It felt like losing, maybe worse …

"What's wrong," Gracie said. "Mrs Plaidt not so keen, or did Konrad burst in on you with a squad of stormtroopers?"

"I'll have one of those – make it a double … Treble," West snapped. The barman nodded. He could feel Gracie's eyes on him, studying him in that detached way of his, waiting for him to talk. Beside them a heavy, balding German, part of a large group of businessmen who had been attending a function in the hotel, was making himself wide, spreading his elbows to force more space by the bar. The barman placed the whisky in front of West and he drained it in a couple of deep gulps. The German dug his elbow in once more and suddenly something West had once heard Kessler say sprang to mind. Something about lebensraum, living space … West made a sharp angle with his elbow and drove it into the German, turning to face him as he did so. Just an old man, smelling of strong pickles and the beer, foam flecks adding to the grey of his moustache, I don't want to fight you in his eyes … But I will, if I have to. Gracie grabbed West by the shoulders and pulled him round gently.

"Steady on there, friend Westbury, what's got into you?"

"Scotch – want another?" Gracie nodded and they drank together for half an hour with hardly a word passing between them. The German plucked up enough courage to try to dig his elbows into West again, but then his friends dragged him away. By that time the crowd by the bar was thinning and the barman's glances at his watch grew more frequent. West waited until he could feel the whisky softening the inside of his head, then he spoke. "Gracie, I want to ask you something," West said, recognising the slur in his voice as the words seemed to catch on his tongue.

"Fire away."

"She thinks it's wrong that I drive for a German team, what with the politics and all that nonsense … I suppose you agree?"

"Hanna thinks that? Good, when there's at least one there's still hope. What about Konrad? Does she think the same of him?"

"I never asked."

"Well, he's here anyway, he has to live with it. You don't. And that's my answer, too – but you know that West. I think that what you do is give them tacit approval at best, and your being here is a distraction from what's really happening in Germany at worst."

"But you were happy enough I was driving for them when it suited you," West said, just a little sulkily.

Gracie suddenly snorted a little laugh: "Do you actually have a clue as to what they *are* doing here?"

West just shook his head slowly.

"I heard a German joke earlier today," Gracie said. "You know why people here greet each other by saying *heil*?"

West shrugged.

"Because no one can remember what it is to have a *good day*."

"Funny."

"You sure? Well, as I said, it's a German joke. But come on West, you're not blind, you must know what's been happening here."

"All I know is that if I am to be with her there is something I need to do."

"Which is?" West let Gracie's question hang in the air for a little while as the barman plucked the empty whisky glasses from in front of them, telling them the bar was closing soon.

"She wants me to give up the drive ... Maybe it's the only way she will believe that I love her."

"Love her!" Gracie made an expression of pantomime shock. "Are you sure you're quite all right, old man?"

"Quite all right. And I'm going to do it."

"*Mmmm*, we'll see."

"Why not? Now Rosemeyer's gone there's no one left worth beating ... I *will* do it."

"Of course you will friend Westbury. But let's see what you think in the morning shall we. Now where can we get another drink?"

*

It had been a blessed relief to peel off the penguin suit, sit in a bath with his pipe clenched between his teeth and then dress in the familiar: creased beige flannels, an old shirt without its collar and the good old cricket jumper. There had been no sleep, but he didn't feel at all bad as he drove through Berlin to the autobahn. In the cold, clear dawn there was a chivalry to what he was doing, he suspected, and it was best to leave it at that rather than think on it too much. Save the sombre thoughts for when you're sitting tall in some ancient Alfa or Delahaye, watching the silver cars disappear into the distance, old chap ...

... While Hanna waits for you.

As he left the city he *saw* things he'd merely looked at before. The propaganda posters with their hideous cartoon Jews; the closed down synagogues, the shuttered up shops, the explicit hate, the early morning paint-out squads obliterating the fresh communist slogans. He'd never taken any of it seriously, hot air from silly men in silly trousers, but now he realised all that silliness had seemed to have had some serious consequences. *Politics. To bloody hell with it.* He paid his mark and took the AVUS autobahn out of the city before heading south-west towards Zwickau, the Horch stuttering on the pissy brew of BV Aral – it had the octane of an orange juice but it was the only pump fuel to be had in this wondrous Reich. It made him realise how important the fuel developed for the racing cars might be, one day. So Gracie had been right about that, too. He wondered if he would ever race on the AVUS again, but he knew if he did it would not be in a streamliner.

A letter would have done it, even a phone call. But somehow he felt that this way was better, part of him hoping that she would get to hear of his gallant early morning drive. He laughed out loud at the thought. But soon the whisky wore off and he stopped for a truly awful coffee and something described as sausage but tasting of sawdust somewhere near Dessau. By then the sun was climbing in the sky and it was turning out to be a bright, windless day.

Once at the Horch works in Zwickau he parked the car in the very same spot he had parked his Lagonda on that rainy day in November a year and a half ago. The same day he had first saw her, and also the day he had almost knocked her off her bicycle, he remembered with a smile. People here knew him well now, he was popular with the secretaries and they all smiled widely to see him as he passed through the offices, some of them would be sorry to see him go, he thought. He climbed the stairs to Feuereissen's office, where he was greeted by the same secretary who had given him a cold welcome all those long months ago, her starched face now cracking into a surprising, and surprised, smile.

"Oh, Herr Holt – he will be pleased to see you!"

"I wouldn't be so sure of that Frau Schmidt …" But she was up and through the door between the anteroom and the office with a speed and style he would have thought impossible from that creaky old body, hardly bothering to pause to tap at the door. He took in the old wood panelling of the anteroom for the last time, how often had he stood here and waited, just for the chance to badger for some extra testing, that extra bit of practice to take him closer to Rosemeyer.

"Westbury, it's so good to see you!" Feuereissen blurted as he came through the doorway.

"Well, wait, I —"

"We've been trying to reach you at the Adlon, we were told you were there?"

"I was, but I checked out first thing. Look, I need to talk to you."

"Right, right, but we have little time. I'll talk as we walk." With that he disappeared back into the office and came back with his hat and loden coat, stuffing the soft hat on his head as he trotted out of the door, Westbury at his heels looking for a chance to get a word in edgeways.

"You see," the team manager said breathlessly, "Konrad is unavailable, his wife says he's ill – has a hangover after celebrating the Anschluss with his Nazi friends no doubt – and we need someone to test something. It's nothing special, we have been planning a small streamlined version of the Type D, but the only driver who had any experience of streamliners was Bernd. We have some new ideas, and we need to test them —"

"But I —"

"I know, I'm sorry, I would have asked you first; but you know how it is, Kessler after every angle, asked me to give Konrad first shot at anything, even though you are the senior driver, but it's getting harder and harder to refuse him, I'm afraid," he pulled his coat over his shoulders as he spoke and skipped down the stairs.

"But you don't —"

"This is not a fast run, we just need to get close to race speeds, not record speeds. We need someone to tell us what happens, now we have lost Bernd there is no one who even knows how these cars are supposed to feel. We just need to test the older body, and then make a few runs with a modified body to see which is best before we commit to the concept for the Type D streamliner. We have obtained permission to close off a section of the Halle-Leipzig autobahn for two hours one afternoon this week and it would be a shame to waste such a good day for it – the weather's perfect." He had opened the door at the bottom of the stairs and the large Büssing NAG lorry with the interlocking rings of Auto Union on its flank stood before them in the yard.

"You have your goggles and helmet, your overalls?"

"I —"

"Not to worry, I'm sure there are spares —"

"But you don't —"

"Oh, forgive me, I've hardly given you time to breathe ... You will do it, of course?"

West tried to choose his words carefully. He didn't like to let the old chap down. Feuereissen waited expectantly, glancing at his watch and looking at the sky once more. "We will be using one of Rosemeyer's old record cars - but at a fraction of his speed, of course," he added.

"Then I'll do it," West heard himself say.

*

West travelled the length of the course in his Horch first, and then drove back to the start line. The near ten-mile stretch of autobahn looked simple enough, except for a long curve, some bridges, and one stretch near a village called Dölbau where there was a turn off and a bridge, with great grass embankments built up to support the concrete structure hemming the road in, so that it almost seemed to be like a drained canal. The surrounding countryside was flat and featureless farmland, a sea of green and brown with lonely villages and sprawling woods off in the distance like far away islands.

By the time he had parked the Horch the mechanics had unloaded the streamliner. It was the old style car, beautiful in its flowing bodywork. The only thing that spoilt its pure lines was the ugly blemish of the swastika behind the cockpit. He tore his eyes from it and looked for Sepp, the youngster saw him but turned away quickly, busying himself with something in the back of the truck. Lick, who was wearing a ridiculous striped cap he'd swiped in a bar brawl with an engine driver the night before – West had heard the tale from one of the other mechanics – handed West some goggles and a white wind helmet, and he wondered where they had come from.

"They're Sepps," Lick said, seeming to read his mind. "He had hoped to be a driver, you know."

"I know. Is he all right, he seems a little distant today?"

"He's to be married," Lick laughed, "and you can bet your last pfennig that that Trudi of his will be wanting a rabbit medal to pin to her tits – it's a big responsibility for a lad."

"Rabbit medal?"

"The Mothers' Cross. It's for best of breeders, pop out a sizeable litter and you get a gong from the Führer."

"I should congratulate him," West said. Sepp emerged from the rear of the truck rolling a spare wheel before him. "Sepp!" West shouted. Sepp carefully let the wheel drop to the floor then disappeared back inside the truck, seeming to ignore the call. West let it go; the lad was obviously in a bad mood. His congratulations could wait, as could that other thing he felt he needed to talk to Sepp about – that other thing he needed to put right. He turned the goggles over as he studied them for any signs of cracks.

"Tell me Lick," West said, "were you here when Rosemeyer tried this thing out, back last year wasn't it?"

"Yes, I was."

"How fast did he go? Do you know?" He tried to load it with as little interest as he could.

"Fast? What does it matter?"

"How fast?"

"Like his arse was on fire as always, he hit 400 for sure."

"400km/h, about 250mph ..." West whispered to himself.

"Why do you ask?" Lick said, a hint of suspicion creeping into his voice.

"Oh, no reason."

"You know this is just a test run?" Lick looked him straight in the eyes and there was a seriousness there that West had seldom seen. "We just need to know how it is at race speeds, about 150mph ... And we do not want to have to scrape you off the autobahn like so much trodden-in shit off a carpet."

"Eloquently put Lick, the image will live with me on the run, you can be sure of that. Now help me into this bloody coffin, there's a good chap."

Lick laughed out loud. Then set to lifting the middle section of the car so that West could squeeze himself in. He tried not to think about the confined space of the cockpit as he lifted his leg over the side of the car and slid between the underside of the hatch and the bodywork. But his heart started to feel like it was pounding at the bars of his ribcage and he had to make a conscious effort to keep moving, gripping at the triangular funnel of the petrol tank just behind the seat to help pull himself through the gap.

"You're not still wearing that old rag are you?" Lick said with undisguised disgust, grabbing a fist of the grubby old wool of West's cricket jumper as he slipped into the seat. "It's never brought you any luck."

"Nor harm, Lick," West said, as another mechanic passed him his steering wheel, which he fitted over the spline of the steering column and gripped tightly to make sure it was securely in place. They lowered the hatch over his shoulders and fixed it shut and the sounds of the aluminium panel sliding into place made his mouth go dry. He felt completely trapped, pinned into the car ... But this was his last chance to beat the man – to beat the *ghost* of Rosemeyer. West took a deep breath and made an effort to relax his grip on the wheel. Feuereissen gave him the thumbs up and he nodded eagerly – *let's get this done then ...*

Other than the all-enclosing bodywork West saw there was little in the streamliner to differentiate it from one of the regular racers, except for the large speedometer that supplemented the rev counter. He looked at one number: 400. 400km/h. "250mph," he whispered to himself. West selected first and pressed in the clutch. He felt the car move beneath him, hearing the hum of the rubber and the slap of the pushing mechanics' shoes on the concrete paving. He gave them time to work up to a trot and then let out the clutch. A lurch, an explosion behind his ears, and then he picked it up on the throttle, kicking in the clutch and revving the engine as the car coasted on. The fuel smells swept over him and the rough breath of the engine reverberated through the body of the car and the sole of his right foot. When he was sure the engine had well and truly caught he gave it some more revs, let out the clutch, and felt the car slither beneath him as it shot off down the road, rear tyres slipping.

He worked it carefully up through the gears, timing his shifts to perfection. The joins in the concrete road surface thumping out a faster beat as the car gathered speed, the bubble windscreen that wrapped round and sloped down either side of his head robbing him of the familiar caress of air resistance, the needle swinging through the face of the clock. Halfway through the run he reached 150mph, there were the expected vibrations, but the car felt good, while the few road cars using the opposite carriageway seemed to be parked, such was the difference in speed – this other traffic used the parallel lane as a regular two-way road. There was a long sweeping right bend, hardly noticeable in the Horch earlier and easy enough now, but on the return run he knew it would be at the point where he should be close to 250. As he passed through it he stole a mark – a lonely tree – some way past the exit, knowing that he would need to turn in very early indeed for this one. He took it over 190. The car felt stable at this speed though the pounding it took from the joints in the road was a worry and his vision was beginning to blur, so much so that it was a conscious effort to keep the car straight – especially under the overpasses. But soon the outward run was over and long before the barrier he let the car slow, not daring to touch the brakes above 160, for he knew that to do so would cause the wheels to lock and the specially made high-speed tyres with their thin, smooth tread, to rip like paper.

Soon enough he had bled off the speed and he brought the streamliner to a halt using the gearbox and gentle braking. He gave the Auto Union men at the barrier his thumbs up and one of them phoned through to the start line. A trolley was placed beneath the car so it could be turned, the long streamliner filling half the road width and more, and West readied himself for the home run, which would be along the same carriageway.

"One last chance Hanna," he whispers to himself. "Just this one last chance to beat him."

He's up to speed. Real speed. Aeroplane speed. By the time the needle nudged 240 he's in a different world, a world in which his senses struggle to get to grip with the new reality. A world in which all that is happening has already happened. A world that rattles his skull to the point that the road in front seems to fork in two ... The steering wheel is eggshell, he shivers it through the palms of his hands in millimetre increments. He tries to aim the car, but the target seems to be on him before he has a chance to line it up; aiming the nose of the streamliner along the thread of road, aiming at the black pinpricks of the bridges. These are the worst, these tiny dark mouths that seem to suck him in, swallow him, and spit him out the other side before he has the time to even register them, the shock wave building up before the car is forced through the gap ahead of him, concrete buttresses within a foot of the roadside. Then – *ka-boom!* Every time he passes beneath the overpasses, the air pressure hitting him like a kick in the chest, driving the breath from his lungs.

He reaches the long curve in the road. The lonely tree's gone almost before he has the time to react to it, a flash on his retina, and then he's out of the curve virtually as soon as he steers into it; a tiny tweak of the wheel that's more instinct than judgement. The engine noise trails far behind him, the *ka-thump-a-thump* of the joints in the road surface now a harsh vibration that threatens to rattle his teeth from his gums. His hands ache from the effort of keeping them relaxed on the wheel, his foot from the effort of jamming it against the accelerator ... Is he driving this thing, is it driving him? He feels he is being flushed through a green funnel of speed – *ka-boom!* – another bridge, another kick in the bloody chest from the displaced air. Bugger it! The wheel shivers in his hand and he thinks he's hit the grass for an instant, but he can't be sure. The fumes are building up in the car, but he can barely risk a breath anyway. It all takes a minute, but lasts a lifetime. Westbury Holt allows himself one glance at the clock. One glance, with one eye – at the clock.

405km/h.

There was no room in his head for the conversion, but he knew it was enough. He oh-so-very-gently eased his foot off the accelerator ... 250, 240, 230, 220, 200mph ... slower, slower, slower ... 180 now, and it felt so slow, as if he could get out and walk. He took a deep breath as the grass-covered banking that led up to the overpass at Dölbau began to fill his peripheral vision. The air was heavy and poisonous through fumes trapped in the cockpit. Sweat was running down his face. Sepp's goggles were not an airtight fit and they had shaken loose during the buffeting of the ride, sliding slightly down West's nose, distracting him. He lifted his hand from the wheel to adjust the goggles.

That next second was somehow split in time and space and stuffed to bursting point. First, his cricket jumper sleeve caught against something. Second, his eyes wandered off the road to see what the problem was. Third, he realised that a hole in the elbow of his jumper had snagged a bracket that held the gear selector rod ... Before he knew it the car was on the central reservation. He gripped the wheel and hauled it over to the right, then, instinctively, he touched the brakes – to a rifle volley of bursting tyres. The nose of the car slewed right and hit the bank and churned up a great wave of dirt as it ploughed to the crest. Then stillness. The streamliner launched itself like an aircraft and all that West could see was the bright blue sky.

Blue turned brown then blue again. Then, after long suspended moments, the nose hit the earth and buried itself into the soft dirt of a ploughed field to a shriek of tearing aluminium. The jolt of the crash travelled the length of West's legs and spine and exploded in his head in all the colours of the butcher's shop. The steering wheel spun through 180-

degrees as the now spat-free front wheels turned in the earth and before he had time to realise it his right arm caught in the spokes. He heard his wrist snap, the sound exactly like that of a dry twig, and at the very same time his head cracked against the steel lip of the cockpit surround.

The car was still now, creaking and ticking loudly. Pain was sending signals from every outpost of his body and he checked them off as they came, trying to find some relief in the all too obvious fact that he was still alive. He felt the bile rise to his throat, and then he was sick. But even over the smell of the vomit, all that good whisky from last night and the bad sausage from this morning, he could still also smell the tell-tale tang of the fuel. He could also hear its drip against hot aluminium, somewhere behind him, but very close. He reached for the dash and switched off the ignition.

Pain or not West knew he had to get out of this coffin. He took a deep breath and grabbed with his good hand on the narrow cockpit surround, greasy with his own blood. Through gritted teeth he heaved ... But the pain was too much. Most of it seemed to come from somewhere in his lower right leg, great burning arrows of it piercing his being, but there was pain from his head, too, and he suddenly felt faint. His last thought was that he was trapped. That he was dead. Then the oil of unconsciousness started to seep within him, and Westbury Holt thanked God for it ... For it, rather than fire.

*

"He just wanted to congratulate you Sepp," Lick said.

"Did he?" What did marriage mean to Westbury Holt anyway? Sepp thought.

"It looked like you were avoiding him."

"He's a fool," Sepp said.

"Arse of Christ Sepp – what's got into you?"

The field telephone rang and all the little conversations around the start line ceased instantly, not one of them could hear its ring now without thinking of Rosemeyer's crash. "All fine," someone shouted, "he's making his way back." Sepp thought there seemed to be a collective sigh of relief, no one was keen on this now, even at low speeds, because it reminded them all of what they had lost. Sepp and Lick stood alongside West's Horch. Sepp had a pair of binoculars slung around his neck so he could study the car as it slowed – it was the sort of thing the team manager trusted him with, and it was one of the reasons they would miss him when he went into the Fallschirmjäger; so soon now. Lick started to tease him about married life again so he pressed the glasses to his eyes and fiddled with the focus wheel until Lick gave up and shut up. The binoculars were Zeiss, good quality, German. He played with them for a while, closing one eye and focusing, then the other, and finding they were both the same. He took this as a good sign, his eyesight was balanced, but such things had ceased to surprise him – now he knew who he was. Perfection was his gift. Perfection was his destiny.

It was because he had the glasses trained on the exact spot that he saw it. Through the filter of lens and distance he could think it nothing more than beautiful at first – just like a flying fish leaping from the ocean. But then he recognised it and the breath froze in his throat. Right then the underside of the car showed up black and ugly as it twisted in its flight, turning again to silver as it dropped out of sight. A split second later there was a great plume of brown dust marking the spot where the streamliner fell to earth.

"He's crashed!" Sepp shouted. He tore at the driver's side door of West's Horch and tossed the binoculars onto the parcel shelf. Lick was with him, snatching at a roll of tools and piling into the passenger seat. The Horch was fast, but it seemed to take an age to reach the scene of the crash. They had a head start on the others and Sepp caught a glimpse in the mirror of a straggling convoy of cars some way behind. The scene of the accident was well marked, thick and sooty skid marks and a great chocolate coloured gash in the embankment pointing the way. Sepp aimed the long nose of the car at the banking, then braked hard, down changed, and then accelerated.

"You're not … Shit!" Lick shouted the last word as the Horch took the embankment at an angle, the rear wheels scrabbling against the grass, the weight of the car threatening to pull it back to the roadside, or flip it onto its roof. But Sepp had judged it well, and he flicked the car down to second for a final burst over the lip of the embankment.

The crash site was within fifty metres and it looked like the streamliner was half buried in the soft dirt. But once on to the ploughed field the Horch sank to its axles and Sepp and Lick were forced to abandon it and run across the furrows. It was only when they reached the car that they saw that West was still inside, his head rag doll tilted to one side, the white wind helmet half scarlet with blood.

"Is he dead?" Lick asked between panting breaths.

"I'm not sure."

"Christ, Sepp, smell that!" He had smelt the fuel already, chosen to ignore it.

"We're in the country Lick, there are always strange smells."

"Fine fucking time to find a sense of humour you have, this thing's going flambé any second!"

Lick stumbled backwards away from the wreck. But Sepp could see the situation: the fuel tank had ruptured and a small pool of fuel was forming in one of the plough furrows, filling it quickly. He knew the car had been fuelled for at least one more run, so there was plenty more in the tank. Once it overflowed there was nothing to stop it running on to the hot exhausts, for the force of the crash had burrowed the car low in the soft earth. The panic was doing strange things to Lick's face, he still stumbled backwards but it was obvious he did not want to leave his friend. At least he had had the presence of mind to bring the roll of tools from the car.

"Throw me the tools." Sepp caught them. "Now stand back, there's no use both of us …" He left the sentence unfinished and hurled himself at the crumpled streamliner. The hatch lifted easily enough, and he could now see that there was also fuel pouring into the cockpit from a rent in the tank behind the seat. He ignored it, concentrating on West. There was a gash in his head, and through the lenses of the goggles he could see his eyes. The only sign of life was nothing, yet something – the sparkle of a fool's gaze. Holt was alive, of that he was sure.

Sepp took the steering wheel off its spline and threw it aside. Then he unbolted and tilted the hatch away and climbed into the cockpit, legs either side of West. He grabbed him under the armpits and heaved for all his worth. But Holt did not move a millimetre, he was stuck fast. Sepp checked the level of the fuel filling the rut, it had risen. Minutes, he estimated, minutes. There was no time for hesitation, he had to get to the root of the problem, he had to free West's legs. He climbed out of the cockpit, then back in head first, crawling under the dash, arching his back as he went, squeezing tight to get past West's legs until he could see his feet, Sepp's own feet poking out of the top of the car behind him. His heart sank at the sight that met him.

The force of the crash had badly distorted the bulkhead, and snapped the brake pedal in two. It was the sharp perforated steel shaft that remained that was pinning West into the car. It had speared through his right foot at an angle – he had obviously been braking hard when the car hit, instinctive for a driver – and it had then gone on right through his ankle after that, before bending back on itself as the pedal rail twisted out of shape. Now it pinned West's mangled foot against the floor-pan. For a moment Sepp fought the urge to throw up, as he grimly studied the problem, realising that there was no way the foot would slide clear. Then he remembered the tool roll. He clambered back out and found the tools.

"How is it?" Lick shouted. Sepp just nodded, there was still no sign of the others and he guessed they would be having difficulty getting up the embankment. The level of the fuel in the rut had risen to within a couple of centimetres of the lip.

"Get out of there Sepp!"

Sepp grabbed the oily tool wrap. He knew the spanners would be no good, the pedal rail was too badly damaged, but there was a chance with the hacksaw at least. He dived back into the cockpit and wriggled his way back down to the pedals. He quickly decided where to cut the metal and placed the blade on that part of the pedal shaft. Just then a further pool of fuel seeped into his line of vision.

"Damn it – a spark will set the whole thing off!"

For the briefest of moments he thought he would have to leave him, but then he knew what had to be done. The only thing he could do …

He placed the blade across West's ankle, quite high up so that he had room to use the tool. He took a deep breath and moved the saw. The cotton split, and then so did skin and flesh. Then Sepp could feel the blade slide against the shin bone. He pressed harder, moved the blade faster, and the tiny teeth of the saw suddenly shrilled, then grated against the bone. Sepp gave it everything, he heard a scream, realised it was West, conscious again, but still he did not let up with his sawing, through tendons then the ankle bone, blood now lubricating his blade, pooling on the floor to mix with the fuel. West punched ineffectively at his sides but Sepp ignored it. When the resistance stopped he guessed that he had passed out again. A few more strokes of the rough blade later and the foot sagged clear of the ankle. One more cut and it slid from the looped shaft of steel and dropped with a meaty thud against the floor-pan of the streamliner.

"Christ Sepp, you have to get out of there!" Lick had ventured close to the car and was pulling at Sepp's ankles.

"I have him clear Lick, help me out!" Lick pulled him out and Sepp dropped to the earth, the bloody saw still in his hands. A finger of fuel burst over the lip of the furrow and spread towards the red-hot exhausts.

"Come on Lick!"

They each heaved at West's underarms and Sepp was relieved when he slid free of the cockpit. They put him between them, arms over their shoulders, and dragged him away from the wreck of the streamliner, his one remaining foot bouncing over the ruts as they went.

The car exploded with a mighty *whumpp*, and the shock wave from the blast broke over them, throwing them face first into the soft dirt, bits of metal whistling past their ears like shrapnel.

Sepp gave himself some seconds to regain his breath as a group of people came over the crest of the embankment.

"My sainted arse Sepp," Lick said breathlessly, "that was the bravest thing I ever saw."

"No Lick. It was simply the right thing to do."

***

195

When I found the streamliner I was a different man. You see, history can change us all. Back then I dealt in futures, but now I deal in the past. History changed me, history took me. But it was Gramps who put me on the trail of the silver ...

Gramps? Father's side. So, a Grace, like me, but he would not have approved of the half-joking sign I then had on my desk in the City: 'Grace – no favours'. He'd grown distant anyway, through three divorces on Pop's part – just another bit of the flotsam and jetsam of wrecked marriages; any love or respect diluted in a vast sea of other people: step-mothers and - fathers, step-brothers, step-sisters; vague relations with little hold on someone as busy as I was back then. Until the old ones come to die, that is, and there's the chance of a step up in the fiscals, some property maybe or – if you like – family silver.

Prostate cancer. I sat with him for an hour, the first time I'd seen him in years. He told me stories: of the war, of before the war. He told me of the things he had seen, of the people he had known, and I nodded and smiled – enough, I thought, to get me into his good books, and on to his will. He'd had a boring war as far as I could see, and I felt my eyelids gaining weight as I was fed with more and more sugar coated memories. Then, quite suddenly, his tone changed, and I felt he was about to say something important, to give me something, even ... Turns out I was right about that. But right then it was just another story.

It was a year after the war had ended. Gramps had been involved in interrogating prisoners of war, to see if they were still Nazi – still *black* was the terminology they used back then. He hinted that there was more to it than that, and part of his job was to talk to those from the east of Germany, find some warm friend for the cold war that was then blowing in. He did a lot of hinting when it came to that secret-squirrel shit, but I never had Gramps down as the James Bond type, so assumed that was a little garnish for posterity, something for me to whisper at the wake.

He was sent to a camp up near Newcastle, where amongst the many he interrogated was a German officer who recognised Gramps from before the war, when he had spent time in Germany. Gramps gave him Woodbines, and the soldier gave Gramps a story in return. It was not the story he really wanted, for he had hoped this soldier might know of the fate of another man, but it was a story that, many years later, would transform the life of a greedy grandson.

The man told Gramps that the Auto Unions had been taken to Russia, a detachment of Red Army troops had found them and they had become spoils of war, he had said, adding that he'd heard that the son of Stalin himself had been their commander – that alone had been worth another Woodbine. All but one car had gone, the man had said, a very special car – a streamliner. This had been saved. Gramps was even given the name of the man who had saved it. The soldier was given a pack of the cigarettes, and his file was stamped with *white*.

It all meant little to Gramps back then, he told me, he'd never been that interested in the racing, and yet he said he had often thought about that car in the years that followed. Right then it had meant even less to me. I often wonder why Gramps even told me. Sometimes I like to believe he knew me for what I was, but perhaps also for what I might become, but that did not cross my mind then, of course. So I made my excuses and promised to visit again. I never did.

I happened to lunch with a colleague a month or so later. He was wealthy enough to race an old Lotus 23 in historic events, and was still risking all on the markets so that one day it might be a Maserati 250F. For something to say I mentioned that my grandfather had seen the German cars race in the 1930s. He knew about the Silver Arrows, and I couldn't stop him talking about them for an hour or so. When I managed to get a word in I asked him how much one might be worth, the question I would ask about everything in those days. He told me of the Ferrari GTO that had just been sold for close to two million dollars; and that prices for such things were escalating fast: a car with history found in a barn was like a Van Gogh found in the attic. An Auto Union, he said, would be worth millions. A streamliner? "Just add noughts," he told me. I never did tell him why I was interested.

Gramps had gone before I could talk to him again. There was nothing for me, except a case of well-thumbed philosophy books that found a good home in a second hand shop … And the secret silver.

I will not bore you with the difficulties of getting into East Germany in the '80s, but suffice to say that a man will fill out his own height in forms when there's silver at stake. And so, in the winter of 1987, when I eventually found the old man in Zwickau, I told him who I was and what I was looking for. I even showed him a photograph of Gramps as he had been in the 1930s. Of course, I didn't tell him I wanted anything other than to see the car – and he understood more than most why someone would merely wish to look at it. So, in the end it didn't take so very much to get him to lead me to it. Not much at all. But then, how was an old man in East Germany to know the worth of these things then, of the madness of western speculation?

Anyway, I have told you of the old man's reaction on seeing it again. I didn't understand that, I will admit, because then I knew little of this story. Besides, I had just stumbled upon a multimillion dollar motor car. So I ignored the tears as his eyes were fixed on the swastika flag behind the cockpit of the streamliner. Stupidly, I had not been carrying a camera when I met the man, but I've always been handy enough with a pencil, so I put my little Maglite between my teeth and flicked its narrow beam of light along that beautiful silver body, sketching in a tiny notebook as I did so. I still have those sketches, with each little bullet-hole marked precisely. But I had hardly finished with my scribbling when, without a word, the old man started to nail the planks back in place. Right then I figured he was regretting that he had ever shown me the car. But I knew there was no arguing with him, so I helped him as best I could, already my mind wrestling with the problem of how I was going to get my silver to the west.

Hiding the car once more was not the work of a moment, for after we had replaced the wooden wall we had to fix the old warning signs that spoke of loose supports and firedamp, the signs that helped to keep people away. Once this was done he led me back to the surface via the long and rusty old ladder we had climbed down some hours before, and from there back towards the river, where I could get my bearings. He looked me in the eyes, reminded me of the promise I had made in my schoolboy German – to tell no one what I had seen – nodded sharply, and then he was gone.

I kept that secret for many years – well, in my own way – and other secrets, too. But now all those secrets can be revealed. Now the silver can shine again.

***

1939

Trudi had caught sight of him on the newsreel, marching as right marker in the fifth rank of paratroopers, eyes snapping right for the Führer, the Fallschirmjäger in the vanguard of Adolf Hitler's fiftieth birthday parade. She was so proud, she had told him, over and over again. "It's hard for me not to smile, my darling," she said now, apologetically, as they walked up the slab-paved path to the entrance of one of the blocks in Zwickau's Heinrich Braun hospital; in the Marienthal district, away from the city's chimneys. That day of which Trudi now spoke, April 20 1939, had been the first time the German people had seen their new parachute force, and they had created quite a stir as they goose-stepped up Berlin's East-West Axis in full jump gear of smocks and harness; it had been the proudest day of Sepp's life. But today he wore his walking out uniform, Luftwaffe light blue with gold-yellow piping on the epaulettes and side cap, and with his wife hanging on his arm as tightly as a rookie at the door rail of a Ju 52 he should have felt almost as proud as he did then. But sometimes it is neither the time nor the place for pride … And he wished she would stop smiling.

"Your sister is on the second floor, go through the ward and there are some private rooms, she is in two-eighteen, Herr Nagel," the receptionist said. He nodded, and noted that Trudi was trying her best to look solemn, then they took the stairs. His rubber-soled jump boots squealed against the steps while Trudi's heels tapped a cold tattoo that echoed up the wide stairwell.

"What should I say to her?" Trudi said.

"Just be friendly," Sepp said. "And it might be better if we didn't mention our news, just for now." She smiled again, briefly, and gently laid her hand on her belly.

There was something wrong with Hanna's baby. That's all that Sepp could take from the message from Konrad passed on to him at the parachute training camp in Stendal, where he had now been made a jump instructor after passing-out top of his class in the autumn. It was early for the baby anyway. Hanna had been arriving in Zwickau with Konrad for an Auto Union function – the first time she had been away from Berlin for many a month – when it had started. That's all that he knew for sure, and that in itself had been a shock, because it had never crossed Sepp's mind that anything to do with Hanna and Konrad's first born should not go exactly to plan.

There was a right turn through some swing doors at the top of the stairs, then they walked through the light and airy ward, with its full length windows and high ceiling, its slight smell of ether, its soft clank of steel on porcelain, and the rasping cough of a sick miner – he'd heard that same cough so often in the Zwickau of his youth. At the end of the ward they pushed through some more swing doors and into a corridor lit by stark white lights suspended from the ceiling. Part way down the corridor a figure was folded on a single chair, forehead resting in his hands, elbows tight to his body. Sepp knew instantly it was Konrad. Two others stood with him, yet apart, deep in conversation. One was in the white coat of a doctor, a stethoscope around his neck, a party badge fixed to his lapel. The other he recognised as Anton Kessler. Neither of the three men seemed to notice Sepp and Trudi and he felt her hold on his arm tighten, but then she was always nervous in the company of important men.

"It's for the best that she did not see it," the doctor said.

"I understand," Kessler said, and Sepp wondered what they were talking about. The harsh light played liquid on the thick lenses of Kessler's spectacles, but Sepp could see that as he spoke he was blinking rapidly. He had seen it before, at race meetings, on those days when the team had met the big men in the Party, and on that cold January morning last year, when Rosemeyer had driven the streamliner instead of Westbury Holt. It was then that Sepp remembered the envelopes, folded and stuffed into the top pocket of his Luftwaffe tunic.

"Ah, Sepp, it's good to see you," Kessler said. Sepp reached out for Kessler's hand. He was not surprised to see him there, for he was always at Konrad's shoulder. Konrad stood and nodded, and almost smiled at Trudi, who shuffled uncomfortably behind Sepp.

"Konrad, is she all right?"

"She will be fine Sepp, fine …"

"And the baby?"

There was silence, and although Sepp could not see their faces he felt that Kessler and the doctor were watching Konrad, waiting to hear how he would answer the question. Then the spell was broken with a sudden crash of a trolley against the swing door down the other end of the corridor.

"Sepp, it is dead," Konrad said.

"Dead?" Trudi said, putting her hand to her mouth as if to belatedly stop the word escaping.

"*It?*" Sepp said.

"Walk with me, Sepp," Kessler ordered, as Konrad crumpled back into the chair.

"I must see Hanna first, is she in here?" Sepp made to open the door of the room marked '218'.

"Not now," Kessler said, clutching at his arm. Sepp, his hand on the door handle, hesitated. "There is something you should know first," Kessler added. With that Sepp's hand reluctantly slipped from the door handle. Kessler and Sepp walked down the corridor a little way and through the swing door before stopping at the top of another stairwell, where there was a window out on to a world of softly scudding clouds which scraped cotton strands against the springtime blue. Outside, a child laughed; a helium chuckle that seemed to float on the breeze.

"Tell me what happened."

"It was a tragedy, the baby was barely human."

"What was wrong?" Sepp said, swallowing hard, part of him not wanting Kessler to go on.

"It was severely malformed, the doctor thinks perhaps it was somehow damaged in the womb – can there be any other explanation?"

"Malformed?"

"No arms to speak of, deformed legs, and its head was strangely misshapen," Kessler said. "The doctor said it would be very unlikely for it to have turned out to be anything less than wholly retarded … Are you all right?"

Sepp felt a lead-like coldness swoop through him, and for a moment he thought he might pass out. But he caught himself; reminding himself how strong he had become, reminding himself that Hanna would need him. Outside the child laughed again, and for a moment it seemed to mock this grown up world Sepp had found himself in. Kessler was still talking, Sepp made an effort to listen. He focused on the eyes of the man, and noticed once more that he was blinking steadily. It was almost as if his eye-lids were a function of his heartbeat, but there was more: the slightest hint of a smile at the edge of his mouth. But no, that could not be …

"You do understand there could be no life for such an infant now?" Kessler went on.

"It … It wouldn't be much of a life, but —"

"It would not be a life," Kessler said, firmly now. Sepp said nothing. There was something hypnotic about the steady blink of Kessler's eyes, so he tore his gaze away, resting his forearms against the narrow sill and pressing his face against the cold glass of the window.

"Fallschirmjäger, yes?"

"Yes."

"So, a Party member." Adding his name to the Nazi list had been a small price to pay to make sure he could wear the uniform of the paratroopers, and Sepp had not minded that. "I am pleased that you are with us, Sepp. I always believed you were just the sort the Party needs. It is men like you that will form the spearhead for the future. But do not think the hard choices – the heroism even – are for the battlefield alone. There are brave decisions to make every day in this new Germany. And perhaps Konrad has taken the bravest decision of all."

"Konrad?" Sepp turned to face Kessler.

Kessler paused for some long moments, as if he was making a

decision, blinking four times before saying: "They would not terminate without the permission of the father."

Terminate. As Sepp took this in he felt curiously detached, as if he was floating above the scene. He tried to imagine a life for this child that would not be. But he could not. Kessler was still studying him closely, Sepp realised.

"Killed?"

"How could it be killed if it did not live, Sepp?"

"But still —"

"Why should it not be killed if it *could* not live?"

"I don't know, it's …" He could not finish the sentence.

"It was no worse than an abortion. You see that, don't you?"

Sepp nodded, but he wasn't sure he did. "It's official?" he said.

"Of course, it was on the highest authority."

Sepp said nothing, and then Kessler smiled faintly, and Sepp felt a shiver rattle down his spine.

"But I don't need to tell you this is not something to speak of, not yet anyway," Kessler said. "The doctor is SS, not from this hospital, we arranged for him to come from Leipzig soon after it was born. Your sister needed a caesarean section, so she was put under, and she was under general anaesthetic when the decision was made and the procedure could be carried out."

"Procedure?"

"Just a simple injection, an overdose of morphium-scopolamine, I believe."

"Does Hanna know it was …?" Again, he felt he could not finish the sentence.

"No, she does not know. She does not know we had to destroy it, and it is better it stays that way, Sepp. Better for her."

Sepp nodded. He knew he had to look at it coldly; he knew from his training that sometimes you have to look at things without passion. Suddenly he was quite ashamed of the child within him; it had made him weak, when he would need to be strong. The doctors had decided, and the doctors know best, what is right, what is wrong. He had to trust them. But he doubted Hanna would be able to look upon this in such a way, and he knew Kessler was right. It was right to keep what had been done from her. It would mean lying to her, and he had never lied to her before. But then it is not always easy to do the right thing.

"Was it a boy, or a girl?" Sepp asked.

Kessler shrugged: "Does it matter?" He was blinking again, a little quicker now. Again Sepp knew he was right. It did not matter, for there could have been no life for this child, and *it* was better than *him* or *her*. *It* also made it easier. Somehow.

"One day it will be different," Kessler said. "One day what we have to do will be acknowledged, celebrated – you see that, don't you Sepp?" Sepp said nothing, he was not sure exactly what Kessler meant. But he was sure that Hanna needed him.

There was the soft tap of shoe leather behind them and Sepp turned to see the doctor approaching. He stopped in front of them and cleared his throat. "Yes?" Kessler said. Sepp thought the doctor was nervous of Kessler. He fiddled with his stethoscope absent-mindedly.

"She is awake now, the drugs have worn off," as he said this his head dipped a little, and his hand moved from the stethoscope to the little round Party badge on his lapel. Suddenly Sepp remembered his sister.

"How is she?"

"She will be fine," the doctor said.

"I must go to her."

Five minutes later Sepp sat at Hanna's bedside. The room was functional, drained of any colour, as if it was somehow an extension of his sister. Her eyes were open, but empty. She had not spoken since Sepp had come into the room. Trudi sat beside him, fidgeting with a handkerchief, squeezing his hand from time to time. Konrad sat opposite, trying to talk to Hanna. It was too warm and the only sound, apart from Konrad's strangely monotone voice, was the soft tick of the radiator the far end of the room, contracting or expanding. There were flowers on the small wooden table beside the bed. Sepp didn't know what they were: white, some yellow …

"You should be up and out of here within a few days," Konrad said, "and then …" But there was no reaction and Konrad let the sentence wither away.

"Would you like some coffee?" Trudi suddenly said.

"She's not allowed it," Konrad replied for Hanna, and Trudi's head dipped in disappointment. "But come Trudi, let me buy you a cup, we will leave Hanna and Sepp to talk."

"No Konrad, you should be here," Sepp said.

"Is that what Hanna wants?" Konrad looked at her as he said it, but she stared ahead. "I will go then – Trudi?" Sepp nodded at her and his wife followed Konrad through the door, unable to hide a look of relief as she left.

"She hates hospitals," Sepp said, in unasked for explanation.

"They killed the baby, didn't they?" Hanna said, turning her eyes to his. It took all his strength to hold her gaze, but he could not find the words to reply.

"They killed my baby."

"It died," he heard himself say. "There was nothing that could be done for it."

"Do you believe that, Sepp?"

He did not answer this time.

"I heard them Sepp, I heard them talking."

"It was just a bad dream, Hanna, you have been asleep for hours, and they have given you drugs."

"Did they kill my baby, Sepp?"

"No," he said.

"Promise me, Sepp?"

He hesitated for a moment, which he covered with a light cough, then he said: "The doctor has told me you reacted badly to the drugs, it is not unusual to have bad dreams with them."

"Promise me Sepp."

"I promise. They did not kill the baby; this is a hospital Hanna, they do not kill in hospitals." The words tasted like bile as he spoke them, for he had never lied to her before. But medicine could taste bad, and he knew she needed the medicine of sweet lies now, and he also knew the damage the truth would do.

"I'm tired now," she said, and closed her eyes. He looked at her for a minute or two and he tried to find the old Hanna, the laughter, the fun. When was the last time he had seen her laugh, even before this? There was an image of her and Westbury Holt in the café at the Berlin Motor Show, well over a year ago now. The memory of the Englishman reminded him of the unopened letters in his pocket, one for him, one for her, as always, which he had picked up from the Zwickau apartments earlier, as he always did on his frequent visits to old Kurt to check up on the rental business.

He unbuttoned the breast pocket of his blue uniform jacket and pulled the folded envelopes from it. The airmail envelopes bore stamps with the English king's head on them, and a London postmark. He had stuffed the letters in his top pocket when he had picked them up, and then almost forgotten about them. He wished Holt would stop writing, would get the message, but then when Westbury Holt wanted something … Sepp looked at his sister again, her eyes tight shut, but he knew she wasn't asleep. There was the sound of whistling in the corridor outside and the squeak of a wheel on a hospital trolley.

He had never opened any of the envelopes, they went straight into the barrack room stove once he had returned to Stendal. But he could always guess what they would say. First, a thank you for him – for saving a fool's life – and he had no need of that. He had heard from Lick how it had gone. Holt's father had arranged for him to be flown home just days after the crash, there was a renowned specialist in London he knew, and could afford, and Holt was too drugged up to argue. There had been complications, infection, and more operations, Sepp's amputation tidied so that it was now further up the leg but still below the knee. Now there would be a slow recuperation, he supposed.

The other letter, to Hanna, could only cause her trouble. That's what he had thought during these past months when she had a baby on the way, after months of trying, and she was content in Berlin, he had supposed. Now, he was not so sure, and he started to ease open the flap of the envelope. Perhaps now the words of a fool could put a smile back on her face? There was a tap on the door. "Yes?" A pretty young nurse walked in.

"Ah, she is asleep, good – it will be the drugs, best let her rest."

"Yes, of course," Sepp placed the envelopes back into his top pocket and scraped the chair away from the bed as quietly as he could while the nurse closed the curtains. But even in the half-light Sepp knew his sister was not asleep.

Half an hour later the letters remained unread, as Sepp tore them into tiny pieces which he fed into the bin in the hospital's cafeteria.

*

The harder he pressed the accelerator the worse the pain. Adrenalin and a small shot of morphine had got him through the first few laps, but now Westbury Holt was hurting bad. He powered the dark green car onto the Members' Banking once more, feeling the rear skip out, feeling the joins in the track surface thudding through the steering wheel, feeling the pulsing burn of his raw stump against the cup of the false lower part of his right leg. They had said it was too early for him to drive a racing car. They had been right. And to make it worse – far worse – he was absolutely nowhere in this race.

West had spent most of what little remained of his money – the foreign currency prize cash from '37 and the proceeds from selling his Horch – on hiring the ERA. The rest of it had gone on rent, on freedom. He might have lived with his father, taken the job at the head office in Uxbridge, forgetting racing – that was the condition – but it would have meant admitting defeat, accepting it was over. And he would not let the old man win quite that easily.

He had not tried out the car before the race, though everyone had said he should. To find out if *it* was quick enough, they had said. To find out if *he* could still do it, he had heard. So West had not bothered with that: because, he had told them, he knew these cars well, and he also knew the Brooklands Campbell circuit well enough. But more truthfully he knew there was a limit to the pain he could take, and the laps he could do. He'd reached that limit far earlier than he'd anticipated, yet still he jammed the accelerator pedal to the bulkhead as the car climbed the slope of the banking.

West had been told it might be possible to fit a hand throttle and a control column brake, but that would take time and money, and it was not his car anyway, so there was a limit to the modifications he could make. More to the point, those sort of changes would also admit defeat – and he had hoped to show them he could still do this pretty much as he had before his prang. And so his false lower leg was strapped tightly in place, with hinged steel rods for bracing that vibrated with the car, tingling to the tune of its shuddering body. He had so far managed to walk on the bloody thing, and he had managed to drive a road car, too. He had done both of these things before the doctors had said he was ready. And he had paid in pain. But then Westbury Holt had never been one to sit around and wait.

There was just enough articulation in his knee joint for him to put pressure on the accelerator and brake pedals, though there was no movement in the ankle part of the false limb, so control was difficult, and he could not blip the throttle on the down-change while braking, the heel and toe movement – but he could always drive around that. Even now the leg had to be locked into place at an angle, and the seat had been modified a little so he could apply a leveraged force on the pedals. It worked, just: but there was little feel, and yet all too much pain. But Westbury Holt raced on, for Westbury Holt still knew no other way.

From a distance the Brooklands banking looked like the inside of a soup plate. From a distance it looked as smooth as china. But up close, at speed, nothing could be further from the truth. The boxy little racing car bucked and kicked as it climbed to the rim, jarring West's burning stump, another flash of pain, a purer pain; he was learning much about the spectrum of suffering this day. West tried to ignore it, selecting the next gear with the lever beneath the dash, before stabbing at the actuator pedal on the extreme left – his legs were splayed either side of the humped aluminium gearbox casing that almost filled the floor of the car. The Wilson pre-selector gearbox then did the work of shifting by itself, as he bent down low to lessen the buffeting of the air, up close to the aero windscreen, which was just an inch beyond the top portion of the shivering, shifting wheel. He felt the porpoising motion of the car beneath him, and the suck of the centrifugal force within him, as the ERA came close to the lip of the banking, raced under the box-girder footbridge, breaking through the dark band of its shadow, the sharply angled curve now spread before him like a fossilised tidal wave.

The car rides the crest of the banking like a ball in the track of a roulette wheel. It's tilted at an acute angle as it clings to the steeply sloped surface, trees peeping over the track's edge flickering it with shadow, as they shine and shimmer in the speeding sunshine. The cockpit is open on both sides and through the corner of his eye the buff-coloured track surface scuffs by in a blur while the noise of the car seems to be amplified by the wall of the speed bowl: the high pitched whine of the supercharger, mixed with the gnashing ripping of the internals of the flat six in front of him, then the fluting resonation through the thick pipe that runs down the side of the car just to West's left, before the final deep metallic crack of its exhaust splits the air. The smell of its methanol-based fuel snatches at his nostrils, cutting through any hint of the spring day air outside of the hot cockpit of the ERA. A fly becomes a blood spot on the surface of his *Protector* goggles. West pre-selects another cog, then, a few seconds or so later, taps at the actuator pedal to engage it, the gear slipping in smoothly.

The big cord-bound four-spoke wheel is juddering in his hands, pulling to the left. On every other lap he has allowed the car to come down off the banking and hit the Railway Straight on the left side of the track, avoiding the worst of the infamous hump, and avoiding the pain of the inevitable jolt. It had saved him some suffering, and cost him no time. But now he's aware of a surge of blood-red taking the space he wants. He holds his line, and the other car is right alongside as they hit the vicious bump.

West had never worried about how a car might fly. A racing car off the deck was natural enough – at the Nürburgring in the Auto Union it sometimes seemed he was airborne as much as he was on the track. But things were different then, and although the ERA flew sweetly for many yards, the sudden jolt of its return to concrete took the pain to another level; as if a burning spike had been plunged into his bloodied stump. West lifted off the throttle involuntarily, a simple reflex, and the car did what any car would do if there was a sudden shift in weight to its nose: it kicked out. He held the brief but violent slide, and planted the burning limb back on the gas, but the other car was ahead now. He recognised it as the red ERA of Lord Caldicot, the car he had passed earlier in the race, back when the pain had seemed almost bearable. Caldicot was long past his best, was too old, too slow. If Caldicot had caught him it meant the pain was slowing West, he knew. The pain was beating him.

Caldicot's ERA was now pulling over in front of West's similar car to take the optimum line for the approaching left hand corner. West pre-selected the gear for the tight Railway Turn. His leg was shaking, he suddenly realised, the nerves in his thigh jumping. He followed the other car close, the warmth of its passage washing over him, its flat metallic rip mixing with the noise from his engine to create a crashing din. Caldicot left his braking as late as he could, the exhaust crackling sharply as the car took on that familiar ERA stance, the tail kicking out as the old-style ladder chassis flexed. West matched the man in front – he knew no other way – feeling the car twist around him, feeling the tramp of the tall tyres as it teetered on the edge, feeling another lightning bolt of pain.

The braking area always seemed to last an age after the near flat-out blast along the banking. Time to think of pain, time to be filled with pain …

Yet pain is simply pain. You accept it, you wonder at it – how those things that are no longer there can hurt so, like a lower leg, like Hanna – but you also fight it. But *feel* is an altogether different thing. More than anything, a racing driver needs feel. He needs it in his fingertips, he needs it in his seat, and he needs it in his right foot; for the delicate balance of accelerating, for the equally delicate balance of braking.

A false foot does not give much feel, and what there was in the stump of his leg was lost in the wash of the agony. He misjudged his braking. The rear of the car started to come around too much, and he hauled on an arm-twisting turn of opposite lock, and came off the burning brake. He held the slide – just – but the car was going too quick, the boat-tail rear of the red ERA was rushing towards him like a poke in the eye. There was not the time to avoid it and there was a muted thud of steel on steel as he hit the sculptured back of the other car.

West watched as Caldicot's ERA looped into a lazy spin, off the track, coming to rest against a low sandbank that was there to stop wayward cars, a great wave of sand flying into the air like the aftermath of an unsuccessful bunker play.

West turned in and then powered the car through the corner in a big slide. His application on the throttle clumsy now, burning bright pain going well with the acrid smell of spinning tyres on concrete as West leant to the left, pressing his buttocks tight to the rear right of the leather seat, elbows out – the natural stance of a man cornering in an ERA – then instinctively leaning right as he corrected the slide.

As he sped on to the next corner he pumped the little knob on the left of the dash three times, enough to keep the fuel pump working, keeping one eye on the gauge, watching for it to reach three lbs – a little ERA chore it was best not to ignore. It was then, in a moment of sharp clarity and piercing honesty, that he decided he would retire the car. He was slow, and getting slower, this was useless …

… And yet at the end of the lap he drove past the pits, and pitched the ERA into Test Hill Hairpin to start another tour. Westbury Holt would not be beaten by pain.

A little later, a lifetime later, West pulled up in front of the pit stalls, the race finally over. Phillip Grace was waiting. This was the first time he had been to a racetrack since the Nürburgring two years before. Gracie looked concerned. West turned off the engine and slumped in the cockpit.

"You all right, friend Westbury?"

"Never better, old boy," West lied. He realised he was shaking. He had been holding the steering wheel too tightly, and now he could barely un-wrap his fingers from its cutting cord binding. He was dimly aware of a sticky feeling around his stump, and he knew it would be raw mincemeat down there. He could feel the heat from the gearbox casing between his legs, and that of the engine in front of him, radiating; soaking him in a fever sweat, but he did not have the energy to remove the old cricket jumper. Over the smell of the methanol and the cooked brakes and the blistered tyres and the *Castrol R* he felt sure he could also smell hot blood, simmering blood. He had bitten his lip, and so he could taste blood, too. But all these things, even the lobster-faced man in white overalls who strode towards him with bunched fists and purpose in his step, were on the misty periphery of the pain.

"Looks like trouble," Gracie said.

"What the devil are you playing at, Holt?" Lord Caldicot shouted. Caldicot was a gentleman, not a player like West, not the sort to take German money, not the sort to *need* to win. He had his name and title on top of one of the pit stalls, had his seat in the club, was of this place: *The right crowd and no crowding* – you'd never see that on the posters at the Nürburgring, West often thought.

"Steady on sir," Gracie said. "Can't you see he's in a bad way?"

"Well, if he's in a bad way he should not be driving – and he certainly shouldn't be driving into me!"

"That's racing," West heard himself mutter.

"I'm sure it was because of the leg," Gracie said. "Isn't that so, West?"

"Well?" Caldicot said.

There was a pause, measured by the ticking steel of the cooling ERA, before West said: "Nothing to do with the leg, old boy. You were simply in my way – what else was I supposed to do?"

Caldicot gave him an icy stare, and then said: "What are you trying to prove, Holt?"

"Just trying to beat the other chap, isn't that the point?"

"You don't drive like a Hun here, got it man?"

West somehow managed to crack a smile, but not quite the cheeky grin he was hoping for, and the good Lord marched off in the direction of the Clerk of the Course's office.

"Well, some things never change," Gracie said. "Come on old boy, let's go and get a drink at the clubhouse before you're barred, eh?"

"If it's all the same to you, I think I'll just sit here a while …"

***

1941

24 April 1941
My dearest Seppi
I am so proud I feel my heart will burst! Feldwebel already and I had only just started to teach Bernd to say oberjager — you naughty sergeant, you must slow down! But he knows your picture and he says 'Daddy' and 'Soldier' and he can almost say 'Führer' too.
I do worry for you but I know you must be brave like all of our soldiers.
I went to see Hanna as you asked. You know she gets some wonderful things from Herr Plaidt, but she never seems grateful. I know it hurts you for me to write of such things but it is my duty to tell you. We are all to be brave and she must forget all that has happened to her but all she does is stay in bed all day and I am sure she cannot still be suffering from it. I shouldn't say this of your dear sister I know but is it the way for a good German wife to behave?
What is more she does not say 'Heil Hitler' but she says 'good day' as if she does not know it is compulsory but she surely does as I have told her myself many times ...

... There was more of this, a whole page more, and Sepp skipped over it until ...

... If you ask me Herr Plaidt would do well to put aside his important work for a moment and put his house in order!
But I must stop writing now before the foolish girl in me asks you to be careful.
Little Bernd cries for me, and for his brave Papa.
Heil Hitler
Trudi

Sepp folded the letter carefully and placed it in the top pocket of his shirt. He knew he should write to Hanna, but he did not know how. Despite all he had learnt these past two years there were still certain things he could not yet do, things like write harsh words to his sister. And so he had not written to her at all, for quite some time. Months, even. She would learn; learn to forget, she would have to. But for now he could not worry about Hanna and her childish behaviour, because for him there was the grown up business of war to think about.

His squad was lying about in various states of undress beneath the olive trees, some stripped to their shorts or completely naked, soaking up the searing sunshine that is late May in Greece. Others worked quietly, stripping their MP 38 machine pistols or clipping ammunition into machine gun belts. There was a strong smell of gun oil and brewing ersatz coffee in the air, overlaid by the sweet tang of the boxes of cherries they had bought from the locals. Every time someone would walk through their small patch of olive grove an insubstantial fog of dust would mark his trail, much of it settling as a film of yellow on the surface of Sepp's black coffee.

It was almost a year since the regiment had last seen action in Holland and Sepp's battalion had faced no opposition here in Corinth, the bloody work already completed by the time they had arrived. The squad's only casualty – sunburn to the shoulder – was being treated by a teasing comrade in one of the dirty, captured English tents they had now made their home. The lads were relaxed, carefree, but then most of them were green, burdened with dreams of glory rather than memories of lost comrades. It could make him feel so old at times.

The grass under the twisted old olive trees had been crushed and pulverised beneath the jump-boots of the battalion. Sepp half lay, half sat, his back against the sinewy-slender trunk of one of the gnarled old trees, his legs in the yellow dust, his head pressed into the padded bowl of his skull-tight jump helmet. The high sun spun a lattice of shadows through the small green-black leaves of the olive trees, painting the tents in dapples of shade and light. Sepp let his eyes drift towards the distant airstrip, a Junkers 52 transport had landed and its three propellers were churning up a huge cloud of dust that soon obliterated the dark mass of the hills in the distance. Closer still and a group of paratroopers busied themselves with filling the long, bomb-shaped canisters with rifles and equipment. The yellow, red and white wheeled containers, each marked with identification rings, would drop when the paratroopers dropped and, it could only be hoped, land somewhere close to them. Where the hard, brittle grass still lay in patches other paratroopers wound long strips of drab parachute silk into bulging bundles. He looked at his own parachute pack and not for the first time he wondered where next: Malta, Cyprus, Egypt? But he had long learned not to pay too much attention to the rumours.

Lick arrived in a flurry of dust and laughter. He wore an English pith helmet he'd found abandoned near the airstrip and dragged a rectangular wooden crate behind him. It was obviously heavy and a corner of it gouged a long furrow in the dry earth. Each man had been given such a crate earlier in the day, in which they placed their personal possessions, attaching a list of the contents to the lid. For safe keeping, they were told, or to be returned to family should the worst happen, the unspoken truth. It had been an easy task for Sepp, just a few bits and pieces, a couple of books, letters from Trudi, and the punch-dagger wrapped in canvas. He had meant to dump the thing, but had somehow never found the time. At least now it took up a little space in the box, stopping the meagre belongings of a paratrooper from rattling around too much. Lick's own box clanked and clinked as he let it fall to the ground. He had that look on his face, sweet innocence, which usually meant that Sepp would have to appeal to the captain on his behalf sooner or later, like the time when he'd lost half his uniform in a game of skat with a couple of infantrymen. Lick lifted the lid off the box and pulled out three beers, winding his fingers around the long throats of the bottles. There were obviously many more inside.

"Where did you get those?" Sepp added a hard edge to his voice, it was always necessary to show the others there were no favours, old friend or not. He'd long since realised that managing to wangle Lick a place in his squad was not perhaps the masterstroke he had at first believed, and it had taken time for Lick to realise that the single sergeant's wing on Sepp's left arm was of more importance than the three years he would always have over Sepp.

"It's off one of the drivers; good stuff – look!" Lick said, as he lifted the bottles higher. It was good, too: *Paulaner*, good Bavarian beer, and Sepp could see the looks of anticipation on the young faces around him. He rarely touched drink, even beer, these days, yet he thought they deserved it, wherever it might have come from. But they had to know it was his decision. They all stared at him, Lick included, eyes pleading. He let them sweat for a few moments, and then tipped his dusty black ersatz coffee onto the yellow earth.

"It will need some cool in it," he said. "Erich, Otto, come on, we'll dig an ice pit for it." He took off his helmet and found an entrenching tool. The other two young men, both of them blond, long muscled and already tanned from days in the sun, followed him, each taking a corner of the crate. Two fighters flew low overhead, their shadows flicking across the olive grove, leaves shivering to their passage, Daimler Benz motors screaming, taking Sepp back to another time when he'd listened to similar engines in the Mercedes racers. The memory came with a too familiar feeling, something close to nausea, and he refused to let the image of the silver car settle on his consciousness. He craned his head and watched as the pair of mottled grey Messerschmitt BF109s banked out to sea, yellow spinners glinting in the sunshine, black crosses vivid against the pale undersides of their squared-off wings.

"Ach, some Tommy is in for a bad time," Erich said.

Sepp nodded, and then looked for a cool spot in the shade to dig the pit for the beer.

*

When the engine finally cut West was within sight of the airfield at Maleme. He could see the white froth of the waves breaking on the beach and the brown Kavkazia Hill with its dark-green streaks of olive groves at the far end of the strip. There was black smoke rising from the field, four or five tall pillars of it, and a bright fire burnt close to the road-bridge over the dried up riverbed. The airfield had been hit again. He had enough height to put the Hurricane into a flat glide and he brought it in carefully, the torn stiff fabric of the fuselage flapping in the slipstream like bunting, the wings creaking and popping, the cockpit reeking of the alcohol-smelling Glycol coolant that poured in through a smoking bullet-hole in the bulkhead. He pumped the undercarriage and flaps into the down position and slid back the hood, the sea air a welcome breath. Then he made a perfect landing, the tyres letting out a relieved little scuff as they kissed the dusty airstrip before the rattle of the undercarriage finally broke the eerie swoosh of the glide.

West brought the Hurricane to a halt close to a gun pit and the ground crew rushed out to meet him, some wearing desert khaki shorts and shirts, others in RAF blue jackets, unbuttoned and flapping, but all of them surprised to see him – because by now he should have been well on his way to Egypt, not back on Crete. He loosened off his parachute and climbed out onto the wing, noting the lazy curl of smoke from the blackened gun channels. Then he jumped down to the ground, forgetting his raw stump, which now sang with pain as it jarred against his false lower right leg. It was terribly sore. It was always hell to jam on right rudder on the bar at his feet as the Hurricane slowly, slowly climbed, or dived at speed, but it was a necessity to counteract the torque, and it caused him great pain; pain he could sometimes forget in the heat of combat, but pain that always came back to haunt him on the ground.

He bit his lip and held the curse inside him. It had become habit that he would never show his injury affected him in any way, because it had been the devil's own work to persuade them he could still fly well enough, and he'd missed enough of the war already. Lucky for him they were short of good pilots, and Douglas Bader had already proved what could be done with *no* legs. He resolved – again – to buy that man a pint one day. West's latest limb – which he called the mark three – had been fabricated in a workshop at Brooklands, lads he'd known in his racing days, and they'd used the best lightweight materials they could find, so it was a mix of wood and metal, just like the Hurricane, with rubber for cushioning and a complicated webbing of straps to stop the bloody thing from falling off. It was a good as it could be, and that just had to be good enough.

"Ran into a couple of 109s," he said, as the ground crew rushed to help him, "but managed to bag a Dornier a bit earlier." He had been told to avoid the enemy, just get the kite back to the airstrip at Gerawla, but the slim Dornier 17 had been stooging along, too tempting a target – in the same way a Hurricane which only has eyes for a bomber can be oh so tempting for a brace of Messerschmitts. *Chalk it up to experience old man, and while you're at it why not chalk up another kill* ... This was number five. It meant he was an ace, if it was confirmed. The problem was the gun camera had not been loaded with film – it was a ferry job, so no need – so he would have to hope someone had seen the 'Flying Pencil' go down.

He looked over the damage. The Hurricane was a sturdy old bus, that was for sure, and many a time in Greece he'd landed one that was all but falling to pieces. Mind you, he'd crashed a couple, too – he might have lost nearly half a leg, but not the Westbury Holt luck. He let his eyes run over the khaki and brown painted Hurricane. Two neat lines of holes ran along the length of the fuselage, intersecting and crossing over just before a large, jagged edged hole where the stiffened fabric covering had been blasted clean away, taking a pie-portion out of the yellow-edged blue, white and red RAF roundel with it. Another chunk had been taken out of the rudder, like the bite of a flying shark, and more hits pockmarked the lower fuselage like big burst blisters. The smaller holes were from the rear gunner in the Dornier, the larger ones from the cannon on the nose of one of the 109s. The same cannon had seen to his engine, too, which smoked and hissed and was now surrounded by a scrum of headshaking erks. He guessed the Messerschmitts had been low on fuel, as they had given up the chase soon after he had dived away, leaving him to limp home.

Suddenly West realised how hot it was down there on the ground as the sweat trickled down from the edge of his leather flying helmet. He peeled off helmet, goggles, Mae West, Irvin flying jacket and cricket jumper, dumping most of it on the floor but tying the sweater around his waist. One of the erks handed him his blue cap with its cloth-covered peak and he placed it far back on his head.

"Can it be fixed?" he asked, once again running his eyes along the length of the fighter, from smoking engine to tattered tail. The fitter just shrugged, as did the rigger. They'd do their best, West knew.

The camp was a short limp away; past the old shot up Fleet Air Arm Fairey Fulmer by the roadside; past the *n*-shaped aircraft pens, formed with sandbags and sand-filled barrels; past the tired looking Royal Marine anti-aircraft gunners servicing their Bofors; past the craters; past the fires. He crossed the road, pausing to allow a lorry load of New Zealand infantry to rattle by, the wheels kicking up choking dust from the road surface. He glanced up at the hill that overlooked the aerodrome, the Kiwis there were well dug in, a battalion of them. He was no soldier, but to him it looked a secure position.

The camp itself was a ramshackle affair, an archipelago of bell tents and an old stone hut on the edge of the rocky, dried up riverbed. To the north was the furthest reaches of the airstrip and the bridge over the River Tavronitis, an iron box girder construction, to the east and overlooking the camp, the lower slopes of Kavkazia Hill, or Hill 107 as the brown jobs called it. The hill was well covered with olive trees, vines and flowering shrubs and was bordered by an irrigation channel that ran into the Tavronitis some way past the camp. West limped towards the operations centre, a place you could get news, and usually a fair cup of char to wash it down with. Someone in the camp was frying up bully beef with onions and its siren smell reminded West that he hadn't eaten anything since yesterday. The front flaps of the large khaki tent were folded back. The radio equipment had been shipped out on the last transport a day ago so there were a number of empty tables. Potter was sitting at one of them, looking at a map of the island, biting what was left of a thumbnail.

Potter was a pilot, but there was some problem with his ears that meant he could not fly, so now he acted as intelligence officer for the squadron. He kept his head down, but then he'd been through a lot in this war already, or so he constantly said. He had a round face, and West thought he was a little overweight, which took some doing after what they had been through in Greece. Under his nose lay a big, fat slug of a moustache, salt and pepper in colouring. He always kept his hat on, perhaps because he seemed to be losing hair by the day, and although he laughed out loud as much as any one of them could bear, his eyes never changed, never a twinkle, as if the iris was a grey dot painted on the white.

"Holt? Thought you'd be in Gerawla by now?" Potter said.

"Ran into Jerry."

"You were supposed to avoid contact and get that Hurry back to Egypt, weren't you?"

"Well, no one told them that."

"Hit anything," Potter said.

"Dornier 17, I saw it go in."

"Well let's hope someone else did, eh, old boy?"

West nodded, then shook his head, knowing it was no use arguing, and just hoping someone at sea had seen the Dornier splash into the Med'. It was part of Potter's job to verify kills, taking in the reports from various sources. West thought he enjoyed it, especially when the kill would remain unconfirmed. It was about the only thing the man did enjoy, and he seldom asked for details of the combat, the sort of info that might have been useful. So for now West could only keep his fingers crossed, for it would be fine and dandy to be on five kills, would certainly show he was good enough, maybe the CO would even recommend a DFC. The next step would be to become the best ...

"Why the smile?" Potter asked.

West shrugged, then turned away. There were two other pilots in the tent, one from West's squadron who had fought with him over Greece, the other a Fleet Air Arm man who had come free with the base. There were many other pilots at Maleme, too, but planes for none of them. West had drawn the straw to take the last airworthy Hurricane back to Egypt, away from the strikes on the bases on Crete that had cost them so many fighters, bombed and shot up on the ground, since the Germans had set up their airstrip on the Peloponnese. The two other pilots were playing a game of chess in the corner, one of them noticed West and gave him a nod and a wide grin.

"What's the gossip Clive?" West said.

"You'll get four to one on an airborne invasion, evens on the sea – brass still looking out to briny," the pilot moved a pawn, then added. "Oh, and there's mail."

There were two letters for him. Weeks old, via Alexandria and then Canea: one from Gracie – now flying a desk in London – and one from Father. There was nothing from her, there never was. But that never stopped him hoping – and it never eased the disappointment. He had stopped writing a long time ago, assuming she had made up her mind, but still he sometimes wondered if there was a chance. He couldn't blame her. He had made the decision. He had driven the streamliner. With that thought the phantom pain where his lower right leg had been burned brighter, so he took the weight off it by sitting on the chair opposite Potter. He stared at the map of Crete and found himself wondering how they could possibly stop Jerry without a single serviceable fighter.

*

The best thing about the blackout was that nobody could see you. Every Berliner was a shadow in a world of shadows, and that suited Hanna just fine. The city was dark so the British bombers would not be able to see, though they had not visited for some months now anyway. She had found her way along Kurfürstendamm by following the phosphorescent dashes painted on the edge of the pavement. There were no longer any street lights and the shop fronts were as dark as the mouths of caves. The only light to be seen were the pissy oblongs of yellow showing through the narrow slots in the headlamp covers of the few cars on the streets – not many had the petrol to drive these days – or the undersea glow of the blue-painted windows of the buses, or the floating fireflies of the cigarettes those other shadows smoked. Hanna liked the blackout.

She came to this particular place to meet someone, but she did not know who she would meet, and she came here because with Konrad away from Berlin she did not feel the need to hide away. And she came here, this and places like it, because now it was all she had: her baby was dead before it had lived and *their* war had taken her Sepp. The place was close to the Kabarett der Komiker, or KadeKo as the Berliners called it. The bar had once been swanky and bright, typical of the Ku'damm before the war, but was now just another dark pocket in the black cloak that covered the city. The windows were blinded by thick roller shutters, and the lighting was dim, failing to lick at the corners of the bar, where shade collected like bundles of night.

The bar was called *Bruno's* after its owner, a big fellow with a heavy face and eyes that fitted the blackout. He did a nice line in misery, but he was a kind man, who always gave the soldiers a free drink, and who constantly worried for his only son, whose panzer division had just shipped out to join Rommel's Afrika Korps. He did not allow war talk, unless it was to ask a tank man if he knew his son, but even in *Bruno's* there was no getting away from what was happening in the world. The back wall was decorated with the flags of many nations, each one painted on a clay tile. As Germany had lost friends Bruno had blacked out the enemy flags. Already it resembled a chessboard and every time she came in she could not help but look at those black flags and wonder where her Sepp might be. It had been four months and two days since she had last received a letter from him.

Hanna greeted Bruno in the old way and he replied with an almost imperceptible nod – but she knew he did not mind the lack of a *heil*. She took a table close to the bar and ordered a cocktail. Bruno had always made wonderful American cocktails. He did a good martini, but his best was Bruno's Bronx. These days he made it with vodka rather than gin, and in place of the hard to come by fresh oranges he used *Fanta* – the drink that had been invented to make up for the lack of *Coca-Cola* syrup, a victim of US trade restrictions. It might not have been wholly authentic, but Bruno loaded his Bronx with more spirit than he did vermouth, so the kick was real enough, while the *Fanta* gave it a pleasing fizz and zest. Drinking alone? It was not a problem in Bruno's, it was that sort of place, where people passed through, thinking their thoughts, drinking their drinks. Hanna thought of little and drank too much, allowing the hours to fuse into a blurred nothingness.

"You are alone?" he asked – a pale creature, skin like a convict, limp and lifeless, a naval uniform, dark eyes like pools of oil. "May I join you?"

"Are you all right?" he said, considerate, gentle; officer of the Kriegsmarine, probably passing through Berlin on his way to some cold, god-forsaken northern port, looking for a little warmth.

"Family troubles?" he said.

"Does it matter?"

"Husband, abroad?"

"I've no idea."

"Children?"

"Dead."

"I'm sorry, is that why you drink alone … Do you grieve?"

"Do you fuck?"

*

The ground trembled to the thunder of the engines. In the near distance Sepp could make out long, ghostly strings of paratroopers making for the dark silhouettes of the aeroplanes, guided by signal lamps and the shouts of the NCOs. Fire barrels illuminated the fringe of the airfield, flames licking at the darkness, throwing grotesque prehistoric shadows of taxiing Junkers 52s across the olive groves. Yes, their buses were ready, their trusty Ju 52s: old 'Auntie Ju', slow but solid. The propellers were throwing up the dust so that it hung in the air and was illuminated by arc lights, wrapping some of the dark machines in an almost golden aura. But even with this gilt-edged trick of light it was an ugly old bird, the Ju, Sepp would never argue with that, what with that incongruous third propeller bristling from its nose and the ribbed Duralumin skin that made it look as if it had been made out of corrugated iron. Yet there was not another plane Sepp would go to war in.

"Feldwebel Nagel!"

"Hauptmann?"

The captain had to shout to be heard over the din of the aircraft: "The Tommy spies will be busy with their gossip tonight, yes Sepp?"

"Yes, sir." Someone shone a torch at them and Sepp could see the light in the young officer's eyes. He had led them well, in Holland, but it had already put age on his face, furrows on his forehead. A crowd of paratroopers soon pressed around them, faces lit pink with glowing cigarettes, all eager for news, some laughing the strange forced laugh of those about to go into battle. The smell of the booze on them was palpable as they had drunk deeply from the beer stocks that night, and had been issued brandy too.

"Have you the orders, sir?" Sepp could hear the excitement in his own voice.

"I have them …" the captain paused theatrically. "It's Crete!"

"Hah! Hand it over boys!" said Lick, the winner of the sweepstake, the captain laughed with them all.

"Operation Mercury," he said.

"A god," said one

"Or quicksilver," said another.

The word reminded Sepp of other things, memories, and disappointment, but he kept that to himself. There was more laughter as Lick pretended to wipe his backside with one of the banknotes handed to him by a sulky private, and then they returned to their preparations, some still cheering, others singing. The songs they sang vied for prominence in Sepp's head, songs of home, not war. Once airborne he would purge them from each and every mind by leading them in the song of the Fallschirmjäger.

Not one of them had slept that night and now some walked through the olive groves searching for their comrades in other companies to wish them luck while others picked at their very early breakfast of schinkenwurst and ersatz coffee. Others simply sat with their thoughts. Sepp had written a long letter to Trudi in the light of a burning oil drum, and also a letter to Hanna, the first one in quite some time. He missed his sister most before combat, and he tried to make the letter friendly, tried not to talk too much about how she should behave. He promised he would visit, soon, and did not use the word *if*. She had changed, he knew, but then so had he. Yet he knew that in essence he was still the same person, and he hoped the same was true of Hanna. But it was not a long letter, for there was little he had to say, while there was nothing about where he was, or where he was going, that he was allowed to tell her.

After he had finished the letters he checked his equipment again, the umpteenth time in an hour, and there were still some hours before the off. Sepp was immensely proud of his combat kit, this that set him and his comrades apart from the other soldiers of the Reich. It was modern, it was paratrooper: from the ankle length jump boots with their side laces and thick rubber soles – much better for grip in the cabin of a plane than the hobnailed footwear of the infantry – to the special rimless helmet. Over his standard Luftwaffe uniform Sepp would wear his water-resistant gabardine, splinter-pattern paratrooper smock, split and buttoned tightly around his thighs with the ammunition bandolier – a canvas strip of twelve pockets containing the five-round clips for his rifle – around his neck and hanging down his chest like a loose and heavy scarf beneath the smock.

His field grey trousers contained his gravity knife in a pocket above the right knee, for cutting the cords of his parachute should he end up in a tree or dragged across the ground by his chute in the wind, and a boot-dagger was clipped into his right boot. The helmet was similar to the coal scuttle infantry helmet but trimmed of ear protection and peak so that it would not snag the cords of the chute, or dig into the ground and break the paratrooper's neck. It gave the men a brutal bullet-headed look, Sepp always thought, but he was glad of that. A camouflage cover was stretched across the helmet and inside it was heavily padded, with reinforced chin-straps added to keep it in place on landing. It was fine kit, state of the art, which had proved itself in the snows of Norway and the fields of the Lowlands. But he knew it would be hell to wear in the heat of Crete in May.

As one of the company's marksmen Sepp had a pair of goggles

hanging around his neck, to protect his eyes during the drop, but his Mauser K98 sniper's rifle was packed away in one of the containers, along with their machine guns and mortars. The only thing Sepp, and most of the rest of them, would carry onto the battlefield would be the Sauer 38H pistol at his waist. They all knew that until they found the containers they would be next to useless as a fighting force.

Suddenly the moon was blotted out by three dark shadows rising slowly from the ground, seeming to seep into the sky like slicks of oil: a Junkers towing two Gotha DFS230 gliders of the Storm Regiment, the tow-plane's engines labouring with its heavy burden. These were the first.

"Sepp?" it was Lick, offering him a cigarette, which he declined. "Tell me old friend; you scared?"

"A little, of course. You too?"

"Shitting my pants."

"You'll do fine, Lick."

"That's not my worry," Lick said. "Is it yours?"

"Take some rest, we will need all our strength."

*

"Where were you last night?" Potter asked.

"Dinner, a show, a club ..." West joked, before swinging his leg half clear of the bunk. By the way the light was playing through the canvas of the tent side he could tell that the sun had recently risen. His boots – the false lower leg within the one – were still in place and his stump itched ferociously. His mouth was dry as parchment so he unhooked a water bottle from the thick centre-pole of the tent, swilling warm water around his mouth. He had gone to sleep in his trousers and cricket jumper and now he looked down to see that the latter was zebra-striped with grease from where he had been helping the erks with the repairs to the Hurricane late into the night. He realised he didn't smell so fresh either.

"Another day, and still no sign of an invasion ... We might still get out of here, don't you think?" Potter seemed agitated. There was a slight tremor in his voice, and as the sleep cleared from West's eyes the shape and the state of the other man grew clearer, pacing and clenching his fists in sharp, nervous little birdlike movements. West had certainly drawn the short straw when it came to tent-mates; Westbury Holt luck, he supposed. He wondered how the lads over in the fighter pen, working on the Hurricane, were getting on – with any luck he might yet have something to fight with. He found his cap and the belt with his holstered Webley service revolver, buckling it up over his jumper.

"Any news on my Dornier?"

"Nothing."

"You sure?"

"As I said, nothing – perhaps I should ask if *you're* sure?"

"I got him, saw him go in. Have you telephoned the other stations? "

"You know, most of us have got far more to worry about than one man's glory right now, Holt."

West grunted, shook his head and forced a wry smile. He would try to ring the airfields at Heraklion and Rethymnon himself later, to see if they had had word on his kill. But before that he would pay the erks in the fighter pen a visit, take them some breakfast. He pushed open the tent flap and strode outside. He yawned widely, for he had managed just two hours sleep, he guessed. The sun was angling in low from across the airfield, lighting up the southern slope of the hillside so that the leaves of the olive trees shimmered an oily black-green. He could just pick out the positions of some of the infantry in the vineyards along the base of the hill. Wild thyme caught at his nostrils, and there was the sizzle of fat in a frying pan from the cookhouse tent. He shook the torpor from his head and took his bearings, stretching his limbs as he did so, the familiar and sharp morning pain in his stump coming alive to the new day. The camp was as it always was at this time in the morning, the big tents throwing their shadows in a jumble of dark geometry – triangles spearing rectangles. The white rocks of the riverbed gleamed like jagged teeth, the black shadow of the iron bridge cast solidly upon them, and the shrubs that dotted the hillside were as still as steel in the tranquil morning air. He heard Potter coming out of the tent behind him.

"You know, I realise what you're up to, Holt, there's oil all over that jumper of yours. You're getting that kite fixed up aren't you? Aiming to clear off, are we?" Potter said.

"Aiming to fight," West replied.

"What on earth ...?"

West heard it at the same time. A dull throbbing sound, growing in intensity by the second; both of them searched the sky, shielding their eyes from the low sun. From over the glistening blue band of the sea a swarm of black specks swelled into an armada of bombers as they watched. They both stood transfixed for a minute or so as they watched it approach, and West began to count off Ju 88s, Heinkels and Dorniers. He was about to say that he had never seen so many bombers together at one time when he noticed that Potter had gone, his soft desert boots kicking up dust as he sprinted for the nearest trench, holding a tin helmet tight to his head and carrying a Lee-Enfield rifle he'd snatched from the tent – many of the ground staff had been issued with them just the day before. By the time the first long stick of twelve bombs was whistling through the air West had joined him, jogging over with painful jarring strides, and leaping into the too-tight slot in the ground. Potter was on the floor of the deep trench, his knees drawn up to his chest, the rifle gripped so hard the white of bone showed through the skin of his knuckles. He was trembling.

Two bombs landed close by, bracketing the trench and showering them with a wave of stone-laced dust. The shockwave of the explosion seemed to punch West in the ears and the ground trembled for long moments after. The bombers' passing shook the sky like a sheet of corrugated iron, their dense formations all but blotting out the blue. More whistles, more sticks of bombs, until each explosion merged with the next like a great rolling stampede across the hillside and the camp. They lay as still as possible at the bottom of the trench as the dry earth was shaken from between the sandbags of the parapet, running onto them in little rivulets. Fragments of bomb casings whistled overhead, clanging against the first hard object they met, and hot air swept across the mouth of the trench like licking flames. It seemed to last an age and West wondered if there would ever be an end to the onslaught of the bombers. He thought he heard a sob from the other man, but then that was drowned by yet another explosion.

West feared for the trench walls, thinking they might collapse, that old childhood terror of small spaces that was always there, ready to ambush him. Anything would be better than being buried alive, he thought, and suddenly he was as afraid as he had ever been in his life. But however scared he was in this grave-like slot in the ground, he knew he would have no chance out in the open and so he tried to put his fears of the earth closing in around him to the back of his mind, as the percussions of the bombs seemed to loosen his teeth and blur his vision.

Finally it slackened. The explosions ceased and the noise of the bombers receded a little, back to that throbbing hum, and West risked a look over the parapet of the trench, coughing and spitting the dry earth from his mouth. A thick blanket of dust covered the scene, but as it settled, a light brown veil falling slowly from the sky, he caught sight of the destruction: tent cloth shredded into beige strips, a dark column of smoke billowing from the edge of the airfield, the torso and head of an airman, lower body severed neatly at the belt, a look of disbelief and shock fixed to his face. West turned away, his head still ringing from the bombing.

"I could use a smoke," he said to Potter, who was slowly lifting his head, like an eggshell man with a hangover.

"Is ... Is it over?" Potter stammered.

West nodded. He realised he had left his pipe in the tent and he hauled himself to the lip of the trench, glad to be clear of the dirty grave. The tent was still standing, though the one alongside had been flattened into a charred ground sheet. He bounded over to the tent with his practised limpy jog, ignoring the jolting pain of it. The air still seemed to quiver from the bombing, like unsettled water after a rock had fallen into it, and he could hear the calls of the Kiwis on the hill as they looked for their own, one mate answering the next in clipped shouts. He found his pipe on the floor by Potter's bunk, the pouch of *Player's No Name* tobacco close by. He thought of the Hurricane in the fighter pen and wondered if the erks were all right, if the kite was all right. It would have been a hoot to get among those bombers, he thought, as he pushed back the tent flap half-concentrating on stuffing the bowl of his pipe ...

The sound was like that of a cricket bat swung through the air, but amplified a hundredfold. He was immersed in its shadow for a dark moment of utter bewilderment and then it passed over him heading towards the river-bed, the wind of its slipstream caressing his face. Then another hit the ground 200 yards behind him with a creak of buckling wood and an ungodly shriek from its belly as it scraped along the rough ground. He looked around to see it skid to a halt in a welter of disturbed stones. Quite suddenly all around him there was the noise of shattering wood and splintering olive trees as the silent attackers crashed to the ground like drunken, giant black albatrosses.

Then one of them demolished the tent he had just stepped out of, the tip of its wing passing within feet of his face like a sweeping scythe as the forty-foot long plane slewed into a half spin and came to a rest with its other wing tip digging into the ground.

"Gliders ..." he said to himself, his mouth very dry as he unbuttoned the flap of his holster and grasped for the checker-plate butt of his revolver. From the riverbed he heard the screams of Germans as one of the Gotha gliders ripped its belly open on the jagged rocks, but his eyes stayed focussed on the body of the glider just ten or so yards in front of him. A large door set in the fuselage broke away to reveal the soldiers inside, shocked and still recovering from the crash landing of the glider. There was a ragged crackle of rifle shots from somewhere far behind him and he saw the mottled green wooden wings flecked yellow as the bullets ripped wounds into the flesh of the wood, while two of the Germans inside crumpled into instant lifelessness. The others started to stumble out of the shattered fuselage from the doors on either side.

He saw his enemy face to face for the first time: fierce, sun-browned, a tuft of blond peeping from under the rim of the tight-fitting helmet. His enemy held a short sub-machine-gun with a long magazine. West raised the pistol, thumbed the hammer, and aimed. His enemy looked groggy, stumbling through the large doorway, shaken from the very crash that he had trained long and hard for. His enemy started to raise his gun. The revolver felt heavy in West's hand. The pupils in his enemy's eyes seemed to swell to twice their size and he levelled the stubby gun at West's torso.

West pulled the trigger, feeling the kick of the recoil as it snapped along the length of his arm, smelling the scorched propellant, and hearing the bullet thudding into the chest of the paratrooper over the air quivering report of his pistol. The German staggered backwards, and West tugged at the trigger a second and a third time to make sure of the kill, aiming below the rim of the helmet, hitting the shock-shaped mouth, piercing the throat. His enemy fell to the ground in front of West, his face a mash of blood and bone, jaw smashed, his last breath taken through shattered teeth, while gushing lifeblood darkened the dust from a large and ragged exit wound in the back of his neck.

Another glider-borne soldier followed, again shaken from the landing, again on the receiving end of three of West's bullets. The revolver was empty. A third paratrooper was levelling his machine pistol, kneeling on the floor of the wrecked glider, revenge and blood lust in his eyes. There was no cover for West to hide behind, but as he desperately searched for an escape route he saw Potter, still at the edge of the trench, his rifle clutched tightly to his chest, the crotch of his desert issue trousers darkened with urine, his face the colour of alabaster.

"Shoot him man!" West shouted, as the German cocked his machine gun, gripping its long magazine tightly. Potter fumbled with the rifle. There was a puff of dirt some yards from his feet, the fall of a stray shot. Potter panicked, forgetting everything except his own safety, dropping his rifle and diving headlong in to the trench. The German smiled grimly, then tightened his curled finger on the trigger.

The angled shot hit him in the eye and came out the other side of his head trailing a ribbon of pink blood. West would never know his saviour, the nameless Kiwi sniper on the hillside, but he knew that he had been given a chance to get to the fighter pens, for the remaining Germans had clambered out of the other side of the glider and were now caught up in other fights.

He ran as quick as he could, ignoring the pain where his stump chafed against his false lower leg, rushing through the camp with its ripping and flapping canvas – like a routed army of tattered ghosts. The air was heavy with lead and he could feel the bullets as they sped past his head, making their little deadly sucking sounds, hissing hot insects – *thsssp-thsssp* – before tearing through the wall of a tent or drilling themselves into the ground in short dentist-drill-like buzzes. A tent he was running alongside suddenly gained a long, neat line of bullet holes, and he could clearly hear the clang and ring of the slugs ricocheting off the iron bridge to his left, along with the chatter of machine guns, the hollow crump of mortars, the staccato crackle of hundreds of rifles, and the rhythmic and steady thump-thump of the ack-ack guns on the airfield. He could only hope that the plane would be ready …

*

"But it's illegal!"

"Only your Nazis could ever think listening to the radio was a crime," Hanna said.

Konrad went to say something else, decided against it, then reached for the dial on the wood and Bakelite casing of the grand *Philips Philetta* radio set, turning it away from the forbidden frequency. Radio crime. That's what they called it.

"It's a damned serious offence, Hanna, you know that. Serious enough for two and half years in prison, even the death penalty if they wanted to make an example of you," Konrad said, an edge of panic in his voice.

"How could they find out?" she replied, calmly. It had been stupid not to reset the dial back to *Deutschlandfunk*, but now she was almost glad, for these days she enjoyed scaring him, though she guessed he was more scared of what Kessler would say if he ever got to hear of it, rather than the possibility of his wife feeling the bite of the Plötzensee guillotine.

"How long have you been listening?"

Hanna shrugged. It had been quite a while, it was the only way she could find out what was really happening in the war, what might be happening to her Sepp, but he needn't know that. It was the maid, Inge, of course, who had realised that the dial was set to the BBC's German service. She would have taken the greatest pleasure in telling him.

"Don't do it again, it's a stupid risk," Konrad said. "Besides, you cannot believe what the English say anyway, it's just propaganda."

She smiled at the irony of that.

"Please Hanna, it's not worth it."

She nodded. But the nod was a lie. She lit a *Kamel*. She had started smoking when they had started their war. It was just something to do; and something a German wife should not do, Kessler had once said. Reason enough to do it, then.

Konrad started to pace up and down in front of the fireplace, stopping once as if to warm his backside, but the fire was out. He was agitated, and she knew it was not just a matter of her radio crime. He wore his smart blue-grey Luftwaffe uniform, rather than the SS one he also had the right to wear, with his Iron Cross from the last war, which Hanna thought might make him feel a little less self-conscious in the crush of soldiery passing through the capital. He smelt strongly of Konrad: cologne and *Murad* cigarettes. Outside Berlin was happy, sunny, boasting its spring. Even the birds, chattering away, seemed to talk of victory, happy times for all. Through the tall windows Hanna could see down into the shared garden space behind the apartment block, where the cherry blossom quivered to the light breeze, a few petals falling to kiss the green lawn – how that fat bitch-in-law of hers had made her laugh out loud: dig it up and plant it with spuds for the Fatherland. Silly cow.

Konrad had just excused Inge, a sly but also triumphant look on her face. The picture of the Führer above the fireplace looked down on Hanna with bulging, disapproving eyes, the ebony eagle with its swastika-gripping talons, looked away. The window frames cast a lattice of sharp morning shadow across the white room, the opened blackout curtains hung heavy like crinkled iron. Hanna sat in an armchair. She wore a long eau-de-nil silk robe, wrapped tight about her. She ached for a drink to go with her cigarette, but it was still too early in the day – too early for Konrad, at least.

"I was close to the front this time."

"Others are closer."

"Still, sometimes I think that madman Kessler wants to get me killed," Konrad said, turning to pace the room again. He had not been quite himself since his short propaganda tour of Greece where, she had learnt, he had been giving inspirational talks to the troops. "I don't understand it, so close to the killing, the death. It's as if he ..." He shook his head: "*madness* ..."

"He was always a peculiar fellow that *friend* of yours," Hanna said.

"He wants more," Konrad said.

"More?"

"*We* are to go to the Air Ministry tonight, that's you and me, Hanna. Göring's hosting a dinner, I think he wants to impress Himmler, Kessler says we —"

"What fun," Hanna interrupted, coating it thick with sarcasm.

Konrad shook his head smartly, glowered, and said: "All you need do is pretend, many are doing far more."

"I cannot. You know I'm still unwell."

"We have to do our duty in the best way we can Hanna ... All of us ... It is time you remembered that. It could all be so much worse, without my position —"

"Your position?" she let out a little snigger. "The Reich has more heroes than it knows what to do with now Konrad, what can you possibly offer?" He looked hurt, and she found she was glad it had stung him.

"The old days, before this – there is still power there, connections I have made. Kessler says —"

"That's shit."

"Look Hanna," Konrad snapped, "all I am saying is that we must get on with our lives. I have built something good for us here, now you must help me." He paced to the window and stared out for a moment, kneading his hands behind his back. She knew what must come next.

"It's time you let go Hanna."

"Like you have?"

"Yes, sometimes it's the only way."

"Yet you have not slept with me for two years, not touched me, not —"

"This is *not* the time!"

"What are you afraid of, Konrad?"

"I am not afraid."

"Yes you are, you have always been afraid."

Suddenly he spun round, his face bulging with anger.

"I will not have you talk to me like that Hanna – I will not!" Hanna found she was strangely amused by the show of temper and she allowed herself to sink deeper into the embrace of the armchair. Konrad composed himself, pacing again, and – she realised with mild surprise – shaking. Not for the first time she wondered what he was really scared of. Failure, fighting, maybe even Kessler? For long moments the room was silent but for the ticking of a clock, even this had a swastika on it, for this room was often used for entertaining – ideal for that, with its over-done Nazi art of nymphs and knights that neither of them ever looked at.

"Have you heard from Sepp?" he said suddenly, catching her unawares.

"No, I haven't, not for a while. I don't even know where he is. There are rumours, of course —"

"But we shouldn't listen to rumour Hanna dear, nor to idle gossip – should we?" his tone was mocking now. "Now if I listened to gossip, where would we be?"

"Better informed, perhaps?"

"Yes, better informed. I might think that my wife is out of here the second my back is turned, even though she is too ill to do the smallest thing for her husband, her country."

"And you would believe *that* gossip?" She shook her head, sneered.

Konrad shrugged: "Look Hanna, all I am saying is that we must all do our best. Think of Sepp, should he worry that you are so sick all the time. Don't you think he will have enough on his mind?"

"Sepp would understand," she murmured.

"Yes? I've been meaning to write to him, you know ..." He trailed off, watching her as the veiled threat sank in. She knew Sepp would always believe what Konrad told him, always had.

"There's no need," she said, quietly.

"Good. Why don't you pop into town, see what dresses they have at the Kaiser Gallery, it's always good to make an impression with these people."

*

227

"Land!"

Sepp just about heard the shout of the co-pilot, far forward in the aircraft, over the buzz of the metal fuselage and the roar of the engines. The last line of the paratrooper song had long since died and each and every one of them had been left with his thoughts. Some of them looked tired. It had been a long day already, with little sleep the night before. When the first of the Ju 52s had returned from the Maleme drop many of them had trailed long banners of thick black smoke, others bore the pockmarks of battle, and two of them landed on their bellies as their damaged undercarriages collapsed on hitting the ground. It had sobered his men, this glimpse of reality before the off, but part of him was glad of that. For there is no greater shock in war than the paratrooper's first taste of battle. In just a few hours the paratrooper goes from the safety of his home base to the thick of the fighting, more often than not behind the enemy lines. It would do them good to be prepared for that little shake up.

In the heat of the morning they had stripped down to shorts and helped with the refuelling of the Ju 52s. The dust had been terrible and by the time they had climbed back into their jump uniforms – dripping in sweat as soon as fabric touched skin – there was just too much of it in the air to allow the planes to take off together. So now they attacked in a long extended line, running late, to be dropped piecemeal over their target.

Sepp turned in his tight seat to get a better view of the island through one of the Perspex panel windows that ran the length of the fuselage. Crete loomed large from the sea, mostly mountains glowing near purple in the lowering sun, some with slender smears of greying snow at their summits. His soldier's eye thought of that high ground and the hills and slopes rising to it, and then the narrow coastal strip on which the paratroopers would have to drop. Intelligence had played down the enemy's strength, but he preferred to trust the evidence of his eyes rather than the back room boys of the Luftwaffe. They were closer to the island now and the plane was put into a shallow bank to the right to follow the coast. His squad fidgeted nervously with the hooks of their cords, one shifted the beads of a length of rifle-pull through fingers and thumb, a rosary for remembered religion. Others mumbled to themselves, their lips hardly moving, just seeming to quiver to the reverberation of the engines. Lick tried to make shouted conversation, a joke about Greek girls, but no one listened.

The paratroopers sat opposite each other on canvas seats, six either side down the length of the aeroplane, a roof gunner towards the rear their only defence against Tommy fighters. Most stared at invisible spots on the Duralumin corrugations of the inside of the fuselage, better that than meet the eyes of a comrade now. Better that than give your thoughts away. Sepp though, looked each one in the face, trying to gauge those who would need his help in the fire-fight to come, and those he could rely on beyond all doubt. The Ju 52 skirted the very edge of the island at less than 150 metres, a lumbering steel bird, good for little more than 200km/h fully loaded, and seeming to be going much slower than that now. The roadside was ablaze with violently pink and yellow flowering shrubs, and every so often dense mats of red poppies would appear in fields like bright rashes on the earth. Sometimes they would fly over a little fishing village, where brightly painted boats sat in the clear water as if encased in green jelly. Once or twice the odd shot clanged against the fuselage, but Sepp thought they would be lucky indeed if that were the end of it.

The dispatcher moved up from the cockpit, a Luftwaffe forage cap set jauntily to the side of his head, the worried look of a man who has seen what lay before them fixed to his face. Sepp hoped he would keep it to himself.

*

It felt good to be in the familiar rubbery smelling cockpit of a Hurricane, and it felt even better to have something more potent than a pistol to fight with. West worked the primer pump five or six times then switched on the main and starting magnetos. The starter churned and the propeller stirred lazily, kicked a little to a whine from the engine, spun again, then once more, then stuttered, then whipped into life with a harsh crackle, individual blades blurring into a silvery disc in front of West's eyes. He turned the fuel distributor cock to main tank and then let the engine warm up. A little while later, once the oil pressure was at sixty, the erks pulled the chocks from the wheels and West let the Hurricane roll out from under the camouflage netting and on to the airstrip. He set the mixture to rich, and waved to the lads, they had done a magnificent job in repairing the kite as the battle had raged on around them throughout the day. Now it was his turn.

West booted the rudder bar and squeezed the wheel brake, turning the plane in the direction of the sea. Some of the German paratroopers at the far end of the airstrip spotted him and bullets raised puffs of dust around the Hurricane, but most of the rounds were robbed of their zip thanks to the extreme range. He opened the hand throttle and felt an instant thrill to the familiar snarl of the 27-litre V12 Rolls Royce Merlin engine. The Hurricane gathered speed along the strip, West urging it on, aching to feel the weight of flight against his controls, scanning the sky above him, because during take-off a fighter is always vulnerable. There was a sudden bump, the undercarriage had hit something that West could not see because of the plane's nose-up attitude, and the tail of the plane hopped into the air a little, then dropped. West glanced in his mirror to see that he had gouged a groove in the corpse of a paratrooper with one of the wheels. He read off the air speed indicator, seventy miles per hour, and then he firmly pushed the control column forward to bring the tail up, centred it again, and then pulled it back when the ASI showed *80* ... Then there was that familiar weightlessness at the base of his belly as the aircraft took flight.

Once airborne he set the prop from fine to coarse pitch, and then banked steeply to the right, his wing tip all but dipping into the sea. West did the fiddly stuff when he was clear of the land, his right hand off the control column spade grip as he worked the levers to pull up the undercarriage, the plane dipping and twisting a little as he controlled it with his left hand. Once his right hand was back on the control column, he pulled and snapped the hood shut, switched on the reflector gun-sight, its glowing red dot within a circle projected onto a glass panel in front of the windscreen. Then he turned the gun button on to *fire*.

Looking through the crazed Perspex of the hood his horizon was full of tall obelisks of black smoke from the shoulder of the Akrotiri Peninsula, and he guessed the German bombers had feasted on Canea. West banked the Hurricane to the left and pulled it round in a long loop that put the box girder iron bridge in his sights. He came in very low and fast, picking out groups of troops on the beach first, a quick three-second burst scattering them and leaving two parallel lines of sand plumes along the shoreline. The smell of the cordite snatched at his nostrils as the plane rattled around him, its nose dipping as it slowed slightly to the recoil of the eight Browning machine guns in the wings. He passed low over the bridge, racing the shadow of the aircraft on the stony white riverbed, and before he knew it he was past the hill and out the other side of the battlefield, climbing hard, using plenty of right rudder to counteract the torque of the engine, feeling the sting of the effort where his false leg jarred tight against his stump. He heard a stray shot rip through the stiffened fabric skin of the fuselage and then strike the armour plate behind his seat with a dull ping.

West decided he'd probably be of more help to those on the ground if he could take out some of the Junkers transports with the paratroopers still on board, rather than hose the men already on the deck, which would more than likely simply keep their heads down. So with this in mind he looped around to find the coast road close to the village of Pirgos near the eastern end of the aerodrome, and then flew out to sea to gain height, always a too-slow process in a Hurricane.

As he climbed the cockpit grew steadily colder and he was glad that he had left his kit with the plane and not in the tent. He searched the sky with the fighter pilot's scan as he had been trained to do, always turning and pivoting his head, eyes never still, never allowing himself to focus on a point in the blue, always searching, always hunting. He was at 12,000ft, turning and heading back over the battlefield, when he saw the Stukas, about 1000ft below him: "Well, now there's a nice surprise," he said to himself, and he pushed the throttle to its stop and the boost to maximum, so as to close the gap as quickly as possible.

The dive-bombers were peeling off to attack the men dug in on Kavkazia Hill by the time West had closed in. The leading planes were just starting their bombing run, a near vertical dive, dive-brakes extended, nose mounted sirens screaming, the oil stains beneath their crooked wings glinting in the sunlight. He chose a Stuka that still had its eggs, letting the sharply creased wings with their bold black crosses drift into the outer circle of his glowing reflector sight, touching left rudder to bring the nose into line with it. West thumbed the firing button on the spade grip and suddenly the Hurricane slowed a little to the harsh, juddering recoil of the guns, the wings shuddering while the shoulder straps of his harness seemed to grip him tighter in that moment of deceleration. The eight guns in his wings were harmonised for 250 yards, and the long white lines of bullets converged on the elongated Plexiglas cockpit cowling of the Stuka, shattering it into crystal and fire as West flashed by his target, before turning tight and watching as the shark-like Stuka spun off a cotton length of white coolant, then black oil smoke, before turning on its back and sliding out of the sky.

West instantly looked for another target, but by now the other Stukas had scattered across the sky and he was met with a lattice of burning red tracer. He ignored the return fire and chose his next victim carefully, intersecting its flight-path and aiming to hit it with a deflection shot, keeping his thumb off the fire button, flying through the tracer from the Stuka's rear gunner – pulsing slowly at first, then zapping past his canopy – and then firing a burst at the piece of sky the plane was about to occupy. He watched as its bomb-load burst beneath the Stuka, and then flew the Hurricane through the fireball that rose above it, before turning hard so that the blood rushed from his head and he trod the grey edge of blacking out. He glanced to his right. All that was left of the Stuka was a disconnected cloud of smoke and a hole in the sky where the plane had once been.

Most of the other Stukas were fleeing out to sea now, one diving away close by. West put the Hurricane in a dive and followed it, feeling the controls grow heavier with the force of the fast air on the surfaces, watching the altimeter unwind like a demented clock. But his speed was too great, the advantage of the Stuka – its very essence – was its slow dive, and West hurtled past at 370mph, never getting the chance to loose off a shot. He pulled out of the dive at about 2000ft, then spotted another of the Stukas as it was coming out of its bombing run about 1000ft above the explosion it had caused. This was an automatic process – because of the risk of the pilot blacking out – and the plane flew itself for some long seconds before its pilot regained control and banked away from West's attack. He put the Hurricane into a half roll and dived at the Stuka, allowing the glowing red dot at the centre of his sight to fix itself onto its ugly snout and the blurring silver coin of the prop in front of it. He fired again, hosing the plane with deft little nudges on his rudder bar, until a piece of metal detached itself from the engine cowling of the Stuka and tumbled into the sky. He kept his thumb hard on the firing button, watching the dancing yellow hits of his bullets on the other plane, but then the guns fell silent.

His fourteen precious seconds of ammunition were at an end and the Stuka would escape. But he had downed two of the buggers, and as he pulled out of the attack and banked out towards the sea he wondered if Potter or the CO had been watching this damned fine show. It was then that he realised that he had lost a lot of height in the fight, and had drifted over the main German positions …

Suddenly West seemed to be flying through a solid mesh of ground fire. He heard the bullets ripping through the fuselage, splintering the wooden formers, and then his view was obliterated as the front of his canopy was covered in oil, while thick black smoke started to pour into the cockpit. Instinctively he pulled up on the controls and gained as much height as he could as the engine faltered. He wrenched open the canopy to clear the choking fumes, and to his left he saw Kavkazia Hill with its shroud of gun smoke and bright pinpricks of fire. The Hurricane climbed a little higher, the engine stuttering. Suddenly the Merlin cut completely and the sound of the rattling prop and the sky rushing past his cockpit, like the beat of the wind against a sail, was the only thing to be heard. Then the flames burst through the bulkhead.

West pulled the pin out of the harness that attached him to his seat and he rolled the aircraft on to its back, at the very next instant kicking out at the control column so that the Hurricane's now inverted nose pointed skywards. He fell from the cockpit like a stone, there was the blur of the passing tail-plane inches from his face and then the rush of the air stinging his skin – but much better that than the fire. He fell headlong for some seconds then pulled at the ripcord at his chest, the canopy cracking open above him, violently tugging his body straight.

It seemed quiet now, seconds later, as he hung in the sky. He turned his head in time to see the blazing Hurricane crash into a hillside, sending a pillar of stones and dust into the air, and then exploding with a whoosh followed instantly by a hollow crump. West felt the wash of the blast across his face, and turned away. He drifted over another valley, losing height all the time. There was a scatter of people waiting below, but the chute was swaying too much for him to make out whether they were civilian or military, friend or foe.

*

"Prepare and hook up," the abstezer shouted above the turmoil of the aircraft.

Sepp nodded, and as a man the squad stood, opening the clips on the karabiner type hooks and closing them over the anchor cable which ran the length of the aeroplane. Sepp did the same, then checked the hook of the paratrooper next to him. The door was opened to a rush of wind that shook the sides of the plane. As squad leader he would be the first to go. The Ju 52 flew by the headland and towards the drop zone, the pilot banking slightly inland as Sepp pulled on his goggles and got into his hunched jump position, his feet wide apart on the door ledge, his hands gripping the two vertical rails either side of the small doorway. The correct stance was vital, get it wrong and you could snag your pack on the doorframe or jump in the wrong body shape, which would send you spinning out of control, tangling the chute. Sepp looked past the wing just in time to see the plane in front hit by flak. It instantly heeled over into its death dive, dragging a long thick pennant of oil smoke out to sea. Two of the paratroopers jumped clear, floating slowly into the bright water, where Sepp knew that their wet chutes would drag them under, drown them.

All around his aircraft the sky was smudged with exploding anti-aircraft shells and Sepp realised that the enemy was firing out of the terraced vineyards on the hillsides, almost level with the plane. All of a sudden small arms fire clanged against the fuselage and pierced it with bright lances of light that had the paratroopers inside crouching low. Sepp made an effort to keep his shape in the doorway – his body more coiled than bent and his head out in the air-stream – an effort to show no fear, and an effort to wait until he could clearly see the light brown stripe of the airfield at Rethymnon before jumping. The slipstream tugged at the belts of his harness and he could smell the exhaust fumes of the engine. A burst of flak rocked the plane, then another, and a continuous volley of shots rang off the flank of the fuselage like hail on a tin roof.

"Jump!" yelled the dispatcher, flicking the switch for the green light and sounding the klaxon. They could barely hear him or the siren over the hammering of the shots against the plane, but Sepp glanced back and spotted the glow of the green light as a bullet whistled past his head.

"It's not time, we're short of the airfield!" Sepp shouted. Two more dirty grey bursts of flak bracketed the aircraft and it yawed violently from right to left, so that Sepp had to jam his feet against the sides of the doorway and grip the hand rails tighter, to stop from falling clear too early.

Then they were hit. A burst of flak caught the middle of the three engines, on the nose of the plane. Hot oil instantly whipped down the side of the fuselage and splashed across Sepp's smock and harness. Suddenly the plane banked to the left, inland. Now there was no time for argument, and Sepp appraised the situation in an accelerated heartbeat and then dived head first, immediately taking the spread-eagled star position. He dropped like a brick for a second until the slack of the nine-metre static line was taken up and the chute was pulled from its pack with a back-jarring snap, pulling him straight.

Sepp just had time to register the cracking and billowing noise of the unfurling chute before he heard the explosion. The force of it shook the dark green silk of his parachute, and a few seconds later a burning meteor of a man plunged past him trailing a cord of flames. The chute was connected to Sepp behind his shoulders, so although his arms were free he hung like a piece of meat swinging off a butcher's hook, and the only way he could get any kind of directional control was to flap his arms, just as he had been trained to do. This helped twist his pendulous body to the left, so that he was facing downwind for his landing. With a turn of his head he was able to catch sight of two others, drifting close by. Then the bullets started to hit. *My God, they are shooting at us as we fall … So this is how Tommy fights his war …*

A parachutist falls fast, at about six metres a second. It's fast enough to sprain your ankles on landing, even break a leg. But it's never *fast enough* in combat, and in this heat they seemed to float in the bullet laced sky for an age. Sepp's chute took two hits, and then a long line of machine gun fire tore past his legs with a string of staccato *phutts*. His descent seemed to speed up and he looked up to see that three of the billowing panels in the umbrella of his canopy had been all but shot away. The ground rushed towards him like a slap, he was speeding towards an olive grove, black-green leaves shining like oil in the low sun, the smell of the hot, dry earth flooding through his nostrils. More shots zipped by, but then he was in the tree, crashing through it like a man jumping into a green pool.

He kept his legs straight and close together and smashed through the upper branches hearing them splinter and crackle as he went, hitting the ground just as the parachute ripped itself into long and thick ribbons behind him. No time to think, instinct and training takes over now. The gravity knife from its specially designed, easy to reach, trouser pocket, is cutting the cords above him, quicker than struggling with the four buckles. He hears the crash of other paratroopers close by, three at least. Sepp pulls off his smock and takes the equipment from beneath it before putting it back on and draping it with his bandolier and re-buckling the belt with its pistol holster. Then he un-holsters his Sauer automatic and darts for the first available piece of cover. He hears a shout in the near distance, it's Lick, and he rushes to join him, hunched over to keep a low silhouette. His friend is trapped in a tree and he helps to cut him free with his gravity knife.

Minutes later three more paratroopers came crashing through the low branches of the grove, the dry grass crackling beneath their jump boots. It was Erich, Otto and Sigi. They were not so much younger than Sepp, Erich older, but at that moment, when he saw their faces, he felt as if they were children. He wondered if others had thought the same of him back in Holland.

"You all okay?"

"Scratches, and Sigi's been hit in the hand," Erich said, in a strange high pitch that at any other time would be funny, "they were shooting at us as we fell, it was murder!"

"They got the plane," Sigi said, "everyone … Hugo burning —"

"Quiet, both of you!" Sepp snapped. He could see that they were shocked, nobody expected to be shot on the way down, they had been told that it was against the rules of war. But maybe Tommy made his own rules. So be it …

There was gunfire to the east, plenty of it, and more from the west, and Sepp guessed they had landed too far inland. Beyond the olive grove there was a large bamboo break, with a dirt track leading down to the main Heraklion-Rethymnon-Canea road, and beyond the road there was the airfield and the sea. From the high ground above and to the south of them Sepp could see the muzzle flashes of the ack-ack guns the enemy had hidden so well.

A group of four Ju 52s passed overhead, spilling their cargo out into the sky. Little blots fell from the planes, trailing cotton behind them before bursting into mushrooms of brown, green, red and white. The air was soon thick with parachutists and canisters – and bullets. They watched in silent horror as a stick of Fallschirmjäger crumpled dead onto the scorched earth, covered with the instant funeral shrouds of their drab chutes. They saw another group of paratroopers drift into the crossfire of two heavy machine guns. There was nothing they could do. Sepp picked out one of them, suspended like a bullied boy on a coat peg, no weapon, and no chance, a helpless marionette dancing on the crest of a British foresight. The machine guns rattled and cut the men and the parachutes to shreds, each paratrooper dying in a mad puppet convulsion like a hanged man kicking out at the gallows drop.

Three more of their comrades drifted towards the bamboo break. The bamboo rose to six metres and more, capped with swaying brushes of lush green leaves. Two of the men were already dead as they landed amidst the bamboo, the long shafts spearing them through like meat on a kebab. The third could do nothing to avoid the break, despite flapping his arms in an attempt to change the direction of the drifting chute, and Sepp knew the scream as a shaft of bamboo impaled him from arse to shoulder would live with his men forever. But he could not let them dwell on it now. He noticed a pillar of red smoke – the canisters set off smoke charges on landing – beyond the bamboo break. "Come on, let's get ourselves some real weapons lads; then we'll show those Tommy murderers a thing or two."

*

Konrad's boots clipped coldly down the long marble-tiled corridor at the heart of Berlin's vast Reich Air Ministry building. Hanna's heels did the same but although she could match his stride she made a point of making sure she was slightly out of step with her husband. Luftwaffe guards snapped nosily to attention as they passed them: blue-grey uniforms spotless, helmets shining, white gloves, rifles and jackboots gleaming in the bright electric light.

"Inge is not so very good you know, Konrad. I am always finding dust that she's overlooked."

"That surprises me my dear, it is not like her to miss a thing."

"So you have said ... But I could do better myself."

"It is not your place. Besides, we are lucky to have her." Another of the guards crashed to attention as they passed. "Forget about Inge. It is time we enjoyed ourselves," Konrad said. "Now you are better."

"I will never be better, Konrad. I am not like you."

They were close to the large doorway into the Hall of Honour by now and Konrad suddenly pulled up, the sole of his boot squeaking against the polished floor. He pulled her arm tight, so that the soft bare flesh above her elbow pinched painfully.

"It was not just bad for you," he whispered, eyes darting from her to the Luftwaffe guards either side of the corridor.

"Ah Konrad, and the lovely Hanna, too; we are honoured," It was Kessler, walking behind them. She wondered how much he had heard.

"Anton ..." Konrad started, almost stammering, letting go of her arm and reaching out to shake Kessler's hand in a heartbeat. Hanna was surprised by the reaction, by the worry flickering in Konrad's eyes. Kessler, wearing the uniform of the SS as he had since the beginning of the war, had her husband exactly where he wanted, she could see. Kessler was in control.

"So, we are well again, Hanna?"

"She is well thank you, Anton." Kessler reached out for Hanna's hand, but she walked on and was into the Hall of Honour before he could kiss it.

"That was rude," Konrad whispered, as Kessler turned to greet someone else.

"He's a snake," she replied, just a little louder. She remembered well the time Kessler had tried it on, and then felt the rake of her nails on his cheek. He had never spoken of that since, and neither had she. But she would never forget the threat: *One day, bitch … One day.*

Kessler finished greeting his acquaintance and walked in after them, glancing at Hanna and smiling his thin smile while she tried very hard not to show she was impressed with the Hall of Honour. Like the building itself, which was said to be the biggest in Europe boasting seven kilometres of corridors, the hall was immense. At one end a huge Nazi eagle, set into the wall with its wings spread, dominated the space, and an entire wall of house-tall windows separated by sturdy square columns ran down one side, letting in the spring light which splashed deep reflections onto the cream and black travertine marble floor. It was an enormous space, but cold and without soul, the sort of room where laughter seems insignificant, drifts away, as if it evaporates.

There had to be 300 people there, at least, but the size of the hall made it seem a thin gathering. There were small knots of field grey, green, black and blue uniformed officers, wreathed in thick cigarette smoke, basking in their long string of victories; groups of wives swapping chit-chat in an archipelago of bright colours; and waiters in white waistcoats balancing silver trays of golden drinks on outstretched fingers, floating across the shimmering marble between the little groups of people, spinning like dancers to offer champagne.

Some of the men stared at her. She was not surprised, for she had done exactly what Konrad had told her to do, she had made an effort: a Lucien Lelong sleeveless satin dress in a blue which matched her eyes. It was just in from Paris – the only worthwhile things to be had in Berlin were from the occupied city – and its hem brushed the marble, while it was sheer enough to cling to her every curve. Konrad handed her a glass of champagne.

"New perfume, Hanna?" Kessler asked, sniffing at the air, it was sort of thing he always noticed.

"No, not new," she lied. The idea of Kessler knowing just how she smelt turned her stomach, and she instantly vowed never to wear the *Houbigant Chantilly*, which she had bought just that day, ever again.

"Have you considered my idea, Konrad?" Kessler said.

"I'm sorry Anton, but I cannot fly again, you know that. I'm old now, and my injuries from racing, they are —"

"I understand, there is no need to explain to me," Kessler said, a knowing smirk creasing his face. "But we will have to find some other outlet for your talents soon, it is not enough to live off past glories." He laughed out loud at that, a girlish laugh that seemed absurdly at odds with his field grey SS uniform. Hanna knew he was teasing

Konrad, enjoying showing the power he had over him in front of her.

Just then the smile slipped from Kessler's lips and Hanna was surprised to notice that a little bead of sweat instantly dotted the pale expanse of his forehead.

"Here he is," Konrad said.

Without any orders the officers and the wives lined the length of the hall to receive the guest of honour. Heinrich Himmler spoke to few of them, but he stopped for Hanna. Birdlike eyes trapped behind thick spectacle lenses flicked from her to Konrad and back again. There was something of the schoolmaster about the man, she always thought, but there was nothing of the master race.

"It has been a long time, it is good to see you again, Frau Plaidt."

"It is a pleasure to see you again, also, Herr Reichsführer," she said.

"Very good," Konrad whispered to her after Himmler had passed by and had gone on to greet Göring.

Once the formalities had finished Hanna found herself alone for a moment, while Konrad spoke to Werner Molders, the fighter ace. She'd hoped she might catch the eye of a fighter pilot herself, but it was Emmy Göring who eventually came to her. She was close to fifty, close to fat, too, but in a wholesome, Nazi, sort of way. She played her part well, but Hanna reminded herself Emmy was an actress of note.

"It is nice to see you, Hanna, how are you?"

"I am well, Frau Göring," were the words that came out. The words that remained unsaid and inside – in protective custody – were: *I am living in a hell on earth.*

"Your husband looks so handsome; you really make the most wonderful couple."

"Thank you Frau Göring." *But he does not touch me, he is afraid it will happen again. I have to take the matter into my own hands, put myself into the hands of others, for warmth, and for a chance that there might still be a baby. What will he say then? He will say nothing, because he is afraid.*

"Oh, but I forgot; you've not been well?"

"I am much better now." *Who is sick now anyway? I feign it so I do not have to meet people like you. This is where the real sickness is* – as she thought that the words from that cruel and short dream came to her. It was the dream she had had on that terrible day in Zwickau, the dream which she had had a thousand times since, a single conversation, between two men, words muted, for even in the dream they were heard through the fog of drugs, or a door ajar, she was never quite sure which.

The termination, is it completed?

It is finished.

Any problems?

No, the process is quite simple.

Do you question it?
No, it is like cutting out a cancer.
The remains?
Incinerated.

But a dream is only a dream. Sepp had promised her that it was only a dream. A drug-fuelled nightmare; and she knew it could not possibly be anything but a dream ... And yet ...

"Are you alright, Hanna?"

"Yes, fine."

"Good," Emmy said, looking for an escape now, as if the gaseous words from the dream had somehow seeped out of Hanna's head. "And it's very good of you to come."

Hanna nodded, smiled. *But I would rather be in the apartment, listening to the forbidden English radio, hoping to find out where my Sepp is ...*

"Oh, but please excuse me, Hanna – there is Erhard."

Emmy went. She had not asked Hanna why she stayed with Konrad, she would not ask that, of course. And Hanna did not know the answer anyway. For comfort? Perhaps. He could get the things others could not, clothes and food, important things. But not quite as important as the respect of the brother who never wrote now, of the little family that was fading from her memory like names written into the condensation of a clouded basement kitchen window, slowly fogging to nothing. Erhard Milch kissed Frau Göring's hand, and Hanna plucked a glass of champagne off a silver tray that floated by.

The next hour passed slowly and her cheekbones began to ache from the insincere smiling, while the inside of her head seemed to soften as if saturated with the welcomingly mind-numbing champagne. She wondered how many others here wore their masks of nylon smiles and she suddenly ached for escape, for a bar, for the grateful arms of a combat soldier. There was the smell of rich cooked food from a nearby dining room. It helped distract her from the lemony, leathery, sandalwood smell of her perfume, the scent which she now hated. Through the tall windows she could see that the sunlight was beginning to fade and the high and bright lights of the hall were now casting their own deep reflections. Like every other dusk, she thought of Sepp, and of where he might be watching the sun go down.

The huge blackout curtains, like velvet sails from a night-dark ship, were closed as she watched, and she was still thinking of her brother when she noticed there was a change in the atmosphere. It was a murmur, passing through the small groups of senior officers like the sough of a breeze in the trees. Some of those in the light blue-grey dress uniforms of the Luftwaffe and the field grey of the OKW were seen making their excuses and rushing off out of the hall through different doorways, escaping down the long corridors. Konrad left her side to ask other officers what was happening.

He came back minutes later, looking confused, corrugating his brow in obvious frustration.

"Something's gone wrong," he said.

"What is it?"

"No one will say, damn them."

She felt someone's breath on the back of her neck.

"It seems," Kessler said suddenly, causing Hanna to jump and turn to face him, "that we may well have bitten off a bit more than we can chew this time."

"Where?"

Sepp's face suddenly filled her inner vision – little boy Sepp, not soldier Sepp.

"No one's saying where," Kessler said, blinking rapidly. "But my guess is that it's hell."

***

Taking up parachuting in the middle of an airborne invasion, now that's what they used to call Westbury Holt luck. It was a crowded sky and the Cretan villagers had mistaken him for a paratrooper and had been ready to hang him from the nearest tree – it had been a *real* German paratrooper that had saved him. The German patrol had left three dead Cretans, and the distinct impression that they had no time for civilians bearing arms. Then they had led their prisoner away.

The Germans had captured the prison in the valley at Agya, a low white structure West had seen many times from the air, which they now used as a base, and to which West had been escorted. The morning after his capture he was placed in a quite large cell with a cold stone floor, decorated with the swirls of Greek graffiti. Two Cretans were sitting sullenly in the corner. The sun had climbed high enough to throw the shadow of the window bars across the floor. The sound of the battle seemed to grow, while German shouts and slamming doors echoed through the corridors of the prison. There was a distinct tang of urine in the air. He felt useless – trapped and useless. There was a rough slot in the thick wooden door and through it West could see into the crowded corridor, where the paratroopers tended their weapons and wounds. Just when he thought things could not get any worse he caught a whiff of cigarette smoke. He patted the pockets of his trousers, but there was nothing, his pipe had gone.

"Bugger it all!" West snapped.

One of the Cretans looked up at him, seemed to understand and nodded, a huge diamond bright tear swelling at the corner of his eye.

That morning was spent trying to talk to the Cretans, watching the shadows cross the floor, and listening to the sounds of the battle and the conversation of the paratroopers when he could. Desperate thoughts of escape entered his head, and as the hours passed he would swear that the cell shrank, its walls seeming to close in around him. At other times he would remember that first German he had killed face to face, and each time the face would morph into that of Sepp's. He wondered if he was on the island, if he was still alive, and then he would find himself thinking of that day at Donington, when the boy's dream had been crushed. How similar that other German's expression had been, all hope lost.

Towards the end of the longest day of West's life the lock in the door rattled and it swung fully open to a creak of old iron hinges. More prisoners, three dejected looking New Zealanders and an artillery corporal. The corporal looked West up and down, noting the wool-lined leather Irvin flying jacket he used as a seat, shook his head with a wry snigger, and said: "Rare As bloody Fairies."

West just smiled, all the RAF lads were used to the jibes by now, had been since the retreat through Greece. Besides, he was just glad that there was someone to talk to. The paratroopers who escorted the prisoners were coated in dust, their faces and uniforms the same dark grey, and West wondered again how the fight went.

"I know you," one of the guards, a slim man with a freshly broken nose and a patch of bandage over one eye, suddenly said, in German.

"Me?"

"Yes, I have it. You are the English racing driver, I saw you once at the Freiburg hill-climb – I'd recognise that ridiculous sweater anywhere."

"Famous racing driver are we? Then we are honoured: Prison Valley, where the stars come to fight," said another paratrooper, an NCO of some kind.

"How is Schmeling?"

"Broke an ankle on landing," said a third paratrooper.

"Shit himself I heard," said the first, to a roar of laughter from the others – West guessed they were talking about the famous boxer, who he supposed must have signed up as a paratrooper.

"You know, we have some Auto Union men in the Fallschirmjäger," the first paratrooper said, now quite enthusiastic.

"Sepp Nagel?"

"Ah! You know Sepp, a good soldier, I was with him in Holland; just the man for a tight spot – and God knows, this is as tight as a nun's snatch."

"He's here?"

"No, he's with the Second, landed down the coast at —"

"Foerster!"

"Sorry Sergeant," the paratrooper said.

"Look," West said. "I understand, but if you bump into him wish him well from me. He saved my life, you know."

"From what I hear saving your life is becoming the number one German pastime," the sergeant said with a sneer.

"I'd appreciate the opportunity to thank him, I never had the chance."

"That would be unlikely," said the sergeant, "the way things are going … But enough of this." He turned and left the cell.

"If I see him I'll tell him you're here," said the first paratrooper as he rushed out behind the sergeant, pulling the heavy door behind him.

"Thank you, there's something else I need to tell him, too, and I think he will be glad to hear it …" the door slammed shut with an echoing boom, "… if it's not too late."

***

West hadn't counted the days. It would have driven him mad. Time just passed as a shadow crossing the floor and climbing the walls, and with the arrival of more prisoners, many more, until the NCOs, erks, privates and the Cretans were turfed out, and this larger cell became an officers-only sort of place, a bit like a London club with its familiar accents, but without the brandy, the cigar smoke and the leather armchairs. He talked cricket with a beached naval officer from Sussex, and rugby with a lieutenant from Auckland. But very soon even this exclusive club began to get a little overcrowded. They were allowed out for an hour or so every day, but that was it, for there were not the soldiers to spare to watch over them, and there were now far too many prisoners, both original inmates and recent POWs. The prison was bursting at the seams.

Each new member to the club had to pass the initiation of news: which meant that each new member was a little less welcome. They heard of the fall of Maleme, how in the fog of the battle the troops had pulled off the hill and gifted the Germans with the aerodrome. They heard how the Luftwaffe had piled its planes onto the strip and the beach, crashing them into a heap of twisted metal in their desperation to get soldiers on the ground. They heard of the long line of British soldiers that was passing through the mountains trying to reach Sphakia on the south coast, where the Royal Navy was saving the army's neck yet again. They heard how the

Stukas had flattened Canea. How the airfields at Heraklion and Rethymnon had held on, how close a damned thing this one had been ... Then they heard how they had lost the battle. Lost the island.

They all sat on the floor now, as there was little room to do anything else, certainly not the room to pace. West felt the crush of the place like an anvil on his chest. The sweat of men was heavy on the stale air, only masked when a miserable Pay Corps officer succumbed to his dysentery. Everyone turned away, made small talk. Gentlemen's club.

"Where do you think they will send us?" asked a nervous infantry captain.

"Germany," the naval officer, a lieutenant-commander named Charlie, said.

"Italy," put in a lieutenant of the Welch.

"I should think they will probably shoot us," said a taciturn tank man, who had had one of the few Matilda 1 tanks on the island 'brew up' under him, his crew burning with it. It was the first thing he had said since arriving, and it hushed the room. There was a nervous cough or two; the club etiquette had definitely been breached.

"What rot!" Charlie said, pushing his white-topped cap to the back of his head.

"Believe it," the tank man said, his voice heavy with bitterness, the fresh and bright crescent-shaped scar on his cheek twisting to his sneer. "Haven't you heard what they did at Maleme, and at the field hospital?" Some nodded sullenly, gossip travels as fast as the bullets in a battle zone. "Human shields ... And I heard they shot a bunch of Fleet Air Arm types in cold blood just because they were in shirtsleeves and they took them for fighting civilians. As if that makes it all right ... Bastards."

"Is that true West, you were at Maleme?" Charlie asked.

"Not for long I'm afraid. But I have to say it sounds a bit rich."

"I have it on good authority," said the tank officer.

"But you didn't *see it* did you. Seems to me you should judge these things on what you see, otherwise we'll be left with all that silly nonsense about them using nuns as bell clappers and eating babies we had in the last show, don't you think?"

"And just what have you seen then fly boy?"

"I've seen them fight, and fight very bravely."

It was all the tank man needed to push him over the edge. He made to stand, his fists bunched, but with a gentle shove from Charlie he was on the floor again, dragged back into the swamp of crossed and crossing limbs. Some of those around him laughed and lightened the mood and then Charlie made his way across the room towards West, making his apologies as he trod on arms and legs on the way.

"I say West, a word?"

"Shoot."

"Your German's good, I've heard?" he whispered.

"It's all right, I suppose."

"It could come in useful … In an escape perhaps?"

"Count me in old man … Count. Me. In."

*

They sat at rough old wooden tables outside the taverna. Lick, remarkably but not surprisingly, had found a crate of beer and the sun felt good on Sepp's face as he allowed himself one, tipping it down his throat, washing away the dust of more than a week of constant battle. So then, the victor … But he hardly felt it. At their back the façade of the taverna was pockmarked with bullet holes and the ground was covered in tiny crystals of broken glass that sparkled in the sunlight and crunched under the wheels of the trucks. The village of Stavromenos sat on the main coast road, just where it started to curl inland around the hill the Australians had held so tenaciously on that first night of fighting. The village had once had an olive oil factory, but now it was a bullet-ridden husk of a building surrounded by the dead – Germans, Greeks and Australians. The Fallshirmjäger had held the factory, and won the battle.

The long line of military vehicles rumbled slowly past them, captured British trucks in the main, many with swastika flags stretched over their bonnets to show the Luftwaffe they were friendly. Lick took great pleasure in holding his bottle high, then drinking to the health of those who passed by on the trucks, before finishing his liquid salute with a gloating belch. The wide brimmed Australian slouch hat he had captured was now decorated with startling yellow and red flowers, their stalks shoved into its dark green band. Some of the trucks were piled high with wounded from the battles to the west, Alpine troops and paratroopers, all exchanging insults with Lick.

"Look at you; you're like an Italian general reviewing his army."

"Ah, Sepp, but my boys have done well – you would think that those shits would smarten themselves up for the olive oil heroes, wouldn't you?"

Suddenly a motorcycle with a sidecar came to a halt just after it had passed the taverna, the skidding tyres lifting a plume of dust from the roadside. A paratrooper jumped out of the sidecar and ran back to them. He wore an eye patch made from a field dressing, his nose was obviously broken, and he looked a hundred years older than the last time Sepp had seen him, in the days before Crete. *Days before Crete* – would it always be that way?

"Sepp, I thought so!"

"Why it's Willi, how are you?" Lick said.

"How is any one of us – did you get it bad here?"

Sepp nodded: "You?"

"Galatas."

"A beer then, for Galatas?" Lick said.

"No, the mountain goat there is in a hurry, and I have papers for Heraklion," he jerked his head in the direction of the Alpine trooper in his ski cap with the edelweiss badge who was impatiently revving the big Zündapp KS 750, "but a message for you too Sepp, from a Britisher."

"Britisher?"

"Yes, the racing driver, Westbury Holt. He's a pilot, we have him in the prison at Agya."

"They gave that one an aeroplane, heaven help us all," Lick said. "Say, Willi, does he still wear that stupid jumper?"

"He does all right!"

"Ach, so he was shot down then ..."

"What does he say?" Sepp asked.

"Says he wants to meet up with you, wants to thank you for saving his life."

"Politeness is a way of life for those fools, it is nothing."

"It might be fun, Sepp," Lick said.

"The past is gone, Lick."

The Alpine motorcyclist shouted for Willi.

"As you wish, take care ... You know I hear they will drop us on Cairo next!" he shouted with a laugh as he rushed back to the sidecar.

"More like they'll shoot us right up Churchill's hairy arse," Lick said, before taking a long slug of the beer.

"Nagel."

"Hauptmann?" The captain had appeared from behind two of the trundling trucks, skipping between them with impeccable timing. He was wearing brand new tropical kit, sand-coloured with a matching soft cap, the yellow tabs on his tunic collar were as bright as buttercups.

"A beer sir?" Lick asked, not bothering to stand. Sepp put his bottle on the table, stood, and saluted.

"Easy Sepp," the captain said, taking the beer offered to him. They watched him as he sipped it. "You men did well. There will be medals, Sepp."

"We only did our duty as Germans and as paratroopers, sir."

"That's right," he took a larger slug of the beer. "But it is not over. There is one more task I must ask of you."

They waited while Lick did his best to hide the beer, then they collected three more paratroopers who were snoozing in the shade of a side street. The captain took them down the slope towards the olive oil factory again. The stench of death hung heavy in the air, mixing with the little beer Sepp had drunk on an empty stomach so that he suddenly felt sick. They walked west for a good way in the heat, down a dusty cart track that led off to little houses at regular intervals. The Cretans were waiting in an olive grove, where the trees were naked from the withering shot and the grass had burnt down to a black scorch. One paratrooper with an MP 38 was watching over them. Most were of fighting age, but two of them were old men, possibly grandfathers, with black-gapped teeth and leathery faces, and there was a woman – nothing to look at, the age of a mother at least. The woman's dress was ripped at the shoulder to reveal the treacherous purple-pink blemish – this was the way to see which of the bitches had used a rifle, the bruise from the recoil always showed. The Cretans all sat on the floor, trying hard to look defiant, and succeeding.

"I want you to see to these people."

"See to them, sir?"

"They are partisans," he said, and Sepp knew at once what he meant.

"But the old men ... the woman ..." She seemed to understand and she spat in Sepp's direction, the phlegm laced gob landing on the track and becoming a grey spot in the dust.

"A woman can pull a trigger," the Captain said, "and an old man can cut the throat of a paratrooper in a tree, Nagel."

"But I —"

"It's an order. These people will not learn otherwise, Sepp. It is the only way, the right thing to do for the good of those Germans who will come after us. It will show these people we are not to be trifled with."

Lick was looking at Sepp, a horrified expression on his face, the Australian hat in his hands so that his greasy red hair glowed in the sunlight.

"It must be done sergeant," the captain said.

"It will be done, Herr Hauptman."

"Good. Leave them where they lie and report to me when it's finished." With that he walked away, the guard who had been watching over the prisoners following him. They waited until the captain was out of sight.

"Fucking typical officer arse-wipe, leaving us to do the dirty work!"

"Lick, give me your machine pistol."

"What are you thinking?" Lick said.

"Give it!" Lick handed him his sub-machine-gun and Sepp gave Lick his rifle in return. "Now, all of you; go back to the village. This is not a job for many hands ... Do not argue with me Lick!"

The others left and he waited until they had disappeared over the rise in the road before unslinging the machine gun with its pistol grip and long magazine. One of the old men looked up at him, eyes like big black olives, gleaming in the oil of ready tears.

"I am sorry," Sepp said, as he slid back the cocking handle.

The MP 38 shuddered in his hands as he emptied it into the men and the woman in short bursts, watching as the fragile, brittle bodies of the old men jerked and danced under the weight of the bullets, snatching the stench of their shit as their bowels vented in death. He emptied two magazines, and then – because it was not possible to make a single shot with the MP 38 – he walked among the bodies, making sure they were dead with clean head shots from his Sauer pistol. Right then it all seemed so very easy. The right thing to do isn't always so easy, he thought to himself. But he did not look at their faces.

Later, back at the taverna, Lick said: "You let them run didn't you? You shot the thing in the air and let them run their little bony arses off, didn't you? I told the others you would —"

"I did what had to be done, Lick."

"Christ, no Sepp … No."

***

The child sat on Hanna's lap. Completely happy … *Complete and happy.* Maybe they were right, she thought, as she stroked his white-blond hair and tickled his chin, maybe there would have been no life for her child, if it had lived? They had told Hanna her baby had been malformed. Hinted that it was a mercy it had died. She had never been able to accept that. But maybe they were right after all …? She sang softly to him, a song she had not sang for such a long time.

"Your Papa liked that song when he was a boy, little Bernd," she said after she had finished.

"What are you saying to him?" Trudi had burst in from the direction of the kitchen, cake crumbs dusting the corner of her mouth. She would have been helping herself to food, feeding off Inge's spicy tongue, too, no doubt.

"I only —"

"Come here Bernd!" Trudi snatched the child from Hanna and he began to cry instantly, as if a switch had been flicked.

"Quiet!" snapped Konrad, who was working away writing letters in the corner of the large living room. "Please," he added, seeming to remember that Trudi and Bernd were guests. Konrad's sudden outburst had shocked the child into silence.

"I'm sorry Herr Plaidt," Trudi said.

"No, I'm sorry Trudi, it's not Bernd's fault. I'm just …" He shook his head. "What time do you want me to take you to meet Sepp?"

"Oh soon, please."

"Then we had better get ready. Hanna, will you be going like that?" He held his pen between two fingers like it was a cigarette. Trudi had a look of concern in her eyes that delighted Hanna. Konrad was right, of course, she would have to change, she was only still wearing her dressing gown because it scandalised Trudi anyway – three o'clock and still not dressed, she could imagine the talk in the kitchen.

"I had hoped, Herr Plaidt, that we might go alone to meet Sepp?"

"What?" Hanna snapped, unable to control her temper, "but he is my brother!"

"And he is my husband. I wish to see him alone first, is it too much to ask … Herr Plaidt?"

"No, of course not Trudi, I will drop you at the station. It's the Anhalter, yes?"

"Please."

"But Sepp will be expecting me!" Hanna said.

"He will be expecting his wife and son," Konrad said, "there will be plenty of time for you to catch up with Sepp later."

"Come Bernd, let us dress in our best clothes to meet Daddy," Trudy said.

Hanna noticed the tug of a sly smile at the corner of Trudi's mouth as she took the child away.

"She has the right to see her husband alone if she wishes," Konrad said.

"But she has no right to turn my brother against me."

"Oh Hanna, you do that yourself, can't you see it?"

*

Sepp was glad that she had put on a little weight. He remembered what the Führer had said about the last war, and how it was lack of food on the home front that had been in part to blame for Germany's defeat, not the lack of will of the troops in the trenches. The Anhalter station was packed, the heat from the engines at its six platforms radiated in warm waves. Clouds of steam curled up to the great curved iron and glass roof high above; a whistle blew from another platform, while another billow of steam hissed from the vacuum brakes of the dark locomotive of the train that had brought him to Berlin. Sepp had to barge his way past other soldiers to get to her and the boy. Some, he noticed, saw the ribbon around his lower left sleeve, Crete stitched out in gold, and those that did gave him and his kit bag plenty of room. The Fallshirmjäger had been told that officers had been instructed to salute those who wore this ribbon, but as yet none had saluted Sepp.

He was with her, at last, and he hugged her and kissed her as the tears streamed down her face. The boy had grown, looked strong for one of his age, but confused by this strange man with the sun-browned face and the Luftwaffe side cap.

"It's Papa Bernd … Oh Seppi, it's so good to see you!" She kissed him again while the boy looked on with big eyes as a black loco spun its wheels against the rails with a squeal.

"You see, he loves wheels – just like his Papa."

"And his namesake," Sepp said. They both laughed at that. "But tell me, where is Hanna?" A shadow seemed to cross his wife's eyes and for a moment he thought the worst – he had seen that same shadow far too often, on far too many faces, just lately.

"Oh, she had things to do," Trudi said, matter-of-factly.

"Things to do?"

"Herr Plaidt is waiting in his car, we have had a lovely time at their apartment, they have such a lovely home, Sepp, perhaps when you're an officer —"

"Tell me Trudi, is she all right?"

"Well Sepp, it's not my place to say, but ..."

*

There was a small damp patch on the pillowslip, from Hanna's tears, and a corner of the bed sheet was twisted tight in her fist. The window was open and she heard Trudi's too-loud voice, floating high from the Bayernallee pavement, gaseous with little girl excitement, telling Sepp of the wonderful things they would have for dinner – Konrad could always get the best of food from Nöthling's deli' in Steglitz, where he and many of his Nazi friends shopped without bothering with the ration cards that restricted others. Hanna lifted her head from the pillow, she thought she should meet Sepp in the living room, but she was still in her dressing gown – they had arrived much earlier than Trudi had led her to expect – and before she had even decided what she might wear she heard them come in to the apartment. She just had the time to wipe the tears from her face when he tapped twice at the door to her room, and then opened it.

Sepp stood in the doorway for a while and she thought he looked taller, his face was tanned to coffee with milk and the hair that showed under his cap was as blond as straw. A black cross was pinned to his tunic, just above his Fallschirmjäger eagle, and rank badges were sewn on his sleeves. There was also a gold ribbon nearer the cuff that read: *Kreta*.

"You look well, Sepp."

"You look a mess."

"I —"

"I had hoped to see you at the station; it's been a long time."

"Yes, I wanted to but —"

"Yes, I see you are still not up." He took the padded chair by the dressing table, running his eyes contemptuously over the makeup and face cream jars and the shining perfume bottles before sitting on the chair backwards, his legs either side, his face balanced on the back of his hands across the top of the wicker chair back. He stared at her without saying a word for some long seconds and Hanna suddenly found she was afraid.

"Trudi tells me you've not been friendly," he said, finally.

"I have been as friendly as I can, Sepp."

"She's my wife, you understand that?"

Hanna nodded, then pressed her head back deep into the pillow. Then something seemed to melt within him and he climbed from the chair and sat beside her on the bed. He smelt of boot polish and *Kondor* soap. He smelt like a soldier, and it was a smell she liked.

"Please Hanna, why won't you try?"

"I do try."

He shook his head, and then said: "Look at you, it's late in the afternoon and still you're not dressed. Is that the way a German wife should behave?"

"Perhaps it would be different if I were a German mother, Sepp."

"Perhaps, but it was not to be." He stiffened and started to fiddle with the black Iron Cross on his tunic, staring down at it as he said: "You have to forget it, Hanna."

She shook her head.

"There might be another child, one day, there —"

"I don't think so," she said, quietly.

"But it's your duty."

She suddenly laughed out loud, a nervous reaction, something beyond her control, and instantly regretted.

"Don't laugh at me," he said, coldly, with no emphasis, with no emotion, just the chilly stare that she found she already feared. Her laugh dried up and she avoided his hard eyes for a few seconds, before turning back to face him.

"Perhaps you should talk to Konrad about duty, Sepp," she said.

Sepp looked a little flustered for a moment, then his features hardened and he said: "Konrad knows his duty, and he knows the meaning of courage, too. I have discovered the meaning of that particular word the hard way, Hanna. Courage is not just about taking a corner at speed, or jumping from an aeroplane, or storming a machine gun nest. There is a far greater sort of courage that you will never understand."

"Sepp, what has happened to you?"

He looked at her, puzzled, then pulled the cap from his head and placed it on the bed, then stood up and walked to her dressing table.

"Trudi tells me Strudel is still living at the apartments," he said.

She shrugged, confused by the change of subject. She had been taking more of an interest in the apartments since Sepp had been away from Germany, for Trudi had little interest in the business, just the money it made.

"Is it true?"

"Yes, of course, where else should he go?"

"There are places for *them*, hospitals."

"Old Kurt has always looked after him," she said, trying to fight off her own cold memories of hospital. "Strudel is his son."

Sepp just shook his head. He picked up one of the little bottles of perfume from the dressing table and shook it lightly so that Hanna could hear the slosh of the precious liquid.

"And what's this for?"

"It hides the stink of Berlin, Sepp."

"But Berlin has never smelt sweeter, Hanna, there's victory in the air." He put the bottle down and found her eyes in the mirror of the dressing table. "I would think a sweet smelling girl like you would be something, for a man just back from the front ... I bet you have to fight them off, don't you Hanna?"

"Ah, so that's it – but I never had you down as a gossip, Sepp."

Suddenly he picked up the little bottle of perfume and threw it at the far wall of the bedroom where it burst in a brandy-clouded explosion, the heady fragrance rapidly flooding the room.

"I do not want people to think my sister is a slut!"

"Even in that sentence *sister* comes first."

"I love you Hanna, but I also know you," he said, before walking out of the bedroom door and slamming it shut behind him.

*

Hanna's behaviour over the next few days could have won her a prize at the Reich Brides' School. Even Trudi warmed to her a little, she thought, as she busied herself around the apartment and smiled her best smile, taking charge of preparing the picnics, and making herself as radiant as the sunshine as they boated at Havelsee. But however hard she tried Sepp still seemed distant, and she could not tell if she was far away from him, or him from her, and that scared her. And the effort she made was corrosive, too, the acid falseness of it all burning inside her, and she needed to live just a little, to ease the pain.

Then there was the dream, the nightmare, the same overheard conversation that itself was just a dream. *Termination ...Cutting out a cancer...Incinerated* ... It always came when she did not drink, always seeming so real, as it always had, from the very first time it taunted her, on that black day when her baby had died.

So, although she wanted to make every second with her brother count, there was still a sort of relief when Sepp, little Bernd and Trudi left for Essen and home – it had become a point of honour for Sepp to make his own way, have his own place, even though they owned the apartments in Zwickau. Also, Trudi was a daddy's girl, and hated to be far from her parents for too long.

Konrad had been invited to Carinhall, Göring's country house in the Schorfheide Forest, and from there he was to go on a tour of airbases in France. Kessler had seemed excited when he picked Konrad up, his eyelids beating harshly, seeming so mechanical that Hanna thought they should clatter and clang. Something was obviously up, but she would not give either of them the satisfaction of asking what. Konrad would not be home for days, she knew, and Inge's mother in the Friedrichshain district of the city had been taken ill. She had asked Konrad for some time off, had gone to stay with her mother for a day or two – never had Hanna felt such joy over someone else's illness. She waited until noon, when Bruno's would open, and listened to records rather than the radio.

It was strange walking to Bruno's in the bright daylight. She noticed that people were crowding around the public loudspeakers on some of the street corners, listening to the feed from the state radio as the sun beat down on them. More paid attention to the broadcast than normal, she thought, but then she was seldom about at this time of the day. Something was happening, that was for sure, but she needed a stiff drink more than she needed news of the war – she knew her Sepp was safe, for now, if not quite himself, so she could let herself forget about news of battles for a little while. Soon she stepped inside Bruno's bar, where she saw the owner talking to a panzer man, asking the soldier if he knew his son.

"Do you know a Gerd Altmann, he's in North Africa now?"

"No, he's not in my outfit, sorry … How about another ouzo, though, to toast Gerd Altmann?"

Something new to drink then, she thought, as she looked for who might be in the bar: sailors, soldiers, some civilians, and flak helpers who didn't look old enough to shave never mind drink, and stuck with Berliner Weisse rather than the ouzo. It wasn't just the painted-over flag tiles that helped the customers in Bruno's bar trace the progress of the war. There was also the stock: if there's ouzo then they'd taken Greece. It would make a change from all the French stuff, she supposed. Without asking Bruno sploshed some of the clear liquid into a little glass, added a splash of water which clouded the drink, before sliding it across the bar to her. He looked no more miserable than normal as he picked up a paint pot and brush from behind the bar. He prised off the tin lid and Hanna caught the sharp earthy smell of the paint, which sat quite well with the aniseed tang of her ouzo.

Bruno took the paint pot across the bar to the wall of tiles painted with the flags of all nations. He dipped the brush in the pot and half of the rectangle of horse hair came out shining black. Then he started to paint over the clay tile that depicted the red flag with the hammer and sickle. Hanna realised that everyone in the bar was silent and all of them watched Bruno paint out the flag of the Soviet Union without emotion. All of them except one, that is, a young man in a good quality brown suit and a black tie. He sat with a cigarette smouldering in long piano-player fingers, his ouzo sitting next to a thin notebook. He was beautiful rather than handsome, but his beauty was of a type: a dangerous beauty, like tracer unzipping the sky during an air raid. He had the blond hair of a Waffen SS recruiting poster, quite long and swept to one side in a wedge, and icy blue eyes that stared with the unblinking focus of a Luftwaffe rear gunner. The target of those eyes was Hanna … She looked away, for those staring blue eyes made her as uneasy as the freshly painted black tile that signified Germany was at war with Russia.

***

1943

The stiff creak of the wooden gate seemed in tune with Westbury Holt's heart. He shuffled through the opening in the wire as the Italian soldiers that bracketed him kept their carbines at the ready. The camp was small, the smallest West had seen – and he'd seen plenty. It was in a snow-encrusted valley with an ice-edged river close by, which needed to be crossed via a rickety old wooden bridge to gain access to the camp. The steep hills that formed the valley walls were pinned in place with a thick bristle of naked trees, each lightly streaked with bandages of bright snow where it had gathered in the crooks of skeletal branches. Some of the old and tired looking tar-coloured wooden huts climbed the cleared lower slopes of the northern side of the valley on terraces, and others lay in orderly rows at the foot of the hillside, while there was also a small cluster of newly built huts outside the wire. The air was heavy with the smell of wood smoke.

There were two wire fences, with a killing ground of thirty yards between them, and West was soon ushered through the second gate. The barbed wire was twenty-feet tall, coiled on top, and overlooked by watchtowers at each corner of the compound. The gate shut behind him with a slam and the now familiar rattle and twang of quivering barbed wire. The guards abandoned him without a *ciao*, rushing off for something warm to eat and drink, he could hardly blame them; it was bitterly cold in this part of Italy at this time of year.

The camp was PG 57 (a), according to the sign painted above the gate, and judging by the time he'd been in the truck West reckoned it had to be around fifty miles north of Trieste, close to the old border with what had once been Austro-Hungarian Slovenia, before the last war. By the look of it this camp hadn't always been for POWs, and that gave him hope, for it was sometimes easier to break out of a place that hadn't been designed as a prison. Westbury Holt was, by now, an expert on such matters.

Some of the prisoners, most muffled and wrapped in whatever bits of clothing they could get their hands on, started to huddle around him. The cold was biting and he began to shiver, already missing the relative warmth of the truck that had brought him here following his latest capture. Suddenly there was a commotion from outside the wire and he turned to see a fat man burst out of what West had taken to be a cookhouse, a cleaver held high above his head, heading for a nearby store hut the other side of the muddy smear in the snow that was the track that led to the camp from the bridge. Two figures tumbled out of the window of the hut. One of the figures was a young boy, just a child, now sprinting ahead, grasping a large red salami sausage tightly, and the other was a girl, light-footed on the icy ground despite a small and lumpy sack that swung from her hand. There was a loud jeer from the prisoners as the fat Italian made to grab the girl. She ducked under his flabby arms, easily avoiding the clumsy swing of the cleaver, and then he slipped as he reached out for her, falling on his fat arse.

There was an exultant cheer from the prisoners, and even laughter from the guards. The girl had bunched her long skirt around her thighs as she ran, thick black hair trailing behind her like smoke from a speeding train, and West's eyes were locked upon her slender legs and the teasing hard line upon them where the sun-browned skin lightened to a creamy, almost ivory, white, slightly tinged dawn-pink with the cold. She was young, nineteen or twenty perhaps, but she was also the most beautiful creature West had set his famished eyes on for many months. More than that, at this moment she seemed the very essence of freedom. This was the greater beauty.

A sergeant shouted and one of the guards on the gate unhitched his Carcano carbine, bringing it to his shoulder with no apparent hurry. But the girl had already joined the young lad in the semi-cover of the trees by the time he let off a half-hearted and high shot that loosed a flurry of fine snow off the branches of the nearest beech, scorching the clear mountain air with cordite. There was more ironic cheering from the prisoners, and West smiled, the first smile in many days. There was no sign of the girl or the boy now, as if they'd melted into the air, and no sign of any willingness on the part of the Italians to go after them, either.

"Those two about the only entertainment we get around here mate," a tall Australian with a thick matted red beard said.

"Who are they?"

"Not sure, no one seems to know. Maybe locals, maybe not; just trying to get a little extra tucker from Fatty Arbuckle's storeroom, I guess. They turn up every so often, take something, then they're gone. They're here enough that the Macaronis know there's little point in chasing them by now, though – they know their way around all right."

"She's —"

"Yeah, mate. Enough to drive you mad."

"Well, we are honoured, Westbury Holt," someone cut in.

"Potter, is that you?" Potter wore a heavy beard and was wrapped in a thick RAF issue greatcoat, but the sarcastic tone of voice was unmistakable. They shook hands.

"My God man, you're like ice. C'mon, let's find you a billet." He seemed in a rush to get him under cover and West wasn't about to argue with that. They climbed up a shale path flanked with patches of dirty, grey old snow and then a flight of icy steps before entering one of the huts. Inside it was mostly unpainted bunk beds, but there was also a potbellied stove in the corner surrounded by an assortment of officers. A strong smell of wood smoke issued from the stove and, judging from the untidy stack of thin planks beside it, West guessed they were burning slats from the beds.

"Clear a space there would you, this man needs thawing out."

The heat from the fire helped the circulation return to his body, and it hurt. But it was a nice hurt, and West closed his eyes to savour it. After almost two years of alternating between being on the run or in captivity he had learned to take, and enjoy, such small pleasures when he could.

"Say Potter, I take it you saw the two Stukas I downed over Maleme?" West had suddenly remembered the kills, which would take his score to six – maybe seven if the Dornier had been confirmed.

"My God, you never give up, do you?" Potter said.

"Well, did you?"

"I was a bit busy that day, as it happens," Potter said, then changed the subject. "When were you put in the bag, Crete?"

"Yes, shot down, we got the Hurricane fixed – surely you must have seen it?"

Potter shook his head, and shrugged. "What does it matter anyway, you're not flying now, the war's over for us."

"Well, that's a matter of opinion, old man. Have you tried to make a break for it yet?"

"Not really had the opportunity," Potter said, and an Aussie near the stove snorted a little laugh. He ignored it. "I suppose *you* have?"

"I managed to break out of Agya with a few chaps, spent some months in the mountains, chasing rumours, looking for boats – looking for just about anything that would damn well float in the end," West said. "Then we heard a whisper of a submarine coming to pick up us strays. But the Germans picked us up on the beach," he shook his head slowly as he remembered. "I was shipped off to Greece, escaped, then got picked up by the Eyeties, and I've been breaking out of camps in Italy ever since."

"How?"

"Usually over the wire, the simplest way's always the best," West said.

"Well, that won't work here," Potter snapped, seeming irritated all of a sudden.

"We'll see."

"Impossible, there's too much clear ground beyond the wire, we've lost men already. Besides, you'll have to clear it with the escape committee, but I wouldn't hold your breath."

"Why not?"

"There's a tunnel under way and they won't allow any other escapes, in case they draw attention to it. Perhaps you could help?"

"Tunnel? No thanks. I'm afraid I get terribly claustrophobic," West said quietly, feeling the sludge of disappointment sinking through his being. A piece of wood cracked in the fire and a glowing ember floated free on the hot air, capturing his attention as it hovered above the flames, then disappeared up the tin tubing of the chimney.

"I'll introduce you to the senior officers later," Potter said. "It's all officers here, Australians for the most part. It's a satellite camp of Campo PG 57 in Cividale. They're a bit pushed for space there, so decided to use this old army camp for odds and sods. It's supposed to be temporary, until we're all moved on to Sulmona, but it's beginning to feel quite permanent now."

"Well, I've seen worse camps. Maybe none so cold, but worse all the same," West said.

"Yes, my thoughts exactly," Potter said.

One of the Australian officers sat around the stove looked at his watch. "Tucker time, I think," he said. The others around the stove drifted away and West made to go with them, suddenly realising just how hungry he was.

"Wait a minute," Potter said, pulling at his arm. "I need to talk to you about that day, at Maleme ..." The others were already through the door.

"Look, we all have off days, forget about it," West said, having already decided not to mention the way Potter had scarpered.

"But it wasn't an off day," Potter replied angrily. "I just had other things to do – important things, vital things, intelligence matters ... Got it?"

West nodded, it seemed so distant now, not two years, but a lifetime too. You couldn't blame a man for wanting to save his own skin, he supposed. Besides, it would be useful to keep Potter on side, always good to have someone show you the ropes. Potter was staring deep into his eyes, but there was little emotion West could see in those lifeless grey dots of his. West nodded again, tried a smile. And only then did Potter seem satisfied.

"Well come on then old man, let's get some grub. It's almost always potato soup at this time of year, but they give us bread, too. It's really not so bad here once you learn to keep your head down, you know."

"I'll take your word for it, but are you sure you didn't see those Stukas go down?"

*

The only break in the monotony of grey sky over snow was the hard black outline of the peasant cabin, its oily timbers dirty against the pure white, a rotten tooth in a glistening smile. Its roof was steeply canted, and the snow that had slid from it, leaving dragged-corpse smears, lay in steep cumulous piles against the stained wood. There was a dark forest beyond the cabin, but nothing else. There was not a sound to be heard; absolute silence. Just as it had been the previous night, right before the treacherous partisan attack that had left two of Sepp's men bleeding to death in the snow. It was time for retribution.

The boy looked at him with expectant eyes. He had betrayed his countrymen, but he had been true to his stomach. Sepp tossed him an unlabelled can of German army meat, because he had promised a reward, and because he was unworthy of a bullet. Besides, he might prove valuable at another time – information on partisan activity was thin here, in the Soviet armpit of Belarus, and intelligence did not strictly have to be intelligent. The boy slithered over the snow bank and dropped down on to the rough, icy track below.

"Can we trust him, Herr Hauptmann?" said the young private at Sepp's side.

"You can always trust the hungry – if you feed them. And he's led us to the right place, I'm sure of it. Look, there are tracks leading to the door, six of them I'd say. But Ivan's been lazy not to hide in the forest, lazy and stupid."

"But there's no smoke from the chimney?"

"No; so perhaps not quite so stupid. But then they must be getting cold, we'll soon put that right." Sepp studied the cottage through the powerful Zeiss Zielvier telescopic sight on his Mauser Kar 98 sniper rifle. This would be the youngster's first action with the Spikes and Sepp wanted to make sure he knew what was what, how the black and white of the Russian front was far starker than the black and white of a *Die Deutsche Wochenschau* newsreel. The private was very young, they seemed to be getting younger all the time. At that age Sepp had been dreaming of racing cars, he remembered, almost as if he were remembering a film he had once seen. But now look at him: a captain, married with two kids. He allowed himself the flashing luxury of thinking of his children: Little Bernd who was getting bigger by the day, far from sight, and Hanna – poor Trudi, she hadn't wanted that name for the baby, but he had hoped it would go some way to bringing his sister close again.

The company was spread out in a wide arc, with the MG 42 machine guns at the extremities where they could give overlapping fields of fire, not that he planned on using them. The MG 42s also covered the back of the cabin, but one of Sepp's men had already scouted close, seen there was no way out. The men had hidden themselves well, for they knew he would be checking: the worst of them just a slight white fold in the ground, and the best of them snow itself. Sepp put the rifle down and pulled the iron sleeve of the punch-dagger over his left hand and wrist. Old Kurt's brutal weapon had become a symbol for the company and although he hated the thing, and it made his silhouette so distinctive to enemy snipers, it seemed good for morale – some of the younger paratroopers had even taken to painting outlines of it on their helmets. The Spikes: the very best in the Fallschirmjäger, any one of them would make the claim.

Sepp raised the white-painted punch-dagger and waved it towards the snow-encrusted cabin. At his signal three white blobs floated clear of the ground some seventy metres in front of him, to the left of the cabin, quickly taking the form of running men swathed in white over-clothes. The hood of the snow smock slipped from the head of one of the men and Sepp recognised Lick's captured Russian fur hat. His best sergeant carried the flamethrower. The two cylindrical tanks, one filled with a nitrogen propellant and the other with the flammable thickened petrol, were strapped to his back, the converging pipes from each held in front of him, the ignition flame of the lower pipe licking lazily from its aperture. The two other paratroopers covered him with their MP 40s.

All along the curved line of hidden men Sepp could now just about pick out the stubby dark barrels of rifles and machine pistols as they bristled out of the snow. His own rifle was swathed in white cloth to soften its outline and camouflage it. He placed the punch-dagger in the snow beside him and reached for the rifle, pressing the butt against his shoulder and the rubber cup of its telescopic sight close to his right eye. The rifle had a double trigger action, and he pulled back on the heavy rear trigger until it clicked, ever so quietly, telling him the front hair trigger was engaged. He curled his finger very lightly around the front trigger and watched the start of the action through the cross hairs of the sight. Lick stood tall, too close to the building: he would have to tell him about that later – it would be stupid to lose a man, his best man at that, on such a trivial operation. There was a *whoosh* and the orange-black flame jumped from the nozzle of the thrower and leapt across a ten-metre gap to lick at the timbers of the cabin, instantly scorching wood and melting snow. The hollow breath of the thrower carried across the emptiness like the howl of a wolf, and Sepp heard the young private at his side gasp. The cabin caught fire almost instantly and Lick and the other two paratroopers withdrew to the cover of the snow banks.

"My God," whispered the youngster, as the fire took hold and the timber started to crackle and spit. Sepp kept the rifle trained on the doorway of the cabin, and waited. It seemed to take an age but Sepp was not concerned, he had learnt the art of patience – it had kept him, and his men, alive. The first two partisans finally burst out of the door of the burning house, their hands in the air in submission. One was a middle-aged woman, she was shouting her surrender through a toothless mouth that Sepp silenced with one well-placed shot to the head, while the report of the rifle's percussion smacked painfully in his ears. The man with her ran to the right of the building as Sepp worked the bolt and engaged the rear trigger again. He squeezed off another shot, turning the man's head into a pulpy mash which stained the snow bright scarlet. None of the other paratroopers fired. As ordered.

"But they are unarmed!" pleaded the young private, as another man came through the door only to be stopped by the strike of Sepp's third bullet, the echo of the shot almost immediately lost in the immensity of the landscape, a pink feather of blood spurting out of the exit wound at his back. Suddenly there was silence again. Sepp kept his sight on the doorway of the cottage as he said: "It is the only way with these people, they do not know how to fight a real war. We must show them that if they hurt us we will hurt them. You must understand that."

"But why do you do all the shooting, Herr Hauptmann?"

"Because I'm the best shot, I rarely miss, so it saves ammunition. It would be criminal to waste rounds on these animals – but you see that, don't you?" The youngster nodded hesitantly and gripped his rifle tightly. "Besides," Sepp added. "It's not easy …"

They waited until the flames completely enveloped half of the cabin, until there seemed little chance of anyone else coming out alive. Part of the roof collapsed and the fire spread along the length of the cabin. Then the door burst open again and the last of the partisans came running out. There were three of them, all in flames: screaming, human torches running towards the line of paratroopers. One, a boy in his teens, carried a Mosin-Nagant rifle that he fired ineffectually into the air, an empty pop in the wilderness.

Sepp lightly tugged at the front trigger and the rifle jolted against his shoulder, the boy fell and the Mosin-Nagant spun away from him. Sepp worked the bolt and took aim at the next, a dancing flame of a woman, who seemed to crumple gratefully to the bullet that met her melting skull. The ejected cartridge sizzled in the snow to Sepp's side and he deftly inserted another five-round stripper clip into the magazine – ordinary ammunition, not the special S rounds for snipers, these targets were unworthy of that – before lining up the last of the partisans in his telescopic sight. The face had already gone, dripping from the head like wax from a candle, eyes just a smouldering white liquid, alabaster sheets of skin falling from the blackening trunk of what was once a man.

"Kill him … Please …" the boy beside Sepp sobbed.

Sepp did not fire. He thumbed the safety and lowered the rifle, and simply allowed the burning figure to sink to the melting snow beneath it. The screams died abruptly. The sickly smell of burnt flesh carried across to the line of soldiers.

"I'm sorry sir," the newcomer said between sobs, "I'm not sure …"

"The bullet saved may well save you. War's not pretty, what is right here may not be right elsewhere. Learn that and you'll prosper in the Spikes," Sepp said. The newcomer was sick in the snow.

He will learn, Sepp thought, as he placed his left hand in the long, cupped gauntlet of the punch-dagger and signalled for his men to move out.

*

The reception was not clear, the volume was necessarily low, and there was a regular clacking sound overlaying the broadcast. But she could hear the names as they were read out, and that's all that mattered. Hanna pressed the side of her head close to the speaker, the mesh of it scratching at her ear, as if the static came to life. The radio set smelt of warm circuitry and of the lacquered wood of its cabinet. Inge was in, so she had to be careful. It did not bother her that the maid might tell Konrad, she could deal with him, but Inge would gossip with Trudi, too – while there were always others someone like her might tell these days. Hanna knew she was taking a risk. And it thrilled her.

The Soviet *Free Germany* broadcast had already started. The male voice spoke in perfect German, reading out the names. It was a very clever way to get the German people to listen to the Russian propaganda, and the British did it, too, whole programmes dedicated to listing the recently captured, which seemed to be getting longer every day. She sometimes half hoped that Sepp might be amongst the names – at least for that rather than the other thing …

Names. Names from every part of Germany, so many names … *"Wolfgang Hoefeld, Edüard Horst, Walter Itzen, Heinrich Jager, Wilhelm Kalow …"* And so it continued … *"Kurt Schulz, Lothar Schuster, Gerhard Sniers, Emil …"* Wait! Lothar Schuster. That was Frau Schuster's son. It had to be, didn't it? He had been with the 6th Army, in Stalingrad, Hanna knew that much at least. The widow would suppose he was dead. Like many others she would have had no news, nothing at all, of his fate after the fall of that cursed city. She would be glad to know he lived, even if he was a prisoner, of that Hanna was certain.

"I must tell her!" Hanna had said it aloud, and loud, and she heard a pan clank from the kitchen. She switched off the radio set and twiddled the tell-tale of the dial. But this time Inge did not look in. She was out of the door and down the stairwell in no time. But then, as she stepped out of the lobby of the apartment block, nodding a greeting to the concierge, the realisation hit her as hard and as suddenly as the cruel cold wind. How could she tell Frau Schuster she knew her son was alive, without giving away the fact that she had been listening to the Russian broadcast? Without giving away the fact that she had committed radio crime. She did not know if the woman was a Nazi, she was kind enough and friendly, but the Party attracted all types, and sometimes it was the quiet ones who were the worst. Hanna stood in the freezing canal of Bayernallee, the icy wind funnelling down it from the east, burning her skin with its ferocity, scudding dark clouds through an iron sky. The bitter cold reminded her of the nightmare she'd had a few nights before; Sepp in the snow, the snow somehow acidic, burning him like white fire ...

"They cannot censor our dreams," she said, and again she had said it aloud. Then she walked quickly in the direction of the tram stop.

The shop on Tauentzien Strasse had been damaged in the bombing in '41 but they had repaired it quickly. Why they bothered Hanna would never know, because despite the display of clothes in the window, clinging to the grey manikins as stubbornly as paint, she knew there was nothing for sale here. Frau Schuster just kept the display behind the brown taped glass to show a veneer of normality. Many of the shopkeepers did the same. Clothes had been in short supply almost since the start, and while most had more than enough ration coupons to buy them, there were simply none to be had. Hanna could always find them, in from Paris, for Konrad was right about one thing, he really did have his uses, his connections. But others had to make do with ersatz clothes as they drank their ersatz coffee and lived their ersatz lives. She had heard they had even started to make clothes from wool spun from wood pulp. The joke in Berlin was of the man who jumped into the Spree to kill himself, only to float to its surface because he was wearing a wooden suit. Berlin still had plenty of that, at least: blackout humour.

She noticed the colour had faded from those few clothes on display. They would have been well out of fashion, if there was still fashion, she thought, as she pushed open the door and stepped into the sparsely stocked shop. It was almost as cold inside the shop as it was outside. Frau Schuster was behind the counter, wrapped in an overcoat and headscarf, her breath showing in icy white feathers. There had once been two others who worked here, for the widow Schuster, but there was not the work for three now. There were never really customers, just visitors, but she carried on like everything was normal. It was the way the city lived. She was not especially old, for a widow, though the benchmark on that was shifting by the day, and yet her hair was greyer than it had been, her skin paler, and she looked almost dusty. But there was no dust in the shop, because she spent most of her time cleaning it.

"Frau Plaidt, how nice to see you," Frau Schuster said – her son, the son now in a Russian POW pen, had been a motor racing enthusiast and had been thrilled to hear the wife of Konrad von Plaidt shopped here – when there had been things to buy – Frau Schuster had once told her. They were not friends, but friendly acquaintances. Friendly enough that Hanna felt she would like to do something for the woman.

"I have news for you," Hanna said as she nodded a greeting.

Frau Schuster's face cracked into a smile, a smile replicated in deep laughter lines that Hanna had not noticed before. There was a gleam in her eye, the only gleam in this shop of old things, as she said: "You have had a dream?"

"How did you know?"

"You are the third person to come in here within the last hour," she said. "The other two both had the same dream, my dear."

"The same dream, but —"

"My boy is alive, yes – a prisoner, but alive?"

Hanna nodded, smiled back. She suddenly felt happy, for the first time in a long while. She felt good because she had found a way to fight back. And she was not alone in fighting back.

She said no more to Frau Schuster, but walked back out into the street. The glacial wind bit at her face, the velocity of it was a thing of wonder, but it was hardly the only one in a hurry to escape from the east, she supposed. As she turned her head, muffling her face with her scarf, she caught her reflection in the window of Frau Schuster's shop. She stared at it for a moment, it seemed more honest than the bright visage that greeted her in the mirror at her dressing table. She thought she looked as pale as Frau Schuster. But it was a shallow, grey day reflection, not good for detail ... And yet the blond hair of the man on the other side of the road seemed as bright as a flare. There was something about that hair, something more than just that it was not under a hat on a day as cold as this, that made her turn to get a better look.

Her breath solidified within her. It was him. The same beautiful young man she had seen in Bruno's almost two years before. Even at a distance of some twenty metres she could make out the cold blue eyes. She had thought of him often to begin with, less so recently, thought about the way he had stared at her on that day the idiots had unleashed Barbarossa. He stared at her just the same way now.

He wore a long leather coat, the sort of coat favoured by the Gestapo, and leather gloves. A bus broke his gaze, coming to rest at a bus stop on her side of the road in a squeak of brakes. Hanna breathed again. But she did not move, as the unseen passengers clumped and shuffled noisily behind the blue painted-out blackout windows.

When the bus had emptied it pulled away in a flak burst of diesel exhaust fumes, but now there was no sign of the young man on the other side of the street, no sign of him anywhere. It was as if he had been plucked up and taken by the cold wind. But the empty space where he had stood somehow seemed as solid as ice, and as much a thing in this world of hers as the shop she had just walked out of. She would never have believed that an area of empty pavement, a space a young man had just filled, could be quite so frightening.

*

"Heard a bored Eyetie chucked a grenade into a latrine at Salonika," the Australian infantry lieutenant with the thick red beard said, warming his hands in front of the potbellied stove, just one in a scrum of prisoners huddled around it, leaning forward in their chairs, hands outstretched and supplicant, as if they worshipped at the black, warm, iron altar.

"That's a one off," Potter said. "The Italians really aren't too bad, much better than the Jerries – isn't that so, Holt?"

"I've not spent so much time in Jerry hands to be honest, but when I have been a guest of the Germans I'd have to say they've been fair —" West started.

"Then you've been lucky," Potter interrupted him. "From what I've heard they …"

West closed his ears to it. The circle of rumour and gossip was the inner keep of every camp he had been in – and the first prison cell he wanted to escape. If it wasn't imagined war crimes it was the chance of macaroni soup, or torture, or Red Cross parcels, they spoke of. He had learned to ignore most of it, and trust only his own eyes.

"… Yes, there are much worse places than this to sit out the war," Potter continued. "I met a pongo who said they went four days without food at —"

"Excuse me, please," West said, as he stood up and pushed his way out of the press of prisoners, giving up his prime spot close to the stove, "I need some air."

"You must be insane man, it's brass monkeys out there."

"It's brass monkeys in here, too," West said, as the floorboards creaked beneath his feet.

"What's his problem," he heard as he opened the door, allowing a gust of wind to rush in, just as if the air itself was escaping the cold.

"Shut that bloody door!" twenty voices shouted in unison.

He slammed the door behind him. Being cooped up in the hut was driving him mad, he longed for activity, and once more he thought about the tunnel he'd been told had been started in Hut 3. Yet the mere thought of crawling through a narrow, dirty passage with just a few old planks to keep the hillside from falling on top of him was enough to bring on a surge of nausea and a sharp jab of panic. He tried to think of something else.

Almost as soon as he had stepped outside he realised he'd made a mistake, for it was bitter cold indeed. But something in him made him want to stay out in the cold for a few minutes at least – there had been too much defeat just lately for a man like Westbury Holt. The wind chopped at his face like it was laced with little icy daggers and he rushed for the sheltered side of one of the huts. Inside he could hear the chat of the inmates and the beat of their boots against the floorboards as they tried to stamp warmth into their bodies. In another hut he could hear the start of a sing-song, an Australian voice dripping with *Waltzing Matilda* melancholy. Wood smoke hung in the air, until the next icy gust snatched it away. His breath froze in a white quill in front of his face and the cold seemed to clutch at his body with icy fingers, rattling his bones.

From here he could see the wire, beyond that the second line of wire, and then snow. Inside the pen the constant walking, walking, walking of the prisoners – there was sod all else to do – had turned the snow to mud that had now frozen into a rough grey-brown crust. There could be no starker contrast than this, no greater demarcation between the captured and the free: beautiful virgin-white snow; shitty, hardened-mud, just the wire between them. He had liberated a meerschaum pipe from a guard at one of the earlier camps. The black shaft of the white pipe was stuck between the weave of his grimy old cricket jumper, which he wore beneath a greatcoat, but there was no tobacco for it … What he would give for tobacco. Just tobacco … and steak and kidney pie, some good Kentish ale, a warm bed, a girl, a hot bath … He ran his fingers through his matted beard. When one wants so much it's difficult to know where to start when it comes to fantasy. But then, he thought, freedom would do.

He looked up at the watchtower that covered this corner of the camp. The guard was bent low behind the split log wall of the tower, just the top of his helmet and the bipod-supported muzzle of the Breda 30 machine gun showing, the glassy lens of the unlit searchlight tilted up to face the gunmetal sky. It would be just a matter of a minute or so for West to scale the wire. But then there was the second wire, and beyond that the land rose steeply to the bare trees, with no cover between, while at this time of the year there were few places to hide even if he could make it as far as that. It would just be hours of free target practice for the Eyeties as he made his way up the steep slope; or maybe just minutes. Long odds, two had perished that way already, and that was in the dark, before he had arrived – and they both had the full complement of legs. And then there was the promise he had made; there was to be no escaping while the tunnel was in progress, nothing to put the Macaronis on their toes. Silly buggers …

"Hey!" The Italian guard had startled him, and for a moment he almost wondered if he had been thinking aloud – he'd found that he was almost always questioning his sanity when shut up in one of these places. The guard seemed to be wrapped in two greatcoats and under his helmet he wore a woollen scarf that covered his head completely, tied beneath his chin in a chunky knot that made him look like a toothache sufferer. He was the other side of the wire, between the fences, scrunching through snow that came halfway up the bandage style puttees wound about his lower legs. His rifle was slung over his shoulder, upside down, and he blew into his hands with rapid steam-engine clouds of breath. West walked towards the fence until he was close enough to it to see the Italian's face through the tight warp and weft of the wire: iced diamonds framing bright, brown eyes set into an olive complexion marred by a cluster of acne on one cheek, eyes that were alive with a childlike excitement.

"So it is you!" he shouted, then went on in rapid Italian, shaking his head in disbelief, before remembering and apologising in stilted English. "I am sorry … But I saw you race at Pescara, it is my home, and then I saw you here, but could not believe it."

"Ah, Pescara," an imprisoned consciousness fleetingly found itself in warm seawater on a starlit night, a beautiful half-naked girl swimming with it.

"You like Pescara?"

"Yes, very much, sorry …?"

"Berardi, Aldo Berardi – it was 1937, *Sì*?"

"Before the war," West said, and Aldo nodded sadly.

"But you were good, in the big silver car … And almost as crazy as Nuvolari!"

"Nobody's as crazy as Nuvolari, and few as fast," West said, and for a moment he thought the Italian would cry, his brown eyes filling, until he wiped them clear with the frost-rough back of a finger-less glove.

"Perhaps Rosemeyer, he was as fast," Aldo said.

"And maybe one other, I think."

"But of course! A racing driver must have confidence," Aldo said with a laugh.

"Then maybe *two* others," West said.

"Heh Berardi!" The Italian looked to the tower where the guard, a corporal, was waving him on. He turned his back on the other guard and then made a secret signal with his thumb through clenched fingers.

"Sorry Signor Holt, I must go."

"Your English is good," West said, to prolong the conversation.

"Before the army I worked in a hotel."

"I don't suppose you have any tobacco?"

"No, sorry," Aldo looked genuinely distressed, "but I have this." He pulled out a large bar of Swiss chocolate and tried to push it through the mesh of the wire, finally breaking it with a loud, frozen snap so it would fit. "I know people all over Italy from my time working in the hotel, there are things I can get —"

"Berardi!"

Aldo waved his hand at the tower impatiently, then said: "One day I will race Signor Holt, when this war is done. We will talk again?"

"Of course, Aldo, and thanks for the chocolate." The Italian scrunched off into the snow, hunching his helmeted head deep into the collars of his greatcoats.

"Oh ... And Aldo," West shouted. "Bring tobacco next time!"

West found that he was smiling when he returned to the hut, and he realised it was the first time in many a day. He snapped up the bar of chocolate, which meant there was half a small block for each man in the hut. Everyone was grateful and West was suddenly very popular. All were happy, except for Potter, who looked at his square of chocolate disdainfully, before popping it into his mouth and slowly sucking it, his eyes closing in relish. Only when it was finished did he say: "You know Holt, it wouldn't do to be seen fraternizing with the enemy too much, old boy."

***

Blue sparks jumped from a passing train on the S-Bahn bringing shadowy figures of men to hard edged life for a frozen moment, like instant cobalt sculpture, before they sank back into the darkness like fast fading afterimages. Hanna walked on. She was always glad of the blackout, but more so tonight, for she had news to pass on.

Bruno's had been forced to close down. They were not content to kill the sons of Germany, now they had come for the fun. 'Total war', Goebbels had called it, as if they had not been quite able to pack enough of it into everyone's lives these past three and half years. They had ordered that all the bars, all the theatres, all the clubs, all the restaurants were closed. Except Horcher's, that is, where the cripple and Göring liked to nuzzle at the trough – the fat one had simply reopened it as a club for Luftwaffe officers. Konrad was there with Kessler tonight. Inge was visiting her mother again. It had meant she could listen to the English broadcast.

Earlier Konrad had asked her to go to the Plaidt family home in the Rhineland, where his mother still lived. It would be safer there, he said, in the countryside away from the bombs. But she knew she could not bear it, the boredom and the stiff formality: she needed to live, and to live she needed Berlin, and the blackout. She thought he wanted her out of the way, but she did not see the point of that, for they hardly talked, hardly even saw each other, anyway. Then he had said Kessler would be pleased she had decided to stay, as if anyone cared a damn, as if he still amounted to anything in a country now so bloody full of bloody heroes, some with crosses on their breasts, most with crosses on their graves.

The back alley would have been dark even without the blackout restrictions, but Bruno had found some phosphorescent paint with which he had painted a big B on the door. The alley smelt of vomit and of burnt wood, where someone had built a little fire to warm cold bones. She had not been able to avoid Bruno's for long, she liked it too much, and she reminded herself she had only seen the beautiful blond man there the once, and that was in the old place, too. He was not a regular, so how could he know of this place? Besides, if he was what she thought he was then to know of it would mean it was shut, with Bruno in the Alex', talking to the cops of the Kripo.

There was a special knock, the tune of the *Badenweiler March*; a good joke, for it was the music they always played when the Führer arrived at a parade or a rally. But it was not Bruno's joke, he was not one for jokes, for smiles. She hoped to change that. She rapped out the start of the march – *tap-tap, tap-tap, tap-tap; tap-tap-tap-tap* – with gloved knuckles and waited. A minute later there was the screech of steel in wood and torchlight shone through an aperture, the suddenness of it in the dark alley forcing Hanna to squint. Hanna was as regular a regular as she could be, whenever she could get away, that is, and Bruno recognised her.

He did not greet her, just led her into the blackout-shuttered backroom that had become the new Bruno's Bar. There were not many people here yet: three soldiers in the far corner, panzer grenadiers hunched over a bottle of vodka, while in the opposite corner a man in a suit had his hand up the skirt of a prostitute who often worked here – people didn't stand on ceremony at this new, even darker, Bruno's. In the other dim corners there were some others, some soldiers and a civilian, but she could not make out their faces. The panzer grenadiers watched with interest as the man started to unbutton the whore's blouse. She did not respond in any way, like one of the manikins in Frau Schuster's shop, wearing the same old clothes for the same old customer. There was no decoration in the bar, no bar in the bar, just a trestle table someone had covered with a naval flag, for no particular reason other than someone happened to have a Kriegsmarine ensign, and no one could spare a tablecloth. There were a few Hindenburg lights, the little candles painting the walls with dancing shadows, but it was far more dark than light – and a good quality dark at that. There was music playing on a gramophone, Lale Andersen, who had once starred at the KadeKo down the way from Bruno's old place on the Ku'damm, singing *Lili Marlene*. Hanna was sick of bloody Lili, but soldiers seemed to need her.

"Bruno, we must talk," she said.

"Must we?" he said, pouring her a measure of vodka then topping it with a splash of *Fanta*.

"It's Gerd," she said.

Bruno's face seemed to collapse, as if a balloon inside his head had suddenly deflated, and tears quickly brimmed in his eyes. He reached out to steady himself against the table. Hanna reached out for him, grasping his shoulder.

"No, Bruno, it's not ... it's not *that*," she said.

"Then?"

"He's safe! He is a prisoner, the English have him – they captured him in Tunisia."

"But ... But how do you know?"

"You know how I know."

Bruno's face began to inflate again, to the same picture of misery, the same unhappy set of jowls that reminded Hanna of a bulldog sucking lemons, while he wiped the tears from his eyes with a corner of his barman's apron. He hung his head, shook it.

"The radio, you fool!" she said.

He looked at her blankly.

"I heard it on the BBC, they read out a list of those captured!" she hissed.

Just then a match flared in the dark corner of the room that was tucked behind the trestle-table bar, and she turned to see the orange glare illuminate the face of a man she had not noticed before. A man with a thin notebook on the table in front of him, lighting his cigarette as Hanna tried to focus on his face. Almost as if to help her see him he touched the still flaring match to the wick of a Hindenburg light and in the new yellow glow she recognised him.

She had not noticed the small scar at the corner of his mouth when she had last seen him, over the road from Frau Schuster's shop on Tauentzien Strasse, for the beautiful blond man had been too far away then. Now though it stood out in ghastly detail in the light of the tiny candle.

It would have been difficult to make this one look more Nazi, but the scar did the trick – for it was almost the exact shape of a single S from an SS *sig* rune lapel flash; instantly bringing to mind jagged glass and punishing lightning. She felt an iron band of fear constrict within her chest as she wondered whether he had been close enough to hear her conversation with Bruno over the scratchy music from the gramophone.

*

West trapped the scuffed old leather football on his chest then let it drop to his better foot – the unnatural left. Aldo slid in with a committed challenge, the heels of his heavy army boots gouging a shallow furrow in the soft ground, a grin like sin stitched to his face. *Nice try Aldo*, West thought, as he dragged the ball back with his heel and watched the young Italian soldier slide by on his arse.

West dodged left, pulling the ball around another sprawling Italian. Now there was just Fatty Arbuckle, standing between the two rusty oil drums, goalkeeper and cook – though both descriptions fitted him about as well as the black sweater stretching itself transparent around his barrel of a body.

The prisoners' team comprised a couple of British, a Kiwi and mostly Australians, who made up for their lack of knowledge of the game with enthusiasm and a desire to even the score with the more brutal of the guards. Thus far it was even: a blackening eye and two sprained ankles for the guards, a snapped tooth and a dead leg for the prisoners. And two goals each. Not too bad for a bunch of under-nourished POWs.

West took aim. Fatty Arbuckle's big eyes seemed to spin in that immense fat face of his, as he panicked and wobbled left then right across a muddy space that resembled the hoof trodden edge of a Serengeti watering hole. For a moment West was balanced on his false leg, and as he kicked with his left an arrow of pain shot up his spine, but still the strike was solid, the aim was true. The heavy leather ball hit the fat cook square in the face and he collapsed back into the goal mouth with a thump that raised a huge splash of smooth mud. As a bonus the ball dribbled over the imaginary line between the barrels. Then the cookhouse bell rang to signal the end of the match. The ranks of prisoners who formed the touch-line cheered, though whether it was for the three-two result or the fact that the cook was sprawled on his back in a pool of mud, West couldn't say.

"Well done, quite a victory," Potter said, dryly, as West and the rest of the team took the slaps on backs that were their due.

"Not bad footie for a bloke with a wooden peg, mate," an Aussie said, his face split in a grin. The Italian team sat by the gate, some nursing their wounds, and West knew that the bruisers among them would not let it rest, someone would suffer. Yet it still seemed worth it.

"You might have at least kept the score level, Holt," Potter said, "there's really no point in antagonising them."

"Not a sports lover, are you Potter?"

"It has its place; preferably England."

"Well, I won't argue with that."

"Westbury!" Aldo barged his way past some of the congratulating prisoners, "Good play Westbury, but poor Luigi!" Aldo laughed as he said it. Luigi was Arbuckle's real name, and he was as unpopular with the guards as he was with the prisoners.

"I tried to miss him, but the man does takes up an awful lot of goal," West said, and Aldo laughed again, it was as natural to him as breathing. Then West looked past Aldo, beyond the wire. There, sitting on a rock at the edge of the trees some way up the slope, was the same girl he had seen on the first day, her legs parted, hands planted firmly on the tops of her thighs. He thought she stared at him. From this distance he could just about make out a dark tress of her hair hanging over her eyes. Her light red dress was rucked up high to show shining pale bronze skin. On her feet she wore a pair of boots, over the dress a black waistcoat. She was beautiful. She was free. She was the very essence of freedom. West's next breath seemed trapped within him, as if it mocked him. The young boy appeared, about twelve, West thought. He tugged at her arm. Aldo followed West's gaze.

"Those two better watch out, if Luigi sees them he will chop them up for Bolognese." West wondered if she had seen him hit Fatty Arbuckle with the ball, hoped she had. But now the girl was leaving and West caught a flash of gleaming flesh on the back of her leg as she stood up off the rock. Even at this distance it caused his heart to skip a beat.

"Who is she, Aldo?"

"Gypsy, I think. But who knows these days, maybe a refugee? Like smoke from the battlefield; as hard to catch as smoke, too." Aldo winked as he said it, and West guessed that the Italian soldiers did not put 100 per cent of their efforts into apprehending the pretty thief. The girl was out of sight now, and West tried hard to snare the image of her in his memory, but Aldo was right, she really was like smoke. He did not even know what she looked like, up close. He only knew that she was free.

Aldo was still talking: "You know, if you can play football as well as that then just think how you would go in a racing car now, Westbury," he said, enthusiasm bubbling through the slight pauses between every word.

"Oh you don't believe all that rot do you?" Potter said to Aldo, elevating his eyebrows.

"Don't mind him Aldo, he's not interested in sport."

"He does not believe you?" Aldo looked Potter up and down, shaking his head. "Don't worry, I will show him. I have —"

"Berardi!" a sergeant, still nursing an ankle as he sat with the other injured Italians by the gate, shouted.

"Ciao Westbury, but I will prove it to him, you'll see!" Aldo said, with another laugh, before running across the temporary football pitch to help his injured team-mates. The crowd around West began to disperse. As it was the first mild and sunny day for a long while most stayed outside, milling around in little groups talking about the game, and teasing the guards. West sat on the steps to the hut, taking the weight off his sore stump.

"Looks painful?" Potter said, sitting down beside him.

"It's not so bad, you get used to it."

"You know, you should be careful with that Italian friend of yours, people are beginning to talk."

"You mean you are beginning to talk," West said.

"What's it to me?"

"Oh, I don't know, seems to me you were happier when I wasn't quite so popular, when you were the old hand, the one with the answers, if not the chocolate – not spoiling your little holiday, is it?"

"That's bloody ridiculous, and you know it!" The claret of anger filled Potter's face and West was glad he'd annoyed him. It helped him take his mind off the pain.

"Yes, bloody ridiculous," he said, smiling softly.

"Anyway," Potter put in petulantly, standing up to get more height over West, "that's not all they say."

"And what else do *you* say?"

"*They* say that for such an accomplished escaper you don't take much of an interest in the tunnel," he whispered it, bending down low so that West could smell his stale breath.

"I've told you, I hate closed in spaces – claustrophobia."

"Right, so that's the word for it now is it?" Potter said, smiling smugly and walking away.

"I wouldn't mind him." It was Henry, the red-bearded Australian lieutenant, just coming out of the hut and now sipping water out of an old bully-beef tin.

"I don't mind him, it's quite the opposite I think – he seems to have developed a bit of a problem with me," West said.

"The poor bastard's had a tough war, just about had enough, I'd say. Some reckon he's lost his nerve, but you know how it is here: talk and talk and a little more talk."

"Well," West said with a grin, resisting the temptation to add to the talk with his own tales of Maleme, "it takes all sorts to make a war."

"You're right there, mate. All sorts."

*

The bombs dropped some blocks away, the explosions shaking the iron bedstead they lay on and causing the paratrooper to laugh out loud. A light powder of plaster fell from around the light fitting above them, dusting their naked bodies. There was the whistle of another stick of bombs and then the deafening, hot-breathed bellow of the explosions. Closer still this time, shaking the bed again, like an echo of their fucking. It had been quite a while since the RAF had dared to bomb Berlin, and during that time they seemed to have improved their aim. Hanna was afraid, but she did not want to go to the nearby public shelter – the Railway Bunker at the station – because times of freedom like these were too precious. Besides, the couple of bottles of Sekt she'd sunk earlier gave her courage enough. Just.

"Tommy's on good form tonight!" the drunken paratrooper laughed again, the bombs did not seem to bother him. Hanna did not know his name, she seldom asked their names, it added to the excitement, while this hotel was used by whores and charged by the hour, so they didn't worry about signatures on a register, or whether the guests broke the law by choosing not to seek shelter from the bombs. She was not even sure exactly where the hotel was, but they had walked the blacked-out streets for ten minutes from the Friedrich Strasse station to get here. She had met him in a small bar someone had set up in a cellar under an office building in one of the tight streets around the station, one of the places she had frequented lately, when she had the chance to get out. She had not gone to Bruno's for weeks. For a little while she had feared she would be arrested for her radio crime, but either the beautiful blond man was not to be feared or – and this she thought more likely – he had not heard her tell Bruno of his son's fate. She did not want to see him again. It was enough to see him in her dreams, her nightmares. For sometimes now it was him, speaking with Kessler; mouths for that same conversation she all too often heard in her dreams:

The termination, is it completed?
It is finished.
Any problems?
No, the process is quite simple.
Do you question it?
No, it is like cutting out a cancer.
The remains?
Incinerated.

The light was not switched on, but the paratrooper had opened the curtains, it made him feel at home to be with his war, he had said. The only illumination crashed in through the window, and came in shivering slabs of orange as the glass rattled to the bombs and guns, while beyond the window the sky was burning blood. There was the clatter of falling metal in the street below, the fall of flak shrapnel, and the pump-pump booming of the anti-aircraft guns punctuated the steady droning hum of the British bombers high above. The night smelt of fire.

"Quite a show," he said.

She let her hand pass over the solid muscle of the paratrooper's chest, then the hard interlacing of the scar tissue down his left side. Then she felt for him. But he was too drunk, and she would have to wait longer before she could have him again. He sniggered, then swung his legs over the edge of the bed and stood up, stumbled and almost fell back on top of her. The flaming sky painted his torso in tiger stripes of orange, while his slim and muscular behind glowed milky white. Even in this light she could see his arms were tanned the same nutty brown as his face, like long gloves, and she guessed he had fought and been wounded in North Africa. He stumbled towards the wardrobe. It was empty, their clothes lay in a mingled pile at the foot of the bed. He opened the doors to the wardrobe then sighed deeply as he pissed. She could hear the stream as it drummed against the back of the wardrobe. He finished, shook his penis, then stumbled back on to bed just as another series of explosions pulsed the room in a strobe of amber light, the percussion shaking their bed once again.

"Why not use the bathroom?" she said.

"It's too far," he replied, but it was just next door. "Besides, a paratrooper, my love," he slurred, "is always able to improvise." She laughed with him. He looked at her spread naked before him, and said: "Are you sure we've never met before?" Perhaps he'd seen her on a newsreel? That still happened sometimes, people would remember her face, from somewhere, some time that seemed long ago now, but was only two years before, maybe a little more. She ignored the question, and said:

"I know another paratrooper."

"I bet you know a battalion," he said, taking one of her breasts and licking at the nipple.

"Sepp Nagel, he's Fallshirmjäger, don't suppose you know him?"

Suddenly the paratrooper stopped licking her nipple. He collapsed back on the bed and stayed silent for a short time. She could hear a woman crying in another room, while upstairs another couple made love with the urgency of the still living.

"You've had Sepp Nagel?"

She said nothing.

"It surprises me ... It really does."

"Why?"

"That one's such a cold fish. So straight, like he has a stick grenade permanently shoved up his arse. I would have taken him for married with kids, and not the sort to fool around, not the sort for fun – not the sort for one like you."

"But you know him?"

"So you have had him?"

Hanna shook her head and they lay quietly for a little while as the single long siren tone of the all clear sounded. She soon heard the jangling bells of the ambulances as they picked their way through rubble strewn streets.

"Yes, I know him," he said suddenly, sounding almost sober now. "But not well. He is a captain now, I've heard, out east with the 1st. A real killer that one, they say —"

"No, that's not Sepp!"

"Oh, then perhaps there are two Sepp Nagels in the Fallschirmjäger? But I tell you, the bastard I speak of is a murderer all right ... and cold with it ... like a machine ...like a killing ..." he trailed off.

"Go on," she suddenly felt chilled and the room seemed to be closing in around her.

"No, I have left all that ... For now at least."

*

The sentry was inches away from him, the muzzle of the rifle sticking out of the embrasure in the small log- and sandbag-built emplacement, his frozen breath whitening a small piece of the night. There was still some snow, lying in hard patches, and Sepp allowed his boot to crunch into a scab of dirty grey ice. It was the first sound he had made in ten minutes – and now he knew for certain that the sentry was asleep. Through the aperture of the emplacement he could see the soft glow of white skin. He crept around the back, through the small opening, and then he unhitched the heavy punch-dagger. When the point of the spike touched the bare skin of the sentry's face he awoke with a start, crying out.

"Quiet!"

"I'm sorry sir, I didn't see you —"

"You were asleep." Sepp waved the spike of the punch-dagger in front of the paratrooper's eyes.

He hesitated, as if he was about to deny it, but then said: "Yes, sir."

"Next time this could be an Ivan dagger, remember that."

"Yes, Hauptmann."

"Good, I will see that you get extra guard duty, but for now go and get some sleep, and there is some hot stew on the go in my bunker – take some and send out Erich in your place."

"Yes sir, thank you, sir." The young paratrooper slid out of the rear doorway of the emplacement.

"Oh, and Weber," Sepp called after him.

"Yes sir?"

"If I find you asleep at your post again, it won't be a court martial. I will cut down on the red tape and kill you myself, with the spike. You understand?"

The youngster went to speak, but could not find words, and simply nodded, before Sepp returned his nod and the lad scurried away towards the log bunker. Sepp took his place, focusing his eyes on the burning seam of Russian campfires that marked the horizon across the lake. The night sky was boiling with cloud, but he thought there was little chance of more snow now. Spring was here, and although it was still cold, the things that would come from that sky would be shells and bombs, and those hellishly shrieking Katyusha rockets – and soon, too.

There was a sudden burst of light from behind, followed instantly by the aroma of the stew. Mutton. Lick had worked wonders once more and he could hear the laughter of the men as they settled down for their meal. The front was quiet, he could see why the lad slept, but he could never excuse it. By right he should have had him arrested; sleeping on sentry duty is a serious offence. But sometimes the right thing to do is simply *not* the right thing to do, Sepp was forever finding out the truth in that. The company was short of men as it was, and there would be little hope of replacing Weber. Besides, he would have learnt his lesson – the touch of the spike was a very good educator – and the shame the man would feel when his sergeant asked him why he was not now on watch would be better still. Young Weber would not fall asleep at his post again.

"My God Sepp, I was about to eat." Erich slipped in beside him.

"Sorry Erich, you are an old soldier now, you must bear the load. I will send some of the food out for you."

"If that fat bastard Lick hasn't eaten it all by now."

Sepp almost smiled, and then clapped the man on the shoulder. He hooked the punch-dagger to his belt and shouldered his rifle. Erich had been with them since before Crete, a good man; all those who had survived Crete were good, and many who hadn't were better. Sepp slid out of the emplacement and took one last look at the Ivan line before going to the bunker. It was one of many, dug deep into the bank of the lake, surrounded by gun emplacements and a wide line of mines and wire on the side that faced Ivan. Sepp levered the heavy, hinge-less door open and the smell of the stew broke over him like a wave, carrying with it the familiar flotsam of smoke, farts and alcohol. He pulled the door back into place, shutting the smells and the cigarette smoke in. There was no effort to stand, just a nod and a smile from the seven soldiers sat around the big pot of stew. The bunker was roomy enough, made of birch trunk, straw-stuffed mattresses lining the walls, and a cooking fire in the centre of the room. Weapons hung from the sturdy rafters and pictures of sweethearts and family marked each man's bunk. Lick was doling out helpings of the stew.

"There is post," Lick said, between ladles, "and I have set you some stew."

"Thank you."

"There was a letter from Eva, she's heard they're thinking of moving all the racing cars from the factory, putting them somewhere safe from the Tommy and the Ami bombs, that's a bad sign Sepp, isn't it?"

"Just a precaution, Lick."

"Christ, to see one of those beauties now, eh Sepp?"

Sepp said nothing, just peeled off his smock and sank onto the straw mattress on his bunk, which was set between the others at the top of the space and doubled as a bench at the head of the table. Trudi and little Bernd smiled down at him from a picture on the wall which he rubbed with the back of his finger. There was still no picture of little Hanna but he hoped there might be something in the letter. It bore the Essen postmark and was propped up on its edge by an enamelled steel mug. He realised the address was not in her handwriting, and that puzzled him. He was hungry and cold as he had been outside bolstering the defences for most of the day, but he ignored the steaming bowl of stew and carefully opened the envelope.

There was no photograph, just a letter, and it wasn't from Trudi. He read the first paragraph in a daze, before his vision misted with tears and he could go no further. He twisted the letter into a tight knot then, without thinking, he made for the heavy door of the bunker. Voices, he heard them, some way beyond the numbness, but they could not cut through, and neither could the cold as he sat outside on a patch of compacted snow, his knees close to his chin. How long had Lick been there, he could not say.

"Sepp, you must come in."

For some reason he could not form the faces of little Bernd and Trudi in his mind. Each time he tried they would morph into somebody else, always one of his many victims, what was left of their faces framed in the scope of his sniper's rifle ... Lick had prised the letter from his hand.

"God, I am so sorry Sepp. Those bomber bastards – what sort of war is this?"

Sepp could not reply. He could not feel the cold and yet he felt frozen from within – and the world of death and Lick and the glow of the Ivan camp fires in the distance seemed outside the block of ice that had become his being.

"They say it was quick Sepp, a direct hit," Lick said, awkwardly, fear in his voice.

"It's what I say too, Lick; in the letters home, when we lose men."

"Please Sepp, come inside, we cannot lose you."

"I will check the defences one more time," Sepp said.

***

Water dripped from the rafters into old tins placed to collect it while the rain bouncing off the roof sounded as solid as gravel. By using the sleeve of his cricket jumper West made a porthole in the condensation clouded window. What had been their little football pitch was now a quagmire and little lakes of chocolate coloured water were forming around most of the huts. The latrines – just logs balanced over open pits – had flooded and the smell of fresh sewage was all-pervading. It had rained for three days, non-stop, and the tunnel in Hut 3 had been discovered on the second day as the water drained into it. Everyone was depressed. On top of all this West had a bad cold; not bad enough to cut out the smell of shit, but bad enough to make even doing nothing an effort. He took to his bunk again and half hid under the coarse blanket.

The stove had gone out and two of his hut mates were busy trying to relight it – it wasn't so cold now but the fire had begun to mean more than just warmth. Suddenly the door of the hut burst open and a sodden Australian artillery lieutenant tumbled in, pursued by a cloud of spray.

"Shut that blasted door!"

"Sorry, urgent business," said the Aussie. "Where's Holt?" The others tilted their heads in the direction of West's bed and he pulled the blanket over his face. *Not another sweet-toothed digger wanting to arrange a trade with Aldo for a slab of Swiss chocolate*, he thought. By now all the bartering of Red Cross parcel goodies was done through West, Aldo would have it no other way, and Aldo was the only one who could get the things everyone wanted, for a price – for the lad had a good business head on him.

"West?"

"Bugger off! I'm not well … I can sort something out for you when the rain stops. If it ever bloody stops."

"It's not that. But I could do with some gaspers?" the Aussie said, his face lifting into a slight smile momentarily at the thought of extra cigarettes, then drooping back into seriousness as he added. "They want you in the big hut."

"The big hut?"

"Best hurry mate, something's up."

"But I'm … Oh, bugger it." West snatched up his greatcoat and a woollen hat then followed the Aussie out into the rain. The ground was slippery under foot and he found it difficult to keep up with the dodging lieutenant as he jumped between the growing brown puddles, slippery isthmus to slippery isthmus. West noticed that the bored guard in the closest watchtower traced their progress through the slanting rods of rain with the barrel of his Breda.

The big hut was, in fact, exactly the same size as all the others. It was called the big hut because it was where they kept the more senior officers, and the escape committee operated out of it. The Aussie pounded up the steps and knocked on the door. Somebody called for them to enter and West rushed in after him, hoping that someone in the big hut had the kit for a brew of some sort.

But a cup of tea was not to be, and instead West was met by a most curious sight. All the bunks had been lined up against the walls and tables had been brought in from other huts – a hell of a job for some mugs in this weather – and they were now formed in the shape of an open sided square with a solitary chair in its centre. Officers sat around the edge of the tables, with the British lieutenant colonel, Stockman-Brace, at the head of it, sitting alongside a usually friendly English wing commander called Chapman. Potter sat at the end of the left bank of tables. The hut smelt of damp clothes.

"What's all this?" West asked.

"Take a seat Flying Officer Holt," Stockman-Brace said, curtly – he was always a sour type, perhaps because he'd *literally* lost his battalion in the desert one night, and had been picked up by the Eyeties while out in a car looking for his men, or so the story went. West took the chair in the centre of the room, looking around him and doing his best to raise a grin as he did so. No one returned his smile.

"Now come on lads … Sir, I know it's a bit of a drag here at the moment but if you are going to play jokes on someone couldn't it be a healthy chap at least?" He sneezed right on cue.

"This is no joke Holt," Stockman-Brace said, a thick vein throbbing at his temple, skin glowing red from too close a shave with too blunt a razor. "You are here to answer very serious accusations."

"Accusations?"

Suddenly Wing Commander Chapman stood up and nodded at West and the rest of the room, and said: "Sorry about this West, not exactly *accusations*, no." Stockman-Brace moved to complain but Chapman stopped him with a little wave of the hand – they were of equivalent rank and no one was quite sure who had seniority. "You know, of course, that the tunnel was found?" Chapman said.

"Yes, I heard."

"And do you know who found it?"

"The Italians?" West said.

"Well, quite, but one Italian in particular – your friend, in fact."

"Aldo?" No one answered, they all waited for the penny to drop, but West could still not quite believe where this was leading. "Now hold on here, you don't think I told him do you?"

"Yes … We … Do!" Stockman-Brace barked, slamming his fist against the table to each word and causing everyone to almost jump out of their seats.

"No, we don't," Chapman said, softly, shaking his head at the lieutenant colonel, "but we cannot afford to take chances … And you have been very friendly with the lad."

"And we have all benefited, I even scrounged some tobacco for you, sir."

"And it was most welcome."

"That's not the point," Stockman-Brace shouted, forcing his way back into the fray, "someone has let us down badly and you look a likely culprit, it's as bloody simple as that."

"Now look here, Aldo's smart enough to find that blasted tunnel himself, the water was flooding into it the other day for Christ's sake, everyone could see that!"

"But he didn't see it, did he? And we were asking ourselves just why someone like you, who says he's broken out of scores of camps, wanted no part in this tunnel?"

"Because I —"

"And that's not all!" Potter shouted, the sudden interruption taking everyone by surprise. "There's this." He held up a black leather bound album, cracked with age and use, and he passed it to West. Stockman-Brace looked livid at the sudden interruption, but the sight of the book seemed to stifle his protest. "Seems your friend was a little too keen to prove what a hero you once were, Holt, the lad even let me borrow his scrapbook," Potter said.

West flicked through the pages of the album, full of blurred but wonderful photographs of racing cars at Pescara, and of already yellowed newspaper cuttings reporting the races. He turned on until he reached the pages marked 1937 and there he was, at the wheel of the Auto Union, guiding it through the twists of Spoltore – right past the little osteria where he and Hanna had dined.

"Something amusing, Holt?" Stockman-Brace asked.

"Sorry, was I smiling?"

"Turn the page," Potter said.

West hadn't thought about Gracie for a long time now. But now his face and his words came back to him, what he said that day in Les Deux Magots in Paris, when he had told him *this* little scene had made the papers: *It's not a joke for millions of people … You need to know what side you are on …* Here was the newspaper cutting, a black faced West all panda-eyed where the goggles had shielded him from the oil and dust, his arm stretched out in a Nazi salute. Trust bloody Gracie to be right.

"Now come on, this was a joke – how was I to know there was to be a war?"

"That may well be so, but this, on top of your friendship with the Italian, does put us in a rather awkward situation," Chapman said, glancing at Stockman-Brace. "I'm afraid we simply cannot take a chance here. You will stay in your hut and we will have someone watch you —"

"But hold on, I —"

"We cannot take the risk, West. Now that's an end to it."

"I always wondered why there never seemed to be anyone around to confirm your *kills*, Holt," Potter said. But West was too stunned to reply to that.

Stockman-Brace and Potter looked grimly satisfied as West was escorted out and then back to his own hut. He was to be imprisoned within a prison, and he suddenly felt a little like one of those Russian dolls; those dolls within dolls. But the thought was much more suffocating than it was whimsical.

*

It was sunny, glorious. The sound of the laughter and the happy shouts from outside mocked him. The hut was empty, except for West and Burt, the young Royal Navy sub-lieutenant who had drawn the short straw today. It was like school detention, and West might have just laughed it off if he could just forget his anger, his disbelief, that they could think such a thing of him. He had stared at this one page of the book for half an hour now, reading and re-reading the same line but never taking it in as he tried to figure out a way he could prove his innocence. It was *Robinson Crusoe*, he could perhaps feel a certain empathy, stranded in a sea of suspicion. Again he tried to read the next line, but it was no good, it was impossible to concentrate. Besides, there was no point, as someone had ripped out some of the later pages for toilet paper – always hard currency here, far too hard.

Bert sat on the bunk alongside West's, his face pushed into the heels of his hands, elbows on knees. He must have been about twenty-one, though he seemed much younger. West thought he looked like he wanted to cry, the blinking eyes and deep swallows of homesickness. If he had been allowed out of this prison within a prison he would have left the lad to it, let him have a bloody good sob and get it out of his system. The only reason he didn't just brush past the diminutive sailor and go outside was because it would get Bert into trouble with Stockman-Brace.

"Look, why don't you have some time in the sunshine? I'll stay put – promise," West said.

"Can't, the colonel said I must stay here with you … Sorry," Bert said, playing with one of the brass buttons on his dark blue monkey jacket and not meeting West's eye, obviously embarrassed. That was typical of the awkwardness most felt about this whole affair, but from the way the whispers had been flying it was obvious they had started another tunnel.

And, while most seemed unable to believe he had tipped off the Italians about the first tunnel, Potter had made sure many had seen the newspaper cutting from Pescara. There was a sharp tap at the window.

"Westbury, Westbury!"

"Is that you, Aldo?"

Bert's face filled with panic and he stared at the grinning and waving Italian through the grimy window.

"Just open it Bert, you'll hear what we say," West said.

"But —"

West strode to the window, the frame was warped and rotten with damp and it took some shifting, finally sliding free with a shriek thanks to the help of Aldo on the other side. The clear mountain air rushed into the stale-smelling hut and West could hear the soothing flow of the Natisone on the other side of the valley.

"So this is where you have been hiding Westbury my friend. What's it all about?"

"Let's just say I've been a bit under the weather Aldo, but it's good to see you."

"The weather?" He rolled his eyes to the blue sky.

"I've been ill."

"Oh, I see. It's not serious?" West shook his head. "I would get you some medicine," Aldo continued, "but I have come to say goodbye, there is little time now." West noticed that Aldo was dressed in his full uniform, a kit bag on the floor beside him. Some of the other prisoners were eyeing them up from a distance, passing comments behind hands.

"You're leaving?"

"Yes, I have been posted."

"I'll be sorry to see you go, Aldo, but at least you'll be getting out of this miserable place."

"So will you."

"Me? I don't follow?"

"All of you, you are all to be moved to Sulmona."

"When?"

"Soon; even tomorrow maybe … But I must leave now."

"Keep safe Aldo," West said, reaching out the window and shaking his hand firmly.

"Ciao Westbury, I will come and see you race after the war, I promise." With that he left, a sad smile on his face.

"We have to tell them, Bert."

"I'll go, I —"

"Bugger that, it's about time they saw that I can get more than just choccy and baccy from my Italian friend, eh?"

West strode through the puddles to the big hut, enjoying the feel of the cool fresh air and the sunlight on his face. Bert rushed after him, two good legs no match for West on a mission. "I thought you were —" one of the other prisoners started, trying to bar his way, but West merely brushed him aside. He strode up the stairs and into the big hut without knocking. There was no one there. Next he tried Hut 5 – hearing the shouted warning and the clamour as they hid the entrance to the new tunnel and the digging equipment as he approached. *Christ, the noisy buggers, the Eyeties needed no mole*, he thought. He barged in through the door. Inside the hut was almost full of prisoners, most of them struggling to catch their breath.

"What the bloody hell do you think you're playing at man?" shouted Stockman-Brace, before succumbing to a fit of wheezy coughs.

"I've news," West said calmly, noticing the tunnel diggers at the rear of the hut hastily washing away the fresh dirt with water from a couple of small tin drums. "Hope I haven't disturbed your afternoon nap, lads?"

"A word of this to your dago friend Holt and —"

"It's too late; they're moving us out." He saw their shoulders sag, those tired men who had almost finished one tunnel and had now started another, all for nothing.

"Why should we believe you?" It was Potter, he was sitting on the bunk to the left so West hadn't seen him when he'd come in.

"That's up to you," West shrugged.

"I can see no reason why he would make it up," Wing Commander Chapman said, gauging the urgency of the situation immediately. "When will this happen, West?"

"As early as tomorrow."

"Where are they sending us?"

"Sulmona, it will be a long trip."

"Your source?"

"My *dago* friend."

"You're not supposed to speak to him," Stockman-Brace said.

"He spoke to me."

"You believe him," Chapman said.

"Yes, I believe him."

"I suppose if it's not true then we just get back to work on the tunnel," Chapman said. "But in the meantime we should think about the contingency plan."

"Shouldn't we wait until he's gone," Stockman-Brace said, nodding at West.

"Don't you think that's all rather academic now? If Holt hadn't given us the news we wouldn't have this last chance anyway," Chapman said. "The important question is: who's it going to be?"

The room was suddenly quiet, shoes shifting on the floorboards the only sound, as the men looked to each other, waiting for someone to say something. It was Potter who spoke first.: "Well, if this is true then it seems to me we are in Holt's debt for letting us know, don't you think?" No one replied. "So why not give him first dibs?"

"That seems generous of you Potter, I thought you —"

"Always willing to give a man a second chance wing commander, and that's what you wanted wasn't it? Besides, he's a loner, and he has roamed the hills before."

"Now hold on a minute, don't I get to know what this is all about?" West said, never wholly comfortable with anything that came out of Potter's mouth these days.

"Of course, it will also give Holt a chance to show us just how keen on escaping he *really* is," Potter added, speaking as if West wasn't even in the room. "While we will no longer need to worry about his loyalties."

The wing commander looked to the men, then to Stockman-Brace, who shook his head glumly, then turned to West and said: "We have planned with this eventuality in mind. We've always known, after all, that this camp is merely temporary. There was always the possibility that we would be moved *en masse* someday."

"Tell me more," West said, noticing that all eyes were fixed solidly on him.

"It's simple really – we will leave you behind," the wing commander said. "First we make it look like there has been a break through the wire by cutting the inner fence tonight, and then we put you down the shaft of the new tunnel. There is about room enough for one there ..." Suddenly the walls of the hut seemed to close in on him, and what felt like an icy iron band tightened within West's chest. Potter's generosity now made sense. For, as far as he could recall, he was the only one who knew of West's claustrophobia.

"... Of course, it's rather risky," Chapman continued. "We don't know who will be here next for a start. And you will have to wait a few days before you show your head as they'll be in the hills looking for you for a while ..." West looked into Potter's laughing eyes – the bastard, he knew there was no way he could do this. He knew that he had him. West could fight fear in all its manifestations, but this one: a tight, confined space for days on end, no light, and little air. It was asking too much to prove a point to people who had no right to doubt him. Asking far too much ... He felt his hands start to shake and he clenched his fists tight to stop it.

"I'll do it," he heard some distant voice within him say, and the sight of the shock on Potter's face was almost worth that cold foetus of fear that turned within his belly.

*

Old Kurt sounded fed up: "Frau Hansen has said she cannot pay her rent on time this month – again."

There was a hiss on the line, and a sudden image of two black snakes, each mirroring the *S* shape of the other flashed in Hanna's mind, causing her to shudder. She did not really believe they listened to every call, but she *could* believe it.

"She also says it's time Strudel went to a special place, says he needs treatment," Kurt continued. "I don't know how she's such an expert, except that maybe she's had some treatment herself, and in which case it obviously doesn't work, but she says she might talk to the block warden about him."

"Don't worry about it, Kurt, just keep Strudel out of sight for a while and let the old bitch pay when she can. It's worth it, isn't it?"

"I'm not sure, Hanna. Perhaps she's right. I can do nothing for the boy now. It sometimes feels as if I don't know him. He never talks – he only ever really talked to Sepp, anyway. You know, it would mean the old prune couldn't threaten us every time rent day comes along. Maybe it would be for the best?"

"Maybe," Hanna said, and was about to go on when the line went completely dead. That happened more and more these days. She sighed and placed the Bakelite handset back into its cradle. She did not think she needed to worry too much about Frau Hansen. She was just a bitter old woman with too much time on her hands, too much hate in her head, too much fear in her heart. She was scared of being thrown out, and if she ever did go to the stair terrier – as everyone called the Nazi block wardens – to tell him Strudel was an undesirable, then she would lose her leverage when it came to rent day. As for Strudel, he knew to keep out of the way of the block warden, for the stair terrier wore the brown shirt of the SA and Strudel feared uniforms. So there was nothing really to worry about other than late rent, maybe a missed month. Simple logic, that. It was the sort of logic she also used when she told herself that one man might be wrong and that, yes, there really could be two Sepp Nagels in the Fallschirmjäger.

She looked at the black telephone, which sat on a low table by the door, as she pulled on her coat. The last time she had answered the phone it had also been bad news. That time it was another old man, an uncle of Trudi, calling from Essen, telling her the house had taken a direct hit. The floor had collapsed into the cellar and on to Trudi, her parents, little Bernd and the new baby who had been given Hanna's name. She had not cried for Trudi, she was too honest for that – and she had felt a little ashamed when she realised she was now free of her – but she had cried for the children and for her Sepp's loss.

Konrad was away, he had left an hour before. His new work, of which he had not spoken, was taking more of his time, and taking its toll. He had aged more in the last year than he had the six before, and he now limped from that old Nürburgring injury almost as much as he had back in the late '30s. The thought of that time brought to mind Westbury Holt. She rarely gave him room in her head, for he had not given her room in his life. He had made his choice, he had driven the streamliner, had crashed it, and now she could not believe she had once thought she loved him. She had not heard from him since his accident, and she sometimes wondered if it might have all been different if she had.

"Are you going out Frau Plaidt?" It was Inge, she had come through from the kitchen, a big white plate held to her chest like a glistening shield, suds speckling her brawny arms beneath the line of her rolled up sleeves.

"Yes," Hanna said, pulling on her gloves.

"And what time should I expect you back?"

"That's none of your business."

"Herr von Plaidt, he —"

"It's my life, not Konrad's," Hanna said.

"But it's my duty ..." Inge started.

That word, *duty*. It bothered Hanna more than most words, for it was the word she most closely associated with Sepp, and so her tone was icy as she said: "I don't think you quite understand Inge. I don't believe Konrad cares what I do, as long as I'm discreet. You should know that this family is not overburdened with morals. I'm surprised you have not found that out yourself, when you sweep the dirt under the carpet. Crowded under there, isn't it?"

She left it at that, knowing that there could be no gossiping letter from Inge to Trudi, gossip that would be passed on to Sepp. Not now. She felt a flush of freedom at the thought. This time there was no guilt. Inge's face reddened, then she simply turned and clumped back into the kitchen, and Hanna left the apartment.

Hanna had still not been back to Bruno's since she had seen the beautiful young man. She had found a new place, in a cellar in a street off Hardenburg Strasse. It was perfect – except for the fact that it wasn't Bruno's – because it doubled as an air raid shelter and the bombs would never interrupt the drinking. She took a tram then walked along Hardenburg, following the fluorescent dashes at the edge of the pavement, looking for a darker patch of dark that marked the turnoff into the side street. She thought of the telephone conversation with Kurt earlier. She had not seen Strudel for a long time, for she had not been back to Zwickau for two years, but from what Kurt said it sounded like he was getting worse. She hated having to give in to the thinly veiled threats of that blackmailing bitch Frau Hansen. Maybe, she thought, Kurt was right? Maybe it would be better for everyone if Strudel was just put in a home, or a hospital? Just the word, *hospital*, caused a shiver to run down her spine, for she had had that same old nightmare the night before.

In the velvet of the blackout she could just about make out the trees that lined the street, and the soft creamy bulk of the cinema, while the flagstones she walked on had a slight silver sheen, like lead. With her eyesight restricted she found her other senses were sharpened, and the few people she passed on the now quiet street were sensory sketches: halitosis and the click of a walking stick, too much cheap perfume and a wet sniff, a mumbled moan about the quality of soap. Each brief cluster of perception passed by, to be replaced with more as other souls floated past in the dark sea of the night. And that creak of leather ...

She realised it had been there for a while now, matching her own step up the cold, leaden pavement. It was new leather she thought, which was a rare thing, but she did not think it sounded like a Wehrmacht boot. She hastened her step, just a little, and listened out for the creak of shoe leather behind her. Sure enough it became more rapid, and she could also now hear the soft cold tap of the shoe sole. She felt a flutter of fear in her chest, but would not allow it to spread its wings, and so she swallowed hard and tried not to think of the rapists and the robbers that, Konrad had always warned her, hunted in the blackout.

Faster. She looked high, to see the junction of roof tops against the scratchy clouds that hung like oily dark rags in the night sky. She heard the squeal of steel on steel and the chuff of an engine in the Zoo Station as she turned into the side street, trying to remember which street it was and where it led, hoping the creaking shoes would walk on down Hardenburg Strasse. It was even darker in this side street, something she would not have thought possible, and with no brightly painted dashes along the kerb she hardly knew if she was even facing in the right direction. She stopped, tried to adjust her eyes to the darker dark. Then she heard the creak of new leather behind her. Following her into the side street ...

Her fear was an expanding fist within her throat, choking her from inside, so that she could not scream or even shout, all she could do was walk on, walk faster, now following a smell of cooking fat from the end of the street. She had gone some way when her toe hit something hard, and she tripped, feeling out into the darkness to stop herself falling. She seemed to hang there in the dark for an age of indecision, where she floated between falling flat or staying on her feet, and then her hands hit the cold and rust-rough metal of railings. She gripped them, and steadied herself, then listened for the creaking leather. It had stopped. She turned. She thought she could see someone, against the backdrop of the slightly lighter opening on to Hardenburg Strasse. The figure was just a pale patch in the night, not quite clear enough to be ghostly. But the man – for she thought it surely was a man – was close.

From high above someone quite suddenly opened a window and

blackout shutter, forgetting the war for an instant, and flinging a patch of light into the dark alley below. It was only for a moment, and even before an air raid warden could shout "lights out there!" the shutters were closed with a slam, the light extinguished to leave a floating yellow carpet of afterimage on Hanna's retinas. But that instant had been enough to see him: the blond hair, the long leather coat – no hat – the blue eyes; and though it was surely impossible she even believed she had seen the small scar in the shape of an SS rune at the corner of his mouth.

At the very moment she recognised him the air raid warning sirens started, those depressingly familiar three long tones of a constant pitch. She turned, and now with an idea of where the street went thanks to the splash of light, she ran.

*

The flak tower was the size of a mighty castle. The flak tower *was* a mighty castle. On its turrets sat fearsome weapons that threw fire at the heavens, within its impregnable walls there was even treasure. But it was not a place of fairy tales, and it was not a place of gallantry. It was a place to hide, from the bombs that fell, or from the beautiful young Nazi with the brand new shoes.

As soon as the sirens had started she knew she had been given a chance. She had headed for the Zoo flak tower. It was close and as she had hoped others had the same idea, and she soon managed to lose herself amongst a group of people rushing for the safety of the public shelters within. She looked back every so often but she could see no sign of him following. But then she could see no sign of anything much, except the tower, for you could not miss the tower, even in the blackout; it was like a vast dark stain on the Berlin night. In daylight the tower was rough green-painted concrete, ugly, and at forty metres high taller than anything else around it for kilometres. The shape of a box, its seventy-metre sides were pierced with tall dark windows that shafted the three-metre thick walls like arrow slits, while its square corner towers were topped with octagonal turrets that supported the guns. Inside there was a hospital ward, the treasures from the city's museums including the bust of Nefertiti, and room for 8000 scared citizens in the public shelters.

As Hanna came closer to the narrow entry channels the crowd thickened, but there was no panic, just an ordered queue. She still expected the blond man to come down the line, to pick her out, but there was no sign of him. She started to think she might have lost him, and she could not believe how lucky she had been that an air raid warning should sound when it did, giving her the chance to lose herself in the crowd. The line ahead steadily disappeared into the bowels of the monstrous fortress in front of her, and she moved closer to the narrow entrance to the tower's public bunker. After the raid at the beginning of March people were now taking the sirens very seriously, and while most would retreat to the cellars of their apartment blocks – as Konrad and Hanna would when he was home – the public bunkers gave even more protection. The soil in Berlin was soft and sandy, so most of the public bunkers were above ground, but none were as big, or seemed quite as safe, as those in the flak towers.

She passed through the thick walls. There was electric light in the narrow corridors within, but on a series of shouts this was turned off and the people had to follow the fluorescent arrows on the walls, or the voices of loved ones. She pressed on, trying to get as far from the entrance as possible, trying to lose herself in the gut of the fortress, following a right-angled zigzag of passageways until she felt she had gone far enough. Like all the Berlin bunkers the tower had been divided into small spaces. The thinking behind this, Konrad had once explained, was that if there was panic then it would not spread – it always amazed her how little faith the Reich had in its chosen people. She found a room and sat on a hard wooden bench to await the end of the air raid, and to hide from the beautiful blond young man. She wondered again if she had lost him, there had been so many people heading for the tower, and many others heading for other bunkers and cellars, and in the blackout he might have taken any one of them for her. Perhaps, she thought, she had even been mistaken.

There was a propaganda poster on the wall, but she could not read its message as the light was poor. Other than the ghostly glow from the fluorescent paint the only illumination was from a small copse of Hindenburg lights on a tiny table in the centre of the space. It was quite warm here in this concrete room, but it was not a pleasant place to be, and in other circumstances she would have rather taken her chances outside – or in a bar, at least.

Others soon joined her but sat on the other side of the room, an old silver-haired couple clutching their most treasured possessions: him a briefcase that might contain a lease and a will, her with a carpet bag possibly filled with clothes for them both. The light was not good enough for Hanna to pick out their features, but from the set of their shoulders she could tell they were tired and afraid. A family joined them soon after, and then she started to hear the muted thump of the mighty Dora flak guns far above them, and the quicker *boom-boom-boom* of the quads. Konrad had told her that the Doras had a recoil force of twenty-five tonnes – it was the sort of thing he would talk about now if they ever spoke – but even that failed to shake the concrete of the mighty tower. Yet she still felt the force of the guns, inside her, as a fluttering in her lungs, a liquid shiver behind her eyes, as if her brain shook like jelly. Hanna swallowed hard and closed her eyes tight, and wondered how long she would have to wait.

She heard the squeak of new shoe leather.

He sat down beside her. Very close, so that she could feel his firm thigh against hers.

"Good evening Frau Plaidt," he said. His voice was lighter than she had expected, not girlish, but almost cheeky.

She went to stand but he gripped her leg with an outstretched hand, those long piano-player fingers seeming iron hard, like a sprung trap. She settled back into her seat, and she noticed that others in the small space looked away, or made false conversation, their voices higher than before.

"Your perfume is distinctive," he said, answering the question she had not asked – and how else would he have found her in this dim place? She smiled a bitter smile, for it had been one of the nice things in life that had been her downfall.

*

By concentrating on the light that filtered through the gaps in the floorboards West could fight the panic. There were six thin bands of it above him and in the daylight they shone like golden rods that he would caress with his fingers. It was a tiny comfort, but he wondered if he could last the night in this tomb without that light.

They had given him an army issue Buren wristwatch – his own Breitling had been taken by a camp guard long ago – and now he could count off the minutes by holding its face to the cracks of light. He had been here for five hours, and during that time he had listened as the others packed their meagre possessions and then formed up outside, and then as they were marched out. His hide was inside the brick pile that supported the corner of the hut, the hollow that was to have become the hatch for the tunnel, but this was as far as they had got with their digging. A hacked out space with *just* enough room for one man, foetal-folded, the false leg unstrapped and stuffed in beside him. He felt like a filling, squeezed into a rotten tooth.

The plan was for him to stay put for some days at the very least and then knock away the sawn-through planks above and make his break for freedom … As long as another bunch of prisoners hadn't moved in, or a regiment of Eyetie infantry, or the bulldozers to flatten the camp … Potter had supplied all those possibilities with thinly disguised glee. The others had supplied the escape kit: RAF tunic and trousers dyed black and cut to resemble the garb of a peasant, a little food, a tin of water, and a map sketched on a handkerchief by a bomber pilot who knew the area from before the war, the latter stitched into the lining of his jacket. But he still wore the cricket jumper, too, for it was bloody cold in this tomb. In the rush he had forgotten his pipe, not that it would be much use now.

The Italians did not search the camp. They had their evidence that one had gone through the wire – someone had risked the searchlights and cut it last night and there was one short at roll call – so he could only hope they would look for the escaper out on the hills for a day or two, and then tire of it. And so he waited.

In time the golden rods of light between the floorboards faded to a porridge grey. He could hear nothing but his breathing and the incessant, strangely slow, ticking of the watch. The camp sounded empty, but he knew he could not risk leaving the cover of the hide yet. His heartbeat was up, sounding to him like the rapid thump of a bass drum, and he could feel the fear creeping within him as if it had a life of its own, as if it readied itself to burst free of him, and of the tomb. Yet only once had he panicked, when they had first shut the boards down on him. He had managed to keep it to himself, biting on his lip until he tasted blood, and sweating and sobbing in the cold hole for the first hour of his entombment.

West held his hand in front of him, so that its outline was stark against the wan light from the joins. When it faded to nothing, he told himself, he would leave the hole, and lie up in the hut for the night. It could do no harm, and it was a risk he would have to take. Suddenly there was the thump of boots on the floorboards. The heavy hobnailed soles shook the boards and West could hear the sound of Italian banter and laughter. There were about three or four of them, he thought. They stopped in a scuff of hobnails against wood. They were directly above him, looking impossibly tall from this angle, one of them holding up a hand, stopping them: "Listen …" he seemed to be saying. West held his breath: had they heard him, could they see him? One of them, a youngster with a sparse beard, looked down, eye to eye with West, as he stared at the floorboards. "Listen," the other said again, and they all stood stock-still, not a sound from any of them, not a breath from the man who lay curled up just inches beneath their feet.

Suddenly the Italian who had silenced the others let out an almighty fart. A rasping, three-part explosion of wind, his face contorted with the relished effort of it. The others laughed and punched him playfully. Someone else shouted from outside, an NCO telling them to get on with their work, West guessed. They shrugged and started dragging the bunks to the doorway, the legs squealing against the plank flooring. It took them an hour or so to move the bunks from the hut. Once the bunks were shifted they departed. It was obviously dark by now and they had lit a lamp, which they did not extinguish.

Ten minutes later West heard a truck pull up outside, the driver crunching the gears. Then the same soldiers started to bring large crates in and West tasted his first tinge of relief that day – *so it was to be a storeroom.* Other than it being left empty, he thought, he could not have hoped for a better result. He guessed it was getting close to dinnertime as the soldiers were working faster now, piling up the crates from the rear of the hut. They looked heavy, two men to a crate, and West looked forward to taking a look at what was inside them: images of canned food flicking through his mind like cinema. But he was also beginning to feel the effects of his day beneath the floorboards. The cramp in his neck was like a knife between the shoulder blades and his left leg was buzzing with pins and needles. *Just a little while longer*, he said to himself, as the soldiers brought in more and more of the wooden crates.

Then the light went out. The sudden darkness startled him and he almost cried out in surprise. He waited for the soldiers to light the lamp again, but they seemed to be unaffected by the darkness, the scrape of the crates against the floor and the thump of their boots the very same as it had been before. He reached up to the floorboards above him, feeling them shudder as the soldiers dropped another crate on to the first crate – that crate that he now realised was already on top of the hatch. The weight of both crates were pinning it shut …

"My God …" he whispered to himself, "… I'm trapped."

*

"Let's find somewhere we can talk, shall we?"

Hanna knew she could not argue with him and so she followed him into the tight passageway. He would be taking her to the Alex', she thought. There would be a black Mercedes 260D waiting outside, the favoured car of the Gestapo, she was sure of it, and the fear lay like lead at the base of her belly, mixed with the dead weight of lost hope. She could still hear the pumping thud-thud of the smaller flak guns on the roof of the tower and she was surprised he did not wait for the end of the air raid. He led her down past some other openings into small rooms in which people waited for the raid to finish, until they arrived at a ninety-degree junction. Then he stopped quite suddenly, taking her by surprise. He leant against the concrete wall and lit a cigarette, the glow of it the only illumination other than the large bright arrow on the wall, its phosphorescent paint glowing dully, giving his skin a jaundiced look, the jagged rune *S* of the scar at the corner of his mouth stark against it. They were now out of earshot of anyone, the thick concrete partitions seeing to that.

"Nice touch, eh?" he said, and she realised he had noticed she stared at the scar, and so she shifted her gaze. He offered her one of his cigarettes and she took it, taking a light from the orange glow of his, getting close enough to smell him over the dank, musty atmosphere of the passageway. He smelt of good soap, not the ubiquitous and all-purpose *Unity* soap. She suddenly realised what he had just said.

"Nice touch?" she repeated.

"Looks just like an SS rune, don't you think? Of course, that wasn't the way it looked when I caught a shard of flak shrapnel – those were the days, eh, when our own anti-aircraft fire was more dangerous than Tommy's bombs," he laughed, and like his voice it was light, cheeky. "I finished it off myself – a fine job, eh?"

She shook her head sharply, she felt he was playing with her, and her fear was beginning to be smothered by a growing anger. "What do you want from me?" she snapped.

"I told you, I want to talk."

"You people do not normally *talk* in places such as this," she said, imagined images of the cells at the police headquarters on Alexander Platz, or in the Gestapo's own building on Prinz Albrecht Strasse, coming instantly to mind, with a spark of sharper fear.

"You people?" he said.

"You know what I mean."

He laughed. "Yes, yes ... I know, sorry, but I can't resist it sometimes." He reached into the pocket of his long leather coat, and then pulled out something insubstantial, a patch of cloth. He gave it to her. It was yellow, triangular, and marked with the Star of David. She knew that it was truly yellow, and that this was not a trick of the false light, for she had seen badges like this before.

"What is this, some kind of joke?" she said.

"It is my pride, and my foolishness, and my memory. It's what I am."

She stared at it for long seconds, hardly able to comprehend. "You do not look like a Jew?" she said, finally. The badge was the Judenstern, the mark every Jew was obliged to wear, sewn upon his or her left breast.

"No, and that is my good fortune. We're not all hooked-nosed and dark-eyed, and *their* science is not quite as scientific as they might think – unless I was adopted, and I'm sure enough I wasn't."

"How do I know —"

"That this is not a trap? If I was really who you think I am, do you think I would have let you go, after what you told Bruno? You admitted to radio crime, that's a serious offence – for such a joke of a crime."

He had heard her that night then, after all.

"So, you're a U-boat?" she said.

"Madam, I am a U-boat ace," he laughed at that and suddenly she found she was laughing with him, it was difficult not to. U-boat was the slang Berliners used to describe those Jews who had dived beneath the surface of the city, those that lurked in its darkest depths, hiding from the Nazis and their restrictions, their persecution.

"Then why are you telling me?" she said.

"Because I need your help."

*

He did not live anywhere, she soon found out. He slept where he could, and often for part of the night he would have to *work* for the right to sleep. He liked his work. The new shoes and his leather coat; all that came from the well off, grateful and lonely women who would give him a bed, and a bath, some money, and not think of their husbands at the front for a night. On the occasions when there was not a lonesome frau to bed he slept in the mausoleum of the opera singer Joseph Schwarz at the overgrown Jewish cemetery in Weissensee, or in a public bomb shelter, or even in bombed out houses. The bombing, he said, had been a godsend. He had found some papers and doctored them, another talent he had. On the few occasions he had been stopped the papers, and the blackout they were inspected in, had served him well. He had an idea he might make papers for others: deserters, other Jews, criminals. There was good money to be made in this bad world, he told her.

Rather than working hard at not looking like a Jew like most U-boats did, he had worked hard at looking like a Nazi. Blond hair and blue eyes were his God-given advantage, but the rest he had done himself, with the help of grateful women who never questioned his circumcision, and a sharp knife that modified a scar to give him the lightning flash of Satan's initial.

His name was Saul. But these days he called himself Max.

They sat in Bruno's new place, for she had no need to stay away now. Max had explained that he had found her thanks to someone here, who had spotted Hanna in the cellar bar off Hardenburg Strasse. Bruno had been missing her, and asking around, he had felt grateful to know his boy was alive. That's when Max had overheard, then went to the other place, only to see her before she went in, and then to follow her to the Zoo tower. Bruno had showed his belated gratitude with a whole bottle of vodka, and Max and Hanna sat at a table in the corner. They had taken three inches out of the bottle already.

"So, *Max*, what is it you want from me?"

He ignored the question, and said: "You know something, I recognised you when I first saw you back in Bruno's old place on the

Ku'damm. I used to be a fan of racing, saw you from a distance once at the AVUS, and in the newsreels, of course."

"Why didn't you talk to me?"

"Your husband's Party, isn't he?"

"Yes but —

"Yes *but* … Maybe I wasn't so confident then. By the time I saw you here, I was plenty confident. But by then you were quite notorious."

"Notorious?"

"I'm not judging you, Hanna."

"No?" she said.

"How can I judge you, I'm a whore — and I'm free because of it," he said.

"It's the same for me," she said. "Freedom."

"I know that, but it's not enough, is it? I've seen you fight against them. I saw this even before you took the risk for Bruno."

"I thought you were Gestapo," she said.

"Yes, that's the general idea." He tapped the thin notebook that sat by the vodka bottle, another prop, she realised.

"But no hat?"

"I find the blond hair works well enough, and then again none of my clients has offered a hat, yet."

"You think I will be one of your clients?"

"As I said, *notorious*. So, I think not."

"Then I ask you again, what do you want from me?" she said, feeling a little disappointed, it had all seemed to be moving in such a deliciously familiar way.

"You know they have been shipping us out, us Yids?"

"Yes, of course. It's ridiculous, criminal."

"Do you know where they send them?"

"East, isn't it?"

"That's what I hear. But that's all I hear. And they have taken my parents." He took a gulp of vodka, as if to burn away the taste of those words. "I did not think we were so close, until they were gone — they say that's always the way, eh? My mother had fair hair, too, you know, but it did not stop them taking her. I *dived* long before all this, of course, I could see where it was going. I can see things like that, I see a lot of things, hear a lot of things … But I can't see beyond Berlin. And I don't know where they are."

"And you think I could help you find them?"

"Konrad von Plaidt …" He left the name hanging in the air like cigarette smoke for a moment, looking into her eyes, but no longer looking like a Nazi, now the veil had been pierced — it was a flimsy veil, a thing or two, once you knew the secret, yet genius all the same, a conjuror's trick.

He continued: "I often see him in the newsreels, in the background, but there: with Göring, or sometimes Himmler, your husband has connections, power —"

"You're on the wrong track here, Max, he has no influence now. Besides, tell me the last time he made *Die Deutsche Wochenschau?*"

He nodded, accepted that. Then said: "But it's my only chance. I need to know they are okay. I heard you talking to Bruno that night, I realised that you could help me. I knew then that you understood what it was like not to know the fate of a loved one."

She thought of Sepp, but it was Sepp from some years back, she realised, not the Sepp she feared. "Perhaps," she said. "But how could Konrad help?"

"Surely it is a small thing for someone like him? These people have records of everything. There must be a way of at least finding out where they are, if they are alive ..." A sudden tear came to his eye, and he turned from her.

"But they are alive, surely they are alive? Why would you think otherwise?" she said.

But when he looked at her again the tear was gone and his face did not look quite so beautiful, and his voice did not sound quite so light and cheeky as he said: "See that ugly ape over there." He nodded in the direction of a darker corner of the dark place, where a walnut skinned face was illuminated by a single candle, so that it almost seemed as if it floated free of a head and a body, like a hovering mask. "He works for the railways; helps send *them* out east. I heard him say it ... You know what comes back from the east, eh?"

She shook her head.

"Stories."

"What sort of stories," she asked, and she felt her mouth dry, reached for her drink, because the way he had said the word had overloaded it with menace.

"Horror stories."

"Go on."

"He has been told they are killing them. He has been told there are *factories* for it. Factories ... It's nonsense, of course. I cannot believe it has come to that – ludicrous!"

She remembered her room in the hospital in Zwickau. She remembered the conversation she was not supposed to hear, the conversation she had been told was just a dream, a dream repeated so often since. She remembered the terminology used by the SS doctor, the words of the laboratory, the words of the factory – *termination ... process ... incinerated* ... She remembered asking Sepp if they had killed the baby, and Sepp had said no. She had believed him, but her nightmares had told her the truth.

Perhaps that was when he had started to change, that first time he lied to her?

"I can believe it," she said.

*

"It's just what that arsehole Hoffman said, that's all."

"And what do you think?"

"I think he's a liar."

Lick had been told that Sepp had requested that the Spikes stay put. They had fought hard, fought well, throughout the Ivan offensive, and they were tired – but the war was not finished. Hoffman worked at headquarters in Kiselli, and Hoffman wasn't lying. It did not matter anyway, as Sepp's request had been turned down. Now they were heading west. Home.

Lick was still talking: "… You wouldn't do *that* to the lads, I know it …"

Sepp had managed to get the men on to the train at Babinitszi. Some had slung their hammocks in the goods cars with the infantry, while Lick had managed to bribe an army transportation clerk so the rest of them had the luxury of a proper carriage. The train had speeded up now. At last the beat of the wheels on the joints had lost the *Trudi-and-Bernd, Trudi-and-Bernd* rhythm, and now bastard Russia was quickly passing the window in a muddy scuff of emptiness. They'd seen Minsk, forests, swamps, the night, and now just hectare after never-ending hectare of grass and muddy fallow. Lick pushed his face close to Sepp's, so that he could smell the tinned sausage on the sergeant's breath. He wore a Russian sailor's hat, God only knew where he'd found it.

"You know Sepp, if I found out that that shit Hoffman was telling the truth I would kill you myself, I swear it."

"Would you really, Lick?" Sepp smiled and the sergeant collapsed back against the hard wooden seat.

"That's the first time I've seen you smile since —"

"We have a job to do Lick, it is as simple as that. We kill these Ivan animals and there is no more war – don't you want to end the war old friend?"

"No … But you didn't … Did you?" Lick half-whispered the last two words, then suddenly turned his head to the emptiness streaking past the window of the carriage. A moment or two later he smiled, and said: "But we're going home Sepp – so Hoffman must be lying!" he laughed at that.

Sepp just nodded, and wondered again what home would mean for him now. He wished that the CO had granted his request, if not the men then him at least. They did not understand, he didn't need this rest they forced upon him. They did not realise he was strong enough. They did not see that the war would not end until the enemy was dead.

The rest of the train was filled with infantry, though it was getting to the point that the difference between the regular Heer and the Fallschirmjäger was just the carriages in which they sat. Since Crete Sepp had not seen a parachute, just snow and mud and death and dirty Ivans. Most of his men were asleep, their rifles and machine pistols at the ready, heads nodding to the jolt and judder of the carriage on the worn old rails.

He glanced out of the window. The sudden thaw had turned Russia into mud, the huge pale morning sky was mottled with dirty clouds, and the only relief to this barren vista was the small village, and the rasping edge of the dark forest behind it. Out of habit he took his Zeiss field glasses from their case and focussed on the village, a jumble of log cabins with dirty thatched roofs. It was unusual for this part of Belarus in that it was still standing, but there was no sign of life. The railway curved slightly so he could now also see the engine, black and dirty like the smoke that billowed from its funnel, pushing a machine-gun equipped flat car ahead of it.

Muted thud. The squeal of steel on steel and the next thing Sepp's thrown onto Lick on the opposite bench, helmets and equipment clatter off the luggage racks and the air is filled with curses and the smooth clicks of weapons being readied.

"Glad to make your acquaintance, my dear," Lick said, as Sepp climbed clear of him. The train was still skidding, the carriages slamming against their couplings, the shriek of the wheels like cat claws on a blackboard. Sepp steadied himself against the edge of the wooden bench seat, his rifle in one hand, the binoculars in the other and the punch-dagger swinging from his belt. The gap in the rails was marked with a plume of smoke, the front of the train about to hit it. Whoever had set the charge had fired it too early. But it would still get the job done.

"Brace yourself lads!" Sepp shouted, and then the carriage seemed to buckle against the one behind it, and a few seconds later the wheels were thumping along the sleepers in a series of jarring crashes that caused the windows to pop and explode inwards, showering the paratroopers in broken glass. An instant later the carriage heeled over and Sepp looked out of the window just in time to see the rough ground coming up to meet him. It hit with a mighty smash that seemed to break the back of the carriage, and Sepp found himself thrown into the curved well of the roof, where he slid uncontrollably before grabbing at one of the luggage racks and holding on as tight as he could. The carriage slid on its side, gouging itself into the earth to the sound of smashing wood, buckling steel and the scream of a man.

Finally the train came to a halt. Sepp checked himself for damage: a gash on his right hand from a shard of flying glass and a strained shoulder where he had grimly clung onto the luggage rack. The punch-dagger had slipped from its loop on his belt and embedded itself into the wooden panelling inches from his face, where it quivered and hummed like a tuning fork. He pulled it clear and tied it back on to his belt. He then found his rifle; the butt was snapped in two, so it was next to useless.

"Lick, you okay?" He heard the pass of two rifle shots outside, both very high he judged. A machine gun at the tail of the train chattered its response.

"I'm fine ..." Lick said groggily, "but Erich's hurt bad."

They spent the next five minutes digging dazed paratroopers out of piles of luggage and equipment. In this carriage at least, the company had been lucky, except for Erich, who had left an arm crushed beneath the side of the carriage and was losing blood quickly. Sepp managed to open the rear door and they gently lifted him through and took him to cover behind the train. The big steel wheels still spun lazily above them, uselessly spending the last of their momentum. The train was ripped in two, but the two other carriages and the cattle trucks still stood upright on the track, soldiers spilling out and taking up positions behind the shallow bank, aiming their rifles between the wheels, while the MG 42 on the flat car at the rear of the train kept up a constant zipping fire. A rifle shot pinged and ricocheted off the wheel above the paratroopers. "That's the first one that's even hit the train," Sepp said, "how's Erich?"

"Bad, he's lost too much blood," Lick said.

"Bloody partisans, I hate these bandits!" Sepp shouted. Most of his men were busy retrieving their equipment from inside the carriage, a line of paratroopers passed out rifles, helmets and packs. None of them were shooting. The heavy smell of axle grease filled the air.

An infantry major, bent double and running, approached from the rear of the train, his eyes swimming with panic as he crossed the open gap between the carriages.

"We have mortars!" he shouted, as a bullet whistled overhead, very high.

"Why bother," Sepp said, coolly, making a point of standing tall, "they are partisans, and useless. Look, they cannot even hit a train." As if to illustrate his point another rifle shot passed with a little phutt some way above their heads.

"And what do you suggest, *captain?*"

"Let's rush them, before they have a chance to escape into the forest – they should not be able to get away with this." He let his eyes rest on the mashed-up red socket where Erich's arm had once been, while a medic started to tend to him, binding the wound tight, administering morphine.

"It is not worth the risk," the major snapped, "the mortars will see to them, now that's an end to it."

"Right you are, *sir*," Sepp said quietly as the major turned and made his way back to the rear of the train, where Sepp could already see the support troops setting up the pipes and base-plates of the GrW 34 mortars some way behind the stricken train. "Come on then, let's get at them lads," he suddenly said.

"But Sepp, the major?" Lick said, eyes switching from Erich to Sepp and back again.

"We are not going to let them get away with this Lick, you with me?"

Lick turned away. Others had gathered around now and most sat on the floor, staring at their rifles or a patch of muddy ground, none of them meeting Sepp's eyes.

"We must attack lads," he pleaded, "we can't let them get away with it, look at Erich!"

"Why not let the mortars get them," someone said, and the rest nodded and mumbled their agreement.

"For Christ's sake you pansies ... Will I have to order you!" he shouted it and heads dipped lower, hands gripped tightly to the stocks of rifles, another shot whistled by, very wide.

"Look! Look I say! They cannot hit a bloody train, not even a bloody train!" Suddenly rage seemed to fill him, as if a tap had been turned somewhere deep inside his being, he reached to the ground and scooped up his paratrooper helmet, throwing it at the underside of the train, where it bounced with a dull clang.

"You cannot order us Herr Hauptmann, we heard the major —"

"Then fuck you, fuck you all, fuck, fuck, fuck you ..." It would have been the first time any one of them, Lick included, had heard him use that word, or had seen him lose his temper, and their expressions ranged from utter bewilderment to true fear – for themselves, and for their leader. Sepp snatched up an MP 40 machine pistol, but left the helmet lying on the ground. "Some covering fire ... That is if it's not too much trouble, sergeant," he shouted, and then he broke the cover of the carriage, and gripping the sub machine gun by the long magazine and pistol grip he ran straight at the village, the mud sucking at his boots.

"Fuck – damn him to hell!" he heard Lick shout, just as a Russian bullet drilled itself into the mud some metres short of Sepp.

*

Hanna liked to return in the early morning, arriving home with the dawn. The raid of the night before was minor and had caused little damage, and what dust there might have been had been washed away by the rain, which had just stopped. She was suddenly quite tired, and cold. The wet cobbles of Bayernallee shone like onyx and the air smelt earthy, of rain-awakened ground. Her heels clicked loudly on the pavement as she walked, and spent raindrops raced down the sleeves of her coat and dripped off the brim of her hat.

Max had still refused to believe it. She offered him some money, which he also refused, but she placed some in the pocket of his leather coat when he went to take a leak. She had told him why she believed. She had told him of the child they had killed. Then she promised him she would try, at least, to find out what had become of his parents. She wondered whether Max was the first true hero she had met in this war. She had not slept with him, but only because he would not allow it. She liked the idea of having his son: brave and resourceful and blond haired, blue eyed. And Jewish. It would be a beautiful boy, a beautiful joke. But Max was too careful to get involved with someone whose husband was well-connected, someone notorious, because these days there were too many people willing to tell tales to get on in life, tales which would change little for Hanna, but would almost certainly cost Max his life. She understood.

Having his baby would have been a long shot anyway. Hanna and Konrad had tried for months, with advice from the best SS doctors, before the child those same bastard doctors had killed had been conceived. It had seemed a miracle, then. But there had been no miracle since; her liaisons had been too few and far between, despite her best efforts, despite her *notoriety*, despite her never insisting that they use a rubber, and she often wondered if she would ever have another chance. She had also often wondered what Konrad would have said, if she had fallen pregnant, but she guessed he would not have cared, so long as it had blond hair and blue eyes. It would just be another ornament to him, just like her.

She realised that Konrad must have agreed to the killing of the baby, surely they would have needed the father's say so at least? But like Sepp, he had also insisted what she had heard was just a dream, a drug-fugged imagining. There had even once been an SS psychiatrist to say the very same thing. She did not think she would ever trust a doctor ever again.

She suddenly found she was thinking of other dead children, little Bernd and the baby that bore her name, and then she was thinking of Sepp. When she was sober she never believed what Sepp had become. When she was sober one man's word meant nothing. But after a few drinks she could believe nothing else. She had written to Sepp since the news of the death of Trudi and the children, but she had not yet received a letter in reply. She could not imagine how the news had hit him, because she did not know him anymore, and she now realised she had not known him for many years, not since he had first lied to her. She turned off the pavement and on to the path that led to the lobby of the apartment block.

She met Konrad on the stairs. He was coming down. She was going up. It seemed right that they were going in opposite directions, she thought, but it was still a surprise. They both stopped on a half landing and greeted each other with a sharp nod. He was wearing his Luftwaffe uniform, carrying a small suitcase, and his breath smelt strongly of booze. He would be noting the same of her breath, she knew. The stairway was cold and clean and dim, what light there was squeezing itself through the frosted glass of the long windows, then dropping, exhausted, into ill-defined lard-coloured puddles on the tiled floor. The elevator had not been working for a week now; it was the sort of thing Germans would fix in an hour at one time. It was the same for the lights in the stairway. It was sometimes these small things – rather than Stalingrad – that made Hanna sure that Germany was dying.

"I thought you were away," she said, her voice amplified by the shaft of the stairway, so that it sounded hollow.

"Evidentially," he said. "Been out, have we?"

She ignored that, and said: "Why are you here?"

"Change of plans, Kessler suddenly had urgent business last night so we postponed our departure until this morning," he said. "You know, it might be better if you come home when it's still dark, people talk."

"People don't have to listen," she said.

"I do not care what I hear, Hanna, but others might."

She nodded, she did not want to argue with him right now. She remembered Max, and the favour she must ask of her husband. She had not expected to see Konrad quite so soon, she thought he would be away for a couple of days at least, and she had not had time to figure out quite how she might broach the subject. But in essence the first question she had to ask was simple enough, and so she asked it: "Konrad, what are they doing with the Jews?"

He wrinkled his brow in surprise, cocking his head to one side, and thought for a moment or three before saying: "You've heard the rumours?"

"I have heard them, are they true?"

His mouth twisted into a cruel smile, but there was enough of the old Konrad left that it should be quite obviously insincere, and she believed there was pain in his eyes when he told her. "They are taken east. There they are stripped naked, put in a shower room and gassed, although I believe there are other methods. Their bodies are burnt, their possessions – down to the fillings in their teeth – are taken for the Reich."

She was ready for it now, so was not shocked, just coldly sickened: "You've seen this?" she said.

"No, but Kessler has. He says it's a 'model of efficiency'."

"All the Jews?"

"Yes, I believe so, eventually – that's the plan."

"Have you said anything?"

"I have said *nothing*," he snorted a derisive little laugh. "There is nothing to say, why would they listen to me?"

"They used to listen to you"

"And I used to think them a joke."

"But how can you just sit there —?"

"There is nothing I can do!" he shouted it, the words splashed back from the bottom of the stairwell in mocking, muted echoes. They stood in cold silence for a little while. When she spoke again her words were softer: "There is one thing you could do, a small thing – it might help."

"Help who?" he said.

She ignored the question, and said: "Could you find out, if someone had survived?"

"I don't see how, why?"

"A friend," she said. She did not want to go into details.

He thought on that for a little while, taking out his silver cigarette case engraved with the details of a long ago race victory and lighting one of his Turkish cigarettes, blowing sweet-scented smoke that seemed to form little question marks in the cold, still air. He offered her a cigarette, but she shook her head, suddenly quite nauseous.

"You friend will be dead," he finally said, snapping the cigarette case shut at the same time, which gave *dead* a fitting full-stop.

"You are sure?"

"Quite sure, yes – ninety-eight per cent sure."

"And is there any way we can check the two per cent?"

"There is not, unless you want to draw attention to the fact that you are friendly with Jews."

"There must be records?"

"Not that I could or would attempt to look at – besides, if your Jew friend is not dead now she – or is it *he* Hanna? – soon will be, that's a certainty."

"They are *all* killed?"

"Some might survive, if they are useful, but that will be temporary."

"Every Jew? Every Jew in Germany?"

"Not just Germany, Hanna, and not just Jews. The Reich is huge now, this corporal has forged an empire – and yet there's still more than enough of this hate to go around."

"Our baby," she said.

"You know?"

"I think I've always known, deep down." For some reason she was not angry with him, the cold air between them, the coldness between them, somehow numbing it. And yet she also realised she had been angry for years, this was, she now knew, why she fought back.

"It was just the start," Konrad said. "But you must know, even if they had let it live, they would have come back for him." That was the first time she had known the sex of her child, for she had never asked before, and Konrad would never talk of it; but knowing was just a twist of the knife. Konrad continued, his tone a little condescending now: "So, it was the right decision, you see. But haven't you ever wondered, dear Hanna, about where all the tramps have gone, the cripples, all those idiots?"

Suddenly Hanna's inner vision was filled with an image of Strudel. She remembered what old Kurt had said about Frau Hansen, about *hospitals*, and she realised at once the danger Strudel was in. She also realised – instantly and instinctively – that someone needed her. With that the nausea seemed to dissipate, and the strength began to seep back into her tired body.

There were some stretched seconds of silence, and then he exhaled a long smoke-laced sigh, and said: "It might have worked, Hanna, if the baby had —"

"But you were too scared to even try again."

"It was too late."

"Too scared."

He did not reply to this. It had been a long time since she had been able to make him angry by calling him a coward, and besides, she knew that he was right. It was far too late, had been for years. He tapped the ash off the tip of his cigarette on the iron rail of the banister, and then said: "I have had my fun, too, you know."

"I'm pleased to hear it."

"Would you like to know who she is?"

"I would like to go home, to Zwickau."

"Why? We are not the only ones pretending, are we?"

"The bombs?" she phrased it like a question, knowing he would have to explain it to Kessler.

"The bombs? Yes, that is good enough."

*

The mud clung to Sepp's boots and slowed him but the marksmanship of the partisans was very poor. Just one bullet came close, drilling wetly into the mud close to his right foot. Fire from the train was heavy and he knew it would be keeping the partisans' heads down, and yet he resented it – he resented them, all of them. At that moment he would have finished the war on his own, all that mattered was that he was able to kill Ivans. The ground firmed beneath his feet and he was able to run faster; he could see the buff backs of some of the partisans' quilted jackets as they ran from the little village and into the cover of the forest beyond. The punch-dagger rattled from his belt, two bullets passed close to his head with a *tsspp-tsspp*. Sepp spotted a muzzle flash in the dark window of one of the cabins. He dropped onto one knee, and then let off a burst from the MP 40 to keep the Ivans from the window, ripping the bark from the logs, opening messy yellow wounds in the wood. He ran on, soon in amongst the cabins, but most of the partisans were gone. He looked back to the train. Lick was running after him, two others followed. The mortars started lobbing their bombs from beyond the train, the first of them landing long, shattering a pine tree at the edge of the forest.

Then there was more firing from the cabin he'd shot up, and little spouts of mud erupted from the ground metres from Lick and the others. Sepp ran to the cabin, easily smashing open the door with a savage kick and felling two of the partisans with an instant belly-high burst from the sub-machine-gun, emptying its magazine. The other partisans were lined up against the far wall, their hands in the air in surrender, two old Mosin-Nagants at their feet ... Just two rifles between the six of them. Sepp walked in.

They were boys, none of them over thirteen he would guess, but they had chosen a man's game. Sepp pulled his Sauer from its holster, its smooth action like the clash of swords in the sudden silence of the log cabin. One of the partisans panicked, rushed for the door: one shot shattered his jaw, the next punctured his forehead as if it was a melon, coming out the back in a pink spray that splashed his comrades. "Next please," Sepp heard someone say, someone who was laughing, someone who had stolen his voice. No one moved, until Sepp shot the next boy in the chest, the bullet socking into him with a rubbery thump. He twitched in a moment of disbelief, his hands covering the wound, before collapsing back against the rough corrugation of the cabin wall. The next boy had pissed himself, a dark patch steadily expanding across the front of his light brown trousers. Sepp levelled the pistol once more, took up first pressure ... Then suddenly changed his mind.

They did not deserve his bullets. The two remaining boys looked at each other, it was their chance to get away, real soldiers would have seen that, Sepp thought, as he holstered the pistol and unhooked the punch-dagger from his belt.

The boy he killed with the punch-dagger was the first to taste old Kurt's brutal steel. He had often wondered where he would aim the thing, if it came to it, but the cowering and squirming of the boy made all that academic. He hit him where he could, and as it turned out he hit him in the eye. There was no initial resistance, just a fine spray of eye juice and pale blood, and then the spike sank deep into the boy's brain until it jarred against the hard bone of the back of his skull. The other boy screamed, then collapsed into a bundle in the corner of the cabin as his comrade fell from the spike, which made a slurping noise as Sepp pulled it clear. Thicker, darker blood suddenly erupted from the wound, gushing like an oil strike, and the boy fell forward onto the dirty floor, landing with a dead thump.

There was noise from outside, big fart-like explosions, mortar bombs landing on soft ground. Sepp could hear Lick shouting, and could imagine him waving at the train, telling them to cease fire, but the mortar line was out of sight, someone would have to pass the message on. Sepp didn't care. For *he* had done it … Cleared the village … All alone … He could win the war alone … Clean up this bloody awful country … Everything was possible at that moment … Right at that moment …

Sepp turned to the last of the boy partisans. He gripped the handle of the punch-dagger tightly, its iron gauntlet had slipped beneath the sleeve of his para smock and for a moment it seemed as if the spike was a part of him, as if his right hand was just the spike of the punch-dagger. The boy cowered on the floor, he was speaking in Russian, pleading, and then he turned his eyes to Sepp, very big and very brown, like polished chestnuts. Sepp had seen eyes just like this before, he thought, as he pulled his arm back ready to thrust with the punch-dagger, but he could not remember where. Another mortar bomb landed outside, causing a great wave of mud to break across the building with a filthy splatter. Yes, it had also been a muddy place … He chose the spot on the boy's head, he had stopped pleading now and was silently awaiting his fate, dribbling and crying, his face dissolved into terror.

Sepp looked into those crying eyes once more and then he was right there again: on the waste ground outside the Horch Works, fighting that bully boy Wolf to save Strudel … Yes, that was it … The boy had those same pleading eyes. Suddenly something seemed to die within Sepp, some sigh that had never sighed, and he let his spiked-arm drop. Tears burnt at the back of his eyes but he could find no way to release them.

It was then that Lick burst through the door, instantly taking in the scene of carnage, the bodies, the smell of recently vented shit and cordite, the thick blood dripping off the tip of the punch-dagger, blinking his eyes quickly as if he fought with himself not to see this. Sepp walked past him, pushing him aside, out into the muddy avenue that ran between those few cabins. The two other paratroopers looked at him, then at each other, one said something, but it was as if it was in another language, spoken underwater. A mortar bomb landed close by and the paratroopers dived for cover. The fall of the bomb coated Sepp in thick mud yet he was barely aware of it. He was half-conscious of Lick at the door to that cabin, throwing up, as he raised the punch-dagger. He heard his friend and sergeant shout, then the whistling fall of another bomb … And then he cocked his head to the left – and punched the long spike straight into the right side of his own skull.

***

West dare not use the matches. The oxygen in this little dark place of his was the most precious thing he had, with very little of it seeping through the small air tube the tunnel diggers had plumbed in. He did not want to burn it up, and so he not seen the face of the watch since the heavy crates had been placed over the planks above him. How long now? Days certainly, perhaps over a week; but it felt like months. The only thing to break the tedium of darkness and pain was the day of the rain – and then the hole had flooded. By then his water supply was finished, so he had been pleased to at least have the dirty, foul tasting water to drink. But then there was his own diarrhoea, caused by the filthy water, and there was nothing he could do but lie in it, nothing for him to breathe but the choking stink of his own bad shit. Now even the supply of dirty water had dried up and he could feel his tongue begin to swell, his throat crack to each rasping breath, and his lips slowly blister and craze.

The food was long finished, as was hope. The only thing in plentiful supply was fear – now of a constant gnawing kind rather than the stark, screaming terror of that first night – plus the burning pain of his tightly constricted limbs, and the hallucinations. The best of these was Hanna, but these were never quite as vivid as the ones that brought green snakes and fire. Sometimes, to pass the time between hallucinations, he would put his imagination behind the wheel of an Auto Union and drive the Nürburgring, Mellaha, Brno, Pescara, Donington … Then he could go back to a time when he could pretend there was never going to be a war.

He constantly listened out for the sound of the Italians returning to the hut. But nobody came, and all he could hear was the regular beat of his heart and the torture tap of water dripping somewhere close by. He bitterly regretted not calling out to the soldiers when he realised he was trapped, when he had the chance, but they had gone by the time he had decided that not even freedom was worth this. Now, it seemed, whatever supplies were here, no one wanted them. So, a game he played: what was in the boxes that trapped him in this tomb? Straw hats he decided once, with absolute certainty – *absolute certainty* – that was the first time he believed he was going mad.

He had thought of escape, but there were no tools in his pack. Once he had tried to dig his way through the side, clawing at the bricks and cement with his fingers, but it was no use, and he soon went back to listening out for the Italians, dreaming of the day he could give himself up again.

Had he slept for any length of time? He could never tell. Sleep down here was like sleep on a bumpy train ride, falling headfirst against your eyelids and waking with a start. He blinked, but it made no difference, there was always nothing but that same velvet darkness, almost solid in its fuzziness. He wondered if his eyes would ever work again. And then there were the rats. He could hear them now, scurrying in the hut above him, the soft brush against the wooden floor, then the creak of the floorboards.

He wondered how big a rat must be to make a floorboard creak ... Then he heard the whispering. There was someone up there.

West tried to shout, but all that would come was a choking gasp that sounded like the soft ripping of parchment. The whispers were sharper now and he could hear the heavy scrape of the packing cases against the floorboards, the squeal of nails in wood, and then the dull, steely ding of something placed on the boards. He tried to shout again, and this time there was a squeak, and the noise and movement above him suddenly stopped. Had the Italians gone? No, there were the whispers again, scared little voices, thinking they had heard a ghost. Then they started to move the packing cases again, but this time with far more urgency, and at the other end of the hut. West put his last effort into his last shout, his last ounce of energy, his last spark of life.

"Help!"

It was a yelp, high and loud in the confines of his stone tomb, and the effort of it seared his throat, as if he'd downed a pint of acid. They stopped again. There seemed to be just two of them, he thought. One seemed bolder than the other and a voice was raised beyond a whisper. They were arguing now and there was the thump of running feet as one of them ran from the phantom beneath the floorboards. The other chased and then both pulled up in a skid of squeaking boots.

"Please ..." West managed to croak, hardly sure if the word had left his mouth. He heard the crates moving again, one scraping against another, but this time much closer: could it be above him? Dust dropped onto his forehead and the floorboards over his tomb began to quiver. Then quite suddenly there was light. It was buttery and insubstantial, hardly filling the cracks in the floorboards, but it was the most beautiful light he had ever seen. He tapped at the underside of the floorboards with his knuckles. A crowbar was jammed between the planks, cold iron close to his face, and then the boards cracked and splintered, then burst apart.

It was Hanna. Another bastard hallucination ...

But no, he blinked, the harsh lamplight was behind her, a shining aura, dazzling his unaccustomed eyes so he had to snap them shut, but she was there all right. She spoke to him in a language he did not understand. "Hanna," he whispered, but she stopped him, a soft finger brushing against his swollen lips. She turned to the short figure behind her carrying the lantern, speaking to it sharply, whereupon there was the scrape of metal on metal and West guessed the lantern had been shuttered. He opened his eyes again. Her face took shape in front of him as he adjusted to the now dim light. West wondered why, how, when, Hanna had joined the Italian army as the texture came to her soft cheeks, the gleam to her eyes, the shine to her hair. She fanned a long, slender hand in front of her face, said something, and the young figure behind, a boy he realised, chuckled. He had forgotten about the stink of this place of his, was used to it and could only smell the oil burning in the bullseye lantern. Now he suddenly felt embarrassed.

They pulled him from the hole, a struggle for them and him, and lay him on the floorboards. In the shuttered light thrown from the lantern he could see that they had opened a few of the crates with the crowbar and the floor was littered with motor parts. They were trying to get him to stand up, but it was difficult and he kept collapsing in a heap on the floor. Hanna smelt wonderful, he thought, but not like he remembered, more like a meadow of wild herbs. She was shorter, too ...

Hanna and the boy helped him strap his lower right leg in place then they finally managed to get him to his unsteady feet and half carried, half dragged him out of the hut. At the bottom of the steps he slipped, but they pulled him onwards, his heels slithering in the mud as he tried to keep his balance. He was dimly aware of light from one of the huts outside the wire, but none of the searchlights were on, and that seemed strange, until he remembered that this was no longer a POW camp. He heard the tinkle of the wire as they passed through a gap he assumed they had made earlier, a barb snatched at his hair, and soon they were at the second fence, and through just as quickly. He could walk just a little better now, as the feeling returned to his legs in bolts of fire, as the boy urged him to hurry in a language he did not understand. But he still did not have the strength to walk unaided and he leant heavily, and guiltily, on their narrow shoulders as they started to climb the steep slope behind the camp, each step a spear wound of searing pain that burst bright in his head as his long-constricted limbs came back to life.

They were soon in among the trees, which grew out of the sharply sloping ground at an acute angle, and West found he could use them to help him along as he felt his way up the slope in the darkness, Hanna always helping, pushing and pulling, the boy a little ahead now, urging them on, finding his way forward with the help of the moonlight that washed the upper branches of the trees a ghostly silver. West's feet slipped in the loose soil, he fell again and again, the pain still twisting in his limbs, but he always lifted himself straight back up onto his unsteady feet, as the realisation started to permeate within him, like whisky warmth, the realisation that he was no longer in that cold hole, the realisation that he was free. He took the air into his lungs in greedy snorts and swallows, the greatest feast he'd ever tasted, and with it came the garnish bouquet of the wood itself; the smoky and earthy tang of wild fungi. The boy was standing on a path that cut across the hillside ahead of West now, just a palely shining seam in the moonlight, he was beckoning frantically for Hanna and West to hurry.

Suddenly a shout shattered the silence of the night. It was Italian, and with it came the sound of twanging wire followed by the thump of boots. West turned sharply, almost losing his balance. He saw the light of a single torch burning a hole in the darkness below, just beyond the edge of the trees. Hanna urged him forward, and the sight of the light below, the sound of the voice, helped him forget the molten steel pain that flowed through every part of his tortured body, helped him climb faster.

The man behind them was alone, that was clear. Maybe there would be more of them asleep in the guardhouse, and maybe they would be braver. But this lone sentry had not risked coming into the trees to follow these unknown intruders. The boy still urged them on from the path, and West now saw there was a donkey with him, a shaggy shadow standing as still as the tree to which it was tied. Hanna was now on the path and she reached down to help West scramble up the last few feet of the climb to it. There was another Italian warning shout from below, and instinctively West turned to see if the sentry now followed. The movement dislodged a rock, which tumbled down the slope. They froze, Hanna and West just touching fingertip to fingertip.

West felt a whip stroke in the air, then a bright flash of white wood appeared on a tree trunk inches from his head, to the ripping sound of shredding bark. An instant later he heard the crack of the rifle shot from below. Just as he was registering that delayed sound as a gunshot there was the poker hot hit of another bullet in the back of his thigh, smashing him forwards against the slope, his nostrils and mouth filling with musky, choking dirt as the slightly lagging report of that second rifle shot reached his ears.

*

The bullet was in deep. In his mind's eye it looked like a red hot rivet, the sort they punch into steel plate at shipyards, and it somehow felt as if its impetus had not been completely arrested; just slowed, as if it still burrowed into him, slowly, painfully, hotly. A lucky shot in the trees and in the night: the sentry had been fortunate, but he had not been brave, and somehow West had managed not to cry out. It meant the soldier did not follow them, persuading himself it was just a deer or a fox or a rabbit, perhaps. His comrades were chiding him now, far below, for spoiling their sleep with his wild shots into the darkness. Meanwhile Hanna and the boy had somehow managed to sling West across the back of the donkey, his stomach on the high wooden cradle-like saddle, arms dangling down one side so his fingers almost brushed the ground, legs the other side. It was, he thought, the way a dead man would ride. West supposed the donkey would have been there to carry their booty. He also supposed that they might have been disappointed to find nothing but carburettors, boxes of spark plugs, and a dog-sick prisoner of war. It couldn't help that that dog-sick prisoner now had a bullet in him, too.

The boy led the donkey along trickle-narrow paths through the trees, its quick little steps scuffing and clopping, the rhythmic creak of the leather that held the cradle in place sometimes lulling West into a fitful doze, but the burning pain in the back of his left leg always keeping him from falling fully asleep. He would have preferred to sit astride the animal, but the wooden cradle and his wound meant that would be difficult, and this hurt his pride almost as much as the fire of the bullet inside him hurt his flesh. But, after so long in the hole, he realised he was pleased to find he still possessed pride.

Soon the boy started to sing, a haunting melody that seemed to call the sun from its hiding place behind the hills, and now, when the path was wide enough, she would walk alongside the donkey. It was not Hanna. He had realised that early on, but he had chosen to cling to the lovely lie of it until the dawn. The truth, he found, was no less lovely.

It was the same girl he had spotted on that first day in the camp, stealing from Fatty Arbuckle, and the girl he had seen outside the camp on occasion. The girl made of freedom. Sometimes she smiled at him and sometimes she talked to him in words he could not understand, but were as beautiful as the boy's singing. It was the first time he had seen her close up. Because of the way he had been bundled across the wooden cradle on the back of the donkey, like a sack of spuds, he had to crane his head to study her, an attitude he could not hold for long, and she would smile at him. She smiled at him as if she had known him all her life, and he somehow felt as if he had known her all his life, too. He did not know how that could be, it was just that there was something in the way she was, something in the way she looked, that touched him in a profound way. Somehow, this girl was someone he had never met, but had always known.

She was beautiful, but in a way that might not work on photographs. Her face was animate, that was the secret to her beauty, he thought. Her slightly upturned nose twitched at the air, as if she wanted to sniff every smell; her ears were a little large and pointed, and curved slightly away from her head, so that she seemed to be always listening out for every sound, too. This was accentuated by the way her long shining ebony black hair was tied back with a red checked bandana into a languid brush stroke of a ponytail. Her eyes were hungry, and big and green; the green of a secluded lagoon, he thought, though there was also a tiny, tiny splinter of yellow-gold within them that seemed feline. It was freedom, he decided. She smiled at him again as he thought it, as if he'd spoken it: white teeth, just one of them slightly out of line, it made her human, playful. He was glad of that, for otherwise she would have seemed a goddess, and maybe then he would think her just another bastard hallucination.

They stopped soon after the sun had come up, after they had crossed the Natisone by way of a wooden bridge. Then they eased him off the donkey. There was shelter in a small abandoned stone farm building of some sort, where they lay him on a grey blanket. He drank cold water from a dish she gave him. She had made sure he had taken sips from a water bottle as they went along, too, and he felt this had saved his life. She turned him on his belly and carefully cut a large, ragged slot in the back of his trouser leg with a knife, and then cleaned and dressed the wound with strips torn from her petticoat, the ragged rips of the cotton tantalizing enough to keep his mind off the pain. Then they helped him back on to the donkey, this time into a sitting position, the wooden cradle now abandoned, to the disgust of the boy. It was better this way, although he had to lean to one side to avoid putting weight on to the wound in the back of his thigh.

The dawn was grey and kind to his starved eyes, and now he fed upon the sight of this beautiful land, and this wonderful girl. They headed north-east. West had done his best to memorise the most important features on the map stitched into the lining of his jacket before he was put into the tomb, and so he was able to figure out that the river they now followed was the Soca, which the Italians called the Isonzo. It was a river that flowed with water of the most extraordinary colour, a shocking hue that almost defied belief. The pilot who had supplied the map had told West it was aquamarine, but he thought it was closer to turquoise, and he knew if an artist was to paint it as true then he would be laughed out of most galleries. When the clouds lifted West was able to see the Julian Alps, pyramidal and imperious in the distance, still crowned with snow, while either side of the broad basin of the Soca Valley the trees clung to the lower slopes before giving way to towering rock faces of limestone, perilously hanging valleys, jumbles of jagged peaks and knife-edge ridges and, at one point, the bright and silver flash of a large waterfall.

When they stopped for the second time she gave him food, a cold potato which he assumed had been baked in its jacket on a campfire the evening before, and he swallowed it quickly. But he could not keep it inside him, for the dysentery still gripped his innards like a sprung trap. The boy started arguing with her then, and he guessed it was over the burden that burdened their beast of burden; the wounded and sick burden, whose liquid shit now trickled through the hole in his trousers to stripe the back of the stoic donkey. West wanted to simply sit in the cold turquoise wash of the Soca, to clean himself and his wound, but the girl, the boy and the donkey walked on. At one point, when they rested again, he tried to ask her name, Tarzan and Jane style. She pointed to her chest: "Roma," she said.

They kept following the river north-east, keeping to the trees that lined its course and skirting the small villages that were dotted along it at a safe distance, though close enough to smell the wood smoke and hear the dogs bark. Then they were climbing up a sharp zigzag pathway that had been cut into a hillside, and then down an equally steep path the other side, where West had to lean back, jarring his wound painfully, to stop himself tumbling forward over the neck of the donkey. He was exhausted to the point of collapse by now, but she would always find some strange foreign word that sounded to him like an incantation, and an encouraging smile, that would persuade him to squeeze a little extra from his spent body.

By the time the sun began to sink West reckoned they had travelled about twenty-five hard miles through that long day and the remnants of the night before it. The sun was going down behind them, so by now they were heading east. They had climbed and descended another wooded slope that reached up to naked limestone heights to the south. Below them the turquoise waters of the Soca were wilder, the valley tighter, but he sensed they were close to the end of the journey because the donkey had upped its pace, despite the gradient and its fatigue, its nostrils flaring as it snorted air into its lungs, its hooves slipping and skidding on the stony ground so that West had to hang on tight. The boy still walked on ahead, easier now as if a load had been lifted from him. They were climbing a very steep, straight and rocky path. The path was quite wide, and the rocks that made up its bed looked to have been placed there, long ago, while alongside it bigger rocks lay haphazard, some of them angular and unnatural looking, like the weatherworn dice of giants. Further up there were bushes of barbed wire caked in rust that looked like dried blood, an old and holed coal scuttle helmet also rusting on the ground, and shell casings stacked in an untidy pile, the burnish of their brass long ago faded. There had been war here, West thought, but it had not been recent.

They came to the top of the slope with no warning, just a sudden levelling off of the climb, and the rocky path gave way to smooth stone that led down an obviously manmade channel formed from closely fitted stone blocks, most stained acid green with lichen, while grass grew in tight tufts through the joins in the smooth stones on the floor. The dark channel was about ten-feet deep, with just about the room for two to walk side by side along it. It very soon turned at a right angle, in the manner of a trench, and West realised it was part of some sort of fortification – not new, but hardly medieval either. Shortly they came to a covered part, where the way was blocked by a rusting iron door, on which a fading red painted double-headed eagle was just about visible. Above the door someone has carved numbers: *2/45. 1916.* A unit and a year, West guessed.

The boy pushed the door, which opened inwards with a heavy creak, then shouted something into the echoing darkness beyond. They stepped inside, tying the donkey to a rusty iron ring set in the wall. West could smell cooking meat and smoke, and hear excited talk in that same strange language. He half climbed and half fell off the donkey, Roma helping him, and then he collapsed against the cold, damp smooth wall within. Suddenly there were many voices, and each one seemed to be shouting, but he heard Roma's above them all. She was still shouting, fighting for him he somehow knew, and clutching his hand tightly, as he drifted into a deep nothingness.

***

They were all Roma, he had learnt that very quickly. But by then it was too late, the girl that fascinated him, filled his days and his dreams, was *Roma*. So he never bothered with her other name, the name they used … They, the Roma: the gypsies. They grew familiar over the next few days, or however long it was, for he would sleep and never really know how many hours, or days, he was out of it as the bullet in his thigh and his time in the stone tomb still took their toll on his ravaged body. Most times he would wake to see her waiting for him, a vision of heavenly beauty against the soot stained log and turf ceiling of the stone construction. At other times he would awake to find a scatter of seemingly disembodied fire-bright faces hovering in front of him, none of which was slit with a smile, and then he would wonder just how ill he really was.

They gave him herbal remedies for his illness and Roma tended the wound with stinging iodine. They also gave him food: sometimes goat in a stew, at other times tinned sardines, stolen, he guessed, from the Italian camp. For days it all went straight through him, for he still had dysentery, and the little tucks of fat that remained on his body after years of captivity seemed to melt away from him. But the bullet, still hot inside his thigh, was a greater worry.

Then the doctor came. He did not seem happy to be there, but he brought chloroform, in a bottle that was of the same vintage as the old stone floor West lay on, and he brought the instruments, gleaming long-handled deep spoons and shining scalpels that West just glimpsed before he drifted into oblivion after inhaling the sweet smelling anaesthetic. When he awoke the doctor was sewing the wound shut and giving Roma instructions West did not understand. Quite soon he was feeling better, and the days became full days, the weeks full weeks, and the gypsies stopped looking at him as if he was about to leave this world.

West had quickly realised this was an old fortification, from the fighting in the last war, when the Austro-Hungarians faced the Italians on the mountain tops. There had been much combat here, most of it bitter, and after the war, and Versailles, this part of Slovenia had been given to Italy. Despite the evidence of the thick stone around him it seemed hard to imagine warfare in a paradise like this. He'd driven through the landscape of the Western Front time and again and had even visited the small corner of Flanders where his uncle had lost his life, his father his sense of humour, but that had seemed different, bleak and unsurprising.

The fortification was not on the old trench-line, so it seemed likely it had been a supporting gun emplacement. There were two bays which would have once housed the field pieces or howitzers, with now rusting steel rails embedded in the stone floor where the guns would have been traversed. They would have covered a spur of the mountain ahead, and the dirty scratch of road that followed the bright river far below. The fortification was on its own spur, with just the one steep path leading to it, and no easy way up, or down, from any other direction – he thought it must have been a bugger of a job to get those guns up here. When the weather was good West would sit in the first of the bays, which now had no roof, and when he had the strength he would stand and watch the valley far below through an aperture that once spat death into this green paradise.

All together there were about forty gypsies living here, and he could only guess at the tragedy that had sent them running to the hills, for tragedy there had surely been. The men – some old, some young – seldom left this place, unless it was to hunt with one of the three ancient rifles they possessed, while the faces of the women were masks of deeply chiselled grief. They went about their work in a trance, hanging up the intricately patterned rugs or rough blankets that separated the sleeping areas in the large rooms that had once been the billets for Austrian artillerymen, and cooking the meals in black iron pots that hung from charred wooden tripods.

There was a fireplace in one of the old billet areas where there was still a chimney, although the atmosphere was still always smoky, as if the big guns still fired. This made for a communal focal point, and there were arguments around that fire almost every evening. They were not now between Roma and the young boy; indeed, he always seemed to side with her now. Rather they were between Roma and a handsome youth with a ponytail, a dagger at his belt, an old Mannlicher rifle forever slung over his shoulder, and an unripe moustache quivering at his top lip. He wore a caramel-coloured leather jerkin, cracked with age, with a grubby, intricately embroidered white shirt beneath it, and tall leather boots that would creak as he paced the space in front of the fire like some captured mountain cat. They called him Ilya. At first West thought he was their leader, but only the four younger men seemed to take much notice of him, and when he was arguing with Roma even they seemed unsure of which side to take. West could never understand a word of these passionate disputes but he guessed, from the amount of times the youth looked his way, that he was all-too-often the cause of it all. He also guessed that this same youth wanted Roma for himself – so then, he was no fool.

After West had been there for three weeks at the very least, his beard now thick, an older man arrived and suddenly calm descended on the place. At first the man said nothing to West, merely nodding, before talking at length with Roma, hearing her side of the story patiently and then doing the same with Ilya, having to calm him on occasion by placing one of his enormous hands on the youngster's shoulder. After that he told his news, everyone listening to what he said without a murmur, as they sat beneath a clear blue sky in the area around the toothless, roofless, gun bays.

He was a big man: bigger than just big, a bear of man, with a dark blanket of a beard that reached to his belt. If the beard had been white he might have looked like Santa Claus, and he was surely old enough that it should be white. His face bore the marks of a man who had lived in the open, with the ploughed, open forehead of the philosopher. He had eyes almost exactly like Roma's, green and sparkling like precious jade-stones, but without the tiny yellow grains of freedom; eyes that were often alight with a humour that just warned you a smile was cutting its way through the undergrowth of his beard. The gypsies laughed with him when he laughed, which was often, and it was then that he managed to smooth the grief from some of those faces.

When the old man had finished he dismissed the others with gentle authority then walked over to West's spot by the old gun barrel aperture, taking a look down into the valley, then sitting opposite him on an old upturned wooden box marked *AM*, which showed it had once belonged to the Italian army.

The old man said: "My name is Nicolai."

West was startled. These were the first English words he had heard in weeks.

"You speak English?" West said.

"Some – and your name is, *West?*"

"Yes." West stretched out his hand and Nicolai took it with a surprisingly gentle, yet firm, handshake.

"And *west* is the way you will want to go?" he asked, the beard parting to reveal a little smile.

"I have not decided yet … I've been ill," West suddenly thought he must sound quite pathetic.

"Yes, my grand-daughter has told me all about you West, she has taken to her stray puppy," he said it with a laugh and West laughed with him. He noticed Ilya glaring from the shadows of the dark stone channel that led to the bay.

"She's your grand-daughter?"

"Yes, and the young boy she was with when she found you is my grandson, her brother." That made sense, West thought, they argued like a brother and sister: hot and fast, then forgotten. "She has fought hard for you, you know?" Nicolai nodded in the direction of Ilya. "That one thinks having you here is a danger, I hope for all our sakes he's not right?"

"I certainly don't intend to be," West said.

"Then that's good, it's what she said. She seems to know you, without even speaking to you. But that does not really surprise me – she is very much like her grandmother, that one," Nicolai said. "I have her strength to remind me of the wife I have lost, the life I have lost …" He let the words trail into a soft sigh.

"I'm sorry," West said.

"It was long ago."

"It's been difficult," West said, "not being able to talk to anyone, could you thank your grand-daughter for me?" He knew she was not here now, for she had left hours earlier.

"I will do this for you," Nicolai said, nodding sharply. "You are a soldier, yes?"

"A pilot."

"Then it is good they did not know," he said, earnest now. "It was a pilot who killed our people, his aeroplane's machine guns feeding on our caravans, our horses, our families ..." Suddenly the old man's eyes shone with the promise of tears.

"What were the markings, on the wings?" West asked.

"Does it matter? Your war, not ours – but it has taken everything from us."

"I'm sorry," West said, once again, for no good reason he could think of, except perhaps that someone should.

"We have been running and hiding for two years. We were in Croatia when the Ustase came to power. They started to persecute our people, and so we moved on, that is the advantage we have over the Serbs and the Jews, it is no difficulty for us to move on. But it is the only advantage."

"When were you attacked by the plane?"

"Over a year ago, but believe me the wounds are still raw. Most will not leave this place now, they are too afraid."

"They have suffered more than civilians should," West said, knowing the horror of an air attack, remembering Crete.

"When there is war the Roma will always suffer, whoever is fighting, and wherever we are. We do not have a country, called Greece, called Italy, called this, called that, for we do not see borders. So, we are always aliens, strangers, we are always the enemy – and wars are a time when hatred is allowed to flourish."

"So, you are hiding until the war ends?"

"Yes, just waiting for the madness to stop – it might take some time."

"It will stop, this place is proof of that, proof that wars end," West said, allowing his eyes to pass over the tight fitting blocks of stone, many of which were stained in leprous lichen, making the emplacement seem much older than the quarter of a century it had been here. "Do you know its history?" he asked, glad of the opportunity to satisfy his curiosity at last.

"It was used by the Austrians when they fought the Italians the last time you people had a disagreement. You know, I sometimes wonder at the work it took to build it. Each and every stone carried hundreds of metres up the hillside, then the guns that were housed here, then the shells, and even the food and water for the soldiers. And this was just one spot among thousands on a general's map. It sometimes seems to me that if they put as much effort into avoiding wars as they put into fighting them, then this world would be a much safer place."

West nodded his agreement, then said: "And is *this* a safe place?"

"It's the best we can find. Not so high in the mountains that we freeze in the winter, but far away from other people, and their hatred. It's our home, for now. There is water close by, there is warmth, and we can hunt for some of our food. Everything else we steal, it's what's expected of us anyway – but you should understand that we only steal when we need to. That's important." He looked deep into West's eyes, looking for a flicker of disapproval perhaps. Then he nodded sharply and continued: "The difference now is that we only steal far away from here, too. This way there's no trouble with the local people, and we are left in peace – this was how Violca found you, the Italian soldiers she takes from are far enough away, and not difficult to steal from. But then Violca is a very good thief!"

Violca was what the others called Roma.

"She saved my life."

"More than once, I think. You were close to death when she found you in that hole, and then there was the bullet. You should know that if I had been here, then I might not have agreed to it – although I do not know how I would have stopped her!" He laughed as he said that, then continued. "It was a risk, bringing a doctor up here, we try not to draw attention to ourselves. But, she has seen something in you, thinks you worthwhile ... She jokes that it is the way you play football?"

West remembered that day he'd floored Fatty Arbuckle with the heavy leather ball, and also remembered she had been watching. That had cost the prisoners, there was a month of food that was even poorer than that which they had gotten used to, but he could see how the girl would have enjoyed watching as her fat nemesis was downed. He wondered if, after all, sport had saved his life. And he smiled.

"It cost her, you know," Nicolai continued. "The doctor would not come here from Kobarid without payment, and there is a great shortage of anaesthetic."

"How did —?"

"There was a necklace," Nicolai cut in, a slight shadow seeming to pass over his eyes. "It once belonged to her mother, she died when the plane came, as did her father. But it had other value. She no longer has it."

"I'm sorry," West said, yet again.

"There is no need to be. It was her choice, and if you stay with us longer you will learn there is no arguing with Violca. Freedom drives the girl, not tradition. She is not like the others. I sometimes think she has the spirit of the ancients, the spirit that put our people on the road in the first place."

Ilya still stood there, listening to words he could not understand, leaning in the tight stone corridor so that it seemed he was holding the walls apart. He suddenly stood straight, to let someone through the narrow gap.

"But here she is," Nicolai said, his smile widening.

Roma walked into the space of the old gun position with a large, bulbous clay water jug balanced on a pad of cloth on the top of her head. It was heavy, it had to be, he had seen how much water it held, and yet she handled it with the poise of a princess. He saw her grandfather's face light up with pride when she came to him and West tried his best not to stare at her. She poured them some water. Most of the water the gypsies had to drink was from a stream close to the base of the slope, carried up the rocky path jug by jug, bucket by bucket, and it looked greasy, tasted brackish. But the water she brought every other day was the sweetest water he had ever sipped, as clean and pure as the air in this high place. He often wondered where she found it, not least because her skin glowed and she smelt of Italian army soap whenever she returned with it.

Nicolai thanked his grand-daughter for West, for all she had done for him, and for the water. She poured a little more of it, this time spilling just a little onto the stone floor, where it splashed itself into a dark patch. Their eyes met over the rim of a tin mug. West thought that he saw the beginning of a blush at her throat, though it was instantly doused by something else, a glimmer of utter understanding in the yellow flecks of those green eyes that was as cheeky as it was animal. The older man smiled again and looked at them both, one to the other, as though he was slowly shaking his head, then said: "The doctor was told you were one of us, you know. Under the anaesthetic you talked, and that helped convince him."

"It helped, how?" West said.

"There was just one word, but you kept repeating it. It was *Roma*."

***

The chickens had shaken the little world in which West now lived. Ilya had not been out for long before he returned with the four dead chickens. If it was meant to impress Roma, which it surely was, then it had gone badly wrong for him. They had had an argument so blazing it seemed to scorch the air – air which still crackled from the heat of those words, none of which West fully understood. Roma had snatched up her clay water pot and left. Nicolai had simply given Ilya the sort of look that non-Roma would take as a gypsy curse, and then sat on the wall of the old fortifications overlooking the valley. He took no part in the preparation and the cooking of the chickens. Others did, for it had been a long time since they had tasted chicken. Ilya had broken the rules, stealing from the local people, but he had gained prestige. Ilya, West guessed, would say that Roma had broken the rules, too, bringing him here, and would use it to his advantage. West wondered what the boy wanted most, Roma, or the respect the others gave to her grandfather.

West sat up and leant against the stone wall of the old gun bay. He was feeling better now, thanks largely to her care, her pampering. In fact he had been feeling much better for weeks – and Nicolai was making his little joke about West heading west all the more often. There had been other arguments, too, Nicolai and Ilya now, and West was beginning to think it was indeed time to move on, head for the Alps and, eventually, Switzerland. He had even thought of joining up with the local partisans, but many of them had been encircled and massacred by the Italians near a village called Kal-Koritnica at about the same time as his arrival. Also, the politics were tricky. Of course, politics were always tricky for Westbury Holt, but some of these partisans were busy fighting future wars already, Nicolai had told him, and it would be difficult to know who to trust. Either way, West knew he was not yet ready to leave. Because he was still weak, yes … But mostly because of the girl made of freedom.

He decided he would go for a walk, the wound in his thigh had almost healed now and he tried to walk a little further every day, building up his strength slowly. If he was lucky he would meet Roma and he could help her carry the water back. He pulled his grubby cricket jumper over his shoulders. Roma had dyed it a rusty-red with henna, which would make it a little less conspicuous when he finally moved on. As his head popped out of the neck he noticed that Ilya was watching him as he sharpened the blade of his dagger over a smooth stone, a strange little near smile tugging at his bottom lip. He sat with the other youngsters on a ledge overlooking the gun bays, where the women cooked in the open. Two of the chickens had been spitted and were beginning to slowly roast, the skin sizzling and dripping, fat flaring the fire, the aroma intoxicating, flooding West's mouth with saliva, filling the faces of the hungry gypsies gathered around the fire with impatient anticipation. West would not eat their chicken. He was not sure

Ilya would offer him some anyway, but he would not eat it because Roma would not eat it, and he owed Roma his life, and his loyalty.

He pulled on his left boot then searched for his loose right limb. It was nowhere to be seen around the tangled pile of old sacking that was his bedding, which he had brought out to sit on. He looked up at the figure dangling his long, thin legs over the top of the wall, Ilya had his head dipped over his work, and the scraping noise of the blade against the stone seemed louder, almost taunting, as did the heels of his boots, drumming lightly against the wall. West searched the area around the old gun bays, then behind a pile of chopped wood for the fire, his hopping causing the wound in his thigh to flare with bright pain, but there was no sign of his false leg. There was sly giggling from the group of young gypsies who sat close to Ilya and then, through the smoke of the cooking fire, West saw Ilya pick up his false limb with the boot attached to it, and toss it down onto the floor. It landed with a thump close to West's foot. The younger gypsies laughed out loud, except for Roma's brother, Georgi, who looked embarrassed. One of them clapped Ilya on the back as he considered his grinning reflection in the gleaming blade of the dagger. West laughed with them, tolerantly, shaking his head in a *boys-will-be-boys* sort of way, before strapping his lower leg into place and walking out of the gun bays and through the connecting corridors and the sleeping space and then out through the iron door.

He hobbled down the steep and rocky path, using the springy trunks of young trees for support, and then, once half way down the hillside he took another path he had not noticed before. It followed the contour of the slope, and it was a relief from the jarring descent that brought pain to his stump and his wounded thigh. After a while he took yet another path that curled to the base of the hill. The grass grew on this path, but was freshly flattened, and that excited him. The sun was already high in the sky and on this side of the hill the rocks that studded the verdant slope were warm to the touch. An eagle drifted on a thermal high above him and he watched it for a while, before walking on into a clump of beech trees that creaked to the light breeze, branches clicking together, the thump of his boots on the root-woven ground making the hill sound hollow. After ten minutes of stumbling progress the path suddenly plunged down into a small hanging valley and he had to hold on to the rock face and the brushy shoots of grass to steady his way. He could hear the soothing shush of water falling onto rock.

The path twisted to the bottom of the valley and he followed it down, using the rocks to help keep his balance. The waterfall was to his left, as yet out of his sight but the splash of it getting louder, and the air he breathed tasted as if it was scrubbed clean. Finally he was at the floor of the tight little valley and there was just one huge lichen-caked flat-topped rock, the size of an Austin 7, between him and the waterfall, an opening to one side of it half choked with a tangled bush. Beneath the rock was the water jug Roma used, and stretched out on the rock was the simple red dress that she had worn as she left the cave that morning. He peeped around the edge of the rock and through the spidery mesh of the bush.

The waterfall fell in a long narrow chute so that, with the sun shining on it, it was almost like a chromium pillar against the backdrop of the smooth, black, coal-shiny sodden rock face. It then flared out into a silver-white fan where it fell into a clear pool – there was not the turquoise of the Soca here – the water then overflowing at one edge to form another pool, or spilling into a faster moving stream. She was in the second pool. Her back was to him so that all he could see was the gentle valley of her spine, the tight crease between her small, rounded buttocks, and the cascade of her black hair, swept to one side so that it covered one of her slender arms. The water was halfway up her well-defined calves and she dipped down to scoop up some of it, letting it drop down over her breasts with a little yelp of shock – he remembered how cold it was even from the jug. Perhaps it was hearing her, perhaps something else, but something broke the spell, and he suddenly became very aware of himself, very aware of this cheap peeping Westbury Holt. He decided to walk back up the path, but then she turned, and nothing – absolutely nothing – could have torn his eyes off her.

She scooped up more water and let it run down her body so that her lovely small and rounded breasts gleamed in the sunlight, the dark nipples nut hard from the cold pool, the frizzy triangle of her sex sparkling with little diamond drops of water. There was not a bite of fat on the girl, just a beautiful collision of sculptured curves, and tightly drawn skin that was almost the colour of dripping honey where the sun had tanned her, a paler, creamier colour where it had not. She took the bar of soap from the edge of the pool and started to lather her body, whitening her thighs and breasts with light suds. It had been ages since he had even seen a naked girl – the army nurse in Cairo was the last, he recalled – and he found he was as hard as the rock he leant against; painfully hard. He shifted a little, for comfort, his shoulder catching the bush, which shivered slightly. It was then he saw Roma's hot stare. She had seen him.

She stood statue still in the pool, letting the suds slide from her body and drip into the water like melting snow. She looked straight at the bush that had hid West, right into his eyes, and he stared back. Then she simply smiled her lovely smile – that smile she smiled when she tended him – and started to wash herself again, with the air of someone who was greatly mistaken, just seeing things. West let the breath that he'd trapped in his chest seep through his lips.

Fool, he thought, as he made his escape, scrambling back up the path, then making his painful way back to the old gun emplacement, which smelt of the cooked chicken all of them, except Nicolai, were devouring. Ilya gave him an interrogating look when he arrived, but he ignored it and sat with his back to the wall of the old gun bay close to where Nicolai also sat, seemingly deep in thought. The climb had exhausted West and it took a while for him to catch his breath, and for the fire in his wound to cool a little. It was then that he realised just how very much she had come to mean to him, because the very thought of offending her had brought a fear to him that was as frightful as the memory of the stone tomb that had almost taken his life.

Half an hour later she returned, the jug of water balanced on the pad of cloth on her head. She smiled at him, exactly as she always did, and scowled at her brother Georgi, who had not been able to resist the chicken. Then she went to her grandfather. After she had spoken to him a puzzled Nicolai said to West. "She wants to know why you did not stay to help her carry the water back?" as Roma grinned radiantly in the background.

***

Roma sat astride West, lifting and lowering her wet warmth along the length of him, the rough surface of the rock digging slightly into the skin of his back. It was the way she liked it, to be on top, as she was not the type to be trapped beneath another – and sometimes even Westbury Holt was a willing prisoner. Every now and then she stroked his beard, or bent down to kiss his lips quickly, hotly. But that was before she was taken from him in a frenzy of absolute passion that seemed to whisk her away from this world ... Then he rode the whirlwind; matching her gasp for gasp, thrust for thrust, and moan for moan, until they had both finished and he felt himself slowly shrivel inside her, while their body sweat pasted them tight together.

"I love you," he said, wondering if she understood him. Then: "I love you," so that it was the third time he had said it in his life, then: "I love you, I love you, I love you, I love you, I love you ..."

"I love you," she said, finally, in exact mimic. Just by the shine in her eyes he knew she understood.

It would be time to move on soon, it had been time for a while in truth, but somehow they had always found something else that needed doing first, usually what they had been doing today. This was how the weeks had passed into months, giving them the chance to slowly grow to understand each other, and to know each other in every way. They peeled apart and lay on the rock on their backs, the pearly October sunlight feeling good on his body – she always insisted they made love completely naked, even now when the air was getting colder. The sound of the waterfall was their special music and they lay still and listened. The hole beneath the hut was a world away, a life away. West was happy.

She kicked softly at the stump where his lower right leg had once been, playing with the ugly mesh of scarring with her toes – it never bothered her as it had bothered the nurse in Cairo. "I will tell your grandfather we will need to leave soon," he said, in a mix of English and Romani, and she seemed to purr her agreement. He just wanted to make sure she knew what was involved, could hardly believe she had finally agreed to come with him. It had taken weeks of persuasion. "It will be a good cover, a husband and wife ..." he went on, breezily, but he knew there was nothing light in this.

They were not married in anyone's eyes except their own. When he first lay with her, on this same long flat rock, she had been a virgin. It was enormously important in Romani society that a bride should be a virgin when she married, and she made sure West understood this, understood that she had committed herself to him. Nicolai had guessed what had occurred between them, he was not the sort to miss a trick, and he made sure West knew the gravity of the situation, too, his eyes sad, even if he said he understood – sad that the old ways were dying in this strange and static time, sad that his Violca would soon be leaving. Sad because she had, in time, chosen West over a future with her people and Nicolai knew he could not stop her, she was far too free to be caged by convention and tradition.

West was not free. He had a *duty* to get back to the war, he knew, and although the word grated he could not ignore it. He had kidded himself he was still recovering, but he should have left months ago. The snow would be coming soon and he could not wait any longer. Nicolai had brought news the week before. Italy was out of the war, they had surrendered. He had heard the news when he had travelled to Trieste. There were Germans in Trieste now, he had said, but the partisans had control of the Soca Valley and Kobarid. West had considered getting in touch with them, they might be able to make contact with the British, but he had heard lots of gunfire lately and was not sure what that meant. Nicolai had warned him that they could not be sure who was on whose side in the confused power vacuum the Italian surrender had created, and they also couldn't be sure if, or when, the Germans would come north. Nicolai had also said he was worried about the partisans and what they might do now they were in control, because Ilya had stolen chickens from the local people once again …

"Ilya!" Roma sat up quickly and grabbed for her dress, using it to shield her nakedness. West followed her eyes, searching for the gypsy on the cliff top above the falls.

"No, a goat," he said with some relief, for Ilya had been burning with jealousy for the past few weeks, and sharpening that dagger whenever West was in earshot. The mountain goat was as dark and woolly as a thundercloud, its silver-yellow curved horns the exact same shape as the moustache of a Blenheim pilot West had once enjoyed a few pints with back in England. The goat bounded from precipitous hoof-hold to precipitous hoof-hold, then edged along a ledge that looked like nothing more than a crease in the rock from where they lay. "Look how he climbs, Roma," West said. "You think the dirty old goat was watching us, eh?" She seemed to understand, and giggled beautifully – softly, like the spill of the water over the brim of the rock pool.

The shot hit with a soft thump before the sound of its discharge echoed through the tight valley. The goat fell from the narrow ledge, bouncing from rock to rock in a succession of hollow thuds, before landing in the pool at the bottom with a heavy splash. A patch of the clear water clouded pink with the goat's blood.

"Klaus, we have dinner!"

The shout was in German and West snatched his clothes from the rock and climbed into them as quickly as he could. Roma shivered the light little dress over her shoulders and then helped him strap his leg in place. The shot and the shout had echoed and West was still trying to decide from which direction it had come from when she took his hand and led him back up the path as quickly as she could. At every turn of the path he thought they might stumble upon the Germans, but she never slowed, pulling him on, back to her grandfather, her people. When they reached the connecting path that followed the contour of the hillside they saw the German soldiers for the first time and West had to dive on top of her to bring her into cover close to the face of the hill. There was a long line of them with more in depth behind, above and below the path, some turning to bring their distinctive coal scuttle helmet silhouettes into West's line of sight. He saw rifles, machine guns, and in the distance, down on the valley floor, mottled green and brown Hanomag armoured half-tracks. She tugged at his hand again and he turned to see the fear swimming in her eyes.

"Keep down," he said, patting his hand against the air to illustrate the point. She seemed to understand and West now took the lead, hugging close to the slope of the hill, bent low out of sight of the German soldiers above and below. They soon arrived at the steep path and climbed it quickly, hearing the German voices behind them now. They reached the old fortification and ran down the stone slit that led to the iron doorway. Nicolai and the others were waiting, probably alerted by the rifle shot that had killed the goat. Ilya had his vintage Mannlicher at the ready. He turned the safety catch at the rear of the action with his thumb and aimed the rifle at West.

*

The rifle wavered inches from West's face, the rust flecked muzzle looking impossibly long. At the far end of the Mannlicher, bisected by the notch of the foresight, one of Ilya's dark eyes shone with hatred and anger. He shouted, and the rifle danced to his words.

"It's because *he's* here!"

West had picked up enough Romani to understand that.

"It's because *you* stole the chickens!" Roma shouted back, grabbing the rifle barrel and yanking it away from West's face.

"Either way, they have come," Nicolai said, calmly now, as if he sighed it, and the others suddenly fell silent. Ilya slung the old Mannlicher over his shoulder and Nicolai turned to West and asked, in English: "Are they close?"

"Very, and they're getting closer," West answered, as Ilya spat his disgust onto the floor. He said something, too quick for West to understand.

"He wants to fight them," Nicolai said.

"What do you think?"

"It would be the right thing to do."

"With that?" West pointed to the antiquated rifle, which he knew was the best of the three they possessed. "You … We … *We* will be slaughtered," West said. The older man clearly understood what West meant, that he would fight with them if it came to it, and he nodded his gratitude. "That's not all," West went on. "The Germans don't believe that civilians should fight, and they would not take prisoners if you resisted. I'm sure of that." He remembered the paratroopers on Crete, those that had both saved and captured him, and what they had done to the Cretans who had fought them.

Ilya was shouting again and the other younger men were beginning to join in, crowding around Nicolai in the narrow stone passageway, each one raising his voice to be heard. The women and the children stood behind them, squeezed into the tight stone channel, all wearing the same mask of fear. West could imagine the memories crowding their thoughts, taking them back to the last time they had come up against automatic weapons, when the plane had strafed the line of caravans. Roma pulled the younger gypsies from her grandfather, managing to shout even louder than they were – it suddenly occurred to West that all this shouting might lead the Germans to them before time. He tried to hush them, raising his finger to his lips and shushing. Ilya spat at his feet, but West ignored it. Nicolai suddenly turned to him again.

"So we must run?"

"But they will shoot you for sure then," West said. "The older people will have no chance, we'll be lucky if half of us make it out alive. And they will follow those that do."

"So what should we do?" Nicolai asked.

West turned from him and addressed the rest of them. He spoke in English, because his few Romani words and phrases would not cover what he had to say. He paused often to allow Nicolai to translate. "There are many of them," West began. "They are bound to find this place, because they have a line of soldiers sweeping the hill … They have automatic weapons, machine guns … You will have no chance against them … They will pin you down … Then they will throw in grenades …" As Nicolai relayed his words he could see the fear in their eyes.

"Look," West said. "You are not partisans —"

"But we are gypsies," Nicolai said, "and thieves."

"Still, surrender is your only chance." There was uproar as Nicolai translated it and suddenly Ilya waved the point of his dagger close to West's throat, shouting at him as he did so, a fine spray of spittle speckling West's face. Roma stepped between them and pushed Ilya away.

"He says it's easy for you, you are not one of us and they will treat you as a prisoner of war," Nicolai said.

"But I want to be with you," West said, looking at Roma who seemed to understand. "I will take the same risk. Look at me now, with my beard;

and with a cap over my hair," he took a hat off a gypsy, "I could pass for one of you easily. Besides, they have not come here for me. No one knows I'm here outside these walls, even the doctor took me for one of you."

Nicolai translated and then West continued: "The only reason I can think the Germans would have come here is that they have already defeated the partisans in the valley, and they are looking for those who fled – and if that is the case you have nothing to fear from them, because you are not partisans, and you should not give them any reason to think you are."

Nicolai translated once more, and Roma took West's hand. But Ilya was still angry, spitting words like machine gun fire.

"He says they will kill us," Nicolai said.

"They will if we fight, or if we run."

"And if not, what will they do?"

"I don't know. But I do know many Germans. I lived there before the war, and most of them are decent people, as decent as any." Nicolai translated again and Ilya shook his head slowly as he replied, more slowly now, wearing an intense expression that drew his eyebrows together.

"He says our people have never known decency – he wants your word."

"I give it to him, to all of you. The Germans I know would not harm innocent people. I can say that and be sure of it. So I will give you my word, we will be safe."

"It is good enough for me," Nicolai said, then he turned to Ilya and some of the younger men. He said something West could not understand. It was obvious that the younger men could run, might get away. But if they did and they were seen by the Germans then where would that leave the rest of them? Ilya seemed to consider it for a moment. He said something to Roma, who was standing close to West. "And you?" he thought it was. Roma said nothing, just nodded and squeezed West's hand. Ilya looked at the others, sighed, then nodded sharply.

They threw the rifles, ammunition and daggers, plus the things they'd stolen from the Italians, down the steep slope on the east side of the hill, and West heard the rip and crack of foliage far below as those dangerous items broke through the branches. Then Ilya walked up close to West, an inch between their noses, his breath smelling sour. He said nothing, just stared, but that stare said plenty: *I will kill you if you are wrong. I will kill you if I get the chance. And I will take great pleasure in killing you.* West understood. There was a shout from outside, German, authoritative enough that its meaning was clear even if you did not understand the language: "Come on out, hands up. We will not fire. You have ten seconds."

West translated and Nicolai immediately led them out with his hands in the air, while West hid amongst the rest of the gypsies with Roma. He wished he could have used the time spent arguing on making himself look more like a gypsy, but what was done was done. There was some rough treatment, Ilya collected a rifle butt to his head for his sneers as he was searched for weapons, but otherwise the Germans treated them with something close to indifference as they led them down the steep and stony path. Roma still gripped West's hand, almost tight enough for it to hurt, but he could not mind that. He tried to catch what the Germans were saying without giving them a clue that he could understand. They were young soldiers, rifles and sub-machine-guns held at the ready, and from what he heard they seemed relieved that they hadn't bumped into partisans. West felt a spark of optimism – perhaps they might just let them go?

The short column of gypsies was led down the hillside by the soldiers and was soon at the bottom of the hill, approaching a camouflaged half-track with a small knot of officers standing in front of it. As the gypsies filed past them one of the officers, a young lieutenant, suddenly locked his eyes on West. He was a strange looking fellow with the smallest ears West had ever seen, and a squashed up nose – his face looked half finished, West thought.

"You!" It was a sudden shout and West instinctively turned his head away. The lieutenant pushed past Nicolai and the others and waved the column to a halt. He grabbed West by the shoulders and spun him round to face him. West stared at him blankly. "No ... But it can't be," the lieutenant whispered, as West did his best to look confused. Then the officer shook his head and waved the column on. West could hear his colleagues teasing him about his gypsy friends as they shuffled past the half-track, and then Nicolai allowed the others to pass him until West was level.

"He seemed to know you?" Nicolai whispered.

"I just have that sort of face, it happens to me all the time," West said, running his fingers through his thick beard, thankful for it.

They walked on. The half-track clattered, squeaked and rumbled alongside them, its shielded Spandau machine gun manned by a soldier who took little interest in the gypsies, its steel rear tracks digging furrows in the unsealed road. They soon approached a cluster of camouflaged tents close to the fast flowing turquoise water of the Soca. For the first time West was almost sure he had done the right thing. The worst that could happen would be a civilian internment camp, he thought, and that would give him far better chances of escape than a POW pen – but he also knew for sure that if he escaped again he would not be leaving the girl behind.

"Wait!" The shout was from behind, and the ragged column shuffled to a halt. West did not turn, but a few seconds later he felt a hand on his shoulder and he was spun round to face that same officer. Suddenly he realised his dyed and tailored RAF tunic had come open as he walked, and the lieutenant with the unfinished face was staring at the grubby cricket jumper. Westbury Holt luck. That's what they used to call it.

"My God, it is you. Here! Wait until the major hears of this – come with me." West played dumb, and Roma squeezed his hand even tighter, but the young lieutenant simply chuckled and shook his head: "Bring him!" Two of the soldiers took West by the arms.

"Wait for me, Roma," he shouted, hoping she would understand, "I will never leave you … I give you my word …" In his panic he had spoken English, and he cursed himself inwardly for his stupidity. Roma clung on to him as they tried to pull him away, but she was no match for a strong soldier and she was thrown to the ground, their handhold breaking. He managed to make fleeting eye contact before he was dragged behind the half-track, and in that moment: in the pain, the defiance, the love, alive in those liquid-jade eyes, he knew she would wait for him. And he also knew that he would never rest until they were together again.

"We have met before you know," the lieutenant said, as West was manhandled to a large tent draped in camouflage netting, set up in a small copse of trees close to the river. "At the Berlin Motor Show in 1938, you gave me your autograph, in the café by the entrance."

"Look, you have mistaken me for someone else, please let me get back to my people —"

"And you speak German, too!" the officer said, seeming to think it a huge joke, thin lips taking the shape of a disbelieving smile. The cricket jumper had been dyed, and was full of holes. If the man had not already had his suspicions he would never have recognised it for what it was. West began to think Lick might have been right about the jumper's curse, after all.

The commanding officer, a major, sat at a map table in front of the tent, under an awning. He was a stout man with an Iron Cross pinned to his field grey tunic and bright blisters of sweat shining on a florid forehead. From the way he looked up from his lunch of sandwiches and wine West guessed the two officers did not get on. "What's this?" demanded the CO, looking at the lieutenant as if he were a cat dragging a dead bird in from the yard.

"An Englander, with the gypsies."

"My god Muller, you waste my time with more nonsense," the major slammed his tumbler of wine onto the table and the liquid sloshed to the brim like a blood rush. "He's as much a gypsy as any of them, look at him!" There were three sandwiches on the major's plate, made, West guessed, from half a loaf of bread. West stared at the food. The sweat of the meat fat had soaked into the lower deck of each slice of bread giving each cross section a marbled strata. The aroma of the pork was unbelievably good, snatching at his nostrils and flooding his throat with saliva, and he realised it had been a long time since he had eaten really well.

"What are you staring at, you stinking animal?"

"Please sir, hear me out," the lieutenant said. "This is Westbury Holt, the racing driver." The major laughed loud at that and then took a gigantic bite from one of the sandwiches, not bothering to close his mouth as he chewed the meat noisily. "I am sure of it, talk to the major, you, talk to him!" the lieutenant prodded West, an edge of frustration in his voice now.

"Please, I am just a gypsy, I only want to get back to my people," West said. The lieutenant looked pleased. But the major was not impressed.

"What does that prove, the animal does tricks?"

"Wait, I will show you." Before West had the time to realise what he was doing the lieutenant was stretching at the collar of the cricket jumper and opening the front of his shirt, tearing at it so that a button flew clear. West tried to back out of his way but a soldier blocked his exit while the lieutenant snapped the cotton cord of his identity tags, a look of undisguised triumph in his eyes.

"You see," he said, tossing the small fibre discs onto the table, "he is an Englander, air force – please read the name, Herr Major." The major stared at the two discs – a round one in red and an octagonal one in green – blinking his eyes in disbelief as he read the name, the number, and the R.A.F at the centre.

"Well," he said finally, "it seems I owe you an apology Lieutenant Muller."

"Please sir, I don't know what those things are," West said.

The major looked West up and down, shaking his head, then said: "I am not a follower of motor racing, so I have not heard of you. No, horses are my game, I go to the Hoppegarten when I can; fine days ..." he trailed off and stared wistfully at the surface of his wine for some silent moments. "But what are we to do with you?"

"He is a prisoner of war."

"In that get up he is a spy, he should be shot." The major snorted a little laugh as he said it.

"Berlin would not be happy with that, he is a hero of the Reich," the lieutenant said. The major glared at him.

"I want to go with the others," West said, "please let me go with them."

"And this hero of yours wants to be a dirty gypsy?"

"It's a ploy," the lieutenant put in, "to escape, that's all. He's resourceful, Berlin will be happy *you* have captured him." The lieutenant looked to West as he said it, and for a moment West thought he might wink at him. He realised Lieutenant Muller thought he was doing him a favour.

"No, I want to be with them!" West shouted.

"Quiet! You are right Muller, it will do no harm to make sure Berlin knows of this, in the meantime keep him out of the way, lock him away in a truck and feed him, he's not one of those animals ..."

There was a ragged volley of rifle fire, quite close by, then two pistol shots.

"There were some trouble makers amongst the younger men," Muller said to the major in unasked for explanation. "The example will knock the fight out of the others." West suddenly made a lunge to get away but was stopped by a rifle butt crashing heavily against his cheek. He fell to the ground, tasting the warm, metallic flood of blood in his mouth while chips of bright light flickered in front of his eyes.

"Is this how you show your gratitude, Herr Holt?" he heard the major say with an ironic sigh. "But then you cannot know what Muller here has saved you from."

***

1944

The thing that had emptied Sepp stood in the centre of the table like a poisoned condiment. The paint had chipped away in shining metallic rashes while the spike gleamed like a filament of light. There was a corroded fringe on the gantlet's edge; rust that looked a little too much like dried blood. Old Kurt knew the weapon well, and now he could not take his eyes off it, Hanna realised, as she flicked her gaze from Sepp to him, then back to Sepp again. Lick had insisted it stayed here, with them, but Hanna thought she would throw it out as soon as he had left, someone could melt it down and turn it into a piece of dirty, bloody panzer as far as she was concerned. Lick looked twice his age, weighed down by the yellow-backed lieutenant badges on his shoulders and lapels. He still made a joke of everything, but the humour was now so dark it was almost opaque, and now that he finally had a grand hat he hadn't needed to steal he didn't seem to want to wear it, so his red hair shone bright in the stark glare of the naked light bulb.

Everything had changed. And yet everything was familiar. They sat in the old basement kitchen; it seemed like the right place. After nine months the Luftwaffe hospital near Munich had suddenly decided it could do little more for Sepp, and it would be better for him to be at home. Now they were all here. Strudel the only absentee, he had been frightened by the sight of Lick in his uniform and had disappeared off to wherever it was that he now disappeared off to every day. Lick slurped his ersatz coffee, a tasteless brew made from roasted malt, washing down the last of the 'balcony pig' stew, and then belching softly – an officer maybe, but a gentleman never. Only one plate of rabbit stew remained untouched.

"Give us that then, Sepp, no use it going to waste," Lick said, and Sepp slid the plate towards him, the same expression of utter nothingness on his face as there was when he had walked into the kitchen that morning, and as there had been ever since.

"No, Lick …" Hanna started.

"Oh balls, can't you see, the man has gone – watch!" Lick looked at Sepp, then barked the order: "Right Sepp, stand up on that chair!"

Sepp went to climb on to his chair.

"No Sepp – sit down!" Hanna shouted. "Please … Lick." Sepp was already on the chair and she thought she might cry, and God she wished she could.

"Get down Sepp," Lick said quietly, then turned to her again. "I'm sorry Hanna, it's the only way. Think of him as he was and you will have no peace, you have to see that Sepp is dead now – this is just a shell."

"No peace?" she whispered, but Lick didn't seem to hear, busy as he was with Sepp's plate of stew. She wondered if she could get used to her empty brother as quickly as he had, but then that's what the front could do, she knew.

"Tell me again, tell me how it happened Lick," old Kurt suddenly said, snapping his eyes away from the punch-dagger at last.

"The punch-dagger, he ... In a fight with an Ivan, the bastard took the bloody thing off him and punched him right in the side of the head with it," Lick said, quietly, staring into the surface of the stew. "The sawbones said he was lucky – if that's the fucking word for it. A mortar shell fell and the Ivan's aim was messed up. The spike slid across his brain; see where it went?" Lick pointed out the neat little round scar on the side of Sepp's head. To Hanna it looked like a pistol wound, or what she might expect that to look like at least. Sepp just stared at the air in front of him, unblinking, almost as though his pupils were painted dots on washed out china beads.

"It's as I told you," Lick said. "It's as though they've emptied him."

"Lick," Hanna suddenly said, clutching at the sleeve of his uniform.

"What?"

"I need to know," she said, "before this, before this happened – was he the same, I mean ... Had my Sepp changed?"

"This war changes us all, Hanna."

"But —"

"He was still Sepp." With that Lick seemed to lose his appetite, sliding the plate away and standing up. He nodded, patted Sepp on the shoulder, seemed to want to say something, but then thought better of it, turning to old Kurt instead. "So, what's the story with that idiot son of yours?"

"Who knows?" Kurt said. "He doesn't tell us where he goes, but he goes out early and clean, and he comes back late and dirty, and sometimes he's out all night. But he's as happy as I've ever seen him. Maybe he has a job?" Kurt laughed as he said it.

"A job? These days he'd more likely see the inside of a camp," Lick said.

"*These days*, anything is possible, my *officer* friend," Kurt spat back, and Lick was forced to smile.

"Well, remember that when you see the bullshit on the newsreels old man, that's how desperate we've become, all the good men have ..." He didn't finish the sentence but simply placed his officer's peaked cap on his head at a jaunty angle and then saluted Sepp awkwardly.

"It could be worse ..." he started, turning to Hanna again, but then seemed to change his mind, shaking his head, then leaving.

"It could be worse," Hanna repeated, whispering it softly.

***

Hanna had placed the old photo album on the kitchen table. A soup of ham bone and dried peas was simmering on the stove and the narrow basement window had steamed up. Sepp's eyes were locked on the blank screen of the condensation. There was nothing there. It was almost as if he was asleep with his eyes open.

"Here, look Sepp," she said as she turned the heavy leather-bound cover of the photo album. "It is Papa …" Sepp did as she said, moving his head slowly to point his eyes in the direction of the page, for *look* would not have been the right word for it. Hanna could not even be sure that the cracked old sepia tinted picture of the man in the tall hat with grand moustaches had even registered.

"… And Mama …" Still no response. "… And here they are both together, do you remember that day, we went on a picnic by the river, you fell in the mud and I had to rescue you. Oh, we both got so dirty," she forced herself to laugh a little. But there was still nothing to suggest he had even heard her. It was just as it had been this past month, nothing but a sort of blind obedience. Sepp would react to commands, but it was mechanical. He even had to be told to eat. She pulled out some other photographs, a fan of them that she had placed between the back pages of the album, having never got around to mounting them. She slid them onto the table in front of him. "Here; what about these?" The first picture was of him in his uniform, arm in arm with Trudi, young Bernd on his shoulders. It had not been so very long ago really, a park in Berlin, and Hanna had not been with them – she had wondered whether that was why Trudi had sent the picture to her, but she hated herself for thinking that now.

"Look, Sepp," she said, and his eyes moved to the picture. But still there was nothing. She stood up and moved to the stove, stirred the soup, despising herself once again for that itch of relief that once more she would not have to face her fears.

"How can I get to you? And who are you now, Sepp? Would I even know the man that would fill that shell?" she whispered to the empty creature across the kitchen. She left the soup to bubble a while longer, getting the last from the bone, though there was barely enough flavour left for the merest hint of an aroma. Then she spent the next half an hour going through the rest of the pictures with him, another album of them and some loose photos from a battered old shoebox. There were just a few she had not passed before his eyes when Kurt stomped down the stairway and into the kitchen. He looked even more tired and drawn than usual and his breathing was irregular and noisy, like a leaking accordion.

"Smells good," he said, out of habit. "How's he getting on?"

"The same," she said, flicking yet another photograph in front of Sepp.

"It's worth a try. I'm surprised you hadn't thought of it earlier?"

Hanna shrugged.

"I will take him to the allotment, if that's all right with you, he still works well as long as I tell him what to do," Kurt added.

"Of course," she said, "the air will do him good." She looked at him again. He was holding a photograph tightly between thumb and forefinger. It was, she thought, the first time he had done that. But she knew it meant nothing. For Sepp was empty now. "Is it better than a picture?" she murmured. "I sometimes wonder." Kurt squeezed her shoulder tenderly.

"Will you have some soup with us later, Kurt?"

"*Hmmm*, is this all there is? Shall I kill another balcony pig?"

"No Kurt, there can't be many left. I've been thinking, I will get on to Konrad, he has plenty – perhaps he can send us some real pork, he can get it in Berlin."

"Real pork?"

"They say there's crocodile now, too, when the Tommies bomb the zoo."

"Pork would do."

"It's about time my husband took care of his extended family."

Kurt was suddenly quiet. She knew he liked to put the food on the table. The vegetables from his allotment down alongside the Zwickau Mulde, or the meat from the rabbits that he bred in his spare room – they were safer there, plenty a thief and otherwise would like to sink his teeth into one of old Kurt's fat Flemish Giants, or 'balcony pigs' as rabbits were now called. But then he smiled, and nodded. "Come on Sepp my lad, let's get digging shall we?" Sepp let go of the photograph and followed Kurt up the stairway.

"It's freezing out. Make sure he wears his coat!" Hanna shouted after them, turning the picture Sepp had been holding through her fingers. She looked at it. It was a racing car: an Auto Union. A streamliner. She thought it was Rosemeyer at the wheel. She remembered it had once stood in a frame at his bedside. A lifetime ago.

***

The parcel was heavy in Hanna's arms, but it was a happy heavy. It was also just a little too big to be easy to carry, so that she would have to stop every now and then to adjust her grip, but she could not mind that. It was not too cold, and the first hint of spring was in the air, today Zwickau was a good place to be, the sky pale but bright. Despite the talk that the bombers must come, because of the city's industry, the buildings here were still untouched by the war, even if most families weren't, and it was almost possible to imagine this were a better time, before it all began. The birds still sang and the trams still clanged their warnings as they clattered down the street. She had been out early to pick up the parcel from the station. Konrad had sent it, it was easy for him now that she was doing something worthy, looking after Sepp; something he could explain to his friends in Berlin, and pass off as a great personal sacrifice on his part too, she guessed.

Good food was valuable, and while it would be safe locked up in the luggage car on a DRG train she would never risk having the parcels delivered from the station, however happily heavy they were, so she would always collect them herself. She wondered what goodies were in the package as she adjusted it once more and made her way up Nord Strasse. Months back Hanna had heard from Max, who wrote to her when he could, about how Nöthling had been arrested and had killed himself in prison, but it seemed Konrad had found another deli' to supply his delights. It was one of the few things he was good for. She hoped there would be chocolate or praline for Strudel, good sausage for Kurt, and whatever it might take to raise a glimmer of life in Sepp, although as much as she would dream of that, she also feared for whatever else it would bring – because she was afraid of what her brother might have become before that spike had drained the life from his eyes.

So far the only flicker of animation she had seen in him was when she had tried to throw the punch-dagger away, and then he had snatched it from her and held it tight to his chest. Now they kept it in the basement kitchen, where they had spent so many happy hours before all this, and where they now seemed to spend so much time again – it seemed the right place to be, these days. She rested again and adjusted her grip on the package. She was close to home. She looked at her watch, she would have just missed Strudel, even the chance of chocolate would not make him late for his daily – and mysterious – business, but just as she was thinking this she saw a figure come out of the front door to their apartment block. She could tell from the walk it was not Strudel, in fact it looked like Sepp, but that could not be: he would never leave the house alone now.

Once at the block she backed her way through the front door and Frau Hansen was ready for her, pretending to clean her portion of the stairs, smearing a foul smelling polish along the banister with an old rag.

"You have started early, Frau Hansen."

"You too Frau Plaidt, a parcel I see?"

"Yes, a parcel." Hanna started to climb the stairs.

"It seems everyone has had an early start this morning."

"Does it?" she said, not bothering to stop.

"I suppose the money the poor boy brings in is useful?" Hanna ignored her, everyone was curious as to where Strudel went almost every morning. "Perhaps that is why your brother has gone after him," Frau Hansen added. Hanna stopped on the stairs, then decided it was better to keep on walking. "Let's hope the simpleton will look after him shall —" It was the last thing she heard the nosey old witch say before she managed to drown out her words with the clip of her shoes against the wooden stairs. She burst into old Kurt's apartment without knocking.

"Ah, sausage, yes?"

"First, I want to know where Sepp is?"

Kurt tried to look innocent, but that never worked with her. "Sepp?" he said.

"Tell me, or no sausage!" The older man's shoulders sagged a little, then he shrugged and smiled. "I just told him to go for a walk, it's a lovely day Hanna, the fresh air will do him good."

"But we have a parcel?"

"More for us then."

"Kurt!"

"All right, all right," he sank into his battered old armchair. Hanna remembered that there were flowers in the pattern of that chair once, long ago, but now it had faded to a muddy brown. It was fitting, all the flowers in Germany had gone, every garden and every park a vegetable patch. Kurt continued: "I told him to follow Strudel, you weren't here and ... Well damn it I'm itching to find out what that little idiot son of mine is up to."

"But he's not well!"

"He's well enough to cross the road Hanna, to look after himself, you know that. There's not much in the way of traffic these days anyhow ... Besides, he's the only one of us who could possibly keep up with the lad."

"But why?"

"I've been worried," Kurt said. "I've always told Strudel to keep his head down, it's the only way to survive this; to keep away from *them* ... It would put my mind at rest to know that where he goes is safe – that's all."

A child shouted in the street below and Hanna found she was drawn to the window. Kurt was right, Sepp would be all right, he was empty, but he could still do things, simple things. Yet that could not stop her worrying for him.

"Sepp won't tell you anything anyway, it's a waste of time, you know he never speaks," Hanna said, watching as the young boy clattered an old tyre-less bicycle wheel along the cobbles with a little stick. She wondered if her own child would have ever played that game, if he'd lived.

"He might show us where he goes, if we ask him to – tell him to," Kurt said.

"You want to know that much?"

"I would like to know my son is not up to something stupid, that's all. Besides, aren't you just a little curious?"

She was. "Well then," Hanna said. "We'll wait until he returns before we open the parcel, shall we?" She thought that she could already smell the sausage in the package and judging by the twitching of Kurt's nostrils, and the sulky droop at the corners of his mouth, he could, too.

*

It was this familiar thing in front of him that had awakened Sepp from that terrible sleep. And now he tried to piece together the jigsaw of the nightmare. Strudel stood beside the familiar thing, quietly awaiting Sepp's reaction, playing with a strand of his thin hair. Sepp dipped his head into his hands, feeling the hard scar tissue of the wound close to his temple, and then he let the memories slowly fill his consciousness, like dark oil seeping into a darker space …

… There was Crete, killing old men and a woman in an olive grove, as he had been ordered … Russia, and hatred of the animals that lived there, people without faces, burning villages … There was an explosion, a train crash, a muddy field and boys, children, nothing more than children. He had hated the children, he had been told to hate them, and he had killed the children he hated. Perhaps that was the first time this had happened, that he had remembered who he was … But then he had tried to destroy himself … Now he recalled the fall of the mortar shell just as he had spiked his head with the punch-dagger, its impact throwing up sheets of mud that coated him wetly, while slanting and spoiling the aim of the spike as he drove it home at what had already been an awkward angle …

Strudel nervously waited for him to say something, those bulging brown eyes shining in the glare of the flashlight Sepp held, eyes that were locked on him, gleaming in nervous anticipation, while one tooth bit into his thin lower lip so that he looked even more rat-like than ever.

… Sepp remembered how Lick had threatened a doctor with his pistol when he was told he would have to wait his turn … Then there was a long train journey home, and hospital … But they could do nothing for him, for they could see no wound but for a small hole in the head … He remembered the hospital, so much suffering, and how he hid from it, and how he had hid from himself …

Just do as you are told, he had thought, then everything will be all right, everything must be all right as long as he did as he was told … They know best … Just as long as he did what he was told then things would be fine …

Then the waking dream of it all: Hanna, had he even said hello? The basement kitchen, had he even known he was there? Kurt, sending him after Strudel …

… Sepp had followed the idiot. He had trailed him up the road, keeping back out of the fool's sight just as Kurt had told him to. Strudel had turned and headed for the Zwickau Mulde, and then he had walked along the riverbank in that slightly jerky way of his, never looking back to see the broken Sepp that followed him … Strudel had walked for a long time, for some kilometres, and he had walked very fast. They had reached some old mine workings and Strudel had slipped through a gap in the fence, a square of cut wire that fitted neatly back into place behind him, held there with a twist of old twine. Sepp had followed.

He had been close to Strudel by now, but still the idiot did not turn. It had not occurred to Sepp then – what, an hour ago, a lifetime ago? – that he might be leading him here. There was a scatter of grimy brick buildings and between them there were square, dirty yellowish patches on the blackened ground where others had been demolished, while rusting parallel tracks criss-crossed the area like sewn up wounds, and oily old timbers lay in piles alongside corroding skeletons of once useful machinery. All of it, including the buildings, was covered in a thin soot of coal dust.

Though this part of the mine was no longer in use they were still very close to the current workings and Sepp had seen the huge black spinners of the winding gear between the buildings, high on their iron-frame tower, spinning in different directions as they lowered cages of men into the dark earth below. But there was another pithead that was closer still, although the wheels of its headgear were no longer spinning, and the cables that led from the nearby winding house were caked with rust. The pithead was enclosed in a grimy brick building, roofed in slanting galvanised iron through which the hoist frame projected into the blue sky, its lattice shadow as sharp as a black-penned technical drawing etched on to the dirty ground. There were a number of blue doors into the pithead building, and Strudel had opened one of these and walked inside. Sepp had walked to the door across black ground that twinkled with crushed anthracite. The blue door had been left ajar, the hinges creaking as it moved slightly in the light breeze, and he too had walked inside.

There had been a large room in which there was a cage with a grille in front of it, plus a dark space alongside it to signify another cage was down below, above the cage and the space he had seen greasy steel cables that were as still and taut as iron bars from the weight of the load that straightened them. There had also been a hatch in the floor, lifted open, through which Sepp had heard the clang of boots on steel rungs. There had been a padlock beside the hatch, sprung open with a length of wire sticking out of the lock. On the floor beside the lock there had been a Daimon flashlight, a small square Bakelite device. It was switched on, casting a tall slanted shadow of Sepp that was diced by the sharp steel of the cage that had once taken miners deep underground. The torch was similar to those he had used in the Fallschirmjäger and without thinking he had done what he would always have done, clipping it to his belt using the stiff steel spring grip.

He had followed Strudel down the shaft ladder. It was a very long climb into the darkness on rungs cold and rough, leprous with rust which flaked off in his hands. Sometimes the brackets were loose and the ladder would sway away from the damp wall, but he had climbed down without a thought, for Sepp was not for thinking just then, he was just following Strudel – as he had been told to do. The clangs of his feet on the iron rungs had answered those of Strudel's like echoes, while the shine from the idiot's torch had been like some deep sea fish glowing in the dark depths below Sepp's feet.

Some way down the ladder there was a landing, and by the time Sepp reached it he had realised the sound of his own steps on iron was the only noise, that and the constant trickle of water down the wall, and the gurgling splash of it elsewhere in the darkness. He had seen the yellowy glow from Strudel's flashlight down a shaft that ran away from the landing in a dark regression of steel supporting hoops. Either side of the shaft's entrance there had been stalls where, he now realised, horses would have once been kept, painted white and still bright against the smother of darkness, while another shaft had headed off at a right angle, inclining upwards, this one older and rougher than the first, and lined with rectangles of timber. He had felt the tickle of air against his skin, a draught from the surface. Then he had followed the tunnel Strudel had taken, which above him was shiny, smooth and black, equally demarcated by thick steel bands and wooden props, with parallel pipes for compressed air and water along the length of it. At his feet the shaft was laid with double rail tracks, on which the coal drams would have once trundled, worn silver with recent use. There had been plenty of headroom and the way was wide, for the passage had been dug for the poor horses they had once used to haul the drams.

He had stumbled on, following the dim light, until there were warning signs to say that there had been a rock-fall ahead, and a stout wooden barrier that had been tumbled aside. Soon he had arrived where Strudel stood, in a wide opening which looked like it had been the scene of a cave-in, for the walls were rough and ragged, as if huge chunks had been torn from them, the passage beyond completely blocked. Strudel had been ready for him, shining his flashlight on that familiar thing.

Yes, Strudel, the idiot, had found it. Found silver. And it had taken an idiot to find Sepp, too.

*

The bell-shaped chamber was covered in thick dirt and spoil, which made the gleam of the familiar thing in front of him all the more startling: like a diamond in the choked pan of a barrack latrine, like a shaft of sunlight in a grey Russian winter sky, like a silver vein in a nugget of coal. The air was very warm, and smelt ashy, reminding Sepp of a fire that had been out for some time, and it seemed shot through with dust, but it was not that which made it hard to breathe, made his mouth go dry. It was this thing that had raised him from his lifeless life.

The half-built streamliner sat on its stands of old oil drums. Sepp had been standing there for a little age, and now he suddenly thought it must all be a mocking dream. But he laid his fingers on the cold bodywork to check it was real, and for a moment took his own trembling excitement for a shiver from the machine.

"How?" Sepp croaked. It was the first time he had spoken for almost a year and the effort of it seemed to tear at his throat, while the word sounded distant, as if someone else had said it. It was strange, this world underground, with its constant noise of water trickling in the rock around them, and he wondered again if he was dreaming. And then it got even stranger ...

Sepp had not heard Strudel talk so very often, and when he had it was usually one word, a yes or a no, or a demand for food, one word of several stuttering syllables. But now his words came out in a torrent, without pausing, without stammering, like a long burst from an MG 42.

"I sometimes went to the works where I helped Herr Fink look after the cars when all the others went to the war like you did and then he was told to take them away in case the bombs came and ..." Sepp thought it made sense, for soon the bombs would fall on the town, on the Horch Works, like they fell elsewhere. Then another part of his brain seemed to spark into life, after so long asleep, and he realised that there might be another reason, realised that some might think that good Duralumin like this would be better used clothing a Messerschmitt. Also, Fink would be sure that Strudel would keep his mouth shut. He always had, until now, so Sepp could see why he would have asked him to help.

" ... We moved them one at a time but we had to hurry because Herr Fink now has to work on making armoured car chassis in the factory and we were told to put them in the buildings in the mine —"

"All of them?" Sepp interrupted, and Strudel snapped his mouth shut, his teeth clacking loudly, as if he was physically cutting off the gush of words.

"Many of them are in the buildings above us where there are Type Cs and Ds and mountain climbers and some spares and —"

"But why is this one here?"

"Herr Fink did not think the buildings were good enough hiding places and he wanted to make sure at least one car would survive the war so we took enough parts to make a streamliner which was my idea as I thought if one was saved then it should be the fastest and we used the old shaft that has not been used for many years and comes down at an angle, which now gives us air, and we took the wood that blocked it shut away ..." Sepp remembered the other shaft he had seen a little earlier. "... and we used a winch which I helped Herr Fink to get working and we put the body and then the chassis on a trolley ..." Sepp followed the flick of Strudel's eyes to a coal dram which had had its skip removed, alongside which was a block and tackle, coiled around itself like a sleeping python, "... and then we brought the engine ..." There was a wooden crate in the corner of the space, Sepp shone the flashlight on it, picking out the four interlocking rings of Auto Union stencilled boldly on to the soot-stained yellow wood. "... Then we blocked the old shaft again and Herr Fink put up warning signs ..."

Sepp went over to the crate as Strudel continued his hosepipe monologue. It was big enough to transport a lion, yet it was the first time he had been aware of anything else in this tight dark space other than the half-built streamliner. There was a crowbar on the floor, and some other tools he now realised, and he eased the tapered end of the bar beneath the lid of the crate, which he then levered off to a harsh squeal of nails sliding in wood. Inside was a V16 engine, its pipes gleaming like the trombones and trumpets of the SS Leibstandarte band. Sepp shook his head, something this beautiful did not belong in a crate.

Strudel still talked as Sepp want back to the car and ran his hand over the beautiful curves of the streamlined body. The cold aluminium seemed to almost quiver beneath his palm, as if it was a pool of quicksilver. He could believe the thing was about to breathe.

"... I have done much of this work alone Herr Fink told me not to come here again but I could not stay away," Strudel said with a grin – and before that Sepp had never even seen him smile before, he realised. He considered the work Strudel had done already; it was good, very good; meticulous. But the car still needed wheels, and tyres, and engine, and gearbox, and ... God knows what else. *But why am I thinking such things?* Sepp lifted his palm from the streamlined body, feeling a little suck of cold metal as if it clung to him, then he shook his head and sighed.

"You know," Sepp said, looking Strudel straight in the child eyes. "What you have done here is wrong?"

"No that's not s-s-so." Strudel shook his head and instantly the smile fell from his face.

"But it's stealing, can't you see that?"

"H-h-how can it be st-st-st-stealing? No one wants this they just want their armoured cars and their w-w-war."

Sepp turned away from him and again studied the beautiful lines of the streamlined body. He fancied he could still feel its smoothness on the palm of his hand, some residue of its clinging form. It seemed a shame that it should not breathe again and a sudden thought came to him: *Wouldn't the real crime be to not let it live?*

"It is y-y-yours," Strudel said.

"Mine?"

"I was b-b-building it for you."

"You have done this for me?" Sepp asked.

"Yes."

"Why, Strudel?"

"You were the only one who helped me."

"Not always."

"S-s-s-sometimes, and you d-d-d-deserve this ... to d-d-d-d-drive it," his stammer was getting worse now.

"Drive it, you're crazy!" Sepp laughed out loud.

"B-b-b-but it is what you always w-w-wanted."

Sepp shook his head, the beam from his flashlight played across Strudel's face, shining on the tears that were forming in his eyes. *Still an idiot.* But he felt for him, because Sepp knew the crush of disappointment.

"I had wanted it, Strudel, but it was not to be. I was not good enough when the time came to prove myself. But thank you." Strudel dipped his head. Sepp noticed he was twisting the fingers of his left hand with his right, as if his hand was a rag to wring dry. *Poor Strudel.* "Besides," he said, as suddenly as the thought had come to him, "where could I drive it?" Strudel shook his head sadly. "It will be enough that we can get it to work," Sepp said, taking hold of Strudel's shoulder and squeezing it gently, "I have long given up wanting to drive these things."

"But we will get it to work?" Strudel said, with a sudden spark.

"Yes, that at least," Sepp said. "That at least is something we can do without hurting anyone ... But it must be our secret." Studel nodded solemnly, and Sepp said: "Now show me how far she has come on, my friend."

***

"Personally, I preferred him the way he was, at least he would have helped out here," Kurt said, turning over some hard earth with his spade.

"Yes, but you see it too don't you, he is a little better now, no?" Hanna said, watching as a crow drifted down to perch on a beanpole on one of the other schrebergärtens, three lots down from Kurt's.

"Perhaps, there is a spark there, I will give you that – but then now we have double the mystery. My God, I would give a field full of cabbages to know what those two are up to." With that he dug into the ground with the spade again, turning it, and although it was cold and hard the earth smelt rich and good.

Kurt's allotment was one small patch in a quilt of mostly brown rectangles that stretched some way along the banks of the Zwickau Mulde, the full flow of the river hidden from view by the tall, grass covered flood banks. Kurt was one of a number of older men digging their plots, pausing to talk and look at the sky for the rain that must come soon, for the clouds sagged heavily. Someone had built a bonfire on one of the allotments and the smoke from it was drifting over them, smarting Hanna's eyes a little as the flames crackled loudly in the relative calm of this haven from bad news. She wore a pair of Sepp's old trousers and a big old woollen pullover that stretched past her thighs – it was one of the good things about *their* total war that a woman could sometimes dress practically. There was not really so much she could do to help, but it was better than sitting in an empty house waiting for her boys to return, and much better than running the risk of having to talk to Frau Hansen.

She thought of Sepp and Strudel again. Two nights before she had stumbled upon them when they were on their way home, both glowing pinkly-clean as they always were on their return – often seeming cleaner than when they left in the morning, which added to the mystery greatly. She had thought they were talking happily then, just like children on the way home from school, but when they had come closer she had realised she had been mistaken, for they were silent, as always. She suddenly recalled Sepp's voice, which she had not heard for well over year now, and with that she remembered happier times.

"You're smiling," Kurt said, as he turned another clod of dark earth.

"Yes, I suppose I am."

"I have not seen it for some time – are we in love again?"

Hanna laughed out loud at that. "You forget that I am a married woman, Kurt."

"Ach, it is so, my mistake," Kurt grinned, then waved to another allotment owner who was leaning against his fork, staring at them. "Look at him. He has not seen such happiness for an age. We should be careful, soon they will be asking me how it grows."

"If you knew that you would be a rich man, Kurt."

"That's true, as long as the witch downstairs didn't tell Adolf, he might want it for the war effort." Kurt laughed as he said it, and Hanna again remembered Frau Hansen's constant questioning. Yes, Hanna had said, Sepp is a little better. No, she had said, of course he would not be going back to the Fallschirmjäger, and yes, Strudel was really very well.

"You should evict her, you know that," Kurt said, thrusting the spade into the ground then rolling the stiffness out of his shoulders, "God, I'm too old for this."

"You're not too old Kurt, and she is harmless. She's just scared, that's why she keeps an eye on us all, so if I were to evict her ..." Hanna shrugged, leaving Kurt to finish the thought himself. They both knew that they could come for Strudel at any time, it would only take a word in the right ear, and while the block warden was friendly enough, would turn a blind eye – mainly because Hanna made a point of dropping some of the most odious names she had had the misfortune of coming to know in Berlin into her conversations with him – others might not be so sympathetic. There was always some little Nazi looking for a tiny victory these days.

"Well, it's your decision," Kurt said, reaching into his tool sack. He pulled out the punch-dagger and slipped it over his right fist. She was shocked and her stomach turned at the sight of it.

"What are you doing with that?" she said.

"It's good for the soil."

"Sepp would not be happy if he saw you with it," she said.

"He's gone for the day, he will never know," Kurt said flatly. With that he began to prod the long spike deep into the earth. And suddenly Hanna realised she was still a little afraid of her brother.

***

The train lurched to a halt with a clank of couplings and a long shriek of metal sliding against metal. West was thrown to the floor between the legs of the two guards. With his hands tied tight behind his back there had been no way of stopping himself from falling, and with his false leg leaning against the wall, there was no way of getting back up unaided. The soldiers who guarded him said it was his own fault for twice trying to make a break for it the day before, and they laughed as they pulled him up and dropped him back against the hard, narrow wooden bench that had become home over the past three days. Through his slot to the world, a tiny gap in the join between the sliding door and the planking of the luggage car, he could see the reason for the sudden stop, the searchlight beams weaving a bright mesh across the dark sky, the separate tones of the distant sirens overlapping, so that they almost sounded like a Cairo call to prayer.

"We'll wait here until the raid is over, I suppose," one of the soldiers who had been given the task of guarding him on this journey said to the other, who nodded. Then he grinned and said to West: "You should be glad you're a gypsy and not a pilot, my friend; the RAF's not popular in these parts." Both of them laughed at that. They thought it a huge joke that West still insisted he was a gypsy, but, of course, they knew full well he was a British pilot; he had heard them tell the SS and police who had checked the papers of the people on this train, time and time again. Yet the two soldiers seemed to have developed a grudging fondness for him, even though he had fought with them twice since being put on the train back in Munich.

The luggage car was enough like a prison cell to be perfect for the use they had given it: square-mesh steel fencing to one side blocking off the corridor that connected it with the rest of the train, solid wooden bench seats facing each other, West on one, the soldiers the other. Besides the three of them there was nothing else in the luggage car except for the soldiers' kit-bags. Their rifles were propped up in the corridor the other side of the steel fence, out of West's reach. The small windows were painted out and the space was lit with a dim and pissy yellow blackout bulb that made the soldiers look like they were suffering from jaundice. They were young, his guards, but looked like veterans all the same, the lines on their yellowed faces showing it as well as the close combat badges on their tunics. The luggage car smelt strongly of sawdust and axle grease.

The guards were waiting for the next desperate lunge that would break the boredom – for him and them. The twine that tied West's wrists behind his back was beginning to bite through the skin, but he would not ask them to loosen the knot, because he knew they would think it a trick. Besides, Westbury Holt deserved the pain. One of the soldiers lit up a cigarette and West thought of his long lost pipe, it had been many months since he had last smoked one, before the hole beneath the hut, before Roma ...

West had lost count of the number of times he had tried to escape since he had been taken from Roma. He had been sent to a prison in Trieste to begin with, where he was interrogated for weeks, but would not admit to who he was, saying nothing except for the few Romani phrases he'd picked up. That had cost him, and only now had he shed the bruising that had covered his body like snake skin. He had tried to climb the wall of that prison in Trieste, and had been lucky that the bullet missed, and then that his fall had been broken by the collapsing corrugated iron roof of a latrine block.

After a couple of months in Trieste he had been moved to Vienna, a slow journey in the back of a closed Einheits-PKW, which offered little chance of escape. This didn't stop him trying, though, nor collecting a few rifle butts in the face. In Vienna he was placed in a cell in the Gestapo headquarters at the Hotel Metropole and the monotonous pain of interrogation restarted. Then, one day, they took some photographs of him. After that he was put back in his cell and, it seemed, forgotten.

But not completely forgotten ... He soon realised someone was looking after him, they were just not doing a very good job of it. He was given just enough to eat and he was allowed just enough sleep – the SS guards took pleasure in waking him when he dozed, with shouts and if that failed with cold water. Also, he was given absolutely nothing to do. The only way to fill the day was thinking of her, and of the mistakes he had made. He felt he was being ground down, very slowly. But, at least the beatings had stopped – unless he would try to escape ...

One of the guards smiled at him, as if reading his thoughts, and West peered through the crack between the door and the planking again. Through this small fissure he had managed to piece together some idea of the route he was taking. He had glimpsed signs for Salzburg, Landshut, and Elsterwerda, and by then he had figured out his destination. He had also realised that the German railway system had been very badly – or very *well* – bombed. It had been a while since he'd thought or cared about what was happening with the war, but he supposed he was pleased the Nazis were getting a good old thrashing. By now the distant sirens had ceased, and through his crack out on to the world he could see the searchlights no longer slashed the sky, but he had heard no planes, no bombs, so guessed it had been a false alarm.

"You want something to eat?" one of the guards asked.

West nodded, he had made a point of not speaking to them, as part of him was still pretending to be a gypsy, the part that hurt the most, but he had been given far more food these past few days since boarding the train before this one in Vienna, and he had been glad of the opportunity to build up his strength for his next escape attempt. The guard unlocked the gate then shut it behind him. Five minutes later he returned with some tinned sausage and a few small rolls of coarse black bread – West got the impression that they were able to get the best of the rations because of their charge, which would account for their cheery nature. The train lurched again, then the car bounced against the coupling of the next carriage and clanked noisily, and then they were moving. One of the soldiers cut the twine to allow him to eat and West gobbled up cold and greasy schinkenwurst and dry bread. Out of the corner of his eye he noticed the soldier had left the key in the lock, and then he quickly switched his gaze from it. But the soldiers had not noticed, far more intent on their tinned dinner. West leant back on the hard bench and closed his eyes. He pretended to fall asleep and he thought he heard a sigh of relief from one of the soldiers. This time they did not tie his hands.

West waited for about an hour and in that time he had not heard the sound of the key being taken from the lock. He had kept his eyes tight shut but had not dozed. The train had now slowed for some reason, perhaps a gradient, and West risked a peep, opening one eye. One of the guards was asleep, the other writing a letter, bending over close to the paper to make out the words he scrawled in the dim yellow light. The key was still in the iron lock set into the steel mesh gate. He felt the train slow a little more, the clunks of its wheels on the rail joints becoming further spaced. West knew that if he could get to the passage he could take the soldiers' rifles, and lock them in the cage. Then he could walk through to a carriage, find a door, and then jump to freedom while the train was still travelling slowly. But first there was the key, and his false leg: he would need to grab that, too, maybe even use it as a weapon, the damned thing was heavy enough, that was for sure. It was a desperate plan, and there were too many *ifs*. But he felt he had to make the attempt. It was all he had left ...

West bounded from his seat and dived for the false leg, grabbing it then reaching for the key while balanced on his good leg. He could not have been quicker, and for a moment he felt the cold touch of the key, a tantalising taste of freedom ... But fleeting, for the soldier was faster still, a strong hand on West's left shoulder, the fluttering sound of writing paper falling to the floor, the grunt of the other soldier awakening ... West spun away from the door, almost toppling over, but the movement had momentum and he was able to swing his false leg at the soldier, the heavy socket end of it cracking against the side of his skull so that he let go of West's arm and reached for his head in reaction to the hit, allowing West to feel for the key again. But by now the other soldier was fully awake and standing, and he swept West's leg from under him with a sharp kick to the shin. West landed on the sawdust-smelling planked floor with a crash that jarred his shoulder painfully, and his dropped false leg clattered to the floor beside him.

"For Christ's sake, can't you just sleep?" the second soldier shouted as he kicked West in the stomach, bringing sausage-flavoured bile to his throat. The other guard stood up too, holding his head in his hands, looking a little dizzy. He drew back his leg ready to give West one hell of a payback kick, right to the face, and he closed his eyes and waited for it. He wasn't afraid of the pain, he was long past that, and part of him even welcomed it – that part that already hurt the most. But there was no kick to the face, just the shout from the other soldier. "Not his face!" And then, slightly later, another sharp kick to the belly that again drove the wind from him like a bursting balloon and left him gasping for breath on the floor.

"Up you get sunshine," the soldier said, seemingly content with the sharp retribution, and West was lifted back on to the bench again, his hands tied very tightly behind his back. It took him some long, painful minutes to get his breath back. Yet all that time what the guard had said was tripping through his mind, *not his face, not his face.* He could not think what it meant but something in the way the guard had shouted it, the edge of stark panic, made him all the more curious. And then he picked up the only weapon he had to fight them with …

West suddenly stood up on his one good leg, bent his head back, and smashed his face against the wire of the cage with as much force as he could muster. He felt the skin above his right eye rupture, and then warm blood began to trickle down his face.

"Fuck!" shouted the guard, and then they were on him once again, this time tying his ankle to the bench with the same biting twine that bound his wrists.

The train rolled on into the night, the night rolled on into the day, and Westbury Holt rolled into Berlin.

*

Strudel had done a fine job. There were only a few things that Sepp had to change, or readjust, and he marvelled at just how much Strudel had picked up from watching the Auto Union mechanics for all those years before the war. They had fitted the engine using the block and tackle, hitched to one of the steel roof support arches, without too much trouble, but it was the small things that had proven to be the biggest headaches. There was only so far they could go with the parts Strudel and Fink had placed down the mine, the rest had taken a bit more ingenuity – and there was still one last ingredient they would need to get it *just* right.

So far rubber hoses, bushes and plugs had caused the most difficulty, as rubber was very hard to come by in Germany these days. Still, they had managed to break in to one of the mine buildings where the racing cars were stored, and had cannibalised what parts they could from the Type Cs.

Then they had crept in to the Horch Works – it was not difficult, Strudel knew many ways in, Sepp had discovered – to find the special speed tyres the streamliner used for record runs. Strudel had not asked why they needed those tyres, and truly Sepp would not have had an answer if he had. He might have said if a job is worth doing then it's worth doing properly. He might have said he made this job as difficult as he could because he feared finishing it. Both explanations might have been true. They found the tyres, and they found something else, a concentration camp near the works, where the chassis for the Sdkfz 222 armoured car was now made. Something in the way those forced to labour looked reminded Sepp of how it had felt to be empty. And he had not wanted to be reminded of that, so they quickly took the tyres, which Fink had hidden away, and they left via a gate Sepp had never even known existed.

And now it was all done. Sepp had also borrowed a roll of good tools from the factory and he was using one of the spanners to run through some final tightening checks as Strudel polished the bodywork. He had gone through the same sequence of bolts at least three times, and he knew this was more than thoroughness. For now that the car was finished what would they do? But at least there was that one big problem to sort out before he had to worry about filling his life again. He stood back from the car, Strudel standing alongside him. He had made a good job of the polishing, which had taken him all morning, and now they shined their flashlights and a lantern on the silver bodywork so that it shimmered like mercury.

"It's beautiful," Strudel whispered.

"Yes my friend, you made it so."

The only blemish on this perfect sculpture was the swastika flag painted above and behind the cockpit. They would have removed it, but then this was the way Rosemeyer had driven this car – or one like it at least – and besides, if they were caught they would be in enough trouble without having to explain why they had erased the symbol of the thousand-year Reich.

"There is just one more thing, Strudel," Sepp said.

"Wash?"

"Yes, I'd forgotten – that too," he smiled as he said it.

They walked back down the shaft and then started the long climb back up the ladder. They washed themselves thoroughly and carefully from a broken standpipe in a disused smithy close to the shaft-head, making sure that every last trace of grease and coal dust was removed. Then, when they were both clean, they started for home, hours earlier than normal. They were careful to make sure they were not seen by anyone in the active pits nearby, and careful to make sure they replaced the wire panel in the fence. Then, as they walked back along the banks of the Zwickau Mulde they talked, or rather Sepp did, and he could not stop himself. Memories seemed to be flooding into his mind with the force of the river's flow: working with Lick on the Auto Unions, driving one for the first time, the disappointment of that test drive in England ... But not even that last memory could dampen his sense of optimism and excitement, and he knew that he was talking very quickly, like the new lads did after their first taste of combat.

Before he knew it they were on Nord Strasse. Strudel walked alongside him, his thin, ratty face contorted with a large grin, his rough old shoes scuffing along the crowns of the cobbles, his big brown eyes shining. Then there was Frau Hansen.

"Hello Sepp," she said, ignoring Strudel completely. She had a basket of provisions hooked over her arm, which she would have traded with one of the men at the allotments for some knitwear, or something equably valuable, he supposed. "Perhaps you could help me with this young man?" He shrugged, he would have preferred not to walk with the old widow, not today – nor any day – but he took the basket anyway and she fell in beside him. Strudel hung back and Sepp could hear the soft brush of his feet along the pavement.

"I must say you are looking much better now, Sepp."

"And so are you Frau Hansen."

"I have not been unwell, Sepp."

"Of course not."

"And I see you have your voice back?"

"My friend and I have much to speak of."

"Yes, of course you have," Frau Hansen said, punctuating it with a sharp, ironic tut. "So, will you be re-joining your regiment soon?" she asked, looking away slightly as she said it, so that it almost seemed as if she was asking the dirty red brick of the buildings they passed rather than the man who walked beside her. Sepp said nothing. "Germany needs all its young men now, all those who are able at any rate," she shot a withering glance back at Strudel as she said it. Sepp caught the sly look, as he was meant to.

"My friend here is more than able, Frau Hansen."

"Yes," she snorted a little laugh, "of course he is."

"And you should be careful."

"Why?" there was an edge of worry to her voice now and her birdy eyes began to dart from side to side.

"Because we are quite insane, my friend and I – and certainly not to be trusted with shopping baskets." With that he stopped and reached beneath the checked cloth that covered the provisions and pulled out a dirt-encrusted onion. Then he bit into it, and chewed noisily, forcing a smile of enjoyment on to his face. Her face filled with shock and wide-eyed fear, and then she snatched the basket from him. Strudel laughed as she made a hasty escape. Once she was a good 100 metres away Sepp spat the partly chewed onion out, skin and dirt included, and started talking about the streamliner again as they walked towards home, Strudel grinning by his side.

*

They had come home early and now they faced Hanna over the table in the basement kitchen, both scrubbed clean. There was potato soup on the stove and its starchy smell was all pervading. By the way Strudel was looking at Sepp it almost seemed as if he was waiting for her brother to speak. But then they had all been waiting months for that.

"What is it?" she said, not expecting an answer from either of them.

Strudel tugged at Sepp's sleeve, slight panic in his eyes. There was more silence, measured off by seven drips of the tap in the sink.

"We need fuel," Sepp suddenly said.

Sepp had spoken. The shock of it was like a zap of static electricity. She stared at him for long seconds, as the shock slowly faded into surprise, and then disappointment, for they were the first words he had said to her in all this time. Then there was fear, a small fear, for now. *Who was this Sepp, this Sepp that spoke to her?*

"Sepp, you talked?" she said, softly, recognising the wonder in her own voice.

"Fuel," he said it again.

"Fuel?" she said.

He nodded.

Fuel. Everyone wanted fuel, everyone wanted everything at this time. But her brother had said he wanted fuel, and it was the first thing he had asked for in an age.

"Fuel for what, have you a car?" she said, playing along, happy – for now – to hear him talk.

"Not just any fuel; good fuel, special fuel, high octane fuel."

"I don't understand, Sepp, what's this about?"

"Aviation fuel – it will do."

"Please Sepp, tell me."

"It's what we need."

Hanna took a deep breath, and then locked her eyes onto those of her brother. There was a spark there, like the Sepp of old, when he talked of his hopes, and suddenly her heart leapt against her ribcage. But she would not let herself get too carried away just yet.

"So you have an aeroplane, have you?" she said, laughing nervously.

"Close," Sepp said, and with that one word there was that rarest of things, a smile from Strudel.

"I need more than that," Hanna said, trying her best to be stern.

"Konrad could get it for us; he's Luftwaffe."

"What, a plane?"

"Fuel."

"And why should Konrad help?" she said.

"Family."

"Family?"

Strudel added the affirmative flourish of a Stan Laurel nod.

"I will need to tell him what you want it for?"

Sepp shrugged.

"So then, you will have to tell me," she said. Sepp looked at Strudel, who nodded back.

"The racing cars are at one of the mines, that's where they have been hidden to protect them, from the bombers. One is now ready," Sepp said, his voice flat and calm.

"Ready?" She stood up and the legs of the chair screeched against the flooring. She looked deep into Sepp's brightly shining blue eyes. "And what will you do with this car of yours?" she said.

"We only want to run the engine," Sepp said.

"Why?"

"Because it is better than other things," Sepp said, and the way he said it she knew that whatever it was that he wanted to do it would be done, with her or without her. She shook her head and sat back down.

"What if you're caught, it would mean trouble?"

"No one is bothered about the cars now," Sepp said, just a little less certain of himself now, she thought.

"You're both mad."

"Evidently," Sepp said, and Strudel nodded seriously.

"Konrad will want nothing to do with this, you know that, don't you?"

"No, he will understand why we're doing this – anyone who has driven a racing car would understand."

"I thought you said you only wanted to start it up?"

"That is so." The room was quiet for some time as Hanna thought it through. "It's only a car," Sepp suddenly said with, for the first time, a hint of pleading. *Only a car*, she thought, nothing was only *only* anymore.

"If I don't?"

"Then I will contact Konrad myself."

"You know he only cares for himself, Sepp."

"That's not how I remember him," Sepp said.

Hanna just nodded, then said: "Then I will do it for you. I will ask him, but please don't be too disappointed when he says no."

Sepp quite suddenly smiled widely, and then said: "Hello sister," the gleaming crystal of a tear at the corner of his eye as he said it. She wanted to hug him, but something in her forced her to hold back, to turn her face away. She stood and walked to the stove, not letting them see the tears that formed in her eyes, too.

"There's some soup," she said.

***

The white-tiled cell was cold and the ammonia tang of his urine hung in the stale air. He knew the cell was on the ground floor, for he had climbed no stairs, and he knew it was on Prinz Albrect Strasse, for he had seen the way they came from the back seat of the Mercedes 260D that had brought him here from the Silesian Station – because, he'd supposed, the Anhalter had been badly damaged in the bombing. He also knew that the headquarters of the state secret police, the Gestapo, was on Prinz Albrect Strasse.

At one time West had dreaded cells like this; but it did not seem such a small space now – perhaps no room would ever seem small after his time in the tomb beneath the hut? He was left alone, only disturbed when it was time to slurp at the thin soup that was provided. He was not interrogated, he was not tortured, but he knew such things went on: hearing the moans and the cries from those they carried down the corridor outside his cell, and sometimes just the drag of a body itself, a living person reduced to nothing more than a wet sack of unthinking meat. He would wait for his turn quietly, and he knew that if it came he would welcome it, for in not being able to do something the least he could do was to have something done to him ... Or at least that's how the scales of justice tipped in his head.

The cell was just three things: Westbury Holt, a hard bench to sleep or sit on, and a bucket to piss in. On some nights, and on some days, he would hear the bombs as they whistled down on Berlin, sometimes landing close enough to shake the wall of his cell. And every night, and every day, he would think of Roma and her people and he would wonder where they were, if they were still alive, and how he could join them again. He gave his solemn word to her again, and again, and again, as he sat on the hard bench, his back pressed tight against the smooth, cold wall of the cell ... And again ... and again ...

When the key rattled in the lock he calmly assumed it was finally his turn for interrogation. The heavy steel door opened smoothly, swung and then slammed against the wall outside, the harsh clang echoing down the corridors. "Come, there is someone here for you," said the lugubrious shirt-sleeved and shoulder-holstered Gestapo man. West nodded and eased himself off the bench that had been his home for the last six days. He was ushered along the corridor and then through a large room, where men in dark suits and crisp white shirts pored over files. In the lobby at the foot of a grand staircase he was handed over to two SS men and taken through a revolving door and into the street. The car, a grey 170V sat at the kerbside, the three-pointed-star gleaming and catching the sunshine on the tip of its bonnet. One of the SS men opened a rear door and pushed West inside. There was Konrad.

"Well?" he said, in English, "are you not surprised?"

"A Mercedes?" West said.

"I mean, are you not you surprised to see me?"

West just shrugged, somehow he wasn't surprised. Konrad was sat on the leather rear seat, his legs crossed in front of him, light Luftwaffe blue trousers spotless and creased to a razor edge, tall leather boots gleaming and reflective – the car seemed a little humble for all that shine, West thought. He still wore the old RAF tunic that had been tailored and dyed to look like an ordinary jacket with his now rust-coloured cricket jumper beneath it.

"Is that the same old rag?" Konrad said, with a dry little laugh. "Well, don't worry, we'll sort you out with something more suitable soon enough." The SS men clicked some latches on the outside of the door and Konrad shrugged with forced embarrassment as they then sat in the front of the car. "Drive on," he ordered. Alongside the driver the other SS guard was cradling a Schmeisser.

"Well West, it's been a long time," Konrad said as they drove through a crumbling square, the driver having to slow and weave between two bombed-out trams. West nodded. "But you do not seem so pleased to see me?"

"I'm not so happy with my lot at the moment, Konrad, nothing personal," he muttered.

"Well perhaps it should be. I have saved your life, you know?" West merely nodded again, then turned to look out of the window. Berlin seemed to be disintegrating before his eyes, crumbling like a city of sand.

"I'd wondered who had gone to so much trouble to make sure I wasn't shot," West said.

"It wasn't easy, believe me, from what they tell me you deserved more than a bullet – but let us hope it was worth it, shall we?"

West just kept his eyes on the broken streets, few of which he could recognise from before the war. At one junction there was a naked apartment block, its outside walls torn from it. A pale ghost of an old woman was knitting on a dust coated armchair on the third floor of the skeletal building, as if the walls were still there, like a little worm behind the glass of a child's worm farm.

"Can you help me find someone, Konrad?" West said.

"One of the gypsies?"

"You know of them?"

"There is a file, of course."

"It's a girl."

"I would have been disappointed in you otherwise, West," he smiled. "But as to whether we can find her ... Let's just say some things are possible, if you know the right people." The Mercedes crunched a narrow isthmus of fallen rubble beneath its wheels, the car lurching a little.

They drove on through the streets of Berlin, through Schöneberg, where children rummaged in tottering piles of debris that were once homes, where families pushed the remains of their possessions on rickety handcarts, where the dust never seemed to settle.

"I am sorry it took so long for you to get here," Konrad said. "Messages do not travel quickly these days, and they do not always find the right recipient. And, as you have seen, the railways are not what they were."

"Things certainly haven't changed for the better," West said, suddenly remembering Berlin in '38, the last time he was there, and with that remembering other things. "How's Hanna?" he asked.

"She is well, I have sent her out to Zwickau; it's safer there."

"And Sepp?"

"Not so good I'm afraid. He was wounded in Russia; it seems it has made him a little ... Strange. Yes, *strange*, but we can hope he will get over it."

"There is always hope," West said.

"Yes, always. But he is living in a different place now. And then perhaps that would be better for all of us, no?" Konrad said. Suddenly a broad smile spread itself across his face. "You know, now he thinks he has an Auto Union to play with."

"Really?" A spark seemed to jump through West's being at the mention of those two words and it surprised him, for he had thought of nothing but Roma since he had lost her, and now he was suddenly reminded of another life; a life of make-believe he once lived.

"That is what he has told Hanna," Konrad continued. "They have asked me to find fuel for it, he wants to run the engine, it seems. They have no idea of the realities of this war, I'm afraid."

"Won't you help them?"

"Of course not. Just because I'm in the uniform of the Luftwaffe it does not mean I go anywhere near aircraft, besides there is a great shortage. It would be quite impossible."

"Have you tried?"

"As I said – quite impossible," Konrad repeated as the car thudded over a fan of fallen telephone cables that lay in the road. They sat silent for a spell that stretched for five minutes and more, as the silver memories sped through West's consciousness.

"Do you remember Donington?" West finally asked.

"In '37?"

"Yes. Before the race, you gave Sepp a try out in the Auto Union?" Konrad nodded, the smile slipping from his eyes if not his mouth. "There is something I have often wondered about that day Konrad —"

"Well, you are right to wonder," Konrad interrupted. "There is no use hiding it now, it all seems so unimportant anyway," he shrugged and looked out of the window.

"So, he was fast then?"

"Very fast. As fast as Rosemeyer!"

"That fast ... He looked it."

"And you knew didn't you?" Konrad said. "Stopwatch or not, you knew."

"Maybe I did, but he trusted you."

"But you did know, didn't you?" Konrad said, triumph in his voice, as West caught his own distorted reflection in the black gleam of the peak of his cap. "I always thought you did. You see we are not so very different are we, when it's survival that is at stake? And neither of us could have survived with another Rosemeyer on the team."

"I'm not so sure you're right about that, Konrad."

"Well, let's hope I am, for if I have misjudged you we are both in very deep trouble."

*

The Focke Wulf 190 swept over them at tree-top height, its slipstream beating against their heads as they stepped out of the Mercedes. West could smell the fumes from its fuel, and it reminded him of his Auto Union days once again. "There is a small airfield close by," Konrad said. "We've had to disperse our aircraft just lately. It can get busy at night, but if they keep you awake you can blame your RAF friends for it." West guessed the fighters would be there to help protect Berlin from the bombers, as they had only travelled for about an hour before they had reached the house, heading south through the suburbs of Wilmersdorf, Steglitz and Lichtenrade before arriving here in Genshagen.

The house was large, with a row of six double windows on the first floor, and it was painted a creamy white, with green shutters and a red tiled roof. It was two storeys, but a row of narrow dormers protruded from the steeply canted roof. Outside the house there was a large gravel-coated parking area bordered by broad lawns, and a single ash tree, its leafless skeleton shivering to the breeze. The tree grew close to the house, its clawing upper branches reaching far higher than the roofline. Konrad gave some instructions to the driver and West took the opportunity to run his escaper's eye over the landscape. The house was surrounded by woodland, and the Focke Wulf, its landing gear extended, was just dipping out of sight beyond the trees. Through a clearing he could see an unfenced camp of small huts, while to the north he could pick out the roofs of factory buildings and a large white house with a tower, perhaps a mansion or even a castle.

"Well, here we are," Konrad said.

"Funny sort of prison," West murmured.

"Not prison," Konrad replied.

The engine noise of the fighter plane had dwindled now and West was suddenly aware of scratchy music drifting by like an un-gripped memory. Then he recognised it, something from before the war, *The Lambeth Walk*. Konrad pushed open the door of the house. The hall was parquet flooring overlaid with elaborate geometric-patterned rugs, with an umbrella stand in the corner, and coat pegs along the one wall, just a quarter of which had field grey German infantry tunics and forage caps hanging from them. There was no wall between the hallway and the living room, just a knocked-through space, and West caught sight of five or six German soldiers sitting in there. Two of them were playing chess, the others lounging in deep armchairs, reading or simply tapping their feet to the music. All of them were smoking so there was a heavy pall of smoke and the aroma of tobacco filled the air. Suddenly West remembered he hadn't enjoyed a good pipe for an age. The music stopped and there was just the harsh, static-laced scrape and click of the needle on the centre of the record.

"Put it on again, Canuck." In English; as broad a London accent as a pearly king ordering jellied eels.

"British Union of Fascists, that one," Konrad said.

"Do it yourself," the Canadian said, in answer to the cockney.

"That one says he's anti-Bolshevik." The soldiers seemed to have suddenly noticed the two of them standing there, West with his jaw hanging slack from the surprise of it all. Two of the soldiers eyed him suspiciously, but one nodded in a friendly enough way.

"They are —"

"Yes, mostly British, there are others too, in the camp down the road, but not as many as we had hoped. Come through and I will explain." He followed Konrad through a door that led off the hall on the opposite side from the living room. Someone put *The Lambeth Walk* back on the record player. "They're treated well, look there is coffee," Konrad said, pointing to the coffee pot, "real coffee!" The room was an office, with another door in

362

the far wall and a row of filing cabinets behind a heavy looking oak desk; clear except for a phone, an in-tray, a letter opener, and a blotter with a pattern of interlocking coffee-cup roundels on its top sheet.

"Yours?"

"No, not mine, it's … but I am forgetting my manners. Here, I have something for you." He pulled the meerschaum pipe out of the side pocket of his tunic and despite himself West grabbed it when it was offered. The pipe was already stuffed and he took the light off Konrad's cigarette eagerly and then patiently went through the old ritual of tamping and relighting it. The tobacco was good and the taste of it filled his head like a soothing balm and he let himself sink into one of the armchairs that filled two corners of the room. Konrad did likewise, then began his explanation.

"Those men belong to a very special unit, the British Free Corps."

"Traitors?"

"We prefer to think that they have seen that the true enemy of England comes from further east than Germany; they come to us in order to fight the Soviets."

"And they come for tobacco, for coffee and comfort too?"

"There's no denying it; we are all human – all too human." Konrad smiled a sad little smile at that.

"How many of them are there, you said it was a corps?"

Konrad seemed to hesitate before saying anything, then shook his head and laughed, taking a deep puff of his cigarette before: "In truth, barely a platoon."

"Will they fight?"

"Who knows? Perhaps. They are attached to the Waffen SS, so that is certainly the idea."

"So why are *we* here, surely you can't expect me to join up with them – can you?" As he said it he heard a car pull up outside, the gravel crunching noisily beneath its wheels, and Konrad swallowed hard. "You really thought I'd join those treacherous bastards?"

"Calm down West, I wouldn't ask you to," Konrad said. "But there is something you will do for me, you have to. I have saved your life, you should know that, now you must return the compliment —" Konrad stopped suddenly, there was the thump of heavy boots in the corridor outside, the music was switched off, then the door of the office burst open.

"Standartenführer Kessler, you are early?"

Kessler cut Konrad short with a flick of his head. "Herr Holt, it's been a long time," he said, looking at his wristwatch, and then at Konrad, who was now standing, almost at attention. Kessler was wearing a field grey SS uniform.

"West, you remember Herr Kessler, of course?" Konrad said, and West noticed a tiny bead of sweat on his forehead, as well as the deference.

West didn't even bother nodding, just lost himself in the veil of pipe smoke that rose before his eyes.

"But he is not ready, where is the uniform?" Kessler suddenly blurted, obviously stung by West's insouciance. "And what's this?" Kessler pointed to the healing welt above West's eye, where he'd butted the steel mesh fence in the luggage car. "There is a cut, bruising?"

"I'm sorry Sir," Konrad blurted, "it was the guards on the train, I —"

"It will have to do, now let's get going."

Konrad shifted awkwardly, then looked from Kessler to West then back again. "I have not explained what we want from him yet," he said, his voice dripping with apology.

"Then do it, but fast." Kessler ignored the armchair Konrad had vacated and sat at the desk, stretching his polished boots out beneath it, and clasping his hands as he considered the scruffy prisoner in front of him with a look of slight disgust on his face.

"It would be easier if you gave us some time alone?" Konrad said.

Kessler simply waved a get-on-with-it and Konrad nodded meekly before clearing his throat and addressing West.

"Let me tell you of my role in this war," Konrad said to West. "Sadly I was not able to fly like you, what with the racing injuries and my age ..." Kessler snorted a little laugh but Konrad ignored it. "But they found a use for me. You see, people still remember me from the good old days, I represent something glorious, if you will, something that everyone can understand and hope to see again – Germany winning." Another fighter passed low over the house, its passage shuddering the glass in the sash window. "So, that's why I have spent much of the war talking, being seen near the front, explaining to the troops why German equipment is better – of course they would prefer a nice pair of legs but they still usually seemed pleased to see me." That was the first time he had smiled since Kessler had entered the room.

"It has worked well, I think, but now they need something different, something a little more —"

"Please get on with it Plaidt, they will be here soon," Kessler made a show of looking at his watch again, and West suddenly realised that they were both slightly agitated. Konrad bit at his bottom lip and nodded.

"German people know you, West," Konrad said.

"I've found that out the hard way."

"It has saved your life."

"It's caused me more misery than you can ever imagine, Konrad."

"But it could work very well for me ... For us," Konrad said. Kessler was tapping a Damascus steel letter opener in the shape of an SS dagger against the desk, the taps getting quicker and louder, in time to his blinking eyes, and Konrad was obviously trying hard to control his patience.

"You have seen that we have some of your countrymen on our side, those that have realised that we are not the true enemy, we are not the danger. Soldiers who hope to fight against the Russians rather than languish in a prison camp."

"Or hope to listen to records and smoke in comfort?" West put in.

"Perhaps you're right, the project has not been a great success; simple soldiers often do not see the bigger picture."

"No, Konrad, they can just see through you, and they can see that it is just a matter of time before Germany is finished."

Kessler suddenly stopped tapping the letter opener against the desk: "Seems to me you have misjudged this one, Plaidt?"

"Give me time."

"There is no time," he stood up sharply and his chair almost toppled on to the floor.

"Please, a little time – and space."

Kessler nodded sharply. "All right. But remember, Konrad, this is your idea, and they will not take kindly to being dragged down from Berlin for nothing. I will leave you friends to catch up," he said, as he left the room.

"Kessler mentioned a uniform," West said. "You didn't really think I would change sides, did you?"

"Just hear what I have to say Westbury, all of it ... Please?"

"You're wasting your time." West took a deep puff of the pipe and stared at an invisible spot on the wall.

"All I am asking is that you put on the uniform and meet a few senior officers. It would make it look like we have had some success. That's all, I promise – and it would get me out of a very deep hole indeed." He was almost pleading now.

"You have got to be joking, Konrad, just because I raced German cars it does not make me a Nazi – have you lost your mind?"

"Close to it West. These people always want results, they always want something to make the soldiers believe again, and it has been years since they have believed in me. I thought that if I could give them a Britisher they had heard of ... And we are old friends, are we not?"

"Bugger off, you knew I was no traitor!"

"But I have saved your life now, don't you see? Without my personal intervention you would have been shot long ago."

"Or I would be with the girl I love," West said softy.

"Ah, that. Yes, that." Konrad paced out the length of the office twice, his hands clasped behind his back, his forehead corrugated in thought. Then an expression of eureka, that was so obviously premeditated that West thought it insulting, spread across his face. "What if I took you to her?"

"You could do that?"

"Yes, it is possible. All you have to do is wear a uniform for an hour and say nice things about Germany to a few fat old officers. That's all."

"And then you will take me to her?"

"Of course."

"Wouldn't you need to check with Kessler?"

"No, I have a certain amount of influence." West could tell he was lying, could tell that this trick had been worked out long before, but that was not the point. The point was that here was a chance. He stared at Konrad through the smoke that drifted slowly from the pipe clenched between his teeth.

"Should I trust you Konrad, you seem desperate?"

"Need you ask that West, we are old friends are we not?"

"Sepp was family."

"Sepp? Oh that … Different," he shook his head. "Much different, believe me West. This is life and death, and not just your life, or your death." It was the closest that Konrad would come to making the threat that had been in the air since Kessler had walked into the room a little earlier. He believed it, but that didn't matter. What mattered was that here at least was a way of seeing Roma again.

"It's just fancy dress West, no one can hold it against you – I will back you up, when this war is over."

"If you are winning, why will you need to?" West said. Konrad smiled a wry little smile. West heard two more cars pull up outside, heavy doors slamming and happy German chit-chat.

"Please West, there is little time – we have a uniform ready for you upstairs."

*

"Have you heard from Konrad about the fuel yet?" Sepp said. Hanna simply shook her head. She could not tell him how her husband had just laughed, before promising to send another food parcel. "Damn it!" Sepp thumped his fist against the kitchen table and the cups rattled in their saucers, black ersatz coffee spilling on to the yellow and white tablecloth. It was the first time Hanna had seen him lose his temper since his return and without realising it she had jumped back from the table, and was now almost in the corner of the little basement kitchen. Sepp was watching her, outburst over, a puzzled expression on his face.

"What is it sister, are you afraid of me?"

"No Sepp, of course not, I —"

"You look afraid – why should you fear me?"

"I don't Sepp, it's just … It's just, there's so much I don't know about you now."

"What is there to know Hanna, I am the same?"

"Tell me Sepp, tell me about it."

"There is nothing to tell."

"I know that's not true Sepp. Tell me Sepp, tell me it all. I need to know, what happened to you?"

He stared down at the little pool of dark liquid on the tablecloth, then at the punch-dagger in its place beside the sink.

"I cannot think about it now, when this is all over I will have to face it again, but not until then."

"When the war is over?"

He shook his head slowly and smiled a faraway smile that failed to reach his eyes. "Hanna," he said, "can't you see? For now, this is me. And I love you as much as I ever did."

*

There was a hot bathtub ready for him in a room at the top of the house and the steam curled temptingly from the surface of the water. West needed no second invitation and he was soon stepping out of his worn-out old clothes and unstrapping his false leg. Konrad scooped up the clothes, a look of comic disgust on his face. West let himself sink into the hot tub, feeling his skin come alive as the grime of the weeks seemed to crack and float away from him.

"You're too thin, we will get you a good meal after it's done," Konrad said, bundling West's clothes into a ball.

"What are you doing with those?" West asked.

"I'll burn them."

"But my jumper?"

"It's only ever brought you bad luck."

"I don't believe in luck," West said, quietly, but the door was already closing on Konrad's back. He heard talking from the landing outside, Konrad giving orders, then he let his head slip under the surface of the water so he missed what was said. For a luxurious half a minute he refused to let a thought enter his head. When he broke surface again Konrad was there, holding a uniform on a coat hanger.

"It's brand new, and we've matched your RAF rank – you're an obersturmführer," Konrad said. West looked at the field grey uniform with its SS lightning flashes at the collar, its silver and yellow shoulder strap rank badges and British Free Corp ribbon and Union Jack shield on the sleeve.

"Very smart …" he started, but Konrad was already hurrying him out of the bath.

"Come on, there's no time, they are all here now and I do not trust Kessler's humour to keep them amused for long." West stepped out of the bath and dried himself with a coarse army towel – Konrad looked at his watch four times in the time this took him. A soldier brought in a chair and filled a bowl with hot water, then proceeded to shave West's beard and cut his hair short, then slicked it back and flat with brilliantine as Konrad paced the room. Half an hour later he was ready. The clouds had descended over the woodland outside and Konrad switched on the light, which threw West's reflection onto the window.

"Well bugger me," he said, with no humour. "What a fine Nazi I make."

"Come, we must hurry." Konrad said, taking him by the arm and leading him down the two flights of stairs. He was rushing now, so much so that West almost tripped, but a soldier who followed steadied him then urged him on again. West was in the hall before he knew it and pushed into the throng as quickly again.

Flash bulbs flared and blinded him momentarily before he had time to take in what was happening. There seemed to be an enormous crush of people and West was dimly aware of a film crew in one corner. Hands were thrust into his and more magnesium flashes lit up the room as Kessler spun him from one senior officer to the next as if he was a dizzy-headed debutante, and then Konrad thrust a card in his hand. He was still in shock as he read it.

"I am very proud to serve Germany once again …" he stopped as he realised what he was saying, Kessler covered for him, then there was another card, this one held up above the senior officers, the photographers and the cameramen. He read again, the flash bulbs flashed once more and a radio microphone was thrust in front of his face. He wanted to get it over with, he wanted to be with Roma, and so he read the card, lies tripping off the tongue easily, as they do in magnesium heated dreams such as these. *The eastern menace … Our German brothers … German sporting excellence on the battlefield … Yes, I feel like I am coming home … That's enough Konrad, please that's enough…*

And then it was over and he was led from the room by Konrad who took him back up the stairs to another room at the top of the house where a plate of diced pork and mashed potatoes awaited him, hot food spiced with paprika, which made the room smell like heaven. It tasted good too, and was as much of a dream as what had just happened. He thought how much Roma would enjoy it.

By the time the last tyres had spun in the gravel of the driveway Konrad and Kessler had joined him. West was still in his uniform, stretched out on the single bed. They both looked down at him, a mix of satisfaction and relief on Konrad's face, while Kessler was blinking at a steady rate.

"What have I done?" West said.

"Saved your life for a start, and made ours just a little more comfortable, too," Kessler said, and Konrad nodded. West had lain there for the last hour trying to piece it all together, how they had rushed him so there was no time to think it through, how they had duped him.

"You never said anything about cameras," he said.

"It's propaganda West," Konrad said, "without pictures it's useless."

West remembered the fuss over the Pescara photograph back in the camp in Italy and silently hoped that none of the pictures would find their way to England … And yet even as he was hoping it hardly seemed to matter, he was about to see Roma again, and somehow anything that had brought that about could not be bad.

"When will I see her?"

"Her?" Kessler looked confused.

"The gypsy girl," Konrad said as matter-of-factly as he could – but with a trace of concern that West instantly detected.

"Gypsy? You're joking, yes?" Kessler laughed out loud and West felt his heart turn to cold lead inside him.

"No – you promised, Konrad!" he heard himself shout as he swung himself up and sat on the edge of the bed.

"Sir, I —" Konrad started but Kessler cut him short with a raised leather-gloved hand.

"Look, if she's not dead yet she will be dying in some camp, like they all are and like they all should be," Kessler said. He was suddenly resting his hand on the butt of his Walther, the holster flapping open, his eyes blinking steadily. "Besides, you are SS now. Do you really think we can have you seen with untermensch scum like that? If you are so desperate, go and fuck a dog my friend."

At any other time West would have gone for his throat, but right now his arms and legs were setting solid with the concrete of shock. Kessler left them.

"I am truly sorry, West."

"Is she dead?"

"I don't know for sure," Konrad said. "But they are killing them; killing them all, the gypsies and the Jews and anybody who doesn't fit – you must see that, they will kill you too if you do not work with them. They would kill me if —"

"Where are these camps?"

"Everywhere West, you could never believe the evil …" his words tailed off and West thought he saw a tear in the man's eyes, then for the first time he realised just how old Konrad had become, just how frightened he was, and always had been. He hated him for it. "I will tell you something West, at one time I laughed at them, men like Kessler, but I made a mistake. Germany made a mistake. I have seen things you would not believe, and they made sure I saw these things, so I shared their guilt. It is a disease West, and it will kill us all."

"Where?" West said, again.

"Everywhere," Konrad repeated in a whisper. "One time I was with Kessler in the fortress at Theresienstadt, there was no need to be there, except that it was a labour camp where skeletons – that's the only way I can describe them – made crankshafts for Auto Union – *our* Auto Union, West. There were two men, the guards were beating them because they would not work hard enough they said, or could not, I suppose, but it was probably for our benefit, now I come to think of it. Kessler borrowed a bayonet and slit the throat of one of them, as casually as a man might cut the tip off a cigar. 'Now watch how the other will work,' he said, blinking – as he does. This was nothing, not there, just normal … And there are other places, far worse than Theresienstadt, places where they are simply killing them. Places that *exist* simply for the purpose of killing them." Konrad shook his head, sharply, as if to shake the memories away.

There was a solid-steel silence for a moment, and then Konrad said: "You can stay here, West. If you give me your word you will not try to escape?"

"My word?"

"Yes, that's all. I know I can rely on it, and it is much better here than other places, you can be sure of that. But if you do try to escape, I will pay for it, you can be sure of that, too."

"My word it is then," West whispered and Konrad nodded, turned his back on him and left the room, pulling the door closed behind him. West listened to his footsteps on the stairs outside the room, three steps, then stop, then three steps back and the rattle of the key in the lock.

"Yes, you have my word Konrad," he whispered to himself.

*

His word. It meant so very little now. *The Germans will not harm you:* that had been his word to them; *I will never leave you,* this had been his word to her, his solemn oath. Everything he had done had caused so much suffering, and every time he had given his word it had caused pain. "It's time to start putting things right, Westbury Holt," he whispered to himself as he tried the lock on the window.

It was fully dark outside now. The glass in the window sandwiched a mesh of wire and the catch was screwed in place. He took a wire coat hanger from the wardrobe and bent it into a more or less straight length which he was able to squeeze beneath the catch, levering it over the head of the screw with a muted pop. He left the window closed, for now, and smashed his empty dinner plate between the bed sheets to cut down the noise. Then he started to un-pick the threads in the Union Jack shield and British Free Corps badges on his tunic with a jagged piece of the china. When the job was finished and all the British badges were taken off he hung the tunic in the wardrobe and lay on the bed, waiting. An hour or so later the knock on the door he had been expecting came. Konrad checking up on him.

"Leave me alone," he said, as sulkily as possible. Konrad waited at the door for a little while, perhaps trying to decide whether to come inside or not, but then West heard his footsteps on the stairs. It might give him until the morning, he thought, it might just give him another two hours. Either way it was time to move. He put the tunic and the peaked cap back on then opened the window as quietly as he could, its little creaks loud against the quiet night. There was a yard or so of steeply sloping roof tiles in front of him, and beyond that a long enough drop to the gravel driveway. In the darkness he could just make out the edge of the roof. He climbed out of the window and made his way along the tiles. One or two of them shifted as he trod on them, letting out little scraping sounds that seemed deafening in the still night. West soon found himself at the point where the tiles met the guttering. Earlier, with the expert eye of the escaper, he had noticed the position of the drainpipe, and now he edged towards it.

To reach the pipe he needed to use the guttering, and trust it would hold his weight. He was not entirely sure it could, but he would not let that stop him. Just then, from below, he heard the scrunch of boots in gravel and peered over the edge of the roof to see the dark smudge of a sentry against the pale parking space, his helmet gleaming in the moonlight. He watched him walk on, then counted off the seconds it took for him to circle the building. When he came around again West waited for him to pass, and now knew exactly how much time he had to get clear of the house. He lowered himself from the roof by the guttering, ignoring the creak and loud snap as he hung from it, then grasped the lead pipe. Then he shinned down the drainpipe, gripping it with his knees. He touched ground with a happy little crunch of gravel. He could hear music and laughter from the living room and a square of light was thrown from the window and across the gravel. He skirted around the edge of the light and on to the lawn, clambering over a fence and then rushing, bent low, for the cover of the woods. He had just reached the trees and turned when he saw the sentry complete his circuit of the house.

Free again. But there was not the usual ecstasy of earlier escapes, rather a feeling of being at the start of something, a journey, and a new life. It had been the easiest escape yet, he mused, but then the flimsy wire of his word was not a difficult fence to cut. He tried to get his bearings as best he could, keeping the well-lit camp where he supposed the traitors of the British Free Corps were housed to his left, and walking as fast as he could through the wood, glancing back every now and then to see if there was any sign of alarm. He believed that with a bit of luck he should arrive at the temporary airfield within a couple of hours.

At first, once he had lost sight of the lights from the camp, he had no way of knowing which way he was heading, and he had soon found himself lost in the woods, fumbling around in hat-snagging circles. But then he had caught the unmistakable raspy rip of an aero engine firing up, and had followed it. Now, crouched at the edge of the field, he could see it was just how Konrad had said: not really an airbase, more of a camp, with tents and heavily camouflaged and widely dispersed fighter pens built out of sandbags. It smelt strongly of fuel. From the trees he could see no sentries, but there was a guard at the gate, through which a truck was now passing, its lights, shining through the slits of the headlamp covers, just pale yellow slashes in the night. Those on the back of the truck were singing, and sounded drunk. While the guard was busy with the truck and its occupants West simply walked on to the airfield. He covered about 100 yards or so of open ground without being challenged before he spotted the sentry with the dog. Both were stood quite still, watching the truck arriving, the Alsatian's ears pricked up in curiosity.

For a moment West's heart stopped. The dog was sure to pick up his scent. Then he remembered the German soap he had washed in, the German clothes he wore, the German food he had eaten, and he knew his smell would not be out of place here. He walked on, making an effort not to up his pace. Some long seconds later he felt a little relieved to be in amongst the tents. He made his way through the jumble of canvas structures, while the truck parked up close by. As the drunken airmen climbed from the truck, they stopped on seeing him. He had guessed his silhouette would be the same as a Luftwaffe officer, with the similarly shaped cap and tunic. He had been banking on it. He touched the peak of his cap, and two of them returned his sloppy salute, before resuming their drunken singing. Then West saw what he had come for ...

The aircraft were spread out in front of him. The FW 190s were tail down beneath the camouflage netting of the fighter pens, each of which was widely spaced the length of the field. But the night fighters were out in the open, ready for scramble. They were Messerschmitt 110s, twin-engine fighters that had been out-flown in the daylight earlier in the war, but had found their role when the sun went down and the Lancasters of the RAF paid their nocturnal calls on the Fatherland. They now wore the distinctive whiskers of radar antennae on their noses and the blotchy grey camouflage of the hunter of the night. He walked up to the night fighters, five in all, chocks jammed beneath their wheels. A fuel tender was just finishing topping up one of the planes, while an armourer was working by lamplight on the rear-facing gun under the long Plexiglas canopy of another, but he barely noticed this lone Luftwaffe officer taking his evening stroll, and West walked on unchallenged. He soon came to the end of the line of aeroplanes. There was a large tent close by and a light glowed within, making a shadow show of the men inside. He could hear laughter, the sort of nervous over-done laughter of the man who is about to go into combat that he recognised so well, and he guessed that this was where the aircrew awaited the call to tell them the enemy bombers were on their way.

The airmen on the fuel truck had finished with the 110 and were unscrewing the hose from the rear of the Opel Blitz bowser. "Evening sir," an airman said, and West touched the peak of his cap. Both airmen mumbled something then closed the double doors on the pumping apparatus and the hose at the back of the Opel. Then they walked away from the aircraft, leaving West alone with the night fighter. He walked behind the tanker out of sight of the aircrew tent. Then he opened the door and climbed inside. The keys were there and the fuel truck started first time.

"Time to start putting things right," he said to himself, before driving the Opel fuel truck away from the line of night fighters and towards the edge of the airstrip.

*

It was not like Konrad to forget to send the food parcel – he only had to remember to tell Inge to put it on the train after all. Often the bombing in Berlin would hold up the train, or the train would not arrive at all, but it was not like him to simply forget to send it. For the first time since this bloody war had started Hanna wondered if her husband had somehow gotten himself caught up in it. But the thought was a cold one, she realised, and she worried more about what her boys, her family, would think when she returned without the parcel. She would ring Konrad later, if the telephone was working again, she decided.

She rushed back to the apartment, all the way wondering what they might have for dinner instead of the longed for treats that would have been in the parcel. It had rained heavily earlier in the afternoon and the cobbles were gleaming wet, the gardens smelt earthy and the tree that overhung the church fence at the corner of the road dripped in time to the fast clip of her heels on the pavement.

Hanna heard Strudel before she saw him, his flat-footed run echoing on the paving stones around the corner of Nord Strasse. Even with the warning she did well to skip out of his way, and he ran on without recognising her. "Strudel!" she shouted, and he suddenly pulled up in a scuffy skid. He had wet himself, a dark patch on the front of his trousers, and there was fear etched deep into his face, she saw it clearly, and others did too, some of them crossing the street to get away from him … These days you steered clear of fear, if you could, everyone knew that, one of the new rules of living – to keep living.

"What is it?" she asked. His big brown eyes seemed to bulge to twice their size and his tongue drooped from his gaping mouth. She thought he had not recognised her. "Strudel, it's me – what is it?" She grabbed at the sleeve of his jacket, but he wriggled and tried to tear himself away, his eyes fixed on a spot down the street, just about where the apartment was. "What is it Strudel?" Now she was shouting, and she could hear the front doors and the windows slamming all around her as the people shut up shop to trouble, locking and bolting doors. Big tears shined in the corner of Strudel's eyes and he trembled violently. She hugged him close and those tremors became a part of her, his thin bones grating against her like a rattling machine, his sobs sinking into her shoulder.

"What is it?" she asked again, softly now, stroking the fine, thin hair of his head while checking down the street for signs of whatever trouble had visited them.

"Th-th-th-they have come f-f-f-for me …" he blurted, and she instantly knew what he had meant. It would be the SS, or the police, they had half expected them for a long time now, come to take Strudel. *That bloody cow Hansen*, she thought.

"Where's Sepp, and your father?"

"D-d-d-down the allotment, they sent me home to get s-s-s-s-sausage."

"Good," she said. It would be better if Sepp was well out of this, she could never tell how he would react to anything, never mind a threat to a friend. "Now listen carefully to me," she held him at arm's length, gripping his shoulders tightly. "You must do exactly what I say, are you listening Strudel?" He nodded, then glanced nervously back down the street. "Go to where you keep the car, it's safe there isn't it?" He nodded again. "Then go, and wait there. I will send Sepp to you when it's clear, hurry now, and try to keep to the back streets."

He was already on his way, the soles of his shoes slapping loudly against the pavement. Hanna strode down the street, she had no idea what she should do, but she knew she should do something. *Wait until Berlin learns of this! Did they know who her husband was? I am a great friend of Reichsführer Himmler's* … she would tell them, all of it, and as she walked she tried to remember all those other ugly old Nazis Konrad had insisted she charmed. The front door was ajar and she flung it noisily against the hinges as she burst into the hallway. Frau Hansen's face was before her, jammed between the door and the doorframe of her apartment, so that her natural ugliness seemed to have found a reason. On seeing Hanna the face disappeared and she heard the sliding of bolts before the echo of the slam had faded. Hanna pounded on the door of the apartment with her fists, hard enough for it to hurt, but then she remembered that that one would have to wait.

"You will keep you poisonous old prune," she hissed at the keyhole, sure that the nosy cow would have her eye against it. She made for the stairs, but something made her look to the door on the right, where the staircase led down to the old basement kitchen. The door was open. She cursed Frau Hansen again, they had known where to look for Strudel all right. The bitch. She swung open the door and carefully made her way down the steep flight of stairs. There was a little noise from the kitchen, a tap running against the basin she realised. An SS peaked hat sat on the table, its silver death's head badge glinting in the harsh light from the naked bulb.

She took a deep breath. Suddenly she realised she was very scared, and her heart seemed to be hammering while at the same time her chest contracted as if an iron band tightened around it. There was just one SS man, an officer she thought, with his back to her, filling a cup with water. She tried to speak but the words seemed to catch in the back of her throat. He turned.

"Hello Hanna."

For long, impossibly stretched, seconds of silence she failed to recognise him. His face had thinned so that his cheeks had hollowed and his eyes seemed to lack the light of old, as if they had retreated into the darker caverns of his eye sockets. He smiled a half smile, just with his mouth, and picked up a piece of stale bread he had cut from the three-day old loaf. "I hope you don't mind," Westbury Holt said. "I'm famished."

*

West had told his story, how he had recovered from the crash and how he had managed to get used to the false leg. How he had flown and fought. How he had been captured and then escaped, and captured and escaped again, and again and again, then how he had been helped by the gypsies and finally ... How he had betrayed them. "Now I will find her," he said.

"But it's impossible," she said, sitting opposite him at the old kitchen table. "they have camps everywhere: Poland, Czechoslovakia, everywhere!"

"They're killing them, aren't they?" he said. He still found it hard to believe – yet he could tell from her eyes that it was true.

"You would not believe what they have done to us all, Westbury."

He nodded, the light was harsh, and shone directly on to her, so he could easily see the thin lines that had etched themselves on to her face over these past six years. To her right, by the sink, there was a strange tool, like a deep beaker with a spike attached to it.

"They have hurt you, too?" West said.

"They killed my baby," she said. He stared at her in disbelief for a little while, not wanting her to go on because of the pain that contorted her face. "It was deformed," she added, then breathed in deeply before saying: "It was a caesarean birth, I was unconscious for the operation, and I never saw him. They told me he had died, told me it was a mercy, too." She thumped her fist against the table.

"You see, it was unfit for this new life of theirs. But it did not die, they killed it. I hid from the truth for a long time, hid from the nightmares that told me the truth, hid in a promise ..." She swallowed hard, and then continued. "Hid in drink and other things, but I think I always knew they had killed him."

"What was wrong —?"

"I'm not sure what was wrong with him, except that *wrong* is the wrong word. There was nothing *wrong*." She started to cry and West reached for her hands across the table, taking them and squeezing them softly.

"But Konrad, surely he —"

"The child was dead to Konrad anyway. As soon as he saw him he knew it was dead. It is the only way, if you want to fit in; don't you know we are building a master race here?"

"I'm sorry," West said.

"What's there for you to apologise for?"

"Blindness, and perhaps they should kill for that, too," he smiled bitterly and felt the anger well up inside him, the monster of hate taking shape, its object an SS man, photographed by the propaganda men of the Third Reich – Westbury Holt ... The same Westbury Holt who saluted from the podium at Pescara ... The same Westbury Holt who drove their Auto Unions – for that could have nothing to do with anything, old man ... The same Westbury Holt who showed them all, here is a place where they do ordinary things, like race cars, things an ordinary Englishman like Westbury Holt could do ...

Suddenly the door at the top of the stairs swung open and he heard the voices of two men. There was no place to hide in the small basement kitchen, and no time either.

"Where is that little idiot, if he's eaten my sausage I swear I'll plant him deep in the allotment." The one voice, loud and teasing as the man clumped down the wooden stairway, soon attached to the animated mouth of a middle- to old-aged man who froze at the sight of the SS uniform. A younger man came down behind him, pushing past; a young man, and yet still a man who looked like he had lived a hundred lives. A man who also looked like Sepp.

*

What could that fool want? Sepp thought. Didn't Hanna realise that they would all be shot if they were found with an escaped prisoner of war? "We will have to turn him in," he heard himself say. "It's our duty."

"Sepp, you can't mean that!" Hanna cried. Sepp shook his head, he had always known that it would be her and a man that would be their downfall, eventually.

"Sister, he is the enemy!"

"Enemy … Enemy? Just who is the enemy Sepp? Who is it that changed you, who does Strudel run from, who kills our children, who has us hiding away and spying on each other for no other reason other than to survive, and survive like animals at that —"

"Enough!" Sepp shouted, and he noticed that Kurt was beginning to back away from the table and walk towards the stairs.

"Kurt, you stay put!" Hanna said, sharply.

"But Hanna …" Kurt looked exasperated. "We cannot risk it – you can bet your last reichsmark, my last reichsmark come to that, that that bitch has a glass to the wall right now!"

"Then perhaps we should all stop shouting then," she said calmly, and then she looked at Westbury Holt, who somehow still looked just like Westbury Holt, but much thinner, much sadder, as though all the joy had been sucked from him. And, Sepp remembered, this one had been so fat with joy.

"This is madness, he must go – or we call the police," Sepp said.

"I'm not here to hide," West said. "I have other things to do – and you need not worry Sepp, the war is not my concern now. I have opted out."

"Me too," Sepp said, quietly. "But that's not the point, you could ruin everything." He said it without thinking and instantly regretted his lapse.

"Everything, Sepp?" West said, elevating an eyebrow a little. "And what would *everything* be?"

"Life, peace, minding our own bloody business, isn't that right Kurt?"

Old Kurt nodded vigorously.

All was still and for a moment, the only noise the drip of the tap in the sink and the cry of a baby in a pram passing by in the street above them.

"I have fuel Sepp – aviation fuel," West said, and Sepp felt his heart leap inside him.

"What would we want with that? It's a bullet in the head!"

"Quiet Kurt," Sepp said, grabbing at the old man's sleeve, then turning back to West: "How did you know?"

"Konrad."

"You have seen him?" Hanna asked.

"Yes, recently. He's well." She shrugged, it mattered little to her now, Sepp could see that.

"Did he send you?" Sepp asked, hearing the excitement in his own voice.

"No."

"Then why?"

"You needed the fuel, didn't you?"

Sepp shook his head, finding it hard to believe the Englishman, but he wanted to, oh he wanted to. "Where is it?" he asked.

"In a tanker, I parked it around the back of the apartment block."

"Are you both mad?" Kurt said. "Isn't helping an Englander dangerous enough without adding stealing petrol to the charge sheet? They will shoot us, my God, they will shoot us all!"

"Shut up you old fool!" Sepp snapped.

"There is more Sepp. First, I owe you, you saved my life, and this is the first chance I have had to thank you … And …" Holt suddenly paused and looked at Hanna before continuing: "I have to put right a wrong."

"I knew all about you two," Sepp said, flicking his head between Hanna and West.

"You did?"

Sepp nodded, one sharp nod, like the fall of an axe.

"But that's not —"

"There was never anything wrong with that anyway," Hanna said, cutting in. Sepp waved her quiet and West continued.

"Remember Donington?"

Sepp remembered the day his dream died, and for the first time in a long, long time it hurt again … How it hurt again.

"You were quick," West said.

"No. Konrad timed me, the watch does not lie."

"But Konrad lied," West shook his head slowly. "And I think I always knew it. I wrote to you, here, to thank you for saving my life, and I hinted at what I suspected, but you never wrote back, so I supposed you never received the letters?"

Sepp remembered the unopened letters he had destroyed, letters to him, letters to Hanna. But he said nothing now, just shaking his head.

"I even tried to tell you once," West continued. "On that day Rosemeyer died – it all had so much to do with Rosemeyer, as it happens."

"Rosemeyer?" Sepp said.

"Yes, Konrad could not have another Rosemeyer on the team, and I suppose the same was true for me, maybe that's the real reason why I said nothing when I could have ... Should have."

"It's not true," he heard himself say. "Konrad would not do that."

"I asked him, and he admitted it," West said.

"I believe it Sepp," Hanna said, then suddenly she held his hand.

"Another Rosemeyer?" Sepp whispered it, the thing he had once known as certainly as the difference between black and white, good and bad, in his then young life, and he knew it again. The words rung in his head, *another Rosemeyer*, and then the images of his years of combat seemed to slide over his consciousness then melt like photos in flames. He felt the tears burning at the back of his eyes; he would not let Kurt see him like this.

"Kurt, could you check he is telling the truth – about the truck I mean?" Kurt hesitated and he could sense that Hanna was making faces at him, silently urging him to do as Sepp asked. Then he heard his heavy garden boots as they thumped up the stairs and down the long passage to the back door. The three of them sat in silence for a while, until they heard the stomp of Kurt's boots again. Sepp did not look up when he came down the stairs and into the kitchen.

"My God, it's true, we will all finish the day in a concentration camp, please Hanna, can't you make them see sense?"

"Don't worry Kurt," Sepp said. "We will be away from here soon enough, and so will the truck."

*

Sepp found West some old Auto Union-badged work overalls and a jacket so that he could get out of the SS uniform. Then they went out of the rear door of the apartment building, where West had parked the fuel tanker. Sepp considered the claw-like marks on the green and brown camouflaged paintwork of the Opel – the scars from West's escape from the airfield, straight through a low hedge and a five-bar gate – and then climbed into the cab as West turned to take a last look at the apartment block. He thought he saw someone at one of the windows and wondered if it was Hanna watching him go. It had not gone the way he had always expected, meeting her again. It had always played so differently in his head. But then that had been before Roma.

Sepp drove slowly along the back streets then turned towards the river.

The Zwickau Mulde was swollen from the recent heavy rain and West could clearly hear its roar over the rattle and ping of the large storage tank fixed to the rear deck of the truck. Soon they were on a rough, unsealed, road and the fuel in the tank behind them sloshed and slapped against the inner baffles as it bounced over the potholes and the ruts. There were mine workings either side of them and huge heaps of black slag, one of which looked like the dark hull of an overturned ship. Eventually Sepp turned the Opel Blitz on to an old, pitted asphalt roadway and drove up to a gate. There were two derelict buildings close to the gate, one of which looked to be half demolished, a wall having fallen away. Sepp clunked the truck into first gear and eased it over the pile of debris, the weight of it crushing the loose timber and tiles noisily under the wheels. He parked it beneath the overhang of the old ceiling, where it would be out of sight.

"It should be safe here, not many come this way," Sepp said. "Come on." He climbed out of the cab of the truck then led West across a patch of blackened ground and along the length of a fence, stopping to untie a panel of cut wire and leading West through the resulting gap. A little later, with the sun now beginning to dip behind the disused winding gear, Sepp led West to another building, which looked like it had once been a workshop. Close by there was a working pit, its headgear turning slowly, the spokes of its contra-spinning black wheels throwing propeller shadows across the red brick wall of the squat little workshop.

Sepp knocked on one of the grimy blue wooden doors, and shouted: "Strudel, it's me, Sepp – and a friend!" There was no answer. "Strudel, open up!" There was a pause and then the scrape of a bolt before the doors were flung open, their hinges creaking loudly. There was Strudel. West remembered him from the day he had shown him a secret way into the Horch works.

"It is all right Strudel, there was no SS." Sepp said.

"B-b-b-but —"

"You just saw the uniform and ran, as you always do. It was Herr Holt, that's all. But listen, he has brought us something."

"Chocolate?" Strudel's eyes lit up.

"Better than that," Sepp said.

"Fuel!" The rest of Strudel's words were lost to West as the background came into focus. Behind the simpleton, inside the old mine workshop, there was a car. Not just any car, but an Auto Union. Not just any Auto Union, but a streamliner. The low sunlight washed over it, picking out the muscular curves of the wheel arches in a watery white, but beneath that bright trick of the light the car was purest silver.

"Well bugger me," West said.

"Still beautiful, isn't it?" Sepp said. West nodded and the three of them walked inside, Strudel bolting the doors behind them. There was little light in the cleared space, but there was just enough to see the car, filtering through the greasy windows high in the walls, and all three stared at it in silence until it was simply too dark to make out anything more than a glimmer of silver shimmer. Then Sepp turned on a small flashlight, careful to mask the beam as much as possible, and they talked.

"But where did you find it?" West asked.

"We built it, or rather Strudel did. I just helped him a little." West gave Strudel a slow nod of approval and suddenly his face was bursting with undisguised pride.

"Marvellous ... Absolutely, bloody marvellous ..." West said, walking slowly up to the car and running his hands over the cold curves of the bodywork.

"We assembled it down in the mine at first, but we knew we had to bring it above ground to fire it up, it would be suicide to start it down there. There is firedamp in these mines and it would not take much to ignite it – if a fire spread to the current workings it could cost innocent miners their lives."

"Firedamp?" West asked.

"Gas," Sepp said. "It would have been madness to start the car down there. So, the only thing to do was to dismantle it and bring it to the surface. There's an older shaft that slopes out, so we did not have to use the lift. It had been sealed, but Strudel and Herr Fink had taken away most of the rubble when they had hidden the body and chassis and the engine. Then they had replaced it, only for Strudel and me to do the very same again. Then we used a winch to haul it out. It was a long job, but time is something we are not short of. But you know, before you arrived I was beginning to think it was all a waste of effort, there is not even the weakest petrol to be found these days."

"But why was it down the mine?" West asked.

"They are all here, in other buildings, most of them in the current workings, to save them from Tommy bombers, or more likely German aeroplane makers," Sepp smiled at that. "Fink wanted to make sure there was at least one that was truly safe. He and Strudel did the rest."

"But you have taken a massive risk here Sepp – surely?"

"*Risk?* That word means nothing to me now."

West simply nodded, he thought then that he understood. "So, will it run?" he asked.

"We will find out tomorrow – thanks to you."

*

Sepp had led Hanna to the old mine, coming half of the way in a tram then walking from the edge of the town, his Daimon flashlight helping to light the way in the darkness. She had insisted on coming. He had carried the basket with the pot of stew and the bowls in it and had handed it to Strudel as soon as they had entered the old building. Strudel had grabbed one of the spoons she'd also brought and was already tucking into his dinner.

"Best make the most of that, my dear," she said, "it is the last of your father's balcony pigs and he's not happy about it." Strudel nodded and took his next mouthful almost comically slowly.

"Hello again," West said.

"I'll get you a bowl of —" she cut off her sentence when she saw it, sitting at the far end of the otherwise empty old workshop, bathed in the light from two electric torches that, from the look on Strudel's face, she guessed had been delicately arranged just for her. She had seen a streamliner before, of course, but right then, in that light, in this place, this was the most beautiful car she had ever set eyes on, and for that moment at least the stupid risk her boys had taken almost seemed worthwhile.

"Well, what do you think?" Sepp asked.

"It's wonderful Sepp, truly wonderful."

"Tomorrow, we will fire up the engine."

"Yes, you have said."

"It is best to wait until morning, when we can see properly," he said it too matter-of-factly, she thought.

"Are you putting it off, Sepp?"

"Perhaps I am," he admitted. "It has been a life, for a while, and it has filled time and hurt no-one." He took a deep breath, then added: "But I have promised Strudel we will run the engine, so that's what we'll do. In the morning we will be able to cut a gap in the fence and bring the truck through."

"But what if you're seen?"

"We will not be seen," he said, then smiled and added: "But you can bet we'll be heard, sister!" Strudel found that funny enough to make him choke on a nugget of rabbit and Sepp had to thump him on the back to dislodge the meat.

"I've told you not to gobble down your food, Strudel," Hanna said, and then she turned her attention back to her brother. His eyes looked bright in the lamplight, and a slight smile tugged at the corners of his mouth. It was like time travel, she thought. But she reminded herself that that was impossible. "It's risky, Sepp," she said.

"It's worth the risk, just to hear the music again … Isn't that right, West?" West smiled and nodded, he seemed to be elsewhere, to have not even have heard the question.

"Then I would like to be here to hear it, too" she said, shrugging her surrender in the face of Sepp's determination, and glad to get the chance to keep an eye on them.

"And miss the parcel again?" Sepp said, after a brief pause to consider her offer. "I think Kurt will be expecting plenty of sausage to make up for boiling his last bunny, sister. Besides, as you said, it is a risk, and there is no use in us all taking it, is there now?" She sighed, there was also no use in arguing when he was in this mood … And it so reminded her of other times that she could not be angry for long anyway. "Well, that's settled then." Sepp said. "Come on Strudel, finish that, we have to go over the final checks."

"But you're only running the engine?" Hanna said.

"We are professionals dear sister, isn't that so Strudel?" Strudel laughed out loud at that, something she had once thought impossible, and clapped his hands in glee, putting his unfinished stew to one side. They both went to the car and started working from the tail, checking the panels and the nuts, all part of an obviously well practised drill.

"Pah! Look at them would you, people are starving all over Germany and they are wasting meat to play with a car – even Strudel!"

"People have given up more than just meat for these things, Hanna" West said. "Much more."

"Well, people make their choices, don't they?" she sighed as she said it, and did not look at him. "But the meat must not go to waste." She took the top off the pot. The stew had cooled enough for some little islands of fat to start floating on the surface. At one time that would have disgusted her, she remembered, but now – after the meat – they were the best bits. She spooned out some of the stew for West plus a bowl for her. They ate in silence for a while, sitting on two old crates in the light from a torch, watching the other two working on the streamliner, the only sound in the cold space the pinging of the tools against the aluminium and West's hungry slurps.

"I knew you would not be able to resist driving it," she said, quite suddenly.

"What?"

"The other one, when you had the accident. They called for Konrad but I said he was out, and that they would find you at the Adlon. It was a test, you see."

"Then I almost passed it," West said. "I wasn't at the Adlon, I was here in Zwickau, ready to hand in my resignation, but —"

"You couldn't resist it."

"No, I couldn't resist it," he said quietly, before popping a piece of potato into his mouth. He ate in silence for a moment or two, then said: "Why didn't you reply to my letters?"

"Letters? But there were never any letters," she said, a part of her wanting to add: *but I had hoped for some letters, for some word, for something …*

"I sent them to the apartment block in Zwickau, I hoped they would be forwarded."

"I never received them."

"That's a pity. But why didn't *you* write to me?" he said.

"You had made your choice, Westbury." she said, remembering all the times she had put pen to paper, only to rip the letter into tiny shreds. Then she wondered what had happened to the letters he had sent. Sepp, she supposed, would have collected them, and Sepp knew of the affair, and would have done what he thought was right, as he always had done. She would ask him about that, one day …

"Perhaps if dear old Papa hadn't been so damned keen to get me back to England after the crash, eh?"

"Perhaps," she said, and then she added: "Would you do the same now? I mean if *she* asked you not to drive?"

He simply shook his head.

"You know," Hanna said, feeling the start of a sob at the base of her throat, a sob that had no right to be there, "it will be difficult for you to find her."

"I know that."

"You have no identity card, there are checkpoints everywhere, and patrols, and even if you did find the camp …" suddenly she had to stop, to carry on would mean crying, and she could not allow it. They ate in silence for a little while longer, until she suddenly, and unexpectedly, heard herself say: "You never really loved me did you, Westbury?"

"Yes, I —"

"Please, not now."

"I'm sorry," he said. "I suppose I never knew what it meant to love, to really love, back then everything was a game to me."

"And now you do know?"

"Pain."

"Yes, that's true," she said, as she turned her head to watch Sepp twirling a plug spanner expertly.

"It must have been very hard for you Hanna," West said. "You almost lost everything." He reached out for her hand and held it in his, squeezing it tenderly, and she noticed that his hand was extraordinarily cold. She searched his eyes for a trace of the man she once knew, but there was nothing.

"Hanna!" Sepp suddenly snapped. "We will go back now." He had been watching them, she guessed.

"I *had* lost everything," she said, as much to herself as to West, "but my Sepp is back." West nodded, seeming to understand.

Then she added: "Do something for me Westbury, keep an eye on him while you are here, especially tomorrow."

"Of course, but if he is back to his old self?"

"That's what's worrying me."

*

It was the rattle of the engine in the Opel Blitz fuel truck that woke West. He had slept in the cockpit of the streamliner, the familiar oily-steely smell of a racing car helping him to nod off, and to dream of other times. Sepp had suggested he spend the night down the mine, where it would be safer, but West had spent enough of his life underground, those days beneath the hut in Italy, so the padded seat of an Auto Union was just fine. The night before he had decided he would leave today, though he had also decided he would stay just long enough to hear the engine run. For one last time, he could not resist that, and he remembered what Hanna had said, the previous evening, of that other time he had been unable to resist the pull of a streamliner – and he hoped that was not an omen.

Dawn had arrived, wrapped in a grey shroud which was stained with darker blotches of cloud. By standing on an old crate West could just about follow the Opel's progress through a roundel-rubbed gap in the grime that coated the high windows. Sepp and Strudel had cut a large portion of fence and the truck was now flattening the diamond mesh into the black ground, the rear tyres buzzing as they spun on the wire. A little later the truck pulled up outside. West unbolted the workshop doors and opened them wide.

Sepp and Strudel both wore light blue work overalls with the Auto Union rings at the breast, just like the overalls West was wearing. It took him back to another time.

"Well then," Sepp said. "Time to wake the beast, eh?"

Strudel chortled at that and they fell into a well-practised drill of lifting the heavy bodywork clear with a hoist attached to the roof beams so the starter could be inserted in the rear of the car. They had oil for the engine, the night before Sepp had explained how they had found old used oil in the works, and had then sieved it well. It would do, West had said to him, if all they wanted was to start it up. They inserted the bulky starter into the rear of the car to pump the lubricant around the block, building up the pressure as Sepp checked the dial in the cockpit. The engine clattered like a printing press, without a spark of life, of fire, the naked car shivering just a little, as if in anticipation of what was to come, the smell of long burnt carbon filling the space, before Sepp was happy and signalled to Strudel to switch the starter off. Then Sepp fitted the sixteen spark plugs, taking his time, making sure every one of them was tightened to exactly the required torque.

"Get the truck," Sepp said to Strudel, who ran to the Opel Blitz in a jerky flat-footed sprint that raised great clouds of black dust.

"Can he drive?"

"Can a maniac run a county?"

"Point taken," West said, "the Führer is an example to us all."

Sepp laughed at that, and it was a warm laugh, full of life – West thought it was the first time someone had really laughed at something he had said for quite some time.

"Actually, he learnt to drive on the quiet, watching others, he learnt quite a bit that way," Sepp said. "And Fink let him drive the truck once when they were hiding the cars." As if to prove it Strudel started the truck and manoeuvred it into place with wheel-spinning panache.

They opened the doors of the large rectangular housing at the rear of the tanker, where the pumping gear was housed, and after a little fiddling they managed to get the hand pump to work, feeding the fuel through the filler nozzle of the streamliner, which was set high behind the driver's seat. Then Sepp parked the Opel where it would be out of sight, behind the building. As he walked back he looked up at the cloudy sky, a slight frown creasing his forehead.

It was time to fire the engine up, and West found he was nervous. But it was a good nervous, the sort of excited nervous of before a race, rather than the sickly fear of before a battle. The naked car was still inside the workshop, its sweeping silver bodywork gleaming on the floor beside it, the double doors thrown open to allow some ventilation. Strudel once more inserted the cumbersome starter into the rear of the engine, and Sepp nodded. The motor turned again, but this time it caught, lumpy at first, as Sepp adjusted the Solex carbs, tuning the engine to match the potent fuel. West had forgotten how loud these things were and as it burst into life he had instinctively covered his ears.

The engine note soon smoothed into a ripping roar that shook the dirty windows and seemed to flutter the air within West's chest. Sepp pressed a screwdriver into a slot on the throttle linkage at the rear of the V16, which he blipped a few times, the doors dancing on their hinges from the vibration, blue smoke billowing from the sixteen pipes. He let it run at low revs for a little while, then started to work the throttle again. If a dragon had ever drawn hot breath, West thought, this was how it would have sounded. Sepp held his hand over the muzzle of each of the vertical exhausts, checking all was right with the engine through the flow of the gases on his hands, his overall sleeve flapping to the warm wash like laundry drying in a storm. The fumes in this small space were pungent and choking, but neither of them stepped outside. Sepp beamed a smile of satisfaction at Strudel, then West, and then gave it one last blast, before Strudel leant into the cockpit to switch the engine off.

When the engine died the world seemed a very quiet place, and West instantly missed that familiar rasp. The sudden stillness seemed to mock them, as if it ached to be filled: by decisions, by action, by repercussions. West knew it was time for him to move on, but he did not know how or where. He could not guess what Sepp would do, now that this thing that had filled his life was over. But for now they were busy putting the body back on the car, neither Strudel nor Sepp speaking a word. West just stood there, and watched ...

Watched as they completed the job ... Watched as Strudel brought a coil of rope from the back of the building ... Watched as Sepp and Strudel attached the streamliner to the tow rope ...

"What's going on?" West said, genuinely baffled.

"A car is not just an engine," Sepp said, a gleam in his eye, the end of the thick rope in his fist. Just then West suddenly understood exactly what was going on, and the shock of it must have shown on his face.

"Well, you didn't think we were really just going to fire it up, did you?" Sepp said. The engine of the Opel tanker turned once but did not catch.

"But you can't, you'll be arrested – It's madness!" West said. "Besides, I promised Hanna I would keep an eye on you."

"Well, come along then, we could use the extra hands – and I would welcome your advice." The engine in the truck turned once more, and then burst into life, a great cloud of black smoke belching from its exhaust as Strudel revved it enthusiastically.

"My God, you *are* insane Sepp," West said, shaking his head.

"Of course, but that on its own was not enough, we needed you to bring the fuel and ..." a graunch of the gears as Strudel found reverse brought an engineer's grimace to Sepp's face.

"*And?*" West asked, as the truck's wheels began to crunch through the brick and coal dust as Strudel backed it up.

"*And* ... the confidence. Now I know I am good enough for it," Sepp said, as he strode forward and thumped on the rear of the tanker with the palm of his hand to stop Strudel before he backed in to the streamliner. Strudel left the engine running and clambered out of the cab. Then he started to hitch the front of the Auto Union to the truck before unclipping the driver's hatch on the silver body and climbing into the cockpit of the streamliner. Sepp closed the hatch tight, so that Strudel's head was all that showed, and then clambered into the cab of the fuel truck.

"This is what we have both always dreamed of, West," Sepp shouted from the driver's seat, glancing back at Strudel, a Christmas child at the wheel of one of the fastest cars ever built. Sepp slammed shut the truck door and the mirror that was fixed to it quivered.

"This will be the last chance to do this, West," he shouted again, through the open window. "For us ... For anybody." West heard the loud creak of the clutch pedal and he saw Sepp draw in breath sympathetically as he crunched the gearstick into first. The towrope suddenly tightened, creaked, then the truck lurched forward, tugging at the heavy streamliner behind it with an aluminium-popping lurch. Sepp eased off the throttle, then accelerated again. The rope slackened, then tightened again, and this time the inertia of the heavy car was broken and it rolled forward, its tyres biting deeply into the coal-blackened ground. Strudel let out a loud shriek of pure delight and the fat barrel-bodied, long-nosed truck – with a sleek record car attached to its tight umbilical, a grinning simpleton in the cockpit – slowly crawled towards the large gap in the fence.

"Bugger it!" West said to himself. "Bugger it and blast it all to buggery!" Then he hobbled after the truck, catching it and jumping onto its narrow running board and opening the door before swinging himself up on to the passenger seat. "Those things are not easy to drive, you know," he said to a grinning Sepp. "You'll need my help."

*

Worry gnawed like a rat inside her. Hanna would have rather been at the old mine, but Sepp had made it clear he did not want her there, and she simply could not argue with him these days. Of course, there *was* every chance that the parcel from Konrad might arrive on today's morning train – though there had been no answer when she had rung the night before to check. But Sepp had never made such a fuss about it before, as he had this morning while they ate their gobbled breakfast of toasted stale bread; in the basement kitchen as always now, since Sepp had returned. She realised she had been spending much more of her time down here now, too, almost as much as she had in the old days. Sepp had also, once again, assured her the risk was small, that they would fire the engine up then that was it: job done. And what then? Well, she worried about that as much as she did about the silly risk her boys were taking.

She put her makeup on in the glare from the single bulb, as the porridgey light that seeped through the slot-shaped window of the basement kitchen was not up to the job. Then she puckered her lips and applied the lipstick. She hardly ever wore makeup and lipstick now, which was ironic because Konrad had always asked her not to, because the Nazis liked their women natural, wholesome. She was supposed to be an ideal Nazi wife. So, back in Berlin, she had always worn makeup and lipstick when she went out, a tiny way she could kick back at them – in the days before she'd rediscovered her little family. But talking to West the night before had reminded her of the girl she used to be, and it would be nice to be looked at again, she had thought, in the way the men had looked at her in Berlin. She had time for a cup of ersatz coffee and the pot was beginning to heat up on the stove. A tram rattled along the street above and then she heard a car pull up outside.

There was the sound of car doors slamming, the fall of heavy boots on the pavement, and the pounding of fists on the door. She stopped suddenly, feeling her heart freeze in her chest, the lipstick indenting her lower lip. She caught her eyes in the little mirror of her compact, pupils spreading like spilt oil, and then she heard Frau Hansen's clucking voice – Hanna had not seen her since the incident the day before and she had assumed the old witch would be trying extra hard to keep out of her way. Then there was the clump of boots in the corridor. There was a moment's deathly silence, the world stood still … And then, quite suddenly, the door at the top of the stairs burst open. There was a stampede of noise and a figure rolled down the steps and fell into the kitchen, arms and legs flaying like those of a tossed rag doll as it crashed into the kitchen table, sending the breakfast dishes flying. There was a strong smell of vomit and a low, creaking moan, and then three more figures followed, slowly walking down the stairs: tall black boots first, then field grey breeches, then drawn pistols, and tunics of the same grey-green. Without thinking she snatched the punch-dagger from its place by the sink and slipped it over her thin hand, gripping tightly at the leather covered brace inside.

"How quaint," Kessler said, as he aimed his pistol at her head, eyes blinking steadily. "Why don't you tell your dear wife to put her toy away Konrad, there is no need for more unpleasantness, is there?" Konrad stared up at her from the spot on the floor where he had landed, a bright, fresh cut on his forehead, slightly older purple swelling around his eyes, his top lip split into a blackening scar. "Do as he says, please Hanna …" Konrad spluttered, through broken teeth.

*

Sepp would not risk towing the low-slung record car along the broken track so he took to the sealed roads as soon as he could. It meant they had to drive through the outskirts of Zwickau, but Sepp kept to those streets that were little used. It was not possible to entirely avoid being seen, though, and many people stopped and stared in disbelief. Young boys on their way to school stood at the kerbside, their jaws hanging slack, men stopped in their tracks and wiped tears from their eyes, a Hitler Youth gave the Nazi salute – and Strudel saluted back from the cockpit of the streamliner like he was the Führer himself. This thing these people saw was a thing from a dream, a thing from a time of dreaming, when this city was at the centre of it all, and everything was possible for Germany, and everything was possible in Germany. A time when they made the fastest cars and built magnificent buildings and wonderful roads, a time when they were at the very start of a new history ... And now, they knew it too, it was nearing the end.

He towed the streamliner out of town, through the village of Cainsdorf, and towards the place he had chosen. Some children in a schoolyard cheered at the sight of the beautiful streamlined silver machine.

"Takes you back, doesn't it?" West said.

Sepp nodded, this was how it was meant to be. Perhaps he had merely dreamed the rest? Now the nightmare was over and he was about to meet his destiny. They saw one policeman, who merely smiled and touched the peak of his shako at the sight of the silver car: perhaps thinking it official for the truck was military and they all wore Auto Union work overalls, perhaps not wanting to get involved, perhaps simply happy to be reminded of better times.

Soon enough they were there. This stretch of the new autobahn had been completed in 1940, after the war had started, and had never been used to test Auto Unions. It was not flat, like the stretch of road between Darmstadt and Frankfurt where Rosemeyer had met his end; the part of the Halle-Leipzig Autobahn where West had crashed; or the length of autobahn near Dessau, which had been specially constructed with record breaking in mind. It was not straight, either. But it would do. It would do for 220mph. Yes, Sepp believed that with a little luck and a lot of skill he could take it over 220mph – and that was the very *least* he would let himself accept.

They took the curling ramp that led on to the autobahn and then Sepp signalled for Strudel to be ready on the streamliner's brakes by waving his arm out of the window before he slowed the truck and stopped at the side of the road. The autobahn was quiet, as few people had the petrol to make journeys these days, and despite the propaganda on the newsreels what tanks there were travelled east by train – the Nazis might think nothing of chewing up good men, but good asphalt was quite another thing.

"You have got to be joking, Sepp," West said, looking up the concrete ribbon that twisted to a filament of grey at the horizon, and obviously guessing Sepp's intention.

"I will take it slow."

"That's rot Sepp, you know it!" West snapped. Sepp just climbed out of the cab and started to unclip the filling hose from the housing on the rear of the Opel tanker. Strudel was already taking up the hatch surround of the cockpit covering and unscrewing the filler cap at the top of the streamliner's large fuel tank. Sepp did not worry that there was not enough fuel left in the bowser, he somehow knew that there would be, and soon they began to pump it in using the mechanical hand pump. It took a good ten minutes and by the time they had finished the tanker was empty. They had been lucky, but then destiny always trumps luck.

"Well, let's get it warmed up again then," Sepp said, and Strudel climbed into the cab of the truck while he slid over the silver body beneath the hatch surround and into the driver's seat. He had sat in this cockpit many times over these last few weeks so it was very familiar to him. He gripped the wheel and all at once he felt completely at home. He flicked the ignition switch and the pumps on and then signalled to Strudel, and the fuel truck took up the slack on the rope. Then, with a lurch and creak, the car was moving forward. Because the bodywork was on they could not use the starter, but they had started it earlier so it fired almost instantly when Sepp lifted the clutch. He knew it would.

Some children appeared at the side of the autobahn, big-eyed and dirty kneed, fingers pressed into their ears as Sepp revved the big V16, thick fuel fumes filling the air, as the kids watched with silent reverence as Sepp kept the engine alive and Strudel went through his final checks.

"Aren't you worried the police will come?" West shouted, over the ripping cadence of the gently revved motor.

"The police were saluting us West – did you not see it? If they come it will be to see this driven as it should be driven; that's all." But West shook his head and gave Sepp an almost pitying smile. "I understand … If you want to get away?" Sepp shouted. West just bit his lip and shook his head slowly, then he leant over the tight cockpit opening to take a glance at the oil pressure gauge.

Sepp shouted out of the other side of the cockpit: "Strudel, take the truck, go and fetch Hanna," he said. "She must not miss this." Strudel and West both looked at him, confused. "It will be too late for her to stop me now, but she must see … It was our dream for so long," he explained.

"Your dream, Sepp," West shouted over the sound of the engine.

"No, our dream … You will see," he smiled as he shouted back.

"Wouldn't it be better if I went for her?"

"No, I need you to give me some idea of what to expect from this."

"On the r-r-r-road? C-c-c-c-can I —?" Strudel started, panic spreading across his face.

"Just drive it Strudel, you know how. Keep to the back roads and pretend the people are not there," Sepp shouted, with his broadest smile, and Strudel nodded solemnly before climbing up into the cab of the Opel Blitz.

"What now?" West asked.

"We wait," Sepp said. "Wait until the car is properly warmed up and big sister has arrived." He looked at his old Fallschirmjäger-issue Aeromatic watch. "It should not take long."

"Provided he doesn't stuff the truck," West said.

"He won't," Sepp answered, with total confidence. Strudel gnashed the gears and pulled off in a flak-like cloud of black diesel exhaust smoke. They watched the Opel as it rattled off up the curling access ramp back in the direction of Zwickau. The children edged closer to the streamliner and in the distance Sepp could make out three more, running across the field from the village school, and beyond that iron-grey clouds, rolling towards them like a sea swell.

"Let's hope Strudel's quick," West said. "It looks like it might rain."

*

Kessler took the coffee pot off the gas hob, but left it alight, the gold-flecked blue flame flickering and hissing. The two SS men stood either side of the stairs, pistols drawn, one pointing at Hanna, the other at Konrad, who had dragged himself up from the floor and was now slumped over the table dabbing his wounded head with a handkerchief.

"Why are you here?" she asked, hating herself for the squeak of fear in her voice.

"Good German neighbours, in the main." Kessler said. "When a party member sees something suspicious, like a petrol tanker in the backyard for example, she tells the SD. The SD tells the Luftwaffe," Kessler smiled, and began to blink slowly. "The rest was down to your loyal husband putting the pieces together."

"What have they done to you, Konrad?" she said. He showed her his face and wearily shook his head. The bruising was worse than she had first realised, plum coloured blotches dappling his face, the swelling half-closing his right eye. When he opened his mouth she could see that his front teeth had been sheared cleanly along a sloping line from right to left.

"Oh," Kessler started before Konrad had the chance to utter a sound, "you should know he told us without any of this." Kessler took hold of Konrad's hair and twisted his head so that Hanna could easier see the damage. "This pretty display is merely a punishment for trusting the Englishman not to escape. You see, the naivety of your husband might yet cause us all a great deal of embarrassment." Kessler took the punch-dagger from where Hanna had placed it on the table and put it on the gas ring, so that the naked flame licked around the spike, scorching what was left of the white paint to black instantly. She watched in horrified fascination as it curled and flaked from the steel. He was smiling. It was the same shallow smile she had seen at Rosemeyer's funeral.

"We have film of our great turncoat hero, but we cannot afford for

392

him to get away and spoil it all now can we? The rewards can be spectacular in this new Germany of ours. But get things wrong and so are the punishments – isn't that so Konrad?" Konrad nodded, and then spat some blood on to one of the breakfast plates. Kessler continued: "This is why you *will* tell us where he is." A thin winding thread of smoke spiralled off the spike where the paint burnt and the acrid smell of it filled the kitchen.

"I have no idea what you are talking about," Hanna said.

"Westbury Holt."

"I knew him, but that was before the war."

"Yes, you knew him well, didn't you? Perhaps I should have guessed he would come here?"

"But he's not here, I have not seen him since —" she started, but then she heard the sound of a truck pulling up noisily outside and she could not help but stop mid-sentence. The engine died with a shudder and the door of the truck slammed shut.

"Sep—" The shout was stopped as Kessler quickly forced his leather-gloved hands over her mouth, pushing her tight against the wall as he did so. She saw him nod to the two SS men at the bottom of the staircase and they stood either side of it, out of sight from anyone coming down.

"Hanna!" It was Strudel, shouting before he had even reached the door to the staircase. "Sepp let me drive the truck!" It was one of the few times she had heard his voice. There was no stammer. He thundered down the stairs and tripped over the outstretched leg of one of Kessler's men. Both the SS men laughed, and Kessler let go of Hanna.

"Strudel, are you all right?" she said, rushing to help him. Strudel looked up, big eyes already swollen with tears, the confusion on his face rapidly melting into fear as he took in the men in their field grey uniforms.

"So you drove a truck did you – well, that is most clever isn't it?" Kessler said. Strudel kept quiet, and then he suddenly seemed to notice the beaten Konrad sitting above him. "Stand up, won't you young man, we must reward you for such cleverness." Kessler smiled that same thin smile as he pulled the punch-dagger from the flickering flame of the hob, gripping it with his thick leather glove at its unheated gauntlet end, and handing it spike first to Strudel.

"Take it," he said, calmly, his steadily blinking eyes seeming to be mesmerised by the glowing orange-red tip of the heated spike. Strudel stumbled backwards, but only into the arms of one of the SS men. "What?" Kessler said. "Will you refuse the gift – hold out your hand!" He shouted the last and Strudel did as he was told. "Take it."

Kessler pressed the red-hot spike against the flesh on the palm of Strudel's hand and Hanna heard the slightest sizzle of searing flesh.

"No!" Hanna shouted, but her shout was immediately lost in Strudel's screams. Kessler let go of the punch-dagger but the hot spike stuck to

Strudel's palm for a few seconds, then the weight of the gauntlet pulled it clear and it fell to the floor with a hollow thump, taking a ribbon of white skin with it. Strudel folded from the pain, collapsing on to the floor and holding his burnt hand away from him and looking at it in disbelief. Konrad buried his face in his arms, muttering something Hanna could not catch. There was a sickly tang of burning flesh in the air. Then Kessler leant forward and picked up the punch-dagger, he seemed disappointed that the red glow had faded a little and he placed it back on the gas hob with a philosophical shrug. "Levers and switches," he said, and then: "So, now will you tell us?" he was blinking even quicker now.

"I've not seen him," she whispered. Kessler nodded at the two SS men and suddenly they started to kick Strudel. She watched, transfixed as blow after blow fell on his face; she saw his nose burst like a red berry and his teeth shatter like crockery. And she saw his eyes, as he looked up at her between kicks, his pleading eyes ... She watched until she could take no more.

"Wait ... Wait!" she shouted. "He was here," she said, a little quieter now. "But he's gone now. I swear it." Kessler looked at her, the edge of his top lip quivering like a rattlesnake's tail.

"Gone? But that would not be so good. But then perhaps you are lying, perhaps you too would like to play with our new toy?"

"That's enough," Konrad suddenly murmured. "She doesn't know ... you can trust her ..."

"You are not a good judge of character, Plaidt." As he said it Hanna followed Kessler's gaze, he was looking at Strudel, who in turn was looking at her with big puppy-dog eyes filled with animal fear. Kessler smiled, and went on: "If you were you might know your wife for the filthy whore she is, most of Berlin knows it."

Konrad said nothing.

"Wait in the car, Plaidt," Kessler said.

Konrad hesitated, then he did as he was told, as he always had, half walking and half stumbling up the wooden stairs. He did not look at Hanna before he left.

Kessler waited until Konrad had closed the door at the top of the staircase behind him before he resumed.

"Ever had an SS man, dear Hanna?" Kessler said, now blinking so fast it was almost mesmerising. "No, well you had your chance, didn't you?"

She remembered that day in the back office of Frau Schuster's shop, the day when he had tried to seduce her, the day she had clawed a vivid fingernail comb on his cheek, and the day he had left a threat that had scarred her consciousness for far longer: *One day, bitch ... One day.*

"You missed a great opportunity that day, dear Hanna. They teach us well in the SS, and the training is very broad; how to be a good German, how to be a good husband. They even show us how to pleasure a woman, where to touch her ..." He took the punch-dagger from the ring of the cooker again and blew on its tip, instantly it glowed cherry red and Strudel cowered tightly in the corner of the room. She saw Kessler glance at him, and smile, and she thought of what he had said: *levers and switches* ...

"Put her on the table," Kessler said, and suddenly both the SS men grabbed her and hauled her on to the kitchen table, on her back, the last of the plates and cups falling onto the floor and breaking into jagged pieces. He nodded and one of the SS men lifted the hem of her dress up over her waist. She tried to struggle, but one of them pushed down hard on her chest and grabbed her hair, pulling her head back, keeping his hands away from her gnashing teeth, while the other held her legs apart. She stared at the ceiling.

"It's all about knowing *just* where to touch, you see," Kessler said, softly, but with a catch of excitement in his voice. She could still hear Strudel whimpering in the corner. She knew Strudel would not tell them, she knew he was too scared to be able to speak. But part of her wished that he would. She focussed on a damp patch on the ceiling, and silently swore to herself that she wouldn't scream. "Yes, you must get it *just* right ..." Kessler said. She felt the heat before it touched her, then smelt the scorching of the cotton of her underwear. "So boy, are you going to tell me?" Kessler said, but all she heard from Strudel was another low moan.

Then Kessler slowly pressed the red hot tip of the spike against her most intimate area, that tiny bud of pleasure.

Her scream was disembodied. It was someone else. It had to be. There was not the room in her for anything but this pain that travelled to every outpost of her body in a burning blink.

"They are at the autobahn, n-n-n-ear Cainsdorf!" she somehow heard Strudel shout through the fat and fuzzy wall of pain, "but leave her, p-p-p-please ..." The spike twitched, she sensed its scorch-tipped movement. Then blackness ... A cool ink poured on to the fire of her consciousness.

*

The ring of children tightened around the streamliner. Sepp gave his best scary stare, which these days could be very scary, and the children in the front rank pushed back against the others. West laughed, and shook his head – he had threatened to leave Sepp to it four times now but still showed no real sign of going. There were now about forty curious onlookers. Not all of them were children, there was one old farmer, red-faced and sausage-fingered, gripping a pitchfork tightly by its shaft. Sepp saw him lean down to speak to one of the children, he seemed to be issuing an order and, after a heartfelt protest the little face drooped with heavy sulk and the child ran off in the direction of the village. There would be more spectators soon, Sepp thought, some unwelcome. *Where the hell are they?* He looked at his watch for the fifth time in as many minutes.

"I'd wager he's crashed the truck," West said, seeming to read Sepp's mind.

"No, he wouldn't … But … Yes, perhaps …" Sepp said. Yes, *perhaps, perhaps* … because he could not face the thought that she didn't want to see this; didn't want to see this dream come true. He fiddled with his goggles. The last time they had been used was when West had worn them when he crashed on the Halle-Leipzig autobahn. He had already drained the Englishman of every memory of that day as they stood by the streamliner and waited for Strudel and Hanna to arrive.

"We're running out of time, Sepp, the whole of Saxony will be here soon," West said.

"Five more minutes." But he knew it had been more than enough time already, and someone in authority was sure to get wind of this before long, while the clouds scudding towards them were looking threatening, fat and billowing folds of iron grey, pregnant with ruining rain.

"Damn it!" Sepp slapped the side of the streamliner and the aluminium rang out loud enough to make the children jump back a few paces. The sharp outburst shocked him, he did not know from where within him it came, he could not control it. But there were things he could control. He nodded, and then slung the goggles around his neck.

"Let's do it!" he said. He thought she, and Strudel, would be there by the time he came to the end of the run. He hoped so. He wanted both of them to see this.

"At least we can put the children to use push-starting the car," West said. Sepp slid himself into the cockpit of the streamliner. He still wore his old Auto Union work overalls, his rubber-soled Fallschirmjäger boots with their side laces, and his own white linen wind helmet, bought seven long years ago, which had lain unused in the bottom of a drawer for most of that time. Now warm, the engine caught straight away, and Sepp gave it a boot-full of revs that had the rear wheels spinning against the road surface and the running kids scattering like a bomb-burst as they let the car go, some falling to the floor, every dirty face split with a huge white grin. He drove the car over the bare strip of packed earth that marked the central reservation and then headed in the direction of Chemnitz, grabbing second and squeezing on more power, the car gaining speed steadily, the sound of the wheels on the expansion joins in the concrete a steady *thud-y-d-dud*, repeated pulse-like through the steering wheel to his fingers, as the fuel fumes caught in his throat and nostrils. He switched his focus to the smudge of grey sky beneath a bridge well down the autobahn. The car felt good as he worked it up through the gears and once he was up to fourth he forgot about Hanna, about Strudel ... Total immersion.

Past 130mph the steering wheel began to shake in his hands, a little quicker and the bodywork sang to the road surface, the thud of the joins now long smoothed out by speed into a buzz that even at higher revs was audible over the trailing noise of the engine behind him, while the smell of the fumes was now swept away by the airflow. The carriageway was not wide, just the space for two-and-a-bit streamliners, he supposed, and there were places where the road curved which he marked in his memory for the return trip – the quick run. There was one concrete bridge crossing the autobahn, all the other crossings went beneath it, and he realised he would be at his highest speed around about here on his return run. He passed a horse and cart and by the time he had glanced in his mirror a second or so later it had diminished to a dot. Then, on the opposite carriageway, he spotted a slow moving truck, and he made a mental note of it, knowing that he was sure to come up on it very quickly on the return run. But otherwise there was no traffic: because of the war, because of the privations it caused, these days the autobahns were quiet roads, and Sepp was glad of that.

After four or five miles he slowed and searched for a spot he could turn the car. Looking far ahead he could see evidence of abandoned building work, a wide apron of gravel that might have been a rest area or a petrol station, if the war hadn't come, but now made for a perfect place to turn the streamliner. He slowed the car through the gears then turned onto the gravel. There were no NSKK lackeys to help turn his car for the return run and he knew it would need a little rough treatment, though the wheel spats meant there was little room for large steering inputs, as the front wheels would foul the covers. But Sepp had been ready for this, and so he braked and steered right on the gravel, which peppered the underside of the car like machine gun fire. He let the rear of the car slide to his left, then gave the throttle a sharp jab, then modulated it, bringing the back of the car around in a wide sweep, overtaking the front, the spinning rear wheels throwing a shotgun blast of gravel against a nearby wooden fence. Sepp guided the car back on to the autobahn facing in the opposite direction. It was a perfectly executed throttle spin, and now he finished his turnaround by once again driving across the central reservation. *Now for the quick run.*

He thought he knew the spot where he would touch 220mph, a little way before the bridge. It was beyond the curves and undulations and it would still give him time to slow before the exit ramp, to come to a stop at the point where West – and hopefully Hanna and Strudel – waited for him. The car accelerated smoothly past 100 and he was up past 150 when it was in the long curves, the tyres squirming against the smooth concrete, kicking out where there were winter-worn imperfections in the surface, Sepp twitching on a touch of opposite lock to correct a slide on two occasions, but always treating the car carefully, just as West had told him to. West had also told him about the vibration, and as the white needle on the speedometer crept upwards, past 180, past 190, the shaking was beginning to get close to unbearable, his vision jellified, teeth chattering, and if he hadn't screwed the thing together himself he would have doubted it could take it. The landscape was rushing past in a scuff of green and beige, the liquid horizon seemed to be squeezed into a blurred space the size of his thumbnail, pinned down by the dark clouds, and he reached it in the blink of an eye – although he could never risk that blink.

As he crested a slight brow at 200 the car went light and flicked against the inner edge of the road. He was dimly aware of a smudge that slid past his right eye like the shadow of a bird, and in his crowded mind there was just the tiniest of niches where it registered as the truck he'd spotted on the outward run. But he had already gathered the car, and himself, by now, and he aimed the streamliner at that tiny portal on the horizon, rushing towards him like a bullet, where the road was pinched tight beneath the bridge. He was holding the wheel tightly now, but somehow he found space in his concentration-crammed consciousness to remember West's advice. He relaxed his grip, treating the wheel like the precious thing it was, his grip on life, his grip on his dream, his grip on destiny.

Then, quite suddenly, the car stopped shaking. All was calm and the streamliner seemed as if it was being sucked towards the seemingly filament thin dark slot beneath the bridge, all the bellow of its engine left far behind. He wasn't driving, he realised, rather guiding the car with some previously untapped instinct, the hand movements on the wheel akin to the microscopic tingles of nerve endings. He almost felt as if he was floating above the road, almost as if he could let go of the wheel and all would be well. And yet complete disaster was but a shiver in either direction. He thought this feeling was what the philosophers, the mystics, spoke of: transcending being, transcending time, floating on time rather than being in it, becoming utterly aware of one's place in the universe. It was the moment he had lived his entire life for. He risked a glance at the clock and saw the white needle as it flicked across the 230mph mark. Even as he looked at the clock, just an inch, just a breath, from death, he knew that no one in this world could ever take that away from him.

Then reality crashed into the moment. The bridge suddenly seemed to jump up in front of him, as if it was a sprung trap, yet the space beneath it still looked impossibly small. An instant later he was somehow through, threading the car beneath the concrete overpass as much by thinking about it as steering, the shock wave of his passage kicking him smartly in the chest to a thundering *ka-boom*, just as West has warned him it would.

After the bridge he carefully started to slow the car, easing slowly off the throttle, but not touching the brakes. Touch them too soon and the tyres will tear like paper, West had told him. Suddenly everything felt very slow. He kept it on part throttle so that he still had control of the car and he watched as the needle slowly swept back to the left. Finally, when he thought it was safe, he touched the brakes, and the streamliner slowed as he took it down through the gears. Speed had stretched his perception so he saw the Opel Blitz tanker parked by the side of the autobahn long before he reached it.

His elation was complete. A dream fulfilled and Hanna there to see it. Just then it started to rain slightly, flecks of water dashed across his windshield. A second or so later and with the needle still slowly nudging to the left he could make out the people standing around the truck. It was strange, but there was no sign of the big group of children. Closer still and he could make out another car in the shadow of the tanker, a grey Mercedes 170V, he thought, and an alarm bell rang in his head. There were three people standing in front of the vehicles. He changed down a gear with a double-declutch, matching the revs with a crisp heel and toe blip of the throttle, and tried to make out who was waiting for him. He could pick out West, then Strudel – why was he holding his wrist? – and was that Konrad? Yes, it was, though he seemed to be swaying on his feet, almost as if he was drunk – *well that explains the Mercedes*, Sepp remembered he had used one for some time. He thought he might speak to him about that Donington try out, but then decided it didn't matter. Not now. By now he was very close, and down in second gear, near enough to see their faces. There were no smiles, and Konrad looked troubled, his shoulders hunched, his face strangely marked.

A cold dread seemed to sink through Sepp's being as the rain began to hammer heavily against the body of the streamliner. "Where's Hanna?" he said to himself. As he said it West twisted to his left and kneed Konrad between the legs ...

*

It was the only way he could give Sepp a chance to drive on down the autobahn; to give him, at least, a possibility of escape. West had needed to flush Kessler and his thugs out of their hiding place behind the tanker, and so he had downed Konrad with a sharp knee to the spheres, and even in the madness of the moment he could not help feeling proud of that kick, of the satisfying *ooomph* that burst like gas from Konrad's mouth as he folded double, clutching at his testicles. But there was no time to waste and now West leapt into the road, waving one hand above his head and pointing to the opposite carriageway with the other, warning Sepp.

Kessler and the SS men reacted instantly and instinctively, and one of the grey-uniformed thugs stepped into the road and was already reaching for his Luger, the flap of the holster unbuttoned, his hand on the angular butt of the pistol. Suddenly everything seemed to be in slow motion: Strudel ducking behind the cover of the tanker, fear large on his badly beaten face, Konrad rolling in pain on the side of the road, the rising pistol in the hand of the SS man – and, above it all, the unmistakable rasp of an Auto Union V16 … Speeding up.

At least I have bought Sepp some seconds to accelerate through, to escape the certainty of a concentration camp, the likelihood of death, West thought. He had been on the point of making himself scarce when he had seen the tanker truck returning, and then he had waited for it. But he had not seen the Mercedes behind the truck until it was too late, and there had been nowhere to hide in that open space. He wondered now whether a streamliner had once again been his undoing. The second SS man levelled his Luger at West, arm extended in a shooting range stance, taking up the first pressure on the trigger …

But then he spun to his left, something about the noise of the approaching streamliner had alerted him, alerted them all, and now Kessler had his Walther drawn, too. But it was too late for the SS man with the Luger, the pinched front of the Auto Union caught him at shin height, the crack as loud as the pistol shot West had expected, and then tossed him high into the air, the streamliner passing beneath him. Then there was another crack, from Kessler's Walther this time, and West heard the zing then the ding of a bullet hitting the body of the streamliner.

"Come on, this is our chance!" West shouted, running to the Opel tanker and grabbing Strudel by the arm, as Kessler and the second SS man stood and fired their pistols in the wake of the streamliner, bullets being about the only things that might catch it. West heard the ringing hit of three more rounds and then the revs of the Auto Union died at the same time as he clambered into the cab of the truck.

Konrad, his voice now a jagged croak of pain, shouted: "They're getting away!"

The truck fired instantly and Strudel climbed in beside West. He slammed it into first then floored it. There was one shot, which shattered the door mirror into a spidery crystal. West drove up the road that curled off the autobahn, knowing they would have no chance of outrunning the Mercedes on the long open road, hoping for twisting lanes where he might be able to shake them. He glanced in the shattered mirror as he worked up through the gears and just caught sight of the streamliner in a clear segment of the glass. It was rolling to a halt in a ploughed field. The mud coated the silver flanks of the car as it came to a stop. West knew Sepp had been hit.

"They sh-sh-shot him!" Strudel shrieked, tears welling in his eyes as he leant out of the window to see.

"Yes, I know," West said sharply. "Now get back in the cab or they'll shoot you too." He knew that Sepp had given them a chance. It would have been easy for him to simply turn across the carriageway and accelerate away. He didn't know whether Sepp was dead or wounded, but he did know that he had to take the opportunity he had handed them.

The road ran straight and narrow between fields for a while, and West hoped for a turnoff before the Mercedes had the scent. It had always felt strange, driving with his false right leg, but even with the tank on its back now drained the truck was slow and today it was less about sensitivity and more about pushing bloody hard on the accelerator, the whole truck shaking like a spaniel out of water, the big round tank popping and clanging, the transmission and engine a shrilling whine, the rain drumming on the steel bonnet in a forest of little white-plumed bursts. But it was no surprise when he heard Strudel's shout.

"They're c-c-c-c-catching us!" Strudel held his bloodied head out of the window again, the rain drenching his thin hair and pasting it to his scalp. Through the slanting rods of water and the halting sweep of the wipers West caught sight of a sign for a junction ahead.

"Where now?"

Strudel pointed to the left. West changed down for the corner. In the broken mirror he could already see the covered headlamps of the Mercedes swelling in size as the car closed in on the lumbering truck. He took the left-handed corner slowly, leaning over Strudel and opening the door on the passenger side and then, before he had time to complain, shoving him clear of the cab, Strudel rolling out and landing on the grass verge. West shouted after him: "Get down in those bushes, there's no point in us both getting caught!" He pulled the door shut and gunned the engine, the rear wheels slithering on the wet paving, kicking the truck into a tail-slide. As he applied opposite lock and eased off the throttle a little, through the corner of his eye West noted the low wall to his right, and from his position high in the cab he could see the heavily swollen river, which he guessed was the Zwickau Mulde, directly beyond it.

Half a minute later the Mercedes was right with the truck, its reflection crazed and jumbled in the shattered wing mirror. West heard a pistol shot as it whistled past the cab, but he knew they wanted him alive, so he guessed they would be careful – besides, they had no idea if there was still fuel in the tanker and they would not want to risk an explosion. The big car pulled out to overtake and West heaved the heavy wheel over to block it, getting a glimpse of those inside the Mercedes. Konrad was in the driving seat and Kessler was alongside him. The car switched to the other side, its tail kicking out in protest, and West mirrored the move. He sensed they were heading into town, there were more houses, stone and slate gleaming with rain. The road was widening and the Mercedes was flashing from mirror to mirror now. It was flat land and West guessed they must have been travelling at close to fifty miles per hour, and he knew the truck could go no faster, acrid fumes from the engine already drifting through the air vents, snatching at his nostrils.

Suddenly the nose of the Mercedes drew alongside. West reacted instinctively, hauling the wheel to the left until he heard the long shriek of metal on metal. Konrad was below his eye-line, but he thought it would have shaken him. He glanced in his mirrors and saw the Mercedes slewing from one side of the road to the other, its fender flapping from the flank of the car like a twisted piece of foil. Konrad held back a little, and then moved to pass again, using the extra space to accelerate and gain momentum. The large tank on the back of the truck hid the Mercedes and West had to second-guess what side Konrad would try, keeping the truck in the centre of the road. He glimpsed left, but guessed wrong, and the grey car swept by in a welter of spray on his right before West had the chance to respond, sparks flying where it scraped the stone wall.

Konrad now carefully manoeuvred the Mercedes in front of the truck and dabbed the brakes, the grille of the Opel kissing the rear of the car. The SS man in the back seat levelled his pistol. West accelerated, rammed the car, using the spare wheel fixed to its boot as a target, throwing the SS man from the back seat with the impact. Looking over the roof of the Mercedes West could see the road kinked hard left ahead, following the river he guessed, the stone wall still marking its edge.

Konrad started to slow the Mercedes for the turn. But West hit the accelerator with all his strength, his false leg jamming painfully against his stump. The truck hit the rear of the car again and pushed it into the corner. All four wheels were now locked on the Mercedes as Konrad had panicked and stood on the brakes as hard as West had stood on the accelerator. Because the wheels were locked Konrad had no control of the car as they came to the turn, and it slithered off the road in a long, wet skid, as the truck pushed it straight on. West could hear the loud sigh of the tyres on the wet tarmac as he shoved the Mercedes before him; his foot still jammed on to the truck's throttle. From his vantage-point in the higher cab he could see that they would hit the wall at an angle, the Mercedes first, and he braced himself for the crash that would sandwich the car between the stone wall and the truck. The car and the truck, now locked together, skidded off the road, across a grassy verge, and towards the wall at an angle of disaster.

At the very last moment West braced himself against the wheel … Then the Mercedes hit the wall, climbed up it a little, then tore off the top layers of dressed stones and disappeared over the lip. The last West saw of it was its grimy floor-pan as it pitched forward on its nose the other side of the wall, and then the wetly gleaming pattern of the tread on the tyres on the still locked wheels as it turned arse over tit and plunged roof first into the rushing river.

West had not banked on that, he had hoped the impact would have put the car out of action against the wall. He had risked all on the truck being stronger, but now he realised it was just too solid, as its heavy momentum took it straight through the stone wall.

The impact took down what remained of that stretch of wall, but also arrested the truck's speed, some of which had already dissipated when the car had hit the wall first in front of it. It also threw West forward, and he heard the sharp snap of a rib as it hit the bone-hard steering wheel, felt its stab within him. Now the front wheels lurched over the edge. For a moment the truck was tottering on the brink of oblivion, the stones from the smashed wall supporting it, jammed under its sump, the boiling current just a few metres below at the bottom of a steep bank, the underside of the Mercedes already disappearing beneath the surface of the wild, brown river. West had cut it damn fine, he thought, as he felt a wave of pure pain from his broken rib surging through his being … *Damn fine …*

Just then a key stone beneath the chassis crumbled or slipped, and the front of the Opel Blitz tottered over the edge and slid into the river. It hit the fast moving water with a force that threatened to smash the glass out of the windscreen, and then the heavy cab and engine dragged the lorry down into the depths of the Zwickau Mulde.

The fast water was thick with mud and silt and West could see absolutely nothing. He grabbed at the door-handle but could not force the door open and then he tried the sliding windows, but they were jammed shut with the pressure of the current.

West was trapped.

He could sense movement, and he guessed the truck was being swept along the riverbed by the force of the water. Somehow he had always known it would end like this: trapped in a small place in the dark. But there was little comfort in him being right. Images flashed before his eyes, not his life, no … But the far too small a portion of it he had spent with Roma.

***

Epilogue

These days I realise this was what I was always really about. I'm much more like Gramps, that book-loving Philip Grace, than I would ever admit back in the '80s. But when the time you live in makes it right to be greedy, well, then it's just too easy to go with the flow. Maybe that's why I can understand ... Maybe.

It had been hard to throw myself back into what now seemed like a mundane life of buying and selling when I had buried treasure to think about. My mind was alive with nothing but the streamliner; it would keep me awake at night, and an hour would not pass without me puzzling over how I would smuggle it out. That was the biggest problem I faced, getting it out of East Germany. There were other problems, many of them, not least ownership. But spoils of war could be sold on, so there were ways around that – when there's big money involved there are ways around most things – and I had a contact in Russia who could supply fakes bills of sale from government offices, so that was a start, as everyone supposed the cars were in the Soviet Union. But, of course, I didn't even know exactly which car this was to begin with. It was not as if I had been able to study chassis numbers and so on; it was not as if I was aware such things existed, back then. And so, in lieu of digging for treasure, I began to dig for knowledge.

I spent days in the basement of a motoring bookshop in Isleworth flicking through old copies of *The Autocar* and *Motor Sport* and it was there, one winter's morning, as I was unscrewing the lid on my Thermos, that my eyes passed over the story of Westbury Holt. The traitor. The old acquaintance of Gramps, mentioned by him just once, and spoke of with a sadder than usual look in his eyes.

A little later I had the idea of writing a book about the traitor, or at least pretending to. It gave me a first class excuse to return to the east without attracting too much suspicion. I improved on my A-level standard German and visited the GDR again early the following year, 1988, but I never saw that old man again, the man who had led me to treasure for the huge reward of a bar of chocolate. I didn't risk going to see the car, not then. I simply started to make the contacts, the people who might be able to help me later – more forms filled, some bribes paid, for that was the way of business in a land without business.

Once back in London my cover story, the amateur historian picking at the bones of the skeleton of a dead traitor, began to take over my life. The motor racing histories were thin on Westbury Holt, but then I suppose he was an embarrassment to the sport in some way: bad egg, and all that. Yet none of that seemed to fit the man I was finding, or the man the people I would talk to had once known at Cambridge or around the race tracks of

Europe. There was one thing, though, a race he had taken part in at Brooklands after his accident, in which he had driven dangerously, or so someone told me – desperately even. That had been his last race.

I devoured everything I could about racing in the 1930s, and while I schemed up a way to get my treasure from the east I also traced Westbury Holt's footsteps. In West Germany I paid my handful of deutschmarks and drove the mighty Nordschleife of the Nürburgring. I visited the memorial to Rosemeyer, a short walk through the trees from a lay-by on the Frankfurt-Darmstadt autobahn. I even found and drove the route of the old road course at Pescara, and by that time my admiration for the men who raced those machines was tinged with honest awe.

Then there was the war: the reading room in the Imperial War Museum, the Public Records Office, and too many gaps. I went to Crete with my then girlfriend and we stayed at a resort: at first she thought this was fabulous, a proper holiday at last. But I spent most of my time touring the battlefields and that was the beginning of the end of that relationship. I well remember standing on the summit of Hill 107, amid the graves of the Fallschirmjäger, looking down on the airstrip at Maleme and wondering what part he had played in it all.

Back in England I traced a former RAF officer who had known Holt on Crete and later at a POW camp. His name was Potter, and it was then that the evidence began to mount up. His memories of Holt were far from positive, and it seemed the war had changed the man, for here was a pilot who claimed kills that were not his – or at least that's what Potter hinted at – and who also refused to take part in escapes. The unpublished journal of an army officer, Brigadier General Sir J.P. Stockman-Brace, who had been the senior officer at an Italian POW camp in which Holt had been incarcerated, merely confirmed what Potter had told me.

Then it got worse. In the MI5 files on the Britischer Freikorps at the Public Records Office there was testimony that he had been seen at one of the pathetic little unit's bases, a Canadian traitor saying he'd been at Genshagen. Then, of course, there was the most damning evidence of all: the recording of the radio broadcast, and the film. He looked strained, and his hair glowed silver-bright with brilliantine, which was hardly his style. I thought then that just perhaps he was forced into it, even into saying what he said. Indeed there was what might just have been bruising above one eye, a dark shadow on the black and white film, and there is confusion on that emaciated face as it's lit by the flashes of the cameras. But I then supposed that was wishful thinking. And after that a strange thing happened. Quite suddenly I felt angry with this man I had never met, this long-dead traitor who had somehow rudely barged into my life. This man who had tarnished my silver.

Anyway, wheels greased with good American dollars slowly turned, and soon I was able to forget Holt and concentrate on my prize. I had settled the legal side of it, or rather the illegal side of it, with faked documents and real signatures, and I'd even picked up the relevant exportation papers – though these were for a Fortschritt tractor, not an Auto Union streamliner, but more dollars would make sure people would not take too close a look. It had cost me everything, including my job, for I had squandered as much time as money, and my employer had owned that time. But by now I did not care. I only cared for the silver.

I will cut a long story short, because it still hurts to even think about it, but the streamliner was gone. I will never forget that night, pouring the *Zwickau Bier* down my throat, and wondering what to do next. I had hired a truck, which I'd filled with all sorts of equipment including a mechanical winch, and a few men who could keep their mouths shut – for the right price – to help me get the car out of the mine and on the road to Rostock, where a container was ready to be stacked on to a Bulgarian freighter. Now I had to pay the men off and send them home. I had staked everything on the streamliner still being there, but the gamble had not paid off.

There was nowhere to go after that, so I stayed in Zwickau for a little while, living off the last of my cash. I had still hoped to find the old man again. If anyone knew where the streamliner had gone it would be him, I told myself, often – always after the second glass of the amber optimism. I asked around the bars, sometimes the name seemed to ring a bell, at other times people gave me the look that many in East Germany would give to questioning strangers. I had one note left in my wallet when I finally made the breakthrough. It was an old woman in the square by the Rathaus, near the statue of Schumann.

"Strudel, yes I knew him."

"Knew?"

"Oh, I am sorry young man, but I am afraid he is dead, the poor thing. An accident, I heard."

I felt the flickering flame of hope die inside me and the old lady read it as grief.

"I am sorry," she repeated, and I nodded and turned to walk away.

"You know, of course," she shouted after me, "he had family ..."

"Family?"

"Well, they were not his real family, his father was all he had, and he died years ago. But they always looked after him."

"Are they here, in Zwickau?"

"Yes, I know them, but not well. They have always kept themselves to themselves ..." she trailed off as she said it and I wondered where her thoughts were taking her.

With her help I managed to find the small apartment block on Leipziger Strasse. It was in good condition, the big front door had recently been repainted in a bold gloss blue. There was an intercom, with names alongside buttons. There was nothing for Sepp and Hanna Nagel but I buzzed the only apartment with a blank.

"Yes?" came a thin voice from the other end of the intercom.

"Frau Nagel?"

"I am not married."

"Oh, I —"

"Sepp is my brother, it is a common mistake – who are you, are you selling?"

"No, I have come to see you." The intercom went quiet except for the fuzzy static, "I am an old friend of Strudel's," I added.

"A friend of Strudel?" she seemed to be laughing, "well this should be interesting." There was a buzz and a loud click and I pushed the door open. They lived at the top of the house. She opened the door to me and smiled warmly. I recognised her as the woman who had once been married to Konrad von Plaidt – there had been pictures of her with him in the books that I'd read. Her face was well lined now, but there was still beauty there, and in the lines themselves, in their stoic symmetry, there was, I thought, great dignity. Her hair was thin and silver, tied back tight to her scalp with a thick black band. She was just into her seventies, then, but those blue eyes had seen a hundred years, it seemed to me. There was a big basket of freshly dug vegetables for me to step over at the door, the roots still caked in black earth.

"Sepp has an allotment," she said, catching my glance. She led me into the main room. I had secretly hoped, during my walk from the town square to the apartment, that it would be filled with racing memorabilia. But there was nothing, just furniture that was tasteful, rugs and a few cases of books, many about gardening, all old and well thumbed. It was only because I was looking for photographs that I realised there were none, none at all: not a son, not a daughter, not a nephew, not a niece, not a wedding, not a memory. She offered coffee, I accepted, and a few minutes later she returned with the cups and a plate of *Russian Bread* biscuits.

"They are Sepp's favourites," she said, offering me a letter-shaped biscuit.

"It's a lovely apartment," I said, by way of small talk, before biting the top off a baked *F*.

"Thank you."

"Have you lived here long?"

"A long time ago I lived here, the street was called Nord Strasse then, and then I returned some years ago. This place has book-ended my life, I suppose," she chuckled softly at that. "But you must tell me, what were you to my Strudel, I have to say I have not seen you before?"

"Oh, well, I only met him the once to be honest, I —"

"Ah," suddenly her eyes seemed to light up. "You were the one who was asking about the Auto Unions, were you not? Mr Grace's grandson?"

"Yes, how did you know?"

"Pah! Strudel met few people, and there are not so very many Englishmen in Zwickau these days." She laughed at that, then seemed to think for a moment, the steaming china cup held close to her lips. "You should know that you caused our Strudel great distress young man."

"I'm sorry ..." I sounded like a naughty kid I was sure, I certainly felt like one.

"You know it's gone," she said.

"What?"

"What you have come for."

"Yes, I know," I said, as there seemed little point in denying it then. "Do you know where?"

"No, Strudel was upset, that's all I know, but *we* were quite glad to see the back of it. No doubt it ended up in Russia somewhere, like the rest of them."

"Yes, no doubt."

"What will you do now?" She asked.

"I'm not sure, I was hoping ... Well, the car is very valuable you know."

"Yes, I know, to Strudel and to my brother it was the most valuable thing in the world."

"Yes, of course," I suddenly felt a little guilty. "I still have my book to write," I said, hoping to salvage a little dignity from the situation.

"A book?"

"Yes, it's going to be about Westbury Holt. Did you know him? I believe there is a story to tell."

"A story to tell? I suppose there is," she said quietly, but she didn't continue. I drank my coffee and ate two more biscuits, an *A* and a *K*, and tried to ask her questions about Holt and the old days which she just brushed lightly aside, skilfully changing the subject. Then I said my goodbyes and told her I hoped to talk to her again soon.

My next step was obvious. I had walked the streets of Zwickau long enough to know where the allotments were, on the fringe of the river, behind the flood banking. I walked up the riverside path, looking at the grey clouds reflected in the surface of the Zwickau Mulde, thinking more about the fortune that had slipped through my fingers than the man I was about to meet. The air was heavy with the sour yeast smell of the brewery. Soon the allotments were spread out in front of me, old men, some well past retirement age, turned the earth with forks or tied beanpoles together with twine, or smoked in their little potting sheds. I had once seen a picture of Sepp Nagel, in one of the many books I had bought, but I could not remember what he looked like. He was just another name in a caption as far as I was concerned, just a mechanic, a bit player. But I knew that this was perhaps my very last chance to find out what had happened to the streamliner.

I clambered down the flood bank and stepped over a low wire fence. Many eyes were on me and I took pains to tread carefully between the plots, almost balancing like a tightrope walker rather than drop a foot in the dark soil.

"I'm looking for Sepp Nagel?" I asked the first gardener I came to, a fat old man, a face slashed with intersecting laughter lines, a fiery mop of red hair stuffed under a ridiculous woolly hat with a bright yellow plastic flower poking through the weave.

"Who wants him?" he asked, suspiciously.

"A friend of a friend."

"Well, he's not here, so best shift your arse out of here sonny boy," he said. I had often come across this in East Germany, and knew what to do. I reached into my pocket and pulled out my wallet.

"Don't waste your money on old Lick," someone said. I turned to see him, a slender figure, another old man, standing in the shadow of the doorway of his potting shed in the next allotment along, a saxophone-shaped Bavarian pipe sticking out of a bushy beard, a tatty old jumper over a plaid shirt and a worn out pair of trousers. He limped into the grey light.

***

The nose of the tanker seemed to bounce off the bottom of the river, churning up another great cloud of silt. West clenched his teeth and shook off the paralysis, then tried once more to open the door. It was no good, so he tried the windows again, but they were the sliding kind and he could not get them to budge because of the pressure of the raging torrent. The water began to shoot in under the doors in freezing jets. He knew the truck was still moving, he could sense it, and he held the steering wheel tight as it swayed violently, coming close to turning turtle.

It was then that the cab broke the surface and he saw the grey sky again. The current had hold of the truck and was propelling it downstream at a velocity that seemed quicker than it had managed when the Mercedes was chasing it. West shook his head in disbelief, and then he realised what had happened. The tank on the back of the petrol truck was empty, full of air: it was as buoyant as a cork, and the truck had simply popped up from the dark depths ...

***

"After that," Westbury Holt said, "I somehow managed to get out of the truck, but then my false leg filled with water and dragged me down, so I unstrapped it and let it sink to the bottom. Then – Lord knows how – I managed to get to the surface and scramble ashore," he laughed as he said it.

I still could not believe I was talking to him, a man who had been presumed dead for over forty years, the traitor who had been linked to my life for what seemed like an age. I had told him who I was, and about the death of my grandfather – to that he had nodded solemnly, and said that he was sorry, Gracie had been a good man, he said. And I think it was because of Gramps that he let me into his life.

He went through it all patiently with me, his English now heavily accented, the man called Lick listening with the air of someone who had heard the story before, but would never miss the chance to hear it again, his colourful curses emphasising the more amazing episodes. The sun had dipped behind the houses by now and Westbury Holt had lit an old lamp that he kept in the little shed, the smell of the paraffin sharp in the cooling air. He refilled his pipe and Lick offered me a cigarette. I took it and soon the shed was filled with smoke.

"But I don't understand – why didn't you try to clear your name?"

"I had lost my name, I suppose … Besides, back then I really thought I was a traitor. I truly believed I had betrayed Roma and her people, I still do."

"Did you try to find her?"

"Of course, I had given my word. First though we had to lay low for a while. But we were lucky, it seemed Kessler and Konrad had not told anyone they were coming here for me, I suppose they were still trying to hush it up. I managed to get back to the flat and then we had to get a doctor for Hanna, she was in a terrible way, poor thing …"

"And the car, the streamliner?" I said, I had to know. "It was the one that Strudel took me to see, wasn't it?"

"Yes, he was always very excited about that, and he found it very difficult to keep it secret. Building the car with Sepp was the best time of his life." West shook his head. "Simpleton eh? He showed us all, my God that was one of the best engineered racing cars I ever saw."

"Did you drive it?" I asked.

"No, it was their car, Sepp and Strudel's. Once I'd kicked him off the truck he went back for Sepp, but it was too late. He pulled the body from the car and later we buried Sepp close to the autobahn. It was an unmarked grave, because I took his identity – I suppose that was meant to be temporary, back then." West shook his head slowly as he said it, then added: "Anyway, we wrapped him in a tarpaulin, with his goggles and wind helmet – I always thought he would have liked that."

"He would have," Lick said.

"But how did the streamliner get back down the mine?"

"Well, that miserable bugger Fink retrieved it and hid it with the others at first, above ground at the colliery. Then he and Strudel broke it up and took it underground again. Things were even worse for Germany by then and Fink was determined to save one – I think Strudel must have persuaded him it should be the streamliner. When the Americans bombed the works Fink was killed, still at his lathe they say. Strudel just built the car again as he had before. Then he blocked off the shaft and added all the danger signs, too – clever bugger, really."

"So it was never found by the Russians?"

"No. When they moved in after the Yanks had liberated the place they started to strip the town of anything of value, including the racing cars. But Sepp's car – that's what Strudel had always called it – well that was safe and sound."

"What about you?"

"I knew nothing about it until Hanna and I came back to Zwickau. All I wanted to do was find Roma. I'd grown another beard and bought some thick glasses. Hanna had a friend in Berlin, Max, who could sort the papers for us. We had a photo taken and he placed it on Sepp's card; he had the tools to emboss it, too. Quite a man, Max. He made it to the west and runs a string of businesses in Stuttgart now, I hear." He smiled at that, and then continued. "Right up to the end of the war I was just about free to travel around Germany as I wished, just another amputee among many – in fact I'm sure my missing leg helped me blend in ..." He trailed off and seemed to stare into the pipe smoke for a little while.

"Was she —?" I started, but he anticipated the question and cut in.

"I never found her. I had no chance, never even knew her surname ... Anyway, I suppose I knew she was dead all along. What I *did* find sickened me though, few people here talk of all that now: the camps, the starving, the dying, the dead. But I think of it every day, I make myself think of it because I never thought of it when I could have done something about it. You should know that. Your grandfather was right."

"You never could have done anything about it you bony arsed old fool," Lick said.

"I could have shown them things were not normal, that this was not a normal place where they do normal things like race cars ... I *was* a bloody fool Lick."

"You know, I bumped into your grandfather after the war," Lick said, changing the subject but still shaking his head. "I was in a prison camp in the north of England somewhere. He didn't recognise me, but I knew him, had seen him at the AVUS with Sepp ... I mean West ... He was the one who said I was no longer a danger to civilisation, as it happens.

Very decent of him, I must say."

"Well, even Gracie could be wrong," West said, with a grin.

"So it was you who told him about the streamliner?"

"Yes, old Kurt told me what had been done when I was on my last leave, before I was picked up with my arse in the Rhine and my hands in the air." Lick said. "There was a letter from him that somehow found me in the camp, too, in which he brought me up to date with the tale. It was a good story; fair play; got me some English cigarettes, anyhow."

I nodded, and then turned to West again: "But I still don't understand why you stayed in East Germany, after the war?"

"I was still looking, and most of the camps were in the east, as were the refugees, and by the time I gave up it was much easier being Sepp Nagel than Westbury Holt. Father was long gone by then, and everyone at home would think me dead, and there was nothing waiting for me in England, except a trial for treason, I supposed," he smiled wryly at that.

"By then East Germany was a police state, anyway," he went on. "It was just far simpler to keep things the way they were. Besides, I was able to travel to other Eastern countries, like Yugoslavia. But there was no sign of her in Slovenia either, no sign of any of them."

"But what about those who had known Sepp?"

"We lived in Berlin until the fellow who was looking after the apartments died in … When did old Kurt die, Lick?"

"About '78."

West nodded: "That was when we moved here, then. Hanna still owns ninety per cent of the property, although it's all in my – I mean Sepp's – name. It's more than most businesses kept when the reds took over, so we've done okay."

"Did no one recognise you?"

"I've worn this blasted itchy beard for years," he rubbed his fingers through the dense mat. "And to be honest no one seemed to remember me, or Sepp – but that's the way it is here now. Too many have dark secrets. After the war we just got on with our lives, people learnt to mind their own bloody business, because for many of them it was very bloody indeed."

"So you have spent all this time with Hanna?"

"As brother and sister, that's all. But not all of it. She was married for a little while, twice in fact, but neither marriage lasted. She had wanted a baby, but it simply didn't happen, so we sort of drifted back together. We had both lost what we wanted, what we needed, and so we were drawn together I suppose. It seemed there was never a chance of her having another baby. But, in a way, she could have a brother again."

"You are her brother now, Sepp."

"I know it, Lick."

"And no one ever said *anything*?"

"Sometimes people whispered, and once or twice we were tipped off that the Stasi were going to visit. But it never came to anything and now I'm Sepp Nagel to everyone – I even spent the last years of my working life at the Horch works."

"Really?"

"Yes, it's quite true; Westbury Holt gluing Trabants together in the very same factory where they once built the Auto Unions."

"And you never felt you wanted to race again?"

"Never. Competition caused all the pain in my life. There is no room for it now, I tend my vegetables and keep my head down ... That way I cannot hurt another person."

He took a long pull on the pipe, then asked: "What will you do now?"

"Tell your story?"

"Can it wait – until I die?"

"If that's what you want," I said, and meant it.

He nodded slowly.

"My arse!" Lick shouted. "It's past seven, Eva will chew my cock off for this!" With that he left the shed, leaving the door swinging against its hinges, creaking quietly. Most of the other old men had gone home, too. There was just one left, a portly sort, kneeling on the ground, who seemed to be whispering something to a marrow.

"Look at that fat bugger Wolf," West said. "If he thinks a little love and tenderness is going to grow him a marrow that will beat mine he's in for a bloody shock."

*

The streamliner? Well, that's still out there. Somewhere ...

THE END

Historical Note

This is historical fiction and as such is a mix between the two: people who have lived and died in real time and space, and people who have only lived in my imagination. West, Hanna and Sepp, are all the latter, as are Konrad, Gracie and Kessler. Rosemeyer, however, was very much a real hero of the age, as anyone with any knowledge of motor racing history will know, though how much he approved or disapproved of the Nazis is still a subject of some speculation. For my part I think he was just a racer, politics were nothing to him – a bit like Westbury Holt, then …

Enthusiasts might wonder about the absence of some names: Varzi, Stuck, Eberan-Eberhorst and quite a few others. Sadly, including everyone was just not an option, as it would be far too complicated for a reader new to the subject. There are non-fiction books out there though; the late Chris Nixon wrote quite a few, while if you want to find out more about the political side to all this I would recommend *Hitler's Motor Racing Battles*, by Eberhard Reuss.

Events that form the backdrop to this drama are all real, including the races and record runs – with the added participation of Westbury Holt – with just the odd change in minor detail, and small shifts in time, added for the sake of the narrative.

As for the espionage strand, there's no doubt that there was a great deal of curiosity about the fuel used by the German racing teams at that time, largely for the reasons given in this work. And with an eye to spicing up a tale, talk of secret brews was just too enticing.

On the other hand, some other things, quite often those that seem all too incredible, are true nonetheless. So yes, a driver did take his girl for a lap of the 'Ring in a Type C Auto Union (Rosemeyer in fact); von Brauchitsch did use his diamond-encrusted swastika to impress *maître d's* into giving him a table in busy Berlin restaurants; and those streamliners really were *that* fast.

The Auto Union racing cars were hidden above ground at a colliery at some time during the war, too, though I'm not sure anyone ever had the chance to run one on the autobahn. Many of the Zwickau racing cars, like the streamliner in this story, also disappeared into the Eastern Bloc afterwards. Those that were brought back from the East were sold for big money. Audi bought a Type D – built from parts retrieved from the USSR – in 2012, and while it's not known how much it paid, the same car had been expected to fetch $10m at auction a few years earlier …

As for Hanna's child, there is a well-known case of a baby killed in similar circumstances in 1939 and there were probably many other cases of infanticide on the quiet at this time. There was also a unit of British soldiers in the Waffen SS (albeit very small); and while I've been a little creative in getting a Hurricane into the air at Maleme on the day of the invasion of Crete, most of the rest of it is as it happened. There were atrocities committed on Crete, too, and it's a fact that the Fallschirmjäger had a very low opinion of partisans.

As to how much the German people knew about the Holocaust during the war, recent research suggest there were certainly many rumours. It's estimated that 28 per cent of Berliners had heard something about it, for instance. BUT, and this is a big but, what they heard was usually still just rumour and many simply refused to believe it. How could they believe that such a thing was happening in their Germany? Indeed, many thought the rumours were enemy propaganda. Now, of course, we *know* what man is capable of. And we must never forget, and certainly never deny it.

One final thing, there really was an Englishman who raced for the Nazi-backed Mercedes team. His name was Richard Seaman, and he's mentioned in this work. He was killed in a crash at Spa just months before the war started. I always wondered how his war might have gone, given the ties he had with Germany, should he have lived. And in the midst of that 'what if' *Pieces of Silver* was born.

Mike Breslin

London, 2014

ABOUT THE AUTHOR

Mike Breslin is a freelance writer specialising in motorsport and motoring. He is originally from south Wales but is now based in London. A former Formula Ford racer – who cleared thousands of pounds of racing debts with one spin of the roulette wheel by betting everything he had on number 11 – Mike has published two other books: *The Unfair Advantage* (fiction, 2000) and *The Track Day Manual* (non-fiction, 2008). Mike loves to travel and when he's not writing he can often be found in his local pub planning his next adventure or road trip. For more on Mike Breslin go to www.bresmedia.co.uk